Always the Bridesmaid
and
It Had To Be You

Sarah Webb worked as a children's bookseller for many years before becoming a full-time writer. She lives in Dublin with her partner and young family.

Writing is her dream job as she can travel, read magazines and books, watch movies and television (she's addicted to *Grey's Anatomy*) – all in the name of research.

Find out more and read Sarah's Launch Lizard blog on her website: www.sarahwebb.ie.

Also by Sarah Webb

Three Times a Lady

Something to Talk About

Some Kind of Wonderful

Take a Chance

When the Boys Are Away

Anything for Love

Sarah Webb

Always the Bridesmaid

and

It Had To Be You

PAN BOOKS

Always the Bridesmaid first published 2001 by Poolbeg Press, Dublin
First published in Great Britain 2003 by Pan Books
It Had to Be You first published 2004 by Macmillan
First published by Pan Books 2005

This omnibus first published 2010 by Pan Books
an imprint of Pan Macmillan, a division of Macmillan Publishers Limited
Pan Macmillan, 20 New Wharf Road, London N1 9RR
Basingstoke and Oxford
Associated companies throughout the world
www.panmacmillan.com

ISBN 978-0-330-51767-6

1 3 5 7 9 8 6 4 2

A CIP catalogue record for this book is available from
the British Library.

Printed in the UK by CPI Mackays, Chatham ME5 8TD

Always the Bridesmaid

To Tanya, who loved this one so much

Acknowledgements

There would have been no *Always the Bridesmaid* without many, many people.

My heartfelt thanks to:

My wonderful family – Mum, Dad, Kate, Emma, Peter, Luan, Charlie and Richard – for all their help, love and babysitting. And thanks for the great illustrations, Kate.

To the men in my life – Sam, for being a star of a son and for making me smile every day, and Ben, my very own 'Steve' and one of the kindest men on the planet.

To Andrew Algeo, Tanya Delargy and Nicky Cullen, my 'youngest' old friends.

To Emma and Peter, for letting me blatantly borrow wedding details. I would like to point out that the Aussie best man, Luke, is in no way based on the lovely Justin, who is an upstanding young man of good character.

To Niamh Hooper, *Irish Independent*, for her introduction to the heady world of wedding fairs.

To Michael Simmonds, bookseller extraordinare. His Exchange Bookshop in Dalkey is an Aladdin's cave for any bibliophile.

To Socky, Geri Maye, Joe Morrison and Sharon Delaney for all the TV research and for letting me be a part of your *Den 2* show. RTE are lucky to have you – true professionals who make work fun.

To my agent, Ali Gunn, for all her enthusiasm, energy and sound advice.

To David North from Macmillan for having faith in me and to Imogen Taylor, my editor, a joy to work with and to hang out with. To Dave Adamson for his enthusiasm and support. And to all the Macmillan gang I met in Galway – *Slainte!*

To all the children's booksellers the length and breadth of Ireland, Northern Ireland and Great Britain. For their tireless promotion of books and reading and their hours of thankless tidying. As I always say – it's not a job, it's a vocation!

To the gang at Eason for all their support and kindness over the years – especially Tom Owens, Adrian White, David O'Callaghan, Alan Johnson, Cathal Elliott and Maria Dickenson.

To all the inner avenue gang in Southampton, especially Mark Jardine and Craig Mitchell, for keeping Ben sane. But please try not to kill him while sailing the skiff and try to keep the sails in one piece, Mitch! To Janet, Louisa and Bob Cooke in Tamworth for wel-coming me into the family. To Dan O'Regan in Bristol – my much loved aunt.

To my writing friends new and old for their support and sense of fun, not to mention the boozy dinners –

Tina O'Reilly, Martina Devlin, Marita Conlon-McKenna, Colette Caddle and all the other 'Irish Girls'.

And almost finally, to all my friends and family whose weddings I've ever attended – they were all inspirational! And most especially to my friends, Jamie Boag and Shirley Robertson, for the unforgettable Cowes experience.

And last but not least, to you, the reader, for parting with your hard-earned cash – I hope you enjoy reading this book as much as I enjoyed writing it!

Life is like a wild tiger. You can either lie down and let it lay its paw on your head – or sit on its back and ride it.

'A GUIDE FOR THE ADVANCED SOUL',
Susan Hayward

Chapter 1

The paranoia all started to kick in when my 'baby' sister Suzi came home from Australia last December at the tender age of twenty-four, with the Golden Delicious rugby-playing Matt in tow. I thought things couldn't get any worse.

I was wrong.

"Suzi, have you told Mum and Dad?" I asked as we were loading my Golf with the bags in the airport car park. Matt had kindly offered to get rid of the baggage trolley.

"About what?" she asked quickly.

"About Matt," I replied. "Do they know he's come to live in Dublin?" She certainly hadn't told me and I'd got rather a shock when I'd seen the whole hunky six-foot-something of him coming through the arrivals gate with his arm draped over my sister's shoulders. Although I must admit that I'd thoroughly enjoyed the firm, muscular hug his brown arms had generously given me.

"Not exactly," she said nervously, "but they'll love him and there's loads of room in the house and . . ."

"The house?" I interrupted, trying to keep my voice level. "You and Matt are planning to live at home?"

"Well, we want to save for a house and I'm sure Mum and Dad won't mind."

"Right," I muttered darkly. First me, now Suzi – it wasn't as if we were Italian. Surely we were supposed to have our own homes at our age.

"Do you think it'll be a problem?" Suzi bit her lip.

"No," I lied. "They're so excited about having you home, I'm sure they won't mind."

Suzi nudged me. Matt was smiling at her across the car's roof.

"Let's go," Suzi said.

"You're very quiet," I said to Suzi who was sitting in the back with Matt as I drove down the motorway. Matt was looking anxiously out the back window at the driving rain and the dark grey sky. She leaned forward and popped her head through the space between the two front seats.

"I'm a bit worried about Mum and Dad. You're right. I should have told them. I just thought I'd surprise them, you know."

"I shouldn't have said anything," I said. I felt bad – I should have kept my mouth firmly shut. I was always putting my Yeti-sized in it.

"Can we go for a drink before going home?" Suzi

asked. She turned her head. "Matt, how are you feeling?"

"Fine," he stated. "Did you say drink?"

"Yes."

"Sounds cool."

"How about Johnnie Fox's?" I asked. "Show Matt a bit of real Ireland."

"Tourist Ireland, you mean," Suzi giggled. "Good idea."

As we drove up the steep, almost vertical, road towards the pub, I thought about the 'lovebirds' and where they would sleep. Although neither of the parents are priests or vicars (unless they secretly belong to some strange sect who only practise early on Saturday and Sunday mornings when normal mortals, myself included, are dead to the world), we live beside the local church, which gives the term 'what will the neighbours think?' new meaning. And directly opposite the house lives Father Lucas. So you can see why Suzi and Matt 'living in sin' might not appeal to Mum and Dad.

When the church sold off some of its land and buildings to pay for a new roof, Dad and Mum bought a run-down, cut-stone Victorian house, originally the rectory. It was described as being 'full of charm and old-world character'. Bloody cold is what it really was. There was no central heating, no hot water as the immersion was on the blink, cold stone-tiled floors on the ground floor and bare pitch-black floorboards in the bedrooms and bathroom upstairs.

At the time we didn't give a monkey's about 'the original Victorian iron fireplaces', or 'the hand-glazed stained-glass window panels' or 'the ancient white claw-footed bath with brass taps'. We were freezing our tits off and destined to be woken every Sunday morning in the wee small hours (well, ten o'clock is very early if you've had one too many the night before) by the deafening clanging peal of the 'original' Victorian church bells!

Mum and Dad had, to give them credit, turned the cold *Psycho*-house on the hill into – as an estate agent would say – 'a delightful residence full of original character and untouched by the scourge of rabid modernisation'. But it had taken over twelve years and a lot of trips to house auctions, antique shops, not to mention rummages in skips and derelict houses. Dad always claimed they were completely derelict but we often wondered. Suzi and I had learnt to spot old pine, original cast porcelain tiles, brass fenders and other weird and wonderful Victorian 'housey bits' at a tender age.

Several years ago Dad opted for early retirement from his job as an architect with the Civil Service and set up The Architectural Salvage Company. A few weeks into the work and he was as happy as Larry and wondering why he hadn't packed in the office job years ago. He was dead right, if you ask me. Life's short and if you're going to spend years of your life working you may as well pick something you like. I should have taken my own advice . . . Anyway, as I said, he loved the work and soon filled the garage and back garden with his 'finds', much to Mum's disgust. Mum used to be an air hostess for Aer Lingus, and she's still always perfectly coiffured and immaculately dressed. She'd look glamorous in a polyester housecoat! I don't know what happened to the rest of the family. Neither does she for that matter.

Mum and Dad make an interesting couple, chalk and cheese really. Dad is never out of his jeans, which are usually covered in rust or mud or paint, his hair is usually in need of a drastic cut and he insists on wearing an old pair of black army boots, although Mum bought him a trendy pair of beige Timberland boots, which live in their box under the bed.

It's funny. Dad stopped working on our own house as soon as he got into the 'business'. I kind of miss helping him painting, giving furniture the distressed look and painting terracotta pots with yoghurt to make them 'mould' and look ancient more quickly.

I used to help my friend Jodie sometimes when she needed a hand. She's an interior designer – the type who will come in and rip your house apart before even starting! So I helped her some weekends when I wasn't in the bookshop – The Wonderland Children's Bookshop in Blackrock.

I really wanted to be . . . it was kind of embarrassing really. I'd never said it out loud to anyone and I knew it would never happen . . . but I really wanted to present children's programmes. On *Den 2*. The girls and guys they have on *Den 2* looked like they were having so much fun. They got to wear cool clothes in really bright colours and act like kids. I used to watch all the time – research, you understand – and they were making little eggshell men, filling eggshells with earth and putting mustard and cress seeds on top. And they had one they'd made earlier – how I longed to say that – 'Here's one I made earlier, boys and girls!' Anyway Damien, the cute dark-haired one, watered his little eggshell man and left him to grow in studio. And as I watched I just wanted to be him. Imagine making eggshell men and introducing cartoons every day – heaven!

"Me ears are popping, mate," Matt exclaimed as we pulled into the car park.

Suzi laughed and nibbled one of his earlobes. I watched them in the rear-view mirror, trying not to let the green-eyed monster grip my heart and squeeze. Suzi's legs were draped over Matt's firm thighs. She curled his hair around her tanned fingers and gazed at him longingly. A black Range Rover blared its horn at my Golf which had wandered, with my mind, onto the wrong side of the road. I waved, mouthed a 'sorry' and pulled the car into an empty space beside the pub's front door. Beside us was a large bus whose signs proclaimed it to be the servant of the Clontarf Rugby Club.

Matt's eyes lit up as soon as he spotted the word 'rugby'. His generous mouth broke into a wide smile, showing two gleaming layers of perfect teeth, honed from years of carnivorous tearing of meat in a rugged, manly way no doubt. Attractive crinkles formed at the sides of his eyes and I gazed, smitten – he was only gorgeous. Suzi glared at me dangerously.

"Amy," she hissed, "stop staring."

"Sorry," I mumbled. But Matt hadn't noticed – his head was full of hookers, oddly shaped balls and tries. I'd always thought rugby was a bizarre sport.

We got out of the car and Matt threw his manly arm around Suzi's petite frame and propelled her through the door. She's five-foot-nothing, with a mane of long silky blonde hair, bright blue eyes and clear peachy skin – your average nightmare! It wouldn't take much to propel her anywhere as she's so tiny. And of course she wears the obligatory 'cute girl' clothes to boot – well, wouldn't you? Belly tops, skin-tight trousers or short leather skirts. I feel like a heffalump beside her. I'm an average sort of size twelve to fourteen, depending on the day and the label. With shortish blonde hair that has to be helped quite considerably to stay blonde, depending on the time of the year. But beside Suzi everyone looks huge. The worst thing is that she eats like a horse, honestly. And I just have to think about chocolate and I put on pounds – it's so unfair!

As we walked through the door our eyes adjusted to the darkened room. Loud cheers were coming from the back, where a group of larger-than-average men had gathered. Matt gazed over longingly. He loped over to the bar to fetch the drinks while Suzi and I flopped onto the huge sofa beside the open fire.

"Bliss," Suzi said as she flipped off her navy Converse sandals and curled her dainty feet under her. Although it was December, her legs and feet were bare.

"Are you not cold?" I asked. She was wearing a purple cotton dress which just skimmed her knees and a white hooded fleece.

"I am a bit," she admitted. "I hope Matt's OK. He's not used to the cold."

"It's not that cold today," I warned. "You're lucky."

"Thanks for collecting us." Suzi smiled and placed her hand on my knee. "It was really good of you."

"Not at all," I replied. "It was nice to get out of the house for a while."

Suzi looked at me carefully. "Are you all right? I was sorry to hear about . . . you know."

"About Jack," I stated firmly. "It's OK, Suzi. I don't mind talking about it."

"It was just so sudden," Suzi continued. "We all thought you two were perfect together. What happened?"

I smiled. Suzi had a habit of coming straight to the point. But it was refreshing in a way. Everyone had spent the last few weeks pussyfooting around me and avoiding asking any direct questions. I guess they all thought that Jack had instigated the 'broken engagement'.

Jack and I had been living together for three years and had begun skirting around the whole marriage thing. Jack seemed to think it was the way forward but

I wasn't so sure. Things hadn't been right for ages. I knew I couldn't marry him in the foreseeable future – it just wouldn't be right if I wasn't 100% sure.

"I don't know where to start, Suze. There was this work party and . . ." I began.

"Here you are, girls," Matt interrupted, plonking the glasses of Guinness down on the table in front of us. "Met a guy from Clontarf Rugby Club. Plays wing like me. OK if I join him for a scoop, love?" he asked Suzi.

"No worries," she replied.

"Great," he grinned. "See you Sheilas later." In a matter of seconds Matt was demonstrating the haka with a rapt audience of adoring Irish and American men and women.

"That's my man," Suzi proclaimed proudly as she watched him waggle his tongue around and slap his thighs.

"I thought it was New Zealand players who did the haka? And I thought Australians hated New Zealanders?" I asked, a little confused.

"It is," Suzi confirmed. "And they do normally. But Matt's special, I guess." She smiled widely. "No one could dislike him. He played for a club in Auckland for a while – that's where he learnt it. Matt's really good, played for his country on the Under-21 reserve team."

"Of course he did," I muttered darkly. "Friend of Jonah's, is he?" He probably had a bloody doctorate in aeronautics too! A right Mr Perfect.

"Sorry?" Suzi asked.

"Nothing. Don't mind me."

Suzi smiled. "Tell me about Jack. What were you saying?"

I took a sip of my drink and stared into the fire. My cheeks were beginning to glow in the warmth and I cast my mind back to that evening, only weeks before.

"I guess the doubts began to set in when Jack's architectural firm had a work party for some of their big clients. They wanted to show how they could use modern technology – Autocad – stuff like that. Anyway before the party each of the established architects was given a 'team' and each team had to produce a design using computer technology. Jack's lot had to design a church using natural materials." I paused and looked at my sister. "Are you sure you want to hear all this?"

Suzi smiled kindly. "Yes. I really do. Go on."

"OK. Jack had been working really hard on this design. I barely saw him at all. When he wasn't in the office he was working on the computer at home."

"That was hard on you," Suzi said.

"That didn't bother me at all, to tell the truth," I said. "I liked it in a way – seeing him so involved in work and so into something. He'd been moaning about being underutilised and this gave him a chance to show what he could do." I took another sip of my Guinness. It was so good to have Suzi back. I needed to talk to someone about Jack. Beth was busy with Tony, and Jodie . . . I loved her dearly but she wasn't the most sympathetic of people at the best of times.

"The night before the presentation he was up to ninety, the design was nearly finished and his team had gone home. He rang me from the office to tell me he'd be late as he was going to try to finish it by himself." I stared at the fire again, watching the flames lick around the red-hot coals. "I heard Jack's car roar into the drive hours later. I was asleep at the time and I remember thinking it was strange as he was usually so careful not to wake me up. He slammed the car door and he made loads of noise stomping up the stairs and fell in the bedroom door." I looked at Suzi and sighed. "He'd been drinking, Suze. I could smell it off his breath. He sat down on the bed and began to talk to me. Asking why I hadn't waited up and ranting about how I never supported him and his work."

"Why?" Suzi asked. "I don't understand. What was wrong?"

"After a while he told me that something had happened to the computer system and he hadn't saved his work properly. Jack went and lost the whole file, Suze. The design his team had been working on so hard for that presentation."

"Jesus!" Suzi said. "Poor man. But why was he annoyed with *you*? It was hardly your fault."

"Because I was there. Because he was annoyed at himself, I guess. And maybe I wasn't as sympathetic as I could have been. I think I told him that it was only work and not to overreact. Something like that anyway." I wondered what exactly I *had* said. I couldn't really remember – I'd been half-asleep at the time and not exactly delighted to be woken up in the middle of the night.

"Did he calm down?" Suzi asked with concern.

"Eventually. And the following day one of the women in the office managed to retrieve the file from the hard drive so it was OK in the end. And to be honest it wasn't even his behaviour that got me thinking."

"What was it?" Suzi asked.

"At the presentation the next evening I was sitting with a group of his colleagues and I just didn't want to be there. The people were nice but I felt so tired and fed up. And as I sat there watching the presentation and listening to Jack's speech, I realised I didn't want to be with him any more. The strange thing is that I couldn't quite put my finger on why – the whole relationship simply felt wrong. It's hard to explain." I stared into space.

"Go on," Suzi urged.

"That's pretty much it, really," I sighed. "The next day I got up early and packed some stuff while he was still asleep. He woke up halfway through."

"What did he say?" Suzi asked.

"He asked me what I was doing," I explained in hushed tones. "I told him I didn't want to be with him any more and that I was really unhappy and that I was moving back home."

"Just like that?" Suzi asked, her eyes wide open in astonishment.

"Yes," I replied firmly. "I knew, given a few days, he'd talk me out of it. You know how strongly he can put things."

Suzi murmured assent. She remembered Jack's 'strong words' at many a family dinner. His was usually the only raised voice at the table as the O'Sullivan family weren't one for arguments.

"That was the strange thing," I said. "He just sat there and looked at me for ages. I started crying and I think I said I was sorry." I started to cry. Suzi put her arms around me. She silently stroked the back of my head.

I took a big gulp of air. "Then he said that I was right, that he'd felt the same way for ages. I couldn't believe it! He didn't want me any more!"

"But, Amy," Suzi said quietly, "you were leaving him. Did you not stop to think that he was only protecting himself? You know what male egos are like. And anyway, why did you care? You were about to walk out on him!"

"I don't know," I said truthfully. "I suppose I wanted him to be still in love with me. For some reason that would have made it easier."

"In the short term, maybe," Suzi said thoughtfully. "But you did the right thing. I know it must have been difficult. Have you spoken to him since?"

"A few times," I grimaced. "To organise picking up my things and to cancel our joint account – that kind of thing."

"But you've never talked about your feelings," she asked, "like how you've both coped with the split?"

"No," I whispered. "Jack did suggest meeting up but I didn't feel strong enough. I knew I'd just cry in front of him and make myself miserable."

"I'm sure Jack has seen you cry before," Suzi smiled gently.

"Um," I murmured. Jack had asked to see me several times in fact but I'd stubbornly refused. I sighed. "I don't know. I'm beginning to think I was a little hasty. Maybe I should give it another chance. Sometimes I think I'm being unrealistic, expecting things to be perfect. Maybe I should have married him and be done with it."

"What are you talking about?"

"Oh, I don't know. I'm a bit down at the moment, I suppose. I'm feeling my age – I'll be thirty in a few months and it's getting to me."

Suzi snorted. "Jeez, girl, would you get a grip! Thirty is hardly the end of the world."

"I know, I know. But I thought I'd be, well . . . married at this stage. With two children and a nice house and a husband."

"I think you need one of those to be married all right!" Suzi laughed.

I smiled. "I'm serious. I had it all planned. Married at twenty-six, a baby girl at twenty-seven and a baby boy at twenty-nine. And what do I have – nothing!"

Suzi laughed. "Amy, I think you're blowing things

well out of proportion. Hitting thirty is no reason to get married. Especially to someone you're not in love with."

"Who says I'm not in love with Jack?" I asked quietly.

Suzi looked at me carefully.

"That's the problem," I continued, tears welling up in my eyes. "I do love him. I just can't stand being with him."

Suzi gave me a hug. "Oh, Amy. I'm sorry. Don't cry. It'll be OK. You'll feel better soon, I promise. You did the right thing."

Chapter 2

"Amy, I know it sounds like a cliché, but it will get easier," Suzi said after coming back from the bar with a pint of Guinness for me and an orange juice for herself. Suzi had decided that she'd drive home as I needed to drink more than she did. Suzi is nice like that – most of the time. She's not bad as sisters go. Although she's a crap driver and I was putting my life in her hands letting her behind the wheel. Still, I did appreciate it.

"Matt's in heaven," she continued, taking off her hoody and draping it over the back of the sofa. "I brought him over a pint but he had three already in front of him. The whole back row were buying him drinks. They already have him persuaded to join their club."

I tried to smile. It wasn't fair on Suzi landing her with all this on her first day back. "Do you have any cigarettes?" I asked hopefully. I didn't really smoke, but now and again, mainly in the pub or in times of dire need, I scabbed one off my friend Beth. Or if things were really bad I bought a pack myself. I always felt guilty buying cigarettes in the shop. And drink too for that matter. It's ironic, I suppose – I'm twenty-nine for heaven's sake and I still worry about being asked my age in the pub. I wish! The last time I was asked for ID was when I put my hair in plaits (very trendy) for Suzi's twenty-first. And that was several years ago.

"Yup, but it's my last pack. I'm giving up. I can't afford to smoke now what with the . . ."

"The what?" I asked.

"Um, the lack of a job," Suzi smiled. "I'm nipping out to the loo. The smokes are in my fleece." She jumped up and walked behind the bar to the toilets, followed by the admiring male eyes of the bar staff. I guess she did look well and a tan was unusual in December. I unzipped her pocket and found the cigarettes and gold Zippo lighter, my fingers grazing something cold. I pulled out the offending object. It was a small metal box. Being a nosy cow I opened it – in it, slipped into the lush red velvet interior, was a ring. Why did Suzi have a ring in her pocket? It looked kind of valuable, the stone sparkled in the dim light almost like a . . . I studied it carefully. It *was* a bloody diamond! Nothing else sparkled like that.

Suzi slipped onto the sofa beside me. "Are you OK?" she asked. "You look kind of pale?"

I held the ring up in front of her face. She blushed

a deep scarlet, visible even under her even golden tan.

"Well?" I asked. "Is this what I think it is?"

Suzi sighed. "I'm sorry. Terrible timing I know, what with Jack and . . ."

I stared at her in amazement. "You mean this *is* an engagement ring?"

"Yes," she whispered. "I was going to wait a few weeks to tell you – when you felt a bit better. I'm sorry."

I felt really bad. Poor Suzi had been listening to me drone on about Jack Daly when she had news of her own. Huge news, the news of the year. The century even.

"Suzi," I leant over and gave her a hug, "I'm the one who should be sorry." Tears welled up in my eyes and I'm embarrassed to admit they were a mixture of tears of happiness for her and tears of regret for me. I was her big sister after all – it was supposed to be me getting hitched first. I tried to stop feeling sorry for myself. It wasn't every day your sister got engaged.

"Oh, Suzi, how exciting! I'm so happy for you." I wiped away a genuine 'happy for you' tear. "I don't know what to say."

"Thanks, sis," Suzi beamed back. She took the ring out of my hand and slipped it onto her ring finger.

"Amy?" she asked smiling at me. "Will you be my bridesmaid?"

"Of course, I'd love to," I lied. I mean what could I say? She was my sister. I'd only been bridesmaid once before when I was eleven at my cousin John's wedding.

I'd worn a dark pink raw-silk dress with tiny pale pink rosebuds sewn onto the puff sleeves. I still cringed when I looked at the photos. Doing my duty once more wouldn't kill me. At least that's what I thought at the time.

Suzi spent the rest of the evening trying not to talk about her wedding. After a while I could see it was killing her not to discuss the plans. She mentioned a wedding dress and then quickly changed the subject.

"It's all right," I lied for the second time. "I'd love to hear your dress ideas."

"If you're sure," she said. "I'm just so excited. I can't believe it – me – getting married!"

I smiled. It was going to be a long evening. Maybe we could join Matt and his new friends. I tried to tune in to what Suzi was saying.

"I was thinking of ivory or even pale pink. I saw this amazing dress in *Vogue*. It was a real fairytale affair with loads of pink net and tiny daisies embroidered all over it. Or maybe tartan, but no, it's not a winter wedding. Or what about light-blue or sky-blue? Maybe not. I think classic white or cream. What do you think?"

"Um, yes," I replied smiling. I hoped it was the right answer. I kept thinking about Jack. I could be planning my wedding now instead of Suzi. And I knew exactly what I wanted. Small wedding – just family and close friends in the local church, big party the following night for the rest of my family and friends. I'd mapped it all out years ago and refined the details until it was perfect. Trendy and fun but classy. I'd decorate the church and the tables myself. With my own vows and my own readings . . .

"Amy? Pink and yellow?" Suzi asked.

"Sorry?"

"About the flowers. Pink and yellow or lilies. Or daisies."

"Wow, I'm not sure, Suzi. It would depend on the dress, I suppose."

She smiled beatifically. "Yes, of course, you're right."

Bingo! Right answer.

"I think Matt is waving at us," I said hopefully. He wasn't, but it was enough to distract Suzi.

"We have been a bit antisocial, I guess," she said anxiously.

I picked up our drinks and stood up. "We should join him. Rude not to," I stated before she had a chance to think about it.

Matt was in the middle of recounting an Australian rules joke as we shoved our way through the crowds towards him.

"Here she is, my beautiful Irish Sheila. All right, Suzi?"

"Hi, Matt," Suzi beamed, wiggling her way to his side. He threw his arm over her shoulder and held her to his chest.

"Hi, babe," he said, kissing the top of her head.

"I told Amy," she bubbled, unable to keep it in for one second longer.

"We're getting married!" Matt informed the whole bar in booming tones, delighted that he didn't have to keep it in any longer. "And you're all invited!"

Suzi dug him in the ribs. "Matt, this is Ireland. You can't say things like that."

I laughed. "She's right, you know. They might all turn up at the wedding!" I kissed my prospective brother-in-law on the cheek. "Congratulations, Matt."

"Thanks, Amy," he grinned. "I'm a lucky man."

"I'm the lucky one," Suzi trilled.

And I'm the unlucky one, I thought to myself darkly.

* * *

Suzi drove us all home at half past ten. We'd meant to leave earlier but the Clontarf boys kept buying us drinks. They'd already installed Matt on the seconds and written his training times and first game on a napkin for him. Suzi was half-delighted and half-dismayed.

"I don't want him to turn into one of those rugby husbands who sees his wife and kids whenever the lads let him," she moaned.

"Kids?" I smiled. The last round – champagne – was beginning to go to my head.

Suzi blushed. "Maybe, eventually." She smiled. "Stop slagging me."

"Wouldn't dream of it," I laughed. It really was good to have Suzi back.

We drove back slowly. Suzi was a bit nervous on the road, not that either Matt or I would have noticed what side of the road my car was on. I hoped Mum and Dad would understand.

"Matt?" I asked as we drove past Foxrock Church. "Do your folks know about the wedding?"

No answer. I looked into the back seat. Matt was fast asleep, head resting against the side window, his warm breath misting up the glass.

"Yes," Suzi answered for him. "They were thrilled. Molly and Dan are great, you'll like them. A little mad but good fun. Matt has a very cute little brother too, Luke."

"Oh, don't you start," I complained.

"What did I say?"

"Sorry, I didn't mean to snap. It's just people."

"What are you talking about, Amy?" My poor sister was confused. But I guess I wasn't making much sense – to anyone other than myself that is. I tried to explain.

"People keep trying to set me up with any old man and I'm sick of it," I said eventually. It wasn't exactly what I meant but it was near enough. "I'm not a basket case. Don't treat me like one."

"A what?" Suzi asked.

"You know – mad. I can get my own men, thank you very much. I don't need help."

"I didn't mean . . ."

I was being hard on Suzi and it wasn't fair. I felt bad – again.

* * *

"Matt, Matt, we're here," Suzi got out of the car, opened the side door and started shaking him.

"High tackle. Run the ball, run the ball," Matt muttered, waking up. He opened his eyes. "Hi, Suzi," he hiccuped, eyes crinkling as he beamed up at her.

"Come on, love. We're here now," Suzi cajoled. She tried to pull him out of the car. I stood beside her, watching the scene. "Give us a hand, will you, Amy?" Suzi asked in desperation. Matt was a hulking sixteen stone or so and there was no way us puny, not to mention unfit (on my part!), lightweights would be able to shift him.

"Matt, if you come inside I'll make you a sandwich," I coaxed. Surely a man that size must like his food. I was right.

"What kinda sandwich?" he asked with interest.

"Meat," Suzi whispered. "Any kind of meat."

"Um, beef," I lied. I knew there was some old, curling-at-the-edges ham in the fridge as I'd thought about eating a slice for lunch before thinking better of it. But he was hardly likely to notice in the state he was in.

"OK," he stated. "Where's the kitchen?"

Suzi and I giggled as he lumbered out of the car and stood up straight.

"He's not used to champagne," Suzi whispered.

The light went on in the hall as we helped Matt towards the door.

"Shit," Suzi said.

Mum opened the door, Dad standing just behind her. The doorstep was bathed in golden light and Matt and I squinted at it from behind Suzi's back. I was trying to appear sober by fixing my eyes on the red and blue stained-glass side-panels on the door. It seemed to stop the swaying anyway.

"Suzi, my darling," Mum gushed, putting her arms around her and giving her a warm hug. Then she noticed Matt who was cowering behind Suzi. He could sense an awkward situation when he saw one. She unwrapped her arms from Suzi and looked at me with a dangerous glint in her eye. "Amy! Tonight of all nights. Have you no sense of decorum?"

"He's not mine!" I wailed before I could help myself.

Suzi smiled sheepishly. "Mum, Dad, this is Matt. My fiancé."

Chapter 3

Matt and I sat at the kitchen table tucking into two huge sandwiches – cheese and tomato for me, and ham and everything I could find in the fridge for him. He had some appetite – he was making proverbial mincemeat of the sandwich and sloshing down a pint of milk which left a cute ring around his manly mouth. I couldn't help myself – I noticed these things even when half-cut. I really had to stop.

I could hear raised voices coming from the living-room where Suzi, Mum and Dad were ensconced. Mum had nearly fainted on the doorstep when Suzi had broken the news. Luckily Dad was behind her to steady her. He had brought her into the living-room and sat her down on the sofa while we all followed behind anxiously. Otherwise she would have come a cropper on the hard tiled floor of the hall. I could just see it now as a headline in *The Star* – 'Mother Struck Dead by

Daughter's Confession'. I was trying not to laugh. I have a terrible habit of giggling when I'm nervous. Matt didn't seem to know what was going on, poor lamb.

As soon as Mum was settled on the sofa, Dad took matters into his own hands. "Amy, bring Matthew into the kitchen and make your mother a cup of tea with lots of sugar." He smiled at Suzi who was quivering in her Converse. "Don't worry, pet. You just gave your Mum a bit of a shock. She'll be grand. Now where's my hug?"

I directed Matt down the three steps into the kitchen. He gave his head a bit of a bang on the door-frame, which is a little low. But he didn't seem to notice.

"Who were they?" he asked in confusion as I pulled two plates out of the wooden drainer above the sink.

I smiled. "Your future parents-in-law."

As we were eating Dad came in. "Is your Mum's tea ready?" he asked.

"Sorry, Dad. I forgot."

"Don't worry," he replied. "I'll do it." He flicked on the kettle and waited while it boiled.

"How's Mum?" I asked.

"Fine. Suzi just gave her a bit of a fright. She explained about Johnnie Fox's and the Clontarf rugby team buying you champagne. I'm not surprised you two are feeling a little under the weather." He smiled at Matt. "Sorry. It wasn't the warmest of welcomes, mate." Dad held out his hand. "I'm Frank O'Sullivan. And you've met my wife, Denise."

Matt wiped his mayonnaise-covered fingers on his jeans before taking Dad's hand. "Matt Street. Pleasure's all mine."

Dad sat down at the table and began to talk to Matt. "Suzi tells us you're a bit of a rugby player. Used to play myself . . ." And they were off. The usual male-bonding session focusing on sport, sport and more sport. I made Mum's tea and brought it up to her.

The door of the living-room was ajar and I stopped for a moment outside. I didn't want to interrupt anything, you understand. They were talking about weddings. It hadn't taken long!

"We'll have to ask Father Lucas about the garden, Suzi. You may have to get officially married in a church or a registry office. But he might give a blessing in the garden."

The garden! She hadn't told me about the garden bit. "Suzi, are you getting married in the garden?" I asked, walking carefully towards the conspiring pair on the sofa, trying to keep the tea in the mug and off the floorboards.

"Maybe, or St Martin's. I did tell you. You mustn't have been listening."

I smiled sheepishly at her. She was probably right.

"Here's your tea, Mum." I handed over the mug.

"Isn't it wonderful news?" Mum glowed. "Suzi and Matt. Who would have thought? I'd heard about the wonderful Matt in Suzi's letters, of course. But finally – a wedding. And this summer. Isn't it exciting?"

I murmured assent under my breath. I was beginning to feel a bit left out if the truth be told. I decided to go to bed and to leave them all to it. I gave Suzi a kiss and said goodnight.

"You're not going already?" Mum asked and then added gently, "Oh my God, Amy, I'm so sorry. I'd forgotten . . . what with all the excitement . . ."

"It's fine. I'm fine. I'm just tired. I have to work tomorrow," I stated quickly. Then it dawned on me. I really did have to work tomorrow. I had to don my Story Princess hat and tell stories to little hyperactive brats for two hours in the bookshop. A nightmare at the best of times, but with a hangover – pure hell!

I staggered up the stairs to my bedroom. As I walked in the door I felt miserable. I was thirty in a few months and I was still living at home, in the same bedroom I'd slept in since I was a child. It had the same yellow walls, Victorian iron-framed bed and huge mahogany chest of drawers. Nothing was different except the bedcovers. Instead of a Garfield duvet cover I now had a plain white one with tiny yellow daisies embroidered on it. It was from the single bed in the guest room of our old house – mine and Jack's. I started crying. I couldn't help it. I pulled off my clothes and crawled into bed in my underwear. I didn't care about my still made-up face. Blocked pores were the least of my worries at this stage. I remembered to set my alarm and then fell soundly asleep as soon as my head hit the pillow.

* * *

I walked into the kitchen in my white towelling dressing-gown the next morning wincing my eyes. My head was throbbing and I felt like death. Mum was chopping tomatoes at the counter, dressed in a perfectly laundered light-blue tracksuit and sparkling white runners. Why did my tracksuit never look like that?

"Morning, love," she said cheerfully. "I'm just cooking Matthew an Irish breakfast. Would you like one?"

My stomach lurched. I wasn't quite sure if it was indicating repulsion to food or hunger. I decided to risk it. I needed sustenance to cope with work. "Thanks, Mum, that would be great. Can I help?"

She smiled. "No, it's all under control. And how are you feeling this morning?"

"A little ropey," I admitted. "Are Suzi and Matt up yet?"

"Matt's out running and Suzi's in the bath."

Running! Was he mad? You can't run with a hangover. It's masochistic.

"Isn't he a nice young man?" Mum asked. "So easy-going and so polite." I couldn't help but feel that she was having a dig at Jack but I decided to ignore it.

"He's lovely," I replied.

"Suzi's a lucky young lady," Mum continued. "He'll make a wonderful husband."

"Um," I replied, opening the Review supplement of *The Sunday Tribune*. You'd want to have rhino-thick skin to live in this house, I thought to myself. I began reading an interesting article on a new children's book.

Suzi walked into the room a few minutes later and sat down at the table. "Amy?" she asked tentatively. "Could we borrow your car today? We're going to look at houses near Clontarf."

"If you drop me into work on your way. I don't have the energy to walk this morning."

"Fine," she agreed.

* * *

An hour later we were driving towards Dublin city. Suzi was at the wheel with Matt beside her and I was in the back. It was quite interesting sitting in the back. I'd never sat there before. I noticed new things about my car, and I even found my pink hairbrush lodged between the upholstery and the side. As we drove past Blackrock College rugby pitches Suzi told Matt about Landsdowne Road and promised to show him the stadium another day. Amazing how sports stadiums could bring out the child in any man, I mused. Jack was into soccer in a big way – Man United were his idols and he had never stopped boring me about the red-jumpered team. It all went in one ear and out the other, of course. At least I wouldn't have to pretend to listen to any of it any more.

I tried to push Jack out of my mind but it was proving difficult. Everything reminded me of him, from music on the radio to certain smells. Especially smells, in fact. Jack had a lemony, clean, boyish smell. It was very attractive and I couldn't get enough of it at one stage. I used to smell the pillows when he'd gone to work and when he was away. I had to stop torturing myself. It was all for the best.

Suzi pulled up outside the bookshop and I hopped out.

"Thanks, Suze," I said. "See you both later." I watched the car drive off. I was trying not to be jealous of my sister but it was hard.

Lynn, the owner and manager, had put the Story Princess board outside the door of the shop. 'Today between two and three the Story Princess will read from *Alice's Adventures in Wonderland* by Lewis Carroll. All welcome.'

I smiled. *Alice* was Lynn's favourite book. Maybe today wouldn't be so bad after all. I mean, reading children stories was hardly 'work', was it? I took a deep breath and smiled again. The shop's window looked wonderful. Lynn had put the Christmas decorations in. A small, real Christmas tree twinkled with white lights. A glorious array of glossy hardback gift-books were displayed against a dark red velvet backdrop. Tiny gold bows adorned each book and handcrafted wooden Christmas decorations hung from the branches of the tree. It looked enchanting.

Lynn was originally from New York, a vibrant and infectiously enthusiastic lady in her early sixties. She wore bright, stylish clothes and always reminded me of a ballet teacher I'd once had when I was in primary school in the way she moved – elegantly and fluidly – with her head held high and her neck and back poker-straight. Good posture you'd call it, I suppose. She had moved to Ireland with her husband, but was now a widow.

I loved working for Lynn. I'd worked for her part-time during college – Arts in UCD – and when I'd graduated she'd offered me a 'proper' job. I hadn't a clue what I wanted to do so I took it. And I'd been there ever since.

As I stepped in the door the bronze bell tinkled. Lynn looked up from the desk where she was reading a new picture-book edition of *The Wizard of Oz*. Perched on her nose were special glasses with green lenses which made the pages glow green, like the Emerald City in the story.

"My, my, you look just like an alien," Lynn smiled. She removed the glasses. "That's better. How are you this good morning?"

I smiled. It was impossible to be in a bad mood with Lynn around. "Grand, thanks. I had a bit of a late night in the end though, so you'll have to go easy on me today."

"And how's Suzi?" she asked warmly. "Happy to be home?"

"Yes," I said. "And wait till I tell you . . ."

"Stop!" Lynn commanded. "Let's get some coffee and you can unravel the whole story."

Soon I had 'unravelled' the whole story as Lynn put it. Matt, Mum and Dad – the whole enchilada.

"It's hard on you, honey. After the whole Jack

thing." I had told Lynn some of the Jack tale. She was a good listener, more like a big sister than a boss.

"I'm fine," I replied. And I would be fine – eventually. "And Suzi's so excited."

The bell tinkled. A man walked in, a large bag over his shoulder and a small, dark-haired girl following closely behind. I stopped talking and went over to help him with the door.

"Thanks," he said as I held the door open for him.

"I'm looking for some books for Zoe," the man said.

"I'm Zoe," the little girl ventured, staring at me intently. She was quite stunning – pale, with huge dark-brown eyes and long black hair which hung in two thin plaits down her back. She was wearing a denim dress, pink woolly tights and tiny red Doc Marten boots.

"Hi, Zoe," I said. "It's very nice to meet you. Now what type of books do you like?"

Silence. Zoe held what I assumed was her Father's hand tightly. He looked at me and smiled warmly.

"She's a little shy today. I think we'll just have a look around for a bit if that's all right." He had a lovely smile. Blond hair, tightly cropped, bright-blue eyes, dressed in black from top to toe like a movie star. He was in his late twenties or early thirties, it was hard to tell, and he had a Southern English accent, soft and attractive.

"Of course," I smiled, trying to concentrate. Things were bad when I started sizing up Fathers! Although he wasn't wearing a wedding ring – I sneaked a look at his ring finger.

Zoe stared at me again. "Are you the Story Princess?" she asked quietly.

"I am," I replied.

"I'd like a princess book, I think," she whispered.

"Let's see what I can find," I smiled. The bell rang as Siobhan Molloy, and her three girls, regular Sunday customers, walked in the door. Lynn greeted them and the girls, all dedicated readers, made their way under the golden arch and into the fiction room at the back of the shop. Lynn had designed and decorated the shop herself and it was a child's heaven, full of nooks and crannies, cloud-painted ceilings and specially crafted bookshelves in the shapes of dragons, the Children of Lir, Matilda and other favourite children's book characters.

I flicked through the picture-books with Zoe by my side.

"Princesses," I murmured. "Let's see. *The Little Princess* by Frances Hodgson Burnett." I pulled out an illustrated edition of the children's classic. "I love this story. It's all about a little girl who's a princess but she has to stay at this boarding-school while her father is away."

Zoe frowned. "Is she a real princess?"

"She is," I replied, trying not to smile. "Or here's another one – *The Thistle Princess* by Vivian French." I opened the book and flicked through the pages. "Look at the pictures – beautiful, aren't they?"

Zoe smiled. "I like the colours. Pink's my favourite, you know."

Her Dad was standing behind us, listening.

"Would you like me to read to you, Zoe?" he asked.

The little girl nodded firmly. Soon their heads were buried in *The Thistle Princess*.

I looked at them and sighed. I loved seeing Dads and their kids but it always made me feel jealous. I could hear my biological clock ticking away at times as loudly as the hands on my ancient bronze alarm clock. It's not that I wanted kids, well, not right then. But I would have liked the option. Jack was never big into children at all. He hadn't much time for them really. It was different for him I supposed. He didn't have fermenting eggs in him. I mused on the unfairness of it all for a few minutes.

"Amy, are you OK?" Lynn joined me at the counter where I was staring listlessly at the computer screen. "You've been staring at that thing for ages. It's not healthy."

I tore my eyes away.

"Sorry, I was in another world."

"Are you ready for the story session? If you're not up to it, I'll do it." Lynn smiled. She really was very kind. But I knew she had Internet orders to process.

"I'm fine, honestly," I tried to appear enthusiastic. "I'm looking forward to *Alice*. I'm going to read the Cheshire Cat chapter."

"Good choice," Lynn enthused. "I'll leave you to get ready."

Lynn sat down on the stool behind the counter and accessed our e-mail to collect the on-line orders. As we were a small specialist shop the Internet was important to our business. We had customers from all over the world, Japan to North America, many of whom relied on Lynn's expertise. She had a doctorate on children's book illustration and was especially keen on the work of the young Irish illustrator P J Lynch who was a personal friend of hers. She was quite a woman!

I fetched the Story Princess hat from the back room and set the little wooden chairs and bean bags in a circle at the back of the shop, beside the Enchanted Castle shelves which held the Irish picture-books. The shop was beginning to fill up. Siobhan's daughters sat down at the front, gazing up at me expectantly. Although they were well able to read themselves they still loved to hear stories told aloud. Zoe and her father sat down behind them, followed by two small boys and several other children.

I began. "I'm the Story Princess and today I'm going to read to you from *Alice's Adventures in Wonderland* by Lewis Carroll." The shop went quiet as all eyes were on me. It was a strange feeling but I liked it.

When I first started the story-telling sessions I felt self-conscious and nervous, but Lynn made me stick with it and I began to look forward to them. Children were an unforgiving audience but an honest one. You had to work hard to hold their attention. "Alice is lost in the woods and she spots a strange cat sitting in a tree above her head. And now I'll begin. 'Cheshire Puss,' Alice began rather timidly. 'Would you tell me, please, which way I ought to go from here?' 'That depends a good deal on where you want to get to,' said the Cat . . ."

After the story my audience clapped and Clara, Siobhan's eldest daughter, a serious girl of eleven bought a copy of the book to read to her sisters at home.

"Thanks, we really enjoyed that," Zoe's Father shook my hand warmly. "Can I buy these?" He handed me a pile of hardback picture-books, including the ones I'd chosen earlier for Zoe.

"Of course, come over to the desk and I'll wrap them for you." I placed the pile on the desk and began to put them through the till. "Oh, I love this one," I smiled as I noticed the cover of *Where the Wild Things Are.*

"It's for me," he smiled. "I love it too. I'm Steve by the way and you've met Zoe."

"I'm Amy," I faltered, blushing. I just couldn't help it. He was so damn nice. Why did they always have to be married?

I bagged his books and gave him his credit card back. And of course I read the name. Stephen J Jones. There had to be some good things about working in a shop after all.

"Goodbye, Steve. And Zoe. See you again." Zoe put her small hand out and Steve grasped it firmly. He smiled. "I hope so."

I gazed out the window after they had left.

"So do I," I whispered. So what if he was married? I could always dream. And maybe he had a nice brother or a friend – who knew? I liked to keep the options open.

Lynn sidled over to me. "Cute, isn't he?" Typical, caught in the act. "You know who he is, of course?"

I stared at her, feigning indifference. "Who?"

"Don't play the innocent with me, young lady," she laughed.

"OK, OK," I sighed. " I admit it, he was nice. So put me out of my misery. Who is he then?"

"Stevie J."

"The Stevie J?"

"Yep!"

"The Stevie J who writes those amazing fantasy books?"

"The very same." Stevie J was an English writer and one of the most famous children's book personalities in the world. His books, based on the adventures of a young wizard called Henry, had sold in their millions and Spielberg was filming the first one.

"And," she grinned mischievously, "he's single and living in Dublin. The little girl is his niece."

"And how do you know that exactly?" I asked amazed. Maybe there was a God.

"Female intuition," she laughed. "And his website!"

Chapter 4

I smiled to myself as I walked down Seapoint Road towards Jodie's flat. Stevie J. I intended to tell Jodie all about my encounter. Not that she would have a clue who he was. But she was always interested in cute guys, no matter who they were. She was pretty much permanently single, by choice and not by design. She'd had one or two 'boyfriends' but they never lasted long. Jodie had unbelievably high standards and wouldn't take any shit from a guy. Which made relationships almost impossible. After all, men and trouble go together hand in glove.

It was nice to think about another guy. I knew I'd probably never see Stevie J again and if he did happen to come into the shop again nothing would happen. What was I going to do – ask him out while he was paying for a book?

"That's ten pounds, please. And by the way how

about dinner tonight?" I didn't think so. Not after the waiter episode. Never, ever again.

"Of course you can ask guys out," Jodie had stated one Sunday in June. "They love it. Remember Liam from Club 92? I asked him out."

"Jodie, he'd already bought you three drinks and you'd been dancing with him all night. And I thought you said he dropped hints all night, like 'What do you do at the weekends?'"

Jodie smiled. "OK, you're right. But I still made the arrangement, didn't I?"

"Um, I suppose," I muttered. Everything was always so black and white in Jodie's world. Life seemed to be so much easier for her than for me. She knew exactly what she wanted and stuck to it no matter what. I was a bit more of a 'grey' sort of person. I didn't find life all that simple or easy at all. In fact some days I found it downright hard to get out of bed. 'Moody', my mother called me. I guess sometimes I thought about things too much. I've always found it hard not to. Made for many a sleepless night as three in the morning seemed my brain's favourite time to think about things. Three in the morning until six in the morning. Then I always fell into a comatose sleep and felt really groggy and crap at seven when I had to get up.

There was this really nice waiter in the Café Java in Blackrock and whenever we went in he always chatted to us and smiled over when he was serving other people. Jodie and I got talking to him one day when the café was quiet. He told us he was a student. After a few weeks he began to sit down at our table and chew the fat for a few minutes. He was really interested in interiors and found Jodie's work fascinating. Jodie reckoned he fancied me. I reckoned he was lonely and liked a natter.

So one day, while Jodie excused herself to go the loo (planned of course!) I mortified myself.

"Um, Joel, I was wondering . . . um, if perhaps you'd, um . . ."

Joel had looked up from his mug of hot chocolate with interest. "Yes?"

I could feel myself blushing. But I couldn't stop now.

"I was wondering if you'd like to go out for a drink sometime?"

Joel seemed very surprised. He gazed at me intently. "You and me?"

I was wringing my hands under the table in embarrassment. "Um, yes."

He had smiled nervously. "That's really nice of you but I guess I should come clean. I'm still in school and . . ."

"What?" I exclaimed, turning heads. I tried to ignore their interested stares.

He continued unabashed. "But if that doesn't bother you . . . I like older women and . . ."

I interrupted him right there. "What age are you exactly?" I emphasised the word 'exactly'.

"Seventeen."

"I see," I cringed. "I'm sorry. I should have realised. You just look so much older. Stupid of me. Forget it."

He looked disappointed. But I guess to most seventeen-year-olds the whole Mrs Robinson thing is dead exciting. Teenagers have too many bloody hormones for their own good.

"Pity," he shrugged his shoulders. "But if you ever change your mind . . . Shit, the boss is staring over. I'd better get back to work."

When Jodie returned I was almost crawling under the table. I had both my hands over my by-now-scarlet face.

"Well?" she asked, sitting down. "Did you ask him?"

"Jodie, can we go now? You pay and I'll settle up with you later." I jumped up and grabbed my bag from under the table. Luckily, Joel seemed to be in the kitchen.

Before she could answer I was out the door. When she found me outside I was still cringing.

"Are you OK?" she asked gently. "What happened?"

"He's seventeen," I whispered.

"Sorry?" she spluttered.

"I've just made a bloody fool of myself !"

She started laughing. "I'm sorry, Amy. I can't help it. I know you like younger men but seventeen . . ."

"He told us he was a student! I assumed he was in college, not school." I stated strongly. "I blame you. You shouldn't have encouraged me."

Jodie was holding her hand over her mouth and trying not to laugh.

Luckily for her I began to see the funny side and began laughing myself. In seconds we were creased up on the pavement, holding our sides.

"I can't believe it," I gasped. "He's so cute."

"Maybe his Dad's available," Jodie said, taking a deep gulp of air to get her breath back.

We didn't go back to Café Java for a few weeks, I couldn't face it although Jodie kept telling me not to be so stupid. And when we did go back Joel had left. Pity really – he was a nice guy regardless of his ineligibility.

I vowed never to ask another guy out for a drink in my whole entire life. So that was out. Stevie J was just a nice distraction, something to think about. I liked having someone on my mind, a cute guy to dream about. I liked to lie in bed and imagine my perfect wedding and it was easier if I had a real face on the bridegroom. Somehow it made it a little spooky if I didn't. Like a black and white horror film – *The Faceless Bridegroom*. I wondered if everyone did this – visualise their future wedding in their head for years and years? Maybe they did. So now Stevie J could take Jack's place in my daydream.

* * *

As I approached Jodie's place I noticed a dark green MG parked in the drive. Jack has the same car, I thought. Damn, I kept being reminded of him.

Jodie lived in this amazing basement flat in an old house that belonged to her granny. Granny O'Connell lived on the ground and first floors. She had given her eldest grandchild the basement floor in a 'living will' six years ago. It all sounded a little morbid if you ask me but I guess it made sense. Jodie had knocked down a lot of the interior walls – except the load-bearing ones, and stripped some of the walls and hefty supporting pillars right back to the bare stone. She created two large bedrooms, a huge bathroom, a study and a massive open plan living-room-cum-kitchen. The whole flat was painted white, with some terracotta on selected walls. Gigantic wall-to-wall mirrors, elaborate floor-standing candelabras and halogen spotlighting gave the living-room a dramatic Gothic look.

In each bedroom Jodie had created a 'four-poster bed' by draping white muslin over self-constructed curving metal hoops which were attached to the ceiling with chain. The wardrobes and dressingtables were old pieces which Dad had recovered from a Georgian house on Merrion Road. Jodie had stripped them down to the bare wood and given them a 'distressed' look with light-green paint and furniture wax.

At the time she was working in an interiors shop in Blackrock. After the flat was finished she had a house-warming party and everyone was blown away by what she had done to the place. One friend of her mum's, the wife of a 'Captain of Industry', asked her to redesign and decorate her house from top to bottom. Jodie transformed the place and it soon became the talk of the town and was featured in *Image Interiors* magazine.

Soon Jodie had more work than she knew what to do with. She packed in her day-job and formed Dream House, her own interior-design company. Jodie had a natural talent but she also worked bloody hard in the first few years. We were dead proud of her, me and Beth.

Jodie would ring me in a desperate state some evenings or weekends. "Amy, I need you! Bring Beth." And Beth and I would be handed a stubby paint-brush and a stencil or a paint-stripper and set to work. It was fun though. Now Jodie had three full-time employees and a secretary. She'd done well. Put myself and Beth to shame really. Beth works as a PA to Louise Keily, the designer. Sounds glamorous but it's not. She likes it though.

I crossed the road and stood at the top of Jodie's steps. I stared at the MG which was parked beside Jodie's Range Rover on the gravel to the right of the house. It was a 2000 reg, just like Jack's. In fact it had a similar number plate – with three sixes. We used to joke that it was the 'devil's car'. Suddenly something clicked in my head. It was Jack's number plate! 00 – D – 29666. Bloody hell. What was Jack doing in Jodie's place? He was hardly visiting Granny O'Connell. They must be talking about me, I thought. I walked over to the car to make sure. It was Jack's all right. His grey fleece jacket was still on the back ledge just where it had been weeks ago.

Just then I heard Granny O'Connell's voice call down from her doorstep.

"Hello, Amy, how are you?" She came down the steps with Laddy, her old black Labrador, sloping along beside her.

"Fine thanks, Mrs O'Connell. And you?"

"Grand. I'm just taking Laddy for a walk." She looked at the MG. "Nice, isn't it? It's been here since yesterday evening. Jodie's new man. She was making him a fine dinner last night. Lucky fellow."

My heart jumped and I suddenly felt sick. I could feel the blood draining from my face.

"Are you all right?" Mrs O'Connell asked. "You look like you've seen a ghost."

Jodie and Jack. Jack and Jodie. She was my friend. How could she do this to me?

"I'm fine, " I muttered. "Just tired. Been working. Have to go now." I scuttled off quickly. It was rude I know but I didn't know what else to do. I didn't want to break down crying in front of Jodie's Granny. I just wanted to be on my own. I ran down the side road which led to the Martello tower. When I felt safely away from Mrs O'Connell I sat down on a wooden bench and gazed out at the sea. My eyes filled with tears and soon I was sobbing my heart out.

Thoughts went rushing through my head. How long had it been going on? While Jack and I were still together? Was she going to tell me? They were probably both laughing at me right now. How could I have been so stupid? He never loved me, he was just trying to get close to Jodie.

I pulled out my mobile phone and rang Beth.

"Beth?"

"Amy, is that you? Are you all right?"

"Nooo," I wailed.

"Where are you?" she asked. "At home?"

"Nooo."

"Are you crying?"

"Yesss."

"Amy," Beth said gently, "tell me where you are."

I tried to talk, but it was hard. I'd been crying so hard that there was a huge lump in my throat and my breath was out of synch. I gulped.

"Take a deep breath, love. You'll be OK. Just tell me where you are."

"The tower . . . in Blackrock."

"The tower?" she asked a little confused. Then it came to her. We often walked along the seafront and she knew I liked the Martello tower. "The Martello tower?"

"Yes."

"Stay right there. I'll be two minutes. OK?"

"OK." I held the phone in my two hands on my knee like a safety blanket. I felt calmer now I knew that Beth was coming. She was brilliant when I was upset. She always knew how to make me feel better. Now and again my bad moods would last days, weeks even and she accepted that. Sometimes more than a bad mood, a touch of depression really. But only Beth and my family knew that. Jack had never really understood and I could never explain to him properly. I just put a brave face on things and hoped the blackness would go away. The doctor suggested pills at one stage but I was loath to take them. Somehow if I dealt with it myself, without medication, it seemed less serious to me – something I could deal with on my own. And a while back, when I'd been really bad, I'd gone for a few sessions of counselling with a friend of Mum's called Dr Shiels and that had seemed to help.

When we were kids Beth had lived across the road from me. We'd known each other since we were seven. We'd grown up together and knew each other back to front and inside out. She now lived in Dun Laoghaire with Tony, a computer programmer from Sutton. I'd first met Jack through him – they were old college friends.

Beth was the kindest and the strongest person I knew. And I needed her right now.

I kept my head down until I heard her gentle voice beside me.

"Amy?" She sat down on the bench and put her two arms around me. "That's it, love. Cry if you want to. Let it all out." She held me as huge sobs racked my body.

I wanted to tell her about Jack and Jodie. About what they'd done to me. But I was crying too much.

When I'd stopped enough to talk I lifted my head and tried to explain.

"It's Jack. And Jodie. They're . . . together."

Beth looked at me carefully. "What?"

"I saw his car and Granny O'Connell said he'd stayed and she'd made him dinner. Dinner!"

Beth was confused. "Granny O'Connell made Jack dinner?"

"No," I wailed. "Jodie."

"Jodie made Jack dinner?"

"Yes!"

"Are you sure?"

I looked at her and she could see the answer in my heartbroken eyes.

Beth was quiet for a second. "I don't know what to say. I'm so sorry, love." She held me close again and sighed. "Let's go back to my place and I'll make you something to eat."

Food was the last thing on my mind but it would be some distraction, I supposed. "OK," I mumbled.

Beth stood up and keeping her arm around me walked me to her car. It was warm inside and we drove in silence towards her house. Beth avoided going past Jodie's house which was probably for the best. In my state I don't think I could have taken any more and seeing Jack's car still outside would have sent me over the edge.

Chapter 5

"Here we are," Beth smiled as she pulled up outside her small redbrick townhouse across the road from Dun Laoghaire library. She and Tony had bought it together a couple of years ago, before the property market had gone mental.

"Tony's playing on the Internet at Jed's house so we have the place to ourselves." Jed was another computer programmer, a lanky South Park fan who I'd never paid much attention to.

I tried to smile but my mouth wouldn't co-operate. "Thanks."

I opened the car door and pulled myself out of Beth's Honda Civic. Why were they built so bloody low on the ground? I muttered to myself, cursing Beth's choice of car ungraciously. I felt exhausted and my head throbbed, but at least I'd stopped crying.

Beth locked the car and smiled hopefully at me again.

"Are you OK?" she asked kindly. I grunted.

I felt terrible for being such an old bag. Beth was being so nice to me and I was being a pain in the ass. The worst thing was that I knew it. I knew how painful and childish I could be when I was in this kind of irrational mood, but I couldn't help it. Luckily, patience was one of Beth's many virtues. She put her arm around me and I tried to shrug it off. But she was having none of it.

"Amy," she stared at me, her brown eyes betraying her concern. "I'm trying to help you. Don't shut me out."

She was right. I was being obtuse and unreasonable. It wasn't her fault I hurt so badly that I wanted to curl up and die.

"Sorry," I mumbled and began to cry again.

"Let's get you inside," she said brightly, "and I'll make you a cup of tea."

"Tea," I spat, glaring at her. "I don't want tea."

Beth sighed. It was going to be a long evening. She opened the yellow front door and stood back.

"In you go," Beth commanded in her headmistress voice. She followed behind me, switching on the tiny halogen lights which were set into the ceiling in the small, narrow hall. She opened the door to the living-room and placed a hand on the small of my back. The room was warm and inviting. Beth flicked on the uplighter in the corner, illuminating the terracotta-painted room with a soft, gentle glow.

"Lie down on the sofa and I'll get you a duvet."

"Don't be thick," I wailed. "I'm not sick."

Beth smiled. "You sound like one of your Dr Seuss books. Don't be thick, I'm not sick. Don't be slow, go, go, go."

I wasn't amused. I glared at her again.

"No," Beth hesitated, "you're not sick. But you are in shock and you need to rest. I'll be back in a second."

I looked around the room from my now bolt-upright position. Beth had changed the curtains, I noticed in my distracted state. They used to be a busy pink floral design which had come with the house. But now heavy cream linen curtains hung in their place. I scowled. Beth should have told me about the new curtains, I thought irritably. Why hadn't she told me? I bet she'd told Jodie. Bloody Jodie . . .

Anyway I was damned if I was going to be treated like a child! I didn't need to lie down. I needed to . . . and in a blinding flash I knew what I needed to do. I needed to hurt Jodie. Physically or mentally – either would do. I needed to smack her smug little face from here to kingdom come. Or tell her what a bitch she was, what a lying, conniving, Cruella de Ville of a traitor. Of course, I thought hysterically. I'll ring her. I pulled my mobile out of my jacket pocket and punched in Jodie's name.

"Hello? Amy?" Jodie asked uncertainly. For a moment I was caught off guard – I'd forgotten that her mobile would recognise mine instantly. I gulped. I was so angry that speech evaded me.

"Amy? Are you there?"

I wiped away my tears with the back of my hand and sniffed loudly.

"Oh Jesus, Amy," Jodie whispered, the penny dropping with a resounding clunk. "Gran said you called by . . . she said you'd seen . . . I'm so sorry . . . I . . ."

"Fuck you," I screamed down the phone. *"You bitch, you fucking bitch . . ."*

Beth lashed down the stairs, dropping the duvet she was carrying on the floor of the hall and pounced on me, pulling the phone out of my shaking hand. She clicked it off and focused on my tear-stained face.

"What are you doing?" she asked, sitting down beside me and taking my hands in hers. "That's not going to make you feel any better. You're in no state to talk to anyone, especially to Jodie." She stroked my hands gently.

I erupted into huge, racking sobs which thundered through my entire body. She was right again.

"Lie down," she commanded in a steely voice and I assented – I was too tired not to. Beth reclaimed the duvet from the hall floorboards and placed it over me, tucking it around my body. She placed a cushion under my head and sat on the floor beside me stroking my hair.

"It will be all right, Amy," she crooned over and over again. "I'm here now, love. You'll be OK."

Later I woke up and opened my swollen eyes. My head throbbed and my body felt like it had been through ten rounds with Muhammad Ali. Although I'd recently seen *Once We Were Kings*, the documentary about the American boxer and I didn't think he'd rate me as much of an opponent. 'Fly like a butterfly, sting like a bee'. I chanted Muhammad's catch phrase over and over like a mantra. He'd had his fair share of troubles, had poor old Muhammad. Yes, I really was losing it.

"Amy?" Beth interrupted my rambling thoughts. She was standing in the doorway with my mobile in her hand. "You should ring your mum. It's getting late and she'll be worried about you."

I sat up gingerly, trying not to move my head too much. I felt strangely hollow, all cried out. I gave Beth a stilted half-smile.

"OK," I nodded.

She eyeballed me carefully. "Jodie rang your mobile a couple of times earlier. I just thought you should know."

My eyes narrowed and I could feel a fiery ball of rage entering my heart once more.

"Amy, leave it," Beth advised. "Talk to her tomorrow. I didn't answer so she has no idea you're here. Why don't you stay the night? Things will seem clearer in the morning."

I glared at her. "Things are crystal clear to me right now, thank you very much," I said, trying to stay calm and giving her a withering look.

"Um," Beth gulped and continued bravely, "ring your mum."

I took the phone from her and thought about screaming abuse at Jodie again. I was sorely tempted but I knew it would disappoint Beth. Although at this stage she had probably despaired of me already.

"Hi, Suzi."

"Amy, where are you? You missed dinner."

I pushed back my sleeve and stared at my pink Baby G watch. Shit, it was almost nine o'clock. I'd been asleep for nearly three hours!

"Oh, yeah," I said vaguely, "I lost track of the time, sorry."

"Jodie was looking for you," Suzi said. "She rang a couple of times and she called in. Is something up?"

Suzi wasn't stupid.

"No," I said without hesitation. "Tell Mum I'm staying at . . . at a friend's house."

I could almost hear Suzi smile. She presumed that there was a man involved, of course. I wish.

"A friend? Sounds interesting. Anyone I know? Is he cute?" she bubbled.

I wasn't in the mood. I sighed. "Bye, see you tomorrow."

"Wait, Amy," Suzi interjected. "What will I tell Jodie if she rings? She said your mobile didn't seem to be working. Will I tell her you'll ring her?"

"No!" I stated emphatically, raising my voice to a dangerous level. "You can tell her to go fuck herself!"

"Oh," Suzi whispered, shocked.

I suddenly felt bad. It wasn't her fault that Jodie had

betrayed me. "I'm sorry," I apologised. "Forget I said that. I'm sorry." I started to cry again.

"What's wrong?" Suzi asked with concern. "Where are you, Amy? Will I come and get you?"

"I'm fine," I sobbed. "I'm at Beth's, but don't tell Jodie."

"OK," Suzi promised. "But I'm worried about you. I'm here if you need me."

"Thanks," I whispered.

Beth left me alone for a little bit while she cooked. She came back into the living-room carrying a large tray.

"Dinner," she stated. "And I'm making you eat it whether you like it or not."

I stared at the tray which she placed on the low pine coffee table in front of me. Lasagne and chips and a large tub of cookies and cream Häagen-Dazs.

I smiled. Comfort food at its very finest. "There goes the waistline," I hiccuped, my tears abating.

Beth handed me a calorific plateful and a knife and fork. "I ran up to the video shop while you were asleep," she smiled, kneeling beside the video with a pile of tapes beside her. "You can choose – *Children of the Corn Part 5, Scream 4* or *Nightmare on Elm Street Returns.*"

"Beth!" I yelled. "Are you trying to kill me?" She knew I hated horror films, especially big-budget ones with no plot.

"I'm only joking," she grinned. "*Rear Window* or *Casablanca*?"

I smiled. Beth was such a sweetie. She'd be much happier watching bad television but she knew I couldn't stand it.

"Beth?" I asked sheepishly. "Do you still have my *Field of Dreams* tape?" I'd lent it to her months ago when she was off work with the flu and bored out of her skull.

"Oops, sorry, I thought I'd given it back to you," she said uncertainly, flicking through the tapes piled neatly in a stack at the bottom of the bookshelf. "Yes, here it is."

She popped it into the video and rewound it to the beginning.

"Do you mind watching it again?" I asked.

"No, I was out of it on Night Nurse the last time I watched it. And anyway," she added, "Kevin Costner looks great in those tight Levis."

I smiled. "Thanks. Thanks for everything. Sorry for being, well you know . . . difficult earlier."

"It's fine," she said kindly. "That's what friends are for." She sat down on the sofa beside me and we munched away contentedly. I didn't much feel like talking and Beth seemed to understand.

Now *Field of Dreams* is hardly a Hollywood classic but I've always loved it. It's basically the story of a farmer from Iowa (Kevin Costner) who hears a voice in his cornfield. And this voice tells him to plough up his corn and build a baseball field on the land in front of his house. Crazy behaviour as he stands to lose his farm – but he does it! I like the film because it says – follow your dreams, do crazy things, don't worry about what other people think even if they call you mad.

We spent the evening on the sofa, eating and watching dreams come true.

At half past eleven Beth started to yawn which set me off too.

"Bedtime, I think," she said, stretching her arms above her head.

"Where's Tony?" I asked.

"He's staying at Jed's tonight," Beth replied. "He'll get a lift into work with him in the morning. He had no idea about Jack and – you know. He said to say he's very sorry."

I was touched. Tony was a decent guy.

"I don't have to be in work till lunchtime, so we can hang out until then. Louise is away and Holly can hold the fort." Holly was one of Louise's young designers.

"Are you sure?" Beth knew I had tomorrow off. I was relieved. I didn't want to be on my own – my brain would conjure up all sorts of conspiracy plots and elaborate revenge plans.

"I'm sure," she smiled.

"Thanks," I said again. "And Beth?"

"Yes?"

"Were you talking to Jodie?" I couldn't help it, I had to know.

"I left the phone off the hook and my mobile off," she said, looking decidedly embarrassed. "I don't want to talk to her right at the moment."

"Me neither," I said. My spirits lifted considerably. Beth was definitely on my side, I thought to myself childishly. Although I'd known them both for years and years I'd always felt closer to Beth. She was more like a second sister than a friend. Jodie liked to think she was my closest friend but if push came to shove I'd save Beth first from a sinking ship any day. And now . . . who needed a traitor for a friend?

I lay in bed in Beth's spare room staring at the ceiling. It had been a long day and I was exhausted. A thin shaft of light pierced the darkness, a streetlamp outside shining through the gap in the curtains. Outside all was still except for the faint rattle of diesel freight-trains clicking over the nearby tracks.

When we were younger someone had told us that the very same night-trains carried deadly chemicals and nuclear waste and if one crashed that it would wipe out the whole population of Dublin city. Funny, the things you believe when you are kids. Maybe it's true, I mused. I tried to focus on things less depressing than mass destruction. But I couldn't think of any.

Chapter 6

I must have fallen asleep eventually because the following morning Beth shook me gently and opened the curtains, letting the grey winter's day into the room.

"Amy," she said quietly, "Suzi is here."

I pulled my weary eyes open and winced in the daylight. My head felt groggy and my whole body ached. Then I remembered and it shot through my whole being like a bad dose of the flu. Jodie and Jack, Jack and Jodie.

"Amy? Amy?" I heard Suzi's voice beside me and I sat up gingerly. Suzi was sitting on the end of the bed, smiling at me warily. "How are you feeling? Beth said you were a bit under the weather."

I tried to smile but my mouth didn't seem to want to co-operate.

"Hi, Suzi. I'm fine, thanks. What are you doing here?"

"I was worried about you. Beth rang me this morning and told me you weren't feeling too well and that you'd had a fight with Jodie. And I wanted to see how you were."

I grimaced. Good old Beth – at least I didn't have to tell Suzi about Jack and Jodie yet. I didn't much feel like going over it all.

"Anyway, you look fine," Suzi continued when she realised I wasn't going to say anything. "I was hoping you'd come shopping with me this afternoon. I have none of my Christmas presents and I was to get something really special for Matt. I see Beth is as organised at usual." Suzi nodded over at the corner of the room. I looked over. Heaps of Christmas presents covered the surface of the dressingtable. Beth's 'theme' this year seemed to be pink and silver and each present was carefully wrapped in metallic paper and adorned with a large pink satin ribbon and bow.

I groaned. I hadn't bought a single present either and it was less than ten days till Christmas! Maybe a good bout of retail therapy would take my mind off things.

"Sounds good," I smiled, properly this time.

"Beth's making us lunch, so I'll go down and give her a hand and you can have a shower."

"Fine."

Suzi walked out of the room and I swung my legs over the side of the bed and onto the cream-carpeted floor. Beth had left a pile of clean clothes on the chair under the window, together with a towel. Tears pricked my eyes. She was so good to me – I didn't deserve it. I promised myself that I'd buy her something really special for Christmas to say thank you.

When I was clean and dressed in a pair of Beth's soft denim dungarees and her red hoody fleece – real comfort clothes – I made my way into the kitchen. Delicious cooking smells were emanating from the hob where Beth was standing. Suzi was sitting at the white pine Habitat table and flicking through the latest issue of *Image* magazine.

"Hi," Beth beamed. "You look great. Fancy some lunch?"

"What's cooking?" I asked, mouth watering. I was starving. "Smells divine."

"Chicken breasts in a cream and Dalkey mustard sauce. And Suzi knocked together a salad."

"It's more Brutus, I'm afraid, than Caesar," Suzi laughed. "I threw in whatever I could find, and I may have gone a little heavy on the dressing. But it should taste nice."

"You guys," I drawled in a heavy American accent, "you just kill me. I love ya."

Suzi giggled. "Who are you supposed to be?"

I threw my eyes up to the heavens. "Joey from *Friends*, of course."

"Ah," Suzi grinned. "I see."

"I hear you two are off shopping, lucky things," Beth said with disappointment trickling off her voice and dropping on the wooden floor. There was nothing Beth loved more than shopping. "They need me in work this afternoon – there's a big consignment of Italian fabrics coming into the warehouse."

I smiled at her sympathetically. "That's a shame. But I promise – the next time you want a spending partner – I'm your woman!"

"Deal!" Beth said emphatically, scooping the chicken breasts onto some crusty French bread and stirring the cream and mustard seed into the frying pan. She poured the rich sauce over the chicken pieces and placed the plates on the table.

"That smells delicious." Suzi licked her lips and helped herself to some salad. "Thanks, Beth." She munched happily on her salad, popping a piece of crisp iceberg lettuce into her mouth with her tanned fingers.

"How are you feeling this morning?" Beth asked me after she had sat down at the table. She tried to keep her voice light and breezy but I knew that she was genuinely concerned.

I took a sip of freshly squeezed orange juice and attempted a 'normal' smile.

"Better thanks. You were right. Things don't seem as dark and hopeless as they did yesterday." I winced, still feeling sick to my stomach thinking about Jack and Jodie.

"Amy," Beth said softly, reading my mind. Sometimes she knew me far too well. "Try not to dwell on it. Focus on this afternoon's shopping, OK?"

"I'll try." I pushed some salad around my plate,

spearing a cube of cucumber despondently. I'd been ravenous a few minutes ago but now a lump had formed in my throat, making swallowing difficult.

"This chicken is delicious," Suzi purred, dipping a finger into the rich sauce and licking it with relish. She glanced over at my plate. "You can't go shopping on an empty stomach," she stated resolutely. "It's against the rules – eat!"

I jabbed a sliver of chicken onto my fork and popped it into my mouth. Suzi was right – it was delicious. I managed to chew and swallow methodically. Beth and Suzi chatted amicably about Australia while I listened. I didn't much feel like joining in. The more I ate the easier it became and soon, much to my surprise, I'd cleared the plate and was crunching on a deliciously cool red apple from Beth's fridge. I felt a little more alive and was even beginning to look forward to the afternoon's retail blitz.

After coffee Suzi skipped off to ring Matt, leaving Beth and me sitting at the table. I stood up and reached over to gather up the sunny yellow plates.

"Leave them," Beth admonished. "I'll tackle them this evening."

"Are you sure?" I asked suspiciously.

Beth looked me straight in the eye. "Yes!" she smiled warmly. "I'm sure. Sit down and relax."

"Beth," I hesitated. She waited expectantly, her brown eyes full of compassion. I blinked back tears. I didn't deserve such a good and kind friend.

"I'm sorry . . . about last night . . . I was . . ."

"I understand," Beth interrupted. "You don't need to say anything else." She reached over the table and placed her hands on mine and held them tight.

"I don't want to feel like this," I continued wretchedly. "I just do."

Beth sighed and squeezed my hands. "I know, love. But you have to move on, leave the past behind. These things happen for a reason. Jack wasn't good for you and some day the right man will come along and everything will click into place."

"My knight in shining armour on his white steed," I muttered, my words dripping with sarcasm.

Beth was a determined romantic and believed wholeheartedly in fate. I wasn't so sure. But at this stage clutching at straws had become second nature.

"Look at myself and Tony," Beth continued, hammering her point home. "Before I met him I'd never had a boyfriend for more than three weeks!"

"I know," I sighed.

"I'm not really helping, am I?" Beth asked resignedly.

I smiled. "You are. I'm just not the easiest of people to help."

"You can say that again!" Beth laughed.

"What are you two giggling about?" Suzi asked as she walked back into the kitchen.

"Nothing," Beth assured her. "How's lover-boy?"

"Grand. He's helping his hooker paint a bedroom today."

Beth and I started laughing again. "Sounds interesting," Beth giggled. "As his fiancée, would his dealings with Dublin's seedy underworld not bother you?"

"Would you two stop?" Suzi insisted, trying to keep a straight face. "The hooker, which for your information is a position in a rugby team, is called Bruce Gorman and he's a painter."

"I'd keep a beady eye on Matt just in case," I hiccuped, holding my stomach which hurt from laughing so much.

Beth continued. "He'll be window-dressing or set-designing with the prop next."

"That makes no sense," Suzi said in exasperation. "Is it supposed to be funny?"

Beth could hardly force the words out. She was in convulsions.

"You know – rugby prop, stage prop."

"That's brutal," Suzi smiled in spite of herself.

"I know," Beth gasped. "I know."

Half an hour later we were on the northbound Dart.

"I wish I was going with you," Beth grumbled as the train drew into Blackrock station.

I kissed her on the cheek and stood up. "I'll ring you later and tell you all about our purchases," I grinned mischievously.

"Don't you dare go into Khan without me," she said dangerously.

"Bye, Beth," I smiled.

Suzi and I waved as the train pulled away from the platform. Ducking a hanging basket full of ivy and bright purple heather, we chatted companionably as we sauntered towards Blackrock main street. The road outside the station was being resurfaced and there was a heady smell of hot tar lingering in the air. The new tarmacadam steamed and hissed as it was flattened into place by the slowly moving roller.

"Hiya, ladies!" a young man shouted as we walked by. "Nice day, thank God."

"He's cute." Suzi whispered. "He looks like the guy from the Diet Coke ad."

"In your dreams," I smiled. "You've been in Australia too long."

As we crossed the busy main street to the Blackrock shopping centre I remembered the last time I'd been here – a few months ago with Jack. We'd been looking for a wedding present for Chris, one of the partners in his firm. Chris was marrying an English girl and the wedding, the second for him, was in Sussex so we weren't actually going. But Jack had wanted to make a good impression.

He had settled on an original glass piece by a young Irish artist, from a small gallery on the main street. It was a vase, a glorious celebration of form and fluidity in the palest green glass – classy yet unusual. Afterwards we had sat in the Californian Coffee Dock sipping cappuccinos, the carefully wrapped vase by Jack's feet.

"What type of wedding do you want?" he'd asked out of the blue, after he had filled me in on the latest Formula 1 controversy.

I hesitated awkwardly. "I'm not sure. I've never really thought about it," I lied. "It would depend on who I'm marrying, I suppose." I smiled.

He looked at me carefully. "What do you mean by that?"

I stiffened. I felt like a deer caught in the headlights of an oncoming vehicle – a pick-up truck with those brutish 'cow-bars' at that.

"Nothing," I said lightly. "I was joking. What were you saying about Eddie Jordan's team?"

"Don't try to change the subject," Jack continued, a serious look on his face. "You have considered . . . us . . . you know . . ."

"Our wedding?" I asked.

"Yes," he said sheepishly, playing with a packet of sugar, turning the small rectangle over and over in his fingers.

"I've thought about it," I replied honestly.

"And," Jack prompted.

"I'm just not ready to make that sort of commitment," I sighed. "It's a lot of work – setting dates and thinking about dresses and flowers and things."

"I'm the one who's supposed to have problems with the C word," he smiled, trying to lighten the mood. For once he wasn't going to start an argument. "People have been asking when we're giving them a day out, that's all. We have been engaged a while now."

"I know," I said, trying not to sigh. "And when I'm ready I'll tell you, I promise."

"Don't leave it too long," he said ominously. Little did he know. "Anyway, it's no big deal." He opened *The Irish Times* on the table at the listings page. "Let's see what's on in Stillorgan. How about the new Bruce Willis thriller? Or there's a romantic comedy with Julia Roberts. You'd like that. Amy, Amy?"

I was miles away wondering why I didn't want to set a date for our wedding. It suddenly dawned on me that maybe I didn't want to marry Jack. Maybe I wasn't nervous of getting married, maybe I was nervous of getting married to him.

That was before the arguments and the tears. And before I finally realised that Jack wasn't who I wanted him to be.

"Amy?" Suzi interrupted my musings and pulled me by the arm into Crowley's Chemists. The chrome, glass and ash-wood interior sparkled under the bright shop lights. Towers of glittering gift boxes were stacked beside the door – bright pink Clinique ones and Gold and Silver Lancôme ones. Every inch of the glass countertops was covered with boxes and bottles of all shapes, sizes and descriptions – all holding wonderfully smelling treats for the senses.

"This is perfect for Mum," Suzi said animatedly, her blue eyes dancing. She held up an Estée Lauder make-up tray. The tortoiseshell tray was filled with all kinds of products, from Re-Nutriv All Day lipsticks to nail-polishes and eye-shadows.

"Oooh," she squealed next, "Matt would love this!" She sprayed a fine mist of Hugo Boss for men into the air and sniffed it appreciatively.

I smiled. It was hard to be in a bad mood with Suzi around. We headed towards the perfume counter and covered our wrists with lots of different scents.

"This is nice. It says it's light and fresh with a flowery bouquet." Suzi sprayed some Anaïs Anaïs on her left wrist. "What do you think?"

"It suits you," I smiled.

She beamed back. "What about you, Amy? Which one do you like?"

"I'm still a Chanel No 5 girl, like Marilyn Munroe," I admitted. I'd worn the fragrance for as long as I could remember.

We left Crowley's laden with plastic shopping-bags. Suzi had bought presents for Mum and Matt and I had bought myself a new Clinique lipstick called Tenderheart – I reckoned I needed a bit of pampering. I bought Dad his obligatory bottle of Old Spice. It always made me feel safe and secure, the smell of Old Spice. It reminded me of Dad so much. I tried to make Jack wear it once but he was having none of it.

"No way!" he'd stated emphatically one morning in the very same chemist's. "It's a corduroy and Labrador man's aftershave. My Dad wears it, Amy."

"So does mine," I'd said softly.

"Sorry?" he'd asked.

"Nothing," I'd mumbled.

In the end Jack had bought Eternity for men – he was always a sucker for clever advertising.

As we walked past Kiddi Kutz on the way up the stairs, *Rugrats* blaring from their bright yellow televisions I heard a familiar voice behind me.

"Amy? Is that you?"

I turned and came face to face with a real blast from the past – Sheena Morris. Sheena had been in my class at St Peter's – head girl, captain of the First XI hockey team, prize-winning debater, A student – you know the type. And she was slim and pretty to boot, with a halo of softly curling brown hair, a generous mouth and a perfect set of *Beverly Hills 91210* even white teeth. Your average nightmare.

"Hi, Sheena," I said, forcing myself to smile. "How are you?"

"Wonderful," she gushed. "I'm married," she thrust her ring-finger into my face. "I'm Sheena Goodyear now. And I have two little angels. They're both in getting their hair trimmed and I just popped into the newsagent's to get the new copy of *V I P*. There's a photo of us in it." She flicked through the glossy pages and planted a long, ruby-red talon on the tiny photograph of a 'glamorous charity media ball'. "Isn't that gas!" she shrieked. "Me, famous."

I studied the photo carefully. For the first time since

meeting her I smiled genuinely. Her husband, Terry Goodyear, was a pig, bless him. He looked about forty-five, with lank grey hair and thick-rimmed, black glasses.

Suzi peered over our shoulders at the magazine. "Is that your husband beside you?" she asked curiously, peering over our shoulders.

"Sorry, Suzi. I'm being rude. This is Sheena, she was in my class at St Peter's. Sheena, this is Suzi, my sister."

"Suzi," Sheena gushed. "Of course I remember you. Always a pretty little thing. Actually the man beside me in the picture is my brother-in-law, Terry. My husband is in the next picture with Pat Kenny."

Of course he was. Drop-dead gorgeous too, with a full head of glossy blond hair, sallow skin and a muscular, athletic build. He looked familiar. I'd seen him on a couple of current affairs programmes on RTE.

"Tasty!" Suzi said, sizing him up from the picture.

"Oh, stop!" Sheena giggled, obviously delighted. "He's in TV so he has to look good. Come and see my little ones, Hannah and Dan." She dragged us over to the window of the hairdresser's where two white-blond-haired children were staring at *Barney* crooning a version of a Frank Sinatra song. Surreal!

"They're beautiful," I said honestly. They really were exceptionally attractive youngsters and perfectly turned out in little matching Osh Kosh denim outfits, dungarees for the boy and a pinafore for the girl.

"Thank you," Sheena cooed. "Hannah's just turned

six and Dan's four. "Are you married?" she asked, turning her attention back towards me.

"No, I'm too busy for that!" I lied. "But Suzi's getting married in May."

"How lovely," Sheena said. "Congratulations."

"Thanks," Suzi replied graciously.

"We must fly now, I'm afraid. Shopping to do, you know . . ." I began. "It was nice bumping into you." I wanted to make a swift exit before the embarrassment of swapping numbers, promising to keep in touch and having no real intention of doing so. Too late. She pressed an elegant, cream business card into my hand.

"Give me a ring sometime and we can catch up properly. Lovely to see you!" She kissed both of my cheeks.

"You too," I said evenly.

"Bye," Suzi said.

Sheena joined her home-made genetic success stories and Suzi and I walked towards the escalator in silence.

"Is that the Sheena who was caught in the showers with the rugby captain?" Suzi asked eventually.

"God, no," I laughed. "That was Sheena Connolly. Sheena Morris was Miss Goody-Two-Shoes."

"Must have done it at least twice though," Suzi smiled. She paused for a second. "Makes you think though, doesn't it. "Married with two kids and she's only your age."

"From her card it seems that she also edits a

specialist food and wine magazine," I said looking dejectedly at her business card.

"Of course," Suzi said, grinning. "And I bet she holds amazing dinner parties for twenty people that would put Darina Allen to shame, is an expert on New World wines, has an immaculate garden and runs the PTA in her daughter's school."

"Obviously," I joined in. "And she buys all her clothes from a little boutique in New York, darling, and only holidays in the most obscure and exotic places."

"Makes you feel a bit inadequate though, doesn't it?" Suzi asked resignedly.

"Humm, I suppose," I replied. "But you know something?" I grinned wickedly.

"What?" Suzi asked.

"Her feet stank in school. We used to make her leave her runners outside the changing rooms on her way out. They were that bad."

"Well, that's OK so!" Suzi laughed. "At least she's not perfect." She linked my arm. "Let's try on some clothes in Khan. I saw an adorable pink Whistles cardigan in *U* magazine and I think they stock it."

"You're on!" I grinned, trying to push all thoughts of wedded bliss, successful classmates and perfect children out of my mind. As if things weren't bad enough.

We crossed the road and gazed at the glittering beaded black and deep-red evening dresses in the window before going in.

"I'd never be able to wear that," I moaned, pointing

at a tiny black slip dress with delicate spaghetti straps and a dramatically low-cut back. "It would show up all my lumps and bumps."

"Don't be ridiculous," Suzi stated. "At least you have the figure to fill it. I have so little chest that it wouldn't stay up."

"Rubbish," I snorted. "You're perfectly proportioned. Don't give me that."

We walked in the door and squeezed our way to the back of the shop to look at the dresses. The small shop was packed with women of all ages – from tall, gangly teenagers with their mothers to immaculately dressed matrons.

"Feel this," Suzi commanded, handing me a dark bottle-green velvet dress with a dramatically boned bodice.

The skirt material was soft and light, and Suzi held it against me with delight.

"Amy, you have to try it on."

I looked at the price tag and smiled. "In your dreams, sis. It's one of Louise's designs and it's three hundred pounds."

"The woman Beth works for?"

"The very same."

"Try it on anyway," Suzi cajoled. "Just to see what it's like on."

"Maybe," I said, hoping she'd forget about it. The way I saw it, there was no point trying on something that you knew you couldn't afford.

Suzi slung it over her arm and moved towards the coats. I followed her, squeezing past a nymph-like teenager who was parading a wickedly tight pink sheath dress for her adoring mother.

"Darling," the older woman purred, "it's just perfect for Aspen. You must have it."

Suzi glanced at me and raised her eyes to heaven. "Hardly much use for skiing," she whispered in exasperation. I smiled.

Suzi found two glorious full-length padded silk coats by Fenn, Wright and Manson, one in metallic grey and one in copper and whisked them off their hangers. She also found the coveted Whistles cardigan. We made our way back to the changing area and waited to use the tiny, curtained-off cubicle.

Suzi became impatient and pulled off her bulky jacket and jumper in the queue, revealing her tiny white vest top and deliciously tanned and well-toned shoulders and arms. I noticed with delight the teenage girl surveying her, eyes flicking green with envy. Suzi had a figure that money couldn't buy.

She looked divine in the cardigan which clung in all the right places, wrapping around her body in an unusual manner and tying at the front with pink ribbon.

"What do you think?" she spun around, almost hitting the woman behind us in the mouth with her shoulder.

"Lovely," I said firmly. "The colour is great on you."

"I have absolutely no clothes to wear over Christmas and I want to look nice when I . . . when we announce the engagement." Suzi's eyes glistened with happiness. "You know what some of the rellies can be like. They'll have me and Matt under the microscope. So I want to look well."

I smiled. She was right – the relatives would be all over herself and Matt like a rash at the parents' annual drinks party and a particular nasty scarlet-fever rash at that.

"I could buy a black skirt in Dunnes and I have a pair of strappy sandals somewhere that never made it to Oz, so they should be still in one piece."

Suzi stared at the price tag hanging from the left sleeve and bit her lip.

"It's a little expensive," she winced, "but it can be my Christmas present from Matt and from Mum and Dad."

"And I'll buy you a skirt," I added.

"Perfect," Suzi beamed, kissing me on the cheek. "You're a star."

The changing room was now free and Suzi pushed me into the brightly lit compartment and thrust the green dress into my arms.

"I'll try on the coats out here," she smiled.

"But . . ." I protested, but Suzi simply closed the heavy linen curtain and ignored me.

I struggled with my fleece and T-shirt, dragging them over my head, and I removed Beth's supremely comfortable dungarees. What am I doing? I asked myself as I carefully guided the luxurious material over my hips. It was easier than I thought it would be – sometimes dresses got caught midway. Thighs were a terrible curse. Mine were white with tiny areas of mottled red veins in places which resembled a London tube map. I spent most of the summer with fake tan on my legs and other selected parts of my body – depending on the weather. I was one of those people who turned lobster with a mere whiff of the sun, so fake tan had been something of a revelation to me. It gave me some confidence to wear skimpy summer clothes which I wouldn't previously have considered. Jodie had introduced fake tan to me, she swore by it and even added a drop to her moisturiser over the winter to give herself a healthy glow. Bloody Jodie . . .

"Amy," Suzi interrupted my thoughts, "how does it look?"

I finished fastening the tiny hooks at the side of the dress and stared in the mirror. I was surprised. The bodice fitted my curves perfectly, giving me a pronounced cleavage and slimming my waist and my hips deceptively. The cleverly cut flowing skirt hung in shimmering folds, lightly grazing my thighs and falling to my ankles.

I twitched back the curtain nervously.

Suzi drew in her breath. "Amy, it's stunning. You're a vision."

A tall, elegantly dressed shop assistant smiled at me.

"It's a joy to wear, isn't it? The colour is perfect on you."

I blushed. I wasn't used to compliments.

"That's an amazing coat," I said, changing the subject. Suzi ran her fingers longingly over the padded silk.

"One day," she said dreamily. She shrugged the coat off her shoulders and handed it to the assistant. "Take it away," she grinned.

I retreated back into the safety of the linen sanctuary and reluctantly glided the dress back over my body. It was beautiful but there was no way I could afford it – not on my salary! Stepping out of the cubicle I joined Suzi who was paying for her cardigan at the cash desk with her credit card.

"I hope I'm not over my limit," she whispered to me surreptitiously. "That would be embarrassing."

The card went through and soon we were walking down the main street towards the tiny jeweller's near The Wonderland Bookshop. I wanted to buy Beth something special for Christmas as a thank-you for being there for me.

Suzi swung her black and white Khan bag jauntily by her side. I decided to check my messages as the phone had been switched off since my psychotic 'Jodie' episode yesterday. The familiar voice told me I had five new messages.

Message one. "Hi, Amy, this is Jodie . . . um, ring me."

I grimaced.

Message two. "Hi Amy, this is Jodie again . . . please ring me. We should talk."

Message three. "Amy, please ring me back. I feel terrible. I really need to speak to you. Um, it's Monday morning. Ring me, please."

Message four. "It's Mum. Will you pick up some

Christmas wrapping-paper for me in Blackrock? Thanks. See you later."

Message five. "It's me again – Jodie. I'm so sorry. I know you're annoyed with me . . . and you have every right to be. But it just happened. We didn't mean it to, honestly. You've got to understand . . . oh, Amy, please ring. I never meant to hurt you. Ring me."

Tears welled up in my eyes. Bollocks it just happened. Jodie could have stopped it happening. I stopped on the street and took a deep breath. Suzi turned towards me and gave me a hug.

"Amy, let's sit down for a second." She gestured towards a wooden bench outside The Coffee Bean and we made our way there and sat down.

"What is it, love? Do you want to talk about it?"

I sniffed and looked at her through blurred eyes. I wiped the tears away with the back of my hand and sniffed again.

"Jodie and Jack are . . ."

"Together?" she asked gently, disbelief on her face.

I nodded.

"Jeez," she whispered.

We sat in silence for a few minutes.

"How do you know?" she asked after a little while. I explained about the car and Jodie's Granny. Her eyes widened in astonishment.

"You poor thing. You must have got a real shock."

"I just feel so stupid. I feel as if they're laughing at me behind my back. And I can't believe Jodie would do such a thing. She's supposed to be my best friend." I raced through my words, barely taking a breath.

"It's all right," Suzi crooned. "Calm down. Let's have some coffee before we do any more shopping."

She led me into The Coffee Bean and we both had a caffè latte, mine laced with oceans of sugar. After I'd taken a few gulps of the strong hot liquid I began to relax.

"You're still in shock," Suzi stated firmly. "You've got to take things easy and give yourself some time." She looked at me carefully. "I think you should talk to Jodie."

"No way," I hissed. "I'm never going to talk to her again."

"I think you should hear what she has to say," Suzi continued bravely, ignoring my dagger looks. "It may make you feel better and it might put things in perspective. Tell me you'll think about it anyway."

I muttered 'right' sarcastically under my breath.

"I'll take that as a yes," Suzi continued. "I'll drop the subject now. But if you want to talk about it I'm here, OK?"

I felt horribly guilty. Suzi didn't deserve my spleen any more than Beth had last night. I was a terrible and ungrateful person and I hated myself for it.

"Thanks," I stapled a smile onto my face. "I appreciate it."

"I know," Suzi smiled. "You mad thing." She punched me playfully on the arm.

Chapter 7

Later that afternoon I sat on my bed fingering the delicate silver Alan Arnduff necklace I'd bought for Beth. A gleaming chain supported a tiny open-fronted embossed silver box in which a heart was suspended. The tiny heart moved from side to side as the wearer moved. I hung the chain over my fingers and watched as the heart swung hypnotically.

It was simple yet beautiful; I knew Beth would love it.

I flicked off my runners and lay back against the Wombles pillow. My head throbbed and I felt tired and achy. Maybe I was coming down with something – flu perhaps. But I knew in my heart of hearts that it was psychosomatic. Maybe Suzi was right. Maybe I should give Jodie a ring.

"Amy," Mum's powerful voice clattered up the stairs and through my bedroom door. "Jodie's here. Will I send her up?"

"Shit," I muttered. OK, so I'd considered ringing her – but seeing her face to face, well that was another matter. I tried to think of a decent excuse but failed miserably. I jumped up and locked my door. I could hear footsteps climbing the stairs. They stopped outside my door.

"Amy?" Jodie knocked gently on my door. "Can I come in?"

I didn't answer. I didn't trust myself not to swear blindly at her so I just stayed stumm.

Jodie tried the door. "Can you unlock the door? Please? I really want to talk to you."

I sat on my bed, bolt upright and eyes focused on the doorknob. It turned once more.

Jodie coughed theatrically. "I'm still here. Open the door, will you? I feel stupid."

"Stupid!" I spat, unable to help myself. "How do you think I feel? Go fuck yourself!"

There was shocked silence for a second before Jodie whispered. "Amy, I'm going now. I'm so sorry . . ."

I listened transfixed as Jodie made her way downstairs. I could hear Mum and her talking in the hall before the heavy front door clunked shut. I expected a telling-off from Mum for being so rude but it was several minutes before anyone ventured up the stairs.

"Amy?" Suzi had been sent to calm the stormy waters. I turned the old iron key in the lock and let her in. As I looked at her concerned face I began to cry.

"Ah, love," she put her arms around me. We sat

down on the bed and she held me in her arms, stroking my head.

The next morning I left early for work. I'd managed to avoid any social interaction the previous evening by staying in my room all night and feigning a headache. Mum was a little concerned but Suzi had smoothed everything over. I assumed she'd explained about Jodie and Jack as Mum was being extra nice to me. She'd brought me some comfort food on a tray – Heinz tomato soup and toast fingers – and the latest Cathy Kelly novel to keep my mind off things.

Work was going to be mental all week. Recommending books for 'brilliant' seven-year-olds – of course they were always 'brilliant', never average or normal. Grandparents were the worst – 'My little Nikki, he's quite brilliant, you know. Reads all by himself. He's very advanced for his age. I want something to stretch him – maybe Dickens or *Treasure Island*.' Poor kids, all they really wanted was *Buffy the Vampire Slayer* and *Goosebumps* and *Harry Potter*. I usually tried to come to some sort of compromise but there was no pleasing some customers. Still, it would take my mind off things.

* * *

The next few days flew by in a haze of Christmas wrapping-paper and 'brilliant' children. All the regulars had been in – Siobhan had spent a small fortune on beautiful hardback books for her girls. I was wistfully half-hoping that the lovely Stevie J would be in again, but of course he wasn't. Before I knew it Christmas Eve had snuck up and thumped me on the head. From eight in the morning (we opened early to get the shop straightened up before the stampede) the place was hopping.

As the afternoon drew in things began to get a little heated and frantic.

"Miss, Miss." Bony fingers clicked in my face. Someone was 'summoning' me.

"Where is the latest Larry O'Loughlin?" a tall woman in a voluminous red coat demanded. "I must have it for my niece. It was reviewed on the radio."

"I'm afraid it's sold out," I said politely. "But we have some of Larry's other books."

"What do you mean sold out?" the woman replied with contempt. "It was reviewed in *The Sunday Tribune*, for goodness sake. You must have it!"

"We had it this morning," I continued, losing patience. "But I'm afraid it's a very popular book and we sold the last copy at lunchtime. Maybe you could try the bookshop in the shopping centre."

She looked at me with disdain. "Ring them and see!"

"Excuse me?" I asked lifting my eyebrows. I'd had quite enough of this rude woman. It was hardly my fault that she'd left her Christmas shopping until now.

"I said ring them!" she repeated, glaring at me.

I looked her straight in the eye. "I presume you

mean 'Would you please ring them for me'?" I asked, staring pointedly at the silver mobile phone clutched in her hand.

Her cheeks began to co-ordinate with her coat and she opened her mouth to respond. Luckily Lynn had noticed the altercation and stepped in, grinning broadly.

"Can I help? I'm afraid Amy is needed at the picture-books." She pushed me towards the back of the shop.

When the customer from hell had left, Lynn squeezed her way to the desk where I was Christmas-wrapping some books.

"What a dragon!" she exclaimed.

I smiled. "Thanks for taking over. I was about to thump her. Wait till we try to close the shop – then the real loonies will come out of the woodwork!"

Lynn opened a bottle of red wine and poured two large glasses.

"We'd better fortify ourselves, so," she grinned, lifting her glass and clinking it gently against mine. "Cheers!"

After we had herded the last straggling customers out of the shop and locked up I walked into Blackrock to meet the gang in Fitzgerald's. My feet ached and I had a sharp pain in my arms and shoulders – repetitive strain injury of the Christmas book-wrapping genre. Lynn had been in flying form – it was the shop's best Christmas yet and she was delighted. She'd even decided not to open until December the twenty-eighth, giving us both an extra day's holiday. Excellent!

I knew Jodie would be in the pub – it was traditional for the three of us – Beth, Jodie and me to meet up every year before the rest of the gang came in. I'd kind of resigned myself to the fact that she would be present; it was Christmas after all. But I didn't want to talk about Jack, and I was doggedly determined to keep off the subject, no matter what. But as I walked in the door and was blasted with hot, deliciously mulled-wine-scented air I spotted Beth sitting alone at a table in the corner, her coat, scarf and bag draped over other seats in a desperate attempt to keep seats.

"Hiya," I smiled, pulling off my coat and hat and flopping down beside her. "Where's Jodie?"

"She didn't want to come."

"Why not?"

Beth looked at me carefully. "She didn't want to ruin the evening for you."

I felt slightly guilty. I knew how much she loved our Christmas Eve drinks. I sniffed. "I suppose she's staying in with Jack so?"

"No," Beth said. "He's going to his family drinks thingy and she's staying at home."

"Oh," I said. If I was a nice, gregarious person I would have rung her and told her not to be so stupid and to get her butt down there. But I wasn't. I was glad she had to stay in on her own. OK, so I felt a little guilty but not enough to spoil my night!

"What are you having?" I asked, changing the subject.

"Mulled wine," Beth smiled.

"Sounds great." I spotted a young lounge boy and ordered four glasses of mulled wine.

"He's cute," I murmured, watching his pert, tight behind moving away in the shiny black trousers.

"Get a grip," Beth giggled. "He's probably still in school. I'm sure those are his uniform trousers."

"I like them young," I smiled. "I dare you to wink at him when he comes back."

"You're in good form," Beth replied. "If I wink at him you have to tell him he looks like Brad Pitt."

"You're on."

The boy walked towards us and nearly spilt the tray on Beth's lap when she winked at him lasciviously.

"Um, who are these drinks for?" he asked nervously, gesturing at the third and fourth glass balanced on his precarious tray.

"They're the standby drinks. For when these run out," I explained. "You can put them down here. Has anyone ever told you you're the split of Brad Pitt?"

The boy reddened from the tips of his ears to his bum-fluffed cheeks. He smiled broadly.

"Jeez, are yer serious? Tanks." He looked me up and down, his brown eyes lingering a little too long on my chest for comfort. "Listen, I'm off early tonight – want to meet me outside later?"

Beth spluttered her drink all down her top. Luckily it was black so the dark red wine didn't show.

"We'll see," I laughed.

"He was well able for you," Beth giggled after he

had left to serve another table. "You're not really going to meet him, are you?"

I stared at her in mock amazement. "I'm not that hard up," I insisted. "But it'll make getting drinks easier if he thinks he's in with a chance."

"You're a wicked woman."

"That's the nicest thing anyone's said to me in a long time," I smiled.

"You pair look well stuck in." Tony approached the table, gave Beth a kiss on the cheek and squeezed in beside her. His friend Jed stood awkwardly beside us. "Jed, get some pints in, will you?" Tony asked. "How's it going, Amy?"

"Grand, thanks, Tony." I knew he knew all about the fall-out with Jodie but he had the decency not to mention it.

"Amy's found herself a toyboy," Beth said.

"Some of my mates from work are calling in later. Does this mean they'll have some competition?" Tony asked smiling.

"I can handle them all," I replied confidently.

"What's that you can handle?" Jed asked, placing two dark velvety pints on the table.

"Don't ask!" Tony said. "Cheers! Here's to a good night and a great Christmas!"

"Cheers!" We all clunked glasses. Maybe it wasn't going to be so bad after all.

* * *

"Amy, wake up," Suzi was sitting on my bed and shaking me hard.

"Wha?" I muttered. "It's early. Get off."

"Mum has breakfast all ready and she wants the whole family downstairs."

"Tell her to bugger off," I said darkly.

Suzi laughed. "I don't think she'd appreciate that on Christmas Day. How's the head?"

"Not good," I admitted.

"I'm not surprised with the amount of drinks you threw back last night. When we arrived you'd already started on a round of tequilas with some of Tony's lot. You drank Jed under the table. Matt was well impressed."

"I didn't do anything stupid, did I?" I asked slowly.

"Well . . . not really."

I sat up gingerly and stared at Suzi. "Go on, tell me."

"You know the bar guy? Brad you were calling him?"

"Yes?"

"You pulled him under the mistletoe and kissed him."

"Really?"

"Yup," Suzi continued smiling. "But the funniest thing was that his girlfriend gave him a belt with her handbag. She was sitting at the bar waiting for him to get off work."

I groaned.

"It was brilliant! I haven't laughed so much for years. Matt and Jed practically carried you home but we were all laughing so much it took forever."

"Jed?" I asked.

"Yes, nice guy. He's not as quiet when he's had a few drinks in him. Single too." Suzi looked at me with a funny expression.

"What are you staring at?" I demanded. "Stop the matchmaking. Leave me alone, for heaven's sake."

"Only if you promise to get up."

"Fine."

I pulled myself out of bed and opened the curtains. It was a manky grey, dull, listless day – an Irish special. No doubt it would start raining later to make it even 'better'. I sighed. As it was Christmas Day I supposed I'd better make some sort of effort to look half-decent. I staggered across to my door, yanked my white towelling robe off its hook and wrapped it around last night's underwear. At least I'd managed to undress before hitting the sack. Yesterday's discarded clothes were straggling inside-out on my wooden floor.

I made it to the shower and soon sharp warm darts were piercing my lethargy. I let the water pummel my body and tried not to think about the headache which was building in my temples. My stomach felt amazingly settled considering the tequila. I was a demon for the dangerous Mexican drink. In college Jodie and I consumed a whole bottle between the two of us one wet, cold afternoon. I can't remember why. Anyway, after hallucinating wildly for several hours, dancing to our own bad singing and dressing up in each other's clothes, getting very confused as to our 'real identities', we passed out and slept until the following day. I'll never, ever forget the hangover. It was the mother of all hangovers – hot sweats, spasming stomachs, jack-hammers in our heads, shaking hands – the works. I've never had a hangover quite like it since – thank goodness!

I stepped out of the shower and grabbed a towel. While drying myself I remembered that I hadn't used any shampoo or soap, so I had to get back into the shower! Eventually I walked back to my room, feeling much more alive, and pulled on a pair of black trousers and a dark red polo-neck. I layered on the make-up, finishing off with some 'Hell Red' lipstick and I was ready to face the world.

Breakfast was already well under way when I entered the kitchen.

"Morning, Amy. Nice of you to join us," Mum said, smiling.

"Late night, was it?" Dad asked while spearing half a sausage on his fork and dipping it into his fried egg.

"Would you like a fry?" Mum asked.

I thought for a second. My stomach seemed OK, so why not? "Thanks, Mum, that'd be great. No pudding though."

Suzi and Matt were holding hands over the table and feeding each other pieces of toast.

"Look what Matt bought me," Suzi exclaimed, pulling up her new pink cardigan and revealing a sexy purple lacy bra. "There's matching knickers too." She stood up to show me.

Dad coughed. "I don't think you need to show us, thanks, Suzi. I'm sure they're lovely."

I laughed. Suzi was great. Matt looked a little embarrassed.

"What did Suzi get you, Matt?" I asked kindly, trying to change the subject.

"Some aftershave," he beamed. "And a season ticket for Lansdowne Road. She's a star."

Dad's ears pricked up. "How did you manage that, Suzi?" he asked. "They're impossible to get."

Suzi smiled. "My new boss."

We all looked at her in amazement. I didn't know Suzi had even been looking for a job.

Mum smiled knowingly as she placed a sizzling breakfast in front of me.

Dad looked at her in amazement. "Is someone going to tell me what's going on?"

"And me," I added, a little miffed that Suzi hadn't said anything to me.

Suzi giggled. "I wanted to tell you all but I didn't want to say anything until I was sure. Matt's coach in Clontarf was looking for a nanny urgently for his brother and Matt suggested me."

"Go on," I urged impatiently.

"Well, I went to meet the family and the kids were great. Katie is five and Simon is seven. So I start in January."

"Tell them who their Dad is," Matt cajoled.

"Oops, I nearly forgot. Their Dad is Brian Lowan."

"No!" Dad exclaimed. "Not *the* Brian Lowan?"

"The rugby guy?" I asked. "The captain of the Irish team?"

"The very same," Suzi replied. "He's a really nice guy and his wife, Julie, is a pet. And I'll get to fly all over the place as he likes his family to travel with him."

"Wow," I exclaimed. I was delighted for Suzi but a little jealous. Everyone seemed to be falling on their feet except for me these days.

Mum kissed Suzi on the head. "We're very proud of you, love. And the Lowans are very lucky."

"They sure are," Matt agreed.

Jesus, I thought. My family have turned into the bloody Waltons. It was going to be a long day.

"Eva's dying to hear all about your wedding plans," Mum continued. "Judy too." Eva and Judy were relatives of some sort – cousins of Dad's or something.

"I can show her my wedding folder," Suzi piped up, delighted.

"Your what?" I asked incredulously.

"Amy, don't be like that," Suzi scolded playfully. "I knew you'd take the piss so I haven't shown you yet."

"Language, please!" Mum exclaimed.

"Oops, sorry, Mum. Anyway, it's a folder of ideas for our wedding." Suzi gazed adoringly at Matt. "You know, colour schemes, dresses, flowers, menus, that sort of thing."

"Um," I muttered. It really was going to be a brutally long day.

Chapter 8

Mum and Dad left for church, followed by two drinks parties, leaving myself and Suzi to begin the Christmas dinner. Matt went for a run, more to keep out of our way I think than from any real desire to pound the local crazy paving that masquerades as pavement.

"I think we're supposed to put the turkey in now," Suzi said in confusion. "But I'm not sure. Dad said it's a twelve-pound bird and according to Mum it needs fifteen minutes per pound – does three hours sound right?"

"I'm not sure," I said nervously. "To be honest I don't have a clue. But I think it went in for longer last year and it was a smaller turkey."

"I'll stuff it anyway. Will you look up one of Mum's cookery books or something? I don't want to poison everyone."

"I'll ring Beth," I decided. "She'll know. She's cooking for her family at her house."

I picked up the phone in the hall and dialled Beth's number.

"Hello?" Beth answered uncertainly.

"Hi, Beth, happy Christmas! How are you this morning?"

"Not too bad considering. And yourself?"

"Getting there. Listen, I need your help urgently." I explained about the twelve-pound uncooked turkey.

"Right, do you have the oven pre-heated?" she asked anxiously – she knew what I was like in the kitchen.

"I think so," I said, trying not to sound as scared as I felt. What if I struck the whole family down with salmonella. On second thoughts . . .

Beth sighed. "Maybe you'd better write this down. Pre-heat the oven high."

"What's high?"

"You have gas, so mark seven. Have you done the stuffing?"

"Suzi's doing that now."

"Fine. Then after she's finished, wrap the turkey in tinfoil and cook it on high for half an hour."

"Right."

"Then turn down the heat to mark three and cook for three hours."

"Three hours! Are you sure?" I asked. "It seems like a long time."

Beth laughed. "Believe me, I'm sure. I've been doing

the Christmas dinner for years. Then turn up the heat again and cook for another twenty minutes. And don't forget to baste the thing. OK?"

I breathed a sigh of relief. I hadn't a clue what basting was but I didn't want to appear a total ignoramus. "Thanks, Beth. You've saved our lives – literally. We might have poisoned the family otherwise. Although that might not be such a bad thing," I added darkly.

"No problem. Is it OK if I call in around seven? I want to give you your present."

"Perfect. I'll see you then."

Suzi looked up from the backside of the turkey as I entered the kitchen. "Well?"

"I have it all here," I said, waving the piece of paper in the air.

"Excellent," Suzi replied, wincing as she shoved more chestnut and apple stuffing into the bird. "Right, he's well filled now." She washed her hands in the sink

"What's basting?" I asked her as we lifted the heavy bird into the oven.

Suzi smiled. "I'm not sure. Is it a trick question? Is it something to do with sex?"

I laughed. "No! It's something to do with cooking a turkey. You have a one-track mind."

I pulled Delia Smith's *Complete Cookery Course* off the bookshelf and studied the index. Nothing on basting.

"Beth?"

"Oh, hi, Amy."

"Sorry to ring again, but what's basting?"

Suzi and I cheered as we heard the front door slamming. Excellent, I thought – Mum was back to take over the cooking. We were sprawled at the kitchen table, exhausted from peeling the spuds for the roast potatoes.

Matt stuck his head around the kitchen door.

"Damn," I exclaimed. "I thought you were Mum."

"Sorry to disappoint you," Matt grinned. "I'm off to have a shower."

"Come here," Suzi said, a wicked smile on her face. She stood up and kissed Matt firmly on the lips. "I love sweaty men." She licked Matt's dripping left temple.

"That's disgusting," I shrieked.

"Yum, salty," she smiled as Matt lumbered out of the kitchen.

"You are revolting," I said, swatting her with a tea-towel. "I suppose we'd better baste the turkey."

The front door slammed again and this time it was Mum and Dad.

"Hallelujah," Suzi shouted. "Mum, we need you urgently."

Mum came into the kitchen, her face flushed. "Hi, girls. How are you getting on?"

"Fine, but we need a break."

"Right, me and your Dad will take over now. Frank!" she called.

We left them to it and retired to the sitting-room,

glasses of chilled white wine in hand. Dad had kindly handed us the whole bottle.

"You keep Eva and Judy occupied and we'll finish the dinner."

"Deal," I agreed.

Several hours later the whole ensemble were seated around the dining-room table tucking into the turkey.

"Beautifully cooked," Judy enthused, cutting her turkey into small, evenly sized pieces.

"Perfect," Eva agreed, piling more cranberry sauce onto her already loaded fork.

"Now tell me all about your wedding plans, Suzi," Judy asked expectantly. "I want to hear all about them."

"Every little detail," Eva agreed. "We're dying to hear everything."

I groaned inwardly. Just what I needed, more bloody wedding talk.

"Might put a fire under your Jack," Judy continued. "It's about time he made an honest woman out of you."

Dad coughed and tried to change the subject. "Um, more turkey anyone?"

I sighed and decided to bite the bullet. "Jack and I broke up, Judy. We won't be getting married, not now, not ever."

There was an awkward silence.

"I'm sorry, Amy," Judy said quietly. "I had no idea . . ."

"It's fine. You weren't to know," I lied breezily. "It's

for the best anyway. Has Suzi told you about her wedding folder?"

Suzi glanced at me and smiled kindly. We were quite used to playing talk-tag to get our parents and relations off a difficult subject.

"I've collected all kinds of things in a folder, Judy. Dress designs, flowers, menus, the works. I'll show it to you after dinner."

"What fun!" Judy exclaimed before launching into a lengthy tale about her own wedding over sixty years ago. Her husband was dead now and they'd never had any children so Suzi and I were kind of her surrogate children. I couldn't concentrate on what she was saying though. My mind kept drifting back to Jack. What had I done? Of course I should have married him. But he was with Jodie now and I'd lost a boyfriend and a best friend all rolled into one. I'd never find anyone else now – I was nearly thirty, for heaven's sake. Who'd want a thirty-year-old with a track record of broken relationships, who had a crappy job and lived at home? No one in their right mind . . .

"Amy?"

The whole table was staring at me.

"Yes?"

"Eva just asked you about work."

"I'm sorry, I . . ." My eyes filled with tears. "Excuse me . . ." I abruptly left the table and thundered up the stairs to my room. I flopped on the bed, tears spilling all over my pillow. Damn, I thought I was fine today.

"Amy?" Suzi was standing over me. "Are you all right??"

"No," I cried. "But I will be." I sniffed. Suzi handed me a tissue. "I'm sorry. It's Christmas Day and I'm spoiling everything."

"Don't be daft," Suzi said gently. "Come down and finish dinner."

"I don't know if I can."

Suzi looked at me sternly. "Don't let Jack-fecking-Daly spoil everything. He's not worth it. In a few months' time you'll have forgotten all about him."

"Maybe," I murmured unconvinced. But I knew Suzi was right. If I could just get through the next few months . . .

"You don't want to miss opening your presents, do you? The bet's still on this year, I presume?"

I smiled. Every year we placed bets on Judy's and Eva's presents. They were creatures of habit but I was convinced that one year they would surprise us both.

"Twenty quid on Judy giving us both BodyShop baskets and Eva giving us Marks & Spencer's vouchers." Suzi was going for the safe bet.

"Fine," I agreed. "Anything else and I win, deal?" I'd lost money every Christmas for the last few years. Maybe my luck would change this year, although it was highly unlikely.

Everyone behaved normally as I returned to the table which was twilight zoneish but blissfully easy to deal with. I had no desire to explain the twists and turns of my emotions, especially not on Christmas Day.

"Christmas pudding, Amy?" Mum asked kindly as I gingerly wiggled my chair under the ancient mahogany table, trying to avoid the strut which I'd crucified my knees on more than once.

"Thanks, Mum," I smiled. Dad refilled my wine glass and stroked my head gently as he walked behind me. The unexpected tenderness made my eyes well up again but I managed to control myself. The rest of the dinner went past in a blur of animated small talk.

"You'll never guess who that singer is stepping out with . . . Simon Strummer," Eve stated with a glint in her eye. She was a great woman for celebrity gossip and lived for her doses of *VIP* and *Hello* magazines.

"Isn't he married?" Mum asked in a disapproving voice.

"Men!" Suzi declared. "Too many hormones for their own good. Except Matt, of course." She gazed at Matt who seemed more than a little overwhelmed by the way that the afternoon had gone. I'm sure my emotional display hadn't helped. He was knocking back the wine like there was no tomorrow.

"I'm sure Matt is full of hormones, aren't you, Matt?" I asked.

Matt turned puce. He had no idea what to say.

Dad took pity on him. "Pay no attention to those two," he said, leaning towards Matt. "I shouldn't have given them so much wine!"

After dinner we brought our drinks into the sitting-room. The fire was roaring in the grate and the tree's white lights sparkled, making the delicate coloured glass baubles glisten. Dad and Matt settled on the sofa beside the fire and began a conversation on Ireland's chances in the Rugby World Cup. It was nice for Dad to have another male in the company. Although last year he'd had Jack to talk to . . . I shivered. I wanted to stop thinking about Jack but it was so damn hard.

"Present time," Mum said, sitting down on the other sofa between Eva and Judy. "Will you do the honours, girls?"

Suzi and I began to distribute the wrapped presents to their owners. Soon the room was filled with oohs, ahhs and shrieks of laughter.

We had various relations who still sent us presents – like Marty, Mum's sister in London, who Suzi and I adored. Every year she treated us to trendy tights, scarves and jewellery she'd picked up in Covent Garden Market. And 'The Canadians' – Dad's brother, the computer nerd and his perfect cheerleader wife and three perfect children, who always sent us perfect presents, professionally wrapped in tissue paper and divine, luxurious gold paper with bows and ribbons – the works.

Chapter 9

This year Marty had sent Suzi a silver silk boa and me a pair of bright pink fishnets – cool! She really was the bee's knees.

"What are those?" Matt had asked from the sofa, his interest suddenly captured by the offending tights which I was pulling out of their plastic packaging.

"Matt!" Suzi exclaimed.

"I was only asking," he muttered sheepishly, deciding to keep his mouth firmly shut in future. He couldn't win.

'The Canadians' had given Mum and Dad a small plastic box and a spiral-bound book. It was called *The Magnetic Poetry Set*.

"It's like Scrabble, " Dad exclaimed animatedly. He had a passion for Scrabble. Poor man, he didn't get out much. He scattered the small white rectangular pieces on the coffee table and began to make sentences. "You make up poems and stick them on the fridge." That was him sorted for the evening. Matt seemed a little lost now that his sofa buddy had been swept away to the land of academia. Poetry wasn't really Matt's thing. Although he did like Purple Ronnie – the guy who wrote those funny, stick-people cards.

Mum wasn't so thrilled. She had hoped for something useful. Fat lot of good some old poems were going to do.

"What the hell is this?" I pulled the gold paper off my 'Canadian' present and wrinkled my nose in disdain.

Suzi giggled. "Looks like a willy warmer!"

"Suzi," Mum spluttered, trying not to laugh.

"Well, it does," she protested.

I held the bright yellow tubular neoprene object in the air. "What do you think Matt? Does it look like a willy-warmer to you?"

"Girls," Mum said in exasperation, "what age are you? What will Eva and Judy think?"

"Don't worry," Judy laughed. "We're not as sheltered as you think. Are we, Eva?"

"Certainly not," Eva agreed. "In fact, we could both teach you a thing or two, I'm sure. And Amy, I think you'll find that you are holding a can-cooler in your hand. And if you've seen willies that size, you're a lucky woman!"

I grinned, delighted.

Dad had chosen to ignore the conversation – he

knew when he was outnumbered. Matt was sitting mouth open in amazement.

Suzi jumped up and planted a fat kiss on his mouth. After a few seconds I could tell that there was some serious tongue action going on there so I tried to keep the attention on the presents.

"This is for you, Judy." I handed her the neatly wrapped (by Suzi) present.

She tore off the Christmas paper like a small child, eyes twinkling, and held up a tiny silver-covered pencil which hung on a delicate silver chain. Her eyes watered. "Girls, it's just beautiful. You remembered."

I sat down on the edge of the armchair. "Of course." Last Christmas Eve Judy had lost an identical necklace at the Concert Hall. It was her favourite necklace, given to her by her late husband.

"Where did you find it?" Judy asked, running her age-spotted fingers affectionately over the tiny pencil and smiling.

"My boss, Lynn, has a friend who owns an antique shop and I asked her to keep her eyes open."

"Thank you," Judy whispered.

"It's a pleasure," I beamed.

Suzi tore herself away from Matt, surreptitiously wiping her glistening mouth on her sleeve.

"Isn't Amy clever?" she asked. "Open yours, Eva."

Eva pulled back a tiny piece of the Christmas paper on her present and then another. A smile came to her coral pink lips. "Is this what I think it is?"

I turned towards Suzi and smiled. She had found the most exquisite natural pearl hairband in Australia for Eva.

"Like in that photograph," Suzi said gently, "with Albert." Albert was Eva's childhood sweetheart and she had shown us old black and white photographs of the pair of them attending a Midsummer's Ball in the Tennis Club. She had worn a cream silk full-length dress that fitted her like a glove and a delicate pearl hairband in her glossy raven black hair.

Eva placed the hairband in her silver hair and closed her eyes. "I can remember that night like it was only yesterday."

It was a surreal moment. The wrinkles on her face disappeared and she looked in complete bliss. There was silence for a few seconds. I looked at Suzi and smiled. For two brain-dead and batty females it was pretty impressive! As Eamon Dunphy would say – *the girls done good*! She winked at me and smiled back.

"This is for you, Suzi," Eva handed her a red envelope. "And for you, Amy." We didn't have to look inside, but we did anyway – rude not to. Yep, M & S vouchers again. Suzi was delighted – she was on her way to winning some drinking money.

"Thanks, just what I need. New underwear, here I come! They have a new Wild West range – I fancy the pink basque, or maybe the bra and string set . . ." Suzi was lost in knicker heaven. Matt's eyes lit up again.

He was lovely. I could see what Suzi liked about him

– he was solid and cuddly. Like a huge big affectionate puppy. But I wasn't sure if I could deal with the predictability.

"Thanks, Eva," I said, plastering a smile on my face.

Judy presented us both with – do I have to say it? – two BodyShop baskets. Not the tiny little cheap ones, mind. Huge, hulking ones, filled to the brim with all kinds of sweet-smelling bubbles, lotions and soaps. And it's a superb present, don't get me wrong. It's just that I hadn't washed my way through last year's basket yet. And it meant I lost the fecking bet – typical. It was obviously going to be another crappy year! The omens were bad enough.

And then Beth arrived.

Chapter 10

"Beth, what do you think of this one," Dad was kneeling at the coffee table, composing 'poems' when Beth entered the room. *"I tell the four corners of the world about you, my love rose."*

Beth smiled. Luckily, she was well used to my Dad. Matt, on the other hand was still looking a little shell-shocked. Judy and Eva had decided to 'take him under their wing', which was a polite and unconfrontational way of saying they were checking out his bloodlines. Suzi was helping Mum in the kitchen, talking weddings no doubt.

"That's clever, Frank. Read me another," Beth encouraged, kindly. Great – encouragement was definitely not what he needed right at that moment.

"How about this – *You ear desire like a poison dart within your heart.* That should be wear but I can't find a 'w'."

"Can I do one?" Beth asked foolishly.

Soon Beth and my Dad were moving the little rectangles over the table like two of the bloody Romantic poets – that Browning lady and Lord Byron. Or like something out of *American Beauty.* You know, where the Dad fancies the girl's best friend. OK, so maybe I was being a little unfair but Beth was my mate and I wanted her all to myself. I wanted to bore her with the details of my weepy episode and I wanted her to analyse it and tell me it would be all right . . . selfish, wasn't I? On Christmas Day too.

"So what did Tony get you this year?" Dad asked, in between poems. Beth was very proud of her *Fireflies glimmer in the garden like my love for you.* Yuck!

Beth blushed and sat up. This was interesting. Maybe Tony had given her some sort of sex toy or something. You couldn't exactly tell your friend's parents that, could you? On second thoughts, maybe Suzi could but not Beth.

"This." She beamed and pulled a tiny blue box out of her pocket.

My heart plummeted. Please, no. Not another one. I couldn't deal with it.

Beth got up and sat down beside me on the sofa. She opened the box. In it sat the most beautiful engagement ring I'd ever seen. A large single diamond was held in a solid platinum band, like a tiny suspension bridge.

"Beth, it's lovely," I whispered. "Put it on."

She took the ring out of the box and slid it onto her

ring. It sparkled in the light and seemed to illuminate her face with its brightness. That was pure happiness of course, not the ring. But it always amazed me how an engagement ring could make even the most nail-bitten or spatula-fingered hands attractive. A monster green dart of jealousy shot through my heart. I tried to swallow it. Tears came to my eyes. And I'm ashamed to say they were not tears of happiness for Beth. I was feeling sorry for myself again. But Beth has such a good heart this wouldn't occur to her and I was relieved that she assumed that they were for her and Tony.

"It's wonderful news," I lied. It was a good day for lies. They were tripping off my tongue like water off the rocks at Powerscourt Waterfall. Pity you can only get away with lying to yourself for a little while.

"How exciting," Dad said. "When's the big day?"

"The first week in May – on the third hopefully if the church is free that day. And if my bridesmaid is free." Beth turned her big, brown eyes on me – what could I do? Say 'no, sorry, I'm busy that week'?

"Of course I'm free!" I gushed. "I wouldn't miss it for the world!"

"Wouldn't miss what?" Suzi asked, coming in the door.

"My wedding," Beth grinned.

"Oh, Beth," Suzi hugged Beth and kissed her on the cheek. "That's excellent. I've just set my date too."

"Two weddings in one summer," I said, attempting a happy, light tone. "Isn't that great?"

"When's yours, Suzi?" Beth asked.

"I haven't told Matt yet." She waved over at her fiancé who was reading a *Calvin and Hobbes* cartoon book. Judy and Eva had completed their interrogation and were now discussing Dolly and genetic engineering. Although it involved sheep, Matt had no interest in their conversation. So Judy had kindly handed him the comic book, one of his presents from my good self. Excellent choice in everything but men.

Matt looked up and smiled. "I'd marry you tomorrow, my love." Jesus, Dad's poetry kit was making everyone barmy, rugby players included. "You just name the date."

Suzi sighed. "Isn't he sweet . . where was I? Oh, yes, Mum and I set the date – May the third."

Suzi's announcement was met with an icy silence. "What have I said?" she asked with concern.

This was a bit more like it. Things going wrong for people who were not me! I know, I know.

Beth coughed and looked around the room nervously. "That's the date myself and Tony have chosen." She gulped. "But I suppose, in the circumstances we can change it. What with Amy being bridesmaid and all . . ."

Typical, I thought to myself. That's right, blame me. I stepped in quickly. "You could always ask someone else, Beth. I wouldn't mind." Please ask someone else, I begged under my breath. I really, really, really don't mind.

"No," Beth stated firmly. "You're my best friend,

Amy. I want you. I'll change the date. It's no big deal. The following week would be fine." She looked doubtful for a second. "I think." She bit her lip.

Suzi was delighted. She slipped over to Matt and threw her arms around him. "Hear that, love. May the third it is." Matt was stuck for words (what's new?) so he just smiled. God, he really did have the most lovely teeth, white and even.

I was beginning to feel like the Ugly Sister at this stage. Unfair, I know, to begrudge the two people who were closest to me in the whole world but hey . . .

Soon the whole room was buzzing with wedding talk. After a respectable interval I snuck off into the kitchen to find more wine. It was dark but I was too lazy to find the light switch. I felt my way to the fridge and opened the door. The light cast a bright yellow shaft over the kitchen table where Suzi's wedding folder lay open. Pictures of wedding dresses insulted my eyes. Pieces of material danced in the dark, silks and organzas flirting on the brown table top.

I pulled a bottle of Australian Chardonnay (in Matt's honour no doubt) out of the fridge and opened it. Pouring myself a large glass, I sat down at the table and looked at the paraphernalia, the open fridge sending an icy chill down my spine. Or was it the fridge? The thought suddenly came to me that maybe Tony had asked Jack to be his best man.

"Amy?" Beth whispered in the gloom. She flicked on the lights. "Are you all right?"

I looked up.

"Not really," I said, attempting to pull my lips into some sort of smile. I failed. "Is Jack Tony's best man?"

"No," Beth said. "Tony asked him, it was only right, but Jack said that in the circumstances he'd have to say no."

I let out a sigh of relief.

"I'm sorry . . ." Beth began. "About the news. The wedding and everything. But I wanted you to be one of the first to know. I didn't mean to upset you."

Dear, sweet Beth. One of the happiest days of her life and I was being a real killjoy.

"No, I'm sorry. It's brilliant news. Tony's a lucky guy." I stood up and held her close.

"Thanks, Amy." We heard a cough behind us and moved apart. Matt was standing in the doorway, blushing.

"Sorry, Matt," I quipped. "Just having a bit of a snog with Beth here. Bit of an Irish tradition if you're mate gets engaged." Beth giggled.

Matt looked more than a little worried.

"Only joking," I smiled. "Although I've always had a bit of a thing for her." I winked at Beth suggestively and licked my lips.

This was too much for Matt who backed away towards the hall. A few minutes later Suzi burst in the door.

"What have you been saying to Matt? Dad sent him down to get the champagne from the fridge and he said he'd interrupted you both. He looked mortified."

"He'd better get used to us," I laughed. "He ain't seen nothing yet!"

"No kidding," Beth agreed.

Suzi looked at us both and sighed. She swung the bottle of champagne out of the fridge and tucked it under her arm. "Are you two coming back up?" she asked suspiciously.

"In a minute," I said. "There's something I have to give Beth first." In all the excitement I'd forgotten to give Beth her Christmas present. I told you I was selfish!

"Here, this is for you," I handed Beth the tiny black suede drawstring bag which had been keeping warm in my pocket.

Beth smiled. "Thanks, Amy. I'll just nip to the car and fetch yours and then we can open them together."

I waited in the kitchen for Beth to come back. I could hear the humming of the fridge, the ticking of the red Habitat clock on the wall and the sound of laughter and glasses tinkling in the sitting-room. Once again I felt achingly alone.

Beth bustled into the room, clutching a large black bin-bag which dwarfed her small frame. "Here you go."

"What is this?" I exclaimed.

"Open it and see," she laughed.

I took the bag from her and ripped open the plastic.

"Jeez, you're such a child." Beth smiled at my impatience.

In astonishment I pulled out a giant bag of multi-coloured pompoms, red and yellow ping-pong balls, a packet of coloured pipe-cleaners, some cardboard insides of toilet rolls, paper glue and craft glue and three plastic tubs filled with glitter, tiny gold stars and tiny red hearts respectively.

I grinned. "What are you like, Beth? What am I supposed to do with this lot?"

"If you want to be a children's presenter you have to start practising. I want to see a whole menagerie of pipe-cleaner animals and loo-roll people the next time I'm around."

"You're joking?" I spluttered.

"No," Beth looked at me straight in the eye. "Amy, if this is something you really want to do you have to take fate into your own hands. No one is going to walk into your shop and offer you a starring role on *Den 2*, you know."

"I know," I muttered. Beth was being a little freaky.

"You've got to take control of your own life. I think you should visit some schools, offer to talk to the kids about books, do some art with them, anything. Get some experience."

"And?" I asked doubtfully.

"And tape yourself interacting with the kids and send it into RTE."

I was silent for a second. She had a point. And maybe it would take my mind off things to do something different, something a little mad. It couldn't be any worse than being the bloody Story Princess, could it?

"I'll see," I said finally.

"Promise?" Beth asked gently.

"Yes, now open your present."

Beth opened the drawstrings and poured the tissue-covered present onto her open palm. She unwrapped the tissue and gasped.

"Oh, Amy, it's beautiful!" She held the necklace up and watched the tiny heart sway in its silver casing. "You shouldn't have!"

"You've been so good to me," I began, tears welling up in my eyes. "I wanted to get you something special."

Beth put her arms around me and kissed me tenderly on the cheek. "Thank you."

We heard a noise behind us and turned around, but the interrupter had gone back to the sitting-room.

"I hope it wasn't Matt," I laughed.

Beth giggled. "God love him."

Later that evening I sat on my bed in the dark and listened to the sounds of laughter coming from downstairs. I had smiled long enough so I'd excused myself and was now regretting it. Feeling sorry for yourself isn't much fun, especially when you recognise it as just that. Beth had gone home – to Tony. Suzi was sticking her tongue down Matt's throat in the kitchen, and Mum and Dad, Eva and Judy were finishing off the champagne and playing with Dad's poetry thingy.

I felt like shite. It was my first single Christmas in a

long time and I wasn't impressed. Last year I'd had Jack to cuddle up to, and to peel and feed me mandarin segments. And now I had no one. It was all most unfair.

And to top it all I had to go back to work on the twenty-eighth. But maybe it was just as well – it would keep my mind off things. Beth had made me promise to go to her engagement party on New Year's Eve before she'd left. Which was something to look forward to, I supposed. It was fancy dress for some reason – namely that Beth loved fancy dress. At least it was giving me something to think about. The theme was Heroes and Heroines.

After two hours of deliberation I'd decided to go as either Kermit the Frog or Ms Indiana Jones.

Chapter 11

"How was work?" Beth asked, opening her front door to me on New Year's Eve.

"Don't ask," I muttered darkly, walking into the hall. I really was in flying form these days. "Stupid people trying to exchange books they bought somewhere else and hoards of bored children looking for the Story Princess."

Beth smiled. "Was the Story Princess available?"

"Yes," I said. "But she read *Struwwelpeter*."

Beth looked confused. "Sorry?"

"They're German cautionary tales about bad children and the things that happen to them."

Beth looked a little shocked. "I think I remember my Granny reading them to me. Was there some boy who had his thumbs cut off 'cos he sucked them? And some girl who burnt the house down with matches?"

"That's the one."

"Are you serious?" Beth asked with concern.

"No," I admitted. "It was *The Secret Garden* this time. But I should have gone with the *Struwwelpeter*."

"Um," Beth murmured doubtfully. "Anyway, you're here now so make yourself useful."

We moved into the kitchen. The table was covered with dishes, bowls and plastic bags of shopping. Long sticks of French bread poked out of one of the bags and I spotted trays of fresh herbs in another. Beth loved throwing parties and never did things by half measures.

"Garlic bread and dips," I said, pulling the shopping out of the bags and placing it on the table. "And lasagne."

"Correct," Beth beamed from the counter where she was making two cups of tea. "You know me so well."

"Hey, isn't that a really bad song?" I laughed. "'I Know Him So Well'?"

Beth began to sing. She had a nice voice, did Beth. Shame about the song.

I joined in.

"Lovely singing, girls," Tony smiled as he walked into the kitchen. Jed followed in his wake, looking embarrassed.

"Hi, Amy," Jed said nervously.

"Hi," I smiled. He was male, wasn't he? With a pulse. And he wasn't all that bad-looking in a computer-geeky sort of way. And if you remember – single. Which is usually all the encouragement I need. "Looking forward to tonight, Jed?" I said, gazing into his eyes and tucking my hair behind my ears. When I had long hair I used to flick it, but, now it was short, tucking seemed to do the trick.

He blushed – bingo!

"Yes," he managed. "Yes, I am."

Tony looked at me strangely. Was he frowning? "We're off to buy the booze. Anything you want in particular?"

Beth squiggled up her nose. She always did this when she was thinking – it make her look like a rabbit but it was cute. Kind of.

"Tequila," I interjected. "And Red Bull."

"No way," Beth exclaimed. "Not after Christmas Eve. No more tequila for you, Amy."

"Ah, go on," I cajoled. "It's only New Year's once a year. What harm can it do?"

Tony looked at Beth and raised his eyebrows. She sighed. "OK, but only one bottle, mind."

I rubbed my hands together. "Excellent. Now where's the garlic? Not that I'll be having any, of course," I reassured the room, looking Jed straight in the eye.

Tony pushed a lobster-faced Jed out the door.

"Look what you did to that poor bloke," Beth scolded as the front door slammed shut. "You'll eat him for dinner."

"I was hoping it might be the other way around."

Beth looked confused.

"I wouldn't mind a bit of nibbling and licking, in the right places of course."

"Amy, you're disgusting!" Beth wrinkled her nose.

"I aim to please."

Beth handed me the garlic-crusher. "Garlic, now!"

"Yes, master."

"Excellent party," Jed whispered in my ear. "Good call on the tequila."

I had spent the last two hours pouring it down his neck and it seemed to have had the desired effect. We were sitting on the sofa beside the stereo and Jed was stroking my leg – which was clad in dramatic leopard-skin hold-ups – enthusiastically. I was hoping he wouldn't create some sort of static electrical charge and burn my lips when we kissed – but I guess you have to take your chances.

"Have some more," I purred, topping up his glass. We'd slugged our way through nearly the whole bottle which was quite an achievement as it was only ten o'clock. I was kind of tipsy but my mind was still sharp – well, sharp-ish. I was mildly enjoying playing with Jed, but it was all a little too easy.

And then Branigan walked in the door.

Branigan was the coolest and hippest guy any of us knew. He ran a club in town, designed his own range of handbags of all things and was at every movie, book or fashion launch in Dublin. And he was drop-dead gorgeous and knew it. Tonight he was wearing skin-tight red plastic trousers, a black T-shirt which clung to his toned torso and outlined his pecs and a black leather jacket. This outfit on anyone else would have looked plain stupid but on Branigan it looked deadly. Well, I assumed he was dressed up as some sort of New Romantic from the 80's, but come to think of it maybe he had just come as himself – I'd seen him in a similar outfit before.

He strode into the room with a pout on his full lips. His short dark hair glistened in the subdued lights. And, sad to say, my stomach lurched. He looked like sex on legs and had a reputation to match. And, praise the Lord, he was alone.

I stood up and tried not to stagger as I sashayed towards him. He looked bemused.

"Amy, how are you, darling?" He kissed both cheeks flamboyantly. "Delighted to hear about Jack. You're far too good for him."

I winced. Obviously the Blackrock old boys' grapevine had kicked in. Unbelievably, Jack and Branigan had been in the same class. I think they had even been some sort of friends at one stage. I could never picture it, they were so different, but maybe they had appreciated each other's selfish streaks.

"Hi, Branigan. How's tricks? Like the outfit – very Simon Le Bon." I should explain that Branigan was Branigan's name. First name that is. Branigan Luce. And it was always said with a drawling emphasis on the 'b'. Bbbbbrrranigan. Like that.

"Thanks. But I dressed up as me. And you look . . ." His eyes wandered languidly over my body, lingering on my legs and chest. "Grrrr." He growled.

I should probably explain at this stage that I'd gone for the Ms Indiana Jones costume – complete with the aforementioned leopardskin hold-ups, short fake snakeskin skirt, brown leather top with tiny shoe-string straps and long black whip (made out of a stick of bamboo painted black with string attached). I'd nicked my father's fishing hat – an Indiana Jones leather affair – and I'd attached fake spiders, bugs and rats to every available surface.

When he growled my legs nearly went from under me. Honestly, I have too many hormones – I should be kept away from men like Branigan.

Jed appeared beside me. "Amy, would you like another drink? The tequila's gone but I've found a bottle of vodka."

I smiled at Jed. He looked at me hopefully. "Thanks, Jed." I turned to Branigan. "Would you like a vodka and Red Bull?" Branigan nodded curtly. "Make that two, Jed."

God, I'm horrible sometimes. When Jed returned from the kitchen Branigan and I were sitting on the sofa which had been nicely warmed up by Jed and me. Like he was the supporting act and Branigan was the main attraction. When Jed saw us his face dropped. He handed us the drinks in silence and sloped off into the hall.

Ten minutes later Branigan and I were playing tonsil-hockey on the same sofa. His tongue was sucking and nipping my eager lips, tantalising my senses. One hand was firmly guiding my head and the other was snaking its way up my leg. Branigan was forceful, manly and, God, I wanted him.

"Hey, babe, I'm on fire for you. Let's go upstairs!"

I peeled my lips from Branigan's earlobe which I had been flicking with my tongue. "Good idea," I whispered.

He stood up immediately and pulled me up off the sofa in one swift, forceful move. I gasped as he held me against him and gyrated his pelvis against mine.

"I need action and I need it now," he said, grinning broadly.

I bit his upper lip – gently, mind, I didn't want to draw blood – and we made our way into the hall.

"Follow me," I said, starting to walk up the stairs.

Branigan followed behind, his hands holding my snakeskinned behind firmly and squeezing now and again. We fell into Beth's room where the coats were piled on the bed. The curtains were open and the streetlamps were lighting the room.

I began to search for my coat, throwing a leather jacket and a long black coat off the pile. But Branigan had other ideas. He launched himself on top of me, kissing the back of my neck and resting his weight on my body. His hands reached forwards and encircled my body, resting on my breasts and kneading gently.

I pulled one of his hands towards my mouth and began to lick his forefinger, popping it in and out of my mouth and caressing it with my tongue.

Branigan was breathing heavily at this stage. He lifted his weight off me and turned me around. He lifted my top, negotiated my bra, unclipping it skilfully with one hand, and kissed my breasts. I began to sigh.

I pulled his head towards me and began to kiss him passionately. His hands moved down my body, pushing up my skirt. He moaned as he caressed the bare thigh at the top of my hold-ups. He slid one of his hands slowly towards my stomach and began moving it down.

I froze. Even in my drunken state it felt wrong. I didn't really know Branigan, not properly. And I was damned if I was going to have meaningless, drunken sex with him just for the sake of it.

"Easy, Branigan," I whispered, placing my hand on his firmly and guiding it onto safer territory. We kissed for a few more minutes before I felt woozy and rolled off him.

I was woken by the sound of Branigan's voice. He was on his mobile.

"Yeah, babe, ten minutes, I promise. I'm on my way."

"Branigan," I smiled.

"Hi, gorgeous," he stroked my cheek. "I'm sorry. I have to go now. I'll ring you, OK?"

I sat up and pulled my skirt down. "Do you have to?" I asked. It wasn't that late.

"Yes, I really do. Bye, princess." He leant over and kissed me on the lips. "Enjoy the rest of the party."

"I'll put my mobile number on your phone," I said desperately, sad person that I am.

"Um, whatever, sure," Branigan muttered, looking a little uneasy. He handed me his chrome mobile.

I punched in my number slowly and carefully. And after watching his back disappear through the door, I lay down on the coats and fell fast asleep.

"Amy, Amy, wake up." Beth was standing over me with a worried expression on her face. "I wondered where you'd got to."

"Hi," I said, dozily. "What time is it?"

"Just before twelve."

"Shit," I exclaimed. "I'm sorry, I must have been asleep for a while."

"Branigan left about an hour ago. Apparently Elena was looking for him."

"Elena?" I asked, puzzled.

"His girlfriend."

"Oh, feck."

"What's wrong?" Beth looked at my face and raised her eyebrows. "You didn't?"

Now I was on the defensive. "No, I didn't. We just kissed a bit. And he didn't tell me about 'Elena'. It's not my fault. Anyway he said he'd ring me. Maybe they're on the way out."

Beth took my hand in hers and held it firmly. We heard shouts and cheers from downstairs. "Happy New Year," she whispered, giving me a hug.

"You should be downstairs with Tony," I said guiltily.

"Don't worry," Beth replied kindly. "He won't mind."

"Is Jed still downstairs?" I asked hopefully. I know, I have no shame. I just didn't want to be on my own right at that minute.

Beth frowned at me and ignored my question. "Listen, it's still early. Why don't you come downstairs and get something to eat."

Shit, with all the drinking and carousing with Jed and Branigan I'd forgotten to eat. No wonder I was out of sorts. I put my arm around Beth. "Sounds good, thanks."

"I kept you a plate of lasagne and some salad, just in case."

Tears pricked my eyes. "You're too good to me."

"I know," Beth smiled.

Tony gave me a dirty look as I walked into the kitchen. He was sitting at the table with Jack and Jodie. Feck it – that was all I needed. My heart lurched as I saw the 'loving couple'. It was the first time I'd seen them together and it cut through my heart like a hot knife through butter.

"Hi, Amy," Jodie said awkwardly.

"Hi," Jack said, his cheeks reddening. "How are you?"

Bloody awful, I felt like screaming. And it's all your fault. But I stood staring at them for a few seconds before deciding to be a mature, together adult. Yeah, right.

"Hi, Tony," I said firmly and ignored the other two completely. I didn't trust myself to speak to them. They didn't deserve my forgiveness and I was damned if I was going to pretend that everything was all right when it very clearly was not.

"Amy . . ." Jack began.

"Fuck off," I finally muttered.

Beth quickly intervened, handing me a plate and ushering me into the hall. I felt like a zombie.

"I'm sorry. I had to invite them," Beth apologised. "I didn't think they'd come. Are you OK? You must have got a shock."

I sighed deeply. We sat down on the stairs. "It hasn't been a good night for me," I whispered. The plate of food sat on my knee getting cold but I had no appetite for it now.

Chapter 12

Fuck you, Branigan. Why haven't you rung?

It was seven o'clock on New Year's Day and I'd waited in all afternoon in case he'd call. I checked my mobile for the umpteenth time. It was working all right.

I was lying on my sofa at home, channel-hopping with the remote control. Mum and Dad had gone on a monster walk, and Suzi and Matt were depressingly (for me) in bed where they had been since they had heard the parentals' car drive away.

Nothing on the box seemed to hold my attention for more than a couple of minutes. I was very, very angsty.

In my heart of hearts I knew Branigan wasn't going to ring. But I was hung-over to shit, feeling very sorry for myself and holding on to the glimmer of hope that someone, anyone liked me.

"Beth?"

"Amy! Hang on a sec," Beth's voice sounded groggy.

"Where did you get to this morning? I went in to wake you and you'd gone."

"I walked home," I explained. "I thought some fresh air might do me good."

"You must have turned some heads in your outfit," Beth giggled.

I laughed. "I did get the odd strange look all right. Listen, what are you doing today?"

"Well . . ." Beth went quiet for a moment. "Why don't you call over this evening?"

I heard Tony groan in the background. They were clearly still in bed. He yelped after his groan – Beth had obviously kicked or elbowed him. I heard her whispering to him. I could make out the words 'depressed' and 'selfish'.

I was mortified. I didn't want to cause trouble for Beth. And I most certainly didn't want to be a burden.

"Actually, we have a family dinner thing, but thanks for asking."

"Are you sure?" Beth asked, sounding relieved. "You could call over after."

"No. I have to work tomorrow but I'll give you a ring."

"Amy, are you OK?"

"Yes, why wouldn't I be?"

"It must have been a shock for you seeing Jodie and Jack. And that business with Branigan . . ."

I winced. "Branigan, who's Branigan?" I asked lightly.

"Amy, you completely ignored Jack and Jodie. That was a bit rude. I know you're upset but . . ."

I took a deep breath. I didn't give a flying fuck about Jack and Jodie. They had ruined my life. In fact, I was never going to speak to either of them again.

"Beth, I don't want to talk about it. I'll ring you tomorrow."

"Listen, they're going away in a few days – why don't you ring Jodie? You don't have to say much . . ."

"No," I interrupted, grumpily. I could be very stubborn when I wanted to. "I suppose you're watering the plants?" It used to be me who watered Jodie's prize rubber plants. Before the betrayal.

"Yes, I am," Beth admitted. "Please. Talk to Jodie. Otherwise you'll lose her as a friend."

"Friend," I spat. "Some friend. There's no way I'm ringing her, ever."

Beth sighed. "I think you're making a mistake."

"I don't care," I said, tears pricking my eyes. "I have to go. I'll talk to you tomorrow."

I put down the phone. I felt bad – it wasn't Beth's fault that my life was in the doldrums at the moment. In fact, if I was honest with myself I'd have to admit that it wasn't really anyone's fault except my own. But it was easier to blame Jack and Jodie. I retreated up the stairs to my bedroom, lay down on my bed and began to cry.

The following day I woke up feeling a little cheerier. A little. I was back to work which wasn't a bad thing – at least it kept my mind off my crappy life.

"Hi, Amy. How was New Year's?" Lynn was sitting in the window of the bookshop, surrounded by sheets of multicoloured perspex, a staple gun in her right hand.

"Great, thanks," I lied. "You look busy, what are you doing?"

"Putting in a new *Wizard of Oz* window. I thought I'd go with an Emerald City theme. I'm covering the lights with green perspex and building a castle with these different *Wizard of Oz* books." She pointed to the pile of large picture-books at her feet.

I smiled. Lynn could make any day brighter. "Sounds great. Can I help?"

"I'm going to be busy here for a while. But the books on the table are from the previous window. Maybe you could find a home for them and keep an eye on the till."

"No problem." I dumped my bag behind the till and stuffed my fleece into one of the large drawers under the computer. The blackboard was leaning against the back wall and I wiped it down and pulled out the box of coloured chalks.

"What story are you reading today?" Lynn asked with interest.

"I'm not sure," I said thoughtfully. I walked over to the picture-books and began to look through them. I pulled out a hardback edition of *Winnie the Pooh*. Pooh always made me smile and I could do with all the smiles I could get at this stage.

"Would you like some help?" Lynn asked from the

window. She was brilliant at calligraphy and always made the blackboard look very professional. My efforts on the other hand always looked like a six-year-old's. I could draw all right but lettering was a completely different ball game.

While Lynn wrote the Story Princess details on the board and placed it outside the door I sat down on one of the small wooden children's chairs, my adult bum squishing over the sides unbecomingly, and began to read. I was lost in the story about Piglet meeting the Heffalumps when I heard a discreet cough beside me. I looked up. I recognised the big brown eyes and neat pigtails. It was Zoe, my young pre-Christmas customer.

"Hello, Zoe," I smiled. "Did you have a nice Christmas?"

"Yes, thank you," she said politely. "Mum says I can choose a bedtime book. We've just finished *My Naughty Little Sister*."

"What type of book would you like?" I asked kindly.

"One about a little girl," she began thoughtfully. "With animals in it."

I walked over to the fiction shelves and pulled off an illustrated copy of *Charlotte's Web*. "I think you'd like this one," I began, handing the book to her. "It's about a little girl called Fern and a pig called Wilbur. They make friends with a spider who saves Wilbur's life. It's very funny."

"*Charlotte's Web* – that was one of my favourite books when I was your age, Zoe. I'd forgotten all about it." A tall blonde woman in black leather trousers and a dark-brown padded jacket pulled one of Zoe's pigtails playfully. "Hi, I'm Rita, Zoe's mum." She held out her hand.

I shook it, smiling. "Amy. Nice to meet you."

"Ah, the Story Princess. Zoe and Steve told me all about their last trip here. It sounded wonderful so I thought we'd visit ourselves. We haven't been in the area long but I can't believe we've missed this place. It's lovely," she gushed in a soft English accent.

"Thanks," I smiled. "It is kind of special."

"Mum," Zoe interrupted, "can we buy this?" She held up *Charlotte's Web.*

"Of course," Rita replied. "And would you like to come back to hear Amy's story later?"

"Yes, please," Zoe looked up at her mother. "We should bring Uncle Steve. He said the Story Princess was one of the most beautiful princesses he'd ever met."

I blushed.

"Did he now?" Rita grinned.

"Yes, and he said he'd bring me here any time I wanted."

Rita laughed. "You seem to have made quite an impression on my brother. We're meeting him for lunch so he may join us here for the story session from the sounds of things."

"Um, how nice," I murmured, my face on fire. I was mortified. Now she was going to tell her brother I fancied him. I just knew it. And I'd be all over the place and I wouldn't be able to read. Disaster. That was all I needed.

Zoe was waiting patiently at the till. She pulled out a small pink purse and counted out seven pound coins onto the counter.

"I think I have a customer." Rita followed me over to the till. I gave Zoe her change and placed the book in the small, brown bag with pink ribbon handles.

"Great bags!" Rita exclaimed. "We'll see you later, Amy."

I walked them over to the door. "Bye, Zoe. Bye, Rita. See you later."

"Bye, Story Princess."

Lynn popped her head over the side of the bookshelf beside the window. "Another satisfied customer," she beamed.

"Yes," I replied, thinking about Stevie J and how embarrassed I would be if they really did bring him.

I walked back to the till and sat down on the stool. I picked at the skin around my right thumb. The bell over the door tinkled. Customers. I tried to keep my mind on the job.

Chapter 13

At three o'clock the reading area of the shop was crammed with children. Their parents stood behind, waiting expectantly for their respective wards to be amused. No sign of Stevie J, thank goodness. I donned my princess hat and stood in front of my audience.

"I'm the Story Princess and today I'm going to read you a story about a bear called Winnie the Pooh. *Once upon a time, a long time ago . . .*"

I was so lost in the story that I didn't notice Zoe edging her way to the front until I'd finished the tale of Pooh and his elaborate plans to steal honey from the bees. As the crowd clapped and began to disperse she came up to me.

"Thank you. That was good," she said quietly.

Then I felt him beside me. Stevie J. You know, when you can just feel someone's presence. Like a fly without the buzz. Not that I was equating him with a fly, but you know what I mean.

"Hi, Amy," he smiled. "I enjoyed that. Pooh is one of my favourite philosophers."

I forced myself to look him in the eye. And, of course, I blushed. He really was cute. But he was a man and men ruined lives. Well, mine anyway.

"Hi." I didn't know what to say. I hardly knew him.

I heard Rita call Zoe over.

Stevie smiled again. "I was wondering if you'd like to go for a coffee with me sometime. I'd love to talk to you about children's books."

"Oh really?" I arched an eyebrow. I wasn't in the mood to be flirted with, even if he was cute and according to Lynn, single. And rich . . ."Is this your usual chat-up line? Let's talk about how rich and famous I am?"

He looked a little confused. "No, I really do want to talk to you. I've written a picture-book and I'm looking for an illustrator. I'd like to use an Irish one if possible. Fresh talent. Someone young and exciting. I thought you might be able to help. I don't really know anyone in Dublin and I thought . . ." he stopped awkwardly.

Now I was mortified. He hadn't been asking me out at all. He really did want to talk about children's books. Now things really couldn't get any worse. I reached up and took my Story Princess hat off.

"It's Lynn you should talk to then. She's an expert on Irish children's illustration. Lynn!" I called her over.

"Lynn, this is Stevie J and he'd like some advice. I think

you could help him." I walked towards the till and left them to it. I couldn't help glancing over towards them though. They were sitting on children's chairs beside the Irish published books. Lynn was showing him different young Irish illustrators. He was gazing at the vibrant colours in a Mary Murphy book and nodding his head sagely.

I sighed. Now I'd really made a complete fool of myself. What was happening to me at all?

"Amy?" Rita was standing beside the counter. "Can I buy this, please?" She handed me a copy of Steve's latest book, *Henry and the Master Wizard*.

"Sorry," I mumbled. "I was miles away."

"I noticed," Rita smiled.

"Your brother's latest," I said, dropping the book into a bag.

"Oh, don't worry about a bag, I'll pop it in with *Charlotte's Web*. I want to get Steve to sign it for one of Zoe's friends. He hates signing books. He says he feels foolish. He's very modest. I don't think he realises how well he writes."

"But he must," I exclaimed. "He's won the Carnegie and the Smarties . . ."

Rita sighed. "I know. But he's . . . I probably shouldn't say this but . . ."

"Are you talking about me?" Steve squeezed his sister's arm affectionately.

"No, of course not." Rita was flustered.

He smiled. "Lynn was really helpful. I think I may

have found my illustrator." He handed me a copy of *Little Penguin* by Mary Murphy. "Look at those vibrant colours, and the black outlines and the movement of the figures – wonderful."

I turned the pages as he talked. He was so enthusiastic about the artwork. I wished I hadn't made such a fool of myself earlier. I would have enjoyed talking to him about children's books. It was so rare to find someone who had any interest and he was a renowned writer to boot.

Lynn joined us beside the till. "Steve has very kindly agreed to a signing session of his new book the weekend after next."

Steve looked a little embarrassed. "I don't usually do many signings, but Lynn has been so kind . . ."

"That's great!" I enthused. "The kids will be delighted. Wait till I tell Siobhan's girls. They love your books."

Steve smiled and his eyes crinkled at the edges. "I'll see both you in two weeks then."

Rita and Zoe said their goodbyes and Lynn saw the group to the door.

"A Stevie J signing, think of it, Amy," Lynn said in rapture. "I'll advertise in the local paper and send flyers out to the local schools. How exciting!"

"We'll be mobbed," I smiled. "I wonder how many *Henry* books we'll sell."

"Hundreds, I hope," Lynn sparkled. "No, honey, thousands! Reach for the stars."

"Amy, this is Jodie. Are you OK? I'm worried about

you. Please ring me back. We're off to Galway later today and I'd love to talk to you before we go."

I grimaced, listening to the familiar voice on my mobile. I was sitting in Lynn's kitchen having a chicken sandwich and some carrot and orange soup. Lynn lived over the shop and always made us both lunch, although we could never eat it together – one of us always had to man the shop floor. She used to close at lunch-time but these days a lot of our adult customers shopped in their lunch hour and we had to stay open to accommodate them.

I didn't mind eating on my own. It gave me some time out from the bustle and noise of the shop. And it meant I had a few minutes to sit and think. Although the way my mind was at present, sitting and thinking was the last thing I needed. I'd remembered the frozen shrimps this morning, stolen from the freezer at home. And the screwdriver. I just wasn't sure if I was going to go through with my master plan. Hearing Jodie's voice, however, pushed me over the edge. What did she mean 'Are you OK? I'm worried about you.'? How dare she? Bitch. I'd felt reasonably all right earlier but now I was slipping into a black mood again. I'd get through the afternoon by throwing myself into some menial tasks.

I had to attend the Wedding Fair in the RDS at the weekend with Suzi and Beth and to say I wasn't looking forward to it was a huge understatement.

I walked back down the narrow stairs, brushing past Lynn's original Niamh Sharkey drawing and making it swing alarmingly from side to side. I put my hand out to steady it. Pity I couldn't steady my mind as easily.

Lynn looked up from a pile of returns. "How was your lunch?"

"Lovely as always," I smiled. She really was very kind. "The soup was delicious – did you make it yourself?"

"Yup, I like making soup. It's very therapeutic – chopping and blending. I have something for you by the way. Wait there." She jumped up and bounded up the stairs. I wished that I had her energy – she was like a teenager. I, on the other hand, felt like an old Granny at the moment. She handed me a white tube. "It's excellent stuff. I used it for the first time a few weeks ago. It's the most soothing mask I've ever had the good luck to find."

"Clinique Deep Cleansing Emergency Mask," I read aloud. "For skin under stress." Tears welled up in my eyes, but I really couldn't help it. Lynne was so kind, I didn't deserve such a nice boss. "Thank you," I murmured, holding the cool tube in my hot hands.

Lynn put her arm around me and gave me a hug. "Amy, I know you're going through a tough time but it will get better, I promise."

"I'm sorry," I began. "Is it that obvious?" I sighed. "It's just . . ."

"You don't have to explain today," Lynn said kindly. "After I've had lunch, why don't you go home? Get some rest. And I'll see you tomorrow."

"That would be great," I said appreciatively. "If you don't mind."

"Of course not."

While Lynn was upstairs I threw myself into taking old price-stickers off the books which we were returning to the publishers. I even managed to avoid any paper cuts which was quite an achievement.

"Off you go now," Lynn said firmly on her return. "See you tomorrow."

I skipped out the door, slinging my bag over my shoulder. I felt like a kid mitching school. It was barely three o'clock and I knew exactly where I was headed.

I lifted the flowerpot to the right of Jodie's door and smiled. She still kept the spare key in the same place. And Granny O'Connell always went to Jodie's Aunts in Cork for a week after New Year's so I let myself in, safe in the knowledge that no one would know I was there. Because there was something I had to do.

Jodie's place looked immaculate as always. The curtains were all drawn, giving the basement an eerie, gothic look. A chink in one of the curtains let in a dart of light, allowing me to make my way to Jodie's bathroom.

I clicked on the switch and walked over to the windowsill where Jodie kept her make-up and potions. I picked up her large bottle of Oil of Olay moisturiser. Jodie, as I had hoped, had been ultra-organised as usual. She always decanted her moisturiser, shampoo and conditioner into small travel bottles when she was going away, leaving the larger versions here – mine for the doctoring.

I put my bag down on the floor and removed my tube of Vichy self-tanning gel. I squirted half the Oil of Olay down the sink and replaced it with the gel. It had a slightly sweeter smell but I hoped the Oil of Olay would drown it out. Then I unscrewed her L'Oreal shampoo bottle, poured half of it down the sink and filled it with Sun-In hair bleach. Just to be on the safe side I did the same with the conditioner. Because let's face it – Jodie was worth it!

I smiled as I thought of her looking in the mirror. Looking back at her would be a brown-streaked face and orange/white streaked hair. As she had a pale complexion and long black hair I thought the effect would be quite stunning!

I put the bottles back where I had found them and washed my hands carefully. I didn't want incriminating brown streaks on my own hands.

Then I went into Jodie's bedroom. My stomach lurched as my eyes fell upon one of Jack's fleeces, draped over the back of Jodie's dressingtable chair. I opened her cupboard. No sign of Jack there, thank goodness. I checked the back of the door. As I thought – two Polo shirts, pink and dark green. I was tempted to cover them in Sun-In and tanning lotion too but that would have been too obvious. And I didn't want to be obvious. God forbid.

I looked at her curtain-rod. Excellent – I was right –

it was brass and hopefully hollow. I pulled the chair over to the window and stood on it. Jack's fleece was under my foot, treatment that was too good for it by half. I examined the end of the rod. It was covered by a brass fitting which looked like a pine cone. I hopped down and took a screwdriver and a plastic bag of now wet and soggy defrosted shrimps out of my bag. I placed the shrimps on the chair beside my feet. The bronze pine cone popped out of its socket after a couple of levers and digs with the screwdriver and fell onto the floor with a bang. I stood still for a few seconds, nervous that the neighbours might have heard me. They hadn't. I reached down and picked up the bag of shrimps. And I began to slowly and carefully feed each shrimp into the curtain-rod.

"Amy, what the hell are you doing?"

Chapter 14

I fell off the chair and crashed onto Jodie's bed, splattering shrimps all over myself and the antique white lace bedspread.

Beth stormed over. "What the hell are you doing? What are these?" She held up a limp pink shrimp in disgust.

It was lucky I'd fallen onto the bed and not onto the floor. "Look what you made me do," I shouted, sitting up and rubbing my leg which had hit the side of the brass bed. "I could have killed myself."

Beth stared at me in amazement, picking the screwdriver off the floor. "What are you doing here? What's this for?" She held up the screwdriver and waved it in my face.

I looked at the curtain-rod guiltily.

"Oh, I get it. You've been listening to too much Gerry Ryan. You were putting those pink things which I assume are prawns . . ."

"Shrimps," I interjected stroppily.

"Shrimps. You were putting shrimps into Jodie's curtain-rod. Amy, how could you?"

I looked at her and winced. "Was it really on Gerry Ryan? I wondered where I'd heard it."

Beth stood in front of me, a fierce look on her face. "Show me your bag."

"Why?"

"Just show me."

"OK, OK," I agreed. I had nothing to lose now.

I handed her my bag. She pulled out the mustard and cress seeds. "You were about to plant these on the carpets, I presume?"

I nodded, blushing furiously.

"And what are these for?" She held up the Sun-In and self-tanning gel.

I smiled. I couldn't help it. "For her moisturiser and shampoo."

Beth stifled a smile herself. "Now that wasn't on the Gerry Ryan show. How original." She looked at me and began to laugh despite herself. "Amy, you're nuts."

"I know," I said, pulling a shrimp off my fleece.

Beth made me buy Jodie new shampoo and moisturiser. And she made me remove all the shrimp from the curtain-rod. It took hours – some of the little buggers didn't seem to want to leave. I had to pull some of the pink squishy bits out with tweezers. It was revolting. It was late before I got home.

Beth saw me to the door. "I've removed Jodie's spare key and I'm going to tell her that it's not safe to leave it there because of burglars. So don't go near the house, understand?"

I hadn't said much all afternoon. I felt ridiculous, to be honest. But it had seemed like a good idea at the time. I didn't like Beth being so disapproving of me. So maybe it was a bit mad and to be honest I was kind of glad in a way that Beth caught me. I didn't want to be labelled as a 'bunny boiler' for the rest of my life.

"Say something, Amy."

"I'm sorry," I muttered.

"What would have happened if I hadn't come along?"

"I probably would have changed my mind anyway," I said brightly, "and taken out the shrimps myself."

"Um," Beth muttered darkly. She didn't seem convinced. "We'll talk about it tomorrow. I don't have the energy right now. Are you still on for the Wedding Fair this weekend? You don't have to come, you know."

"I'm coming," I said firmly. I was in a sadomasochistic mood. I might as well make myself even more miserable. Hell, Jodie and Jack might even be there. Now wouldn't that be nice?

That evening I curled up on the sofa and watched *The Runaway Bride* with Suzi and Matt. It was that or *Muriel's Wedding* or *Four Weddings and a Funeral* again. Worryingly all Matt's choices. But I'm sure he was just trying to get on Suzi's good side. Not that he needed to bother – if he hadn't worked out that she was a sure thing by now he needed his brain tested.

At least things weren't exactly going to plan for Julia Roberts on the wedding front. She wasn't called 'the Runaway Bride' for nothing. Pity about the ending though. Why did they have to ruin a perfectly acceptable film about marital evasion by slapping on a happy ending? I won't tell you what happens because you may want to watch it at some time in the future – I'm not that mean. But it wouldn't take a genius to work out that it's saccharinely happy.

The next two days of work dragged along at a pedestrian pace – a ninety-year-old pedestrian. Lynn was very kind. She let me avoid most of the customers by setting me stockroom tasks and sending me into town to collect art and craft supplies for our new window. Stevie J hadn't seen the completed work of art – when he'd been in all that was in place was a background of purple material, crepe paper and lights – he was in for a surprise. Beth hadn't rung since the shrimp incident and to be honest I didn't blame her. And I was too embarrassed to ring her myself. I hoped that she'd forget all about it and never mention it again. Hell, a girl can dream, can't she?

Suzi bounded into my room on Saturday morning and sat down on my bed. Tigger from *Winnie the Pooh* had nothing on her. Her dogged optimism and good humour were beginning to annoy me. What right had she to be in such damned fine form? It was raining outside, she was stony-broke and . . . and . . . actually, come to think of it, things were pretty rosy for Suzi at the moment. She had a man who loved her to death and who would fight lions for her, an impending marriage to same said man and a size-eight body which was still on the Australian side of white. And regular sex. Let's not underestimate the power of regular sex.

"Hey, Amy, are you ready? Beth's downstairs," she said, smiling.

I groaned inwardly. Now I remembered – this was the Wedding Fair day.

"Do I look fucking ready?" I muttered from beneath my warm, snuggly duvet.

"Don't be like that," Suzi frowned. "I'll bring you breakfast in bed. How about that?"

My ears pricked up. "Sausages?" I muttered.

"OK, I'll cook you sausages. I'll even make you a banana smoothie."

I looked at Suzi and tried not to smile. It was very difficult to be annoyed with her. She was too nice.

"Right, you stay here and have a doze. And I'll bring up breakfast when it's ready." Suzi flitted out the door and down the stairs. I rolled over and clamped my eyes tight shut.

A few minutes later I heard footsteps on the stairs. That was quick, I thought to myself. I hope she didn't microwave my bloody sausages, I liked them grilled or fried, not bloody microwaved.

"Amy?"

Shit, it was Beth. I wasn't in the mood. I pretended to be asleep.

"I know you're awake." She sat down on my bed, squashing my arm into the bargain.

"Ow," I yelped.

She jumped. "Sorry, I didn't see your arm there."

"Yeah, right," I muttered, my eyes still closed.

"I don't suppose you're in the mood to discuss the other day?" she asked quietly.

"No."

"Look at me, Amy."

I opened my eyes slowly. Beth's concerned face peered down at me. Sympathy. I hated it.

"I think you should talk to someone about all this. What about that nice lady you went to before – Dr Shield?"

"Dr Shiels," I corrected her.

"Well?"

I winced. Dr Shiels had been very kind to me. I'd gone to her before when things had been a little out of control. But that was when I was having panic attacks, for goodness sake, not revenge attacks. Highly provoked revenge attacks, I might add.

"Amy?"

"What?"

"Will you go to Dr Shiels again?"

It would have been easy to say yes, of course, I will, Beth. You're right. I need help. I can't cope with how I feel about Jack and Jodie. I am behaving in an inappropriate manner and I recognise that. I'll make an appointment first thing Monday morning.

But I didn't. "Fuck off. There's nothing wrong with me. Stop being such a moan!" Nice, Amy. Swear at your best friend who's only trying to help.

Luckily Beth had a very thick skin. "Amy. You leave me no choice then. I'm going to talk to your mum."

She knew she had me now. The last thing I wanted was for Mum to get involved. I'd be watched morning, noon and night. She'd have a diet and exercise plan made out for me before I could say boo. And to top it all Dr Shiels was a friend of hers so they'd have 'casual' deep discussions while I was in the room. Morag Shiels would never betray her Hippocratic Oath, of course, but when she was calling in to Mum for coffee I was fair game.

"Amy, tell your mum what you told me about your fear of being alone," Dr Shiels would say. Or "Amy, ask your mum about that incident when the boy next door locked you in the toy-cupboard . . ."

No. There was no way I wanted Mum involved this time. I was perfectly capable of dealing with this myself. I'd talk myself out of my bad mood and into a good mood. It was January after all. And come to think of it, I hadn't even made my New Year's Resolutions yet. No wonder I had no sense of direction these days.

This afternoon I'd sit down and write out my resolutions starting with 1) fuck up Jack and Jodie's life.

"Amy?" Beth interjected, breaking into my racing thoughts. "Are you listening to me? I'd said I'd have to talk to your mother."

"I heard you." I took the easy way out this time. "I know you're worried, Beth. And I don't blame you. But I recognise I have a problem and I'm going to deal with it. I promise. So you don't have to worry any more."

Beth looked at me carefully. "Does this mean you're going to go back to Dr Shiels?"

"Yes," I lied.

"Promise?"

I crossed my fingers under the duvet. "Promise."

Just then Suzi, bless her little heart, pushed open the door with her shoulder and came in.

"Breakfast," she said, smiling, "for my favourite grumpy sister. Matt made you some scrambled eggs with salmon, just how you like them."

I had to smile. "Thanks," I said gratefully. God, I was being such a ratty bitch. I didn't deserve such kindness. I sat up straight and Suzi placed the tray on my lap. She pulled over a chair and sat down beside the bed.

"So, are we all set for the Fair?" she asked. "It's going to be such a laugh."

"You think?" I asked incredulously, mouth full of sausage.

"What was that?" Beth asked. Luckily neither of them could understand my garbled question.

"I said you're right," I lied.

Beth smiled and patted my leg. "I'm dying to see the wedding dresses. And I want to find a gold silk waistcoat for Tony."

"Ooh, I saw some great waistcoats in one of my wedding magazines. I'll run down and get it for you." Suzi bolted out the door.

Beth and I sat in silence waiting for her. I munched my way half-heartedly through my breakfast. Sometimes, when I was emotional and not feeling myself, eating went out the window. Food just didn't taste of anything and I found it hard to swallow. It was better when someone was with me – to encourage me along.

Beth was twisting her engagement ring around and around her finger. She seemed deep in thought.

I swigged the last piece of sausage down with some orange juice. "Beth," I asked, "are you all right?"

"I just worry about you, that's all. You're overreacting to things. The business with the shrimps . . ."

"Do we have to talk about the bloody shrimps again?"

"What about shrimps? Are you talking about wedding starters?" Suzi asked as she came in the door laden down with an armful of glossy wedding magazines.

"Not exactly," Beth replied looking at me darkly. "Now, show me these waistcoats."

Soon the two affianced women were discussing colour schemes for grooms' clothes and I slipped discreetly out to have a shower.

Standing under the warm darts of water I tried to block all negative thought out of my head. Focus on the positive, I told myself. Count your blessings. But the only 'blessing' that I could come up with was that I wasn't dead yet.

We took the Dart to the RDS. Beth quite sensibly pointed out that it would be a nightmare to find parking. I moaned a bit as I liked being driven around – but I knew I was being stupid.

As we approached the RDS the area outside the main entrance was heaving with people. There was a queue snaking back towards the gates and well-dressed women and bored-looking men stared apprehensively at the body-jammed doorway.

"We'll be queuing for hours," Suzi said in dismay.

Beth smiled and waved three blue tickets in front of our noses. "I don't work for one of Ireland's top designers for nothing," she stated, walking confidently towards the top of the queue. We were ushered in immediately. Things were looking up.

But as we walked in the door, all my worst nightmares became real.

Chapter 15

The RDS was wall-to-wall shiny, happy wedding people. I'd never seen so many engagement rings in one place in my life. Beaming brides-to-be, excitement oozing out of every pore. A large catwalk ran down the centre of the hall. To either side, stalls of every size, shape and description were pushing their particular nuptial wares. We gazed around in awe.

"It's huge," Suzi exclaimed. "Where are we going to start?"

Beth, Little Miss Organised, had a plan as usual. "I've studied the hall layout and pinpointed stalls that I thought might be worth visiting." She pulled a catalogue of the Fair out of her bag. "I've highlighted those in pink." She certainly had. The map of the hall was dotted with pink splodges. And blue and yellow ones too. "The blue stalls are ones Suzi might be interested in. They specialise in home weddings – marquees, table hire, that sort of thing. And the yellow are Amy's ones."

I stared at her in bemusement. "Sorry?"

"Bridesmaid dresses."

"Ah," I decided not to question this. I'd rather fancied a Karen Millen number or something from French Connection. There was no way either of them were getting me into a traditional bridesmaid full-length flowery thing. No way!

"I thought you could wear fuchsia pink," Beth smiled. "Something quite classic, off-the-shoulder maybe. With turquoise shoes and silk flowers in your hair."

I realised that I didn't have much choice in the matter. It was her wedding after all. And at Beth's wedding Tony's sister, Stella, was also a bridesmaid. Stella was nearly six foot, with flowing dark hair all the way down to her bum and clear sallow skin. Your average nightmare. She was seventeen and still in school. And she had a stunning boyfriend of twenty-seven who ran a successful computer magazine called *Online News*. I'd look like one of the Ugly Sisters from Cinderella beside her. I hated her already.

"Stella said she was happy with whatever we picked."

"She'd look good in a bin-liner," I pointed out gloomily.

"No," Beth replied calmly. "She tried wearing one at her Christmas party. Didn't suit her. Black isn't really her colour."

I smiled despite myself.

"I thought you could wear pink at mine too!" Suzi said excitedly. "Light pink though, baby pink."

I tried not to wince.

Suzi continued. "You know how much I like pink. I was thinking of something long and slinky. Maybe with a scooped neck and a little diamante tiara. Or a ballerina skirt thing, you know, like a tutu."

My sister was mad. Quite, quite mad. I'd look ridiculous.

"What do you think?" she asked.

"Um," I said, noncommittally.

Beth brandished her multicoloured map. "Let's start on the right-hand wall and work over to the left. There's a wedding-dress fashion show on at two – that should be good."

"Can't wait," I muttered.

Beth dug me in the ribs. "Stop that," she said admonitorially. "As bridesmaid to both of us, you could at least be a little enthusiastic. If it was the other way around and you were getting married I'd be Miss Enthusiasm."

"Fat chance of that," I said, trying to hide my bitterness. "But you're right. Roll out the bridesmaids' dresses. I'm ready." She had a point, I was being a pain in the rear. I decided to try a lot harder. I pasted a smile on my face and determined to keep it there all day.

Beth took matters into her own capable hands. "Why don't we stick together to start off with?" she asked.

Suzi nodded. "Suits me. I really want to find a wedding dress. Can we look at those first?"

"Of course," Beth agreed. "My plan exactly. I saw a Lynn Carr dress I really liked in *Brides Today* magazine and I want to check it out in the flesh. "

"I'll just tag along for the laugh, will I?" I asked, biting my lip as soon as the words had snuck out of my mouth. "Sorry," I smiled, trying to make it look genuine. "I'm only joking, I'd love to look at wedding dresses. Pay no attention to me."

We began walking down the left side of the hall. I tried to feel like I belonged here, not like some sort of leper.

We made our way from stand to stand – The Bridal Suite, Loreto Brides, Bridal Beauties, Brides of Ireland, Wedding Belles, Pronuptia. That name always made me smile – Pronuptia – it reminded me of sex? Sad really, isn't it. You know – Pronuptia, prenuptial, wedding night.

Soon I became convinced that everyone was glancing at my wedding finger and pitying me for not having a ring. Eventually I slipped my plain silver ring onto my wedding finger. I thought it might make me feel less conspicuously unmarried. Didn't really work though. I remembered that I could have had a real engagement ring on my finger if I hadn't been so damn fussy. OK, so Jack wasn't perfect, but he was male and breathing. I tried not to think about him. But this wasn't exactly the ideal atmosphere to forget about boyfriends and weddings.

There were wedding dresses everywhere – white

puffy ones, grey satin ones, slinky ones, ones that looked like nighties and lacy ones. But none of them seemed quite right for either Suzi or Beth. They both saw shoes they liked though. Suzi's were little satin ballet pumps with a pinkish shimmer and light-pink satin ribbons. Beth's were more traditional, open-toed sling-backs in cream satin with tiny cream flowers along the straps and a kitten heel.

And Suzi found a tiara – a gorgeously frothy affair in silver wire inlaid with tiny pink beads. Like a fairytale crown. It suited her perfectly. But still no dresses.

"How about this?" Beth asked doubtfully, fingering a linen dress with corset type lacing down the back.

"For you or me?" Suzi asked in confusion.

"Oh, you. Definitely." Beth replied, smiling.

"I don't think so," Suzi said. "It looks like some kind of old-fashioned underwear."

"What type of dresses are you both looking for?" I asked, trying to be helpful.

But it wasn't that simple it seemed.

"I'm not sure," Suzi answered. "Something romantic. White, I guess. With lace. I'll know it when I see it."

"And I want something very classy. In silk or satin. Flowy," Beth added.

"Sorry?" I asked.

"You know, flowing."

"Right." God, I was bored at this stage. We'd been window-shopping, or stand-shopping should I say, for nearly an hour now and neither of them had seen a dress that they were remotely interested in.

Suddenly Suzi gave a little gasp. "That's it," she whispered. "That's my dress."

Beth and I followed Suzi eyes and gazed at the lace, net and satin creation before us on the Sharon Hoey stand. And it was beautiful.

"Try it on," I suggested. An immaculately made-up sales assistant swanned over to Suzi.

"Can I help you?" she asked in a clipped South Dublin accent.

"Can I try on this dress, please?" Suzi asked politely.

"Certainly, madam," the assistant replied. She looked Suzi up and down appraisingly. "I think you may find it a little on the large side though. It's a size twelve. I'll get some pins."

She ushered Suzi into the makeshift changing cubicle and took a plastic box of dressmakers' pins from a table top in readiness.

Less than a minute later Suzi stepped out.

This time it was my turn to gasp. She looked quite amazing. Tears pricked my eyes. My baby sister was really getting married. Although the dress was far too big and swam on Suzi's tiny hips, she still looked a million dollars. The long net skirt floated just above the floor. The lace bodice had tiny cap sleeves and white satin flowers cascaded over the surface, each flower's centre embellished with a small light-pink sequin. The overall effect was quite breathtaking.

"It's just lovely," Beth gushed. "It's perfect on you."

The sales assistant buzzed around, taking in tucks of material around Suzi's hips and pinning them down. Eventually she stood back to admire her work.

"It's called the 'Daisy'. A classic ballerina skirt with a modern lace bodice. For a fresh, young look," she pitched.

Suzi gave a twirl and the skirt followed her movement effortlessly. "How much?" she asked gingerly.

"Nine hundred and fifty pounds. With fittings, of course," the assistant replied.

Suzi bit her lip. "It's a lot more than we'd budgeted for," she said disappointedly. "Sorry."

I intervened. "Suzi, it's the dress for you. I just know it. What's a few hundred pounds anyway? You won't find anything else you like as much."

"I know, but it's so expensive. Maybe I could get something similar made . . ." she added hopefully.

Beth smiled and put her hand on Suzi's shoulder. "Amy's right. It's gorgeous on you. But go home and think about it. Take your Mum to see it. Don't make any rush decisions."

Suzi beamed. "Of course, you're right." She turned to the assistant. "Can you give me your shop details, please? I'll be back."

"Great," I smiled. "Now you're turning into Arnie Schwarzenegger, that's all we need."

Suzi smiled and skipped back into the changing cubicle. Beth and I waited, flicking through the rails of dresses.

"She's going to make a beautiful bride," Beth said.

"So will you," I said, smiling. I could be nice when I wanted to, after all. I was relieved.

"Thanks," she replied, squeezing my hand.

Beth found the Lynn Carr dress she had seen on the very next stand. It was very 'Beth'. It also turned out to be the dress Melanie in *Eastenders* wore at her marriage to Ian Beale. I hoped Beth's marriage would last longer than the ill-fated soap one – Melanie did a scarper after a mere eighteen minutes!

The dress was called the 'Olivia'. It had a long, flowing satin chiffon skirt and a satin fitted bodice. Beth tried it on and it suited her down to the ground.

"What do you think?" she asked as she twisted her body to survey her bum in the full-length mirror. "You don't think it makes my bum stick out?"

"No way," Suzi enthused. "You look slim and elegant."

"Right answer," Beth grinned gratefully. "I'll have to go on a diet though," she added wistfully. Beth, like me, liked her food.

"Me too," Suzi piped up. "I'm going on this protein diet. It's not supposed to be very good for you, but it's the one the *Friends* girls use apparently. And your one, the lawyer from *Ally McBeal*."

Within seconds Beth and Suzi were discussing the merits of different diets – the Cabbage diet, Food Combining, the Dine Out Lose Weight diet (now that one had possibilities) . . . if Suzi was any skinnier she'd fall down a drain – honestly the girl didn't have a pick of fat on her. Beth shouldn't have beeen encouraging her.

Jack used to drop hints about diets to me now and again. He wasn't exactly the most tactful of men. Bloody Jack! I really didn't want to think about him, or him and Jodie. I tried to shut him out of my mind. Jodie wasn't exactly slim. She was at least a size fourteen, for goodness sake. I wondered if he dropped hints to her about the gym and cutting out fat in your diet. I doubted it. She wouldn't stand for that kind of nonsense.

Beth went back into the cubicle to change and Suzi and I leaned against the back of the stand waiting for her in silence. I was exhausted. If I saw another wedding dress in my life again it would be too soon.

My thoughts were interrupted by the tannoy.

"Ladies and gentlemen, the Wedding Fair Fashion Show will commence on the main runway at three o'clock. A large selection of wedding dresses and bridesmaid dresses will be shown by some of Ireland's top models including the current Miss Ireland, Celia Davitt. Men's wedding attire will also be featured. Thank you."

"Come on, girls," Beth grabbed my arm and pulled me reluctantly along. Suzi followed behind us. "It's show-time."

Brilliant, I thought to myself murderously. Bloody brilliant!

Chapter 16

After half an hour of white, cream, grey, gold and more white my eyes were accosted by bright pink. Two tall, leggy blonde freaks of nature were modelling the most in-your-face bridesmaids' dresses I'd ever seen. The bodices were raspberry-pink, with tiny shoe-string straps. And the skirts, well the skirts wouldn't have looked out of place in a circus. Acres and acres of light pink net were layered on top of each other. And the worst thing was I just knew what Suzi was going to say. And I was right.

"How pretty! Amy, you would look darling in that," Suzi trilled.

I sighed. It was her wedding after all. Who was I to upset the apple-cart? To be honest I was beyond caring at this stage. My feet hurt and I could feel a headache coming on. If I said yes at least it would mean I wouldn't have to look at any more dresses. I mean there's only so much even I can take.

Beth glanced at me questioningly. I shrugged.

"If you like it, Suze, that's good enough for me," I said graciously.

"Excellent. Beth, can you jot down the details?"

Beth wrote down the name of the Dublin shop, Beautiful Brides, (even the name sent shivers down my spine) on the side of the programme.

We watched some hunky men parade down the catwalk in an assortment of suits, black tie and morning dress. Both Suzi and Beth decided then and there to put their men in morning suits. Suzi was adamant that she wanted Matt in cream, to set off his tan. Beth was thinking along more traditional lines, surprise, surprise – dark jacket, pinstripe trousers and gold waistcoat.

I wondered what Jack would have looked best in – something classic with a modern twist. Being an architect he would have gone for a wacky waistcoat or a red velvet jacket or the like.

"Amy," Beth asked. "What's up? You're miles away."

"Sorry," I mumbled. "Just thinking about something."

"The show's over. We were going to have a look at the wedding stationery. Are you coming?"

"Um," I replied. "Yes, I mean."

Suzi powered on ahead towards the right side of the hall.

"Where does she get her energy?" Beth asked.

"I don't know," I replied, "but she has Matt worn out too!"

"Amy!"

"Well, it's true," I insisted. "He doesn't seem to mind though," I added.

"I'm sure he doesn't," Beth smiled. "Do you really like that pink dress?"

I scrunched up my face. "What do you think?"

Beth stared at me. "Why don't you tell Suzi? It's not too late, you know."

I sighed. "I don't really mind what I wear, to tell the truth. So if it makes her happy . . ." I shrugged again.

Beth smiled. "You and Stella can choose what you'd like to wear at my wedding. The decision will be up to both of you."

"Thanks," I said gratefully. Beth was the kindest girl in the universe. "And I'll make sure we choose elegant and flowy dresses."

"Are you making fun of me?" Beth asked with a twinkle in her eye.

I raised my eyebrows. "Would I?"

Two hours later we had chosen Suzi's wedding stationery – delightfully wacky cream cards with tiny cartoon characters of a bride and groom, designed by an Irish company called Big Leap Designs. Beth had found a website which helped you organise your big day – www.weddingsireland.com. And we were all fit to drop.

We dragged ourselves out of the RDS into the dying daylight.

"God, I'm knackered," Suzi complained, rubbing

her shoulders as we made our way to the Dart station.

"Think of what we achieved though," Beth stated in her own inimitably positive manner. "We got a hell of a lot of the more difficult things done. And loads of ideas for other things."

We arrived at the Dart station, put our return tickets through the machine and made our way to the southbound platform. We sat down on a wooden bench.

Beth pulled out an A4 sheet and a pen and began ticking things off on a list.

"What are you doing?" Suzi asked curiously.

"This is my wedding checklist. I'm seeing what I still have to arrange."

I peered over her shoulder with interest. "I didn't realise wedding were such a hassle," I said.

"Only if you're not organised," Beth scolded. "I still have to arrange flowers, music, your dress, Stella's dress, lingerie, veil if I want one – I haven't decided yet, my wedding style . . ."

"Your what?" I asked incredulously.

"You know, what type of decoration and colour schemes we want – for example, Suzi's style, and correct me if I'm wrong, Suzi, would be young and fun, the flowers would be spring flowers in pinks, yellows and blues, freesias for example, and the wedding colour would be pink."

Suzi beamed. "You're right. Although I think I'll go for daisies instead of spring flowers. I'm impressed."

Beth continued. "And my style is elegant . . ."

"And flowy," I added with a wink.

"Amy, I'm being serious," Beth chided.

"Sorry," I mumbled.

"My style," Beth resumed, "is elegant and traditional. My flowers will be lilies and roses."

"And your colour is cream," Suzi added.

"Precisely," Beth said.

"I get you," I nodded. "Very interesting." Yeah right!

Just then the crossing gates over the tracks lowered with a clatter and our train approached. We stepped on and fell into the green seats.

"I'll sleep well this evening," I said.

"We all will," Beth agreed.

"Thanks for coming with us, Amy," Suzi said. "It can't have been much fun for you."

"It's OK," I smiled. "Anything for my two favourite brides-to-be. It was a laugh." And the strange thing was that it was kind of fun in a way. A giant shopping trip. And miraculously, I was starting to feel better.

The following Thursday evening Suzi dragged me to into town for her first dress fitting. She'd tentatively shown Dad the picture of the 'Daisy' dress the evening before and told him how much she loved it and how happy it would make her to wear it and how it would make her big day just perfect.

Dad had smiled and asked "How much?", winced and given in.

"If it would make you that happy . . ." he'd trailed

off lamely. Mum was less enthusiastic, asking could Suzi not shop around and consider some other dresses but at the end of the day it was Dad's chequebook that was paying the deposit and her sensible words fell on deaf ears. Dad was a bit of a pushover at the best of times, especially when it came to his little princess Suzi, or so it always seemed to me. As I'd expected, Mum and Dad generously (as they were paying for it!) conceded that a wedding was a once-in-a-lifetime experience and that they might as well get used to the idea that the whole thing was going to cost them a king's ransom.

As we walked down the steps to the Sharon Hoey showroom Suzi grabbed my arm.

"This is so exciting," she gushed. "It's all really happening. Thanks for coming with me, Amy."

"Not a problem," I said. "It'll be . . ." I fished for the right phrase but words escaped me, "interesting."

The assistants in the showroom were lovely. Kind and patient. They clucked over Suzi like mother hens, taking her measurements, showing her tiaras, shoes and underwear that would suitably accompany her dress.

"You've made the right choice, love," the older woman who had identified herself as 'Bronagh' said. "The Daisy is perfect for you."

Suzi smiled appreciatively. "Thanks."

It took nearly an hour for me to drag Suzi out. She was caught up in trying other dresses on – just to reinforce how 'right' the Daisy was for her. I blamed

Bronagh, she was definitely encouraging her. The woman seemed to love her job a little too much for my liking. In fact she was positively wedding-obsessed. I guess it was probably hard not to be in that line of business.

Finally Suzi made another appointment. I hadn't realised the dress would entail so much work. I presumed that they'd measure you, make the thing and Bob's your uncle, it was all yours. But, oh no, it wasn't as simple as that. It would take six fittings or more! Seemed like a bit of a waste of time to me, but I supposed if you were shelling out nearly a grand for one dress you'd want it to fit all right!

I rang Beth on Friday evening. There was a film I wanted to see in the multi-screen in Dun Laoghaire, a bodice-ripping costume drama. I knew it would be just Beth's cup of tea as Hugh Grant was playing the lead and she had an inexplicably large (and very sad) crush on him. I'd already asked Suzi to go but 'we', otherwise known as herself and Matt, were 'staying in'. Mum and Dad had been invited to a book launch by an author friend of theirs. It was sad when your parents' social life was more exciting than your own. Embarrassing really.

"Hi, Amy," Beth answered, sounding a little flustered.

"Are you in the middle of something?" I asked.

I could hear Beth sigh. "We're having a discussion. Hang on a sec. Tony, Tony . . . come back, don't be like that . . . Tony . . ." I heard a door slam and Beth came back to the phone. "Sorry about that." She sounded more than a little shaken.

"Is everything OK?" I asked carefully.

"It's just the whole wedding thing. I think it's begun to get to him. He's refusing to wear a morning suit. He says he'll look like a ponce."

I tried not to laugh. It sounded like the sort of thing Tony would say all right. "He'll come round," I assured her. "Once he's tried one on and seen how handsome he looks."

Beth sighed again. "I hope you're right."

"I don't suppose you want to come to the cinema tonight?" I asked hopefully. "The new Hugh Grant has just been released."

"I'd better wait for Tony to come back. Sorry. We're supposed to be sorting out the guest list tonight."

"That's OK," I replied, trying not to sound too disappointed.

I put down the receiver and stared at the phone. I couldn't think of anyone else to ring except Jodie and there was no way I was ringing her. All my friends were living in wedded or cohabitual bliss. I'd given up on most of them, especially the ones with babies who never, ever seemed to go out.

Everyone I knew seemed to be a 'we' and not a 'me'. I sat down on the stairs and stared at the front door. I suppose I could have gone to the film on my own but I would be dead embarrassed if anyone saw me. They'd think I was Billy No Friends, and the sad thing is that they'd be right! I could feel tears pricking my eyes and I began to feel very sorry for myself. I could hear Suzi giggling in the living-room. Matt seemed to spend his life making her laugh. Lucky cow.

I retreated into the kitchen, piled a tray full of crackers, two packets of Tayto cheese and onion crisps, a huge packet of dry roasted peanuts, a tub of Philadelphia cream cheese (with chives), a tub of garlic and lemon mayonnaise dip, two Diet Cokes and half a tube of Pringles and headed up the stairs. After all, I reasoned, I needed extra salt to replace all the salt lost in my tears.

Chapter 17

I sat down on my bed and started to eat. I piled a cracker high with cream cheese and bit down hard. Crumbs scattered all over my bed. I munched away, trying to take my mind off my sad and lonely life as a spinster. My eyes rested on a bright blue book which was lying on my bed. I picked it up and read the title – *The Power is Within You* by Louise L Hay. I figured Mum had left it there for me – she was mad into popular psychology books. Her favourite was called *Happiness is a Choice* by some American guy. She was a firm believer that you could make yourself happy or unhappy depending on your state of mind. Followed logically, this means that she believed that I made myself miserable. Which I think is a bit insulting and over-simplistic myself. When I was feeling crappy and down I didn't need her leaving bright-pink sticky notes on my door saying 'Embrace your fear' or 'Life is a journey. Travel light'. Or her reading positive affirmations to me over breakfast – 'Love yourself. You are a child of the universe', 'Be free to be yourself', 'Every day in every way I am stronger and stronger'.

As I had nothing else to do I picked up the book and began flicking through it while shovelling peanuts down my throat. I nearly choked when I read 'Stuffing food into our bodies is another way to hide our love . . . often we use food and diets to punish ourselves and create obesity.' I snapped the book shut and opened a packet of Taytos.

Half an hour later, after demolishing most of the food on the tray I began to feel a bit sick. I put the tray on the floor and lay back on my bed.

I woke up later and groggily looked at the clock beside my bed. It was ten past three. I wrapped the duvet over me and went back to sleep. Another exciting Friday night.

Work flew by on Saturday. We were inundated with calls, e-mails and faxes about Stevie J's signing session the following weekend. Children and parents alike were madly excited to be meeting their hero. RTE's *Den 2* were sending a roving reporter to cover the event and the newspapers were also sending out interested signals, which was very unusual in itself. Usually the papers couldn't give two hoots about children's books except at Christmas, or so it seemed to Lynn and me –

we were always trying to get them to cover children's events in our shop.

We took reservations for over three hundred signed books over the phone from places as far away as North America. Stevie fans had found details of the event from our website and were anxious to secure a rare signed copy. Not to mention the fact that Stevie's signature alone tripled the value of the book instantly.

Luckily he'd agreed to come in both days – Saturday and Sunday. I wondered if he'd stamp the books with a custom-made rubber signature block, like I'd seen some lazy authors do. Or just produce an illegible squiggle?

I hoped he'd forgotten my rude rebuff the last time I'd seen him. I was such an idiot.

After work I staggered home. My feet were killing me from rushing about all day and I had a throbbing headache. At least I had Sunday off. Beth had taken pity on me and postponed bridesmaid-dress shopping for two weeks, until Stella had finished some sort of weekend webdesign course. Of course, Stella's some sort of computer genius, as well as being young, gorgeous and in happy coupledom with Mr Rich and Successful.

I had dinner with Suzi and Matt. Mum and Dad were off at some friend's housewarming party. I never saw them at the weekends – they were always doing something. I retreated to the living-room when Suzi started spoon-feeding Matt ice cream. I watched crap television for a while – some sad people pretending to be even sadder 'famous' people, and some couples fighting after expensive sun holidays had been wasted on them.

What was I doing with my life? I should be out having fun with my huge gang of trendy and fun mates, not stuck in on my own – again.

I'd spoken to Beth earlier and she and Tony had made up. Which was good but it also meant that they were going out to dinner tonight, just the two of them. Which left me on my tod.

Uncharacteristically for me, I decided to do something positive – to tidy my room. Since I'd moved back from Jack's house I still hadn't unpacked the black bin-bags that contained many of my prized possessions. In fact some of my favourite clothes were still lurking in a suitcase under my bed. I pulled myself off the sofa and plodded upstairs.

As I fished the suitcase from under the bed, I also pulled out another slightly dusty black bin-sack. I peered inside and smiled. It was the craft materials that Beth had given me for Christmas. Funny old Beth. She really thought I could do something with them.

I pulled out the multicoloured pipe-cleaners and started playing with them. The bright green ones reminded me of Kermit the Frog and I began to twist the furry wires into a frog shape. It was quite good fun and very – therapeutic, I suppose. An hour later I had made a yellow duck, a black cat and three tiny white mice.

Beth had supplied some 'goggly eyes' – you know, the ones that move when you shake them. The bag contained 'over a hundred eyes for all your craft needs'! They looked very strange in the plastic bag – disembodied eyes caught in all kinds of weird expressions – but made my animals really come alive. Beth, bless her, had thought of everything – glue, glitter, felt, foam, pom-poms, coloured feathers – you name it. A veritable treasure-trove of materials. I began to run my fingers over the feathers and think about what I could do with them.

"Amy," I jumped as Suzi bounded through the door, "what are you doing?"

She looked at the bed where I'd lined up my little pipe-cleaner menagerie.

"They're brilliant. How did you make those?" she asked. "I like the rats." She picked up one of the white and pink mice and popped it onto her palm.

"They're mice," I smiled. "Do you really like them?"

"Of course. They're excellent. You know me – if they were crap I'd tell you."

I laughed. "I guess you would."

"You used to make things all the time. Your room used to be covered in things – clay people, candles, weird pasta jewellery, remember? And you used to make up stories and embroider pictures on cloth with feathers and bits of material, remember?"

I ran a bright purple feather over the cat's back. "I always liked making things."

"You should have been an art teacher or something," Suzi said. "Anyway we're about to put on a video. Do you want to come and watch it with us?"

"No, thanks," I replied. "There's something I have to do."

"Was someone up in the attic?" Dad asked the following evening during dinner. The whole family were gathered around the kitchen table, enjoying Mum's lasagne. "The hatch hasn't been closed properly."

"Sorry," I explained. "That was me."

Dad looked at me with interest. "What were you looking for?"

"Just some old things, nothing in particular." I didn't feel like telling them all I was looking for my old clay figures and little cloth books for some reason. It would trigger too many questions and I wasn't in the mood. "What evening are we doing the bridesmaid dress thing?" I asked Suzi, blatantly changing the subject.

"Thursday, if that suits. They're open late. Maybe Mum would like to come." Mum had missed the Sharon Hoey expedition.

"I'd love to," Mum assented.

"Thursday's fine," I said. "I'm sure Lynn will let me off early as I'll be working all weekend."

"That Stevie J guy is in your shop, isn't he?" Dad asked. "*The Irish Times* had something about it in the books section last weekend."

"That's right. He's signing all weekend. It'll be mobbed," I sighed.

"Is he cute?" Suzi asked. Typical Suzi.

I tried not to blush. I supposed he was kind of cute. "I guess so," I replied. "He wouldn't be my type though," I added, just to cover myself.

"I think I'll call in on Sunday," Suzi smiled.

Matt glared at her from across the table. "I like his work," she assured him. "And Simon loves his books, I've been reading them to him. Kate listens too, but I'm not sure how much she understands – she's only five after all."

Matt grunted. "I'll come with you."

Suzi grinned at him. "That would be great. You can look after Kate while I bring Simon to meet Stevie J." Matt frowned. That wasn't exactly what he'd planned for his weekend.

"How's work going?" I asked Suzi. She'd been with the Lowan family for a couple of weeks now.

"Great," she enthused. "Julie still models part-time, so she's out a lot. Kate and Simon are both little dotes, no trouble at all."

"And is Brian around much?" Dad asked. Brian Lowan was one of his rugby heroes. The charismatic Irish captain had been widely credited for turning the team around. Ireland was now one of the most highly respected teams in the world, and one of the youngest. Brian had been responsible for encouraging and nurturing talented young players, some still in school.

"Sometimes," Suzi replied. "He's mad busy though. But he's brilliant with the kids, and when he is around he plays with them non-stop. I don't know where he gets his energy."

Matt smiled. "Suzi's asked Kate to be flower girl and Simon to be pageboy at the wedding."

"Will Kate be wearing pink too?" I asked cautiously. I wasn't sure I liked the idea at all.

"No," Suzi said. I breathed a sigh of relief. "I saw a darling little dress in Monsoon, plain white cotton with little pink flowers embroidered on the bodice."

"Sounds lovely," Mum beamed. "It's no time away now, only fifteen weeks."

Dad caught my eye. "Thank goodness," he mouthed.

I smiled at him. At least I wasn't the only one bored with the wedding already. Roll on, May.

* * *

I looked in the mirror. I expected to see a large light pink meringue, but I was surprised. My bridesmaid's dress didn't look too bad really. I'd expected to look really ridiculous and I only looked a little ridiculous. And the way my life was going these days I could live with a little ridiculous.

The assistants in Beautiful Brides were nice enough. They helpfully suggested some foundation underwear to 'smooth out the lines', a tactful way to say 'to lessen that pot belly'. The size fourteen dress fitted almost perfectly. They just had to take in the bodice a little and shorten the skirt – which was depressing as I'd previously been living in a size-twelve fantasy world. In recent weeks I'd had to wear a belt on my jeans as the button wouldn't do up, but I thought that was just post-Christmas tummy and would magically melt away in January. No such luck. I reluctantly decided I'd better go on some kind of diet. I felt sorry for Suzi too – I'm sure she wanted a slim and attractive bridesmaid. She probably felt like she had to ask me as I was her sister.

Suzi stood beside me and smoothed down the top layer of net. "It's lovely, Amy," she smiled. "Really lovely."

"Thanks," I said, trying to hold in my stomach.

When I woke up on Saturday morning I was a bundle of nerves. I'd spent most of the second half of the week making Valentine's cards to decorate the shop. Although Valentine's Day was weeks away Lynn wanted to make the shop as interesting as possible. So as well as Stevie J's posters, cardboard cut-outs and mobiles, we had 'love' shelves in each of the different book areas.

In the picture-book corner I'd made giant pink and silver cards with pompoms. Copies of *Guess How Much I Love You?* with its cute hares nestled among the oversized cards. In the fiction area I'd made huge cardboard hearts and covered them with multi-coloured feathers. And in the Irish section I'd made a huge mobile of red foam hearts sprinkled with gold glitter which moved gently, twinkling in the lights. Beth's goody-bag was proving very useful.

I managed to eat a slice of toast before walking into work. It was a mild enough day for January and the sky was clear for once. The odd cloud puffed by but otherwise it looked like it wasn't going to rain.

As I reached the top of Blackrock Road I gasped. Outside The Wonderland there was a whopping great queue. As I drew closer I stared in amazement at the crowd which was increasing right before my eyes. The queue snaked along the path, against the windows of the neighbouring shops and houses.

Lynn had placed the blackboard outside the shop and as I walked towards the door a little girl pulled my fleece.

"It's not open yet. We were here at seven o'clock this morning," she said quietly.

Her mother smiled at me. "We drove up from Cork last night. She's a huge Stevie fan."

"I work here," I explained levelly. "I'm not skipping the queue."

"That's OK then," the little girl said.

Lynn came to the door and opened it just enough to let me in.

"Hi, Amy," she said when I was safely inside. "Am I glad to see you! Isn't it crazy out there?"

"You're not kidding!" I replied. "And it's not even nine yet. Heaven knows what it will be like later."

"Jess is coming in to help and she's bringing three friends from college." Jess was a student who was training to be a primary school teacher.

"Great, we should be fine then. I hope Steve doesn't get mobbed on the way in."

Lynn grinned. "I've already rung him. He's going to drive up the back lane and come in the delivery door."

"Good thinking," I said. "I'll just go and dump my stuff upstairs."

When I came back down Jess and her friends Frank, Paul and Lucy had arrived. Frank and Paul were nice and tall and Lynn immediately assigned them to crowd control, Frank outside and Paul inside. Jess would be in charge of the door with Lucy, leaving Lynn and me to man the signing.

The PR woman, Rachel, from Steve's publishers arrived next with the Dublin sales rep. They offered to help sell the books.

Steve arrived at ten to nine. He seemed a little shell-shocked.

"Mate, did you see the kids outside?" he asked me as he stepped over the boxes in the goods-in room. "Must be hundreds of them."

"Popular guy," I smiled. "I hope your hand is up to it."

"I'm wondering that myself," he smiled back. He really was very cute. Then it occurred to me that he was highly unlikely to be interested in me – I'd made a right wally of myself the last time we'd met. In fact, I'd been downright rude. He was being dead nice though – maybe he'd forgotten all about it.

"Can I get you a coffee or anything?" I asked.

"You mean now or are you asking me out?" he laughed.

Shit! He hadn't forgotten. I could feel my face getting redder and redder. I didn't know what to say.

"I'm sorry," Steve said. "I didn't mean to embarrass you. I just couldn't resist it."

"It's OK," I mumbled.

At that moment Lynn bustled in, saving me from further mortification.

"Steve, I'm delighted to see you. I presume you saw your fans outside?"

"Sure did, mate," he replied. "Scary stuff. I hope you have lots of books."

"Absolutely!" Lynn assured him. "I'll show you your signing desk. Can I get you a coffee?"

Steve smiled. "Amy's already kindly offered."

I looked at him and smiled. "Milk and sugar?" I asked.

"Black," he replied. "One sugar. Thanks."

The morning flew by. From the first little Cork girl, Steve was the epitome of charm. He signed each book with a smile, often writing a special dedication. He chatted to the children, answered their every question and also talked to the parents. Mid-morning, I spotted Siobhan and Clara making their way to Steve's desk, ably shepherded by Paul and Jess.

"Hi, Amy," Siobhan smiled when she spotted me over the sea of heads and squeezed over. "How's it going?"

"Brilliantly," I said enthusiastically. "Steve's a star. I've never seen anyone write so quickly."

Clara moved forward, towards Steve and passed him her book. I moved behind him with Siobhan,.

"I've seen you before," Steve said to Clara, kindly. "At one of Amy's Story Princess sessions."

"That's right," Clara replied, delighted that he'd remembered her. "Amy's cool. We love her."

At that moment I nearly cried. I could honestly feel tears prick the back of my eyes. It was the nicest thing anyone had said about me for a long, long time. And when I heard Steve's reply . . . I couldn't remember feeling so happy.

"She is, isn't she?" Steve smiled at Clara. "And don't tell her, but I think she's really pretty."

Clara giggled. "I won't," she promised, "but she's right behind you."

"Ah," he turned his head and smiled at me. "Hi, Amy."

I laughed. "Hi, Steve. You're all right. I didn't hear anything."

"That's OK then," he smiled again.

I spent the rest of the day walking on air.

At lunchtime I went upstairs to grab a bit of lunch. Lynn had made sandwiches and wraps for everyone and they were delicious. Steve had taken a ten-minute break, thrown some food and coffee down himself and gone back to the fray. Brave man! He figured he'd have to get stuck in if he was going to meet every child. And as some of them had travelled long distances to meet him, he didn't want to disappoint anyone.

Jess popped her head around the kitchen door as I had just bitten into a chicken tikka wrap.

"Amy, there's a woman from RTE who wants to talk to you. Can I bring her up?"

"Sure," I nodded. Lynn had nominated me as the Wonderland press person. Only because she didn't want to do it – I was famous for my lack of tact so it was an odd choice.

Jess returned with a tall, slim woman with cropped black hair. She looked really young and trendy and I was intimidated already.

She bounced towards me on shiny, red DKNY trainers. "Hi, I'm Helen. I work for *Den 2*. I just wanted to find out who did the Valentine's cards downstairs?"

I winced. She obviously thought some child had done them. How embarrassing. I bit the bullet.

"Hi, I'm Amy." I thought about offering my hand but decided against it. She looked too cool to be into handshaking. And anyway, I had tikka sauce on mine. I wiped them on my jeans just in case. "I made the cards."

"No way," she gushed. "They're so cooool! So original. I love them."

I was taken aback. She wasn't here to slag my feeble craft attempts. She really liked them.

"Um, thanks," I mumbled.

"I'm putting together the Valentine's set at the

moment for *Den 2*. Would you be interested in making some more for me?"

I nearly fainted. Me? Make things for television – and *Den 2* no less? Was she kidding?

"Of course," I spluttered. "If you really think . . ."

"They'll need to be even bigger but I love the colours and the styles. So if you could make six for me, poster size?"

"Two of each style, A0 size?" I asked, wanting to get it right.

"Exactly!" she exclaimed. "And we'll cover all your expenses and give you a design fee. I'm afraid we don't pay that much, but how does one hundred pounds sound?"

Like music to my ears, I thought.

"That sounds fine," I said.

"Cool!" She pulled a gleaming black personal organiser out of her jacket pocket and began to play with it. "I'll need them by the end of next week. Delivered to the television centre, if that's all right."

"No problem," I said in a daze. "I'll have them done by Friday."

"Cool! Friday afternoon is perfect. Give me a ring when you get to reception. Great to meet you," Helen held out her hand and shook mine firmly. "I look forward to seeing your hearts." With that she bounded back down the stairs, leaving me staring in her wake.

Amazing, I thought to myself. Quite amazing. I immediately began to worry – what if I can't do it, what if they turn out crap, what if I catch some disease and I'm in bed all week . . .

Jess called up the stairs, interrupting my musings. "Amy, are you finished? Paul and I are dying for a cigarette."

"Just coming," I yelled down, slurping down some orange juice and rinsing my hands under the tap.

Chapter 18

The afternoon was a little less frantic. The queue outside had abated – it was now only twenty or thirty children long. Steve was exhausted by the end of the day.

"Blimey, mate," he said as we shut the door behind the final customer at half past six, "I thought I'd be here all night. I can't believe I have to do this again tomorrow."

Lynn smiled. "We've sold over six hundred books today alone, not including the mail orders. That's incredible!"

Steve whistled. "That's a lot of books all right." He chatted to his publishers while Lynn and I cashed up the till. Jess and her friends were straightening up the shop, which looked like a bomb had hit it.

"We'd like to take you and your staff out for drinks and dinner tonight, if everyone's free," Rachel said, walking across the room towards us. "Where's good around here?"

"The Italian on the main street is nice," Lynn said. "Or there's a couple of places in Dun Laoghaire and Dalkey."

"How about Coconut Street?" I suggested. "It does Caribbean food and it's always a good laugh."

"Sounds perfect," Steve said, joining us.

"Coconut Street it is," Rachel pronounced. "How many can come? Lynn, Amy, Jess?"

"Count me in," Lynn smiled.

"I can't," Jess replied, "and Lucy's baby-sitting but Paul and Frank might be able to – how about it, boys? Free for dinner tonight?"

The boys nodded enthusiastically.

"How about you, Amy?" Rachel asked. I tried my damnedest not to look at Steve. But it was no use. He smiled at me.

"You have to come, Amy," he encouraged. "It wouldn't be the same without you."

"OK," I agreed. "I'd love to. Right, who's on for pints beforehand?"

"Good idea," Steve said.

We made our way to the Purty Kitchen. Steve was adamant that he wanted to walk. He said he needed some air to clear his head after the day's session. I kindly offered to walk with him. Anne, the sales rep, took Lynn and Paul, and Rachel insisted on giving Frank a lift in her car, a rather nifty-looking red two-seater BMW. The PR woman seemed to have taken a shine to Frank, although I'm sure he was at least ten years younger than her.

"It's not a bad evening," Steve commented.

"No, it's grand," I replied. I thought it was a little chilly myself, to tell the truth. But after his gracious comments about me to Clara earlier I was willing to brave the sub-zero temperatures of the Arctic for him.

"Thanks for walking with me," he continued. "I need some fresh air before tonight's session."

"That's OK," I smiled. "Me too."

As we walked past Jodie's house I shivered. I hadn't thought about Jack or Jodie all day, we'd been so busy.

"Are you cold?" Steve asked kindly. He started to take off his leather jacket.

"I'm fine. Please, put your jacket back on. You'd freeze in your shirt. Someone just walked over my grave, that's all."

"Ghosts?" he asked gently.

"Sorry?" I asked, confused.

"Ghosts of the past?"

"Something like that."

"Want to talk about it?" he asked.

I hesitated. I would have loved to talk about Jack and Jodie and how hurt and alone I felt but I didn't want to put him off. I was starting to really like him. "No, thanks though."

He stopped suddenly and wheeled around to face me head on. "There's something I wanted to tell you. I think I was asking you out that time. I was just afraid you'd say no. Which you did." He paused. "It's funny," he continued. "When I'm writing, words come out so easily and I have no trouble expressing anything. But when I'm with real people it's a different story."

"You're doing fine," I reassured him. "But what are you trying to say?"

"That I like you. That I want to get to know you," he said honestly. He looked at me intently.

"OK," I said.

"OK, yes," he asked, "or OK, no?"

"What are you asking exactly?"

He blushed. "I guess I'm asking do you like *me*?" He blushed even more furiously.

I was delighted – that blushing was something other people did and not just me, that he liked me and most of all that he wanted to get to know me.

"Yes," I said, "I like you." I tried not to giggle. I felt like a teenager.

He blew out a breath. "Phew, that wasn't so bad. Now let's go drinking. I could murder a pint of Guinness."

We began walking again and he put his arm around my shoulders. I could feel the side of his body moving against mine beneath his jacket. He smelt warm and male, a mixture of faded aftershave and leather.

We chatted amicably about the signing – the noise and mayhem of the morning, the delighted children, the unbearably pushy parents. As we passed the Martello tower at Monkstown I remembered the day, not that long ago, when I had cried my heart out on a bench beside the tower. I could still feel the hurt like it was yesterday.

"Amy," Steve said, "I asked you a question. You're miles away."

"Sorry," I mumbled. "What did you ask me?"

"About Dun Laoghaire pier. How old is it?"

I tried to keep my mind from wandering. "I'm not sure exactly. I know the rock used came from Dalkey Quarry. They used to bring it on tracks down a pathway called The Metals from the top of Dalkey Hill. You can still see the tracks in some places."

"Is the quarry still there?" he asked.

"Yes, but it hasn't been used for a long time. It's popular for rock climbing these days. There's The Purty." We rounded the corner and the cream building came clearly into view – you couldn't miss it.

"Just one thing before we go in," Steve stopped in his tracks and put both his arms around me. My stomach gave a little lurch and I closed my eyes. I was disappointed when I felt a soft kiss on my forehead.

When we walked in the door we spotted Anne, Lynn and Paul at the bar starting into their drinks.

"What are you having, guys?" Anne asked. "The night is on your publishers, Steve, so drink away."

"In that case I'll have a bottle of champagne and a Guinness to start with," Steve grinned.

"Is the champagne just for you or can anyone join in?" I asked. He patted me on the head.

"Don't be such a muppet. It's for everyone," he smiled.

"I'll have champagne, so. And what the hell is a muppet?"

Steve began to explain. While he was talking Lynn grabbed my shoulder and pulled me towards her.

"What's going on between you two?" she whispered, nodding towards Steve. "You look very chummy."

I smiled conspiratorially. "That would be telling."

"Dinner is booked for eight," Anne reminded us all. "So don't get too cosy."

"Where's Rachel?" Steve asked with a mischievous grin.

"Good question," Anne replied.

Rachel and Frank appeared at seven. Frank's hair was tousled and his cheeks were flushed. Rachel was in high spirits. She draped her camel cashmere coat over the back of Steve's chair. She had changed out of her black trouser suit into a black dress. Her make-up had been immaculately re-applied, her blood-red lips standing out on her pale face. In fact, she looked just like a Billy girl from *Ally McBeal*.

"Sorry, darling," she gushed, kissing Steve dramatically on both cheeks and leaving striking red lip-marks. "We got caught up." She looked at Frank pointedly. He smiled sheepishly, blushed and looked at the ground. "Excellent, champers. Another bottle, please," she called to the barman, waving the empty bottle in front of his face. "Actually, make that two."

At eight o'clock we made our way towards Coconut

Street. The Irish among us – myself, Frank and Paul – insisted that eight meant eightish and that we had time for another bottle of champagne, but we were outnumbered by punctual foreigners.

"Honestly, they won't be expecting us on time," I told Steve as we staggered towards the restaurant. Luckily it was only a few minutes walk. The cold air was making me feel quite tipsy.

Rachel and Frank, who had been flirting quite shamelessly for the last hour, were walking in front of us. Rachel's hand was planted firmly in Frank's back jeans pocket and she was whispering in his ear. Actually it looked more like nibbling than whispering. Paul, Anne and Lynn were enjoying a good discussion about the marginalisation of children's books in the Irish media. Paul was an English Literature student in Maynooth and was writing his thesis on the famine books by Marita Conlon-McKenna, a popular Irish children's writer. The conversation sounded way too serious for me.

"Are you working tomorrow?" Steve asked me.

"Yes, unfortunately. We'll all be the worse for wear, I'd say."

"Good," he smiled, squeezing my shoulder. His arm was around me again. "That means I get to see you again."

The outside of the restaurant was lit by huge orange lanterns. As we walked in the door a waft of warm, spicy air hit us. As we waited to be seated I looked around. The walls were a warm orange, decorated with large, bright modern paintings. The lighting was subdued and every table was packed with people. The place was humming.

Our table was in the back of the large main room. It was already laden with dips and home-made breads which we laid into without ceremony.

"Good choice, Amy," Rachel said approvingly. "Great place. I hope they do champagne."

We all laughed. A young American waiter took our drinks order – red and white wine and two bottles of champagne – and left us to decide on our food. Soon we were all busy chatting and laughing. The poor waiter had to come back several times before we'd all even looked at the menu. He was very good-tempered about it though.

"I don't know what to have," Lynn said. "It all sounds wonderful. What are you having, Amy?"

"Jerk chicken, I think. Or Calypso chicken. And yam sticks to start with."

Finally we placed our orders. The food came swiftly and we were soon tucking into our starters. Steve was sitting beside me. Rachel and Frank were opposite us. Rachel's hand kept disappearing under the table. Frank didn't seem to mind though.

"Where do you live, Rachel?" Lynn asked, oblivious.

"West London," Rachel replied. "I have an apartment. I'm not there much though. There's always some launch or function on."

"Do you have to travel to Ireland much?" Frank

asked hopefully. At twenty, his libido was the foremost thing on his mind.

"Yes, lots," she replied. "I'm over here a lot and in Edinburgh, Bologna for the Children's Book Fair, Frankfurt, that kind of thing."

"Sounds very glamorous," I said enviously.

Rachel smiled. "It can be, I suppose. But sometimes I'd just like to be at home, curled up on the sofa with a video and some ice cream. Launches can be a bore."

"Remind me not to invite you to any of mine," Steve laughed.

"Yours are never boring, honey," Rachel smiled.

Soon our main courses arrived. I'd decided on the Jerk chicken, a deliciously spicy dish.

"What are you doing later?" Steve asked.

I smiled lazily. This was more like it. "That depends."

"Would you like to share a taxi?"

I'd like to share a lot more than a taxi, I thought. But I decided I'd better not scare him off.

"Sounds good, thanks," I said graciously.

After dessert – deep-fried fruit fritters with cream all round – it was time for Irish coffees and flaming sambucas. Even Lynn had a sambuca.

"How are you feeling?" I asked Steve, putting my hand on his leg under the table and leaning towards him.

"Drunk and very, very full. And you?"

"The same."

He put his hand on mine, lifted it towards his lips

and planted a kiss on it. "I've had a great evening. You're good company, Amy."

"Thanks," I smiled. I wished it was just the two of us at that moment. It was difficult to be romantic at a table full of people. Although Rachel and Frank seemed to be managing it. Frank was nuzzling Rachel's neck with his lips.

Rachel stood up. "Bedtime for me, I'm afraid. Early start in the morning. My hotel is just around the corner so Frank is walking me back."

We all smiled knowingly and said our goodbyes.

"Don't do anything I wouldn't do," Paul told Frank with a wink.

Frank grinned back. "See you tomorrow."

Anne, Lynn and Paul left next, sharing a taxi, leaving myself and Steve alone. This was more like it.

Unfortunately the waiter signalled over to tell us our taxi had arrived.

"My lady," Steve said, helping me on with my fleece jacket, "our carriage awaits." We climbed into the taxi.

"Monkstown. and . . ." Steve looked at me expectantly.

"Oh, Blackrock," I said. When he said he'd take me home I presumed he meant to his house and not literally. I was disappointed. Maybe he didn't like me at all. Maybe he'd gone off me during the evening. Luckily I wasn't too drunk, otherwise I probably would have lunged at him in the taxi. I tended to do that when I was feeling insecure and needy.

I told the taxi driver my address and sat back in the

seat. Steve held my hand. We sat silently until we reached my house. It was terrible – I couldn't think of anything to say.

"This is me," I said. I fumbled in my pocket for some money.

"I'll get it," Steve said. He leant over and kissed me on the cheek. "See you tomorrow." He let go of my hand.

I stepped out of the taxi and walked towards my front door. The car waited until I'd opened the door and then drove away. It was after one and I was exhausted and faintly disappointed. It had been quite a day.

Chapter 19

The next morning my alarm trilled, waking me out of my dead sleep. I'd had the foresight to set my alarm last night, proving that I couldn't have been too drunk. I pulled open my eyes. It was ten o'clock. Luckily the shop didn't open until eleven on Sundays. I lay in bed for a few minutes thinking about Steve. If he really liked me, in a romantic way, last night would have been different. He obviously liked me but wasn't attracted to me – typical!

I showered and pulled on some clothes. Sitting at the breakfast table I contemplated my hangover. I had a pain in the back of my neck and my head throbbed. I'd been poisoned by drink again and I had no one but myself to blame.

As I pulled the car out of the drive the rain pummelled down. It was a miserable day, dark and cold as well as wet. It matched my mood. The roads were completely clear and I arrived at work well before eleven. There were no crowds outside today – the rain had put them off no doubt. Lynn was piling *Henry and the Master Wizard* behind the signing table.

Steve arrived next, by the front door this time, followed by Rachel and Frank. Frank had yesterday's clothes on which Jess, Lucy and Paul took delight in pointing out as soon as they arrived.

"Your shirt could do with an iron," Lucy laughed. "It looks like it spent the night on the floor."

"Maybe it did," Paul said. "Where did you sleep last night, Frank? Care to tell us."

Luckily Lynn and Rachel were in the kitchen at the time, making coffee.

"Shut up," he blushed. "You're just jealous."

"Damn right," Paul said. "Rachel's a fine-looking woman."

"No way!" Jess exclaimed. "She's ancient."

Charming, I thought to myself. Rachel was a year older than me. I left them to it and began to check the new e-mails. Steve stood at the desk watching me.

"Anything interesting?" he asked.

"There's a message here for you," I smiled. I decided I'd try to keep my distance with Steve today. After all, I wasn't sure what was going on or if he liked me.

He stood beside me and read the e-mail over my shoulder. It was from a young boy in Cork who was sick and couldn't make the signing. But he wanted to ask Steve what his favourite football team was.

"May I?" Steve asked. I nodded. He leant over the keyboard and typed in a reply.

"My favourite team is Manchester United. Thanks for asking. I hope you get better soon. Keep reading, Stevie J."

As soon as he'd finished I got back to work. He stayed beside me.

"Amy? Are you OK?"

I looked up from the screen. "Sorry?"

"You're ignoring me."

"I'm not ignoring you. I'm just busy," I explained.

"Have I done something wrong?" he asked.

"No," I said, trying to make my voice come out evenly. I wasn't in the best of moods and I wanted to be left alone. "I told you. I'm just busy."

"I'll go and sit at my table then."

"Here." I handed him the sheet of e-mail requests for signed books. He took it from me in silence.

The day went slowly. We were all nursing hangovers and a shop full of excited children and associated adult hangers-on didn't help. Frank and Rachel disappeared for a long lunch at two. Lucy and Jess were a godsend. They took over much of the work, helped by Paul, whose hangover didn't seem as bad as us 'ancient' people's.

At four Suzi, Matt, Simon and Kate arrived. Kate was sitting on Matt's shoulders and had to duck to come in the door. Luckily The Wonderland had a very high ceiling.

"Hi, Amy," Suzi called as they spotted me behind

the till. Simon joined the queue to meet Steve, and Matt was directed towards the picture-books by Kate. He whisked her off his shoulders and plonked her on the floor. Kate handed him a copy of *Can't You Sleep, Little Bear?* and Matt, looking a little startled at first, began to read.

"He's a natural," Suzi laughed, watching her fiancé. "Kate has really taken to him and Simon adores him."

"Sweet," I said darkly.

"You're in a good mood," Suzi said.

"Sorry," I mumbled.

"What's up?" she asked.

"Nothing," I muttered. "I'm woefully hungover."

Suzi put her hand on my shoulder. I shrugged it off. "I'm in later," she said. "If you feel like talking."

I felt bad. I was being irrational again, I knew the signs. I just couldn't help it.

"Stevie J's lovely," she said, running her eyes over him appreciatively. "Nice shirt too." He was wearing a dark-blue shirt which I had to admit really suited him.

"Um," I grunted non-committally.

"He's about to sign Simon's book now so I'll just go and say hello," she squeezed into the queue beside her ward.

I watched as she smiled at Steve and asked him a question. He smiled and nodded and looked over at me. Suzi said something else and he beamed. What the hell were they talking about? I stared at the screen in front of me.

Finally it was six o'clock and we ushered the last remaining customers out of the shop. Steve sat back in his chair and sighed.

"I'm glad that's over, I'm exhausted."

"Me too," Rachel said.

Paul guffawed in the background. Frank threw him a dagger look.

"That went brilliantly," Lynn said. "I can't thank you enough, Steve."

"It was a pleasure," he replied graciously.

I went upstairs to collect my jacket. I heard footsteps on the stairs behind me. It was Steve.

"Amy, would you like to do something tonight? Maybe the cinema or a drink?"

"No, thanks," I said stiffly. His face fell. God, I could be such a bitch sometimes. He was just being nice. "Maybe some other time."

"OK," he smiled. "I'm sure you're tired. Can I ring you?"

What's the point? I thought to myself. "Whatever," I said, trying not to catch his eye.

There was silence for a second. "Right," he said, making his way back down the stairs. "Whatever."

I stood at the top of the stairs. I'd upset him. I knew it, but I didn't care.

That evening I was lying on my bed staring at the ceiling. Suzi came into my room.

"Thanks for knocking," I muttered.

She sat down on my bed and ignored my comment. "You didn't come down for dinner."

"I wasn't hungry," I said. It was the truth – I really wasn't hungry. I hadn't really felt like eating at lunchtime either. I had managed half a cheese and salad roll but the food had tasted of cardboard.

"I brought you up a mug of soup – it's tomato."

I sat up slowly. "Thanks." I took the mug from her and placed it on my bedside table. I could always pour it down the sink later.

"Steve seemed nice. He's quite taken with you," Suzi smiled.

"What do you mean?" I asked suspiciously.

"I told him I was your sister and he said he hoped he'd be seeing more of me in the future," she explained.

"Did he?" I asked in amazement. Then I remembered how rude I'd been to him after that. "It's unlikely you'll ever see him again," I stated baldly.

"Why?" Suzi asked gently. She could sense that I wanted to talk but she didn't want to push me. Closing up like a clam was one of my specialities.

"Just because," I couldn't be bothered to explain, and anyway I didn't understand it myself.

"But he seemed really keen. What's going on?"

I sighed. I thought I might as well tell her so she'd get off my back. "We were getting on really well last night and then he dropped me home. So I guess he just wants to be friends."

"Amy, not everyone jumps into bed on the first

night. Some people like to get to know each other first."

I reddened. "That's not it!" I lied. "I didn't mean I wanted to . . . you know. I just don't think he was interested in me in that way. He barely kissed me."

"Was he being affectionate?" Suzi asked thoughtfully.

"He held my hand and put his arm around me, that sort of thing," I admitted.

"But he didn't kiss you?"

"No. Only on the hand and the cheek which hardly counts."

Suzi began to giggle.

"What are you laughing at?" I asked angrily.

"You!" she exclaimed. "You've met a decent guy who likes you and you're annoyed because he didn't hop on your bones."

"That's not true," I said defensively.

"Really?" Suzi asked.

"Well, maybe it's a bit true," I admitted painfully. "But I blew it anyway so there's no point dwelling on it."

"What happened?" she asked.

I told her about my 'whatever' remark. She frowned and bit her lip. "He might still ring," she said, trying to sound hopeful.

"Yeah, whatever," I muttered.

The following week was unbearable. The usual waiting for the phone to ring lark. Steve was no different from any other man, I decided. Allergic to the phone. But I figured I'd scared him off with my Jekyll and Hyde impersonation.

Lynne sensed something was up and she went easy on me at work. Luckily I had my *Den 2* hearts to keep me occupied in the evenings. I threw myself into it – cutting, colouring and gluing like billy-oh and trying to keep my mind off Steve. Steve, Jodie, Jack, weddings – the whole damn lot.

And my thirtieth birthday was creeping up on me with alarming speed. Not that it mattered anyway – I had no one to celebrate it with (although I think commiserate would be more the thing). Even Suzi and Beth had forgotten – they were too tied up in their bloody weddings to think about me.

I delivered my hearts to Helen in RTE the following Friday. She bounced into the reception area down the sweeping stairs with the energy of a young puppy.

"Hey, Amy, these are amazing," she enthused. "Perfect. Can you give me a hand up with them to the set?"

"Of course," I smiled. I was feeling a little better, less hormonal and mad, thank goodness.

We made our way through the narrow corridors and up the stairs towards the *Den 2* studio. The room was much smaller than I'd imagined. There were all kinds of props all over the floor and walls – toys, books, huge toothbrushes, giant Pokemon figures – the works. The set had been covered in swathes of pink and purple net material which reminded me of my bridesmaid's dress.

"This is the Valentine's Day set," Helen explained. "Or Valentine's week I should say. What do you think?"

I looked at the set carefully. It was, well, it was boring. I could see why they needed my hearts to jazz it up. "It's nice and bright," I said finally.

"Missing something, isn't it?" Helen asked. "Hopefully your hearts will liven it up a little. I'm going to put them up now."

"Would you like me to give you a hand?" I asked.

"Are you sure?" she asked. I nodded. "If you're not doing anything, that would be fabbo, thanks."

It turned out to be a more difficult job that Helen had anticipated. The hearts were quite heavy and were threatening to pull the material off the walls. So I suggested suspending them from the ceiling. Finally we had all the hearts in place. I'd found some silver and gold spray in the corner of the studio and gave the pink net a metallic layer which made it shimmer in the strong studio lights.

Finally, after almost two hours we had finished. The set now looked amazing, like a romantic pink wonderland. The hearts spun slowly on their suspending wires, catching the light.

We went outside to look at the set on the television screen. Helen introduced me to Mary, the producer, and a tall young man. I blushed as I realised it was Damien, the presenter from *Den 2*. I felt like I knew him from watching the programme so much but he was much better-looking in real life.

"Hiya," he said, smiling broadly. "Like what you've done with the set."

"Thanks," I murmured nervously.

"He's right," Mary added. "It looks brilliant. Helen, you must get Amy in to help with the Paddy's Day set."

"Good idea," Helen agreed. She turned towards me. "I'll see you out. It's a bit of a rabbit warren in here."

As we walked back through the corridors Helen showed me the offices of the various departments.

"Listen, I'm sorry it took so long to fix up the set," she said. "We'll pay you for your time, of course."

"It's no trouble. It was fun," I smiled.

"I'll give you a ring in two weeks or so about the Paddy's Day set. I can get you at The Wonderland, right?"

"Yes," I beamed. Maybe things were finally looking up.

Chapter 20

I tried to push Steve out of my mind but I was finding it nigh impossible. Working in The Wonderland didn't help. There were vivid reminders of him in every nook and cranny. Huge posters of his smiling face hung on the walls, there was constant barrage of e-mails thanking us for bringing him to the shop and his books were selling like proverbial hot cakes. We were finding it hard to keep them in stock. The latest – *Henry and the Master Wizard* – was now out on CD. The full unabridged story was available to play in our shop and boy did it play – over and over again. And guess who was reading this fine recording? Yes, none other that Steve himself. So not only were my eyes assaulted with his image, I had to listen to his calm, hypnotic and sensual voice as well. It was all driving me crazy. And it all meant that I couldn't forget him even if I wanted to.

Suzi asked about him one evening and I bit her head

off, so she didn't mention it again. Beth had been lying very low. In fact I'd only had very brief conversations with her over the last two weeks. I hadn't even filled her in on the whole Steve thing, not really. She claimed she and Tony were up to their tonsils organising the wedding, but I'm sure she was simply fed up with me and all my complaints. Who wouldn't be?

However, Beth did deign to call over on Wednesday evening , just when I was getting settled into an episode of *Dawson's Creek*. I'd become quite addicted to this American teenage soap as the characters in it had even more problems than I did. Although they were all unrealistically good-looking and eloquent. Far too philosophical too, especially that Joey one. I also identified with Andie, the kooky blonde one who suffered from depression and found life a trial.

"Hi, Amy," Beth smiled as Suzi led her into the sitting-room.

"Hang on," I said, jumping off the sofa and grabbing a blank video tape off the shelf. I placed it in the recorder and pressed record. I didn't want to miss the end.

"What are you watching?" Beth asked in amusement. "It's not *Dawson's Creek*, is it? Stella loves it. She has a big crush on the Pacey guy."

"I'm not surprised," I smiled. "He's very cute. More her age than mine unfortunately."

"I feel like I haven't seen you for ages," Beth said.

"You haven't," I replied, trying not to sound bitter or accusing.

"I know, and I'm sorry. It's just all this wedding stuff. And, to be honest, Tony and I, I guess we're feeling the strain a little. We've been having arguments. And you know how much I hate arguments."

I felt terrible. It hadn't occurred to me that Beth might be having problems of her own.

"I'm sorry," I said gently. "I had no idea. Do you want to talk about it?" I asked.

"I'm being stupid. It'll all be fine. There are just so many things to arrange and organise. We never seem to have time to ourselves. And then Tony gets moody and storms over to Jed's and they spend all evening playing with the bloody Internet. They've decided to start up their own website design company and I'm so worried. We could lose the house if it doesn't work out. And I'm so tired all the time. I think I may be sick." Tears pricked Beth's eyes.

I gave Beth a hug and sighed. She was always so strong and together. It was strange to see her like this. But it made me feel a little better. At least I wasn't the only one who couldn't cope at times. And maybe this time I could stop feeling sorry for myself and help someone else.

"Beth, there's no point worrying about things that may or may not happen. Tony and Jed have been in the computer business for long enough now to know the risks. And they work so hard – you're always telling me so. I'm sure they'll be sensible about the whole thing. When are they thinking of leaving their jobs?"

"Next September."

"And they'll be able to bring some of their clients with them, I presume?" I asked.

"I think so," Beth said thoughtfully.

"And will they be running an office?"

"No, they'll be using Jed's house to start with."

"Beth, I really don't think you have to be concerned. They are starting off small and their overheads will be tiny if they're not running an office. Trust them."

Beth smiled. "You're right. I should stop worrying, but it's hard."

"I know. And you're probably just tired because of all the stress. You've been running about like a blue-assed fly getting everything ready. And worrying takes a lot of energy too. Believe me, I know all about it." I gave her another hug. "And you and Tony will be fine, you're made for each other. It will all slot into place, you'll see."

"Thanks, Amy. I feel a bit better now. Sorry for unloading all this on you."

I laughed. "Don't be ridiculous. It's usually you listening to me. It's the least I can do. And Beth, if you're really worried about your health, why don't you ask your GP to do some tests, just so you can be sure. You should probably have a check-up before your wedding anyway."

"That's a good idea."

"And maybe you should try to get away for a few days before the wedding. For the weekend or something. To relax."

"Amy, that's another good idea, thanks. I'll talk to Tony about it later."

"I aim to please," I smiled.

Beth smiled back. "Now, rewind that *Dawson's Creek* and let's have a look at this Pacey guy! I want to find out what kind of taste in men Stella has."

Later that evening Beth rang me.

"Amy, I was talking to Tony and he had an idea. He and Jed are taking a week off work next month to finalise their business plan and he'll be pretty tied up. He suggested that I take a week's holiday then."

"Sounds great!" I enthused. "Where will you go?"

"I'm sure you thought I'd forgotten but I haven't."

"Forgotten what?" I asked in confusion.

"Your birthday. The big three – o."

"I was trying to forget," I grimaced. "But what has that got to do with your holiday?"

Beth was silent for a brief moment. "I want to take you to Rome for your birthday. I know you've always wanted to go."

I gasped. I'd dreamt about going to Rome ever since I was a highly impressionable child and I'd heard all about the fountains and the architecture from Mum. It was her favourite city, and she and Dad had honeymooned there. But I couldn't let Beth pay for me – with the wedding coming up she couldn't possibly afford it.

"Amy, what do you say?"

"It's a lovely idea but . . . Beth, I couldn't let you pay

and I'm afraid I can't afford it at the moment," I said, disappointed.

"Amy, I insist. And it won't cost that much. Louise has given me a holiday voucher as a wedding present. With Tony and Jed's business starting up we can't really go away for long. So that will cover the flights. And Mum and Dad have friends in Rome we can stay with. Remember Lucia?"

"Your Italian au pair?" I giggled. "Vaguely, we were quite young at the time."

"She now lives in Rome with her husband and daughter and she's always saying how much she'd love us to come over. Her husband's Irish – remember Pat?"

"The son of your next-door neighbours. I'd forgotten they'd got married. And Olivia is their daughter." Olivia had stayed with Beth's family one summer to improve her English.

"Exactly. She's seventeen now and she e-mails me sometimes. She'd love to show us around."

I gave in. It all sounded so perfect. Rome in the spring with my best friend. What could be nicer?

"Beth, it sounds perfect. When are we going?"

* * *

Valentine's day loomed closer. I was in much better form now that I had a holiday to look forward to. We had settled on the third week in March and I couldn't wait. Helen from *The Den* had rung and we'd talked about on large green shamrocks and huge, dancing leprechauns for the St Patrick's Day set. I was going to make the shamrocks out of lots of different materials – tissue paper, feathers, glitter, card and foam. I had two weeks to finish everything and I was getting stuck in already.

The girls in the art and craft shop in Dun Laoghaire shopping centre were very helpful. I'm sure they wondered why I needed a large bag of green feathers but I'm sure they were used to unusual requests.

I was sitting at the desk in work on Monday morning, thinking about the best glue to attach feathers to foam, when a familiar voice startled me.

"Hi, Amy."

I looked up. It was Steve. He had a strange expression on his face. I couldn't quite make it out. Hard, I suppose you'd call it, business-like.

"Is Lynn here?"

"No, it's very quiet so she's gone to the bank. She'll be back in a few minutes."

"Right, I'll call back later then."

"Stay," I said suddenly, surprising myself. "I'll make you some coffee."

He looked at me carefully. "I don't think so, Amy."

"Is something wrong?" I asked blithely. I knew damn well there was.

He looked at me again. "You and me and . . . *coffee* . . . let's just leave it."

"What are you talking about?" I asked defensively.

"I don't really want to have this conversation." He

started walking towards the door. Luckily there were no customers in the shop to overhear.

I jumped up and followed him. "Why? What are you talking about?"

"Are you being smart?" he asked. I flinched. I'd obviously really hurt him. I was ashamed of my previous behaviour. His hand reached out to open the door.

"I'm sorry," I began, putting my back against the door.

"Amy, can you stand back please, I'm trying to leave."

"And I'm trying to apologise," I said agitated. "And . . . and . . . you never rang. You said you'd ring!"

"What?" he asked, raising his voice. "I asked could I ring you and you said 'whatever'. Remember? You acted like you couldn't care less about me. You were bloody rude to tell the truth. We spent a really nice evening together and I thought . . . let's just forget it."

And then I started to cry. I couldn't help it. I threw my hands to my face and ran towards the stairs.

"Amy?" I heard Steve's voice after a few minutes. I presumed he'd gone. I was sitting in the middle of the stairs, trying to compose myself. How embarrassing, I thought. He must think I'm a right idiot.

He sat on the step below me. "Don't cry. For heaven's sake, I didn't mean to upset you."

"It's not you," I hiccuped. "It's me. I always fuck things up."

I looked down at him. He was smiling.

"It's not funny," I stated. And then I began to laugh. I guess it was a little funny.

We sat on the stairs for a few minutes while I caught my breath.

"Hell, the shop," I stood up when I'd stopped crying.

"I locked the door and put the closed sign on it," Steve said.

"Thanks," I said. I was now feeling very, very stupid. I had no idea what to say.

"Amy," Steve said gently, "how about we start again?"

"Sorry?" I asked.

"You and me."

I smiled and sniffed. "OK."

"Amy, can we go out for coffee sometime? I'd really like to get to know you."

I smiled again. "That would be nice. How about Friday afternoon? It's my day off."

"Friday is perfect. Can I ring you?"

"Yes," I nodded. "I'd like that."

Chapter 21

Mum had been videoing *Den 2* with my set on it for the last week. I kept trying to explain that it was unlikely to change but she insisted on getting a shot of it every day. Beth had rung during the week about it. I was quite proud of myself really – it looked very striking and professional. Not bad for a rank amateur.

Suzi asked me to visit the Montessori where Kate went to make things with the kids. It sounded like fun and it would be good practice for my future television career. Right! Like they'd ever in a million years want me in front of the camera. I'd probably break the lens. But a girl could dream.

I decided to make Valentine's cards with them as Saturday was Valentine's Day. The class were all four and five, junior infants, so I decided to do lots of collage – cutting and sticking. Not all little ones could draw or write and I wanted them all to feel involved.

Wee Place Montessori School was in Blackrock, near our house. At ten o'clock on Friday morning I knocked on the bright yellow door and waited. The windows of the school were framed with the pupils' work. Outside there was a fenced-in playing area with a wooden climbing-frame and a slide painted red.

A large, grey-haired woman opened the door. She looked familiar. She was wearing a raspberry pink velour track suit and a wide smile.

"Hi, you must be Amy. I'm Nancy. Welcome." Nancy held out her hand. I balanced the cardboard box I was carrying on my hip and shook her hand.

"Let me help you with that," she said kindly.

"There's another box in the car," I said, handing her the box. I fetched the other box and she showed me into the front room. Lots of tiny, round faces stared up at me expectantly.

"Boys and girls, this is Amy. Say hello to Amy," Nancy said loudly.

"Hello, Amy," chorused the children.

"Now, playtime for ten minutes while Amy gets ready. Una, will you bring them outside?"

"No problem," said a tall young woman who was standing at the back of the room. "Coats on, everyone. Line up. No pushing, Luke."

We watched as the children snaked outside.

"Now you'll have a little peace and quiet for ten minutes," Nancy laughed. "Can I get you tea or coffee?"

"No, I'm fine, thanks," I replied. I looked round the

room. The walls were covered with art work of all kinds. Mobiles hung from the ceiling and there was a large nature table under the window. Low bookshelves held hundreds of books of all shapes and sizes. Posters displaying the alphabet and numbers adorned the walls.

"This is a lovely room," I said.

"Thanks," Nancy smiled. "It used to be the dining-room and the sitting-room. Suzi tells me you work at The Wonderland."

"That's right," I nodded.

"I love that bookshop. We get a lot of our books there. Picture-books especially. You have an amazing range."

"I knew I recognised you from somewhere," I smiled. "I think I helped you order some Richard Scarry books from the States last year."

"That's right," Nancy smiled. "You were very helpful and the kids love the books, especially *Busy, Busy World*."

"I'm glad," I smiled.

"Would you like to use this desk?" Nancy asked kindly. "I'm sure you'd like to set up now, before the little monsters come back inside."

"Great," I said, putting down one of the boxes on the desk. Nancy put the other box down beside it.

"You're very good to come in," Nancy began. "Suzi didn't mention your fee. I hope this covers it." She handed me a cheque.

"I wasn't expecting anything . . ." I said lamely. "I . . ."

"Take it," Nancy smiled. "Please. I know how much art materials cost, believe me!"

"Thanks." I put the cheque in my pocket.

I began to lay out the materials – large sheets of coloured card, glitter, pipe-cleaners, feathers and tissue paper.

Una and Nancy brought the children back in and they sat down excitedly at their desks.

"Hi, I'm Amy," I began tentatively. "And I'm here to make Valentine's Day cards with you. Now who would like to tell me who you'll give your cards to?"

A sea of tiny hands were raised in the air. I smiled at Kate who was waving her arm around in front of my face.

"Kate, who will you send your card to?" I asked.

"My Mummy, my Daddy and my Suzi," she said sweetly.

"I guess you'll have to make three cards then," I smiled. "In that case we'd better get started. "I'll hand round the coloured card first and then I'll show you the different cards you can make."

I spent a happy hour with the children. One they were engrossed in making their cards they were mercifully quiet.

"They seem to be enjoying themselves," I said to Nancy as she helped me dole out feathers to the children.

"You're very good at explaining things," she said. "You have great patience. Some people take it for granted that they will understand everything. You made sure that every child knew what to do before you went on."

"Thanks," I smiled. "My sister Suzi often brings Kate to our house, so I guess I'm used to five-year-olds."

"Suzi tells me you made the wonderful hearts on the *Den 2* set. I was watching it yesterday afternoon with my son."

"Miss, did you meet Dustin and Socky?" a little boy with sandy blond hair asked.

"Were you eavesdropping, Kevin?" Nancy asked, trying not to laugh.

"Sorry, Mrs Carver," he said contritely. "But did you, Miss?"

"Amy," I smiled. "Call me Amy. And no, I didn't. But maybe I will next time."

"You're so lucky," another little girl said. "I'd love to meet Damien and Geri May. They're so cool."

"Yes, I am lucky," I agreed.

That afternoon I walked into Blackrock village to meet Steve. He'd rung the previous day to arrange the 'date'. I was tired after the morning's session in Wee Place but I'd really enjoyed it. I was looking forward to meeting him but I was also very nervous. What if he didn't like me when he got to know me? I knew it was pointless worrying but it was hard not to.

As I walked into Angel Café he was already there, sitting at a table by the window writing into a small spiral-bound notebook.

"Hi," I said, walking towards him.

He stood up and gave me a kiss on the cheek. "Hi, Amy. Nice to see you."

Steve looked great. His blond hair had been freshly cut and was now very short, giving him a young, boyish look. He was wearing a white, long-sleeved T-shirt and dark blue denims. His leather jacket hung from the back of his chair. I felt dowdy and uninteresting in comparison in jeans and a pink fleece.

"Writing your next masterpiece," I smiled, looking at his notebook.

"I wish," he grinned. "List of things I have to do, I'm afraid – find a tiler, choose a colour for the hall, buy a new notice-board. Boring really."

I ordered a cappuccino from the waitress.

"When do you write?" I asked with interest. I'd always wondered how it worked.

"Depends on the day really," Steve said thoughtfully. "Sometimes I write from ten to four, with a break for lunch. Sometimes I write all day and all night until I'm tired out. At the moment I'm taking a break."

"A break?" I asked.

"Yes. I'm on book six in the Henry series and I find it takes over my life sometimes. So I've told my publishers that there won't be another book until the year after next. I want to do other things, picture-books maybe. Or even something totally different. I'm not sure."

"How long have you been in Dublin?" I asked. I realised that I knew nothing about his 'real life'.

"Not long, nearly four months now. My sister Rita, you've met her, she's married to an Irish guy and she loves it here. I needed a change and I thought it would be a nice place to live. And, once I'm a resident, I don't have to pay any tax in Ireland," he grinned.

"Are you serious?" I asked.

"Yes, artists' exemption."

"I knew I should have been an artist," I joked. "And do you like it here?"

"I miss my friends in London." Steve rubbed his chin. "And it's not that easy to meet people really. But things are looking up." He looked at me and smiled.

"And was there anyone special in London?" I asked before I could stop myself.

Steve was silent for a few seconds.

"I'm sorry I'm being too nosy," I said. "Ignore me."

"No, it's all right," he said. "There was someone. Ella. We lived together for a few years but we broke up last year. We decided that we weren't going to get married. We were just too different and we wanted different things in the end. It was for the best. But it's hard."

"I know," I said quietly. I told him about Jack and Jodie. And it felt so good to talk to someone who had been in a similar situation. He understood how you could still love someone even though you couldn't live with them. And he was a bloody good listener.

The light outside was fading by the time we looked at our watches. The staff had begun to clear up around us.

"Time to go," Steve smiled. "I hadn't realised how late it was." It was well past six.

"Thanks for the coffee," I said, standing up. We walked outside.

"I'm this way," I smiled. "I'll . . ." Steve interrupted me with a kiss. And this time it was on the lips. A gentle yet firm kiss.

"Come home with me," he said. "I'll cook you dinner."

"I'm not sure. I have to . . ."

He kissed me again.

"Please, Amy. I'd really like you to."

"OK," I smiled. "If you insist."

That evening, over plates of pasta in Steve's kitchen, we talked like old friends who had known each other since birth. He was easy to be with. We had so much in common and seemed to have the same warped sense of humour. There was just one thing holding me back. And that was myself.

"You can't like *Goodnight Moon*," I screamed during dessert – strawberry icecream.

"What's wrong with *Goodnight Moon*?" Steve asked, laughing. "It's a damn fine picture-book, bright, modern illustrations, simple text . . ."

"Exactly," I interrupted. "The text is far too simple. In fact it's downright sleep-inducing."

"No, it's not," he argued. "I think I have to warn you that my own picture-book is pretty simple. I hope it won't put you to sleep too. And anyway – that's the point of *Goodnight Moon*. It's supposed to put little kids into a relaxed state. It's a bedtime book."

He had a point. "Fine," I smiled. "You win. Can I read your book?"

"After what you've just said I'm not so sure." He stood up, picked up the empty dessert bowls and put them in the sink.

"Please," I begged. "I'll be nice. I promise."

"I'll only let you read it if you're honest, not nice," he said seriously.

"Deal."

I stood up and followed him into the hall. Steve's apartment was on the first floor of a large Georgian house. It was set back off the road and had a garden full of mature trees and rose bushes. It reminded me of Jodie's Granny's house.

"Sorry about the mess," Steve said as we climbed over a pile of paperbacks which had fallen and spilled all over the floor of the living-room. "I haven't really done much to the place since I bought it. The walls need to be repainted and I've no curtains anywhere."

"I doesn't matter," I said honestly. "It's beautiful. I love the high ceilings and the space."

"That's the main reason I bought it," Steve explained. "I wanted somewhere that wasn't too big but that still had a sense of space."

In the window bay of the sitting-room was a large glass-topped table on which stood a black computer screen and keyboard. On either side of the table were waist-high wooden bookshelves where copies of Steve's books nuzzled against dictionaries, a book of quotations, a pocket encyclopaedia and books on ancient Greek and Roman mythology. To the right was a notice-board on which photographs, illustrations, letters and all kinds of newspaper and magazine cuttings were pinned. I spotted a feature about The Wonderland signings from *The Sunday Tribune*.

"This is where I work," Steve said. He sat down at the desk and switched on the computer. "I'll print out a copy of the picture-book text for you to read, if you're still keen."

"I'd love to read it," I smiled. "Really." I sat down on the cream sofa and watched him. After a few minutes he handed me the freshly printed story.

"It's about a little mouse who is adopted into a cat family," Steve explained, sitting down beside me. "I wanted to explain racism to children without being too heavy-handed or preachy. It's about accepting differences and loving each other."

"Sounds good," I smiled.

"I'll go and make some coffee while you read." Steve stood up and I pored over the printed pages.

A few minutes later he came back in.

"Well?" he asked nervously.

"It's good," I stated firmly. "In fact, it's better than good. It's great."

He smiled. "Thanks."

"It has just the right mix of seriousness and fun. The mouse, Ernie, is a lovely character and I think kids will have no problem identifying with him. Who are you getting to illustrate it?"

Steve sighed. "I'm not sure. Lynn had suggested Mary Murphy but I contacted her through her publishers and she wouldn't be able to do it for about two years. She's really busy with her penguin and koala books. So any suggestions would be gratefully received."

We talked about illustrators for a while. Steve than asked about my *Den 2* work – Lynn had told him about it when he'd rung for me.

"So do you draw?" he asked slowly.

"Sorry?" I asked.

"You're obviously very artistic. I've seen your work in the shop – the embroidered banners over the picture books are yours, aren't they?"

I was nervous as to where this was heading. "Yes, I guess they are. I don't draw but I sew and I used to make things all the time . . . but not any more."

He looked at me carefully. "How about trying some embroidery illustrations for my book? I think they'd work with the text."

I laughed. "There's no way I'd be good enough to illustrate a Stevie J book!" I laughed. "Are you mad?"

"How do you know if you haven't tried?" he asked. "I tell you what – I won't even look at them. We'll send them to the publishers and see what they have to say. How about that?"

"Are you serious?" I asked.

"Deadly," he grinned.

I thought about it for a second. He was right – I had nothing to lose. The worst that could happen is that they would get rejected. The fact that he suggested it at all gave me confidence. "You're on. Give me your story and I'll have a go."

"Excellent! I'll drop a copy of the manuscript into the shop – I've a few changes still to make." Steve smiled. "We'll make an amazing double act, you wait and see."

I hope so, I thought to myself. What had I let myself in for ?

Chapter 22

Unfortunately Steve had to catch a ridiculously early flight (five am) to London the following morning for another book signing, this time in Waterstone's on Charing Cross Road and other London bookshops, so we ended the evening at twelve.

As we waited for the taxi I tried not to worry that he hadn't kissed me all evening, or that he hadn't asked to see me again. After all, we'd talked and laughed all afternoon and evening. I was pretty sure he liked me – maybe. And he'd asked me to illustrate his books – which showed – I wasn't quite sure what it showed but at the very least it meant he thought we'd know each other for a while at least.

As for my own feelings, I really liked him, but I wasn't sure that I could fall in love with him. Jack had been so much more forceful and passionate and manly. I was used to loudness and disagreements. They were par for the course with a man, weren't they? I just wasn't sure that Steve was my type. He was so damn *nice.*

We heard a car pull up outside the house.

"That'll be the taxi," Steve smiled. "I had a great evening, Amy. Thanks." He leant over and kissed me once on the lips, a lingering, firm kiss. He held me close for several seconds before drawing away. "I'll ring you when I get back on Tuesday."

"OK," I smiled. I was half tempted to give him a big smooch but I decided against it. I didn't want to scare him off.

In the taxi on the way home I thought about Jack. The terrible thing was that I missed him. I missed the excitement, the unpredictability. Or at least I thought I did. It seemed easier and easier to remember the good bits and forget the bad bits. Selective memory.

I had to work the next day so I went straight to bed after saying goodnight to Suzi and Matt, who were sitting in the dark in the living-room. Bless them. I could hear the faint tinkle of Suzi giggling from my bedroom. I rolled over and tried to sleep. But the image of Jack's face kept appearing. Jack. Eventually I feel into an exhausted sleep.

"Where were you last night, Amy?" Mum asked as she pottered around the kitchen the next morning, watering the house plants.

"At a friend's house," I said, hoping she'd leave it.

"Anyone I know?" Mum continued. She wasn't going to let it go that easily.

"A children's writer. He wanted some advice on picture-books."

"He?" she smiled. Shit, I should have said she and Mum would have lost interest.

"Is there any more Special K?" I asked, shaking the box. Since the bridesmaid-dress fitting with Suzi I'd tried to make an effort. Although all it had amounted to really was stealing some of Suzi's Special K in the mornings. Still, it was a start. I'd just have to starve myself for a few days before the wedding. Sorry, weddings.

"In the cupboard beside the fridge," Mum said. "Was it that young man from the book signing? Stevie K?"

"Stevie J," I corrected.

At that moment Suzi came in the door. Typical. Was I to get no peace?

"What's that about Steve?" she asked. "Were you out with him, Amy?" she grinned.

"No, I wasn't 'out' with him," I stated firmly. "We were just discussing books, that's all."

"Oh, yes?" Suzi raised her eyebrows. "Is that what they call it these days?"

I'd had enough. I wasn't in the mood. I stood up and pushed the chair into the table with a clunk. Mum looked at me anxiously.

"Are you not going to have some cereal, love?"

"No, I'm running late, I'll get something in work," I replied.

I left the room and collected my bag from the end of the stairs. I could hear Mum telling Suzi to go easy on me as I walked towards the front door.

"Bye, love. See you later." Mum's voice wafted up the hall towards me.

"Bye," I shouted gruffly. And good riddance.

It was a clear enough morning and I walked into work. It was Valentine's Day on Monday and everywhere I looked I was reminded of the fact. Card shops, posters, hoarding, bus shelters, they all seemed to have gone Valentine's-mad this year.

I hated Valentine's Day even when I did have a boyfriend. Last year Jack had taken me to an Italian restaurant. He'd left it late to book so we could only get a table for ten o'clock. I hated eating late and I made a bit of a fuss. When we got there the place was teeming with happy couples. There were pink and red helium balloons in the shape of hearts at every table.

From the moment we sat down Jack moaned and complained. The waiter didn't come quickly enough, his garlic bread wasn't hot enough, the white wine wasn't cold enough. Eventually I asked him to stop griping and try to enjoy himself. Then he started laying into me instead.

"It was you who wanted to go out for dinner, not me," he muttered. "I was quite happy to stay in."

I decided it was better to stay quiet. I knew what Jack was like when he was in one of his moods.

"We should have had an early night. God knows it's been long enough." He looked at me accusingly.

"Excuse me? That's unfair!" I spluttered. That was a bit below the belt – literally. "Don't blame me. You've been tired too."

"At least I don't fall asleep the minute my head hits the pillow," he continued. "A man has needs, you know."

I'd had enough. "It's not the time nor the place to have this discussion," I said firmly. "Drop it."

"When are we going to talk about it then?" he asked, an unpleasant sneer on his face. "Maybe I can book an appointment with you sometime, Amy. Because it sure as hell won't get talked about otherwise."

"Jack, it's you who works late all the time, not me," I reminded him.

"But it's you who has to work at the weekends. I've told you to ask Lynn for time off. Or leave the bloody place. It's not as if it's well paid. You're always moaning about it. You're tired all the time, I try and deal with it and you get all moody and snap my head off."

"That's not fair. I like my work!" I said enraged. "And the weekend work won't go on for long. She's asked a student to cover one of the days."

"One of the days!" Jack exclaimed. "We'll still have no time together. It's a shitty job, Amy. I make enough to support us both. Why don't you just leave? I'm sure you'd find part-time work in another shop."

"The Wonderland is not a shop!" I said. My blood was beginning to boil. "It's a bookshop. And I'm not bloody leaving. You leave. Work at home. Lots of architects do."

"Now you're being pathetic," Jack sighed. "I earn a fortune where I am. You're brain-dead sometimes, do you know that?"

"Stop it, Jack," I whispered. I'd had enough. This was supposed to be a romantic dinner not a cat-fight.

"And another thing, I thought you said you'd ring the electrician. My shaving-light still doesn't work."

I stared at him in amazement. "Don't be so petty. Stop picking on me or I'm leaving."

"Yeah, right," he laughed.

That was it. I finally snapped. I stood up, said sorry to the waiter as I brushed abruptly past him and ran out of the restaurant. I began to walk home.

Jack didn't appear until after twelve.

"Where were you?" I asked as he came into the sitting-room. I was curled up on the sofa waiting for him. I felt bad. It was Valentine's day after all and we shouldn't be arguing.

"Having dinner," he said evenly. "And getting some peace."

"You stayed in the restaurant?" I asked in amazement.

"I'm going to bed now," he replied. "I presume you'll sleep down here. Goodnight."

Nice night. One of many similar nice nights.

As I approached The Wonderland I thought about calling into the card shop and buying a card for Steve. But I decided against it.

I knocked on the door and Lynn answered. "Hi, Amy. And how are you this good morning?"

"Fine, thanks," I replied.

"How did your date go yesterday?"

"How did you . . ."

"Steve told me when he rang – that you were going out for coffee."

I smiled. Lynn was as nosy as I was. "It went well, thank you. But I wouldn't exactly call it a date."

"Rendezvous then. We've got a busy day ahead of us. The Puffin and Random House new titles have arrived and they need to be received and priced. And there's a large order to be boxed for Wee Place. Nancy was in yesterday and bought some American picture-books. She said you were a big hit with the kids."

"Did she?" I smiled. "I'll just dump my bag and jacket and I'll get straight into the Puffin order."

"Are you sure?" Lynn asked. "I don't mind doing it."

"No, it's fine." It would mean I was hidden in the back room, far away from any pesky customers.

The day flew by. Lynn was right – there was a lot of work to do. I went home pleasantly exhausted.

The next day – Sunday – Steve rang.

"How's my favourite artist?" he said.

"Where are you?" I asked.

"In The Mayfair Hotel. I though I'd give you a ring and see how you're doing."

"How are the signings going?"

"Really well, I think. I did the two big Waterstone's yesterday and I'm in Borders and Ottakers in the Science Museum today."

"Sounds hectic," I said.

"It is a little," Steve said. "But I've a few more shops tomorrow and then I'm back home."

"Home?" I asked. Was he staying in London?

"Dublin," he replied.

"You call Dublin home?"

"At the moment. You know what they say : 'Home Is Where the Heart Is'." Steve laughed. "Listen, I have to go. I'll ring you when I get back."

"I look forward to it," I said.

On Monday morning my life fell apart – again.

Chapter 23

I woke up on Monday morning with a feeling of dread. Valentine's Day. God knows what Suzi and Matt would be like, and Beth and Tony, and Mum and Dad, and Jodie and . . . I tried not to think about it.

There were no cards for me on the hall floor – surprise, surprise. I had, however, received a mobile-phone bill, a credit-card bill and a junk mail flyer advertising thermal underwear. Great!

I went into the kitchen, and I was just in time to catch Mum and Dad exchanging cards and kisses. I said my hellos and goodbyes and left their post on the kitchen table.

Suzi and Matt were still in their beds. Or bed, I should say. Although they ostensibly had separate rooms they weren't fooling anyone. At first they'd been discreet about it but you could still hear Suzi's light creeping footsteps most evenings as she made her way into Matt's room. It was all for appearances. We all knew damn well they were not exactly saving themselves for their wedding night.

I showered, pulled on a pair of clean combats, my favourite cream fleece with the hood, and smeared some Clinique Almost Make-Up on my face, to protect my cheeks from getting any redder than they already were. Red cheeks and broken veins ran in the family, unfortunately. Mum had luckily made Suzi and me wear protection on our faces, even in the winter. So we were saved from the ignominy of looking like Noddy every day.

It was another clear day so I decided to walk to work. I pulled on a jacket and a fleece hat as it looked cold enough outside.

I was right, there was a nippy breeze, cutting into my face and chilling my hands which I thrust into my pockets. As I made my way into Blackrock I tried to think about nice things – Steve, *Den 2* . . . that's all I could think of. But it was a start.

As I crossed the street to buy a bottle of water before I went into the bookshop a large hoarding caught my eye. What really caught my eye was the small crowd of punters who were congregated under the hoarding, looking up, pointing and laughing. It was not even nine o'clock in the morning. What the hell were they doing?

I bought my bottle of Ballygowan and walked down the street towards the crowd. As I grew nearer I could see what looked like a radio crew gathered on the path.

A young man held a tape recorder and another appeared to be talking into a microphone. A young woman was interviewing a large, aproned woman who I recognised as one of the sandwich-makers from Sam's Sandwiches.

And then I read the hoarding. Written in huge letters at least ten foot high were the immortal and heart-crushing words –

Jodie R , I Love You. Will You Marry Me? Jack D

The blood drained from my face and I felt sick. I began to shake.

"Amy? Are you all right?" Lynn appeared beside me. She put her arm around my shoulders.

I looked at her. I was dumbstruck. Large tears began to pour down my face.

"Come with me," she said gently, leading me away. She brought me into The Wonderland, up the stairs and sat me down at the kitchen table.

"I'll just go and put a notice on the door. I'll be back in a second."

I nodded. I sat statue-still until she returned.

"You've had a bit of a shock," she soothed. "I'll make you a cup of tea."

I would have protested that tea wasn't going to help me but I didn't have the energy to open my mouth, I felt completely drained.

"Did you have any idea about . . . about a possible engagement?" Lynn asked eventually. She was sitting at the table opposite me, with a look of concern on her face.

"No," I mumbled.

"I'm sorry, Amy, but I'll have to open the shop. Would you like to go home?"

"No," I decided. I wiped my eyes on the sleeve of my fleece. Lynn jumped up, tore a piece of kitchen roll from the dispenser on the counter and handed it to me.

"Thanks," I said. "If it's OK with you I'll stay. I don't really want to go home. Mum will be there and . . . I'd only think about it too much."

"I understand," Lynn said. "Come down whenever you're ready." She went downstairs. After a few minutes I heard the doorbell tinkle – our first customer of the day.

My mobile rang in my bag. I looked at the screen. It was Beth.

"Amy, I was listening to Gerry Ryan and they were talking about this hoarding in Blackrock. And then I realised. Oh, love, I'm so sorry. Are you all right?"

"I'm not sure," I said honestly. I'd stopped crying and I just felt numb.

"Is there anything I can do? Where are you?"

"In work."

"Will I come and collect you?"

Beth was such a sweetheart but I couldn't drag her out of work again. "No. Maybe you could call over this evening."

"Of course," Beth said. "But I have a better idea. Why don't I collect you from work and make you dinner?"

"Won't Tony mind?" I asked quietly.

"Na," she insisted. "I'll send him over to Jed's. He won't mind." I hoped she wasn't crossing her fingers. Tony must be getting really fed up with me by now. "I'll see you around quarter to six."

"Thanks," I said again. I didn't deserve her. She was too good to me.

I checked my eyes in the mirror on the back of the kitchen door. They were a little red but nothing too vampirish. I took a deep breath and went downstairs.

Lynn was talking to Gwen, who worked in the Blackrock library.

"I was just asking Lynn had she seen the hoarding down the road. Some guy called Jack was proposing to . . ."

"Yes, we both saw it on our way in," Lynn interrupted. She put her hand under Gwen's elbow. "Now, which Roald Dahls did you need to replace? And did you want hardbacks or paperbacks?"

Soon the two women were firmly ensconced in the fiction room, leaving me blissfully alone. I realised that everyone in Dublin would have seen or heard about the hoarding by the end of the day and I had better get used to it. In fact I was surprised that Mum or Suzi hadn't . . .

My mobile rang in my pocket. It was Mum. I turned the phone onto messages and put it on the shelf under the till.

I threw myself into tidying the picture-book stands.

They were always in a state after the weekend. There were large colourful books scattered on the floor in front of the stands and nothing seemed to be in its proper alphabetical order anymore. I pulled every single book out of the stand and placed them in piles around me on the floor. Then I began the tedious job of re-alphabetising them. Usually I dreaded doing this, but today the laborious job helped keep my mind off Jack and Jodie.

I tried not to admit it to myself but the reason I was so upset was that I was jealous. I didn't want to marry Jack myself but I sure as hell didn't want him to be happy with anyone else. And especially my ex-best friend. *I* wanted to be happy. I wanted a man who loved *me* enough to proclaim it to the whole world.

I kept myself very busy all morning doing jobs that Lynn and I had put off forever. Taking the stock-taking stickers off the top shelves, taking the blu-tack off the ceiling, dusting the mobiles, cleaning the windows.

Just after twelve the bell rang at the door. I looked up from the computer screen where I'd been checking on an overdue order. It was Steve. My heart sank. I should have been pleased to see him but I was so tired and so emotional I didn't think I could bear talking to him.

"Hi, Amy," he beamed. "I'm back!"

"So I can see," I said evenly.

He leant over the desk and planted a kiss on my cheek. I tried not to wince. Why today? Why couldn't he have called in tomorrow or in a few days when I was in better form?

"Is everything all right?" he asked carefully.

"Of course, why wouldn't it be?" I replied.

"I just thought . . . never mind. Are you free for lunch?"

"No, sorry." Which was the truth. Lynn had gone to the art shop to pick up some supplies for a new window display and wouldn't be back for ages.

"How about this evening?" he asked.

"I'm having dinner at Beth's."

He seemed disappointed. "Are you sure there's nothing wrong?" he asked again. "Have *I* done anything wrong?"

Why didn't I tell him – about the hoarding, about how upset I was, that I really wanted to see him but just not today or tonight? I don't know. I guess I wanted to forget about it all. And I certainly didn't want to break down in tears in front of him – again!

"No, of course not. I'm sorry . . ." I shook my head.

He looked at me for a couple of seconds, as if deciding whether to pursue the conversation. "I'll go then. Bye." And he walked towards the door without looking back.

I know. I should have gone after him and apologised and explained that it wasn't anything to do with him. But I'm stupid and I didn't. I just watched him leave and got back to my work. It was only later that I realised what I'd done.

"You let him leave?" Beth asked after dinner when I told her about Steve's visit. "He's going to think you're mad!" She paused for a second. "Sorry, I didn't mean . . ."

"It's OK. You're right. My behaviour isn't exactly sane at the moment. Poor Steve." It was beginning to sink in that he'd never, never want to go out with me again. And as for illustrating his book . . .

Beth looked at me and smiled gently. "But you're doing well, Amy. Do you remember the last time, when I had to collect you from the Martello tower?"

I nodded.

"You're dealing with this really well."

I was pleased. Beth was right. I know I'd had a bit of a weep in the shop but I had got a terrible shock. And it still hurt – a lot. But at least I hadn't taken to my bed this time. Maybe I was getting stronger. And maybe I was finally getting over Jack.

"Thanks," I smiled. "I don't feel great but I also don't feel suicidal."

Beth grimaced.

"Sorry," I said. "But what am I going to do about Steve?"

"You'll have to apologise to him and try to explain," she replied.

"I suppose so," I said warily. But perhaps it would be easier to just leave it. After all, men were a lot of trouble. And the last thing I needed right now was trouble.

On Thursday evening I met Stella outside the

Powerscourt Townhouse Centre to look for bridesmaids' dresses. I hadn't heard from Steve all week and I wasn't exactly surprised. I hadn't rung him either and I was trying to banish him from my mind.

Beth had told me that Jodie had said yes to Jack. She had hated being the bearer of bad news but thought I'd prefer to hear it from her than someone else. The 'happy couple' had set their date for – get this – the second week in June. A month after Suzi and Beth's weddings! It was just as well we were no longer speaking to each other. Think of it – I might almost have had to be a bridesmaid three times in one summer. Lucky escape if you ask me! At least Jodie hadn't had the audacity to ask me regardless. She wasn't that thoughtless.

Stella was standing outside French Connection as I approached the centre. She was wearing her bottle-green Loreto school uniform but she still managed to look stunning. She waved as I approached.

"Hi, Amy. Good to see you." She gave me a hug. "Isn't this exciting?"

"Um," I said. "Where will we start?"

Stella overlooked my lack of enthusiasm. "There're some great dresses in Karen Millen I want to show you first. Or we could try Brown Thomas's or Pia Bang. I had a look around earlier, I hope you don't mind."

"No, that's fine," I said. The sooner this was all over the better. I wasn't a big shopping fan at the best of times. I never had any money. When I lived with Jack he had liked to buy me nice clothes. But I hadn't bought myself anything really since then.

"Is Beth coming in?" Stella asked as we walked in the entrance of the centre.

"No," I replied. "She said to put aside anything we liked and she'd come in and pay for it."

"Sounds like my kind of shopping!" Stella laughed.

"Do you not have a rich boyfriend to buy you things?" I asked acidly.

Stella looked at me carefully. "I don't like accepting presents from James. Especially not clothes. He's always trying to buy me smart little suits and dresses. I'm more comfortable in combats and runners."

"I'm sorry," I said contritely. "I didn't mean . . ."

"That's all right," Stella said. "Everyone presumes I'm with James for the money and the parties and everything. But when we first met I had no idea who he was. He treated me like an adult and he listened to me."

"And now?" I asked, noticing the past tense.

"Things have changed. I've become some sort of accessory that he hangs on his arm when it suits him. We never seem to spend any time alone together. We're always going out and I'm getting a bit sick of it."

"What do you want?" I asked. Maybe Stella's life wasn't so perfect after all. "Someone fun, who makes me laugh," Stella explained. "And someone I can stay in and watch videos with."

I smiled. "Don't we all?"

As we walked into Karen Millen's Stella pointed to a bright blue dress.

"What do you think?"

I unhooked the coat hanger and held the dress in front of me. It was long and slinky, with tiny shoe-string straps. Heavy lace hung over shimmering lycra.

"It might be a bit clingy on me," I said nervously. "I'm not exactly a size ten."

"I think it would look great," Stella said encouragingly. "Try it on and see. I'll try one on too."

She grabbed what I presumed was a size eight and we headed to the changing rooms. I gently pulled the dress up over my hips in the generously sized cubicle and was pleasantly surprised when it didn't get stuck. I wiggled the dress around to zip it up and pulled it into place again. I looked in the mirror.

"What do you think?" Stella's disembodied voice asked.

The dress hugged my curves and accentuated my chest. I wasn't exactly huge – a size 36C – but the bodice gave me a great cleavage. And my hips didn't look that huge. My stomach curved worryingly though – I really would have to diet very soon. The Special K alone didn't seem to be doing the trick.

"It looks OK, I think," I replied.

"Can I see?" she asked.

"Sure."

She pulled back the curtain. "Wow, I wish I had your cleavage! I'll have to wear a Wonder Bra."

I smiled. "You look great. The colour really suits you."

"Thanks," Stella said. "Do you think Beth will like them?" She turned in the mirror and surveyed her tiny bottom. "They're quite tight."

"I'm not sure. Why don't we put them on hold and she can come in. We can have a look in BT's and Pia Bang's and see if there's anything we like more."

"Good idea," Stella agreed.

Two hours later we were sharing a pizza in Gotham City. We'd tried the other shops but hadn't seen anything we both liked.

"God, I'm exhausted," Stella said, sipping her Diet Coke. "And I have school tomorrow."

I laughed. "I keep forgetting you're still in school."

"Thanks," she smiled. "I take that as a compliment."

We chatted about Beth's wedding for a while. Stella was debating whether to ask James or not. He hadn't exactly been all that interested when she'd mentioned it to him.

"There's this boy, David, who works in the video shop. I've met him in the pub a couple of times and he seems really nice," she said. "He asked me out once a few months ago but I was mad about James at the time. I was thinking I might ask him. Who are you bringing?"

Good question. I hadn't thought of that. "No one," I said lightly. "I broke up with someone a while ago and there hasn't been anyone since, not really." Steve's face briefly flitted thorough my mind but I brushed it away.

"You know," Stella said thoughtfully, "I think you're right. I don't think I'll bring anyone. Two single, attractive bridesmaids could have great fun, couldn't they?" She raised her eyebrows.

"Dead right," I agreed. I'd changed my mind – Stella was great, it wasn't her fault she was so good-looking.

Chapter 24

The family had tactfully decided not to mention the hoarding, ever. Suzi and Mum had both briefly questioned me about it but I assured them both that I was, if not exactly fine, dealing with it. So I guess I couldn't blame Mum too much for letting Jodie in. I mean, how was she to know?

"Amy," Mum called up to me on Sunday morning, "there's someone here to see you."

I looked up from the large, furry St Patrick's Day hat I was making for Damien. I'd decided Damien, Socky and Dustin would look great in green hats that matched the *Den 2* set.

"Send them up," I yelled, assuming it was Beth. I stood up and opened the door.

And there to my horror was Jodie. Her hair had grown since I'd last seen her and I hate to say it but she looked really well.

"What do you want?" I asked nastily, rooted to the spot.

"Can I come in?" she asked gingerly.

"I suppose," I muttered. "It's a free country."

"I know things between us have been a little . . . strained," she began.

I snorted.

She ignored me and continued. "But I really want you to be OK with me and Jack."

"And why do you think I give a shit?" I spat. "It's not as if I know either of you. It's not as if you're my friend or anything."

She winced.

"Amy, this is all really upsetting me. I don't want to lose you . . ."

"You should have thought of that before you stole my boyfriend!" I exclaimed.

"That's not fair," Jodie said, raising her voice. "You'd broken up. You weren't right for each other. You said it yourself at the time. You didn't want him."

"That's not the point," I shouted. "You were supposed to be my friend. Friends don't marry your ex-fiancé."

"Amy, you're being ridiculous," Jodie said in exasperation. "You're not being logical."

"Life isn't logical," I retorted. "Love isn't logical."

"I guess I'm wasting my time then," Jodie sighed loudly. "I thought that maybe you'd cooled off."

"After that bloody hoarding rubbing my nose in it?" I sneered. "What do you expect?"

"That wasn't my idea," Jodie said defensively, putting her hands on her hips. "And it's not my fault if you're jealous . . ."

"Jealous," I screamed. "Of what? Jack is bad news, Jodie. Don't come running to me when he chews you up and spits you out."

Jodie went deathly silent. I could hear Mum calling up the stairs. "Are you all right, girls?" As we had stopped shouting I presume she'd figured it was safe to let us get on with it.

"Jack Daly is a good man. He treated you well, Amy, and you know it. Although I wouldn't have blamed him if he hadn't. You're a complete bitch. I don't know how he put up with you for so long."

I listened to her with my mouth open.

"We've been friends for nearly fifteen years now," Jodie said. "I thought that might mean something. I'm sorry I hurt you. I really am. But I've had enough of this 'poor me' shit. I'm going now."

Tears streamed down my face as I listened to her walk down the stairs and bang the front door behind her.

Suzi walked in. "I was in my bedroom. I heard the shouting. Are you OK?"

"I don't know," I cried. "I don't know."

Early March went by in a blur of wedding details. Final dress fittings, wording for invitations, guest lists, missals for the service, booking string quartets and bands. I hadn't realised there was so much to do. I tried to keep well out of it, but with both Beth and Suzi quite obsessed it was hard. Mum was the worst. She wanted to get every detail right. Because the reception was being held in our house, well, in a marquee in the garden, she'd had painters, tilers and gardeners in to make the place look perfect. We now had a newly terracotta-tiled floor in the washroom which was to be the men's toilet, yellow instead of cream walls in the hall and ready-grown shrubs and flowering plants would be planted in the garden at the end of April. Dad, like myself, was trying to keep a low profile. He'd had to clear the garden of all his 'bits' as Mum had disparagingly called his architectural salvage. Every fireplace, Victorian brick, marble statue and iron fender had been hauled off to a friend's workshop in Thomas Street. It had been quite a job and the garden hadn't looked so neat and tidy for years.

He'd also been to Woodie's more times then he cared to remember to pick up garden lanterns, garden candles, varnish for the garden furniture, grouting for the downstairs bathroom – you name it – he'd bought it.

Beth was holding her wedding in West Cork. She'd decided to limit it to family and close friends only. Her mother was from Cork and all her aunts, uncles and cousins lived there. The venues she liked in Dublin were all booked out so she'd decided on the South instead. Tony didn't mind. He was happy to marry Beth wherever she wanted. In fact he was quite relieved that the wedding was going to be a small affair. He didn't fancy the world and his wife seeing him in the morning gear which he'd reluctantly agreed to wear. Jed was to be his best man but I was trying not to think about that too much.

I hadn't heard from Steve at all and I was too embarrassed to ring him. And as for Jodie, according to Beth she was really upset but had resigned herself to the fact that I wouldn't be attending her wedding!

I'd finished the new *Den 2* set and helped Helen set it up. The boys loved their Paddy's Day hats. Helen had asked me to design the Easter set. In fact she'd asked if RTE could keep me on a retainer. I was delighted.

My birthday was getting nearer and nearer and I was so glad I was going away with Beth. Whenever anyone asked me was I having a party I could tell them that I'd be in Rome! Lynn had given me the *Rough Guide to Rome* and I'd spent countless evenings poring over it, deciding where to go. There was so much to see – St Peter's, the Colosseum, hundreds of cool churches, the Pantheon, the stone mouth thingy that Audrey Hepburn had put her hand in with the very attractive Gregory Peck by her side . . .

The days dragged a little but finally it was holiday D-Day. Tony very kindly dropped us to Dublin airport.

Poor pet, our flight was at seven in the morning

which meant collecting me at five. Lovely! But he was very good-tempered about it. I think he was secretly looking forward to ten days without any wedding talk. He and Jed could immerse themselves in their own geeky world of digital cameras, mini-disks and sound cards or whatever new gadgets they could get their hands on.

Beth and I had decided on ten days. We could sandwich our holiday in between Good Friday and the weekend before Suzi's hen night, which obviously we couldn't miss. Suzi had arranged the entire thing herself – holiday chalets, pony trekking, dinner, dancing, local farmers . . . only joking! We were going to stay in a holiday complex just outside Arklow, eleven of us – Suzi, me, Beth, Stella (my suggestion as Beth had decided not to have a hen), Martha and Jan, old school friends, Siobhan and Deirdre who used to work with Suzi in Tiny Tots Crèche, Julie Lowan, and Amber and Polly (our unfeasibly good-looking and incredibly posh English cousins). Suzi had decided to have the hen nice and early so we'd all have lots of time to recover. Knowing Suzi and some of her friends it wasn't a bad idea – it could easily take a month! Beth wasn't having a hen so the Rome trip would be special for her too – her last holiday as a single woman.

From the moment Tony dropped us off at the set-down area I was buzzing with excitement. I hadn't been away on a proper holiday for ages. During college we'd spent each summer working away from home: first year – London; second year – Paris; third year – New York. The last time I'd been on an aeroplane was with Jack. We'd spent a weekend in London. He never wanted to go on holidays – the most I could ever tempt him away from the office for was three or four days. He thought he was indispensable.

As Tony and Beth smooched beside the car, I looked around. There were people everywhere. Brown people coming out the heavy glass doors and white people going in.

"Bye, Amy," Tony kissed me on the cheek. "Have a good time."

"I'll try," I smiled. "And I'll keep the Italian men away from Beth."

Beth giggled and elbowed me in the ribs. Tony shuffled on his feet nervously.

"Only joking," I said quickly. "It's a man-free holiday!"

Beth laughed. "That's not what you told me."

"Ah, but it's different for me, I'm young, free and single."

"Bye, love," Beth kissed Tony again. "See you on Sunday week."

As soon as Tony's car had driven down the ramp we turned towards each other.

"Dark-haired Romeos, here I come!" I grinned.

We picked up our bags and headed in the glass doors. The place was hopping. We took the lift to the Departures Hall and located the Aer Lingus check-in desk.

"This place is like a madhouse," Beth said. "I can't believe it's so busy – it's not even six yet!"

We waited in line behind an immaculately dressed woman. She was wearing a jet-black suit with a tiny skirt, and dangerously high heels. Gucci sunglasses were perched on the top of her chignoned dark brown head.

"Italian women always make you feel so underdressed," Beth whispered.

"Look at her luggage." I pointed at the matching Gucci brown leather case, vanity bag and handbag.

We watched in awe as the woman hoisted the case onto the conveyor belt and handed the ground steward her ticket.

"An aisle seat please," she said clearly in a strong Galway accent.

"Jeez, she's Irish," I whispered to Beth.

"I know," Beth groaned. "That really puts us to shame."

When we'd checked in our luggage we made our way to the Hughes and Hughes Bookshop and browsed.

"This looks interesting," Beth said, holding up a book with a serious-looking female face on the cover. " 'The latest book by this award-winning author,'" she read aloud from the blurb on the back of the book. "'An epic love story set in contemporary Ireland, the tale of two women and their tragic lives.'"

"Very cheery," I interrupted. Beth put the book back on the table. "How about this one." I held up a bright green book with the picture of a smiling woman on the cover. "'Molly is fed up. She's tired of her job in a stuffy insurance company and she longs for some excitement. But when Arthur Dillon comes on the scene, with his sexy smile and his immense fortune, things begin to look up.' Now that sounds more like it."

Beth took the book from me and looked inside the front cover. "It says here that the author is from Dublin and used to work in a bookshop. OK, I think I'll get this one. What about you?"

I scanned the bestsellers table for something that stood out. Finally I settled on the new Marian Keyes and the latest copy of *Cosmopolitan* – purely because it had an article on living without men in it. I needed all the help I could get.

"I hate the boarding area," Beth complained. We were sitting at our gate, waiting to be whisked away to warmer climes. "The seats are so bloody uncomfortable." She wiggled around on the dark-blue upholstery. "Why do they make them so hard?"

"Maybe it's to stop people from falling asleep," I mused. I took a glug of my Ballygowan and flicked through my magazine. An article on sexual positions caught my attention.

"Have you ever tried that?" I asked Beth, pointing at an illustration on one of the glossy pages.

"Amy," she hissed, "stop trying to embarrass me."

"I'm not," I replied. "It was a genuine question." I tried to figure out how the woman had leant back so far while in that position. Surely her legs would snap or at the very least she'd strain a muscle or two? I turned the page upside down. That way it looked a little more feasible.

Beth looked over my shoulder.

"I thought you weren't interested," I said.

She smiled. "I guess I might pick up a few tips before my wedding night."

"How about that one?" We studied a position called the 'Cosmo Angel'. It involved a lot of stretching and exertion. "Maybe not," I continued. "Looks exhausting. What about the 'Starfish'? Now I could see Tony liking that."

"Stop it!" Beth shrieked. "If he only knew what you were saying about him."

"He'd be delighted," I assured her.

"Ladies and gentlemen, we are now boarding the E121 flight to Rome. Please have your tickets ready."

We jumped up and joined the queue.

"Thanks, Beth," I said as we waited.

"For what?" Beth asked.

"For this," I smiled. "For everything."

She squeezed my arm. "You're welcome."

Nearly two hours later we stepped off the aeroplane and into hot, balmy sun. And it was only ten o'clock local time.

As our feet touched *terra firma* Beth turned her face to the sun. She smiled languorously. "Bliss," she purred.

Lucia and Olivia were standing waiting for us in the

arrivals hall. Both had dark-brown hair and warm, chocolate-brown eyes.

"Olivia, you've grown," Beth smiled, kissing her on both cheeks. "You're taller than me!"

Olivia laughed. "You won't be able to call me 'Little Olivia' any more."

"Beth, Amy, welcome to Rome," Lucia said. "We are so happy to see you."

"Thank you for having us to stay, Lucia," Beth said.

"It's our pleasure," Lucia smiled, her eyes full of kindness. "Your Mamma was so good to me. I'm happy to be able to repay her."

Lucia drove us to their apartment in the suburbs. I stared out the window while Beth filled them in on all the wedding details. Soon we pulled up outside a white apartment building which was surrounded by trees. Hundreds of white and grey birds perched in the branches and the warm air was filled with their gentle chirping.

Olivia showed us to our quarters, a deliciously cool room with a white marble floor and two beds with matching light-blue duvets and insisted we made ourselves at home. A slatted wooden blind hung on the large window. We dumped our bags and collapsed on the beds.

"I love Rome already," I smiled.

Chapter 25

After a light lunch of delicious Italian bread, salad and fruit (very healthy – I felt more full of vitamins than I had for ages!) Olivia took us to the Spanish Steps which led down to the Piazza di Spagna.

"It's so beautiful!" Beth exclaimed as we stood at the top of the steps. At either side of the steps were pots of bright pink flowers. It was a bright, clear day and the sun shone gently.

I pulled out my camera.

"I'll take a photo of you both," Olivia said smiling.

"I have a better idea," I said, looking around for someone to take a shot.

Olivia frowned. "Be careful. Don't give your camera to an Italian."

"Why?" I asked with interest. "Are they lousy photographers?"

Olivia laughed, her brown eyes dancing in the sunlight. "No, silly. There are a lot of thieves around. They offer to take photos and run off with your camera."

I chose an innocent-enough-looking English tourist, a woman in her late fifties, who was happy to oblige.

"How old are these steps?" Beth asked Olivia.

The young girl shrugged. "I think they were built in the eighteenth century sometime. But you'd have to ask Mamma."

We began to walk down the steps, trying to avoid the hordes of other tourists who threatened to trip us up. The place was packed; everywhere we looked there were Japanese tourists with tiny digital cameras. They travelled in packs and each group had a 'leader' who held an open umbrella in the air so he or she could be seen. It was quite a sight, crocodiles of tourists following along like the rats after the Pied Piper.

"This is the Fontana della Barcaccia," Olivia said as we passed an oval fountain. We continued along the street and turned right. "And this is the Via Condotti. Shopping heaven!"

"Dangerous," Beth said as we spotted an Armani store. "Better lock up my credit card this week I think. Or else the wedding won't be paid for ."

I smiled. At least Beth could still use her credit card. Mine was hovering precariously just under its limit. I hoped I didn't have to use it – there was nothing worse than your card being refused in a shop. The assistant always looked at you with such an accusing air, as if you were a jewel thief or a pickpocket. Believe me, I know.

Beth bought a simple but stunning cream top in Armani, which set her back a bit but she explained that it was 'an investment', and we spent several happy hours browsing in the other shops, guided by the ever-patient Olivia.

"So, girls," Lucia asked as we walked in the door of the apartment into the cool, white hall, "how was your day? You must show me what you've bought."

Beth opened the smart black paper bag and held up her new top.

"Che carina!" Lucia said, feeling the soft, luxurious material. "Tell me about your day." She showed us into the kitchen and we sat down at the table. Olivia poured us all welcome glasses of water from the fridge and kicked off her runners.

"Olivia, put your runners in your room," Lucia scolded. The teenager picked up her shoes and pretended to frown.

We told Lucia all about our window shopping, browsing and eating (there had been one or two pit stops for ice cream along the way).

"Olivia was so kind to show us around," I smiled. Olivia was now sprawled on the sofa in the adjoining sitting-room, listening to U2.

"She's a good girl," Lucia said, "and it's nice for her to have you both here. I think she'd have liked a sister, but . . ." she paused for a second, "Pat and I were only blessed with one."

"Do I hear my name being mentioned?" A tall, dark-haired man walked into the room. He was dressed in a dark suit, with a crisp, white shirt. He looked more Italian than an Italian. "What have I done now?"

Lucia jumped up and kissed him on the cheek. "*Ciao*, Pat, I didn't hear you come in. This is Amy and you know Beth."

"Beth, how nice to see you again! My girls have been so excited about your visit." He smiled at his wife and at Olivia, who had just come back into the kitchen. He leant down and kissed his daughter on the forehead. Beth stood up and he hugged her warmly. "I'll leave the kisses," he laughed. "We are Irish after all. And Amy," he shook my hand warmly, "lovely to meet you."

"Thanks for having us," Beth said as we sat back down at the table.

"And now," Lucia smiled, "Beth, tell us all about the great wedding. Every detail."

I groaned inwardly. I couldn't get away from it, even in Rome.

That evening we went to a pizza restaurant in the centre of town. Rome at night was bright, lively and exciting. Like a warm, exotic Temple Bar without the stag and hen parties. Everywhere you looked people were zipping around on scooters, weaving in and out of the fast, excitable traffic. Teenagers loitered on the streets, chatting and laughing. Although it was only March, the air was blissfully warm.

The restaurant was brightly lit, with long wooden

tables and simple, functional glasses and cutlery. Pat told us that it was family-run and that Lucia's family had been coming here for generations.

"What are you having?" Pat asked, as I read my way through the blackboard on which the menu was clearly listed – in Italian. "Can I help?"

"Please," I smiled.

"I could do with some help too," Beth laughed. "We Irish are so un-lingual. You guys put us to shame."

I nodded. "In Ireland your average seventeen-year-old has maybe a little French or Spanish. A few are fluent but only if they have been abroad while they were at school. Olivia, your English is amazing."

"Thank you," Olivia said, "but you must remember that I'm in an International School and some of our classes are taught in English. And of course Papa is Irish."

"That helps!" Pat laughed. "Now let's order."

An elderly waiter, wearing a black suit and a voluminous white apron, stood patiently by our table while Pat and Lucia deciphered the dishes for me and Beth. As we waited for the food, Pat asked us about Ireland, the recent political scandals, the 'Celtic Tiger', and, of course, the house prices.

I looked around the room and my eyes settled on a young couple in the corner who were feeding each other pizza. Jack and I had always meant to visit Rome. In fact we had always meant to visit a lot of places but his work always got in the way.

"Amy," Lucia asked, "were you the *margherita* with mushrooms and pepperoni, or with spinach?"

"Mushrooms and pepperoni," I replied, taking the huge plate from the waiter. I bit into the first slice. It was incredible. Nothing like the pizza at home. The cheese was rich and tasty, the tomato sauce zinged with flavour and the base was deliciously thin and light. "Delicious!" I exclaimed.

Pat smiled. "We try not to eat here too much," he patted his belly, "but it's difficult. I'm a total pizza addict."

"That's why he married me," Lucia quipped. "I make good pizza."

That evening I slept more soundly than I had for a long, long time.

"Amy?" Beth had whispered, just before I'd fallen asleep.

"Yes?"

"Do you feel like a child here or is it just me? You know – being looked after so well, and being taken out and shown around, and having a sleepover with your best friend?"

I thought for a second. "I do a bit." I smiled in the dark. "But, you know, I kind of like it."

"Me too," Beth said. "In fact, I like it a lot."

The week flew by in a blur of sightseeing, shopping (Beth), browsing in bookshops (me), eating, drinking, talking and laughing. I toyed with the idea of looking for an Italian man – searching the bars and nightclubs for worthy specimens but after the first two days the idea no longer had any appeal. I was having too much fun spending 'quality time' with Beth and with Pat and his family.

I tried not to think about my fast approaching thirtieth birthday – after all it was no big deal, not really. Who am I kidding – of course it was a big deal, it was a huge, all-encompassing big deal. By thirty you were supposed to have life all mapped out – your mate firmly bagged and ringed, one or two doting children, a blistering career and an involvement in a children's charity, your children's school's PTA or both. Leaving your carefree, live-life-to-the-full twenties is not easy.

I'd considered shifting the goalposts a little. As Oscar Wilde once said 'No woman should ever be quite accurate about her age. It looks so calculating'. Maybe I'd stay twenty-eight forever. And in my late forties fix my 'age' at thirty-four. I'd have to get Beth in on the act. At least I no longer had to deal with Jodie's resolute single-minded determination to tell everyone her exact age at every opportunity. She didn't believe in growing old gracefully. She turned thirty last autumn and made sure everyone knew about it. Beth, on the other hand, was a little ambiguous about the whole age thing – like me her thirtieth birthday did not fill her with relish. At least she had another few precious months of twenty-something denial. Her birthday wasn't until September.

Lucia mothered us constantly and we loved it. Olivia was delighted – it meant her mother didn't notice her as much, and she managed to avoid the usual interrogation before leaving the house. She was on her Easter school break, so spent a lot of time alternating between showing us around and sneaking off to meet her 'older' boyfriend who her mother didn't approve of.

I wasn't surprised that Lucia didn't approve of Flavio – he was a shifty-looking character, with a fine red scooter and a pierced eyebrow. But he turned out to be a sweetie and even offered to introduce me to his older brother, Emilio. Surprisingly, I declined the kind offer.

There was one major problem with Rome. The weddings.

There was no getting away from weddings in Rome. Everywhere you looked there were young, attractive dark-skinned couples fawning over each other – in full wedding attire, black suits, whiter than white dresses, veils, the works. The Trevi Fountain was the worst. It was positively riddled with happy couples. Apparently it's a Roman tradition to be photographed in your full garb at the fountain. And photographed they were. By the official photographer, friends, relations and passing tourists.

And don't get me wrong, as settings go it's pretty spectacular – cascading water, dramatic white sculptures of Neptune and Tritons (information kindly supplied by Lucia). Beats the feebly foliated arch in the local Irish hotel any day. But I'd hoped to get away from weddings and instead they seemed to be following me.

Of course Beth squealed with delight when she saw her first Italian newly-wed couple. She turned towards Lucia. "Lucia, is it OK to take a picture do you think?"

Lucia smiled broadly. "Of course, in Italy the bride and groom love being the centre of attention. In fact, it's considered very good luck to kiss the bridegroom."

"I dare you, Beth," Olivia said wickedly. "Go on. He's very cute."

Beth blushed. I had a good look at the bridegroom. "Olivia's right. He is cute," I smiled. "Go on, Beth, I won't tell Tony. I promise."

"I couldn't," Beth sighed. "I'd be too embarrassed." She stared at me. "But there's nothing stopping you. I double-dare you."

"So do I," Olivia encouraged.

Lucia laughed. "They say if you kiss the bridegroom you'll meet the man of your dreams within the year."

"In that case," I smiled, " it's worth a try. I feel like we're on a school tour. I haven't been double-dared for years."

"What about the New Year's Eve before last?" Beth giggled. "Do you not remember the chandelier incident?"

I grinned. I had forgotten that.

"Tell us, Beth," Olivia begged.

Beth continued. "Amy decided she could swing from our friend Jodie's chandelier. So I dared her and she managed to pull it out of the ceiling. It smashed onto the tile floor and our friend wasn't impressed."

"I'll never forget her face," I smiled. "Poor Jodie, she loved that chandelier."

"Kissing that nice young man is easy compared to that," Lucia said. "You'd better hurry. They are getting ready to leave." The couple had been sitting at the edge of the fountain and were now picking up the bride's long, flowing train. I took a deep breath and made my way through the crowds towards them. The groom was taller than I'd expected. I gulped.

"Mi scusi?" I asked in my best evening-class Italian. *"Posso?"* I raised my eyebrows and pursed my lips. He turned towards his bride who smiled and nodded. He then kissed me gently on the cheek.

"Tanti auguri," he whispered.

I felt a warm glow spread from my tingling lips right down to my toes. In that split second the thought went through my head that maybe finding love was possible, even for me.

I floated back to the others.

"Well done, Amy," Beth said, beaming. "I have it all on camera."

I smiled. "Great," I said sarcastically. "What does *tanti augun* mean?" I asked Olivia.

"Tanti auguri," Olivia grinned. "Good luck. Maybe I should try," she said.

Lucia put her hand on the young girl's shoulder. "Not so fast, Olivia."

We watched the bridal party leave and sat on the edge of the fountain watching the water. I dipped my fingers into the clear, blue water. It was pleasantly cool.

"Penny for them," Beth said, as I moved my fingers through the water.

I looked up at her. "Weddings," I replied honestly. "I was thinking about weddings."

That evening I dreamt that I was at the altar in a huge, white stone church. All around me were unfamiliar faces, all dressed in black, with dark-skinned, Mediterranean faces. The young man from the fountain was at my side.

"Don't worry," he whispered in my ear. "You'll find him soon."

Chapter 26

On Friday morning I woke up with a deep-rooted feeling of dread. I knew I should be worried or wary of something, but I couldn't quite remember what that something was. I lay in bed staring at the ceiling. Suddenly it hit me with a bang. I was now officially thirty. I gently fingered the skin around my eyes. No new crows' feet had etched themselves into my skin during the night. Not yet anyway. I did, however feel a brand new spot bumping up the skin under my left eyebrow. It was throbbing a little and I cursed plucking my eyebrows last night. I'd obviously poisoned my follicle and caused a new spot. I wondered absently would it turn into a whitehead and would I have to pop it? I quite enjoyed popping spots sometimes. It gave me a certain sense of control.

When I turned eighteen I thought in my innocence that my spots would clear up. Then I thought they'd disappear on my twenty-first birthday. But slowly I began to realise in horror that I was destined to have the offending blemishes forever. And now, in my thirties, I had spots and wrinkles to beat the band. My weight would start to pile on next and I'd . . .

"Amy?" Beth interrupted my gloomy thoughts. "Happy birthday, love." She sat up and smiled. "So how does it feel being thirty?"

I moaned. "Don't remind me. I was just pondering on the unfairness of having spots and wrinkles at the same time."

Beth laughed. "You don't have either."

I pointed to my newly acquired lump. "What's this then?"

Beth surveyed my eyebrow. "An eyebrow?" she suggested helpfully.

"No, the thing under it," I said, in exasperation.

"Amy, that's tiny, hardly a spot at all. And anyway, in a few years when we all have real wrinkles you'll be thanking your lucky stars for your skin. Mine's so dry I'll definitely get mega-wrinkles."

"You have lovely skin and you know it," I said. "Don't give me that."

Beth reached down beside her bed and pulled out a small package. She got up, sat down on my bed and handed it to me.

"Happy birthday," she said, kissing me on the head. I sat up and smiled.

"Thanks." I ripped off the bright-red wrapping paper.

Inside was a small black box. "Is it jewellery?" I asked with interest.

"Open it and see," she said.

I opened the velvet-covered box. Inside was a small silver angel brooch. It had a long body embossed with stars and hearts. On the angel's head was a delicate crown.

"It's beautiful, Beth," I whispered. "I love it, thanks." I took it out of the box. On the back was engraved 'May this angel watch over you and keep you safe'.

"So, birthday girl, what would you like to do today?" Beth asked.

"I'm not sure. There's so much more to see. But I guess the Colosseum would be top of my list."

"Perfect," Beth smiled. "And I think Pat and Lucia have something organised for tonight, just to warn you."

"Tell me," I begged. "What have they planned?"

"No way," Beth was adamant. "I shouldn't have told you anything. I just didn't want you to think we weren't celebrating tonight, that's all."

I let her away with it. After we'd both showered I sat by the dressingtable as Beth put her hair up. "Beth?" I asked.

"Yes?"

"Are you sure about your hen? That you don't want one, I mean."

"Positive," she said. "It's not really my kind of thing. I'm happy to spend this time here with you and I can have a few drinks at Suzi's hen."

"If you're sure," I said doubtfully. I felt bad. As bridesmaid I felt honour bound to get Beth very drunk and wearing a plastic 'willy' hat and veil. I'd spoken to Stella about it and she'd been disappointed too. But Beth had made up her mind.

"Honestly," Beth looked me in the eye. "I'm not into all that chocolate willy and silly clothes business, or streeling around the pubs and clubs blind drunk."

I winced. Maybe it was just as well I'd abandoned the 'willy' hat idea then. "If you're sure."

"Yes!" Beth exclaimed. "Absolutely sure. OK?"

I decided to drop the subject.

We joined Lucia and Olivia for brunch. Pat had left earlier for work at one of the banks where he was in charge of the IT department.

"Hi, girls," Lucia beamed as we sat down at the table. Gentle sun shone in through the window, throwing shafts of light into the room. "How did you both sleep?"

"Very well, thanks," Beth said.

Olivia passed me a long black box which was decorated with a bright yellow ribbon and an envelope. "For your birthday," she smiled.

I was touched. "You shouldn't have," I stammered. "It's really kind of you."

"Open it," Olivia insisted. "I chose it."

I slid off the ribbon and opened the box. Inside was a pink Swatch with tiny gold angels on the straps and watch face. "It's lovely," I said. "Really lovely." I placed the watch on my left wrist and fastened the strap. "You won't believe this, but Beth gave me an angel brooch." I pointed at my T-shirt on which I'd pinned the silver angel.

Lucia whistled. "Must be fate," she said. "Your guardian angel is sending you a message."

I opened the card. It was a picture of David by Michelangelo. On the front was a red arrow which pointed to David's tackle. 'Wow, David!' It read.

Lucia laughed. "Olivia chose the card too!"

"I thought so," I said. "Thank you both."

"What would you like to see today?" Olivia asked.

"The Colosseum," Beth said.

"Cool," Olivia said. "I'll come with you. Mamma's shopping and meeting Dad for lunch, I think." She looked over and her mum nodded. "So it's just the girls."

"I nearly forgot," Lucia said. "Your Mum rang. I didn't want to wake you."

"Is it OK to ring her back?" I asked.

"Of course," Lucia said, "I'll write down the codes for you." She handed me a scrap of paper and I punched the numbers into the phone followed by my own number.

Mum answered the phone. It was nice to hear her voice.

"Hi, Mum, it's Amy."

"Amy, love, happy birthday. Are you having a nice day?"

I smiled. "Yes, really nice. Lucia's family are being so kind and we've seen so much. We're off to the Colosseum today."

"Your Dad wants to say hi," Mum said.

"Amy, happy birthday. How does it feel being thirty?" Dad asked.

"Twenty-eight!" I pointed out.

Dad laughed. "I see. Twenty-eight again. Your Mother was thirty-five for years. It must run in the family. Anyway have a great day. Suzi and Matt send their love."

"Thanks, Dad," I said. "See you on Sunday."

Walking towards the bus stop from the apartment after lunch, Olivia turned towards us.

"I told Flavio to meet us there. I hope that's OK."

"Of course," I smiled.

"How long have you two been together?" Beth asked.

"Nearly three months," Olivia replied proudly.

I was impressed. At seventeen that was quite an achievement.

A warm breeze rustled through the trees which lined the small suburban street. It was another deeply pleasant day, weather-wise.

"I wonder what Irish people would be like if they had nicer weather," I pondered aloud.

"What do you mean?" Olivia asked.

I tried to explain. "It's always raining in Ireland. And if it's not raining it's grey and overcast."

Olivia looked at Beth quizzically.

"It's true," Beth assured her. "But we do get the odd nice day."

"In May," I said. "Or September. And we never get more than two or three days on the trot. In fact, it can be sunny in the morning during the summer and pouring from the heavens in the afternoon. It plays havoc with your wardrobe. Some days you just don't know what to wear."

Olivia laughed. "Sounds terrible. I don't remember it raining when I was in Dublin." She paused for a second. "Not all the time. Maybe sometimes."

"See!" I said. "Anyway, I think that if we had a bit more sun and general brightness Irish people might be in better humour most of the time."

Beth smiled. "Gerry Ryan thinks the weather affects our feelings too."

"It's a proven scientific fact." I was on a roll now. "There's a name for it – SADD, I think."

"That's right," Beth nodded. "Now that you mention it, I remember reading about it somewhere. Seasonal adjustment something."

Olivia laughed. "OK, I believe you both."

"Sorry," I grinned. "The weather or lack of it is a bit of an Irish preoccupation."

"That and Man United," Beth added.

The bus was very like an Irish single-decker bus, except it was blue instead of green. We settled into our seats, letting Olivia deal with the driver. She had the right number of tickets in her pocket which had to be bought before you stepped onto the bus. She plonked herself down on a seat in front of Beth and me and began to tell us about Flavio.

"It's so nice to be able to talk about him," she explained, her brown eyes shining. "He used to go out with one of my best friends, Maria, and I haven't told her about us yet, so I can't talk about him with anyone really."

"What does he do?" Beth asked. "Is he in college?"

"No," Olivia replied. "He's in a band with his brother and a few friends. They're called *Eco Eco* after an Italian writer."

"Umberto Eco," I interrupted.

Beth raised her eyebrows. "Aren't we the intellectual?"

I laughed. "He wrote a film Christian Slater was in called *The Name of the Rose*. Stop slagging me."

"Amy works in a bookshop," Beth explained. "And she's a movie freak."

"Less of the freak, thank you very much," I smiled. "A movie fan."

"So am I," Olivia enthused. "I love films. My favourite is *The Sixth Sense* with Bruce Willis. Did you see it? It come out a few years ago."

"Sure did," I said. "I brought Beth and she spent the whole time clinging onto my arm. When the ghosts appeared she wouldn't look. She missed half the film."

"It was bloody terrifying!" Beth exclaimed. "Thinking about it still gives me the shivers."

"We're here," Olivia said, jumping down from her seat. "Come on, you two. Watch your step, Granny Amy."

I glared at her. "I'm not dead yet, Olivia."

We crossed the busy road, avoiding the mad Roman drivers. And in front of us was the famous Colosseum.

"Holy cow," Beth exclaimed as we drew closer. "It's huge!"

"There's Flavio." Olivia waved at her boyfriend who was leaning against the outside wall of the Colosseum, smoking, one leg propped against the weathered red wall. He was wearing immaculate-looking denims, a white T-shirt and a black leather jacket, doing his best James Dean. He threw his cigarette to the ground as we approached him, grinding it into the ground with the heel of his black leather boot.

"Ciao, bella." He swung Olivia in the air and kissed her on the lips.

"Put me down," she giggled. He placed her carefully on the ground beside him.

"Hi, Beth and Amy." He cocked his head to the side and smiled. "How are you pretty girls today?"

"Fine, thanks," I said, delighted that he'd called me a girl.

"Ready to see the mighty Colosseum?" he asked. Just then a tall boy, dressed in similar garb walked towards us.

"Ah," Flavio said. "This is Emilio, my brother." Emilio smiled, showing his beautifully white and even teeth. He had a wonderfully cheeky smile. My heart lurched.

"Emilio, this is Amy and Beth – Olivia's friends from Ireland," Flavio said.

"Ireland, I love Ireland. U2, Van Morrison, yes?" Emilio asked, cocking his head.

I smiled. "That's right."

He kissed both our hands. I could feel the blood rush to my face as I felt his cool lips against my skin. He then turned to talk to Flavio.

"This could be interesting," Beth whispered in my ear. "He even looks a bit like your man from *Gladiator*. Imagine what he'd look like in that leather tunic thingy."

"If I get lost later, send him to rescue me, will you?" I asked.

"Absolutely," Beth smiled.

As we wandered round the ancient amphitheatre I was overcome by the sheer scale of the building, the mammoth columns and arches. Flavio and Olivia disappeared early on, leaving Emilio as our tour guide. He didn't seem to mind too much.

"The Colosseum was built by the Emperor," he explained, as we explored an internal corridor behind the tiered stadium of the amphitheatre. "They had wild animal fights here and gladiators."

Beth nudged me. "Gladiators," she grinned.

"Which emperor?" I asked with interest, ignoring her.

"I'm not sure," Emilio answered truthfully.

Beth flicked through the pages of her travel guide. "Here it is. 'Rome's Colosseum was commissioned by

Emperor Vespasian in 72 AD. At the first games in 80 AD over 9,000 wild animals were killed. The immense building could seat over 55,000 people,'" she read.

Emilio smiled. "We'd better find my brother and Olivia now. I'll ring him." He pulled out a stylish chrome mobile.

Everyone in Rome seemed to have a mobile, from young children to old grannies. They talked on them incessantly, yabbering away, while they were walking, riding their scooters or eating. It was quite a sight.

Emilio talked for a few seconds, and then turned towards Beth and me.

"They will meet us in the Café Vesta," he said. "Let's go."

"Can I take a picture before we leave?" Beth asked. "Of yourself and Amy."

I stared at her. What was she up to?

"You make a lovely couple," she continued.

I could have killed her. "Beth . . ." I began murderously.

Emilio didn't seem to mind. He grinned and put his arm around me. "Smile, Amy," he insisted, holding me closely. I could feel the leathery coolness of his jacket against the bare skin of my arms. It reminded me of Steve.

"Amy," Beth commanded, "smile!"

She clicked the shutter. "One more," she said, clicking it again. "That's great. Thanks Emilio."

"My pleasure," he said, looking me in the eye. He left his arm draped around my shoulder. I wiggled free and strode towards the entrance. Beth caught up with me.

"What's the matter with you?" she asked in confusion.

"Stop trying to push me at Emilio," I hissed.

"It's only a bit of fun," she whispered back. "Anyway, I think he likes you."

"Yeah, right," I muttered.

"I'm serious," she said. "He's been watching you all afternoon."

"Really?" I asked, beginning to be interested.

"Wait for me," I heard his voice behind us. "You girls walk so quickly. Take your time."

He was nice, and maybe Beth was right. He did seem to be smiling at me a lot.

"The café is on the Piazza del Colosseo. Follow me," he said.

We left the building and followed Emilio as he wound his way through the traffic and stopped outside a restaurant. Olivia and Flavio were sitting at a table outside, holding hands and gazing into each other's eyes. They hadn't noticed us – yet.

Emilio put his fingers in his mouth and gave an earth-shattering whistle, startling the star-crossed lovers as well as myself and Beth.

"Emilio!" I laughed, punching him on the arm.

He grinned and held my clenched fist. "You have quite a punch." He unfolded my fist and brought my hand to his lips. He kissed my fingers, lingering over each digit.

I shivered deliciously.

"Emilio," Flavio's voice drifted towards us. I looked over and realised that Olivia, Flavio and Beth were watching us with interest.

"Stop flirting, Emilio, and join us," Olivia laughed.

I blushed.

Minutes later we were sitting at the table, watching the world go by. I was sipping a large cappuccino and Beth and Olivia were sharing mineral water. The boys were tucking into large plates of gnocchi with relish, washed down with large glasses of red wine.

"Did you like the Colosseum?" Olivia asked, as the boys rattled away in Italian about some football match.

"It was amazing," Beth enthused. "You could almost see and smell the people and the gladiators. It's so steeped in history."

Olivia nodded. "I love it. I've been so many times but I still can't get enough. And Amy? Did you like it?"

"Oh, yes," I assured her. "It was a real experience."

Olivia leant over towards me and whispered. "And Emilio, what do you think?"

I raised my eyebrows. "He's very nice, Olivia."

"No, I mean . . ." she continued. Beth leant her head down and listened.

"I know what you mean," I said.

"Well?" Olivia asked again.

"She likes him," Beth interjected.

"Beth," I hissed.

"What are you girls talking about?" Flavio asked.

"Nothing," Olivia said.

"Tanti auguri a te," the strong singing voices of the Italian waiters drifted towards us from inside the restaurant. The singing grew nearer and nearer.

"Must be someone's birthday," Olivia smiled. "How nice."

We watched as the waiters came outside. They made their way towards our table, one of them holding in his hands a small, chocolate-covered cake on which birthday candles flickered. They stood at our table and continued to sing.

"Happy birthday, Amy," Olivia giggled, her eyes sparkling.

The cake was placed reverently in front of me and each leant over and kissed me on the cheek. I was mortified but delighted.

When they had stopped singing the whole restaurant clapped and said *"Buon compleanno."*

"They're all wishing you a happy birthday," Olivia explained.

"Thanks, Olivia," I smiled, when the commotion had stopped. I was embarrassed but delighted. "Now who would like cake?"

Chapter 27

"I don't know what to wear," I moaned. I was standing in our bedroom in my underwear, a growing pile of discarded clothes on my bed. We were back at the apartment and Beth was sitting on the other bed, watching me. It had taken about ten minutes for her to get dressed, fix her hair and put on some make-up.

Beth, Olivia and Lucia still refused to tell me where we were eating. We were meeting Flavio and Emilio afterwards, although we couldn't tell Lucia and Pat.

Just before leaving the restaurant earlier, Emilio had kissed my cheek and said "Until later, bella Amy." And I hated to admit it but I was really looking forward to seeing him again. I kicked myself for not agreeing to meet him earlier in the week.

"How about your red dress?" Beth suggested. We'd already ruled out trousers.

I held it up in front of me and stared at my reflection in the full-length mirror. "I don't think so. It's too long."

"The turquoise then," she said.

I pulled it out of the large, white wardrobe. Another dress caught my eye. "What about this one?" I held a white dress up for her attention.

"How many dresses did you bring?" she asked in amusement.

"It's best to be prepared," I said. I stepped into the white dress and looked critically in the mirror.

"I prefer the turquoise," Beth said. "That one's a bit . . . boring."

"Thanks," I said, sarcastically.

"You want me to be honest, don't you," she replied.

"I suppose," I said doubtfully. I tried on the turquoise lycra dress. It clung to every lump and bump and made me feel very self-conscious. "I look fat in this," I said, twisting my head to look at my backside.

"No, you don't," Beth sighed.

"It's hopeless," I cried, flopping down on the bed on top of my rejected outfits. "I've nothing to wear."

Beth was well used to my histronics. "Why don't you wear this? I'll find something else," she gestured at the black dress she was wearing.

"I couldn't," I stammered. I loved the dress, it was one of Louise's. Perfectly cut in black linen, it was a dream to wear – I knew 'cos I'd borrowed it more than once.

"Go on," Beth cajoled, unzipping it. "I don't mind. It's a good excuse to wear my new Armani top."

"Are you sure?" I asked.

She handed the dress to me. "Yes. If you'll let me borrow your black trousers."

I put her dress on. It was still slightly warm from her body heat. It looked great. I threw a dark pink cardigan over my shoulders and slipped my feet into my dark pink mules. "What do you think?" I asked her.

"Stunning," she smiled.

"You look great too," I said. Her new purchase shimmered in the light. "That top is beautiful."

There was a gentle knock at the door. Olivia popped her head in. "Are you ready?" she asked.

"Nearly," I replied.

"Papa's home," she explained. "We'll be going in a few minutes."

"Are you going to tell me where?" I said.

"You never give up!" Olivia asked. "You'll find out soon enough." She looked at me carefully. "I love the dress, Amy. It really suits you."

"Thanks," I smiled. "It's Beth's."

Minutes later we were all piling into Pat's car. I felt like a child being taken on a trip by Mum and Dad. It was a warm evening and Pat opened the sunroof to let some air in.

"You all look beautiful," he smiled. "I'm a lucky man." Olivia and Lucia had also dressed up for the occasion – Olivia in a tiny white top and matching skirt and her mother in an elegant navy linen dress with a cut-away back.

We drove towards the city and Pat parked the car and insisted on holding the doors while we all got out.

"We're nearly there," he assured me, looking with concern at my kitten heels. "Just around the corner."

It was nearly eight o'clock and the light had faded, leaving the sky a dusky dark blue. As we walked through the small twisting streets, I could hear the strains of music coming from the near distance.

"This way," Pat said, leading us around an old building.

As we walked around the building, Beth and I went ahead. And before us was one of the most spectacular sights I'd ever seen. I caught my breath.

"Wow!" Beth exclaimed.

We had stepped into a wonderland of huge, artificially-lit fountains which threw white water into the sky, a long piazza of monumental buildings, churches and buzzing restaurants, ice-cream parlours and cafés. There were people everywhere, tourists, street entertainers – mime-artists, puppeteers, singers, actors, and all kinds of Italians, young and old, enjoying themselves. It was quite a sight.

Pat led us through the throngs. He stopped outside a restaurant about halfway down the piazza.

"Here we are," he smiled. " The *Navona*. One of our favourite places to eat."

The waiter led us to our outside table. There was a large outside brazier to keep the chill out of the air and above our heads was a white cotton umbrella. Tiny pink roses grew on a trellis over the door of the restaurant. It was heavenly.

"It's lovely," Beth said, smiling. A mime artist was entertaining the crowds and the diners just in front of us.

The waiter handed out menus and Lucia ordered the wine.

"Red and white, I think," she smiled. "And water for Olivia."

"Mamma," Olivia complained.

"Maybe one glass of wine," her mother said kindly.

There were so many delicious dishes on the menu it was hard to choose. Eventually, with the help of Olivia, I decided on suppli di rosa, fried rice croquettes stuffed with cheese, and spaghetti alla carbonara.

As we waited for our food we watched the mime artist.

"What did you see today?" Pat asked, munching on some crispy bread-sticks.

"The Colosseum," Beth said. "It was amazing."

"Tomorrow we'll visit St Peter's," Pat smiled. "It's a pity you don't have more time. There's so much more to see."

"How long have you lived in Rome, Pat?" I asked.

He thought for a second. "Let's see, Olivia's seventeen and we moved here when she was one. We'd been living with Lucia's parents just outside Naples. So nearly sixteen years."

"Pat moved over when he was nineteen to be with

me," Lucia smiled, squeezing his arm. "He couldn't live without me."

"I never thought I'd end up living here," Pat said. "But now I wouldn't live anywhere else. I love it."

The waiter arrived with the starters. We tucked in with relish.

"What's that?" I asked Beth, who was licking her lips.

"Focaccia," she replied. "with olives and tomato. It's delicious, try some."

I pulled off a piece, covering my fingers in warm olive oil. She was right, it was delicious. "Try one of these," I said, cutting one of my rice balls in half, spearing the half with my fork and placing it on her plate.

"Thanks," she said.

"How are the antipasti?" Lucia asked.

Beth looked at me quizzically. "The starters are great, thanks," I replied.

We sipped our wine and listened to a young man singing to a guitar. He was sitting on the side of the main fountain, right under one of Bernini's river sculptures.

"What's he singing?" Beth asked. "It sounds familiar."

"It's called 'Nel Blu Dipinto di Blu'," he said. "Which means 'In the Blue Painted in Blue" – not a very catchy title. Most people call it 'Volare'."

"It's lovely," I smiled. I looked at the singer. He looked very like Flavio.

The singer then launched into 'That's Amore'. Olivia kicked me under the table and winked.

As Pat and Lucia ordered more wine, Olivia

whispered "It's Flavio. He sings here some nights to make money. Emilio will be here later too."

I smiled. And Olivia was proved right. Halfway through eating our main courses, Flavio was joined by his brother and they launched into a version of Chris De Burgh's 'Lady in Red'. Emilio was an excellent singer, even if his choice of music was a little suspect. 'Take My Breath Away' was next, followed by several Frank Sinatra croons.

"Is it OK if Olivia shows us around later?" I asked, after we ordered ice cream or *il gelato* all round. "I promise we won't keep her up too late."

"Well, I'm not sure . . ." Pat began.

"Papa," Olivia interrupted, "it's their last night. Please? I have my phone and I can book a taxi on your company's account."

Pat smiled despite himself. "Oh, you can, can you?"

Olivia grinned at her father. "You know it's the only way to get a cab in this city, Papa."

"I suppose it would be all right," Pat began.

"They're big girls," Lucia assured her husband. "They'll be fine. There's no need to worry."

"You're right," Pat said. "But home before one, Olivia. Understand."

"Yes, Papa," she smiled, delighted with herself. "I promise."

Later, as we said our goodbyes, Pat still looked a little apprehensive. It was obvious that Olivia was his little princess and he was very protective of her. I felt a little guilty that we were hoodwinking him and Lucia. But Flavio was a nice young man and Emilio . . . Emilio was also a nice young man, very nice indeed.

The two brothers were still singing by the fountain and we made our way over. They broke into another rendition of 'That's Amore', Flavio getting down on one knee, holding Olivia's hand and gazing up at her.

Beth and I laughed. Olivia was blushing furiously but enjoying her boyfriend's attention. As he finished the song the crowd clapped and cheered. Coins jingled into Flavio's open guitar case.

We listened to the boys for almost an hour. Now and again one of them would sing alone and the other would come and talk to us, taking a cigarette break at the same time.

"What do you think?" Emilio asked on one such break. "As good as U2?"

"Better," I stated. "Much more romantic." The wine was beginning to go to my head.

"I will sing a song for you next, my bella Amy," he promised, taking one long last drag from his cigarette. He kissed me on the cheek and returned to Flavio.

"The next song," Emilio told the crowd, "is for a beautiful Irish girl. *Buon compleanno,* Amy." They began to strum their guitars and the opening strains of U2's 'With or Without You' rang out.

Beth turned towards me. "It's your favourite song," she smiled. "Did you ask him to play it?"

"No," I whispered back. "No, I didn't."

Beth put her arm around my shoulder and we swayed together to the music.

Olivia joined in. Soon other voices from the crowd did too.

I looked around me. Lots of happy, smiling faces enjoying the music. Emilio winked at me and blew a kiss when the song had finished. I couldn't remember ever feeling quite so relaxed and content.

The boys had to play two 'encores' before the crowd would let them stop. When their audience had finally dispersed we approached them.

"That was amazing," Olivia smiled. "You're going to be a big star, Flavio."

He kissed her on the forehead. "Thank you, Olivia," he said genuinely.

"I think she's right," I smiled. "You were both brilliant." I turned to Emilio. "Thanks for the U2 song."

"*Niente,*" he said, grinning. "Would you like to go for a walk, Amy? There's something I'd like to show you."

Oh yeah? I thought to myself cynically.

"Well?" he asked, cocking his head to one side. "Will you come?"

I looked at Beth. She shrugged and smiled. "Go," she said. "I'll stay with Olivia and see she gets home OK."

"And I'll look after both of these beautiful girls," Flavio promised.

"*Benissimo,*" Emilio smiled, offering me his arm. "This way, Amy."

I put my arm in his and let him lead me away.

"See you later," I called to the others, but they were already locked in conversation. Flavio had an arm around each of the girls. He was in his element.

Emilio's guitar was slung over his back and it bumped gently against me as we walked.

"Where are we going?" I asked nervously. My feet were killing me.

"You'll see," he said. "It's only around the corner."

We walked for a few minutes talking about Flavio and Emilio's band and their hopes of breaking into the music scene in Rome. The road became steeper and we took it slowly, Emilio pulling me along.

"Come on," he encouraged. "We're nearly there."

"It better be worth it," I said.

"It will be," he said, his eyes twinkling. He stoppd outside two large, pale-blue gates. "Here we are.We'll have to climb in, I think."

I looked at the high gates and surrounding railings. "You're joking."

"Don't worry. It's easy," he assured me. He swung the guitar off his back and hung it carefully over the railings, dangling down on the far side. He then placed one foot firmly in the grid of the railings beside the gate and hauled himself up. He straddled the railings – precariously as there were long spikes along the top.

"Careful," I said in alarm.

"It's fine," he smiled. "Now put your foot there and

give me your arm." He pointed to the side of the gate where there was a flat horizontal bar.

I took a deep breath and did as he said. He grabbed my waist.

"You'll have to lift up your skirt," he grinned, "or you might rip it."

Unfortunately he was right. Beth wouldn't be too pleased if I ruined her good dress. I hitched it up.

"That's better," he said. "Now move your other foot over the railings here." He helped me as I swung my leg over the top of the railings. "Now put your other foot here and lean on me." I moved my other foot over and placed it safely over the spikes. I was now safe.

"Well done," he congratulated me. "Now wait and I'll lift you down." He jumped down onto the grass and held out his arms to help me. I fell into them gratefully. He held me against him and I breathed in his warm, musky scent.

I looked up and smiled. "Thank you," I whispered.

"Fa niente," he whispered, gazing into my eyes. My stomach lurched. I was surprisingly nervous. I knew he liked me and I wanted him to kiss me. But something was holding me back.

He seemed to sense my unease and loosened his embrace. "Follow me," he said, leading me along a rough, pebbled path. We were in a small park which was long and narrow and led towards a waist-high wall. As we approached the wall I began to see why he had brought me here.

Over the wall, stretched out in front of us as far as the eye could see were hundreds and hundreds of lights. We were on top of a hill looking down on the city which sparkled and twinkled beneath us. It was quite a sight.

"It's beautiful," I said, beaming.

"It's my favourite place," Emilio explained, "especially at night. I often come here and just watch the lights."

"I can see why," I said. He put his arm gently around my shoulder and drew me towards him.

"May I kiss you, Amy?" he asked softly.

"Yes," I whispered, my stomach knotting in anticipation.

He brushed my hair off my face and kissed my forehead. Then he kissed my eyelids, delicate, butterfly kisses and made his way down my face, kissing the tip of my nose. My mouth was crying out for him and I closed my eyes and sighed happily. I felt his cool, firm lips on mine and we kissed slowly, savouring the sensation. Our lips and tongues moved together, exploring each other's mouths. He nipped my top lip playfully and whispered *'Amy bella'* in my ear. He nuzzled my neck and kissed my earlobes.

After what seemed like a delicious eternity he pulled back. "Can I sing for you?" he asked, smiling.

"Yes," I smiled shyly back.

He began strumming the guitar softly. I looked out over Rome and listened as Emilio played Italian love songs. It was the perfect end to a perfect birthday.

We didn't talk much for the rest of the evening. We kissed and he sang and played his guitar.

Emilio was the perfect gentleman and just after one o'clock he insisted on bringing me back to the apartment on the back of his scooter which he had left at the Piazza Navona.

"I must bring you home now or Olivia's father will worry," he smiled as I protested half-heartedly. "Flavio tells me Pat worries a lot."

"You're right," I sighed. "I'd better go back."

He pulled a spare helmet out from under the seat of the silver Vespa and handed it to me.

"To keep you safe," he smiled. He pulled his own helmet over his dark hair and smiled broadly at me. "I won't go too fast, I promise."

I hopped on the back and he started the engine. It purred loudly and soon we were zipping along the Roman backstreets. The fresh, invigorating air brushed past my face. I clung onto Emilio, my arms wrapped tightly around his waist.

All too soon we chugged up the familiar road to Pat and Lucia's apartment.

"Come on, *piccola*," Emilio encouraged his Vespa which didn't seem to like inclines. He pulled up outside the apartment. "Home," he smiled, hopping off the scooter and helping me down. He flicked the stand and the scooter stood by itself. He held me against his chest and kissed me firmly.

"It's been a wonderful night," he said. "I will never

forget you, Amy. If only you lived in Rome . . ." he sighed.

I smiled. I knew it was probably just a line but it was nice to hear anyway. "I know," I said. "But it's been lovely. Thank you." We kissed for several more minutes. The stars were shining in the sky above us and in the distance I could hear the sounds of the city.

It had been a magical night. I didn't want it to end. Eventually I pulled away from him. "I'll have to go now. I'm sorry. Bye."

He smiled and blew me a kiss as I waved from the doorstep. Then I realised I'd have to wake the family to get in. Oops.

I rang the bell nervously. Olivia answered the door smiling. "We've just got in," she said. "We told Papa that you were in the garden, looking at the stars."

"Did he believe you?" I asked.

"I'm not sure." Olivia waved at Emilio. *"Ciao, Emilio,"* she said. He started up his scooter and rode away.

I watched his back disappear down the road.

Pat's voice startled us. "What are you two doing?" he asked sleepily.

"Watching the stars," I lied. "It's a beautiful night."

He looked out. "It certainly is," he said. "Now I'm going back to bed!"

Chapter 28

The next day Lucia and Pat brought us to St Peter's. They'd wanted us to visit it last. Beth and I were both tired and a little hungover but we wanted to make the most of our last full day in Rome. Olivia had managed to wangle her way out of it and planned to meet Flavio in town. I told her to say 'hi' to Emilio.

"What happened last night?" Beth had asked as we dressed that morning. "You should have woken me up."

"You were sleeping like a baby," I smiled. "It seemed cruel."

"Well, go on," Beth cajoled. "What's Emilio like?"

"You've met him," I stalled. "You know him too."

"But not intimately," Beth laughed.

I raised my eyebrows. "It wasn't like that," I assured her. "He was a real gentleman, very sweet. We walked to this park at the top of a hill. It was beautiful, Beth.

You could see the whole of Rome from there, all lit up like fairyland."

"Sounds romantic," Beth said. "Did you kiss him?"

"Of course I did," I smiled. "He's a good-looking guy and I'm on my holidays. I'm not that stupid!"

Beth laughed. "It's nice that he's Flavio's brother. It makes him sort of safe, if you know what I mean. You couldn't go for a walk with an Italian man you'd just met otherwise. It wouldn't be right."

I smiled. "You're always so practical, Beth. But I suppose you have a point."

"Are you going to keep in touch?" Beth asked.

"No, I wouldn't think so," I sighed. "He's a lot younger than me and, to be honest, I much prefer Irish guys. The Italians are too good-looking. It makes me nervous."

"Nervous?" Beth asked.

"You know," I began to explain. "They might go off with someone else or decide I didn't tan quickly enough."

"You're talking rubbish," Beth giggled. "What about English men then? They tend to equal Irish men in the non-good-looking stakes." I knew she was referring to Steve.

"I'm sure they'd all be delighted to hear you say that," I laughed. I tried to change the subject. "Will we give Lucia and Pat their present today or tomorrow?" I asked. "And we should get Olivia a present too."

Beth thought for a second. "Tomorrow morning, I think. I bought a necklace for Stella but I know Olivia would love it. Why don't we give her that and I'll buy Stella some perfume at the airport?"

"Sounds good," I replied.

"You'll see why I told you to leave St Peter's till last when you step inside," Pat said as we approached the cathedral. "The sheer scale of it is out of this world."

Lucia smiled. "Pat loves St Peter's. He'll give you all the statistics if you let him." She put on her best tour-guide voice. "The dome is one hundred and ten metres high. It was designed by Michaelangelo, but he died before it was completed."

"Stop making fun of me," Pat laughed. "Lucia's right, I do tend to bore her and Olivia with the details. The dome is one hundred and thirty-six metres wide, by the way."

Beth laughed. "Don't worry. I'm used to it. Dad's the same. He just loves all those details."

We made our way up the steps of the huge church and walked past the black-suited security guards.

"They stop anyone whose shoulders aren't covered," Pat explained. "Or anyone in shorts."

"Heavens!" Beth exclaimed as we stood just inside the doorway. "It's massive. I had no idea."

"This is the Pietà that was damaged in 1972," Pat explained. "Some hooligan took a hammer to it and now it's kept behind glass."

"It's by Michelangelo too," Lucia added.

"Are you girls on for a bit of a climb?" Pat asked. "The view from the top of the dome is amazing."

"How many steps?" I enquired, trying to sound casual.

"Five hundred and thirty-seven," Pat smiled. "But we'll take it slowly."

He was right, the view from the top was spectacular. But getting up there wasn't.

"Think of it as penance," Lucia said as we puffed and panted our way up each step. The walls and the steps got narrower and narrower as we ascended. I felt distinctly light-headed when we reached the top.

Stretched out in front of us was the whole city.

"Over there are the Vatican gardens," Pat explained, pointing to an expanse of green. Small fountains were surrounded by perfectly kept hedges, trees and shrubs.

"The colours of the buildings are so different to Ireland," Beth commented. "We're so used to grey, and here they are all warm reds or oranges, even the roofs."

"Over there is the Vatican Museum and the Sistine Chapel," Pat continued. "The queues for the chapel are unbelievable. You can be waiting for more than three hours to get in."

"I think we'll give it a miss then," Beth said. "I hate queuing. I have no patience. Unless Amy wants to go."

"No," I said. "I hate queuing too. I'd prefer not to if that's OK. Life's too short. We can see them next time we're here. I'm definitely coming back."

"Me too!" Beth exclaimed.

"But there is something you must do," Lucia said firmly. "If you dare."

"What's that?" Beth asked with interest.

"'Bocca della Verità'," Lucia said cryptically.

"Mouth of something," I translated. My Italian was a little sketchy.

"You'll see," Pat smiled.

"Are you sure you want to go through with this?" I asked Beth in a serious voice. "You know it's supposed to bite off the hand of liars?"

We stood in front of the huge stone medallion, the 'Bocca della Verità', or mouth of truth. It was in the portico entrance of a small church and it was the sculpture we both knew from the Audrey Hepburn and Gregory Peck film.

Pat and Lucia were standing behind us.

"Go on, Beth," Pat encouraged. "We can always sew it back on."

Beth scrunched up her eyes tightly and shoved her hand into the mouth.

"Phew!" she said, drawing it out quickly. "Now you, Amy."

I felt a little nervous. I knew it was only an ancient superstition, but still. I needed my hands, both of them. I shook myself, I was being silly. I took a deep breath and plunged my hand into the gap. The mouth was cool and worn smooth from the millions of hands which had rubbed past its lips. I pulled it out again.

"Well done, girls," Lucia smiled. Pat put his arm around his wife and we all walked back to his car.

"They're a lovely couple," I whispered, as they walked on ahead.

"I know," Beth replied. "I hope Tony and I are as happy together."

"Of course you will be," I assured her. "Sure, aren't you happy now?"

"Yes, I know," Beth said, "but they say marriage changes everything."

"Only if you let it," I replied.

"I guess you're right," Beth smiled. "I guess I'm just nervous about the whole thing."

"Marriage?" I asked.

"Marriage, the wedding, the future . . ." Beth sighed. "It's a big step."

"Beth," I said gently, "you and Tony were meant for each other. He's a great guy and he makes you happy. How long have we known each other?"

"Forever," Beth replied.

"Exactly. I know you inside out. And I genuinely think that Tony is perfect for you. So stop worrying."

"Thanks," Beth smiled gratefully.

"You're more than welcome," I smiled and gave her a little hug. "And I for one am really looking forward to the wedding," I lied. "It's all going to be perfect."

"I hope so," Beth said.

Getting up at seven am on Sunday morning to catch our flight was a killer. Luckily we'd all had an early night as exhaustion had started to finally kick in after the previous busy day.

We'd spent all week lying in, pottering around the

house in the morning, relaxing and taking our time. It would be hard to get back to life in the real world. At breakfast we gave Lucia and Pat a small marble statue, a copy of a Bernini, an Italian sculptor whom they both admired, for the garden.

"Oh, you shouldn't have," Lucia said, unwrapping the white tissue from around the statue. We were sitting at the kitchen table for our last breakfast in Rome. "It's perfect."

"You've been so kind to us," Beth said. "We've had a lovely time."

"We've enjoyed having you," Pat smiled. "And Olivia has too." Olivia was still in bed, her door ajar. Moments later she popped her head around the door. Her hair was ruffled and she smiled sleepily. "Bye, Beth. Bye, Amy," she kissed us both on the cheek. "Safe trip home."

We handed her the present. She opened it eagerly. "It's beautiful!" she exclaimed, placing the necklace around her slender neck. The silver glistened against her sallow skin. She fastened the clasp expertly. "What do you think, Papa?" she asked.

"Bellissima," Pat said.

Olivia kissed us both again. "It's been fun. I really enjoyed having you both here." There was a twinkle in her eye. As she kissed me she whispered in my ear. "Emilio said he had a wonderful night and to thank you, his beautiful Irish girl."

I smiled to myself. Emilio – what a nice memory.

Pat drove us to the airport. I stared listlessly out the

window while he and Beth talked about Tony's new venture. I really didn't want to leave. We'd had such a chilled-out time. Meeting Emilio had been an added bonus but I knew we wouldn't keep in touch. I hadn't even asked him for his address or number. I was happy to leave it as a glowing Roman memory.

Now it was home to the same old things – to work, to all Suzi's wedding preparations and to Steve. He'd been lingering at the back of my mind all week. Being back in Dublin meant that I'd have to face him again. I'd been so rude and irrational and he deserved an explanation. I wondered if I was brave enough to contact him. Or if he'd even talk to me.

Arriving in Dublin airport, I felt deflated. Tony was waiting in the Arrivals Hall and he'd brought Beth a huge bunch of stargazer lilies, her favourite flowers.

He took my bags off me, slung them onto the luggage trolley and put his arm around Beth's shoulders.

"How are you, Amy?" he asked kindly. "Did you have a nice holiday?"

"Great," I smiled. "Rome is amazing. I definitely want to go back."

"Did Beth behave herself?" Tony asked, only half-joking.

"Of course," I smiled. "There was a bit of an incident with a bridegroom but . . ."

"Amy!" Beth interrupted. "That was you!"

"That's your story," I laughed. Beth glared at me. "OK, OK, I admit it – it was me, Tony."

"Sounds interesting," Tony said, relieved. "You can tell me all about it in the car."

"I'd be happy to," I said. "And about Beth and the waiter at my birthday dinner."

Beth scowled at me again.

Tony laughed. "I presume that's another joke," he said uncertainly. "You're certainly in flying form, Amy."

"Um," Beth muttered.

We made our way to the car and Tony slung our bags into the boot. Men did have their uses after all – slinging bags, not to mention putting out the bins and cutting the grass.

As we drove towards Dun Laoghaire Beth and I told Tony all about Rome – the fountains, the shops, the churches and the food.

"Did you have a good birthday?" Tony asked as we crossed the East-Link Bridge.

"Yes!" I exclaimed. "It was perfect. From start to finish."

"Especially finish," Beth smiled.

Tony looked at me quizzically.

I was more than happy to tell all. "We went to the Colosseum during the day and then to a café and these waiters sang 'Happy Birthday' to me in Italian."

Tony laughed. "You wouldn't get Irish waiters doing that."

"Too right," I said. "We all went out for dinner in the evening in the Piazza Navona and were serenaded by two Italian guys. And then I went for a walk with one of them who showed me Rome by night."

Tony smiled. "Sounds very romantic. And where were you, Beth? I hope you weren't with the other singer."

"No," Beth smiled. "He's Olivia's boyfriend. We all went for a wander around the Piazza and watched the world go by. It was a lovely evening."

Tony whistled. "It's been cold and wet all week. You didn't miss much."

"Did you get much work done?" Beth asked.

"Yeah, loads," Tony assured her. "In fact, I think we may be almost ready to start taking on clients."

"I thought you were going to wait till after the wedding?" Beth asked, a little worried. "We have a lot to organise still – the flowers, the seating plans . . ."

"Beth," Tony interrupted, "once word gets out about what Jed and I are doing we'll lose our jobs. And we can't afford to live on air. If and when it happens, we'll have to move fast."

Beth went silent for a second. "I see," she said. "We'll talk about it later." She stared out the window.

Poor Beth. She had been looking forward to finishing all the wedding plans with Tony's help. Now it looked as if she'd have to bear the brunt of it herself.

I tried to lighten the mood. "I hear Jed's your best man," I said.

"That's right," Tony said carefully.

He obviously hadn't forgotten my behaviour at the New Year's party. Oops. Another touchy subject. And as it was my fault he couldn't have Jack, who he'd really wanted, I'm sure I wasn't exactly Tony's favourite person at the moment. "I met Stella, Tony, and we chose our bridesmaids' dresses," I continued, trying to steer myself onto safer ground. "She's great. We're going to have a laugh at the wedding."

"Beth said something about it, all right," Tony said. "What are the dresses like?"

"They're light blue, with heavy lace over lycra," I explained.

"Lycra?" Tony asked. "Is that not the tight, swimsuit material?"

Beth turned to look at me and winked. "The dresses are great, Tony. I went in to see them with Stella. Really tight, with no back and tiny, shoe-string straps. And low-cut at the front. You'll love them."

Tony was bemused. "Are you sure they're suitable, love? Don't bridesmaids usually wear something a little more . . . um . . . traditional?"

"We thought we'd go for something different – a little more racy," I said, enjoying winding Tony up. "Wait till you see Beth's red dress. Talk about sexy!"

Tony's eyes widened. "Are you serious?" he asked in a mixture of shock and delight.

Beth laughed. "Don't mind her, Tony. It's not red. But it is very sexy."

"I'm looking forward to it," Tony said, smiling.

Beth asked Tony about the West Cork acccommodation plans. I half-listened. There was a Sunday newspaper on the back seat and I flicked through the Arts supplement. On the Books Review page a familiar face caught my eye. It was Steve. The article was entitled *My Writing Day*. I began to read. *'At the moment, with a new Henry book out and the associated promotional work involved, I am doing very little actual writing. I recently spent a whole weekend in 'The Wonderland Bookshop' signing copies of the new book and meeting young readers. It was very enjoyable but exhausting . . .* ' He went on to talk about his new work – a picture-book about a little mouse called Ernie which would be illustrated by Cath Brennan, a young and upcoming Irish artist.

So he'd asked someone else to illustrate his picture book. I can't say I was surprised. I stared at the picture of Steve. It was a professional black and white photograph, very tasteful. Steve stared out, a wry smile playing on his lips. I wondered what was going through his mind as the photographer was snapping away. He looked like he'd been thinking – "Get me out of here!"

I folded up the paper and thought about Steve. I really would have to ring him.

Chapter 29

"Here we are, Amy," Tony said, pulling up outside my house.

"Thanks," I smiled half-heartedly. I reluctantly stepped out of the car, lifting out one of my bags and plonking it on the pavement beside me. Tony lifted my heavy red suitcase out of the boot.

"I'll bring this in for you," he said kindly.

Beth got out of the car. She put her arms around me. "It's a bit of an anti-climax being home, isn't it?" she asked. "I'll miss all the late mornings and the pasta."

"I know," I agreed. "It's going to be a killer going back to work tomorrow. But we have the hen next weekend – that'll be a good laugh."

"Yes," Beth smiled uncertainly. I looked at her carefully. "What's up?"

"I just hope it doesn't get a little out of hand," she explained. "Suzi's friends can be a bit wild."

"Don't you worry," I assured her, mentally crossing my fingers. "I'll take care of you, I promise."

Tony was waiting for us on the doorstep.

"I'll walk you to the door," Beth said.

Tony rang the doorbell and in a few seconds I saw Suzi's shadowy figure approach through the tinted glass. She flung open the door.

"Amy! Welcome home. Did you have a good holiday?" she asked, hugging me warmly.

"Yes, thanks," I grinned. Suzi grabbed the bag I was carrying and bustled me into the hall.

"You look brilliant. Mum and Dad are in the kitchen waiting for you. Go on down," she commanded. "They'd love to see you, Beth. Why don't you and Tony pop down too?"

"Sure," Beth smiled. She turned towards Tony. "Is that OK, love?"

"Of course," Tony replied.

I began to get a little suspicious as I heard loud female laughter coming from the kitchen. Mum's laugh was gentler and less raucous. In fact, it sounded a lot like Eva. I opened the door gingerly.

"Happy birthday!" Dad shouted as I walked into the room. I looked around. Sitting around the table were Mum, Dad, Eva, Matt and Judy, all grinning widely. The table was decorated with a red paper tablecloth with Happy Birthday emblazoned on it in huge yellow letters. There were balloons hanging from the light-fittings, streamers wall to wall and a pile of wrapped presents in the centre of the table.

I laughed. "What are you all like?" I asked. I was embarrassed but strangely touched.

"You didn't think we'd forget to celebrate your birthday?" Mum asked. "Sit here, Amy. And over here, Beth and Tony."

"Beth," I spluttered, "did you know about this?"

"Yes," she said, sheepishly. "Your Mum made me promise not to say anything."

"I'll kill you," I hissed.

"Amy," Mum interrupted, "would you like to open your presents while I serve? Frank, can you carve?"

Suzi jumped up with a bottle of wine in each hand. "I'll pour the wine," she offered, splashing generous amounts into the newcomers' glasses. She winked at me as she filled my glass to the very brim.

Eva pulled her present out of the bundle and handed it to me. It was a slightly plump envelope. More M&S vouchers, I figured.

"Happy birthday, Amy," she smiled. "You look so well. Rome must have agreed with you."

"Thanks, Eva," I said, accepting her present. "You're right, I loved Rome."

"I was there in my twenties," Judy joined in. "Such a beautiful city. Did you see the Trevi Fountain? Isn't it spectacular?"

"Sure is," Beth agreed.

I pulled a teddy-bear card out of the envelope and opened it. Inside was a gift voucher for Susan Bunting's exclusive lingerie shop on Dawson Street.

"Thanks, Eva," I grinned. "I've always wanted some La Perla and maybe now I'll be able to get it." I jumped up and planted a kiss on her cheek.

She blushed. "I thought I'd get you something different. It is your thirtieth after all."

"Help yourselves to dips while you're waiting," Mum said, plonking two large plates at either end of the table. Colourful strips of red and yellow peppers, carrots and celery were arranged around small terracotta bowls of garlic and herb cheese dip. We tucked in eagerly, loading the vegetables with as much of the high cholesterol dip as gravity allowed.

Judy passed me another wrapped present and I opened it eagerly. It was a set of Lancôme beauty products – anti-ageing cream, fine-line cream for around the eyes and firming cream for the thighs. I wasn't sure whether to be insulted or delighted.

"Thanks, Judy," I smiled, kissing my fingers and blowing the kiss across the table.

Lynn had dropped in a cream silk dressing-gown, Suzi and Matt had given me a silver bracelet and Mum and Dad a gift voucher for Station House Beauty and Health Farm. I was overwhelmed. They had all put so much thought into my presents.

"Thanks, everyone," I smiled, lifting my presents off the table and putting them on top of the kitchen counter.

Mum and Dad passed out plates laden with chicken.

"Help yourselves to vegetables," she said. "There's gravy and butter in the middle of the table."

"This is delicious, Denise," Matt said, loading his fork with potato, carrots and chicken.

Mum smiled. "Thanks, Matt. Anyone for extra stuffing?" Matt and Tony nodded eagerly.

"How does it feel being thirty?" Suzi asked me.

I glared at her.

"Amy's still only twenty-eight," Dad interjected. "Didn't you know?"

"Sorry," Suzi said to me, contrite. "I was only slagging you."

"I know," I muttered. "And that smile will be on the other side of your face in a few years."

"Tell us about St Peter's," Mum said hastily.

We talked about Rome and Italy for the remainder of the lunch. It was a safe subject and no one wanted to upset me.

"How are the plans for next weekend?" Judy asked as Dad and Suzi cleared away the plates.

"Good," Suzi grinned, a dangerous glint in her eyes. "It's going to be a crazy few days."

I glanced at Beth whose eyes were getting wider.

"Any male strippers?" Eva giggled.

"No," Suzi said. Beth looked relieved. "But we've lots of other things planned."

"I thought the bridesmaid was supposed to organise the hen?" Dad asked, confused.

"I'm helping," I assured him. "Suzi wanted to organise some of it herself," I explained.

"So what's planned?" Matt asked nervously.

"That would be telling," Suzi winked at him.

Tony shifted nervously in his seat. Beth turned to him and smiled reassuringly.

"And what do you have planned, Matt?" Dad asked him.

"Just a few drinks with the Clontarf lads," he smiled. "A quiet night really."

I snorted. "Quiet! The Clontarf rugby team, I don't think so! How about you, Tony?"

"I'm off to Amsterdam with the lads the weekend after next," he smiled. "Jed organised it."

"Is he your best man?" Suzi asked feigning innocence.

"Yes."

"Amy, that means you have to kiss Jed. It's traditional – bridesmaid and best man."

Her comment was met with stony silence as I glared at her. She knew all about New Year's Eve – I'd told her myself.

Beth stepped in. "Maybe Stella will take to Jed, you never know," she said diplomatically. "What are you wearing to Suzi's wedding, Eva?"

Eva and Judy described their planned outfits while I kicked Suzi under the table. "I'll kill you," I hissed under my breath.

"Sorry," she mouthed back. "Couldn't resist it."

"Um," I muttered darkly. I was dreading the whole

bridesmaid thing enough without the whole world knowing myself and Jed's short and ignominious history.

Mum carried over an ice-cream cake covered in tiny pink candles. "Happy birthday, love," she smiled, placing it in front of me.

"Happy birthday to you," the table sang as I cringed. *"Happy birthday to you, Happy birthday, dear Amy, Happy birthday to you."*

I felt six years old. I blew out the candles and made a wish. And sad female that I was, before I could stop myself I wished for a boyfriend. Talk about wasting your wishes.

After lunch we retired to the sitting-room. Judy and Eva interrogated Suzi about the hen but she was staying stumm.

"There's some post for you," Mum said. "A few cards, I think. And Lynn dropped in a letter for you which had been sent to the shop." She handed me an assortment of envelopes – the usual clear-windowed bills, junk mail and two handwritten ones.

"Thanks," I smiled, putting the bills aside. I opened the first handwritten envelope which had a Canadian stamp. It was a card from 'The Canadians' and a gift cheque. I smiled. I really was getting great presents this year. The other envelope, addressed to me at The Wonderland had a British stamp. I pulled out a typed letter and began to read.

Marra International Press
2 Kew House
Moss Garden
London SW2 9PE

16 March 2001

Dear Ms O'Sullivan,

Steve Jones asked me to contact you regarding picture-book illustration. We are always looking for new illustrators and would be happy to put your portfolio on file. Steve tells me that you have great talent and we are especially interested in young Irish authors and illustrators for our children's list.

Please read the following guidelines regarding portfolios carefully.

Kind regards,

Serena Rudd
Children's Editor.

I put the letter back in its envelope. Steve had contacted his publishers for me, after all my batty behaviour. I didn't know what to think. He'd found someone else to illustrate his own book – so he obviously didn't want to work with me himself. But he'd told his publishers that I had talent and he hadn't even seen my work. Apart from windows and display bits and banners at The Wonderland, but they hardly counted.

"Are you all right?" Beth asked, sitting down beside me. She nodded at the letter. "Bad news?"

"No, not exactly," I said. I handed her the letter. "Read it."

She scanned the letter and placed it back in the envelope. "But that's brilliant. They want to see your work. Hey, you could be famous one day. My friend, the illustrator."

I winced. "You don't think I'm sending them anything, do you?" I asked incredulously.

"Of course," Beth said. "Why ever not?"

"Because," I said slowly, "I'm not good enough."

Beth stared at me. "You've always been brilliant at art. Give it a try anyway. The worst that can happen is that they'll send it back."

"Maybe," I said doubtfully.

"And the *Den 2* sets have been amazing. RTE are hardly paying you if they don't like your work, are they?"

"I suppose not," I said reluctantly.

"Why don't you give it a go?" Beth encouraged. "Show Lynn some of your work and see what she says."

"No way!" I said emphatically.

"Why?" Beth asked gently.

"She'd be too honest," I explained, "and I don't think I could cope with that."

"Amy," Beth began, her face looking serious, "one day you'll wake up and regret not taking every opportunity you were offered. By then it may be too late. You have to seize the day."

I smiled. Beth was off on her *Dead Poets' Society* kick again. But perhaps she was right. Maybe I should take life by the reins and see what happened. Starting tomorrow.

I stood outside The Wonderland and stared. Lynn had changed the window in the last week – it now had a wedding theme. Lots of pink net, dolls dressed in tiny wedding dresses and books celebrating love and marriage. As if I hadn't been getting enough at home. I put my hand over my eyes and looked in through the rain-splattered glass on the door. Lynn was behind the till, the end of a biro in her mouth. I knocked on the door. She looked up and smiled.

"Hi, Amy," she said opening the door. "Come in out of the elements. How was your holiday?"

"Brilliant," I smiled. "What's with the window?" I stuck my umbrella in the stand beside the door and ran my fingers through my damp matted hair. I'd washed it that morning but the hairdryer was on the blink. So I was destined to have mad, windswept hair all day.

"Do you like it?" she asked, smiling. "It was that or yellow spring chicks," she explained. "I couldn't think of another spring theme."

"Right," I said non-committally. "It's different anyway."

We walked upstairs and Lynn poured me a large mug of fresh coffee.

"Get this inside you," she said. "It's so wet and damp today. I hope the weather improves for your sister's wedding."

"It's not for a few weeks." I said, "Hopefully it will have cleared up by then. Has it been busy?"

"On and off," Lynn said. "There were a few big school orders last week and Saturday was manic. I hope you're ready to get stuck in. The picture-books are in dire need of some attention. Mrs Potter from Blackrock National School cleared us out of Babette Coles."

"Lynn," I began. I was going to ask her if she would have a look at some of my illustrations but I chickened out.

"Yes?" she asked.

"Nothing," I said. "I'll get stuck into the picture-book order."

I brought up the ordering programme on the computer and punched in the code for the picture-books – PICT. I winced as the screen brought up over two hundred titles, all of which had been sold and had gone out of stock since I'd gone away. I began to key in the re-order quantities, three copies of *Can't You Sleep, Little Bear*?, two of *Dogger*, five of *Princess Smartypants*. I continued down the screen until the order was finished. While I worked, Lynn served a few rain-dripping customers.

I jumped up from the desk at one stage to check how many of *The Grumpy Goldfish* were in stock. Walking towards the picturebook stand I had the sudden realisation that I'd been doing the same thing every Monday for as long as I could remember. Ordering books on the computer, processing special customer requests and tidying the books – and it was time for a change. I loved the bookshop and I enjoyed working with Lynn but I needed more. And Beth was right – I had to grab the bull by the horns and try and make a go of illustration. I had the *Den 2* money to keep me going. And as I was living at home my costs were minimal.

And working at the bookshop left me open to bumping into Steve again – although, thinking about it, he wasn't likely to come in here again, not after . . . I tried to push him out of my mind, but it was hard when he was the bestselling children's author and every few phone calls were still about his bloody signed books.

On holidays I'd told myself I'd ring him, apologise and try to explain. But as the days went on it became harder and harder. I'd pretty much decided to just leave it at this stage. Put it down to experience, push him out of my mind.

I mulled over things all day. Lynn asked me several times if I was all right. I just smiled and nodded. I'm sure she put it down to post-holiday blues.

After lunch the phone rang. "Hi, Amy, it's Helen from the *Den*."

"Hi, Helen, how are things?"

"Good, thanks. Listen, I know this is a bit sudden but we've got a new children's art and crafts show for the autumn and I was wondering would you be interested in doing some research for it?"

"Tell me more," I said cautiously. "What would it involve?"

"You'd be working with Darren Shaw, the presenter. Coming up with ideas for shows, making the props, buying the materials, that sort of thing."

"Sounds interesting. How much time is involved?" I asked.

"It would be pretty much full-time, I think." Helen said. "But you could do a lot of the work at home. You'd be on a short-term contract."

"Can I get back to you?" I asked. "I'll have to think about it."

"No problem," Helen said.

"What's the show called?" I asked.

"*Sticky Fingers,*" Helen said. "Give me a ring in the next few days. Bye . . ."

I placed the phone back on the receiver and stared at it, biting the skin around my thumb.

"Everything all right?" Lynn asked.

"Fine, thanks," I said.

The afternoon dragged by. I couldn't get Helen's offer out of my mind. I was dying to get home and ring Beth. I needed advice on what to do. I knew it would be risky leaving work for a short-term contract. But it sounded fun, and I knew I could do it. At least I thought I could.

By the time I'd got home I wasn't so sure. I'd tried ringing Beth on the mobile on the way home but hers was powered off.

As I walked in the door Suzi came bounding down the stairs.

"Hi, Amy. Your bridesmaid's dress is ready. I'm going in on Thursday night to collect it. Do you want to come?"

I didn't really. I was hoping the dress would disappear into a puff of smoke at the last minute and I'd have to wear my jeans. "Yes, of course," I lied.

"Excellent. How was your first day back?"

"Fine," I murmured, picking up another mobile-phone bill from the hall table, where they seemed to breed. "See you later," I said, walking up the stairs towards my room, leaving Suzi standing alone in the hall.

"Oh," she said, disappointed. I could tell she wanted a chat but I wasn't in the mood.

I pushed open my bedroom door with my shoulder and sat down on the bed. I tried ringing Beth again. Her mobile was on this time but she wasn't answering it. I left a message and tried her house. No answer.

Suzi's head appeared around the door. She was brave. "Are you really OK? What's up?"

I sighed. I figured I might as well tell her. "I got a call at work today. Helen from RTE offered me a job doing research for a kid's show."

"That's great!" Suzi exclaimed.

"Maybe," I muttered. "I don't know what to do."

"Why?" Suzi asked. "Surely you're going to take it?"

I shrugged my shoulders.

"You'd be mad not to," Suzi said. "And Lynn would understand. In fact I'm sure she'd have you back if it didn't work out. Or you could work part-time for her, just in case."

"I suppose so," I said doubtfully. Maybe Lynn *would* keep my job open. I could always ask her.

"You should have more confidence in yourself," Suzi said. "You're great at art. I wish I had a quarter of your talent."

"Thanks," I said gratefully.

"So you'll take the new job?" she asked. Suzi wasn't one to give up.

"I'll think about it," I smiled.

"Good," she said. "Now I have to talk to you about the weekend. I thought we'd go into Ann Summers after picking up the bridesmaid's dress." She unfolded her costume plans for the weekend.

"What do you think?" she asked. "Is it too much?"

I grinned. "Not at all. It sounds good to me."

"Excellent!" she beamed. "I hope Beth won't mind."

"Don't worry about Beth," I smiled. "I think she'll surprise us all."

I talked to Beth that evening and you'd think herself and Suzi were in cahoots.

"I'm sure Lynn will understand," she assured me. "You've been working for her for years. I'm sure she'll hold your job open for you or let you work part-time or something."

"That's what Suzi said," I smiled. And thinking about it – they were both right.

Chapter 30

The following day I talked to Lynn about Helen's offer. She was scarily blasé about the whole thing.

"You've been a gem, Amy, but it may be time for you to move on," she'd said kindly. "But you know there's always a job here for you if you want it."

"Thanks," I said, genuinely touched.

"I'll ask Jess to work full-time during her holidays and we'll see where we are in September."

I rang Helen. She was delighted that I'd decided to join her team.

"That's cool, Amy," she gushed. "Welcome aboard. When can you start?"

"How about the middle of June?" I asked. The weddings would create havoc with work before then.

"Excellento," she said. "Let's have a meeting before that to sort out the details. I'll talk to Darren and get back to you. And can you start . . . say the fifteenth of June?"

"Perfect," I said. "Thanks, Helen."

Friday came all too quickly. Lynn had kindly given me a half-day as she knew Suzi's hen was in Arklow and we had a party planned for that evening.

Polly and Amber had arrived the previous evening and had terrified us with their plummy accents and designer clothes. They'd brought a huge suitcase and vanity bag each, crammed full of expensive, trendy clothes. They were clothes-obsessed, especially Polly, and insisted on showing myself and Suzi all their gear.

"These are my Manolo Blahniks," Polly purred, holding up a pair of shockingly skyscraper-high pink suede sandals.

"And this is Prada," Amber boasted, pulling out a glorious silk-chiffon dress in chocolate brown.

"I've seen one of the Corrs in that," I said, running the luxurious fabric through my fingers enviously.

"This skirt is fab," Suzi squealed, holding the shimmering silver and blue mermaid-like fabric against her.

"It's Clements Ribeiro," Amber said smugly.

"Last season," Polly added even more smugly.

"You're so lucky," Suzi said enviously. "I'd love some designer clothes."

"Honey," Polly crooned, "you'd look good in anything. When you have hips and thighs like mine you need expensive clothes."

I laughed. Polly was a riot. And she hadn't even had a drink yet.

Amber and Suzi went downstairs to make coffee.

"How's work?" I asked Polly as she hung her clothes up in the spare room. Amber and Polly both worked for *Marie Claire* magazine, Polly as Fashion Editor and Amber as Health and Beauty Assistant. They were great fun and visited Ireland at least once a year, usually with their mum. Polly was small and pretty, with a rounded size-sixteen figure (which she never stopped moaning about), and long dark hair which was usually pulled back into some sort of top-knot and secured with the latest accessory – today's being a huge bright-pink silk lily. Amber was tall and blonde, white blonde – like the Swedish-looking Timotei girl off the ads, bitch.

They were both so painfully stylish that I dreaded to think what they would think of my bridesmaid's dress which I'd collected that very evening. Luckily it was hiding safely on the back of my door in its heavy white plastic wrapping.

"What are you wearing to the wedding?" I asked Polly.

"I'm not sure, really," Polly began. "It's a toss up between my new Pucci in purple and black or a dark-pink and purple-spotted Whistles dress. I haven't quite decided yet."

"Whistles is a bit down-market, darling, isn't it?" Amber said, walking into the room and handing her sister a mug of coffee.

"I know," Polly agreed, "but spots are so now."

Suzi followed her holding what looked like my bridesmaid's dress. I looked closer and cringed: it was my bridesmaid's dress.

"Look what Amy is wearing at the wedding," Amber said, pointing at the frothy pink creation. "Isn't it simply darling?"

Polly stood up and cast her eye over the dress. She handed me her mug, took the dress from Suzi and held it up against me. I dreaded what she was going to say. Polly wasn't a style-guru for nothing.

"Yes," she said thoughtfully. "Gaultier meets the Sugar Plum Fairy, I like it."

"You do?" I asked cautiously.

"Yes!" she replied. "Very now."

I breathed a sigh of relief. Maybe I wouldn't look so tragic after all.

On Friday afternoon I rushed home to join Beth. She was giving Polly and Amber a lift down to Arklow in her Civic. It would be a bit of a squash but we'd persuaded the cousins to decant their clothes into one suitcase. They insisted on bringing the two Gucci leather vanity cases which they perched on their knees. I sat in the front with Beth.

Amber and Polly put on their red-tinted frameless Prada sunglasses and spritzed their faces with water.

"Travelling is so dehydrating," Amber explained as we pulled out of the drive.

Julie was driving Suzi, Stella, Siobhan and Deirdre in

her Range Rover Jeep and Martha and Jan were making their own way down on Saturday morning and meeting us there.

"It's like planning a bloody military manoeuvre," Suzi had said as she waited for Julie at the door. I was talking to her as Beth was loading the car in our drive. Stella was talking to James on her mobile. We could hear snatches of 'Of course I won't. What do you think I'm like?' and 'It's only two nights. Don't be so bloody selfish' and 'James, stop being so stupid'.

"Are you ready?" Beth called over when she'd settled the cousins in the back. Trendy dance music was blaring out of the speakers (courtesy of Polly).

"Absolutely," I smiled. I kissed Suzi. "See you down there," I said.

The journey down was a panic. Polly's vanity case turned out to be crammed full with bottles of champagne, small airline style. We glugged the frothy liquid down like it was Coke. All except Beth.

"We'll keep you some, darling," Polly promised as she popped another plastic cork, "I promise."

"That's OK," Beth assured her. "I'm not a big champagne drinker."

"Nonsense," Amber laughed. "Everyone's a champagne drinker."

Every time we passed a good-looking (and this was a very broad term which encompassed seventeen-year-olds playing football and grampas) we yelled out the window. Polly was unstoppable. Pulling up to traffic-lights on the Wicklow road she flirted unmercifully with the man in the Volvo beside us. Unluckily for him, his front passenger's window was open so he could hear everything. He had two baby seats in the back of the estate car, over which a huge golden Labrador was romping freely. He began to redden from his cheeks to the tips of his ears and down his neck as he listened to Polly.

"That's a darling car you have there," Polly purred, sticking her head out Beth's window and nearly strangling herself in the process on the seat belt. "I love estate cars. You must have rather a lot of money and I hear men with estates are awfully well endowed." We all shrieked with laughter at this gem. "And dogs just do it for me, with their big, brown eyes and their warm, lapping tongues and . . ."

Luckily for the Volvo driver the lights changed at this stage. He looked over as he moved away and stared lasciviously at Polly.

"Poor love," Polly smiled as we pulled away from the lights, the Volvo tearing along the road in front of us in a blatant display of male testosterone, "probably doesn't get much at home."

"Speaking of men, how's Arthur?" Amber asked her sister. "Arthur's her latest," she explained to me and Beth.

"Arthur?" Polly asked vaguely. "Oh, Artie! Sorry darling, you lost me there for a moment. Haven't seen Artie for weeks. Got bored of him really. No dress sense for a start and an annoying way of laughing. Frightful job too. Some sort of politician or something. Awfully boring parties."

Amber and Polly went through men like hot dinners. There seemed to be a never-ending supply in London. Amber had been married to a millionaire lord at one stage but it had only lasted a few months. He'd turned out to be incredibly stingy.

"Jazz is the latest. He's a hat designer, terribly talented. Amazingly good with his hands," she smiled wickedly. "Genius with his fingers, in fact."

"Polly!" Amber scolded. "Amy's used to you but Beth . . ."

"It's fine," Beth interrupted, laughing. "I don't mind at all. Tell us more Polly."

"Well," Polly began, "he gives the most amazing massages. He uses some of the feathers from his hats." We all listened, enthralled. "He starts off running the feathers over my back and then cools his hands on ice and traces his fingers over my spine. Then he warms his hands in hot water. It's bliss."

There was deathly silence in the car for a few seconds as we all imagined the sensations.

"Lucky bitch," I said, laughing. "You wouldn't get Irish men doing that kind of thing. It's more wham, bam, thank you ma'am."

"I don't know," Beth said slowly. "Tony can be very inventive when he sets his mind to it."

"Go on," I encouraged.

I looked at Beth smiling. She was blushing. "I couldn't," she stammered.

"Wait till we ply you with some shampoo," Polly assured her. "You can tell us then."

"Go on, ya good thing!" I yelled out the window at an electrician who was halfway up a lamp post, nearly deafening the car.

Beth sighed. "It's going to be a long weekend. I hope I'm able for it."

"'Course you are," I slurred, the champagne beginning to kick in with a vengeance. "I think that's the roundabout Suzi was talking about. Turn left here."

Beth drove the car up a smaller, windy road. To the right was a sign for the Arklow Holiday Centre.

"We're here," I said, turning my head and looking at Polly and Amber.

"How rural," Amber smiled.

"Very quaint," Polly agreed. "But what's that smell?"

"Silage," Beth smiled.

We pulled up outside a stone-walled cottage with a large wooden reception sign on its wall and Beth and I helped the two girls out of the back of the car. They stood on their heels uncertainly, finding it hard to balance on the gravel.

"Hi, girls," a stocky blond man came out of the building smiling. "The hen party, is it?"

"That's right," Beth nodded.

"None of you look old enough to be getting hitched," he said.

"You charmer," Amber giggled.

"I'm Tim," he explained. "I run the centre. I'll be taking you riding . . ."

Polly giggled.

He took a deep breath and continued, "and teaching you archery and shooting."

"Darling," Amber drawled, "we've been shooting since we were tiny."

"Sounds like a challenge to me," he replied grinning.

"I look forward to it," Amber purred. She ran a hand through her hair, flicking it from one side of her perfect face to the other.

"There are definite sparks flying there," I whispered to Beth. Tim was gazing at Amber with undisguised admiration.

"I hope you have some other shoes packed," Tim laughed, staring at Amber and Polly's heels.

"Darling, we have everything packed. Leather cat-suits, nurse outfits, the works. We *are* on a hen party." Amber looked him straight in the eye.

Tim stared back for a few seconds in awe before breaking the silence. "Can I join you?" he grinned.

"We'll have to wait and see, won't we," Amber smiled.

Beth coughed. "Can you show us where we're staying?" she asked the distracted man.

"Of course. Sorry. Follow me," he said. "You can park over there, beside your cottage." He pointed at a gravelled area beside a yellow-painted bungalow. "I'll help you in with your bags."

Beth parked the car. Amber and Polly tottered towards the cottage, whispering to each other and staring blatantly at Tim's behind as he walked in front of them.

He opened the door, lifted the bags and boxes of drink in from the boot of the car without a word and handed the key to me. "Here you are," he smiled, "Primrose Cottage. If you need anything I live over there." He pointed at the reception building.

"With your family?" Amber asked with interest. I stared at her. How direct could you get? I wish I was that brave.

"No," he smiled, his eyes lingering on her face, "on my own."

As he walked away Amber grinned. "What a darling man."

"He seems quite taken with you," I said.

"Poor misguided soul," Polly beamed.

"Polly," Amber squealed, thumping her sister on the arm.

We made ourselves at home, choosing our beds and jumping up and down on them like children.

Polly took charge of the drinks, whipping up some dynamite vodka and Red Bulls with her 'secret ingredient' – tequila.

"Are you trying to kill us?" Beth asked as the strong alcohol hit her stomach.

I lifted a large cardboard box in from the hall. "We'd better get decorating," I said. "Suzi will be here soon." Julie had promised to stall Suzi by stopping for drinks along the way. But we still didn't have long. Not in the state we were in when it would take us twice as long as usual to do anything.

I pulled out the large roll of card. "Beth, you'd better do the photographs." I handed her a brown envelope, some PrittStick and a large black marker. "I'll decorate it when you've finished. And Amber, you can help Beth with the captions." I rummaged in the box and found the streamers and balloons. "Will you help me with these?" I asked Polly.

In less than an hour we had transformed the cottage's living-room into a hen's paradise. There were phallic balloons in the shape of large pink willies hanging from the walls and ceilings. Streamers hung wall to wall and willy-candles lit the room, dripping their pink wax suggestively down their stems. Coloured and flavoured condoms had been placed in a bowl on the mantelpiece above the fireplace, 'just in case'. One wall was covered with pictures of Suzi, each shot ably captioned by Beth and Amber. *'Our Suze always had her finger on the pulse of fashion'*, one read. Suzi was wearing a very dodgy pair of white leggings, a pink shirt and a wide white leather belt with layers of silver studs on it. *'Her taste in men has improved'* read another, under a picture of poor Gary Simmons, a spotty teenager with gappy teeth and spiky hair, one of Suzi's ex's.

"It's finished," I sighed, collapsing on the sofa. "More drink, Polly." I waved my right hand which held an empty glass.

"Coming up," Polly smiled, bringing over a jug and pouring me a large glass of an orange drink.

"What's this?" Beth asked innocently as Polly handed her a fresh glass.

"Sex on the Beach," Polly grinned. "You'll love it."

Beth giggled. "Sounds good."

"I think that's Suzi," I jumped up, hearing the gravel crunching under tyres outside. I looked out the window. "Here they are!"

Beth opened the front door and we spilled onto the gravel, waving our glasses.

"It's the hen," Polly squealed as Suzi staggered out of the jeep.

"I'm plassstered," she slurred. "Those lot were pouring drink into me."

"Well done, girls," I smiled.

"Our pleasure," Julie laughed.

"Hi, Amy, nice to see you again," Siobhan said. She was small and dark-haired, and she and Deirdre looked so alike most people thought they were sisters.

"Are you still in the crèche?" I asked her. Siobhan and Deirdre had worked with Suzi in Tiny Tots Crèche in Foxrock before Suzi had gone to Australia.

"Yes," Siobhan said, "we're both still there." Deirdre walked over. "For our sins," she added.

"How's it going, Amy?" Deirdre smiled. "This is a grand place. We're going to have such a laugh."

Stella plonked a willy hat with a white net veil on Suzi's head. "Suits you," she giggled.

I pushed Suzi in the door and into the living-room. "Guys," she exclaimed as she saw the decorations, "you shouldn't have." She looked at the captioned photographs carefully. We all stood behind her, pointing and laughing. "Gary Simmons!" she shrieked. "He was so ugly! You really shouldn't have!" She was laughing so much tears were pouring down her face.

"Love the dress," Siobhan pointed to Suzi's bright blue ruched satin debs dress.

"Do you mind?" Suzi said. "It was the height of fashion."

"Who's that thing beside you?" Deirdre asked.

"Don't be so rude," Suzi grinned. "That's Des. Shit, I can't remember his second name. He was from Blackrock College. Nice guy, shame about the face."

"No kidding," I smiled.

"He was a rugby player," Suzi continued. "He had a great body."

"Always one for the rugby players," Julie laughed.

"Look who's talking!" I exclaimed. "Mrs Rugby herself!"

"I think I need a drink," Julie said quickly, "or I'm going to be in a lot of trouble."

"What's Brian like in bed?" Polly asked wickedly. She been told all about Brian by Matt the previous night over dinner.

"Polly!" Amber shouted. "Stop it."

Julie laughed. "Have you ever seen him on the rugby pitch?" she asked.

Polly nodded. "Against England last year."

"Honey, he's twice as good in bed."

We all hooted and clapped.

"Good on you, Julie!" Suzi yelled. "You're well able for them!"

Chapter 31

A lot of drinks later we were sitting around the table, sharing filthy jokes. Julie had kindly offered to provide the food for the weekend and tonight's meal was lasagne and chips.

"This is delicious," I said, dipping a chip into some tomato sauce. "Just what we need to soak up all the alcohol."

"Good girl, Julie," Suzi said. "Toast to Julie."

"To Julie!" we all yelled, clinking our glasses dangerously hard.

"Toast to the hen!" Julie said. "The best girl in the world. Matt's a lucky man."

"To the hen," yelled Siobhan, Julie and me. "To Suzi," yelled Stella, Beth, Amber and Polly. "To Looly," yelled Deirdre, who was the most drunk of us all. We clinked our glasses again, this time spilling lots on the table.

"To the bridesmaids," Suzi shouted, "Amy and Stella."

"To the bridesmaids," we all yelled. The table was by now covered with drink.

"To women," Stella yelled, "without men!"

"To women without men," we all yelled.

"I like men," Amber stated loudly. "That Tim, he's all right. I'm going to snog him."

We all cheered.

"Who's Tim?" Suzi asked.

"The rather hunky guy who runs this place," I explained.

"Tim, Tim, Tim, Tim," the table began to chant.

Amber stood up and clambered onto the table. "Tim, Tim, Tim," she chanted, waving her arms in the air.

Suddenly she jumped down off the table and ran barefoot towards the door. "I'll just go and get him," she shouted.

We all laughed hysterically.

"She's only messing, isn't she?" Stella asked.

Polly smiled. "No, I don't think so."

We watched the door expectantly. There was no sign of Amber.

"Do you think she's OK?" Beth asked, a little less drunk than the rest of us.

"It's Tim we should be worried about," Polly assured us.

"Let's play 'Bunnies'," Polly shouted. "Everyone get a full drink in front of them and I'll explain the rules."

"Rules?" Siobhan asked. "Is it complicated?"

Polly thought for a bit. "It is a bit. I know, I'll make up a new game. It's called boys' names. You have to think of a boy's name and shout it out when it's your turn. If it's a crap name you have to drink your whole glass. OK?"

"Yes!" everyone yelled.

"What kind of names?" Suzi asked. "Would Matt be good or bad?"

"Good," said Polly definitely.

"What about Tony?" Beth asked a little worried.

"Good!" Polly yelled.

"Cedric?" Siobhan asked.

"Bad!" Polly shouted.

"Kevin?" Deirdre asked.

"Bad!" Polly yelled.

"That's my Dad's name," Stella said.

"Sorry," Polly apologised.

"That's all right," Stella assured her. "I don't like it either."

"Have we started the game?" I asked in confusion.

"No," Polly said, "but we will now. Around the table, Suzi first."

"Matt!" Suzi yelled.

"You already said Matt," I laughed.

"I'm saying it again," Suzi giggled. "I'm the hen. I'm allowed."

"Quite right too," Polly said. "Next!"

"Adam," Stella yelled.

"Good!" Polly said. "Next."

"Brian," Julie shouted.

"Bad!" Polly said.

"Why?" Julie asked, a little perturbed.

"I'm just trying to get you drunk," Polly explained. "It's a nice name really."

"That's OK then," Julie said, knocking back her drink.

We continued yelling out good and bad names, getting more and more drunk. In the middle of the 'game' I staggered out to the loo. Hearing a noise outside the house I opened the front door to investigate. It was Amber, her arms draped around Tim's shoulders.

"Hi, Amy," she smiled, "look who I found."

Tim grinned sheepishly. "Hello again."

"I'm not sure you want to go in there," I warned him.

"I'm a big boy," he said. "I'll be fine."

Coming out of the toilet I heard loud shrieks and shouts. As I walked into the living-room I saw what all the noise was about. Tim was in the thick of it. All the girls were circling around him trying to pull his jeans down. He was holding onto his denims for dear life.

"Now, girls, stop that," he was shouting ineffectually. "Ow, careful!" They'd already succeeded in removing his fleece and T-shirt which had been thrown onto the floor. Hands pawed at his chest, stroking his six-pack.

"Who's a big boy then?" Polly said.

"Look at those muscles," Julie said admiringly. "Almost as good as my Brian's."

Amber was a little concerned. "Maybe we should leave him alone . . ." she began.

"Why don't we play 'Spin the Bottle'?" Polly suggested.

I giggled. "You can't play with only one man," I said.

"We could kiss each other," Siobhan added helpfully.

"Don't be gross," Suzi said. "I'm not kissing my sister. Or any girl for that matter."

Tim was finally left alone after Polly arrived with another jug of some sort of lethal cocktail.

"What's this one?" Amber asked.

"Don't know," Polly admitted. "I just chucked everything in really. Tastes divine though."

I nearly choked after taking a sip. It was pure rocket fuel. I could taste gin and tequila and after that I didn't want to know.

"Let's have a sing-song," Tim suggested carefully. He was either very brave or very stupid to stay in the room, considering our state. Sitting on the sofa, still bare-chested with one arm resting over Amber's back he obviously had more hormones than sense.

"I nominate 'Two Shy' by Kagagoogo."

"Ya what?" Deirdre asked from the floor where she had raised her head for the first time in several minutes. She really was a little under the weather.

We launched into a bizarre rendition of 'Too Shy' followed by an even more dodgy version of 'Wherever

I Lay My Hat That's My Home', one of Polly's favourites.

At half three I just couldn't take it any more. My head was spinning, I felt decidedly nauseous and very, very sleepy. I decided to call it a day. I snuck upstairs to my bed and lay down fully clothed on the soft duvet. I was out like a light.

The next morning I woke up to the sounds of music blaring from downstairs. I could also hear laughter and shrieks. I sat up slowly and looked out the window. I hadn't closed the curtains and it was bright outside. Stella was crashed out on the bed beside me, also fully clothed.

I staggered downstairs holding my head in my hands. I needed painkillers and water fast. My temples were throbbing like nobody's business and my stomach felt like a tiny bunch of gremlins were punching the lining from the inside. Not to mention the definite presence of a dead rat in my mouth.

"Hi, Amy," Polly yelled from the sofa. The curtains were drawn and Polly, Siobhan and Deirdre were sprawled on the large sofa covered in duvets. "Wanna drink?"

Were they mad? "No, thanks," I muttered. I stared at them carefully. "How long have you been up?" I looked at my watch. "It's only half eleven."

"Up?" Siobhan giggled. "We haven't been down."

"You stayed up all night?" I asked incredulously. They were barking.

"Yep," Polly stated proudly. She took a long slug of her drink. "Thanks to my amazing cocktails."

The gravel outside crunched and someone knocked on the door. I opened it. Martha and Jan stared at me with a worried expression on their innocent faces.

"Are you OK?" Martha asked. "You look a little ropy."

"I'm fine," I assured them. "Come in. It's good to see you both. Suzi's asleep, I think."

They followed me into the living-room.

"Hi, girls," Siobhan shouted from the sofa. "Fancy a drink?"

"It's a bit early, isn't it?" Jan asked.

"Never too early," Polly hiccuped.

At two o'clock Amber arrived at the door barefoot with a grin plastered from ear to ear. Apart from Polly, Siobhan and Deirdre who had taken to their beds for the afternoon, we were all sitting at the table (freshly cleared away and cleaned by Julie or 'Mammy' as we'd started calling her, much to her disgust) eating toast and drinking large mugs of coffee.

"Where were you, Amber?" I asked with a grin.

She smiled. "With the lovely Tim, of course."

"Tell us all about it," Stella demanded. "Every little detail."

"To be honest I can't remember much, thanks to my darling sister's cocktails," she laughed, "but he's very sweet. He's on his way up here to bring you all riding."

"I don't think I'd be into that," Suzi winced. "All

that up and down motion. I don't think my stomach would survive."

"You're probably right," Julie agreed.

"Then how about shooting?" Amber asked. "That wouldn't affect your stomach."

"It's very noisy though," I muttered. My headache was getting worse.

Amber sighed. "I know," she said brightly. "Archery. That's not noisy."

"Maybe," Stella said. "Is it hard?"

"Not really," Amber said. "It's good fun."

Tim came bounding in the door. "Are you all ready?" he asked.

"Do we look ready?" I asked, glaring at him. He was for too perky for this time of the morning. He stood behind Amber and I could see his hands lingering on her pert buttocks before slotting around her waist.

"I think archery might be the best choice, darling," Amber said, nuzzling his neck.

"Would you two stop that!" Suzi exclaimed. "This is supposed to be my hen weekend. No men allowed."

"Sorry," Amber giggled. "Irish men just do it for me."

"Are you mad?" I asked. Tim glared at me.

"Right, gang," he stated, all gung-ho. "Everyone on their feet. You'll need sensible shoes, no heels please. And bring a jacket. It can get quite cold up by the targets. I'll collect Jasper and meet you outside in two minutes."

"Who's Jasper?" I asked Amber after Tim had left.

"No idea," Amber admitted. "Maybe it's his dog."

We pulled on runners, Nike and Adidas for all of us except Amber who had bright blue Power Girl ones. Jackets and fleece hats followed. Julie had brought spare jackets and hats, bless her.

"Julie, you're too good to us," I smiled as she handed me a grey fleece hat.

"I'm so used to standing on the sidelines I have hundreds of warm jackets and hats," she explained.

Tim smiled as he saw us gathered on the gravel in front of the cottage. "That's better," he said. "This is Jasper," he said, introducing a young man in combats, black fleece and Timberland boots. "He'll be helping me today."

"Cute," Stella whispered in my ear.

"I'll just warn you, this lot are dangerous," he told Jasper. Amber pouted. "Except Amber, of course." The blonde woman beamed and blew him a kiss with her perfectly manicured hand. "This is Stella, Suzi, Amy, Beth, Julie, Martha and Jan," he introduced each of us in turn, delighted that he'd remembered all the names.

"I think I can handle them," Jasper said. He had a deep, throaty voice.

"I wouldn't be too sure," Stella flirted.

"Follow Jasper up to the targets," Tim said. "I'll be there with the bows in a few minutes."

"I'll go with you," Amber trilled.

"This way," Jasper commanded, leading us behind the buildings and towards the top of an open field. In the far corner six large targets came into view, coloured circles on heavy straw backgrounds. Each target was the size of a large dustbin lid.

"That doesn't look too bad," Martha said as we approached them. She was a bit of a Sporty Spice – she'd always won everything in school, I remembered. Jan didn't look too sure.

"Have any of you done archery before?" Jasper asked as we huddled together, waiting for Tim and Amber.

"No," we all chorused.

"There are a few things to keep in mind," he continued. "Firstly, the bows are heavy. You need to hold them firmly and strongly . . ."

"Oh, yeah?" Stella quipped. Jasper smiled at her.

"As I was saying, hold them firmly. I'll show each of you the correct position when Tim arrives with the bows."

"I wouldn't hold your breath," Suzi laughed.

Jasper looked a little worried. The prospect of entertaining us without bows wasn't too appealing.

"There are two bows and plenty of arrows here," he said, pointing over to a large black box. "So maybe we'll get started with those. "Who would like to go first? I need two of you."

"I will," Martha offered.

"Me too," Julie said.

"Put these on your wrists." He handed them leather

pieces with Velcro-fastening straps and helped them secure them. "These are to stop the string catching you."

Jasper then lined them up, facing sideways towards the targets. He handed them a bow each and showed them the correct way to hold them.

"I'll load the arrows for you this time. Next time you'll be doing it yourselves. The green plastic piece needs to be on the top." He slotted the arrow onto the bow. "Now comes the hard part." Stella nudged me in the side. I tried not to giggle. It was great fun being so childish. "Pull back the string, keeping the bow steady. Good, Martha. Stella . . ."

"Julie," she corrected.

"Sorry, Julie, you need to pull back harder. Like this." He stood behind her and helped her pull back the heavy string.

"Now let the string go." Martha's arrow shot towards the target, landing at the edge with a whack. Julie's arrow landed at her feet.

"Oops," she laughed. "I'm not much good at this."

"Not to worry," Jasper said kindly. "It takes a while to get the hang of it."

Julie and Martha had a few more goes before it was Suzi and Stella's turn. I had 'kindly' offered to wait with Jan. I was more then happy to just watch. If Julie couldn't do it I didn't have a hope in hell. I was one of those kids who was always picked last for teams in school. Sport of any kind just wasn't my thing.

Suzi was good. She hit the target every time, several

times in the red 'bull's eye'. Stella wasn't bad either. I'm sure she could have been a lot better but she seemed to like Jasper showing her how to do it.

"Amber's taking her time," Jan said, smiling.

"You should have seen her last night," Julie said, rubbing her upper arm. "She was all over Tim."

"Poor lad," I said, "he was lucky we didn't strip him fully."

"Sounds like I missed a good night," Jan smiled.

"Tonight will be even better," I promised her.

"Here's Amber," Suzi shouted. "Hey, Amber, what were you doing? Your fleece is inside out."

Amber looked at her fleece and giggled. Tim was carrying an armful of bows and handed them out, ignoring our slags.

"Now you have one each. If you've all had a bit of a practice, Jasper will keep the scores. I'll split you into two teams."

"There's an odd number so I'll watch," Julie said.

"Are you sure?" Amber asked.

"Yes," Julie replied. "My arm's a bit stiff anyway. You go ahead."

Amber jumped up and tested the string on her bow. She looked very professional.

"Have you done this before?" Martha asked.

"A little," Amber said.

Martha was fiercely competitive and didn't like to lose. "You're on my team, so.

"I think I'll pick the teams, " Tim decided. "Just to

make it interesting. Martha, you take Suzi and Amy, and Amber, you take Jan and Stella."

"OK," Martha agreed. "May the best team win."

Amber turned out to be exceptional. Which was just as well as Jan and Stella were hopeless. But not as hopeless as myself and Suzi who laughed our way through the competition. Much to the annoyance of Martha.

"You could put some effort in," she grumbled. "Concentrate a bit."

We lost spectacularly.

Tim was well impressed with Amber. He gave her a big hug after the competition and lifted her into the air.

"I think we'll have to ban Amber this evening," Suzi grinned. "She'll bring your man and ruin everything."

"Maybe we could invite himself and Jasper over after dinner," Stella eagerly suggested. She'd taken a liking to the other young instructor.

"After we've dazzled the men of Arklow with our talent, of course," Suzi smiled. "I can't wait to get into my costume."

We trekked back to the cottage, peeled off our fleeces and jackets and collapsed on the sofa and chairs.

"That was fun," Julie said. "Amber, you're bloody good. Where did you learn archery?"

"One of Polly's ex's was a big archery fan," she explained. "He had a target in his back garden and he taught us both."

"Where's lover-boy?" Stella asked.

"He's gone back to his house," Amber said. "He's going out with Jasper and the riding instructor this evening. I might see him tomorrow but tonight is Suzi's night."

"Damn right!" Suzi exclaimed. "Maybe we can hook up with them later," she said kindly. "I wouldn't mind."

Amber smiled at her warmly. "You always were my fave cousin."

"What about me?" I asked in mock disgust.

"You too," Amber. "You're both my favourite cousins."

At six o'clock, after a few glasses of wine and beer – we'd decided to leave Polly's cocktails till later – we trooped upstairs and changed after waking Polly, Siobhan and Deirdre. The three girls were decidedly chirpy in the circumstances.

"How was your afternoon?" Polly asked, stretching her arms over her head and yawning.

"Great," Suzi said. "We did archery and your sister's team won."

Polly smiled. "Amber's rather super at archery. Now, what are we wearing tonight?"

"We're going for dinner at a local restaurant," Suzi explained. "It also has a nightclub called 'The Copa'."

"The locals call it the 'cop-a-feel'," I explained helpfully. "It's a bit of a dive but it'll be a laugh. We have divine costumes for Suzi and Beth that should raise an eyebrow or two."

"And the temperature," Suzi added.

"I'm wearing a skirt and a little top," I said. "And my kitten heels."

"I think it'll be my little pink dress then," Polly said. "Now accessories, let me see . . ."

An hour later we waited in the hall for Suzi and Beth. Everyone looked stunning. Lots of little dresses, skirts and leather trousers. Arklow wouldn't know what hit it. Body jewellery, courtesy of Polly, and the latest sparkly make-up, courtesy of Amber. The second vanity case had been full of sample cosmetics and hair products from all the top trendy companies I'd only ever read about in *OK* and *Now* magazine – Urban Decay Nail Enamel, Philosophy Never Let Them See You Shine powder, Bumble and Bumble Thickening Hair Spray. We were all in girlie heaven.

"Here we come, girls," Suzi shouted as she appeared at the top of the stairs. "Ready or not."

She was wearing a black latex rubber imitation leather cat-suit that clung unforgivingly to every curve. Luckily Suzi had the figure for it and looked stunning. A little sleazy but amazing none the less. Amber had piled her hair on the top of her head and made up her face to perfection. She was wearing high red sandals.

"Wow," Polly drew her breath. "You look just like Michelle Pfeiffer's Catwoman. Amazing."

"Thanks," she said. "Beth, come down."

"No," Beth wailed. "I look ridiculous."

"Beth," Julie yelled up the stairs. "I'm sure you don't."

"Hen," Polly and Amber shouted.

"Hen, hen," everyone joined in, yelling louder and louder.

"OK, OK," Beth finally shouted. As she stood at the top of the stairs we all gasped.

Chapter 32

I'd never seen Beth look so . . . so . . . well, it just wasn't Beth. She was wearing a red snakeskin printed 'leather' bra top which clung to her generous breasts like a second skin. The matching red skirt rested just above her knee but was slashed up the sides to reveal her legs. Black leather high-heeled boots completed the outfit.

"I feel like a porn queen," she complained as she made her way nervously down the stairs.

We were all stunned. Amber had straightened her normally curly hair and used bright, strong colours on her lips and eyes. Her arms and cleavage had been dusted with sparkling bronzer, which danced in the light.

"You look amazing," Polly said admiringly. "You'll stop traffic, darling."

Beth seemed unsure. "Maybe I'll go up and change. They might not let me into the nightclub . . ."

"You're joking," Siobhan said. "They'd definitely let

you into any nightclub in the world – even Hollywood looking like that."

"You're any red-blooded male's dream girl," Martha agreed.

"Pamela Anderson eat your heart out," Suzi said.

"I'm not sure," Beth said.

"Grab her, girls," Julie commanded. "We're off!"

"Get off me, you mad things," Beth squealed as we pushed her out the door and into Julie's jeep. Julie was leaving her wheels at the restaurant and would collect them the following day.

We all piled in on top of Beth. It was quite a squeeze but what was a mouthful of hair between friends?

"Are we there yet, Mammy?" Polly asked as we crunched down the gravel drive.

"Stop calling me Mammy," Julie said.

"Yes, Mammy," we all chorused.

We piled out of the jeep and into the 'Eden Tree' restaurant. They had quite sensibly given us a large table at the back of the room, looking out onto a brightly lit courtyard.

"Beth and Suzi at the two ends," I said. "And everyone else pile in."

There was much giggling and squeals as we seated ourselves.

"What if I need to go to the loo?" Deirdre asked. "I'm a bit boxed in here."

"You'd better let her sit on the outside," Martha suggested, "just in case."

As Deirdre had shown her lack of staying power the previous evening, Siobhan kindly offered to swap with her.

"I'll crawl under," Siobhan said. "No need for anyone to move." She wriggled down her seat and ducked her head under the table.

"I'll give you these," a young male waiter began, handing out large laminated terracotta-coloured menus, "and would you like to order drinks?"

"A 'Flaming Orgasm' for me, mate," came Siobhan's voice from under the table.

The waiter jumped. We all laughed as her head popped up from between Stella and Martha's chairs.

"I'm not sure we have those," the waiter said nervously.

"A 'Sex on the Beach', so," Siobhan smiled. Deirdre popped out of her seat and began to crawl the opposite way, towards Siobhan's old seat.

"I don't think . . ." the waiter began, staring at Deirdre's disappearing behind in amazement.

"How about a vodka and Red Bull?" she asked.

"Yes," he said, gratefully, "one vodka and Red Bull."

"Me too," said Beth and Suzi in unison.

"Beth!" I exclaimed. "You don't drink spirits."

"It's a special occasion," Beth smiled, "and I think I'm going to need something strong."

"Quite right too, darling," Amber smiled. "Same for me, please."

The waiter came back several minutes later with a tray of eleven vodka and Red Bulls.

"Have you decided on your food yet?" he asked.

"Food?" Deirdre asked vacantly. "Oh, yes, food."

"Come back in a few minutes," Julie said kindly. "We haven't really looked at the menus yet."

"And bring another round," Polly instructed, "same again."

"And three bottles of champagne," Amber said. "No, better make it five. The bubbly's on me."

"Go, Amber," we yelled, waving our arms in the air in true Rikki Lake style. "Go, Amber, go, Amber."

Eventually the waiter managed to extract our order. Garlic bread was the favoured starter, except for Stella and Amber who got slagged mightily for ordering melon instead.

"Snoggers," Siobhan shouted, "snoggers, snoggers."

"Do you mind?" Stella asked in mock disgust. "I have a boyfriend."

"Don't let that stop you!" Beth yelled.

"Beth!" I smiled. "I think the drink has gone to your head."

"I think so too," she grinned sloppily. "Iss lovely stuff. *More vodka!* Vodka, vodka," she yelled, banging her knife and fork on the table.

At this stage heads were turning and the waiter scuttled over to us.

"I'm afraid you'll have to keep it down," he insisted. "Other diners are complaining."

"Sorry," Julie said quickly. "We'll behave."

"For now," Polly added, a dangerous glint in her eye.

Luckily our food arrived quickly and soon we were all (except Stella and Amber) tucking into delicious hot garlic bread which was topped with mozzarella cheese and sun-dried tomatoes.

"This is very good," Julie said enthusiastically, licking dripping butter off her fingers. "How's the melon, snoggers?" Polly asked, grinning.

"Very good, thanks, smelly-breath," Stella smiled.

"Will we order wine?" Julie asked, a little anxious at the effect the Red Bull was having on the crew. Even Deirdre was bright-eyed and bushy-tailed. In fact she was very bushy-tailed, her pupils were definitely dilated and she looked a little crazed.

"What happened to the champagne?" Amber asked. We'd forgotten about it.

Just then her question was answered. The waiter carried over two silver buckets, followed by another waiter with a tray of long champagne flutes.

"Sorry about the delay," he said. "We don't get asked for champagne much. I'll bring the other bottles in a minute."

He placed the buckets in the centre of the table and began to pour the sparkling liquid. When all our glasses were filled Amber stood up.

"A toast to the two hens, Suzi and Beth," she said loudly, smiling.

"To the hens," we all clinked our glasses and took a sip.

Suzi jumped up. "To Amber for the champagne," she said.

"To Amber," we toasted.

"Not again," Julie giggled. "This could go on all night. Let's leave the toasts till after the food."

"Good idea," Beth agreed. "Now who's going to give that champagne bottle a blow-job?"

"Beth!" I spluttered, spilling a mouthful of champagne down my silver top.

"I will," Siobhan said, licking her lips. She placed the top of the champagne bottle between her lips and began to slide it in and out of her mouth.

"Go, girl!" Polly said.

Luckily no one appeared to have noticed what we were doing.

"Do you still do that when you're married?" Deirdre asked Julie, pointing at Siobhan.

Julie smiled. "Of course," she said, "and more."

"Tell us," Beth encouraged.

"I will not!" Julie said. "That's between me and the hubby."

"How long have you been married?" I asked, trying to steer the conversation onto safer ground.

"Ten years nearly," Julie smiled. "We met at school."

"Childhood sweethearts," Stella said. "When did you realise that he was, you know, 'the one'?"

"I'm not sure," Julie smiled. "It happened gradually, I suppose."

"How about you, Suzi?" Stella asked. "When did you know you wanted to marry Matt?"

Suzi smiled. "From the moment I saw him, I think.

We were at this party and our eyes met across a crowded room. I know it sounds like a cliché but it was like, bang, that was it."

"Once you can be yourself with someone, and they put up with all your funny habits and still love you, that's when you know," Beth smiled.

"You're both so lucky," Amber sighed, "I'd love to be getting married."

"Your turn will come," Julie said. "You never know, Tim might be 'the one'."

Amber laughed, "I don't think so, but I'm having a good time testing him out."

"Are you really?" Polly said. "And what would that involve, exactly?" she asked.

When the waiter arrived with the food the conversation had taken a downward spiral into the world of favourite sexual positions and the weirdest place anyone had had sex.

"I don't believe you," Suzi was saying as her steak was placed in front of her. "Those aeroplane toilets are tiny. I thought that was just an urban myth."

"No, honestly, darling," Polly insisted. "It's the most fun."

By the end of the dinner we were all flying on clouds of alcohol and good food.

"Desserts, anyone?" the waiter asked as he cleared away our plates with the help of two other waiters. Polly pinched his bum. He jumped and moved quickly away from her.

"I'd love some ice cream," Amber said.

"Banoffi pie for me," Julie said, handing back the menu.

"Anyone else?" he asked.

There were no other takers.

"Coffee?" he asked.

"No thanks," Beth trilled. "More vodka please."

"Another round of vodka and Red Bull," Polly smiled, "honey." She winked at him and he scuttled away, blushing.

"Are you making a speech, Suzi and Beth?" Amber asked after her ice cream.

"Go on, dolls," Polly smiled. "Speech."

"Speech, speech," we all yelled.

The waiter stared over and we lowered our voices.

Suzi stood up. "Thank you all for coming this evening. It's great to see you all here. Especially Polly and Amber who've travelled a long way to be with us . . ."

"Pleasure, darling," Polly interrupted.

"I'm so excited about getting married. I don't know what to say. I love Matt to bits and I hope all of you find your own Matt."

"Not a doormat, though," Deirdre quipped.

We all groaned.

"That's all really. Oh, and thanks to Amy for being my bridesmaid. I know she's not over the moon with the idea but she's been great." She leant over and gave me a kiss. "So have a good night, everyone."

We clapped and cheered.

"Your turn, Beth," Julie said.

Beth got to her feet. "This is really Suzi's night, I'm just tagging along. So firstly thanks to Suzi for letting me share this evening." Suzi smiled. "And to my bridesmaids, Amy and Stella. Amy is great to do it twice. As most of you know our weddings are only days apart so I really appreciate it."

"You know what they say," I smiled grimly, *"always the bridesmaid, never the bride."*

"That won't be true for you," Beth continued. "You're lovely. I'd marry you myself, if I was a boy."

"So would I," Suzi agreed, "if I was a boy and not related to you."

"I would too!" Polly exclaimed.

"We all would," Stella shouted.

I laughed. "Thanks, guys. If any of you ever get a sex change, look me up!"

"That's all I have to say really," Beth finished. "Now have fun!"

Paying the bill was interesting. Julie took charge and split the bill nine ways, paying for Beth and Suzi. Amber covered the champagne which was just as well. Not all of us lived on London salaries.

The doormen at The Copa were very impressed with Suzi and Beth's outfits, as predicted.

"All right, love?" a burly redhead asked Beth. "Doing anything later?"

"Getting married," Beth replied. "First thing in the morning," she lied.

"Bloody hell," he muttered, "the good ones are always feckin' married."

"Hasn't stopped you before, Dirk," another bald bouncer joked.

"True," Dirk answered.

"How about it, sweetheart?" he asked Beth. "I'm off at three."

"No, thanks," Beth laughed. "I appreciate the offer though."

The Copa was very dark inside. The walls were painted matt red, and mirrors and glitter-balls sent broken, reflected light around the room. The dance floor was generously sized and as we walked in the dulcet tones of 'Come on, Eileen' rang out.

"Excellent," Julie shouted over the noise. "It's an eighties night."

It turned out not to be – the DJ just had very strange taste in music which encompassed the eighties, the nineties and some dodgy modern 'hits' from Steps and Billie. He even played slow sets.

We found seats beside the dance floor and settled in. Polly, Amber and Siobhan immediately started dancing to Fatboy Slim, showing a ridiculous amount of energy and enthusiasm.

"Are ya dancing?" a voice beside me asked as I sipped my bottle of Ritz.

"Are ya asking?" I replied, thinking he was joking, looking up at a bum-fluffed cheek. The tall, gangly male in front of me was all of seventeen.

"I am," he said humourlessly, holding out his hand.

"I dare you," Suzi hissed at me.

I glared at her and stood up gingerly, the others giggling and poking each other behind me. I held his clammy palm as he pulled me eagerly onto the dance floor. Just my luck – the music changed and Celine Dion's *Titanic* song bellowed out.

Please don't let him try and kiss me, I thought to myself.

The boy put his arms around me. "What's your name?" he asked.

"Poppy," I lied for some reason.

"Like the flowers?" he asked.

"Yes," I nodded.

"That's nice. I'm Owen," he said resting his head on my bare shoulder.

We shuffled around in circles to the music. It reminded me of school discos. After our one dance the music changed – more eighties this time – he walked me back to my seat, thanked me and walked away.

"Amazing," I said to Stella. "He was the perfect gentleman. Maybe chivalry isn't dead after all."

But Stella was paying me absolutely no attention. Her eyes were fixed on the doorway.

"Look who it is," she said, a smile spreading from ear to ear.

Tim, Jasper and a tall blond man walked in. She jumped down and went over to the threesome. Tim had already stopped Amber on the dance floor and in seconds everyone was waving their arms in the air to 'YMCA'.

"I love this one!" Julie yelled over the music to me. "Let's dance. Come on, girls, follow us," she said to the others.

We all jumped to our feet except Deirdre who had fallen asleep, her head resting on the table in front of her.

"I'll stay with her," Beth said kindly. "I'll mind the bags."

"Are you sure?" I asked.

"Yes," she smiled. "I'll have fun watching you all making wallies of yourselves."

"Thanks a lot," I grinned.

"This is Justin," Tim yelled over the music, introducing his friend who was dancing beside me. "He works at the centre."

"Hi, Justin," I smiled. "I'm Amy."

"Nice name," he smiled back. "You all look like you've been having a good time."

"No kidding," I said loudly.

"And now . . ." the DJ's swarthy voice came over the speakers, "by special request from the Dublin hens for Suzi and Beth – 'Like a Virgin' by Madonna."

We all surrounded Suzi and Beth and made them dance in the middle while we clapped and cheered. Jasper and Justin seemed to be entering into the spirit of things with gusto. Tim and Amber had disappeared.

"Where's Tim?" I asked Justin after a while.

"I think he's gone back to the house," he grinned. "He's mad about your friend. He has a bottle of wine in the fridge apparently."

"I see," I smiled. "Lucky Amber."

"Lucky Tim more like," he grinned. "She's a babe."

"She's my cousin," I smiled.

"Must run in the family," he said.

The nightclub closed at three and we were all there till the bitter end. Deirdre slept through most of the night and Julie, Jan and Martha didn't look far off comatose themselves. They were sitting slumped in their seats when the lights came on.

"I hate when they turn on the lights," Justin said to me. "It's such a jolt. Back to the real world."

"And everyone just looks tired," I said. "The girls have mascara-panda eyes and the boys have sweat dripping down their faces."

"You look even better in this light," he smiled, brushing my hair out of my eyes.

My stomach lurched. I realised that Justin was flirting with me. It hadn't occurred to me before – maybe I was too drunk to notice. But now I was just nice drunk, warm and relaxed without feeling out of it. I looked at him. He was very attractive – dark hair cut very short, green eyes and a wide, crooked smile. He looked a little young, twenty-two or three maybe, but I wasn't going to let that stop me. He was legal after all. I was single and there was no one else to think about, not really. Steve's face briefly flitted through my drunken mind. But that was over, finito.

"We've loads of drink back at the cottage," I smiled, trying to appear cool. "You're welcome to join us."

"Sure," he smiled, "sounds good."

"Hey, Jasper," he shouted over at his friend whose arm was around Stella's waist. "Are you going back to the girls' cottage?"

Jasper looked at Stella who nodded. "Yes!" he exclaimed.

Justin, who was a local, managed to order us three taxis and we arrived back at the cottage within twenty minutes.

"Where do you live?" I asked him.

"Down the road from here, with Jasper. And you're from Dublin, I presume."

"Yes," I said. "Blackrock." I didn't feel like going into any details, to be honest. He was cute and nice but I was really only after his body.

Chapter 33

When we arrived at the cottage the lights were on and music was playing. Not just music – Abba's 'Dancing Queen', Suzi's favourite song.

Amber and Tim met us on the doorstep. "I found *Abba's Greatest Hits,*" she shouted over the music.

Suzi jumped out of the taxi and ran inside. "Let's dance, girls," she yelled. "Follow me."

Within minutes everyone, including Deirdre who had woken up, was dancing. Justin, Tim and Jasper included.

"Everyone off the floor," Suzi commanded, as the strains of 'Waterloo' hit the air.

"Sorry?" Justin asked. He watched in amazement as we all scrambled onto chairs, the sofa, the table and kitchen chairs.

"Come on, boys," Suzi yelled. "Off the floor."

Justin climbed onto one of the windowsills, Tim sat

on the top of the fridge and Jasper joined Stella on one of the armchairs.

"You're all mad!" Tim yelled over the music. "I'm not supposed to allow any noise after twelve." He grinned. "Luckily there's no one in the other cottages this weekend as they're being painted."

"So we can make noise all night," Beth shouted.

After three more Abba songs I was exhausted. I hadn't had so much exercise for years. I staggered out into the hall and plonked myself down on the stairs.

"Are you OK?" Justin asked, following me out and handing me a glass.

"What's this?" I asked, sniffing the glass suspiciously.

"I'm not sure," he smiled. "Polly gave it to me. It tastes sweet though. Try it."

He took a sip and handed it to me. I stared at his moist lips. I took the glass from him and placed it on the stair above me. "I think I'll taste yours," I smiled. I leant over and ran my tongue over his lips seductively. "Umm, nice," I smiled.

He took a sip of the drink, put his hand behind my head and pressed his lips firmly to mine. As my mouth opened he allowed the sweet, warm liquid trickle into my mouth. He then started kissing me, gently at first, brushing my lips with his, softly and slowly. I began to caress his tongue with mine. He responded immediately, taking my lead. Soon our bodies were entwined on the stairs, the carpeted edges jutting into our backs.

"Let's go upstairs," I suggested. He followed me

without a word, holding my hand tightly. We fell onto my bed, kissing passionately.

"You're amazing," Justin whispered in my ear as he nuzzled my neck. His cool, firm hands moved over my bare shoulders and across my back. I pulled his shirt out of his trousers and ran my fingers up and down his spine. He pulled his shirt over his head, ignoring the buttons, and threw it on the floor. His hairless, muscular chest shone in the moonlight.

"What age *are* you?" I asked him, coming up for air as his hands caressed my back.

"Does it matter?" he smiled, kissing me.

"Not really, I was just wondering," I said.

"I'm nearly twenty," he replied.

Bloody hell, I thought to myself. What the feck am I doing? I could be his mother – well, not quite, but almost.

"What's wrong?" Justin asked. "You've gone very quiet."

"What age do you think I am?" I whispered.

He sat up. "I don't know, twenty-four, twenty-five? But don't worry, I like older women."

Yes! I thought. He thinks I'm twenty-four. Yes!

"What age are you?" he asked.

"Twenty-four," I lied.

He smiled and kissed me gently. "Shut up and come here, gorgeous."

He rolled over, pinning me under his body. He carefully pulled my top over my head and removed my bra. I was glad I'd worn my fairly new, pink lacy bra. Shit, I muttered to myself, am I wearing the matching knickers? Amy, I thought as he kissed my breasts, are you seriously thinking of sleeping with this guy? But what harm would it do?

At this stage I should explain that I'd never, ever had a one-night stand. In fact the nearest I'd come to it was the unfortunate Branigan New Year's Eve debacle and you know how that turned out. I'd had sex exactly twice before Jack. Once with a guy called Martin Bowler when I was nineteen. We'd been together for nearly three months and I was mad about him. I was also dying to lose my virginity – it was like an albatross around my late-teenage neck. The sex was mediocre to say the least.

Number two was Ryan Ahearne, my first 'real' long-term boyfriend. I'd just broken up with Martin (he went off with Kelly, the local bicycle, who he kept telling me was 'mad for it', unlike myself apparently) and I met Ryan in town outside the William Tell pub. We were together for years, literally. Almost four. And the sex was good, but not very good. With Jack it was different. I was older and I had oodles more confidence. I liked my body enough to let him see me naked in semi-darkness (never daylight!) and it made me feel close to him.

So, as you see, one-night stands hadn't really come into it until tonight. Sure, Justin was young, very young. But it was uncomplicated and, feck it, fun.

Justin sat up and looked at me. "You seems miles away," he said with concern. "Do you want me to stop?"

"No," I said, "I just don't normally do this . . ." I shrugged.

"You're on your holidays," Justin smiled. "Relax. We won't do anything you don't want to do."

"How did you get to be so nice?" I asked.

"Practice," he grinned. He began kissing me again, concentrating on my lips and neck and then running his lips down towards my breasts. I revelled in the sensations and began to relax. I moved my hands down over his back towards his pert buttocks. I started to unbuckle his belt using both hands. He sat up slightly, allowing me to unbutton his jeans and slide them down his thighs. He kicked off his shoes and deftly removed his socks with either foot. He then helped me pull his jeans down his legs and pushed them off the bed onto the floor.

He began kissing me again, his hands moving my knee-length skirt towards my waist. As his fingers skimmed over the lacy top of my hold-ups, I moaned. He teased me through the material of my knickers and my body began to respond to his touch. His fingers danced at the edge of the lace, skimming my skin and sending darts of pleasure up and down my spine.

I ran my hand up and down his hardness. He breathed heavily. "I really want you, Amy," he groaned.

"Do you have any . . . you know?" I asked. The word 'condom' just wouldn't come out of my mouth.

"Shit, no," he muttered. "Sorry."

"Wait there," I whispered, remembering the stash on the mantelpiece. I pulled down my skirt, threw my top back on and ran down the stairs. Luckily everyone was too drunk or too asleep to notice me helping myself to a handful of Durex. Stella and Jasper were lying asleep on the couch, her head on his knee. Polly, Siobhan, Martha, Jan and Beth were dancing, still to *Abba's Greatest Hits*. Beth, Julie and Suzi were sitting at the table talking, about husbands and weddings no doubt. Deirdre was asleep on an armchair and snoring loudly. Amber waved over to me from the sofa.

"Hi, Amy, bet you're regretting that garlic bread now," she said.

"Justin doesn't seem to mind," I smiled and went back upstairs. Justin was lying on the bed in all his naked glory. He beamed at me as I opened the door.

"Hi, princess," he said. "Any luck?"

I held out my hand.

"Well done," he smiled. I sat down on the bed. He rolled over and bit my bum through my skirt.

"Hey," I squealed, dropping the condoms on the floor.

He picked one up. "What have we here?" he read the wrapper. "Strawberry – my favourite. Will you do the honours or will I?"

I blushed. "You," I whispered. I watched open-eyed as he opened the packet carefully with his teeth, spitting out the edge of the foil onto the floor. He removed the latex sheath and began to roll it on. I'd never seen a guy putting on a condom before. They'd usually done it under the covers or I'd shut my eyes tightly. With Jack I was on the pill so the process hadn't come up. So to speak.

"I hope you like strawberry," he grinned, pulling me towards him.

"I do," I smiled, "and mint."

"Are there mint ones?" he asked.

"There are," I assured him.

"We'll try one of those next, then," he said.

Thank you, God, for younger men, I prayed. Thank you.

When I woke up the following morning I felt remarkably fine considering the copious amounts of alcohol I'd poured into myself. Justin was lying on his back beside me, snoring gently. Julie and Suzi had diplomatically slept downstairs I presumed, as their beds were empty. It was grey outside and fat raindrops were running down the windowpane. I'd forgotten to draw the curtains again.

Justin opened his eyes and looked over at me. "Morning," he smiled. He kissed my cheek gently. "How are you this morning?"

"Good," I smiled.

He looked and his watch and groaned. "Damn, I have to go now. I have to take a group of American tourists trekking." He stared out the window in dismay. "Typical, rain. Can I call in and see you later?"

"Sure," I smiled. It would be nice to see him but I wasn't too bothered one way or another. Which was good. No – which was bloody excellent. We'd had great sex, a real laugh and I was happy to leave it at that. Love them and leave them – it was a strange new feeling to me.

He jumped up and threw on his clothes. He leant over and kissed me again. "Thanks, I had a great night."

"My pleasure," I smiled, meaning it.

As soon as I heard the door slam, Suzi and Beth bounded into the room.

"I don't believe you did that," Beth giggled. "He's only nineteen."

"Nearly twenty," I grinned.

We spent the day lolling around the house. Tim called in and suggested a hike and we laughed at him. He ended up sitting with us all afternoon watching bad television and eating junk food. Hangover city. Deirdre was quite chipper as she'd slept most of it off in the nightclub – everyone else was dying.

"I thought this was supposed to be a healthy, outdoorsy weekend," Tim smiled. "Lots of fresh air and exercise."

"But some of us *have* had lots of exercise," Polly insisted, grinning at myself and Amber.

"How was the weekend?" Mum asked as Suzi and I staggered in the door on Sunday evening.

"Great," Suzi said, dumping her bag in the hallway.

"Brilliant," I agreed.

"Matt's in bed," Mum said. "He didn't get in till nine this morning. He had a shower, he was covered in shaving-cream and lipstick."

"I don't want to know," Suzi smiled.

"Lipstick writing," Mum insisted. "Not lip marks."

"I think I'll join him," Suzi said, yawning. "I'm bushed."

"Me too," I said, putting my head on my sister's shoulder.

"You can tell me all about it tomorrow then," Mum smiled. "I'll bring your bags up." She swung the bags onto her shoulders.

"I'll help you, Mum," I said, taking my bag off her.

"We'll tell you some of it," Suzi said, winking at me. "Not all."

"There are some things even a mother doesn't need to know," Mum smiled.

Chapter 34

"How many steps?" I asked Suzi. "Three or four?"

She bit her lip. "Four, I'm not used to walking in such a long dress. We'll have to go slowly."

"Did you hear that, Dad?" I asked, "four steps to the end of the aisle from the door, not three, OK?"

"Sure, love," he said distractedly. He was listening to RTE 1 on his Walkman.

We'd been in the church for almost an hour now and he was getting a little bored. Katie and Simon, Julie's children – the flower girl and pageboy – were getting a little twitchy too. But Suzi wanted to get everything just right.

The last few weeks since the hen had flown by. I couldn't believe that Suzi's wedding was in two days. She and Mum had been up to ninety getting all the last-minute details organised. The marquee had been erected the day before as it needed some time to 'settle' into the ground according to the company. It was magnificent – a huge white rectangle with pink and white striped awnings inside. The roof was covered with white chiffon and huge imitation crystal chandeliers hung from the ceiling. The wooden floor had been covered with a green carpet except for the dance area which had been left bare. There was a small catering tent to the back and a side tent, opening onto the main tent, for the bar. The fold-up tables and chairs were stacked on the floor, waiting to be erected.

"What music are you using for the procession?" I asked Suzi as we waited while Father Lucas talked to Matt and his brother, Luke, who was his best man. Matt's family had arrived from Perth that morning and poor Luke was looking a little shattered as he'd come straight from the airport.

Luke was tall and well built, like his brother, with a shock of blond hair, blue eyes and a wide, toothy smile. Your average Australian hard body. He was also just twenty-two, which after Arklow didn't seem all that young any more. Tragic, aren't I?

"'The Trumpet Tune' by Purcell," Suzi said. "Matt chose it. He originally wanted 'Sympathy for the Devil' . . ."

"The Rolling Stones' song?" I asked incredulously.

"Yes," Suzi smiled. "It's his favourite."

I laughed. "What did Father Lucas say?"

"He didn't think it was appropriate in the circumstances."

"Quite right too," I smiled. "They use it as the funeral song in *The Big Chill*."

"I'd forgotten about that," Suzi mused. She smiled. "But I don't think that was what he meant. Anyway Matt settled for trumpets instead."

"Ladies," Father Lucas said loudly from the front of the church, "ready to proceed?"

"Yes, Father," Suzi smiled.

"And one," Father Lucas began, "two . . . keep your head up, Amy. Mr O'Sullivan, full attention, please. Simon, hands out of pockets, please."

"Sorry," Dad mumbled, taking the earphones off his head and slipping them into his pocket. Simon took his hands out of his jeans and clasped them in front of him.

We walked up the aisle, slowly and remarkably together.

"Suzi, you stand beside Matt," Father Lucas instructed as we reached the altar, "Amy drop back behind her with Katie and Simon by your side. Matt and Luke stay put. Good, good. That's perfect."

"Can we go now?" Dad whispered to me. I smiled.

"Mr O'Sullivan, hand your daughter over, good, good, and take your place in the pew. Perfect." Father Lucas beamed. "Nicely done. I think that's it until Saturday. There will be two ushers though?"

"That's right," Matt nodded. "They're playing in a rugby match today, but they'll be here on Saturday."

"Unless there's another bloody rugby match," Suzi muttered under her breath. "Can we practise the readings?" Suzi asked Father Lucas. "Luke's here, he's reading the poem and Siobhan is doing the Mark Chapter Ten one. She's not here though."

Luke butted in. "It'll be all right, mate. I don't need to practise." He was dying to get to the pub with Matt and catch up. Another minute in the church would do his head in. He'd said he couldn't remember the last time he'd been in one.

Suzi seemed doubtful. "I suppose, if you're sure . . ."

"That's it then," Matt grinned. "Who's coming to Fitzie's?" Fitzgerald's Pub was just down the road.

"Matt," Suzi began, "we have to talk to the girl from Mad Flowers and help Dad with the garden."

Matt looked distraught. "But Luke wants to see a real Irish pub, don't you, Luke?" He elbowed his brother in the ribs.

"Please, Suzi," Luke said imploringly, "we'll only stay for one, I promise."

I tried not to laugh.

Suzi's face softened. "OK, but I want you back in one hour, do you hear me?"

Matt nodded.

I had a brainwave. "Why don't I go with them, Suzi, to keep an eye on them?"

"Good one, Amy," Luke smiled. I sensed trouble.

"As long as you're back later to finish the seating plan," Suzi said. "Promise?"

"Of course," I said. "Anyway it's nearly done, I just have to stick the leaves on and spray it again."

"And the place names?" Suzi asked.

Yikes, I thought. I'd forgotten all about those.

"I'll do them tomorrow. How many people are there exactly?" I asked, trying not to appear nervous.

"A hundred and thirty-two."

I whistled. "That many," I said. "I'd better get a few more gold pens."

I'd decided to write each guest's name on a gold-sprayed real leaf. The table plan would also be gold, with each table's names on a separate large leaf – these ones were fake. It was taking rather longer than I'd originally planned. I'd have to get up early and start writing the names on leaves – all one hundred and thirty-two of them!

"Are you married, Amy?" Luke asked as we walked down the road towards the pub.

I spluttered. "Married! Me? No way!"

He smiled. "But you're so pretty – I can't believe no one's snapped you up yet."

"Mate!" Matt interrupted. "Stop flirting with my sister-in-law."

Luke grinned. "Can't help myself, sorry."

"Luke's the womaniser of the family," Matt explained. "Pay no attention to him."

But I intended to pay attention to him, lots and lots of it. He was just what I needed, more good-looking distraction. After Justin I was hooked.

As we walked into Fitzgerald's my heart suddenly lifted and then sank lead-balloon-like to the floor. In the corner, chatting animatedly, was Steve. Beside him was a dark-haired woman in a flamboyant black and purple dress. I tried to peel my eyes away from them but I couldn't. They were smiling and laughing. When Steve took her hand in his and kissed it, I decided I'd had enough.

"Let's go," I said hurriedly to Matt and Luke who were standing at the bar by now. "I'd forgotten how much I disliked this pub."

"Are you joking?" Luke asked, looking around. "It's great."

"We've already ordered," Matt said levelly.

"Right," I said, moodily. "I'll find somewhere to sit."

"We can go if you like, Amy," Luke said kindly.

"No, it's fine," I said quietly. "Ignore me. I'm being stupid." I sat down at the far end of the pub, making sure I couldn't see Steve and he couldn't see me.

Stupid, stupid, stupid. What did I expect – that Steve still held a torch for me? That we were 'soul-mates'? That he'd notice me over here, run over and declare undying love? I wasn't living in a Mills and Boon romance. I'd be lucky if he even said hello to me . . .

"Hello, Amy."

I raised my head. Steve was smiling down at me uncertainly.

"How are you?" he asked. "I thought I saw you come in."

"Fine," I snapped. You know what they say – attack is the best form of defence.

He stared at me for a few seconds. "Can I sit down?" he asked.

"It's a free country," I said.

"Is there something wrong?" he asked gently. "You seem . . ."

"How would you know how I seem?" I asked.

"If you're going to be like that," he stood up.

"Steve," I began. I took a deep breath, "I'm sorry, sit down, please."

He sighed. "Listen, don't worry about it. I only wanted to . . ."

"Steve," a voice trilled down from above our heads, "Are you ready?"

Steve stood up. "Amy, this is Ella – Ella, Amy."

"Hello," I said stiffly. Ella? My mind went into overdrive. The ex. It was obvious. They were back together. Maybe they'd been together all along. I was such an idiot. My eyes rested on her left hand. She was wearing a bloody huge hulking diamond on her ring-finger. It was impossible to miss it. As Hugh Grant would say : fuck, fuckity, fuck.

"Amy works in the children's bookshop I was telling you about," Steve explained.

I stood up. I couldn't take this any more.

"I'm sorry, I must join my friends," I smiled falsely. "Please excuse me." I walked over to the bar where Matt and Luke were talking to the barman.

"Hi, guys," I smiled, putting my arm around Luke's back and holding him close to me.

Luke smiled. "Here's your drink, Amy." He passed me a pint of lager. I turned my head to see if Steve was watching. He was standing by the door of the toilets, his eyes fixed on me. His fiancée was nowhere to be seen.

I held Luke tighter.

"I like the Irish hospitality," Luke beamed at me. "Very welcoming."

Suddenly I felt a tap on my shoulder. "Amy, can I talk to you for a minute?"

Steve was standing beside us, glaring at me.

"She's all yours," Luke said, unravelling himself from my arms and picking up his pint.

I was caught. I didn't want to appear rude in front of Luke so I nodded. "Let's go outside," I suggested.

"Fine," Steve muttered.

We walked out of the bar and into the sunlight. It was a warm and bright day and I wished I'd brought my sunglasses.

"What's wrong with you?" Steve asked again.

"What do you mean?" I asked innocently.

"That was really rude in there. Ella doesn't know what to think," Steve began.

I sighed. I wasn't in the mood for this. I wanted to get back to my uncomplicated Aussie and my pint.

"Well," Steve continued, "an apology would be nice."

"Sorry," I mumbled. "Can I go?"

Steve stared at me and the edges of his mouth began to curl.

"What?" I muttered. "Are you laughing at me?"

"Might be," Steve grinned. "You're just so impossible. You're like a petulant child."

"I beg your pardon?" I asked.

"You heard me," he said.

I scowled.

"Anyway, I wanted to tell you that I'm moving to Bath in little while, that's all," he said calmly.

This information took a few seconds to sink in.

"Bath?" I asked. "Why Bath?"

"I have friends there," he began. "And it's easier for work, nearer London."

"Fine," I said. "You've told me now." I turned away from him, towards the door. I didn't know how to feel so I blocked everything out and concentrated on Luke and pints. Luke and pints.

"Amy," Steve grabbing my arm and stopping me, "you really are impossible. Do you have nothing to say?"

I'd had enough. "What the hell do you want from me?" I asked loudly. "You're engaged to your ex and about to move back to England!"

Steve began to laugh. "I'm not getting married," he stated. "Ella is though. She came over from London to tell me. But that has nothing to do with me moving back to England. And anyway, I haven't definitely decided to go."

"Why did you say it then?" I asked. And he was calling me mad.

"I was trying to get a reaction, I suppose," he shrugged.

"I don't care where you go or what you do," I said firmly. "So goodbye."

"Amy," Steve said, exasperated, "I also wanted to say I'm sorry about Jack and Jodie."

I narrowed my eyes. "What?"

"I saw the hoarding . . . and I put two and two together."

"You and the rest of the world," I muttered.

"I know it must be hard on you. I found out about Ella the same week."

"Really?" I asked.

"Yes," he sighed. "It was a real blow. I didn't want her back or anything, I just didn't want her to move on before me, I guess. I understand how upset you must have been. I was going to ring, but as the days went by I didn't know what to say."

I softened. He was being so nice. And he really did seem to understand. "I'm sorry for being rude that day . . ." I began.

"Valentine's Day," he grinned.

"Um," I nodded. I decided to be brutally honest for once in my life. I had nothing to lose. "I didn't want you to see me cry. I was in bits. I didn't know how to deal with it."

"Bad timing," he smiled.

"Sorry?" I asked.

"You and me," he said gently. "Bad timing."

"Yes," I smiled.

"Steve," Ella pushed the door open and walked towards us. "There you are. I thought you'd done a Houdini on me."

"Hi again," I said. "Sorry for rushing away earlier."

"That's OK, chuck," she smiled. "No hard feelings. Steve, I have to find a phone and ring Earl and then I'll be back out to you, love."

"You can use my mobile," I offered.

"That's all right," she smiled, "I have loads of change I have to use up. Thanks anyway." She went inside again.

"Earl?" I asked. "Who's he when he's at home?"

Steve grinned. "Earl's her fiancé. He's a musician."

I smiled. "Where were we?"

"You were apologising," he said.

"I'd finished that," I said, raising my eyebrows. "So what next?"

"Who was the tanned guy in the bar," Steve began, "the one you had your arm around?"

"That's Luke," I said, "Matt's brother. From Australia."

"Over for your sister's wedding?" Steve asked. He had a good memory, I thought.

"Yes," I said. "He's the best man. The wedding's the day after tomorrow."

"Pity," Steve said.

"Why?" I asked.

"I was going to ask you out."

"Again?" I asked in amazement. "Are you serious?"

"Yes," he smiled. "Third time lucky. I haven't stopped thinking about you."

I began to blush. "I thought you were moving back to England," I said.

"Not yet," he said. "How about later in the week?"

"For moving back or a date?" I quipped.

"A date," he said.

"I'm sorry, but I have Beth's wedding then," I said.

"That'll be fun," he smiled. "Busy week for you then. I'll give you a ring."

"Tell you what," I smiled. "I'll ring you." I leant over and gave him a kiss on the cheek. He put his arms around me and held me gently. "I'd better go," I mumbled, relishing the hug. "Bye."

"Bye, Amy," he smiled, releasing his arms.

I joined Matt and Luke at the bar.

"What kept you?" Luke asked. "Who was that man? We were about to send out a search party."

"He's a friend," I said softly, "from work." I picked up my pint. "Now where were we?"

I regretted the pints the following morning while sprawled on the floor of my bedroom writing each guest's name onto a leaf. Suzi had killed me for bringing Matt and Luke back half-cut, but when I'd told her about Steve she'd mellowed a bit.

My gold pens were acting up, clogging and blotting something terrible and some of the leaves had crumpled overnight, forcing me to spray some more replacements.

My mobile rang and I swore as I noticed that I'd misspelled Siobhan's name. Another leaf bit the dust.

"Amy, it's Beth."

"Hi, love, how are things?"

"Fine, I was just checking things for Tuesday – you know – the wedding practice."

"Stella and I are driving down in her Mum's car and we'll get there around lunchtime," I said.

"What time are you leaving?" Beth asked.

"As close to six a.m. as we can," I grimaced. The things I did for my friends.

"I'll arrange the practice for three," Beth said, relieved. "That should give us plenty of time."

"Perfect," I smiled. "And Beth?" I was going to tell her about Steve. And ask her about Jack and Jodie.

"Yes?"

"Nothing," I said, deciding I didn't have the energy to talk about either. "I'll see you tomorrow."

I clicked the phone off and sat back on my heels. That morning Mum had told me she'd heard on the grapevine that Jack and Jodie's wedding had been postponed indefinitely. I wanted to ask Beth about it so much that it hurt.

My mobile rang again.

"Amy, it's Beth again."

"Everything OK?" I asked.

"You were going to ask me about Jack and Jodie, weren't you?" she asked.

"How did you . . . ?" I began.

"Because," she said, "I know you. Basically it was a mutual decision. Jodie rang me yesterday but she wouldn't talk about it. She sounded upset."

"Really?" I whispered. This wasn't quite what I expected.

"They're coming, by the way," Beth added.

"To what?" I asked in confusion. This was turning into a strange morning indeed.

"To the wedding," Beth continued.

"Your wedding?" I asked. I was in total shock now.

"Yes," Beth said, a little confused. "My wedding. You know I invited them. I think they could do with a weekend away together, to be honest."

"But I thought . . ." I couldn't finish my sentence. I was upset, angry and tired all rolled into one.

"I know," she said. "They changed their minds. I don't know what to say."

"Tell them not to come," I said, my voice dangerously loud. "I'm the bridesmaid. Tell them to fuck off!"

Beth sighed. "If you really want me to, I will. But you know how long Tony's known Jack."

"You'd tell them to fuck off?" I asked in astonishment.

"Not exactly," Beth replied. I could hear her stifle a laugh. "I'd use different words. Why don't you think about it and ring me back?"

"OK," I mumbled.

I put down the phone and sat staring into space. Jack and Jodie had postponed their wedding. What did this mean? With Suzi's wedding on the near horizon I didn't have time to think about it. Which was probably just as well, all things considered.

Chapter 35

Denise and Frank O'Sullivan
would like

Amy O'Sullivan

to join them in celebrating the marriage of their daughter

Susan
with
Matthew Street

at St Martin's Church, Greendale Road, Blackrock
on Saturday 3rd May at 3.30pm
and afterwards at
48 Greendale Road, Blackrock

RSVP 48 Greendale Road, Blackrock, Co Dublin

"Can you pass me the hairclips, Amy?" Jenny, the hairdresser, asked, "one by one."

"Sure," I smiled. I watched as she took small handfuls of hair in her fingers and twisted them expertly, securing each section with a hairclip. When she had finished the front of my head she tucked pink and white feathers into the twists.

"Suzi," she called over to my sister, who was waiting patiently at the basin, flicking through magazines nervously, "what do you think?"

Suzi jumped up, putting down the tatty old copy of *Hello* on the black leather seat and stood behind me looking in the mirror.

"Perfect," she beamed.

"I'm going to put the back up too," Jenny said, "or would you prefer it down?"

"No, up is good," Suzi said thoughtfully. "But maybe pull down a few tendrils to soften the effect around her face."

I felt like a prize heifer on show.

"Good idea," Jenny smiled. "I'll be finished in five minutes. Martine," she said to the junior who was picking the skin around her nails at the till, "could you wash Suzi's hair, please?"

When my hair was finished I had to admit it looked pretty spectacular. One hair-do down, one to go.

I waited while Jenny dried Suzi's hair and began to twist it on top of her head, in a similar style to mine. Finally on top of the bride's blonde locks Jenny placed the delicate pink and silver tiara.

I caught my breath as I looked at the final effect – Suzi looked amazing and she didn't even have a scrap of make-up on yet. Jenny's sister, Ciara, was doing that next in the beauty salon upstairs.

When we walked in the front door two hours later Dad whistled.

"You both look amazing," he smiled. "Now go upstairs quickly before Matt sees you." Matt and Luke had stayed at our house last night. Their parents were staying at Blackrock Castle Hotel.

"I'm so nervous," Suzi said, sitting down on her bed. "I hope everything goes OK."

"Of course it will," I reassured her. "It will all be perfect. Now let's get you dressed."

Suzi peeled off her tracksuit and revealed her wedding underwear.

"What do you think?" she asked, surveying herself in the full-length mirror which had been borrowed from Mum and Dad's room for the day. The white balconet bra and briefs were deliciously lacy and frivolous. Suzi picked up a matching suspender-belt from the dresser and began to roll pale white stockings over her slim legs.

"I can never do these clippy things," she complained, catching her fingers in the small metal hoops.

"Let me do it," I smiled. I clicked the clips into place over the stockings. "There you go."

I then helped her as she stepped into her wedding dress. I fastened her up and straightened the seam. Tears came to my eyes as I looked at the final effect.

"You look beautiful, Suzi," I said. "Just beautiful."

Mum knocked on the door. "The flowers are here, love. Can I come in?"

"Sure," Suzi said.

As Mum walked into the room she gasped. She put the bouquets on the bed and put her hands to her mouth. "My little girl," she smiled. "You look like a princess. Frank," she called, "come here."

Dad walked in the door and stared at Suzi. "I don't believe it," he said in his best Victor Meldrew voice. He kissed Suzi on the forehead. "I can see the dress was worth every penny, Suzi. It's lovely."

"Thanks," Suzi beamed. I felt a little left out. I took my dress off the back of the door and unzipped it from its plastic cover.

Hearing a car pull up outside, Mum and Dad went back downstairs to dispatch Matt and Luke to the church.

I stepped into my dress and Suzi did me up.

I looked in the mirror and was pleasantly surprised. I looked all right. My hair really suited the dress and Ciara had done a bloody good job with the old slap. Amazing what make-up can do these days. We both slipped on our shoes.

"Give us a hand with the ribbons, will you?" Suzi asked. She was finding it hard to bend down in her dress. I wound the white ribbons of her ballet-type slippers around her ankles and tied them carefully in two small bows.

Suzi picked up the bouquets from the bed and handed me the two smaller ones. One for me and one for Katie, Julie's daughter, who we were meeting at the church. The bouquets were made up of white and pink flowers including roses and lilies.

Suzi kissed me on the cheek. "Thanks for being my bridesmaid, Amy," she said.

"It's a pleasure," I smiled back. "I'll just see if it's safe to go downstairs now." I poked my head out the door. "Mum," I shouted, "are the guys here?"

"No," she shouted back, "they've just gone. They're meeting Eamon and Andrew at the church." Eamon and Andrew were the two ushers, friends of Matt's from rugby.

"Are you ready?" I asked.

Suzi took a deep breath. "I think so," she smiled nervously.

Mum, Dad, Suzi and me arrived at the church in a cream vintage car. Suzi had insisted on being driven around the block a few times – just to get the whole wedding experience, car and all. Pulling up outside St Martin's, Suzi grabbed my hand and squeezed it tightly. She looked anxious.

"You're fine," I whispered. "Matt is waiting for you."

"Yes, you're right," she smiled.

We waited outside the church for a few minutes, arranging Suzi's dress and veil and composing ourselves. It was a bright day and the sun was threatening to shine through the clouds very soon. Julie rushed towards us dragging Simon and Katie by the hands. Simon was wearing a black morning suit with a cream silk waistcoat, which looked sweet on his small, slim frame. Katie's dress was white with tiny pink roses embroidered on the bodice and on the hem and the edges of the sleeves.

"Sorry we're late," Julie gushed. She tried to flatten Simon's cowlick with her hand. Brian Lowan followed behind her, walking at a slower pace. He took his wife's hand.

"Leave the kids with Suzi and Amy," he smiled, "and come inside." He leant over and kissed Suzi on the cheek. "You look lovely," he smiled. "Good luck."

"Thanks," Suzi said. "Now take your places, Katie and Simon," she said kindly. "Katie, you hold Amy's hand until we get in, OK?"

Dad popped his head inside the church. "That's us," he said. "Eamon gave me the nod."

He took Suzi's arm and I stood behind her holding Simon's and Katie's hands. We began to walk inside. Simon dropped behind us and Katie walked beside me, looking at her feet carefully, determined to get it right.

"Head up," I whispered to her. She smiled at me a little anxiously. "I won't let you trip," I assured her. "I promise."

I was incredibly nervous as we made our way up the aisle. I could see Matt's back, resplendent in a dark cream silk morning suit. It looked amazing against his sallow skin. Luke, Eamon and Andrew were wearing black morning suits with cream waistcoats, like Simon's. I kept my head up and tried to look straight ahead. It was hard not to glance at the guests though.

"Amy," I heard Beth's voice whisper. I turned my head and saw her beaming at me from one of the pews near the front. I smiled. There were tears in her eyes – she was such an old softie. Tony wasn't coming until later, so she was sitting with Judy and Eva.

The service flew by. One minute we were 'gathered here today' and the next minute Suzi and Matt were 'I do-ing'. As we retired to sign the register in a small room to the side of the altar, Suzi let out a huge sigh.

"What a relief," she smiled. She and Matt sat down at the desk and signed the huge black leather-bound register. Followed by myself and Luke as witnesses. As I leant over him in the cramped room to sign the book, Luke placed his hand on the small of my back. My skin tingled deliciously. Temptation.

"Now it's legal," Father Lucas smiled. We all cheered.

Suzi and Matt beamed. Matt grabbed Suzi and kissed her passionately. Father Lucas cleared his throat.

"Everyone looking this way," the photographer commanded. "Say sausages."

"Sausages," we chorused.

Mum and Dad and Matt's parents squeezed into the room, obstructing the photographer. "Careful," he complained, as Mum knocked his arm with her elbow.

"Sorry," she beamed.

He softened and smiled. "One more. Flower girl and pageboy – look this way please. Best man, eyes front, please. Stop checking out the bridesmaid!"

We all laughed. Warm waves of anticipation slithered up and down my spine. Then I thought of Steve and how kind he had been. Maybe I'd . . .

"Amy," Suzi said, "you need to move so we can get out."

"Sorry," I mumbled, moving towards the door and taking Katie's hand. As we came out the heavy wooden door the guests all began to clap and cheer. Suzi and Matt led the way down the aisle, smiling broadly. It seemed to take forever to walk back down the aisle. I had to pay attention or I'd end up on top of Suzi. Luke walked beside me. Eamon and Andrew brought up the rear with Katie and Simon.

The sun had broken through the clouds outside and was beaming down. Mum handed Simon and Katie plastic bottles of bubbles in the shape of white churches as soon as we got outside, and they began to fill the air with tiny transparent spheres which drifted in the gentle breeze.

Beth joined me outside. "That was a beautiful service," she smiled. "You look lovely. And that Luke's a bit of a hunk."

"No kidding," I grinned. "But wait till you hear about Fitzie's. I completely forgot to tell you. You'll never guess who I bumped into. Go on, guess."

"Um, oh, I don't know, tell me," she squealed impatiently.

"Steve," I grinned again.

"No!" she exclaimed. "What happened?"

"Well," I began, "first of all I thought he was engaged – he was with his ex . . ."

"The English girl?" Beth interrupted.

"Yes, Ella," I continued. "Then he said he was moving back to England, and then he said he thought about me all the time and we kind of made up."

"Really?" Beth asked. "That's great. But I thought you were rude to him . . ."

"Amy!" Matt shouted over at me. He was standing under a tree with Luke and staring over at me expectantly.

"I'll fill you in on the details later," I promised, touching her arm gently. "Right now I have a date with a photographer."

We left the church after the photographs. Luke and I shared a taxi with his parents. I was dying for a drink, but stopping at a pub was out of the question. This bridesmaid lark wasn't the best for one's enjoyment quota.

I perked up when Luke reminded me that we could lay into the champagne early. He was dead right. I just hoped he could open bottles – I hated the bang they made and always refused to do it.

The balloon man had visited the house while we were at the church and the outside of the house was covered in clumps of huge white balloons.

"Looks like Disneyland," Luke quipped as we made our way under a balloon arch and into the house.

"I'll be back in one second," I promised as I nipped upstairs. I checked my appearance in Suzi's room. My hair was still in place, my make-up hadn't run and I had nothing stuck in between my teeth – perfect.

"Here you go," Luke handed me a still fizzing glass

of champagne as I joined him in the garden. The string quartet had begun to play and the guests were beginning to arrive. Suzi and Matt had decided to make the most of the vintage car and had gone on a short drive around the neighbourhood.

Siobhan and Deirdre bounded over to me. "Hi, Amy," Siobhan smiled. "How are you? You look great!"

"Thanks," I smiled. "This is Luke, Matt's brother."

"Hi, Luke," the girls smiled, giving him appreciative looks.

"Have you both recovered from the other weekend yet?" I asked.

"Just about," Deirdre said. "It was great though. And how's that young man – Joseph, was it?"

"Justin," I corrected her.

"Have you seen him since?" Siobhan asked. Luke was listening with interest.

"No," I said, anxious to change the subject. I didn't want Luke to think I was that sort of girl. Not that I was and, to be honest, in the circumstances I was sure 'that sort of girl' was probably exactly what he was looking for. "Here come Suzi and Matt," I said, grateful for the distraction. We all watched them step into the garden, Matt with his arm protectively around his new wife's waist.

"Don't they look sweet together?" Deirdre asked.

I was whisked away from the girls for another round of posed photographs, 'The O'Sullivan Family', 'The Wedding Party', 'The Bride and Bridesmaid', 'The

Bride, Bridesmaid and Flower Girl' . . . I hoped my smile wasn't too lopsided.

The photographs seemed to go on forever and ever. "Smile," "Say cheese," "Sausages." Finally we were allowed to escape. Matt and Suzi weren't so lucky – the photographer took them further into the garden for some romantic shots.

"See you all tomorrow," Suzi laughed as they walked away.

"Amy," I heard my name shouted across the crowd.

Chapter 36

It was Polly, standing with Amber in the shade of the large cherry tree. I made my way over, squeezing through the guests carefully. As I drew closer I noticed a familiar face beside Amber.

"Hi, girls," I smiled, "hi, Tim. I didn't know you were coming."

Amber blushed slightly under her golden St Tropez fake tan. "I rang Suzi. She said it was all right."

"Oh, sorry," I apologised, realising that I'd made her feel awkward, "I didn't mean it that way – it's a nice surprise, that's all."

"Justin was asking for you," Tim grinned. "He's quite taken with you, poor lad. Amber told him what age you really are . . ."

Amber dug him in the ribs. "Hey," he complained. "What was that for? Anyway, Justin didn't seem to mind.

In fact he thinks it's way cool. Real Mrs Robinson stuff."

"And who is Mrs Robinson?" I heard Luke's voice ask from behind me.

"Amy's been seducing toyboys," Polly laughed.

"This is Luke, Matt's brother," I introduced the grinning man.

"Nice to meet you," he beamed, his gaze lingering on Polly's cleavage. I felt a dagger of jealousy shoot through my bones.

"This is Amber and Polly, they're my cousins, and this is Tim . . ."

"My Irish boyfriend," Amber piped in.

"Amy," Mum's voice rang out across the guests' heads from the back door of the house.

"Coming, Mum," I shouted back. "Have to go, guys," I said reluctantly. "A bridesmaid's work is never done. See you all later."

"And where are you staying?" I heard Polly ask Luke as I walked towards the house.

"Take these," Mum said, a tone of urgency in her voice. She handed me the box of leaves. "The waitresses said they'll help you put them out."

"But I thought the caterers were doing that . . ." I began.

Mum put her hands up in exasperation. "Don't ask. They said they couldn't find them. Please, Amy?"

"Sure, Mum," I smiled. Poor Mum – she looked rather frazzled. "I'll do it right now, OK?"

"Thanks, love," she said gratefully. "Now I have to

ring the electrician. The electricity in the tent is on the blink."

I walked around the edge of the garden, waving to friends and relations and trying not to get caught up in any conversations.

"Is there anything we can do?" Judy asked as I passed herself and Eva. "You look very busy."

"That would be great," I smiled. "Follow me."

In less then twenty minutes we had managed to put out most of the place names successfully. I'd managed to tweak Suzi and Mum's seating plan a little so that Polly was sitting in between Andrew and Eamon (both single and real charmers) – just in case she'd taken a shine to Luke.

I sat down at the top table and rested my head on my arms. Judy handed me a large glass of champagne which she'd procured from the bar.

"Thanks," I smiled gratefully.

"It's hot out there," Eva said, "noisy too. Not that I'm complaining of course. It's nice and peaceful in here."

The caterers buzzed around us, putting out the starters.

"It looks like the breakfast will be soon," Judy said.

"Breakfast?" I asked confused. "Surely this would be lunch or dinner or something."

"The wedding food is traditionally called breakfast," Eva explained.

"Eating breakfast in morning suits," I laughed. "Makes sense. Here comes the crowd." We watched the guests piling into the marquee, making a beeline for their seats and plonking themselves down. My seating plan was outside the tent and seemed to be doing the trick. I moved to my correct seat, beside Luke, and waited in anticipation.

Luke walked into the tent with the ushers and beamed as he saw me.

"Hi, Amy," he said, "I was looking for you."

"I've been in here for a little while," I explained. "Come and sit down." I patted his seat with my hand.

"Beside you?" he asked. I smiled. "Excellent, this gets better and better."

"I hope you have your speech ready," I said, raising my eyebrows.

"Absolutely," he grinned, patting his breast pocket. "Safe and sound."

"I look forward to it," I said.

"I'll just announce Matt and Suzi," he said, standing up and removing the microphone from its stand in front of him. He switched it on and tapped it lightly with his forefinger. "Ladies and gentlemen, please welcome the bride and groom . . ."

The guests stood up and clapped as the happy couple entered the tent and sat down.

Luke continued. "And now I'd like to ask Father Lucas to say grace. Father?"

Luke handed the priest the microphone.

Halfway through the main course of salmon, new potatoes and salad, Luke asked me about Justin.

"So you like younger men?" he said, his eyes lighting up.

The champagne was beginning to take effect so I was watching what I said. "That depends," I replied, hedging my bets, "on the young man in question."

"I see," Luke beamed. He speared a sliver of salmon on his fork and brought it up to my lips.

"Luke," I chastised. "Behave!"

"Oh, behave," he said in his best Austin Powers voice. He put his hand on my thigh under the table and I jumped.

"Stop," I said. "I'm serious."

"I will," he promised with a twinkle in his eye, "for now."

I looked up and saw Beth watching me with interest. She had a bemused expression on her face. I shrugged my shoulders and continued eating.

Suzi and Matt cut their French-style profiterole cake and the waitresses handed the gooey chocolate and cream-filled pastries to each guest. I tucked into the deliciously sweet concoction with relish. Luckily between eating and reading over his speech Luke was too busy to accost my legs again.

As the coffee was being poured, Luke stood up.

"Here goes," he whispered at me, smiling. "I'd like to introduce my new sister-in-law, Suzi Street." Everyone clapped.

Suzi stood up, smiling nervously. "When Matt asked me to marry him I had one major decision to make," she began. "And that was whether to take his name or not. After all, Suzi Street does sound a little funny – like Easy Street or something. But I got over it and I hope you all will too." Everyone laughed gently. She was right – Suzi Street did sound a bit twee. I thought of Beth and Tony – Beth was keeping her own name so there wouldn't be any problems there. And Jack and Jodie, maybe that would never happen . . . I concentrated on what my sister was saying. "I'd like to thank you all for coming today. It means a lot to both Matt and me to see so many of our friends and relations here. Special thanks to Matt's parents Molly and Dan, and to the rest of the Aussies for making the long trip."

"Hear, hear," yelled my Dad who was certainly getting into the spirit, spirit being the operative word. He was on large brandies at this stage – ostensibly to calm his stage nerves.

"I'd like to thank my parents – Denise and Frank," Suzi continued, "for making this day so special and for letting us use the garden. Mum and Dad have been wonderful parents and have always supported me in everything I do. I love them very much." Suzi sniffed and wiped a tear away from her left eye with the back of her hand. "Sorry," she smiled. Mum was crying too and I was just about holding back the tears – what a family! "Amy, thank you for being my bridesmaid and for being a great sister. And thanks Katie and Simon, my wonderful flower girl and pageboy. And finally to Matt." Suzi turned towards Matt who was gazing up at her in open admiration. "Matt, you've made me so happy today – thank you. I look forward to all the years we'll spend together." She sat down and kissed him firmly on the lips. We all clapped and cheered.

Luke jumped to his feet again. "Father of the Bride – Mr Frank O'Sullivan."

Dad cleared his throat and stood up. "I'm not a man for public speaking," he began, "so you'll have to be kind to me. I count myself lucky to have three beautiful and talented women in my life, my wife, Denise, and my two daughters, Amy and Suzi. When Suzi came back from Perth with Matt and broke the news of the engagement to us we were shocked but overjoyed. She seemed so happy and we knew that Matt was the right man for her. Matt is everything a man could want in a son-in-law – he's strong and fit, perfect for all those jobs around the house and garden I don't want to do." Everyone laughed. "He plays and follows rugby, so we'll never run out of conversation. And finally, he loves my daughter more than anything in the world and that's good enough for me."

"Aah," I sighed.

Luke smiled at me. "Bit of a softie is your dad."

"I know," I agreed.

"Suzi has brought Denise and me years of joy," Dad went on. "I'm delighted to welcome Matt and the Streets into our family." He raised his glass. "To Matt and Suzi Street. May they always live on easy street."

I stood up along with the rest of the marquee and raised my glass. "To Matt and Suzi." Luke clinked his glass against mine. "To the O'Sullivan girls," he whispered.

Luke stayed standing. "I'd now like to introduce the groom."

Matt stood up and took the microphone from his brother. He looked very nervous. Tiny beads of perspiration had formed on his temples.

"I've never done this before," he began, his voice faltering, "spoken in public, I mean. So you'll have to bear with me. Laugh at my jokes and stuff." Everyone laughed gently. Matt turned to face Suzi. "When I first met Suzi in The Irish Bar in Perth I couldn't talk. She was so pretty it took my breath away. So she did most of the talking that evening. I can't believe I'm here today, married!" Matt looked around at the guests, beaming. Everyone clapped and cheered. "I don't know what to say. I suppose I should thank my Mum and Dad and my rellies for being here. And Luke for being my best man. And everyone involved in making today cool – Father Lucas, the caterers, Mad Flowers, Denise and Frank. And anyone else I've forgotten. Oh, and thanks for all the great presents. And thanks to anyone who planted a Child of Prague in their garden. For the Aussies here, that's a little religious statue that's supposed to keep the rain away. As you can see it worked!" Everyone laughed.

"I don't think you plant them, Matt," Dad shouted. "They're not flowers."

Matt grinned sheepishly. "That's about it, then." Matt gazed at Suzi again. "I love you, Suzi. And I'll make you the happiest woman in the world, I promise. I'll look after you and love you till I die. You're my world." He leant over, kissed her forehead and sat down.

There wasn't a dry eye in the house at this stage. Who would have thought that Matt was such a sentimental old rugby player?

Luke jumped to his feet. "My brother, the big romantic," he began, smiling. "Who would have thought? Married at his young age. In his prime you might say. What would Rosie O'Grady say?" Luke looked around the room, grinning. "Who was Rosie, I hear you ask?" The crowd hooted and cheered. "OK, OK, I'll tell you. Rosie was Matt's first girlfriend. And it was very serious. In fact, I believe he asked her to marry him? Isn't that right, mate?"

Matt smiled. "Yes, but we were only six!" he insisted. The guests clapped and laughed.

"Next there was Hannah," Luke continued.

Matt groaned.

"Matt was obsessed with Hannah. He followed her around everywhere. He bought her treats. Talked about her incessantly. But there was an age issue. She was ten years older than him."

I stared at Matt. Who was this? Matt was smiling. "She was my baby-sitter. And he's right, I was mad about her when I was seven."

"But I'll stop there," Luke said. "Because although there were a few more girlfriends they all pale into insignificance beside Suzi."

Luke tapped his watch. "Table Ten, how am I on time?" He smiled over at one of the tables which was full of Clontarf rugby players and their partners. "Am I over or under? They're timing my speech," he explained.

"You're under," Andrew yelled. "Keep going."

"Right," Luke said. "What can I say about Suzi?" Suzi covered her face with her hands and squealed. "The first time I met her was at a barbie at Matt's house. She'd had a few tinnies too many and she was lying on her back in the garden looking up at the stars."

"You can stop there, Luke," Suzi shrieked. "No one wants to hear this."

"Yes, we do," I shouted. This sounded interesting.

Luke grinned wickedly. "Suzi looked up at me, bleary-eyed, and said 'You're cute. If things don't work out with my boyfriend I'll have you. What's your name?' So I sat down beside her and said 'Luke, Luke Street'." Everyone laughed. "She looked at me and said 'That's funny, my Matt's name is Street too. Is that a common name in Australia?' And then Matt came over and introduced me as his brother. Suzi was mortified."

"I can't believe you told them that," Suzi giggled. Luckily she had a good sense of humour.

"So, if things hadn't worked out," Luke continued, "this could have been me and Suzi's wedding!"

Everyone clapped.

"But I don't think I'd be able for her," Luke admitted. "Irish girls are a real handful." I thumped him on the leg. "Thanks, Amy," he smiled down at me.

"There's no need for violence, love. But seriously, I think Matt is the luckiest man in the world. Suzi is wonderful and they are obviously madly in love. And I wish them years and years of happiness together." He raised his glass. "To the bride and groom," he toasted.

"The bride and groom," the guests joined in.

"Now how am I on time?" Luke asked. "I'm officially finished."

"Turbo O'Hara won," Andrew shouted. "Four minutes, thirty seconds." A large man sitting to Andrew's right jumped up and cheered. Turbo, I assumed.

"Enjoy the evening, everyone," Luke said, sitting down and clicking off the microphone. A hum of conversation and laughter took over the room.

"I'm glad that's over," Luke smiled, putting his hand on mine. "I can concentrate on other things."

"Luke," Polly trilled, making her way past the tables, her eyes firmly fixed on the Australian prize, "you were wonderful. Well done." She leant over and kissed him on the cheek.

I gave my cousin a dirty look but it was wasted on her.

"A touch of indigestion, Amy?" she asked sweetly.

"No," I muttered. I gave up and decided to leave her to it. "I'm just going to find Beth." I stood up and felt a little dizzy. The champagne and wine must have gone to my head.

"Are you OK?" Luke asked with concern. "Maybe I should come with you."

"I'm fine," I assured him. "Thanks anyway."

I decided to get some air.

"Amy," Matt called as I walked past him. Suzi was nowhere to be seen. "Join me."

"Where's Mrs Street?" I grinned, making my way around the table, excusing myself past Father Lucas and sitting down beside Matt.

"Simon and Katie dragged her outside," he smiled. "They wanted to talk to her apparently. I think they're a bit worried that she won't be going back to looking after them, now she's married."

"She is though, isn't she?" I asked suspiciously. I hoped Matt wasn't so neanderthal as to suggest his wife couldn't work.

"Of course," he beamed. "She loves it and the Lowans are really good to her."

"That's all right, then," I said, relieved. "I liked your speech, well done."

"Thanks," he said, gratefully. "You don't think it was a bit short?"

"No," I said honestly. "You said everything you needed to say. Luke was good too. Must run in the family."

"Um," Matt murmured. An anxious look darted across his face.

"What?" I asked.

"Nothing," he said, trying to cover up.

"There's something on your mind," I prompted.

"It's Luke," he said quietly.

Chapter 37

"What about Luke?" I asked with interest.

"I just thought you should know," Matt said, "he has a girlfriend at home – Finn. They've been together nearly three years now."

"A girlfriend?" I asked in amazement. This was the guy whose hand had been on my leg a little while ago and who had been flirting with me shamelessly for the last two days?

"Yes," Matt said. "I'm not sure what kind of relationship they have, to be honest," he said gently. "I just don't want to see you get hurt. I know he's my brother and everything but you're my sister now. Kind of."

"Thanks," I whispered. Typical, bloody typical. Justin probably had a girlfriend too – a slip of a thing – all of eighteen or nineteen. Not that I cared, of course. What the hell was I doing?

"Amy?" Matt asked. "Are you OK?"

"Sure," I said. "Just a little disillusioned with men. Don't worry about it."

But Matt, bless him, did look a little worried. "We're not all like Luke," he said earnestly. "Some of us meet the right woman, fall in love and devote our lives to her. Look at me."

I could have hugged him. All along I thought he was, well, a bit dim to tell the truth. But he wasn't. He was a kind, decent, loving guy. And bloody good-looking, of course. The type of guy I'd like to love me and to take care of me. Sure, I'd take care of him too, but you know what I mean. I wanted hugs when I'd stubbed my toe getting out of the bath, understanding when I was pre-menstrual and crying at *Eastenders* . . .

"Amy," Matt smiled, interrupting my musings, "Suzi told me about that writer guy. He's nice, isn't he?"

I looked at him carefully. "What did Suzi tell you exactly?" I hadn't realised my private life was not so private after all.

"Everything," he said sheepishly. He paused for a few seconds when I hadn't said anything. "I'm sorry," he said, looking at me carefully. "Maybe I shouldn't have mentioned it. He just sounded like a good bloke, that's all."

"It's fine," I replied. "Don't worry about it." I thought for a second. "You know, you're right. He's nice. Bloody nice. Excuse me." I jumped up and walked quickly towards the house.

I walked in the kitchen door, past the caterers and ran up the stairs as fast as my dress would allow me. I picked up my mobile from my dressingtable and searched for the saved number.

"Hi, Steve," I said, "it's Amy."

"So what made you ring?" Steve and I were sitting in the garden, behind the marquee on a wooden bench. The band inside the tent were giving it wellies – their own rendition of favourite Abba songs as requested by Suzi, and Doors and Rolling Stones songs as requested by Matt. It made an interesting mix. 'Light My Fire' followed by 'Momma Mia'.

Steve's arm was draped around my back and we were sharing a bottle of champagne.

"It was my new brother-in-law, I guess," I smiled. "Suzi had told him the whole story and he said you sounded nice."

"Nice?" Steve asked with disgust. "I'm not sure I like that."

"There's nothing wrong with nice," I insisted. "It's a hell of a lot better than nasty, dishonest or violent. And anyway, I'm not so sure you are all that nice."

"Hey you," Steve pinched my arm playfully and then studied my face. "You've been badly burnt along the line, haven't you?" he asked gently.

I nodded.

"But we're not all like that," he continued.

"That's what Matt said," I interjected.

"He's right," Steve stroked my hand. "Let's just be very, very nice to each other and see what happens." He kissed me on each eyelid, his warm lips sending a shiver down my spine.

"Suits me," I whispered as his lips found mine. His tongue gently but firmly explored my mouth, teasing my senses and warming my whole body. His fingers caressed the nape of my bare neck, feather-like and sensuous.

"Amy," he whispered into my ear, his soft breath tingling my earlobe, "in case I've forgotten to say it – you look beautiful."

We kissed for what seemed forever before we parted and he held me close to him, his fingers running up and down my arms in light, hair-raising movements.

"I'd better go inside," I sighed. "Suzi will be wondering where I am. I'm sure I was supposed to dance with the best man at some stage."

"Your sister will understand," Steve assured me, "and Matt sounds like a decent chap. I'd like to meet him."

"I'll introduce him," I smiled. The strains of 'Knowing Me, Knowing You' came thundering through the tent.

"I love this," I squealed. "Let's dance."

"An Abba freak!" Steve grinned. "What have I let myself in for ?"

As we walked inside I caught my breath. Polly and Luke were sitting just inside the door, Polly balancing precariously on his knee. One of his hands was halfway up her Gucci skirt and they were eating the face off each other energetically.

"Charming!" Steve laughed.

"That's the best man," I grinned, glad that I felt nothing. After all, up to a few hours ago I had been harbouring feelings for him – of lust perhaps, but they were still feelings.

"You're kidding?" Steve raised his eyebrows.

"No," I smiled, "that's Luke and the girl is Polly, my English cousin."

"Those English people," Steve joked, "no sense of decorum."

I pulled him towards the dance floor. The chairs and tables had been moved towards the back of the tent and the 'walls', leaving plenty of room for dancing.

"Amy!" I heard my sister's voice yelling from beside the band. We made our way towards her. "Where were you? I was looking for you. Polly had to dance the first dance with Luke instead of you."

"Sorry," I said contrite. I leant over and whispered in her ear – loudly as the music was deafening. "I was outside with Steve."

Suzi beamed. "In that case, I forgive you. But don't let it happen again." She grabbed my hand in hers and started to dance.

"Come on," she shouted to Steve. "Shake a leg." Steve took her in his arms and spun her around, flipping her into the air like she was as light as a feather and swinging her from side to side.

"This one can dance," Suzi exclaimed when he finally put her down.

Matt came lumbering over, looking a little worse for wear.

"Hi, mate," Steve shook his hand, "you must be Matt. I'm Steve."

"Nice to meet you, Steve," Matt grinned, putting his arm around Suzi's waist.

The band began to play 'Dancing Queen' and we all threw ourselves around the dance floor. Mum and Dad, Beth and Tony, Eva and Judy, Eamon and Andrew, and Julie and Brian joined us, as well as some of the Street family. Luke and Polly had disappeared.

"I was going to ask you where you've been," Beth shouted at me while we were dancing together, "before I spotted Steve, that is."

I grinned guiltily.

"Good on you, Amy," she laughed. "You only live once."

Steve swept me away and held me in his arms.

It was a night to remember.

At two o'clock Dad reluctantly asked the band to stop playing. He didn't want to upset the neighbours, although he and Mum had invited them all to the afters to smooth over the waters. If they hadn't, our deadline would have been more like twelve o'clock.

"What are you doing now?" Steve asked as we made our way to a table at the side of the tent and sat down.

"I'm going to bed, I'm afraid," I said. "It's been a hell of a long day and I'm knackered."

"I'm sure you are," he said, taking my hand in his. "Can I see you tomorrow? I know you'll be busy clearing up but . . ."

"I'd love to," I interrupted. "Why don't I ring you at lunchtime? It would be nice to get away from the demolition site." I gestured towards the garden. The tent was staying till Monday but I'd promised to help tidy up tomorrow. Black-plastic-bag-land – here I come.

Steve stood up. "I think I'll get going."

I was disappointed. I was hoping he'd stay for a little while. But maybe it was just as well. I really was knackered. Suzi and Matt had already left for Blackrock Castle where they were spending the night before flying to Paris for a week the next day. I hadn't really seen Beth all night, let alone Siobhan, Deirdre and the rest of the girls from the hen. But it didn't really bother me. I'd had an amazing night. The best for a long, long time.

The following morning I felt remarkably fine, considering. I woke up with a smile on my face and I found it hard to stifle it. I was full of happy beans.

I could hear noise from outside and I padded towards the window and opened the curtains. Mum, Dad and Matt's parents were sitting outside, drinking coffee and laughing amiably. Luke wasn't with them, thank goodness. The sun was shining down gently and reflected off the white tent, making my eyes squint in the intense light.

I had a quick shower, threw on a T-shirt and shorts and joined them, making sure to bring my sunglasses.

"Morning, Amy," Dad smiled as I walked through the kitchen door, past the leftovers which adorned every available surface. "Would you like a glass of Buck's Fizz?"

My stomach lurched. "No, thanks, Dad. I'll have the orange though, on its own."

He poured me a glass and passed it to me.

"How are you this morning?" Molly Street asked.

"Fine, thanks, Mrs Street," I said.

"Please call me Molly," she laughed. "We're family now, after all."

"And I'm Dan," Mr Street smiled.

"So tell us," Molly continued, "who was that nice young man with you last night?"

"Yes, do tell us," Mum smiled wickedly.

I could feel myself blush. "He's a friend from work," I said quickly. "Um, who caught the bouquet by the way? I missed that bit."

"Stop trying to change the subject," my Mum said cruelly. "What's his name?"

"Steve," I muttered.

"Not that Stevie J guy?" Mum gasped.

"Yes, Mum," I said. "Now, drop it."

"That name sounds familiar," Molly mused. "Was he in the papers recently?"

"That's right!" Dan exclaimed. "You're right. He was. He's some sort of children's writer who's made a fortune on witch books."

"Wizard books," I corrected. "Now I really must be going." I jumped up. There was no way I was going to be put through the grinder today.

"But you haven't finished your juice," Dad said. "And I want to hear all about this Steve."

"See you all later," I said. I rushed up the stairs and grabbed my phone.

"Steve, it's Amy. Come and save me."

Chapter 38

Stella sang along with James Taylor's 'Carolina in my Mind' which was playing on the radio.

"You've a great voice," I said when she'd finished crooning away.

"Thanks," she said. "I love singing. So tell me all about your sister's wedding, I want to know all the gory details."

"I don't know where to start," I smiled. We were sharing the driving and I was taking the second shift as I knew the directions. Getting to Cork wasn't a problem, the roads were mostly quite reasonable and clearly signposted. But finding Castlehaven was more of a problem. It was only sixty miles west of Cork City but the roads were small and narrow. Stella's mum had very kindly (and a little foolishly I thought) lent us her black convertible Golf. As it was only just after seven in the morning we hadn't put the top down – yet.

Stella turned off the M50 and onto the Cork road. "Start at the hairdresser's."

"Are you sure?" I asked.

"We have hours to fill," Stella laughed, "and I want to find out everything about being a bridesmaid from the expert."

"Thanks," I said glumly.

"Have I said something wrong?" Stella asked with concern.

"No," I said. "I'm just a bit paranoid about being the bridesmaid all the time."

"Twice!" Stella giggled. "Hardly all the time, you nutter." She bit her lip as she overtook a lumbering tractor.

I smiled. A few months ago I would have picked up on the word 'nutter' and wondered did she really mean it. Now I knew that she was only slagging me. I felt a whole lot better and stronger in myself. I knew that it could be a temporary thing – that any day now I might feel bad again. But I'd started to recognise the signs – feeling tired and run down, getting upset over insignificant things, obsessive behaviour. At the end of the day, I was bloody lucky and I was starting to recognise it and not curse the day I was born every time something went wrong. Although maybe last night's phone call was, in some ways, putting storm clouds on my horizon again. I'd have to wait and see.

"Amy?" Stella interrupted my musings. "Left or straight on, do you think?"

I recognised the road straight away. "Straight on," I said. We'd spent many summers in Schull as children and the drive was still familiar to me.

"So," Stella insisted, "you said you'd tell me everything. Go on."

"OK," I laughed, "OK. We got our hair done in Blackrock." I described our 'up-styles' (Jenny had told us this was the official hairdressing name for putting hair up) and our make-up.

"The feathers sound wicked!" Stella grinned, pulling out slightly to avoid a cyclist. "Do you have any photos with you?"

"Give us a chance," I laughed. "It's all been a tad busy at chez O'Sullivan!"

"Sorry!" Stella said. "And then you got dressed."

"Correct," I smiled. "I helped Suzi put on her dress and then we went to the church. It was all quite exciting really."

"I'm really excited," Stella bubbled. "I've never been to a wedding before."

"You must have," I said incredulously.

"Honestly," Stella said. "This is my first. I have no idea what happens."

"Beth has told you about the breaking of the glasses and the plates after the meal?" I asked, keeping a deadly straight face.

"No," Stella replied doubtfully. "Is that not in Greece or Italy or something?"

"It's optional at any wedding," I continued,

warming to the subject. "And after the speeches the bridesmaids are carried around the tables by the best man and ushers and any single man can kiss them. But they have to throw a few pounds into a bridesmaids' kitty."

"No!" Stella said, her eyes widening.

"It's true," I insisted. "And at the end of the evening the man who has put the most money into the kitty gets to go home with the bridesmaid of his choice."

"Amy!" Stella laughed. "You're making this up."

"I can't believe you took me seriously," I smiled.

"What's the best man like, anyway?" she asked. "Jed. I've met him once or twice, but I've never really talked to him."

"Why," I said, "are you interested?"

"Might be," she replied. "Depends."

I thought for a minute. "He's quiet," I began.

"And," she said.

"Nice-looking, I guess," I continued. "Tallish, a bit skinny. He wears glasses. Twenty-five, I think. A bit old for you."

"You're not making him sound very attractive," she said. "Maybe you're after him yourself."

"Jed?" I laughed. "I've already . . ." I stopped suddenly.

"You've what?" she asked. "Kissed him?"

I shouldn't have opened my big, fat mouth. Typical. "Yes," I admitted. "Briefly, on New Year's Eve. So it doesn't really count."

"Was he a good snog?" Stella asked with interest.

"He was, I suppose," I grinned. "Very tender and kind. I just wasn't ready for kind at that stage."

"Well, I am!" Stella stated firmly. "I've finally broken up with James."

"Oh, I'm sorry," I said.

"Don't be," Stella insisted. "He was a selfish creep. He didn't deserve me."

"Good attitude." I said. "What about Jasper?"

"He was just my transitional man," she said airily. I looked at her face. She was smiling. We both burst out laughing.

As we drove I told her about the wedding service, the food and the speeches. She listened in rapt attention. It was nice to have a captive audience.

I took over the driving at Cashel. Before we swapped front seats we decided to take the roof down.

"May as well make the most of the wheels," Stella grinned. "Might pick up a few hard-bodies along the way too. Like in *Thelma and Louise.*"

"We're unlikely to find Brad Pitt on the side of the road in Ireland," I giggled. "More like Anto Pitted, knowing our luck, but we can give it a go."

With a bit of puffing and panting as it was rather stiff, not to mention awkward, we managed to take down the roof and fold it away.

"I thought you pressed a button and the roof put itself away," I moaned, sucking the top of my finger which one of the metal roof hinges had caught. I hoped it wouldn't turn black – Beth would kill me. She hardly wanted an incapacitated bridesmaid.

Stella looked at my finger, unimpressed. "You'll live, you big baby," she smiled. "And I think you've been in one or two Porsches too many, my love! Not too many roofs do that in real life."

"Hardly," I smiled. "I've been watching too many American soap operas."

Stella laughed.

We buckled ourselves in and I put my foot down on the accelerator. The Golf moved off smoothly, purring like a kitten. It was a joy to drive, responsive and nippy.

"Slow down, Amy," Stella said loudly as we took a corner a little too fast. I glanced over at her. She was holding onto the side-door handle for dear life.

"Sorry," I said. I reduced speed and prayed for an open road and a sleeping Stella. I fancied myself as Eddie Irvine, burning rubber in Monaco, hordes of babes at my beck and call (male ones for me, of course).

Stella reached into the back and pulled a CD case out of her bag. "What do you fancy?" she asked.

"Something poppy," I smiled. "Something we can sing along to."

"How about some early Madonna?"

"Perfect," I said.

Stella pulled out *The Immaculate Collection*. "'Holiday' is first," she said, "then 'Lucky Star'."

"Is 'Like a Prayer' on it?" I asked hopefully.

"It most certainly is," Stella confirmed. She slipped in the CD and we began to sing along.

"This is great!" I laughed as we tore down the road. Although we were only doing just over sixty it seemed much faster.

In no time we had reached the outskirts of Cork City and decided to stop for sandwiches at a roadside pub. Luckily we could park the car right outside so we didn't have to grapple with the hood again.

"Did you meet anyone new at the wedding?" Stella asked as she bit into her roll. We were sitting on wooden picnic benches outside.

"Not exactly," I smiled, pulling a large piece of red onion out of my sandwich and putting it on my plate.

"What do you mean?" she asked with interest.

"Have I told you about Steve?" I asked.

"No."

"Well, Steve is an English guy who writes children's books. You might have heard of him – Stevie J?"

"I don't think so," Stella admitted.

"Henry and the Master Wizard?"

"Oh, yes!" she exclaimed. "There was an article about the film in *Empire*."

"That's Steve's book," I continued. "Anyway I met him when he came into the bookshop I work in to do a signing."

"And?" Stella said.

"We kind of hit it off and we went out a couple of times," I skipped over the embarrassing messy bit in the middle. Although Stella was only seventeen I still wanted her to think I was reasonably 'cool' and together. Not a complete moron. "And he was at the wedding."

"And you kissed him?" Stella asked with interest.

"Um," I nodded, my mouth full.

"Are you seeing him again?" she asked.

"I think so," I began, taking a sip of my Fanta. "But things have changed a little in the last few days. So, to be honest, I'm not sure now."

"Why not? What things?" Stella said. "Do you like him?"

"It's not as simple as that," I said. "There are other factors involved."

"Like what? Someone else?"

"Not exactly," I said hesitantly. "Well, maybe. I'm bit confused."

"You're confused!" Stella laughed. "I'm baffled. You're being very cryptic."

"Sorry," I said. "I'm not really sure I want to talk about it."

Stella looked at the traffic passing by. After a minute she turned back. "That's OK. I understand. I get like that myself sometimes." She smiled. "Tell me about the band at the wedding. Were they good?"

We talked about Suzi's wedding for a few more minutes before returning to the car. In just under two hours we pulled into Castlehaven. We pulled in outside Trudi's and climbed out of the car.

"I'm so stiff," Stella complained, stretching her arms above her head and yawning at the same time.

"Me too," I said.

"Amy, Stella," Beth came running out of the pub and gave me a huge hug. "It's so good to see you. You're early."

"Amy's a nippy driver," Stella smiled.

"Come inside," Beth said. "Tony and Jed are in the garden at the back. We're about to have lunch. Have you eaten?"

"Not really," Stella said, "we just had a sandwich on the way. I could definitely eat again."

"It's OK for you," I moaned. "You don't have a problem with your stomach sticking out. If I don't stop stuffing myself, I'll look like a pregnant bridesmaid tomorrow!"

"Don't be silly," Beth laughed. "You'll both look great. And the food here is lovely – loads of fresh seafood and salads."

"Well, maybe I could have a salad," I said doubtfully.

Beth led us inside, through the pub and into the garden.

"This place is amazing," Stella enthused. "I love all the low beams and the old wood bar."

Beth smiled. "We were lucky to find it," she admitted. "It's owned by friends of Mum's who retired down here a few years ago. They don't normally do weddings but they made an exception for us."

Tony and Jed stood up as we approached. "Hi, girls," Tony smiled. He kissed us both on the cheek. "Good to see you. Stella, this is Jed, my best man. You've met before."

Jed smiled shyly at Stella. "Only briefly. Hi, Stella." He held out his hand politely.

"Nice to finally meet you properly," Stella smiled.

"And you know Amy," Tony said wryly.

"Um, yes," Jed stammered.

"Hi, Jed," I smiled. I decided to be nice to him. He was a decent bloke and anyway, I didn't want to cause any hassle today of all days. Beth's wedding was only a day away after all.

We sat down and looked at the menus which were on the white metal table in front of us.

"Can I take your order?" a waitress with an American accent asked us.

"I'll have the steak sandwich with chips," Tony said. "And another pint of Guinness."

Beth gave Tony a disapproving look. "What?" he asked.

"It's not even one o'clock," Beth pointed out.

Tony reached over and took Beth's hand in his. "We're on our holidays, love," he smiled. "And I'm only keeping Jed company."

"Don't blame me," Jed said quickly.

"Do you not want another pint?" Tony asked.

"Of course I do," Jed assured him.

"Well then, point proven," Tony said.

We all laughed.

"I'll have the same," Jed smiled at the waitress.

"Scampi for me," Beth said, "and a glass of cider."

"And me," Stella piped up. "But make mine a pint."

"And yourself?" the waitress asked me. I studied the menu carefully. "A Caesar salad," I replied, "and a pint of cider."

"Good on you," Tony smiled.

Beth seemed a little worried. "We have the practice at three. I don't want the wedding party half-cut, thank you very much."

"We'll be fine," Stella assured her. "A couple of drinks won't do us any harm. And we don't have to drive again today, do we?"

"No," Beth said, "I suppose not. Your guest house is across the road."

"Are you staying there too?" I asked.

"Yes and no," Beth said. "Tony's staying there tonight and I'm here. And tomorrow we're both staying here. They have a little guest house which is a converted stables. It's lovely. We're going to stay down for a few days after the wedding to recoup. Then Tony has to get back to work."

"We'll take a proper honeymoon in the New Year," Tony said, "when work's a little less frantic."

"How's it going?" I asked. Tony and Jed's computer company had been up and running for over a month now.

"Really well," Tony said. "We've more work than we

can handle right now. We may need to take on another person soon."

"That's great," I smiled.

"What do you do, Stella?" Tony asked quietly.

"I'm studying at the moment," Stella told him. "I mean, I was. I've just finished my Leaving Cert. I'm hoping to get into college this year. I'd like to study computers."

"Really?" Jed asked. He and Tony began to discuss the various college courses with her.

I put my head on Beth's shoulder and sighed. "Computers mean nothing to me," I said. "I can just about use the re-order programme at work. And send e-mails. That's about it."

"I know what you mean," Beth said. "At least you don't have to live with a computer nerd," she whispered.

I lifted my head. "When are the other guests arriving?" I asked, trying to sound casual.

Beth looked at me carefully. "Most of them are arriving this evening. Tony's mum and dad are here already. They went into Skibbereen with my parents for lunch. They're all staying in the Skibbereen Grand Hotel. They'll be back for the rehearsal."

"How about your friends?" I asked.

"You know about Jack. I believe you were talking to him," she raised her eyebrows.

"Last night," I mumbled.

"And there aren't that many others really," Beth continued, pretending not to notice my awkwardness.

"Just Owen and Gloria, Louise and Hal, and Eithne, Joe and Colm. They're all staying in Skib, I think." Owen, Joe and Colm were friends of Tony's from school and college. Gloria was Owen's wife, and Eithne was a school friend of Beth's.

Beth and Tony had decided to have a tiny wedding – best friends and direct family only. And Louise, Beth's boss who she was very fond of, and her partner Hal who owned a chain of clothes shops.

Neither Beth nor Tony were into big occasions and they wanted their day to be spent with the people they loved the most.

And, as one of Tony's oldest friends, Jack was going. Because last night, on the phone, I had told him to.

Chapter 39

"Amy?" I nearly dropped dead at the vividly familiar voice. I was out of breath as I'd been racing around my room packing for Beth's wedding. Myself and Stella were leaving in the wee hours of the following morning, I had no clean underwear to my name and I couldn't find my wallet.

"Jack?" I faltered. I sat down on the floor. My head was racing. Why was he ringing?

"I'm sorry," he began slowly, "is this a bad time? Will I ring you back?"

"No, no," I said, "it's fine. I'm just packing for Beth's wedding."

"That's why I'm ringing you," he said.

"Oh?" I asked.

"Beth called in. She asked us not to go to the wedding. She said it would cause too much trouble."

I smiled broadly. I knew it was awful but I'd asked Beth to talk to them. After mulling it over I'd told Beth that I was her best friend, not Jodie, and that if she loved me at all she'd ask them not to go to the wedding because it would hurt me too much. Talk about giving someone a guilt trip.

"She told me," I said. Isn't it great? I wanted to say. Beth likes me more than Jodie. It's me she chose. Me, me, me. But I wasn't that stupid. He went silent. I decided to tread carefully. "I'm sorry," I lied, "but it had nothing to do with me."

"Beth said it was her decision and that Tony had reluctantly gone along with it. I don't want to spoil her day. Or your day, I suppose," he added.

"Um, thanks," I murmured. I was beginning to feel a little awkward. Then it hit me. Of course I didn't want *them* there, rubbing my nose in it, but Jack on his own – now that was a different matter. I could show him how great I looked, tell him all about Steve, and Suzi's wedding. Let him know how much better my life was without him. If nothing else it would make *me* feel better.

I could hear the cogs turning over in his brain. "Amy, did you ask Beth to talk to us?"

"No!" I lied shamefully. "I wouldn't do that."

"Sorry," he apologised. "I shouldn't have said that." He didn't sound all that sure.

"Jack," I sighed deeply and audibly, "listen, why don't *you* go, Tony would want you to be there. You've know each other forever."

"On my own, without Jodie?" he asked quietly.

"Yes," I whispered.

"No, I don't think so," he replied, "and anyway, things are a bit difficult at present." He fell silent for a moment. "Actually, you know, that might not be a bad idea. Are you sure you wouldn't mind?"

I gulped a breath. My heart was pounding faster than ever. I tried to keep my voice level. "No," I said. "It would be fine." I gulped. "Fine."

"Really?" he asked doubtfully. After all, the last time we'd seen each other I'd told him where to go in no uncertain terms in front of everyone.

"Jack," replied, "I'm seeing someone else now. And even if I wasn't it would be all right, honestly."

"But you still haven't spoken to Jodie," he said levelly.

"No," I agreed, "I haven't. But I will."

"When?" he asked.

"Soon."

"Um," he mumbled, sounding unconvinced. "Who's this new bloke anyway?"

I smiled. So he'd heard. "Oh, just a writer," I said nonchalantly. "No one you'd know."

"Is he going to the wedding?" Jack asked.

"No," I said. This was all very strange.

"I have to go now, Amy," Jack said. "I'll ring Beth and check it's OK with her and Tony."

"Wait," I said.

"Yes?"

"I just wanted to say that I was sorry to hear about yourself and Jodie, you know, the wedding and everything . . ." I trailed off lamely.

Jack coughed nervously. "Thanks," he murmured.

"Are you all right?" I asked.

"Me?" Jack asked. "Yes, I'm grand. It's . . ." He went silent for a few seconds. "Listen," he whispered, "I'd really like to talk to you about it. That's why I rang really. Maybe we can talk at the wedding."

"Right," I said in astonishment. "I'll see you in Cork."

I held the phone to my ear for several seconds after he'd clicked off his phone. Jack wanted to talk to me. Alone. And his wedding had been practically cancelled.

It suddenly dawned on me – he wanted me back. Yes, that must be it.

I wasn't sure how I felt about this. I sat down on the side of my bed and thought it over. Images of the past came rushing back to haunt me – myself and Jack walking on Brittas beach, myself and Jack painting the spare bedroom and covering each other in light-blue emulsion before sharing a bath and washing the paint out of each other's hair . . . it would be so familiar and so easy.

I decided that it would be simple to sweep all the bad things about our previous relationship under the carpet. Better the devil you know, as Kylie once said. I'd tried to push Jack out of my mind but he'd always been there lurking in the subconscious depths.

I'd had enough of being on my own. I was finally ready to marry Jack.

I had meant to ring Steve that evening but my mind was so full of Jack that I'd forgotten. I'd spent the last few days with Steve and we'd been getting on famously. But now everything had changed.

I sang to myself tunelessly as I threw some jeans into my suitcase. This was going to be one hell of a wedding.

* * *

"This is the most beautiful church I've ever seen," Stella said in a reverential whisper. Stella and Jed and I were standing at the entrance of the church looking towards the altar. "It's so quiet." Beth and Tony had gone on ahead while we'd finished up our drinks.

We stepped inside, practically tiptoeing into the cool, still interior. The walls of the simple, rectangular church were painted stark white and the well-worn mahogany wood of the pews and the altar looked hundreds of years old. The floor, which felt cold under my feet even though I had shoes on, was covered with dark copper-coloured tiles, and huge brass chandeliers hung from the high wooden-beamed ceiling. The sun shone in through delicately blue and dark-pink coloured glass windows which showed scenes from the Nativity and three tall, willowy saints.

"You're right," I agreed.

Beth and Tony were sitting silently in one of the pews to the left of us. They turned and smiled when they saw us.

"Hi, girls," Beth said in a low voice. "Reverend Elmes will be with us in a few minutes. And Mum and Dad are on their way."

I shimmied into the pew beside Beth. "It's so peaceful in here," I smiled.

"Isn't it lovely?" Beth asked. Trudi suggested it. The church was five minutes down the road from the bar which was very handy. "I haven't met Reverend Elmes though," she continued. "I hope he's nice. We did our preparation with Reverend Howe from the local church in Dun Laoghaire but he was taken ill at the last minute and couldn't travel down, unfortunately. He arranged Reverend Elmes for us."

"Welcome, welcome," a loud voice boomed from the back of the church. Myself and Beth jumped. A large woman with short dark hair was making her way towards us, arms outstretched. "Which of you are Beth and Tony?"

We all stared at the woman in astonishment. She was wearing a green T-shirt and a billowing flowery skirt.

"Is this the woman who's doing the flowers?" I whispered to Beth.

Beth looked worried. "I'm not sure . . ." she began.

"I'm Clare Elmes, or Reverend Elmes," the woman introduced herself. "This is my parish."

I started to giggle. I couldn't help it. It must have been the cider. I set Stella off too. Beth glared at us before seeing the funny side.

"Sorry, Reverend Elmes," she said, trying not to laugh, "We thought you were a man. I'm Beth."

"Not at all," the smiling woman said. "I'm used to it. And call me Clare. I'm delighted to meet you."

"I'm Tony," Tony stood up and held out his hand. And this is Jed, my best man, and Amy and Stella, the two bridesmaids." We all said hello.

"I'm delighted to see everyone in such good spirits," Clare said. "A wedding is a glorious occasion and certainly one to enjoy. My own wedding was many years ago, of course, but it was a splendid day."

Jed looked at her in astonishment. "Is that allowed?" he whispered to me.

"It is in the Church of Ireland," I smiled.

"That's great!" Stella said quietly. "Getting married by a woman and a married one at that. How cool!"

Beth's dad walked in the door, followed by her mum and Tony's parents.

Beth walked towards them before they had the chance to ask any questions about Clare.

"Hi, everyone, this is Reverend Elmes, or Clare as she's asked to be called. She's the Rector here."

Tony's parents looked a little shocked but took it well. Everyone introduced themselves.

The practice went swimmingly. Clare was a panic and made us all collapse around the church laughing several times. In fact I was looking forward to the ceremony – Beth and Tony had chosen all the readings and music themselves and it would be a very personal service. And a little too interactive for my liking. I wasn't used to singing out loud!

"Did she just say we all had to sing?" Stella whispered. "Is that normal?"

"I think so," I smiled. "Don't worry. At least you have a nice voice." I'd been to a few Church of Ireland weddings and the congregation liked to belt out the hymns like there was no tomorrow. 'Onward Christian Soldiers' and all that.

"Have you seen *Four Weddings and a Funeral*?" Jed asked Stella. "There's lots of singing in that. Some hymn about 'Old England'."

"Oh, yes!" Stella said. "I do remember now."

After the practice we went back to Trudi's. Owen and Gloria had arrived and were sitting outside enjoying the sunshine with their young son, Milo.

"Hi, guys," I said as I approached their table. "Beth and Tony are inside. They'll be out in a second."

"Nice to see you again, Amy," Gloria said. Milo pulled out of my skirt and stared up at me. He had white-blond hair, huge blue eyes and sallow skin.

"Hi, Milo," I smiled. "What age are you?"

"He's not really talking much yet," Owen explained as I sat down beside them. Milo was still hanging on to my skirt. "He's only eighteen months."

"And he's a bit shy," Gloria said. "But he seems to have taken a bit of a liking to you."

"Mook," Milo said. "Choo-choo." He handed me a book with a train on the cover.

"I know this one," I beamed. "*The Little Engine That Could*. Would you like me to read it to you, Milo?"

"Mook!" Milo nodded. "Read mook!"

"He calls books 'mooks'," Gloria laughed. "He'd

love a story but don't feel you have to. It's not a busman's holiday."

"I don't mind," I said honestly. "It's one of my favourites." I lifted Milo onto my knee and began to read the familiar story.

Halfway through the second animated rendition of *'I think I can, I think I can'* I felt a hand on my shoulder.

"Hi, Amy."

I glanced up. It was Jack. My stomach lurched. I could feel my face reddening. Typical, I was pretending to be a steam-train, with my cheeks puffed out and my eyes open wide. Talk about timing!

"Hi, Jack," I said. "How was the drive?" He looked really well. He was wearing a white T-shirt and light blue denims. He had gained a little weight and his jowls had got jowlier but it suited him in a 'not-a-little-boy-any-more' sort of way.

"Not too bad, thanks," he smiled. I tried to hold his gaze but he turned towards Owen and Gloria. "Milo's huge! The last time I saw him he was tiny. He must have been only a few months old."

"Has it been that long?" Gloria asked thoughtfully. "I suppose it has. Where have you been hiding yourself? You and Amy haven't been around these days." Owen glared at his wife. "Oh, sorry . . ." Gloria faltered, embarrassed.

"It's OK, Gloria," I said, trying to smooth things over. "It's fine. Jack and I are the best of friends now, aren't we, Jack?"

Jack seemed unsure how to deal with this comment. He decided to nod and move away. "Just going to ask Tony something . . ." he mumbled and went back inside. I was disappointed he'd hadn't stayed to talk to me but there was all weekend to catch up, after all.

Owen was restless. He was dying to go inside and join 'the lads' at the bar. Tony, Jed and now Jack were all watching *Baywatch* on satellite. Or 'Babe watch' as Tony liked to call it. Much as he loved his wife and son he had a craving for a few snatched lads-only minutes. "Drinks, Amy, Gloria?" He stood up.

"I'm fine, thanks," Gloria beamed, "for now." I shook my head. He disappeared swiftly.

"I'm sorry, Amy," Gloria said as soon as he'd left. "I didn't mean to . . ."

"Honestly, I'm OK about it. Please don't worry," I assured her. "We're both with other people now." I thought for a second. It wasn't strictly true on my part but it sounded better than admitting that I was on my own. It was easier, I suppose. "And you know Jack and Jodie are together?" I asked, stroking Milo's silky head. But not for long, I thought to myself.

"I'd heard," Gloria said. "Beth told me. That must have been hard."

"It was," I agreed. Bloody, devastatingly hard.

"And tell me about your new man," Gloria said. "Beth hasn't filled me in on that one yet."

"Did I hear my name being mentioned?" Beth smiled. "The boys are all watching *Baywatch* and the bikini and swimsuit comments are getting to me. I thought I'd come out and join the normal mortals." She sat down at our table. "Hi, Milo," she kissed him on the top of his head. "He's being very good," she said.

"Don't speak too soon," Gloria replied. "He's bound to break a couple of glasses and terrorise the cat in a few minutes." Trudi's big, fat tabby was sunning itself on the wall beside us and sure enough, Milo's eyes were fixed on the sleeping moggy. "I was just saying you hadn't told me about Amy's new man," Gloria continued.

"New man?" Beth asked in confusion. "Emilio?"

"Steve," I interrupted, staring pointedly at Beth.

"Oh, that new man," she said. "Because he's new on the scene I wasn't sure if Amy wanted people to know about him, that's all." She smiled at me. "He was at Suzi's wedding. Lovely guy. Seemed a little preoccupied that night though, I didn't really get to talk to him."

I kicked her under the table.

"So tell me," Gloria asked. "What does he do? Have you a photo? You know I rely on these things to make my suburban life more interesting."

"Suburban life, my ass," Beth giggled. "Jeez, you have the life of Reilly. Having the day to yourself with only a few nappies to change. Get a grip."

"It's not easy being at home all day," Gloria insisted. "Milo's a real handful. And it's a bit boring to be honest. Most of my friends are out at work all day. And

I'm getting a bit tired of *Barney* and *Bear in the Big Blue House* to tell the truth."

"Isn't Milo going to playschool in September?" Beth asked.

"That's right," Gloria said. "I was thinking of going back to work part-time after that. In a shop or something."

"You were in publishing before, weren't you?" I asked.

"Yes," Gloria nodded. "I was in the editorial department of Puffin Books in London, before we moved back. I was in charge of the children's picture-book list."

"You know," I said slowly. "I just might have the right job for you. Lynn is always looking for good part-time help. How would you like working in The Wonderland?"

Gloria smiled. "That sounds perfect. Do you think Lynn would hire me?" she asked hopefully.

"Without a doubt," I said. "With your experience. Are you joking? Picture-books are her big thing. I'll talk to her next week."

"Thanks, Amy," Gloria said gratefully. "You may have just saved my sanity."

"I can't believe we've been here all day," Beth giggled, sipping on a glass of red wine.

"All day and all night more like," Stella smiled. "It's nearly twelve."

"No way!" Beth squealed, plonking her glass down on the table in front of her. "I'm getting married tomorrow. What am I thinking of? I need my sleep. I have to go. Where's Tony?"

Tony was sitting in the corner of the bar, one arm around Jack and the other holding a pint of Guinness.

"He looks well stuck in," I grinned. "Good luck to you. Where's he staying?"

"In the same guest house as you tonight, remember?"

The whole wedding party, those that had arrived that was, had eaten in the bar. There was a restaurant upstairs but we were leaving that till tomorrow night, as that's where we'd be eating after the wedding. We'd lost count of the wine and after-dinner drinks we'd consumed. Tony's and Beth's parents had retired for the evening, followed by Gloria and Owen, a gently snoring Milo in his arms. Unlike Dublin pubs, Trudi's was supremely child-and-parent-friendly.

"Let him sleep over there," Trudi had told Gloria at nine o'clock. She'd pointed at a small, wide bench beside the back door. The bench was covered in a long, flat cushion and was out of the way of the smoky bar. Gloria had been carrying Milo out the front door. "I'll get him a rug and he'll be happy as Larry. Means you can stay and enjoy yourself, love."

Gloria had been so grateful she'd nearly cried. "Thank you so much," she'd gushed. "I don't get out much, you see."

"It's a special occasion," Trudi had said gently, "and

I know what it's like with small children. I've grandchildren myself."

"Right, come on, you," Beth commanded, standing in front of Tony. "We're off. I'll drop you back to your guesthouse."

"Just a few more minutes, love," Tony insisted, slurring his words slightly. "Have to talk to Jack about . . ."

Beth sighed. "Please, Tony. It's late."

Tony looked up at her and beamed. "For the future Mrs O'Leary, anything." He got up slowly. "Bye, old friend," he said to Jack. "See you tomorrow."

"Cheers, Tony," Jack grinned. "Get some beauty sleep. You need it!"

My eyes lingered on the seat vacated by Tony. "Excuse me," I said to Stella and Jed, standing up.

Chapter 40

"Amy," Jack said as I sat down beside him. He didn't say any more and we sat in silence for a few minutes. The bar was beginning to thin out and the gentle strains of 'Have I Told You Lately' filled the air.

"Van Morrison," Jack said finally. "Every pub in Ireland must have a Van Morrison CD."

I smiled. "Remember this one? We used to dance to it in the kitchen."

"In the early days," Jack murmured.

"What's that supposed to mean?" I asked.

"Forget it," Jack said, running his finger up and down his pint which was sitting on the table in front of him. "I'm just a bit . . . oh, I don't know. Tony and myself were talking about old times, when the four of us used to do things together."

"Do you miss them, the old days, I mean?" I asked slowly.

He looked at me carefully. "I suppose I do," he said, shrugging his shoulders. "But things change. People change."

"I miss those days too," I began, taking a deep breath. "I miss you." There, I'd said it.

Jack put his hand on mine. "I know, Amy," he said gently, "and I miss you too. I hope we can be friends now."

"Friends?" I blurted out. This wasn't quite what I'd expected.

"You're right," Jack said. "It's probably a bit too soon to be friends. I'm sorry."

What the hell was he talking about? I tried again. "What did you want to talk about, Jack?" I asked, trying not to sound impatient, and attempting to make him move quickly to the point. He took his hand off mine.

"Jodie," he said softly.

"Jodie?" I asked. "What about Jodie?"

"She's going to kill me for telling you this."

"What?" I demanded. This 'talk' wasn't going as planned.

"Listen, we've both had a few drinks. Let's discuss it tomorrow, OK?"

"No!" I exclaimed, "I want to talk about it right now. You can't start telling me something and then cut off like that. It's not fair. You've broken up, is that it?"

"Sorry?" he asked in confusion. "Whatever gave you that idea?"

"Don't act the innocent with me," I began, raising

my voice. "*First* you postpone your wedding, and *then* you ring and tell me you want to talk to me. And *then* you ask me if I'm coming here alone and you show up without Jodie. What in God's name am I supposed to think?"

Jack sighed and put his head in his hands. "I'm sorry," he murmured. "I'm so, so sorry." When he raised his head there were tears in his eyes.

"But you want me back," I whispered. "I know you do."

We sat in silence for several minutes. I could feel tears pricking my eyes and there was a large lump forming in the back of my throat.

"I'm sorry if you got the wrong idea," Jack said finally. "Postponing the wedding has nothing to do with you, honestly."

I stared at him. "But I love you. You love me."

"You're not making sense, Amy," Jack said gently. "Let it go. We'd never have made it to the altar anyway. We weren't right for each other."

"What do you mean?" I asked emotionally. Tears began to roll down my cheeks. Jack handed me a red paper napkin from the table, left over from dinner.

"Here," he said kindly. "Don't cry. You'll be fine."

"Why?" I asked him. "What was wrong?"

"I don't really want to talk about this right now," Jack said, gulping back some of his pint.

"You feel guilty, don't you?" I muttered. "For treating me so badly."

"Guilty!" he spluttered, nearly choking on his drink. "OK, Amy, if you want to talk about it, let's talk about it. Starting with your unbearably moody behaviour. Or your obsessive jealousy. Do you remember almost giving me a black eye the evening after Owen and Gloria's party because I'd spent the evening talking to Eithne about computers?"

"I was drunk," I sniffed. "I didn't mean to hurt you. And you were flirting with her!"

"I used to come home from work knackered and you'd be moaning on about your job and how you wanted to do something else. And we'd spend hours talking about your future and then you'd ignore all my advice and stay at that bloody bookshop."

"I've got a new job now," I said defensively. "I'm going to be working for RTE."

"Good!" Jack said, mellowing slightly. "I'm glad, about time too. What will you be doing?"

"Research on a children's art show," I said. "So you see, I have changed, really."

Jack smiled gently. "Amy, I'm not trying to argue with you. But I'm with Jodie now and we're happy."

I gulped back the tears. "But we were happy too."

"I know," he said. "But I couldn't deal with you. You need someone with more patience. Two moody people in one house just doesn't work. I used to get so annoyed and frustrated with you."

"Was I that bad?" I asked.

"Not all the time," he said. He sighed. "Sometimes.

And I used to yell at you and I'm sorry for that. But I never treated you badly, Amy. Jodie said . . ."

"I shouldn't have said that to her," I said. "I'm sorry." Tears were pouring down my face. Jack put his arm around me.

"You'll be fine," he said, stroking my head. I breathed in his familiar smell. "It was you who left me, remember?"

"I know," I mumbled. "But that doesn't make it any easier."

"Amy, we've never really discussed this properly," Jack said.

"What?" I asked.

"You, me, breaking up, everything. You just shut me out. We should have talked it through."

"I know," I sniffed. "I just wasn't strong enough and when I found out about you and Jodie . . ."

"We never meant to hurt you," Jack interrupted. "I'm sorry you had to find out like that. It must have been terrible. We wanted to tell you. We were just waiting for the right time."

"I don't think there ever would have been a good time," I frowned. "I felt so betrayed and so bloody stupid."

"I can understand that," Jack said, "but I promise you, nothing happened between myself and Jodie until way after you and I broke up. We met at a work do and the rest is history."

I sighed. I didn't know quite what to say. I still hated

them both for putting me through all the heartache but Jack was right – it was time to move on.

"It's in the past now," I said, attempting a smile. "And I'm sorry for telling you to fuck off at New Year's."

"That's OK," Jack grinned. "And maybe I deserved it. I should have just kept quiet."

"No," I grinned back. "In the mood I was in I still would have yelled at you in some form or another. I wasn't exactly the life and the soul of the party that night."

"And now?" Jack asked gently.

"I'm better," I said. "Things have been a little topsy-turvy but they'll sort themselves out."

"Well, you look great," Jack smiled. "But then again, you always did."

I smiled at him gratefully.

I'd painted him as a monster in my mind over the last while – mainly because it was easier that way – but he was a decent guy. "You don't look so bad yourself. Jodie must be feeding you well."

"She is," Jack agreed. "Anyway, tell me about your boyfriend. The writer. "

I thought about Steve for a moment. I didn't know him the way I knew Jack, yet Steve seemed to understand me.

"His name is Steve, Steve Jones. He writes children's books," I said.

"Sounds ideal," Jack smiled. "You won't ever run out of things to talk about then."

I smiled. "No."

We listened to Van Morrison sing. I felt tired and emotionally washed out.

"That's Jodie's song," I said finally, "'Brown-Eyed Girl'."

"Yes," Jack said softly, looking into space. "There's something I wanted to tell you. Jodie's going to murder me but I don't care."

"What is it?" I asked. Jack's face was ashen-pale.

"I don't really know how to say this." He took a deep breath. "Jodie's mum has cancer. She's quite bad. The doctors don't know how long she has left."

"Oh my God," I whispered in shock. I didn't know what to say. Jane Ryan was a lovely woman, full of life and great crack. "I'm sorry," I began, starting to cry once more. I couldn't believe that I'd been so selfish – worrying about my love life when Jodie was losing her mother.

"It's OK," Jack said, holding my hand. "Jodie wanted to tell you herself, but the way things have been in the last while . . ."

"I've been such a bitch," I cried. "Poor Jodie."

"She's dealing with it really well," Jack said. "But you can see why we postponed the wedding."

"Of course," I whispered.

"The family don't want everyone to know. They want to deal with things quietly and in their own time," Jack continued. "Jodie's been staying at home a lot, to help her Mum."

I felt so bad. Whatever had happened she was still one of my oldest friends. "Where is she this weekend, Jack?" I asked softly.

"She's at home. Jane's staying in our house this weekend to get some peace and quiet and some rest."

"I'll ring Jodie first thing in the morning," I said firmly.

"I don't think . . ." Jack began.

"I have to," I told him. "It's about time I apologised. She needs her friends around her now. I hope she'll forgive me."

"She will," Jack said. "She has a big heart. Like yourself."

"Thanks," I smiled through the tears.

"Listen, it's been a long night," Jack said. "Why don't I walk you back to the guesthouse?"

"That would be nice, thanks," I smiled. We stood up and made our way towards Jed and Stella's table.

"I'm walking Amy back," Jack said to the couple.

"We should be joining you," Jed replied. "Big day tomorrow after all."

Jack offered me his arm. "Come on, Amy," he whispered. "Let's be friends. For Beth and Tony."

"And for Jodie," I added.

I slept remarkably well that evening. Talking to Jack must have had a cathartic effect. I'm sure the drink helped too.

Stella and I were sharing a large room in 'The Oaks'

guesthouse. Jack and Jed had rooms across the hall, and Tony had stayed in another room on the ground floor for the night. Our beds were supremely comfortable, high, brass beds with cool, white linen embroidered quilts. The room was an eclectic mix of the old and the new – an antique dressingtable was furnished with a funky steel mirror, and the wardrobe had been given a lime-green distressed look. Our bridesmaids' dresses hung ready on the back of the door.

I opened my eyes and sighed in relief as a shaft of bright sunlight was visible through the white curtains. I lay, cossetted in the soft warm bed, thinking about Jack, Jodie and our conversation the previous evening. It hurt like hell that he'd moved on but in a strange way it was a relief. Now I knew I had to get on with my own life, without Jack. And as for Jodie, I just hoped that she'd talk to me after all that had happened.

"Penny for them," Stella smiled. She was sitting up in her bed, her hair a messy dark halo around her pretty face.

I smiled. "Forget about me," I said. "What about you and Jed? You were getting on very well last night."

Stella grinned. "He's a nice guy. We were talking about computers. Anyway, I'm sure he thinks I'm a bit young for him."

"You're nearly eighteen," I said, "I wouldn't worry about that. You'll have to make the first move, though. He's very shy."

"You said that before," Stella mused, "but he didn't

seem shy to me. We were chatting for hours. He has a great sense of humour."

"Maybe he's just met the right woman," I said.

She threw a pillow at me.

"What's that for?" I squealed.

"Maybe he has. Stop slagging me," she said. "I'm going to use the shower." She jumped up and loped over towards the en-suite bathroom. "See you in a minute. How are we for time, by the way?"

I looked at my watch, which was beside my mobile on the bedside table. "Grand," I said. "It's nearly ten and we have to be over with Beth at twelve."

"Perfect," she beamed, closing the bathroom door behind her.

I picked up my phone and held it for a few minutes before finding the familiar number.

"Amy?"

"Sorry, did I wake you up? It is pretty early."

"Not at all. It's fine. I was up."

"What are you doing today?" I asked.

I made one more phone call before lying back against the pillow and closing my eyes.

Chapter 41

Helen & Ivan McNally

request the pleasure of the company of

Amy O'Sullivan

at the marriage of their daughter

Elizabeth to Anthony O'Leary

at St Bart's Church, Castlehaven, West Cork

on Wednesday 10th May at 4.00pm

and afterwards at

Trudi's Restaurant, Castlehaven, West Cork

RSVP 22 Elgin Road, Donnybrook, Dublin 4

"I'm not sure if I should have had that champagne," Stella whispered to me.

"You'll be fine," I assured her. "Just think of Jed at the altar."

Stella giggled. "I'm only seventeen. It's a bit early for that, I think."

I laughed. "You know what I mean."

"What are we waiting for?" she asked.

"Beth, you ninny," I whispered. "She'll be here with her Dad in a second."

"Right," she said.

I looked towards the church gate. She'd want to get a move on. She was almost over the obligatory fifteen minutes and Tony would be getting worried.

"Here she is," Stella whispered.

Beth made her way up the church steps towards us, her Dad, Ivan, at her side.

I could feel the waterworks again. Her Dad hadn't been well recently and he was taking the steps slowly. We'd spotted Tony, Jack and Jed this morning having breakfast in 'The Oaks' with Tony's parents. The lads had all looked a little worse for wear.

Stella and Beth and I had had a lovely morning getting ready. First a slap-up breakfast with Beth's parents, and then Beth did her own make-up and hair, with my and Stella's 'help'. Then we lazed around in the huge hotel room and drank champagne.

"Beth," Stella waved excitedly.

"Hi," Beth smiled nervously. "This is it."

"Tony's waiting for you inside," I said.

"Will I give Clare the nod?" Ivan asked.

Beth took a deep breath. "One minute, Dad." She brushed away a tear with the back of her hand. "Oh, my make-up is going to run."

"No, it won't," I said gently. "You have waterproof

mascara on, remember? And anyway, what does it matter?"

"I'm just so happy," Beth smiled. She squeezed my hand. "Thanks for being here."

"My pleasure," I said. "Now we really had better get going. Tony will be bricking it."

"OK, Dad," Beth said.

Ivan popped his head inside the door.

"Take my arm, love," he said kindly to his only daughter.

The strains of violins filled the church.

"What's that music?" I asked. "It's beautiful."

"It's Mozart," Beth smiled. "Tony chose it. We weren't mad on the usual 'here comes the bride' stuff."

As we entered the church I looked up the aisle. Louise had arrived and was wearing the most amazing purple hat and matching dress. Her partner, Hal, was resplendent in a cream suit. All eyes turned towards Beth.

And in the pew in front of Louise was Jodie, standing at Jack's side, in a flowing lilac Ghost dress.

"Jodie's here," Beth turned to whisper to me.

"I know," I whispered back. "I rang her and begged her to come."

"Oh, Amy," Beth smiled. "Thank you."

As I walked up the aisle towards Tony and Jed a glowing feeling came over my whole body. It felt such a magical, happy day. All the people Beth and Tony loved most in the world were gathered in this special place to wish them well.

When we reached the top of the small church Clare said, "Please be seated."

"We are gathered here," she began, "on this wonderful, sunny day for Beth and Tony's wedding. I would like to begin the service by welcoming you all to St Bart's. I know you have all travelled to be here today and I'm delighted to share my church with you all, regardless of your religious persuasion. And now we will all sing the first hymn – 'All Things Bright and Beautiful'."

Stella smiled at me as she began to sing, her sweet voice ringing out. Jed, surprisingly, also had a wonderful voice, deep and mellow. I mouthed the words, not wanting to ruin things.

"Please be seated for the first reading," Clare said.

Beth made her way up to the bronze lectern. "This is for Tony," she said.

"'He Wishes for the Cloths of Heaven' by William Butler Yeats."

As I listened to her voice ringing out softly but clearly in the hushed church a wave of emotion washed over me. There seemed to be a real presence in the air. It was hard to explain. A religious person would say that God was in the church, touching everyone's lives and filling everyone with his divine love. I just felt filled with a sense of calm, wonder and, for the first time in as long as I could remember, peace.

Beth finished, gazing at Tony. His eyes in turn were fixed on hers.

"Thank you, Beth. That was splendid," Clare said. "And now we have a reading from Tony."

Tony approached the lectern and coughed quietly. "Um, this is for Beth," he said nervously.

"This is from the Book of Ruth. *'Wherever you go, I will go; wherever you live, I will live; your people shall be my people and your God will be my God too. Where you die, I will die, and there I shall be buried beside you. We shall be together forever, and our love will be the gift of our lives.'*"

I'd never seen Tony cry but there were definitely tears in his eyes at that moment. Beth was smiling through her own tears. In fact, there wasn't a dry eye in the house.

"Wonderful. Thank you, Tony," Clare said. "And now we'll begin the wedding ceremony.

"Dearly beloved, we are gathered here in the sight of God and in the face of this congregation, to join together this man and this woman in holy matrimony . . ."

As I listened to Tony and Beth exchange their wedding vows I wondered how Suzi and Matt were. I missed my sister already and she'd only been away a few days. But when they moved out of Mum and Dad's I'd have to get used to not seeing her as much. I'd have to start putting together my own new life, new job and all. I was nervous but, as Jack had pointed out last night, it was about time.

Beth's mum read the lesson, all about love and loving one another. And then we all sang 'Be Thou My Vision'. Stella winked at me as she began to sing.

As we made our way into the side room to sign the register, Stella smiled. "That was so lovely," she sighed. "I never thought it would all be so . . . so emotional."

"They're not all like that," I smiled back. "Some weddings are boring, to be honest. It's different when you're a bridesmaid. You're more involved."

"I suppose you're right," she said. "The voice of the experienced bridesmaid speaks."

I glared at her and began to laugh.

"Did you see the cute blond guy who snuck in after the first hymn?" she asked.

"Amy," Clare interrupted, "can you sign here?" I was ushered towards the long mahogany table before I had a chance to ask Stella what the man looked like. But I knew in my heart who it was.

Outside the church I spotted him immediately. He was wearing a dark blue suit and a white shirt with a lemon yellow tie. It was sunny and he was sporting metal-framed sunglasses that made him look like a movie star. My heart leapt. I made my way towards him.

"Steve," I grinned. He kissed me tenderly on the cheek.

"You look so beautiful," he smiled. "It was a beautiful service too. I loved the Yeats poem."

"Me too," I agreed.

"Sorry I was a bit late," he said, taking my hand. "It's one hell of a drive."

"I know," I said. "It was good of you to come on such short notice." I was overjoyed that he had driven the whole way down here to be with me.

"Thanks for asking me," he beamed, taking my hand in his. "I've never been to an Irish wedding. It's a new experience for me." He brought my hand to my lips and kissed it gently.

"I want to introduce you to a few people," I said, guiding him towards Tony and Beth. "Beth, Tony, this is Steve."

"Great to meet you," Tony shook his hand warmly.

"Steve," Beth smiled, "I've heard so much about you. I'm delighted you could make it." Beth had squealed with delight when I'd told her that morning that I'd asked him. I felt a bit bad as it was supposed to be close friends and family only, but Beth has such a giant-sized heart she didn't mind one bit.

Jodie and Jack joined us. Jack smiled at me gently. Jodie was hopping from one foot to another and seemed very nervous. We looked at each other for a few seconds. And the funny thing was, I didn't feel angry with her any more. In fact, I missed her. I gave her a hug and whispered, "I'm so sorry" into her ear.

She whispered, "It's OK. I'm sorry too" back.

"We'll catch up later," I promised her, trying not to cry.

"Yes," she smiled. She also looked on the verge of tears.

I knew things could never go back to the way

they were, but maybe, in time, we could be close again.

"Jodie, this is Steve, my boyfriend." Steve took my hand, squeezed it and smiled at me.

"This is Jodie," I continued, "one of my oldest friends."

Chapter 42

Three Months Later

> Jane and Desmond Ryan
> request the pleasure of the company of
>
> Amy O'Sullivan & Steve Jones
>
> at the marriage of their daughter
> *Jodie Ryan* to *Jack Daly*
> at St Paul's Church, Booterstown
> on Saturday 14th August at 3.00pm
> and afterwards at Blackrock Castle,
> Blackrock, Co Dublin.
>
> *RSVP 2 The Elms, Rathgar, Co Dublin*

"Are you all right?" Steve asked as we sat together in a taxi on our way to Booterstown. "You look a little pale."

"I'm fine," I lied. My stomach was churning and I felt decidedly faint.

"Are you sure you want to go through with this?" he asked. "You don't have to."

"I know," I smiled wanly. "But I want to. Honestly."

He squeezed my hand. "I understand." He looked out the window for a few minutes and then turned towards me. "There's something I wanted to ask you."

"Shoot," I said.

"Will you go to Ella's wedding with me? It's at the end of September."

I smiled. "I'd be honoured. Where is it?"

"Southampton," he said. "I'll book a hotel. There's a lovely one down by the sea."

"Sounds nice," I smiled.

"Here we are," the taxi man said, pulling up in front of St Paul's. Steve paid the fare. He also jumped out of the taxi, held the door for me and helped me out.

I put on my large black hat, which had been resting on my knee in the taxi, and took a deep breath. "Let's go in," I smiled.

Steve gave me his arm and supported some of my weight as I'd insisted on wearing my new black kitten heels which I hadn't really mastered walking in. They looked great, though, and today of all days I wanted to look my best. In my new green dress which Beth had given me for being her bridesmaid (the one I'd loved so much in Khan), black mules and black hat I was pleased with the effect.

It was a sunny day and I popped my sunglasses on, grateful for the opportunity to be somewhat incognito.

"There's Beth," Steve said, pointing to the right side of the church entrance.

"Well spotted," I said. Being tall had its advantages. As a squirt, I knew this only too well.

Beth smiled as we approached. "You're here," she said beaming. "I'm glad. I wasn't sure if you were going to come."

"I wasn't going to," I began, "but Jack and Jodie rang me last night and begged me to come. It's what they both wanted." I squeezed Steve's arm. "And I've Steve here with me for moral support. I'm only going to stay for the ceremony."

"Then I'm taking her away for some stiff drinks," Steve smiled, his blue eyes twinkling.

Beth beamed. "It's great that you're here, Amy. Really, really great."

The guests began to move inside and we followed the crowd. Jack and Jodie's family had already taken their seats towards the top of the church. Jodie's mum looked thin and tired but there was a huge grin plastered on her face. She was a determined woman and she was responding well to the chemotherapy, much to everyone's delight. Jack and Jodie had decided to go ahead with the wedding at her request. So it really was a very special day for her family.

"Let's sit here," I suggested, gesturing towards a pew at the back of the church.

"Do you not want to go a bit further up?" Steve asked gently.

I shook my head.

As I shuffled into my seat I stared at Jack's back. He was wearing a dark red velvet jacket and matching trousers. He looked handsome. As I watched him he turned slowly and caught my eye. He looked at me intently for a long second, smiled and then raised his hand in a small wave. I took a deep breath, smiled and waved back. He turned back towards the altar.

"Penny for them," Steve whispered.

"I was just thinking about myself and Jack. The past, you know," I whispered.

Just then the church went deathly silent and all eyes were glued on the door. The music began, the same trumpet music as was played at Suzi's wedding, and Jodie appeared at the entrance. She looked stunning and very, very happy. Her cream ivory dress suited her to a T, and her elegant bouquet of lilies was simply perfect. Her two sisters, the bridesmaids, were dressed in dark red satin, the same colour as Jack's suit.

As she walked slowly in the door on her father's arm, I whispered, "Good luck, Jodie."

She looked over and our eyes met. She smiled fondly. "Thanks," she mouthed. There were tears in her eyes. And in mine.

"Here," Steve said, handing me a huge, clean white linen handkerchief. "I think you'll need this."

One Year Later

(On RTE's morning television)

"Hi everyone, it's *Den* 2 and I'm Amy O'Sullivan, your new presenter."

"Does that mean we have to be nice to you?"

"Yes, Socky. It certainly does."

"Is it a bit like the boys' and girls' first day at school when they're really nervous?"

"That's right, Socky. It's just like that. And before *Scooby Doo* I'd like to say 'hi and welcome' to baby Aran, my little nephew who was born the day before yesterday and his Mummy and Daddy, Suzi and Matt."

"That means he's only two days old!"

"That's right, Socky."

"And who's on Den 2 later, Amy?"

"That's a secret, Socky. But here's a clue – he writes magic books."

"Amy. I know, I know. It's Stevie J and he's your boyfriend, isn't he? And I heard you're getting married at Christmas!"

"Socky!!"

"It's true, isn't it, Amy? Amy?"

THE END

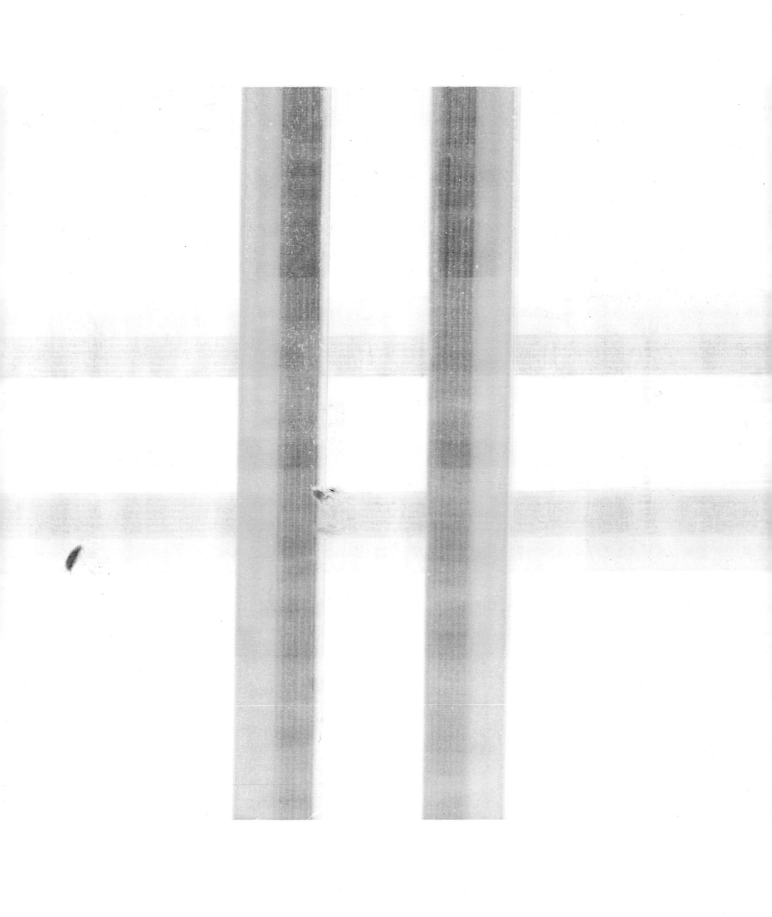

It Had To Be You

This one's for my sisters, Kate and Emma.

Thanks

To all my family and friends, especially Mum and Dad, Kate and Richard; Emma, Peter, Luan and Charlie; Ben, Sam and Amy-Rose; Nicky, Andrew and Tanya.

To my agent Ali Gunne, for her advice and enthusiasm. And to Milly Gosworth for all her help.

To all in Macmillan – especially my editor, Imogen Taylor, David North, Emma Bravo, David Adamson and Trisha Jackson. And to Cormac Kinsella in Repforce.

To Councillor Mary Elliott and Deputy Fiona O'Malley for the invaluable insights into the world of local councillors and Irish politics.

To the staff at Dalkey library, especially Trish Byrne and Niall Brewster for all the help in finding just the books I needed for my research, and for never asking why I desperately needed information on dating, shoes and pregnancy all on the same day!

To all my writing friends – especially Martina Devlin, Martina Murphy, Clare Dowling and all the Irish Girls. It's a pleasure knowing you and thanks for all the fun lunches, dinners, e-mails and phone calls.

To all those in the Irish book trade who have always been so encouraging – especially Tom Owens, Eoin McHugh, David O'Callaghan, Alan Johnson, Maria Dickenson, Cathal Elliot, Bert Wright and all the Eason gang.

And to all the booksellers I met on my last book tour – especially Seamus Duffy in Westport – thanks for all the support and kindness.

And finally to you, the reader. I hope you enjoy reading *It Had To Be You* as much as I enjoyed writing it. I love hearing from my readers so do drop me an e-mail. You can contact me through my website – www.sarahwebb.info.

After writing *It Had To Be You*, my sister, Emma, told me about an area near Greystones, Co. Wicklow called 'The Burnaby'. I've become so attached to my own fictional village, Burnaby Village, that it would break my heart to change it – so Burnaby Village it stays. But, for the record, there's no Happily Ever After in 'The Burnaby', or anywhere else in Ireland for that matter – and more's the pity!

'Make good use of bad rubbish'
Elizabeth Beresford

Chapter 1

Molly

The minute Anita walked through the door of Happily Ever After bookshop that fateful Monday morning, Molly knew that something was up. Although Anita looked perfectly normal – her long red hair tied back in its customary loose chignon, her floor-sweeping black jersey dress clinging in all the wrong, bumpy places – there was a strange expression on her face. Her usual Monday wrinkled brow looked a little less furrowed and her gait was loose and almost girlish, unlike her more normal heavy-footed loaf. She smiled at Molly as soon as she swung open the door, sending the small bell into wild reverberations.

'Hi Molly, how are you this fine morning?'

Molly studied her boss carefully. Was Anita *really* smiling? It suited her: more's the pity that she didn't do it more often.

'Anita. You're early. I wasn't expecting you until lunchtime.'

Although Anita lived in an apartment directly above the bookshop, she wasn't know to be an early riser. She rarely lifted her head from her anti-allergy pillow until after ten, and without exception never made it down the stairs and through the shop door before noon, though she was usually just in time to be taken out to lunch by whichever publisher's rep was currently courting her. Anita was crotchety and ill-tempered at the best of times but she also had an unerring talent for spotting bestsellers. Every day she received at least ten couriered packages or jiffy bags containing manuscripts and proofs from various publishers – some from as far away as America and Canada. She was the best-kept secret in Irish bookselling and, as publishers had been telling her for years, she'd missed her calling as an editor. What they didn't know and what she'd never divulged was that she *had* worked as an editor for a large British publisher many moons ago and the experience had been enough to put her off the publishing business for life.

Anita sniffed. 'Yes, well, I have some news. Where's the other poor unfortunate?'

'In the back going through the Eason's order.'

'I see,' Anita said dreamily.

Molly looked at her carefully – Anita was behaving most strangely this morning.

The bell on the door finally stopped ringing and Molly breathed a sigh of relief, grateful for the peace once again. As if to compensate, Anita picked up a stapler off the counter and began to play with it – pressing it together and watching as closed staples fell uselessly onto the fake pine with whispery rattles.

Molly coughed. Anita looked at her. She knew how much Molly hated her fidgeting. They'd had many minor arguments about it over the past few years. Molly had been working in Anita's bookshop for nearly six years now – ever since she'd left college – progressing from lowly part-time assistant to the lofty heights of shop manager. She and Anita were like chalk and cheese and it was amazing that they hadn't killed each other yet.

Molly brushed the wasted staples onto her right hand and dropped them purposefully into the bin under the counter. She resisted the temptation to pull out the duster to polish the fake pine. It was only ten o'clock after all and they'd only just opened. Not even one greasy customer fingerprint to warrant such action yet.

'Felix came in especially early this morning to get the new orders processed,' Molly said. Felix was the other full-time staff member. 'It's really busy at the moment what with the Rosemary Hamilton reading and the Book Club meeting, both on the same day.' She looked at Anita pointedly.

Anita ignored her and instead picked up yesterday's copy of the *Sunday Ireland* newspaper and began to flick through it. Molly sighed and went back to cutting up *The Times* book pages, continuing her usual Monday morning review selection for the bookshop's large notice board. Anita had booked Rosemary to read and sign, forgetting that it would clash with the Book Club, which met religiously on the first Saturday morning of every month. And by the time Molly had realized the mistake, it had been too late to cancel Rosemary's event. Meaning yet more work for Molly. Still, she was looking forward to meeting the popular American writer.

Rosemary Hamilton was starting to break through in Ireland and the UK. She wrote big, generous, kind-hearted romantic sagas, exactly the kind of books that both Anita and Molly liked to read. It was one of the few things that they actually had in common. Rosemary had been described as an 'American Maeve Binchy' and there had been terrific response to the event which they'd advertised in the local press and which had been picked up by some of the nationals, even the *Irish Daily* who weren't exactly renowned for their love of romantic fiction.

Anita Vickers had opened Happily Ever After to cater for readers like herself – voracious readers of popular fiction, especially romantic fiction, thrillers and crime novels. And although the shop had a decidedly female slant, including its very own pink-couched 'Romance Room' packed full of all kinds of women's fiction from Mills and Boon to Jane Austen, they also had many loyal male customers who travelled to Burnaby

Village, to find books by their favourite American crime writers which were difficult to come by in mainstream bookshops.

Happily Ever After was just off Burnaby's main street, tucked between Coffee Heaven, and Slick Harry's – Irish floral-design legend Harry Masterson's shop which specialized in unusual plants and shrubs and catered to the well-heeled market. Burnaby Village, nestled on the south Dublin coast, was a Mecca for shoppers with a taste for the unusual. Hidden within its windy, cobbled laneways was the tiny yet perfectly formed print and art gallery, Halo; Presents of Mind, a gift shop crammed full of all kinds of delights including a miniature stone Buddha carved from pink, black and white marble; funky American cloth bags decorated with Andy Warholesque prints for the discerning grocery shopper; not to mention Baroque, the uber-trendy shoe emporium stocking everything from Converse and Camper, to Gina and Jimmy Choo.

The bell rang and Molly looked up. Their first customer of the day.

'Morning.' She smiled at the tall, white-haired woman.

'Hello. Have you got the new Ivy White book? I believe it came out today.'

'You might be in luck. We've just received an order of new titles and it should be in one of the boxes. Let me check for you.'

'Thanks,' the woman said gratefully. 'I'm going on my holidays today and I was hoping to take it with me.' Molly went into the back room to find it for her.

'It's good,' said Anita thoughtfully while the customer waited. 'She writes wonderfully about affairs of the heart, don't you think?'

'Yes.' The woman nodded. 'Quite.'

Molly came out smiling, holding the spanking-new book out in front of her. 'Here we are. The very first copy. We haven't even priced it yet.'

After the woman left, happily swinging her dark pink

Happily Ever After bag by her side, Molly looked at Anita. 'What were you saying about having news? I got distracted by a scathing review of Paddy O'Hara's new thriller.'

'I'm not surprised, it was very harsh indeed,' said Anita. 'And completely undeserved, poor man.'

'Your news?' Molly pressed.

'Ah, yes. I was just coming to that. Can you get Felix?'

'Can't you tell me first? Please.'

'Of course.' Anita smiled easily, unnerving Molly yet again. 'I've just sold the shop.'

'You've what?' Molly stared at her incredulously.

'Sold the shop.'

'You can't have.'

'Ah, but I did.'

'To who?'

'To whom, you mean?'

'Anita!' Molly was reeling with shock and didn't need a lesson in grammar right now.

The bell on the door rang again and Molly cursed inwardly. This was unbelievable. Anita *was* Happily Ever After, the bookshop wouldn't exist without her. And Anita almost wouldn't exist without the shop – the shop was her whole life.

Molly heard a discreet cough. Anita was staring at her. Patricia Simons, the Trinity publisher's sales rep was standing in front of them, glammed up to the teeth as usual in a perfectly-pressed navy suit with cream and red pipe-edging, a dazzling sheen on her immaculately bobbed blonde hair and her lips painted a perfect rosebud pink. 'Penny for them,' Patricia smiled.

Molly looked at Anita's face which somewhat unnervingly wasn't betraying any emotion at all, and back at Patricia. 'Sorry, I was miles away,' she said. 'Anita just told me some rather surprising news.'

'Oh, really?' Patricia's eyes lit up. She loved news, and she loved being the purveyor of it to all her customers. Nothing like a juicy bit of gossip, ahem, news to make the day go a little faster.

Anita glared at Molly. Had Molly taken leave of her senses? Telling Patricia anything guaranteed that it would be all over town in the blink of an eye. Bush fires had nothing on this publisher's rep.

'Well?' Patricia tapped her red nails on the counter-top impatiently.

Molly could feel the heat of Anita's stare and chose to ignore it. She wasn't stupid – she knew exactly how big Patricia's mouth was and she had no intention of telling the woman anything. She just wanted to make Anita sweat. 'Harry Masterson is thinking of opening a lap dancing club in the basement of Slick Harry's. What do you think of that?'

'Really?' Patricia asked with unabashed interest. 'But that's just beside you. It could bring in some interesting new business, I suppose.'

Molly laughed. 'Could do. But I'm only joking! Harry isn't exactly the lap dancing type.'

Patricia frowned. Molly often poked fun at her expense and she didn't like it one little bit. She sniffed. 'He's a business man though. It wouldn't be the worst idea in the world.'

'Would you like some coffee?' Anita interrupted. She knew there was no love lost between the two women.

'Love some,' Patricia smiled gratefully. 'But why don't we pop next door? My treat. I have a manuscript that I'd love you to read. A young Irish author straight out of college that Trinity's looking at acquiring.'

Anita looked at Molly who shrugged her shoulders. 'We'll have that meeting as soon as I get back,' promised Anita. 'I won't be long.'

'Fine. I have plenty to be getting on with.' Molly turned

towards Patricia. 'Are we doing the order for the December new titles today?'

'I'll do the order with Anita if that's all right. There's nothing of much importance, to tell the truth. December is a pretty dead month for us.'

'Fine,' Molly said curtly. It was her job to order the new titles for the shop from the sales reps and Patricia knew this. Patricia was no fool. The experienced rep knew she'd get a far larger order than was strictly necessary from Anita – who always got carried away in the face of glossy new fiction titles and blew their budget for the month with one single publisher. Which was precisely why Anita and Molly had agreed years ago that Molly would do all the 'front list' or new title ordering.

As soon as Anita and Patricia had left the shop Molly picked up the phone and dialled nine for an outside line.

'Paige? Pick up if you're there. It's Molly.'

Paige, a Burnaby County Councillor and Molly's best friend, was notorious for screening her calls. She said it was a necessity in her business when all the local nutters had both her work and home numbers and were likely to call at all hours of the day to complain about anything that took their fancy – from blocked drains and leaking pipes, to noisy neighbours and dog poo on the streets.

'Hi, Molly. How are you this fine morning?'

'Do you have me on speaker phone again?'

'No.'

'You do, don't you?'

'Well yes, but I'm in the middle of typing a document and . . .'

'No buts. I demand your 100 per cent concentration. It's important.'

Paige picked up the receiver. 'OK, you have it. Now what's up?'

'I can't believe you never told me about Anita selling the shop.'

'Happily Ever After?'

'Yes! What other shop would I be talking about?' snapped Molly.

'Keep your shirt on. I didn't know. I would have told you if I'd heard anything.'

'But you know everything about Burnaby!' Molly protested. 'That's your job.'

'And you're sure she's sold it?'

'Yes! She told me herself only a few minutes ago.'

'Why didn't you ask her who she sold it to then?' Paige said trying not to sound condescending. She regretted the question as soon as she'd asked it.

'I would have if she hadn't left the building. She's gone out for coffee with Patricia Simons who walked in as soon as Anita had broken the news to me, bloody nuisance of a woman. And she'll be gone for a while I imagine. I'm dying of curiosity here. I thought you might be able to put me out of my misery.'

Paige sighed. 'I'm sorry I can't be more help. It must have been a private sale. But it seems a bit out of the blue. Two weeks ago she was telling me about her plans for the October events. Is she selling it as a going concern?'

'A what?' Molly was confused.

'You know – will it still be trading as a bookshop?'

'Goodness, I hadn't even thought of that.' Molly sat down on the stool behind the counter and began to run her left fingers up and down the coiled flex nervously. 'You mean the new owners might close the shop? And I might lose my job? I'm hardly qualified to do anything else. That would be terrible. What would I do?'

'Stop right there,' commanded Paige. 'There's no point worrying about things that may never happen. Anita's no fool. There's no way she'll see you out in the street – or Felix for that matter. Talk to her as soon as she comes back. I'm sure she'll put your mind at rest.'

'You're probably right. But what if . . .'

'Molly!'

'Sorry. Listen, I'd better go. I can see a customer approaching out the window.'

'Ring me when you've talked to Anita.'

'OK.'

'Promise?'

'Promise.'

'And Molly?'

'Yes.'

'Stop worrying. I'm sure your job is safe.'

The bell on the shop door rang, interrupting their conversation.

'I'll try. I have to go.' Molly put down the phone and smiled at the man in front of her. 'Hello, how can I help you?'

'Are you Molly?'

She studied the short, shiny-headed man in front of her. He was wearing an expensive-looking black wool polo neck and dark brown cords and as he held out his hand, a heavy gold bracelet slid down his wrist towards his hairy hand. She nodded. How on earth did this stranger know her name?

'Yes, how can I help you?'

'I'm Milo Devine, the new owner of this shop, since you ask. And the question is – how can I help *you*?'

Molly stared at him without saying a word. She could feel the blood drain from her face and her palms began to feel cold and clammy.

'Are you all right?' Milo asked with concern. 'You seem a little pale.'

'Um, yes, fine,' she mumbled.

'I'm sorry, my dear, has Anita not told you about me?'

Molly shook her head. 'No. Not a word.'

'Ah, I see.' He looked a little embarrassed. 'Maybe I should have waited . . . but still, now that I'm here, why don't you show me around? Tell me about the kind of books you stock. I'm not much of an expert on romance I must admit, but I have seen *Gone With the Wind*.'

Molly had been decidedly unsettled by Milo's unannounced visit and, in Anita's continued absence, had rung her friend Paige again to discuss it. Paige had sighed, saved her half-written document on the computer and picked up the receiver. Molly gave her a description of the man – gold chains, wide Hollywood smiles and all – and told her what he'd said in one breathless gasp.

'Milo Devine, first of all, what kind of name is that?' Paige scoffed when she'd heard the details. 'Sounds like a dodgy American detective.'

Molly laughed. 'It does rather, I suppose, but he's actually Irish. He gives me the creeps to be honest. He reminds me of a wide-boy car salesman – all smiles and platitudes but always on the make. I have a bad feeling about him, Paige, I really do. He mentioned a few of his plans for the shop, but it's what he didn't say that I'm worried about.'

'When's Anita back?' asked Paige looking at her watch and biting her lip. Much as she loved talking to Molly she really did have rather a lot of work to do today.

'Soon, I hope. I have a lot of questions to ask her.' The bell rang again. 'Damn, I have to go.'

'Ring me later,' Paige insisted. 'But not for about an hour if you don't mind, I have to get this bloody document finished before lunchtime. This is better than *EastEnders*. I'm dying to hear more.'

'Excuse me. Have you seen my dad?' a deep, treacle-rich voice asked Molly as soon as she'd put the receiver down.

Molly looked up. This day was getting stranger and stranger. There in front of her was the face of an angel – a rugged, no-shoes and dirty-faced kind of angel, but an angel nonetheless.

His dark blonde hair hung in messy curls around his strong square face. Molly had read about 'chiseled cheekbones' in many of her romantic novels but she'd never come face to face with them in real life. His must have been carved by Michelangelo – they were that sharp and that perfect. One of his front teeth was slightly chipped and his full dark-pink lips were lopsided – all adding to his attraction in Molly's eyes.

Stop staring and say something, she told herself.

'Um, your dad?' Brilliant, Molly, just brilliant. Inspired.

'Milo Devine?' The man smiled. 'I was supposed to meet him in here but I'm running a bit late.' He coughed nervously and glanced at his watch. 'Well, very late actually.'

The new owner's son. This was all she needed. 'He was here but he left a while ago,' Molly said. 'Sorry.'

'I see. I'm Sam. And you are . . . ?'

'Oh, sorry.' She could feel hot prickles running up the back of her neck and spreading towards her cheeks. 'I'm Molly,' she managed eventually. 'Molly Harper. I'm the manager.'

'Ah, yes, of course. I've heard all about you from Anita.' He smiled again.

Molly noticed that the pocket on his dark blue shirt was torn and had an irrational urge to touch it, and an even more irrational urge to offer to take it home and mend it. What was happening to her?

'This must all have come as a bit of a surprise to you – the shop being sold and everything,' he said kindly.

She nodded. 'Yes.'

'But Dad's only going to make one or two minor changes. And I'll just slot in – you'll see. You won't even notice me. Of course I'll need your help at first – I've never run a bookshop before. But I'm sure I'll get the hang of it quickly enough.'

Molly felt decidedly faint. What did he mean – run a bookshop? She was the manager here. Did he not know that? She'd had enough. Was no one going to tell her anything? Wait until she got her hands on Anita, she'd had an emotional roller coaster of a morning thanks to her.

'Have I said something wrong?' He looked at Molly carefully. She was staring at him and her large blue eyes seemed to be swimming with moisture.

A large tear dropped from her right eye and twinkled down her cheek. She wiped it off swiftly with the back of her hand, mortified. 'Sorry,' she murmured. 'Something in my eye. Excuse me.' She brushed past him, pushed open the door at the back of the shop and stepped through it.

Felix looked over. He was sitting outside the back door catching a few surreptitious rays of morning sun.

He stood up quickly. 'Are you all right, Molly? I'm just waiting for the Macmillan delivery. The driver rang to say he was on his way.'

'I'm fine, thanks. I don't want to disturbed.' Molly walked past him and into the office, closing the door behind her.

Felix shrugged his shoulders and sat back down. He'd been working in the bookshop for almost five years now, so was well used to Molly and knew to keep out of her way when she was angry or upset. After a moment, he heard a knock on the door which led on to the shop floor. 'Hello, is anyone there? Molly?' A tall figure walked through the doorway and blinked in the brightness. Felix stood up again. 'Can I help you?'

'Do you know where Molly went?' the man asked.

Felix gestured towards the wide open back door. 'She went out, mate,' he lied smoothly. 'Gone to get a coffee, I'd say. I'm just on my way in to look after the shop. Can I help you?'

'No, never mind,' he said. 'Tell her Sam said goodbye.'

'Sam. Sure thing.'

Sam turned swiftly on his heels, took one last lingering look at the dark pink bookshelves and left the shop, the bell ringing loudly behind him.

As soon as Molly heard the bell she gingerly opened the office door a slit. 'Is he gone?' she asked Felix in a low voice.

'Sam?'

'Yes.'

Felix nodded. 'He said to say goodbye.'

'Thanks,' she said. What a relief. The tears had stopped just as soon as they'd started and she felt stupid. It was just a reaction to the sudden news, she told herself, nothing to worry about, just shock. She still felt a little funny though.

'I'll look after the shop for a while,' Felix said, noticing the slightly manic look in her red-rimmed eyes. 'You stay in the office. I'm sure you have work to do.'

'Thanks.' She smiled gratefully. Felix never asked questions, that was one of the reasons she liked him so much. A silver-haired early retiree from the civil service who had got bored at home, he'd been working in Happily Ever After for almost as long as she had, pottering along at his slow yet solid pace, getting everything done and rarely making a mistake.

Half an hour later Anita opened the door of the office and found Molly rifling through one of the drawers of the tall grey filing cabinet – the top drawer where Anita kept all her private papers.

Anita coughed quietly. Molly jumped.

'I was just looking for . . .' Molly began and then stopped.

'For what?' prompted Anita.

Think of something, Molly willed herself. Anything. She couldn't – her mind had gone completely blank. 'I was looking for information about the sale,' she said truthfully. 'About Milo and his son. About my job.' She stared at the dark blue carpet tiles, bit her lip and willed the tears away. Could this day get any worse?

Anita put her hand on Molly's shoulder. 'I'm so sorry,' she said. 'Sam rang my mobile and left a message. He was worried that he might have upset you.'

Molly pushed her back against the drawer, sending it clattering home. 'When were you going to tell me about the new owner?'

'This morning,' Anita said gently. 'You know that. Milo just pre-empted me, that's all. He's quite . . . um, how will I put this?'

'Pushy?' Molly suggested.

'Not exactly the word I was going to use. Forthright I suppose.'

'Pushy,' Molly said again.

Anita ignored her. 'His son seems nice though – Sam. Did you like him?'

'Sam, the new manager, you mean?' Molly glared at her.

'Is that what he told you?'

Molly nodded silently.

'I see. You'd better sit down.' Anita waved at the sofa opposite the desk.

Molly did as requested.

'Sam will be working here with you. You will be the Book Manager – in charge of everything to do with the books and the events – just as you are now. Sam will do what I've been doing – staff rotas, holidays, the accounts, tax returns, that kind of thing. His official title will be Shop Manager, but it doesn't mean he's over you. Not at all. Milo promised me that we'd all keep our jobs and that the shop would stay as it always has been with one or two minor changes, nothing drastic, he promised.'

'We?' asked Molly. 'Are you staying?'

'Yes, I'll be working at the weekends and on Thursday evenings. Just to keep my hand in. And I'll still be living upstairs so you'll see me all the time. Now do you feel any better? I'm so sorry you've had such a stressful morning, my dear. I didn't mean for it all to come out this way.'

'I understand. But you should have told me earlier.'

'I know.'

Molly cocked her head to one side. 'One more question. Why did you sell to him?'

'He offered me a good price,' said Anita honestly. 'He's taken early retirement and has always wanted to own a bookshop in the area.'

'And?'

'And what?'

'Don't give me that, Anita. There must be another reason. You love this place.'

'No other reason, honestly.'

'There is, and I know it. And if you won't tell me I'll find out anyway.'

Anita smiled. 'You'll be disappointed.'

'We'll see.'

'Feeling better now?' Anita asked. She put her hand on Molly's shoulder and gave it an affectionate squeeze.

'Yes,' Molly said. 'Much better. But please tell Felix before Milo or Sam get to him, OK?'

'I'll tell him right now.' Anita smiled. 'I promise.'

Chapter 2

Kate

Kate looked up, sipping her lukewarm coffee and saw the man she assumed to be her new client, Angus Cawley. He'd described himself on paper as 'tall and dapper, with an eclectic dress sense'. Eclectic, she thought, looking him up and down, more like downright bad. He was wearing what she presumed were once black jeans but which had now turned an unsavoury shade of greeny-grey, a grey cotton polo neck and the pièce de résistance – a black silk waistcoat decorated with what looked like bright red cherries. To top it all he was also wearing red suede brothel creepers on his large feet and some of his hair was greased back in a type of poor man's duck's-ass, the rest falling lankly around his face. Kate sighed. She had her work cut out for her with this one.

Kate had been running 'Dublin Dummy Dates' ('Dummy Dates' for short) for over six months now and it hadn't been quite the 'nice little earner' she'd imagined when she'd set it up. In fact, most days it was downright disheartening – there were a lot of sad lost male souls out there all too in need of her services. After an initial consultation, like this morning's meeting, she took men out on dummy dates and put them through their paces – from grooming and clothes, to conversational openers (otherwise known as 'chat-up lines') and learning to listen without interrupting – building their confidence and preparing them for future 'real' dates. Many of the men on her books had gone on to have successful 'real' dates and one, Ken, had even announced an engagement a month after meeting his 'ideal woman', a dog groomer from Rialto, which, although it had been cancelled after three weeks, still counted as an engagement (on Kate's promotional blurb anyway).

Her plan had been to start the company, get it running smoothly and then fade back into a purely administrative role, allowing her hand-picked employees to deal with the actual dates. But herein lay the problem. The company hadn't actually made enough money for Kate to employ anyone, so she'd ended up taking out all the clients herself, which wasn't exactly ideal. Alex and Matty O'Connor, the sibling owners of Coffee Heaven where she held most of the initial meetings with the prospective dates, thought she was some sort of compulsive man-eater until Kate had explained what her work entailed.

In the afternoons and on Saturdays, too, Kate worked in Baroque, the local designer shoe shop, but mornings and evenings she turned into Ms Dummy Date. She advertised her services in the local newspaper, *Burnaby People*, and in several Dublin magazines. The phone hadn't stopped hopping from the second week on after she'd appeared on the Brenda Jackson morning radio show talking about her services. Brenda had been intrigued and had sent her intrepid reporter Missie O'Donaghue along on a dummy date with Kate and one of her clients – a rather showy man from Howth called Bryan – 'Bryan with a y, mind, not an i, mind'. Bryan had turned out to be a compulsive liar, the most sexist man either woman had ever encountered and was basically a lost cause. Awful as he was, he had made compulsive radio listening and the company had gained the best free nationwide advertising ever. After the show, Kate had been interviewed by *Sunday Ireland*, the *Irish News* and the *Dublin People*.

She raised her hand and waved at her new client who was looking around the coffee shop anxiously. He caught her eye and smiled. Kate smiled back. He made his way towards her, tripping over a buggy and slopping a mug of coffee all over a table. 'Sorry,' he murmured to the owner of the coffee who was glaring at him.

Kate tried not to sigh. An awkward, socially inept specimen – she'd seen it all before. He probably had a stutter or a stammer and voted Green Party to boot. Stop it! She chastised herself. That's not nice. You are here to help this man, not to make fun of him. Just because you had a disagreement with Trina already this morning doesn't mean you can take it out on this poor individual, even if he is pathetic.

Trina was the rich and rather batty owner of Baroque whose taste in shoes was, as Kate liked to say rather crudely, 'up her ass', and who couldn't tell a Manolo Blahnik from a Gina Couture – quite a failing in a designer shoe buyer. She had far more money than sense and Kate was convinced that Trina's husband, Dublin and London property magnate Farrell de Barra, only bankrolled the shop to keep his darling wife out of his hair and away from his office. Trina ran the shop with the help of her 'VBF', Cathy Philips, another trophy wife, married to snooker hall and leisure plex owner 'Flames' Philips. Unlike Trina, who was Burnaby old-money born and bred, Cathy was from Limerick and had worked as an Aer Lingus air hostess for three years before serving 'Flames' champagne on a memorable trans-Atlantic trip. He'd whisked her away from her life in green, but after two children ('Axel', boy and 'Lolita', girl) she'd decided she needed to get out of the house more and going into cahoots, otherwise known as 'business' with Trina seemed like a good idea at the time.

Shoes, after 'Flames', were Cathy's great passion – and the

more expensive the better. Kate had no complaints about Cathy's taste, it was Trina who had chosen the bright orange '70s inspired wedge sandals and the chunky 'Bjork' inspired white tap dancers with the thick dark brown heels and soles for this season, when all their customers were clamouring for was sexy dark pink stiletto sandals and neat '50s peep-toes with kitten heels.

Angus stuck out his hand in front of her face. 'Kate, I presume? Sorry I'm late.'

'Not to worry. Please sit down. I've ordered you a coffee.'

He pulled the chair back from the table, catching the back legs on the wooden floor with a loud dragging noise. 'Sorry. I'm a bit nervous.'

'No need to be.' Kate said kindly. 'I'm here to help you. Think of me as your sister.'

'I haven't got a sister,' he admitted as he sat down.

'Your aunt then.'

He shook his head again.

This man was beginning to annoy her and he'd only just arrived. 'Your mother then.' She fixed a smile on her face. 'You have one of them, don't you?'

Angus looked down at the table. 'I did. She died last year.'

Kate's heart sank. Please let him not be a crier, she pleaded. I couldn't deal with that today.

'But she was a great woman,' he continued looking up and smiling back.

'You have nice eyes,' she said, studying him properly for the first time. His quiff had collapsed, dark brown hair tumbled shapelessly around his face. His steel-rimmed Germanic glasses did nothing for him, but his dark brown eyes shone brightly and intelligently from his slightly sallow skin. Maybe Angus wasn't going to be such a difficult nut to crack after all. She glanced at her watch and jotted down the time at the top of her foolscap sheet. 'Bang on quarter past ten – let's get started shall we?'

'Fine.'

Alex arrived at the table with a large mug of coffee and placed it on the table in front of Angus. Terminally nosy, she always enjoyed having a look at Kate's latest client. 'Enjoy,' said Alex looking him up and down. She wasn't impressed. Too skinny and what was with that hair?

'Thanks,' he said, oblivious to Alex's critical gaze.

'Thanks, Alex,' added Kate.

Alex lingered within hearing distance, flicking a cloth ineffectually at the table beside them and rearranging the milk jug and sugar bowl several times. But Kate was having none of it. She waited patiently until Alex had sniffed audibly and retreated into the kitchen, allowing Angus to take a few calming sips of his coffee before continuing. She promised her clients absolute confidentiality and that was what she gave them.

'I just need to get one or two details from you before we begin our session,' she said poising her pen at the top of the page. 'How old are you, Angus, if you don't mind me asking?'

'Not at all,' he said. 'I'm twenty-nine.'

'Really?' she raised her eyebrows. Her clients had a habit of stretching the truth a little and he looked a lot younger than that.

'OK,' he admitted, 'I'm twenty-six. But I much prefer women who are a few years older than me, so I usually say twenty-nine just to be on the safe side.'

Kate looked him in the eye. 'Let's get this straight from the very start. I'm here to help you. You're paying me to be honest with you. The process won't work unless you tell me the truth – do you understand?'

He nodded. 'Yes, I'm sorry, I understand, really. Please continue.'

She tried not to laugh. He really did look rather contrite; his head hung low, almost disappearing into his shoulders and his hands were clasped on the table in front of him.

'Do you work?' she continued.

'Yes, um, well no.'

'Which is it – yes or no?'

'I'm not sure. I went back to college to take my teaching diploma which I've nearly finished. I'm working part-time in a primary school at the moment as work experience – does that count as work or not?'

'Yes, I guess so. Are you training to be a primary school teacher?'

He nodded sheepishly.

'You're embarrassed by this?' she asked.

'A little.'

'Why?'

He shrugged his shoulders. 'Not very manly is it – teaching four- and five-year-olds?'

'I don't know,' Kate said thoughtfully, 'some women like men with a sensitive side. It's a very useful job and you're obviously not in it for the money.' She looked him in the eye. 'Why are you in it exactly?'

He held her gaze for a few minutes and then looked away. 'My mother was a primary school teacher. I like children and I think I'll be a good teacher. I know it's not very fashionable and to be honest, I get more than my fair share of snide comments from people who don't know me, which frankly I find a little upsetting. Implying . . . well, things.'

'I can imagine,' Kate said. She was ashamed that she'd been thinking along the same lines herself. 'I'm sorry, but I need to get to know you a little so that I can help you.'

'I understand. But honestly, I want to be a teacher for all the right reasons. Trust me.'

Something in those eyes made her believe him without

question. She scribbled some preliminary notes on the foolscap pad. In this job, her two years studying psychology in UCD came in extremely useful – not that she could remember many of the technical terms. *Training to be primary school teacher*, she jotted down. *Wears heart on sleeve. Over sincere? Could be a problem. Too intense? Scaring women away? Mother complex? Oedipus thingy?*

'What are you writing?' asked Angus.

'Just notes, nothing for you to worry about.'

'I'll stop trying to read upside down, then.'

She smiled. 'Yes. Better not to. Where are you studying?'

'Trinity College.'

'And your last date was?'

'Excuse me?'

'Your last date – when was it exactly?'

'That's a bit personal isn't it?'

'Angus, it's only me you're talking to.' She lowered her voice. 'Kate from 'Dummy Dates', remember? I'm not here to judge you. I'm just trying to help, honestly.'

'Sorry,' he murmured. 'I know. OK, it was last year.'

'Can you give me some of the details? How do you feel it went?'

'Terribly. We had nothing to talk about and halfway through the meal she excused herself to go to the Ladies.' He stared at his hands.

'And?' Kate asked gently.

'She never came back. I waited for half an hour and then left. I never saw her again.'

'Right,' Kate said a little more brightly than she'd intended. 'That does happen. Two of my other clients have had exactly the same experience. One in a cinema and one in Wales.'

'In Wales?'

'Yep. They went over to Wales on the ferry to spend a romantic weekend in a hotel. My client's date excused herself while they were having a drink in the hotel bar and Bob's your uncle.'

'What happened?' he asked with interest.

'She'd gone upstairs, packed her bag and got the last ferry back to Dublin.'

'No!'

'Honestly. He was devastated. Poor man.'

'I can imagine.'

'But he got over it. In fact he got engaged to a lovely girl only two months later.'

'Really?'

'Yes, really. So, you see, there's hope for you all.' She thought it prudent not to mention that the engagement had been broken after only a few weeks.

Angus considered this for a brief moment. 'For us all, you mean?'

'No, for you all. All my clients.'

'Have you already found your own true love then?' he asked.

'My own true love?' she repeated slowly. She had a right one on her hands here.

'Yes, you know, your soulmate.'

Kate smiled indulgently. 'Let's crack on, shall we?'

'Maybe you'll tell me later?'

She raised her eyebrows and ignored him. 'Can you tell me a little about your previous dating history? Before the one who did the legger.'

'OK, point taken. We're here to talk about me not you, right?'

She nodded curtly. 'Dating history?'

'Right, well, there hasn't been a huge amount of it to tell the truth. I find it very difficult to talk to women. I tend to get nervous and clam up.'

'You're talking to me,' she pointed out.

'But that's different. You told me to pretend I was talking to my mother.'

'True. Sorry, continue.'

'There was Sandy in school, we went out for two weeks just before the debs. She was in the Computer Club with me.'

'And what happened?'

'She dumped me at the debs for a guy from the debating team. Then there was Dina.'

'Dina? Tell me about her?'

'She was from Bangor. I studied Computer Science in college and I met her there. We were together for two years. Dina was special.'

His voice became wistful and Kate allowed him time to collect his thoughts.

'She married my best friend last summer. I'd asked him to keep an eye on her while I was in Germany for two months working on my Master's. I never believed he'd betray me like that. Anyway he did and after that, there was the legger woman as you called her and that's about it.'

Let down and hurt badly by friend and ex-girlfriend ('Dina'), Kate jotted down, *self-esteem problems?, honest, seems sincere.*

'Thank you for sharing that with me,' she said, putting down her foolscap pad. 'And now can I ask you – what are you looking for in a woman? What qualities do you find important?'

Angus considered for a moment. 'Honesty,' he began hesitantly. 'I'd like someone I can trust, and someone kind. She'd have to like children, I guess, and have a big heart. Someone a bit pretty maybe, but I'm not too bothered.'

'You said you liked older women?'

Angus shrugged his shoulders. 'I don't know why I said that to tell the truth. I just thought someone a little older might be less inclined to judge me and might accept me for who I am.'

'And is that important to you – acceptance?'

'Of course, isn't that what everyone wants – to be accepted and loved for who they are?'

'I suppose so.'

He stared at the table and then looked up again. 'This isn't how I thought it would be, you know.'

'What?' she asked.

'You, I suppose. All this. I thought you'd just give me some hints on how to dress and some killer chat-up lines.'

'But you could get that from a book or a magazine. I try to get a little deeper, get down to the root of the problem.'

'And what's my problem, Doctor?'

'I'm not sure yet,' she said honestly. 'You seem a very decent young man and . . .'

'Why did you call me that?'

'What?'

'Young man? You can't be much older than me.'

'I don't know why,' she replied. 'I don't suppose I am.'

'To establish professional distance?' he suggested.

'Maybe.'

'What age are you anyway?' he said. 'If you don't mind me asking.'

'Actually I do. And as I keep reminding you, I'm not the one we're here to talk about, am I?'

'Sorry, I just find other people far more interesting than myself, I guess.'

'So do I. But I get paid for finding out about other people and you don't. So let's move on.' She glanced at her watch. 'We only have another ten minutes before this session is over.'

'What's next?'

'I'm going to advise you on your appearance and then we're going to set up a dummy date so that I can get a feel for how you behave on a first date. Then I'll give you a full report with some recommendations.'

'And then?'

'It's up to you to use the information I've supplied.'

'And will the dummy date be with you?'

'I'll have to check my diary. I think all my employees are pretty much booked up for the next few weeks. I presume you'd like the date as soon as possible?'

'Yes.'

'Well then it will be me all right.'

'Good.' He smiled.

'So, appearance,' she said trying to veer the conversation back onto safer ground. 'What do you think women like men to wear?'

'I'd say they like them to look smart and coordinated. And clean,' he added as an afterthought.

'Good. And what type of clothes do you wear generally?'

'This kind of thing,' he said gesturing to his chest. 'Although I keep this waistcoat for special occasions. Normally it's just the polo neck or maybe a checked shirt.'

'I see.' Kate bit the top of her pen.

'You don't approve of the waistcoat, do you?'

'No.'

'Why not?'

'Honestly?'

He nodded.

'It's too loud. And not very fashionable.'

'Oh. Mum made it for me. It's my lucky waistcoat.'

'Right.' She could hardly tell him how awful it was now.

'If I said it was a post-modernist joke would I get away with it?' He tilted his head to the side.

'Not really.'

'I see. I won't wear it again then.'

'I didn't say that. Just don't wear it on the first date, OK?'

'Understood. And how about the shoes? You don't like them either, do you?'

'Truthfully?'

He nodded again.

'No, I think they're terrible,' she said.

'They're going in the bin then. I've no major attachment to them and besides they're not all that comfortable. What about the jeans?' He looked at her face. She was wrinkling her nose slightly. 'Another no-no. So give it to me straight – what should I be wearing?'

'On a first date you want to look smart yet not too formal. Clean, classic, ironed clothes always impress. As you're twenty-six I'd suggest something fashionable but not too over the top. Think Next or TopMan rather than cutting edge. A nice white shirt, a pair of jeans that fit properly – Levis, or something like that, not cheap chain store jeans, girls hate them; brown or black boots, and, if the budget will stretch to it, a nice simple well-made leather or suede jacket. And you'll need to get a haircut and maybe think of changing the frames of your glasses for something less severe.'

Angus whistled. 'Serious make-over stuff. I'm way off the mark, aren't I, Kate?'

'Just a little,' she admitted.

'And does all that really make a difference – the haircut and the clothes?'

'Yes, it really does. Most people judge on first appearances whether they admit to it or not. It can make or break a first date.'

'Well, I'll have a go. I have jeans that might be OK and runners, are runners acceptable?'

'Not really. They can be a bit scruffy.'

'I think the budget might just about stretch to a pair of boots and a haircut. I have a white shirt – I'll get it pressed in the dry cleaners. And I have contacts instead of the glasses, should I wear those?'

'Definitely.'

'Then I'm pretty much set.' He smiled widely. 'This is going to change my life, Kate, I can feel it in my bones.'

'Great. Your time's up, I'm afraid. When would you like your dummy date?'

'How about next Wednesday night?'

'Fine.'

'Where would you suggest?'

'It's usually best to go somewhere casual on the first date. I wouldn't always suggest dinner, unless you're confident that you can eat and talk without getting too nervous. Women do like to be taken out to dinner but sometimes a drink can be a little less intimidating for you both. Arrange it for the early evening – say sevenish – and if you're getting on well with your date you can always suggest dinner after the drink. Or maybe she'll even suggest it – if she's interested.'

'And how will I know that?'

'I'll explain how to read the signs on the dummy date.'

'Great. So how about seven in O'Connor's pub on Wednesday?'

'Perfect. I look forward to it.'

'Really?'

She smiled at him. 'Sure. Now I'm afraid I have a lunch appointment so you'll have to excuse me.'

'A date?'

'Angus!' She laughed. Maybe she should try setting him up with Alex – they were as bad as each other.

'Sorry.' He stood up and held out his hand.

She took it in hers and shook it. His grip was surprisingly firm. 'Bye, Kate. See you on Wednesday.'

'See you.' She watched as he walked towards the door, managing to reach it safely and without incident this time.

Alex buzzed over to Kate's table as soon as he'd left. 'Well, what's he like?'

'As always, Alex, I'm afraid I can't tell you. Client

confidentiality and all that. But I would like a Chicken Caesar Salad and a fresh cup of coffee, thanks.'

Alex sniffed. 'Fine,' she said and flounced away.

Kate reached into her bag and fished out her *Irish Times*. She loved Thursday's edition – the property pages and the new film reviews – lots to interest her. She began to read about a bijoux cottage in Burnaby, which sounded about as big as a shoebox, which was selling for over three hundred thousand euro. She'd never be able to afford to buy in Burnaby at this rate. The townhouse she shared with Molly was tiny and they spent the whole time trying not to get under each other's feet – which was difficult as there wasn't even enough room to pass comfortably in the hall and they shared a tiny shower-room. Damn, she remembered, I promised Molly I'd get a new bulb. The bathroom had no window and they'd been having showers by candle light for the last two days – romantic but not very practical. She got on well with her housemate but sometimes Molly could be a little anal about cleanliness and tidiness. It was best just to keep out of her way when she was on one of her regular 'spring, summer, autumn or winter' cleaning sprees.

Kate had arrived back in Dublin nearly a year ago, after ten years living and working in Boston. But that was all in the past. Her new life lay in Burnaby – making enough money to buy a house in the area that felt like home, near her beloved Granny Lily. She got on fine with her mum and dad who had moved to Connemara after her dad had retired, but it was Lily who she'd always felt closest to. Her parents had had a rather tempestuous marriage when Kate was growing up, and she had loved staying in her granny's peaceful and cosy Burnaby house, away from her parents' continuous arguments and shouting matches. Her father, Billy, had always been a bit of a bully, with a furious temper, which had mellowed with age, thank goodness, and Cleo, his wife and Kate's mum, had walked out on him several times over the years. But she always came back and they'd stayed together, mainly for their daughter's sake. Now, in their early sixties, they seemed to have come to some sort of strained truce.

Kate had written to Lily every week when she was in the States, and once her granny had learnt how to use the Internet at evening classes there was no stopping her. They conversed every day on-line, sometimes several times a day. In fact, it was Lily who had advised her to come home to Ireland before 'all the good men are snapped up', as she'd put it. If only Lily knew the whole story. Kate had no intention of letting a man get close to her ever again – American, Irish or any other nationality for that matter. But she was enjoying being home and knew she'd made the right decision. Besides, Lily hadn't been all that well recently and Kate wanted to be there for her – especially as she was her only grandchild.

'Here you are,' said Alex.

Kate moved the newspaper to allow Alex to place the steaming mug of coffee and large white plate in front of her. The plate was heaped full with light green lettuce, croutons and strips of juicy looking chicken. The dish was topped with a generous amount of Parmesan shavings and dusted with freshly ground black pepper – just the way Kate liked it.

'Thanks, Alex,' she said. 'That looks great.'

'Have you any more clients coming in today?' asked Alex hopefully.

'No.' Kate smiled.

'Pity,' Alex said, walking away.

Kate tucked into her salad with relish and thought about Angus. He was an interesting one all right. She really was quite looking forward to Wednesday to tell the truth – in her professional capacity of course. She wondered what he'd look like with a haircut and contacts. As she speared a piece of chicken with her fork she remembered that she'd have to talk to Trina again today about the shoe lines that weren't selling. She'd tried talking sense into the woman earlier this morning, but they'd ended up arguing. Kate had pointed out that it made no sense waiting until the end of the summer season to sell skimpy sandals and white shoes – they might as well cut their losses early. Maybe that way they'd shift them all before July was out but Trina was having none of it, control freak that she was.

Sometimes Kate wished she had Molly's job – books could be returned to their publisher with no questions asked. Light bulb! she thought suddenly. She'll kill me if I forget again. She pulled a blue ballpoint out of her bag and wrote the word in capital letters on the back of her left hand. *LIGHTBULB!!*

Chapter 3

Paige

'What do you mean you're closing "Little Orchard" for August?' Paige demanded. 'You can't close for a whole month – what will I do?'

Clodagh sighed. 'I'm sorry, Paige, but we can't get staff to cover us in August, and me and Ethel badly need a holiday.'

'What about Connie? Will she not be around? You must be able to do something!'

'Connie's going back to Sydney for the month. And before you ask, Marta's English isn't good enough yet to run the place. Even if it was, she's only been here three months and she'd need at least six staff to keep the place open. We just can't do it – I'm sorry – we have tried, believe me.'

Paige felt bad – it was hardly Clodagh's fault she had to close. 'No, I'm sorry. I didn't mean to jump down your throat. It's just I rely on you to be able to work, that's all.'

'I understand, honestly. But there's nothing we can do.' Clodagh, who ran the crèche and after-school club had had this exact conversation with many of the parents. But her hands were tied – she had to give her staff holidays. She couldn't afford to pay them as well as she would like to, so a month's holidays in the summer was the least she could do.

'Do you have any suggestions?' Paige asked. 'Is there somewhere else open that you can recommend?'

'Not really,' said Clodagh. 'You could try Nora Hilton's place in Sandybay but I think it's full to tell the truth.'

'Do you have the number? I'll give it a try.'

Clodagh flicked through the large desk diary, wrote down Nora's number on a yellow sticky note and handed it to Paige.

'Thanks, I appreciate it,' said Paige. 'And you're open again . . .?'

'Monday the third of September. The first day of school for most of the older children. I've booked Alfie and Callum in already – Alfie into the baby room and Callum into Montessori and afternoon care – is that right?'

'Yes.' Paige nodded. 'We'll see you on Monday. And sorry for being short with you.'

Clodagh smiled. 'Not to worry. I know how busy you are, Paige. I read all about the proposed refugee centre on Burnaby Crescent. Good luck with it anyway.'

'Thanks. I hope it gets resolved soon. Everyone's getting a little heated about the whole thing.'

'But the Crescent would be ideal for the families wouldn't it? I know a lot of them have young children and it's just beside the park. I can't really see what the problem is.'

'Not everyone sees it like that,' Paige said evenly. 'I have to represent all my constituents and they have all kinds of views. Especially the Crescent residents.'

'I can imagine. Mrs Calloway from the gallery lives there, doesn't she?'

Paige nodded but said nothing. Connie Calloway was the current thorn in her side and the over-opinionated woman was calling into Paige that very evening – a prospect that didn't exactly fill her with joy. 'Anyway, I'd better collect my little monsters before they think I've abandoned them.'

Clodagh led her towards the baby room at the back of the building. Paige looked through the glass at the top of the door and studied the row of baby seats, looking for Alfie. She spotted him almost immediately. He was crying and Marta was crouching beside him, offering him a bottle. He hit her hand away, sending the bottle flying across the room.

'He's been a bit cranky today,' said Clodagh leading her in. 'Teeth coming through I expect.'

Paige sighed. 'Tell me about it. He was like a demon last night – wouldn't settle at all. His poor little gums were sore and he was dribbling like a dog. We didn't get a wink of sleep. I was hoping he'd be better today.'

'You never know,' Clodagh said kindly as they walked towards him. 'He might be all right by this evening. Fingers crossed.'

Paige bent down, unclipped Alfie from his chair and lifted him up. 'There, there, little man. What's bothering you?' He'd obviously been crying for a while – his face was red and blotchy and his breath was uneven. Paige felt a stab of guilt pierce her heart. She shouldn't have left him here all day. He hadn't been happy this morning when she'd got him ready and he'd cried all the way to 'Little Orchard'. She was a terrible mother. She held him close to her.

Marta handed her another bottle. 'Try this one,' she said gently in her accented English, 'it's nice and warm.'

'Thanks, Marta.' Paige swung Alfie around so that he was nestled in the crook of her left arm and put the teat in his mouth. He sucked immediately, his crying forgotten.

'He would have been the same at home,' said Clodagh, as if reading Paige's mind. 'He's just having a bad day. Marta's been great with him – rocking him in his seat and walking him around the room in the buggy. He was in good hands.'

Paige could feel tears prick the back of her eyes. Clodagh really was a find – she knew exactly the right thing to say at exactly the right moment. 'Thanks,' she murmured gratefully.

Clodagh smiled. She knew how difficult it was for working mums. 'That's what I'm here for. Now, let's find Callum, shall we?'

Clodagh helped Paige gather together all Alfie's bits – baby bag, bottles, food containers, buggy and baby seat. She clicked the seat into the buggy expertly and pushed it in front of Paige who was still holding Alfie.

As they entered the other, larger room Callum came crashing towards them and hurled himself at his mother's legs.

'Callum!' she scolded. 'You nearly knocked me over and I'm holding Alfie.'

'Sorry, Mum.' He looked up at her, beaming. 'Can I see Alfie?'

'Sure.' She bent down and showed Callum his brother's face. 'Now don't poke him or anything, he's not a very happy camper today.'

'Why not?' asked Callum. 'Does he have a poo in his nappy?'

'No, he doesn't!' Paige tried not to laugh. 'His little teeth are coming through his gums, that's all. But if he did have a smelly nappy I'd make you change it.'

Callum wrinkled his nose. 'Yucky!'

'Let's get you both to the car,' said Paige. 'Say goodbye to Clodagh now and go and put your coat on, there's a good fellow.'

'Bye, Clodagh Woda,' he shouted as he ran towards the coat pegs. 'See you later, alligator. Not too soon, you big baboon.'

'Hey, that's my line.' Clodagh laughed.

'Sorry,' Paige said. 'His manners are getting really bad.'

'I'm quite used to it. He's by no means the worst. He's just lively.'

Paige smiled. 'I'd love to ask you who was but I'm sure you wouldn't tell me.'

'Try guessing,' Clodagh suggested with an evil glint in her eyes.

Paige lowered her voice. 'I'd say Axel and Lolita Philips, am I right?' naming the ultra-spoilt children of one of Burnaby's best know socialites, Cathy Philips, co-owner of Baroque shoe shop.

'I couldn't possibly say.' Clodagh gave a tiny nod and grinned widely.

'You've made my day.' Paige laughed. 'I'll see you on Monday morning.'

'Bright and early.' Clodagh opened the main door for Paige and helped her down the three steps with Alfie's buggy.

'Bye poo-face,' Callum said loudly as soon as she closed the door behind them.

Paige glared at him. 'I hope she didn't hear that. You are a very rude little boy and there'll be no telly for you this evening. Do you hear me? Tea, bath and straight to bed.'

'Muuumm!' he moaned. 'That's not fair.'

'Quiet!' she snapped. 'Mummy's tired and she won't take any more nonsense from you, young man, do you hear me?'

He nodded.

Alfie began to cry again.

'Now look what you've done.' Paige pushed the buggy down the gravel drive towards the car. Callum trailed behind her. 'Sorry, Mummy. Can I have a treat on the way home?'

'What do you think, Callum?'

'Yes?' he asked, his little face upturned hopefully.

She ignored him, unlocked the car, unclicked Alfie's seat from the buggy and lifted it onto the back seat, all the while listening to his ever-increasing roars. 'Please, let me just get home sane,' she murmured. 'You're OK, Alfie,' she soothed, lodging his bottle into his mouth and cupping his plump pink hands around it. 'Here's your bottle. There's a good boy.' He looked at her for a moment, contemplating whether to continue crying or not, then decided he was actually quite hungry and began to suck. 'Thank you, baby.' Paige let out a sigh of relief. She turned around to tell Callum to get in beside his brother but he'd disappeared. She put her hand to her head. Not again. Callum had a habit of playing hide-and-seek at the most inopportune moments. Her nerves were frayed enough as it was today, she didn't know if she could take any more.

'Callum!' she shouted. 'Come here right now or there'll be trouble. Do you hear me?'

She leant her back against the car. It was just as well that she wasn't premenstrual or she'd have started crying right about now. In fact, she thought suddenly, have I had my period this month? I must have had, but I don't remember it. She heard gravel crunching on the far side of the car.

'Come on, Callum. Get into the car, please.'

'Boo!' He jumped in front of her and waved his hands above his head.

'Very funny, now what have I told you about wandering off?'

'But I was beside the car, you just couldn't see me. I was doing good hiding.'

Paige held him by the arm to stop him running off again.

'That hurts, Mummy!' he protested. 'Leave me alone.'

'I'll give you hurt if you don't get into the car this instant, young man, do you hear me?'

He climbed in and sat on the booster seat.

'Keep still, I'm trying to fasten your seat belt.'

'I hate seatbelts!' He wriggled again.

'The guards will arrest you if you don't wear your seatbelt,' she threatened.

'They never wear theirs,' he retorted. 'I've seen them.'

'Yes, they do,' Paige lied, thinking that her son had a point. 'Most of the time anyway. But sometimes they need to be able to jump out of cars quickly to catch robbers and things, that's all.'

'I need to catch robbers,' he said, wriggling again.

'No you don't,' she said firmly. 'And for the last time, stay still.' She finally managed to click him in, tucking the seatbelt clasp under the upholstery of the back seat just as her husband Tom had shown her. It was the only way to stop Callum unclicking himself as soon as she started driving. They'd had to use duct tape over the clasp up until last weekend when Tom had made the loose upholstery discovery while cleaning her car for her.

As Paige sat behind the steering wheel and turned the key in the ignition she could feel pressure building behind her temples. Great, she thought, a tension headache. Just what I need before a meeting with Madame Calloway.

'Tom, are you in?' Paige shouted as she walked into the hall. 'Tom?'

'In here.'

She walked into the kitchen. 'Be an angel and give me a hand with the kids, will you? They're still in the car and Connie Calloway will be here any minute.'

He groaned. 'Could she not have met you earlier or this evening? Dinner time is not exactly convenient, is it?'

'I know, and I'm sorry. But she insisted on meeting me today and she has some kind of gala charity do later this evening.'

'So as usual you're expected to bend over backwards to suit her, is that it?'

'Something like that.' Paige smiled wryly. 'I'm sorry. But with the elections coming up soon . . .'

'I know, she's a well respected member of the community with a lot of contacts, I understand. But the sooner the bloody elections are over the better.'

'Not long now,' Paige promised. 'The polling date is due to be announced any day, it's only a matter of time.'

'Good! I've saved up all my holidays to help you, but at this stage I'm getting itchy feet.'

'I know and I really appreciate it, my love. You'll make a great campaign manager.'

'I don't know about . . . is that Alfie screaming?'

They ran outside the house.

'Callum, what are you doing?' asked Tom.

Callum quickly took Alfie's bottle out of his mouth and hid it behind his back. He smiled sheepishly. 'I was having a drink, I was thirsty. Mummy wouldn't get me a treat in the shops.'

'Give your brother back his bottle this instant,' said Paige testily. 'Will you take Callum inside, Tom? I'll deal with Alfie.'

'Sure.' Tom unbuckled the seatbelt and let Callum free. Callum jumped up, sprung out of the car and ran into the house. Tom immediately followed him. Callum on the loose in this kind of humour was no joke.

'He's not allowed any telly,' Paige shouted to their disappearing backs.

'Come on, little man,' she said to Alfie, 'let's get you out.'

'Connie, how nice to see you, won't you come in?'

Connie Calloway stepped over the bulging baby bag which had been unceremoniously dumped in the hall, past the litter of outdoor shoes and overcoats heaped to one side and noted the broken radiator cover that was hanging from the wall by a single hinge.

Paige led her into the sitting room to the right. Connie studied the seat of the leather sofa carefully before she sat down. She took in the small painting beside the window – a reasonable attempt at a still life, practically worthless, of course, but pleasant enough, and the random pieces of rather fine antique furniture – gifts from relatives no doubt. She wouldn't have thought of Paige as a collector.

'Would you like some coffee?' asked Paige politely.

'Please, black, no sugar.'

As Paige walked into the kitchen she frowned. Callum was

sitting at the kitchen table, eating some toast and watching television.

'Sorry,' Tom said sheepishly. 'I said he could watch one episode of *Rugrats*. I need to get Alfie ready for bed.' Alfie was sitting in his little chair with a fresh white Babygro and vest by his feet.

'Don't worry about it,' Paige said mildly. 'I probably would have done the same myself.' She flicked on the kettle, luckily still warm from Tom's cup of tea and put some biscuits on a plate. 'I was talking to Clodagh today. They're closing "Little Orchard" for August. She can't get extra staff to cover the holidays.'

Tom whistled. 'Not good news for us. Any ideas?'

'She gave me the number of a place in Sandybay, I'll try that tomorrow.'

'Otherwise?'

Paige shrugged her shoulders.

'My mum might help if we asked her,' Tom suggested. 'She'd take Alfie anyway.'

'That would be great but Callum's the problem,' said Paige.

'I'm not a problem,' Callum insisted.

'Little pitchers and all that.' Tom smiled. He turned towards Callum. 'No love, we were talking about another Callum.'

'Oh.' Callum accepted this immediately and went back to watching *Rugrats*.

'Would there be any students around for the month do you think?' asked Tom. 'We could pay them well.'

'I'm not sure,' Paige said doubtfully. 'Do you think they'd be able to cope?'

'You never know. If we found the right person.'

'It's a possibility. I'll put an ad up in the supermarket tomorrow. Can you type something up for me later?'

'No problem. I have a bit of work to do anyway after dinner.'

'Not again,' Paige sighed. The kettle boiled, she poured the steaming water into the cafetière, lowered the plunger, pulled out a tray and put the coffee, two mugs and the biscuit plate on it.

'Sorry, love. August will be quieter, I promise.' Tom was a manager in the Castle Building Society in Dun Laoghaire, in charge of the mortgage department. It was a highly responsible and very busy job, and one he was becoming less and less enamoured of as time went on. He'd love to spend more time with the children but it just wasn't possible these days. He had to cover their own mortgage after all. Not to mention the bills. As a local councillor, Paige was only paid a nominal salary. She got reasonably generous expenses on top of this but, in total, it didn't even cover the crèche fees. It was Tom's salary that supported the household, a fact he never alluded to, being the kind and decent man that he was.

'Into the fire.' She kissed him on the cheek before picking up the tray.

'Here you go, Connie,' Paige said, walking through the door.

'Thank you. I thought you'd forgotten all about me.'

'Sorry, had to wait for the kettle to boil.' Paige placed the tray on the coffee table, sat down in front of it and began to pour.

Connie said nothing.

'So,' Paige opened, 'you wanted to see me.'

'Yes. And I'm sure you know exactly what it's about.'

'The refugee centre?'

'Precisely. We just can't allow it to happen in the Crescent. You understand that, don't you, my dear?'

Paige refused to be drawn. 'Why don't you explain your objections and I'll just jot them down.' She took a notebook and pen from the desk by the window.

'Right, first of all, they're all foreigners, aren't they? We don't know what kind of diseases they may have brought with them, do we?' Connie sniffed.

'Objection number one: foreign diseases. Any foreign diseases in particular, Connie, or just diseases in general.'

Connie looked at her. Was Paige trying to be funny? She wasn't smiling but Connie got the distinct impression that she wasn't exactly taking this matter as seriously as she should. 'Aids, my dear girl, for one. And malaria and typhoid, things like that. And smallpox.'

Paige wrote everything down.

Connie continued, 'And the Crescent doesn't have the car parking spaces for lots of extra cars. It's already a big problem.'

'I don't think the refugees will own many cars, to tell the truth,' Paige said evenly. 'Most of them won't have been in the country very long.'

'Well then,' said Connie, 'they won't even have any English, will they?'

'Probably not. The centre would offer English lessons to all age groups, including children.'

'Another problem. Children. It's a busy road and there's no pedestrian crossing to the park.'

'And will I put down house prices?' Paige suggested.

Connie stared at her. 'That isn't one of our main reasons, but it is a factor, yes. The residents are worried that it would affect the value of their properties.'

'Especially you, I would imagine, as you're right next door to the proposed centre.'

'*All* the residents,' Connie stressed.

'And is everyone in agreement on this?' Paige asked. 'The objections, I mean.'

'Everyone except one or two,' Connie admitted. 'But they're new to the area, they don't really count.'

'Who are new?'

'Harry Masterson and Darcy Wallis.'

'Darcy has lived in Burnaby for years,' said Paige. 'She's hardly a newcomer.'

'But she's only been on the Crescent for three,' Connie pointed out. 'Making her a newcomer.'

'Right, I see.' Paige glanced at her watch. She was starving. 'Any more objections, Connie? I know you have a dinner to go to later.'

'My dear, I've only just started. The dinner can wait. This is far more important.'

Paige sighed inwardly. It was going to be a long evening.

Chapter 4

Molly

Molly slipped the key into the lock of Happily Ever After and turned it. She stepped inside, closed the door behind her and quickly made her way to the office where she disabled the alarm. It wasn't even eight yet and the rest of the staff wouldn't be in for at least another hour but she'd slept really badly – tossing and turning all night and finally waking up for good at six a.m. She'd lain in bed for a while but had only got to worrying about the future of the bookshop and about last night's rather unnerving phone call from her ex-boyfriend, Denis – both good reasons for her fretful slumber.

Molly sat down at the desk she shared with Anita. She'd come in early to try to get some writing done. For several years now she'd been cutting her teeth on a succession of short stories – building up her confidence and learning how to make her characters and stories come to life. What she really wanted to write was a big, romantic saga, like *Gone With the Wind*, only set in nineteenth-century Ireland, encompassing all the sweeping political and social changes that had taken place at that time. She had a main character in mind – a feisty heroine who would start off as a kitchen maid and go on to become actively involved in the 1916 Easter rising, finally meeting and marrying a fictional tragi-hero, not unlike Michael Collins. She even had a title – 'The Price of Gold'.

Molly had only told two people in the whole world about her writing – Anita, who had been hugely supportive and had offered to read her work at any time, and Denis, who had laughed, patted her on the head and said 'Stick to the bookselling, Molly, you're not a writer. You don't have it in you'.

After fifteen long minutes staring at a blank computer screen, Molly gave up and pulled a blank yellow-sheeted foolscap pad towards her. If she couldn't write, she may as well do some work instead. She found a pen in the top drawer and wrote 'Saturday 12th July – Book Club Meeting and Rosemary Hamilton Event' on the top of the first sheet in large capitals, intending to make a list of all the things she needed each member of staff to do as soon as they all came in. She then put the pen down, sat back and sighed. Her brain just wouldn't click in this morning. Coffee, she thought, that's what I need, strong, black coffee. Matty would definitely be in Coffee Heaven baking or making soup or something, even if they didn't open till nine. He always was. You could set your watch by him. She stood up, took her wallet out of her bag and walked out of the office. She decided against setting the alarm – she'd only be a few minutes after all.

'Morning, Molly, I was wondering who was banging so insistently on my door,' Matty smiled. He brushed his sandy-blonde hair out of his eyes, sprinkling flour onto his freckled temples in the process.

'Sorry, Matty,' said Molly. 'Hope I wasn't interrupting anything.'

'Just the usual early-morning scone-making, nothing important. Coffee is it?'

She nodded and smiled. 'How did you guess?'

'Come on in. I've just put on the first brew of the day – Columbian all right?'

'Perfect.'

He poured the rich steaming-hot liquid into a large paper cup, popped on a plastic lid and handed it to her.

'Thanks, how much do I owe you?'

He waved his hand at her. 'Nothing. On the house.'

'Are you sure?'

'Yes. Sorry I can't stop and chat but I have soup to prepare.'

'That's OK. Thanks again.'

As she unlocked the bookshop for the second time she got the distinct feeling that someone was watching her. She turned around and looked up and down Burnaby's main street. It was completely empty. She must have been imagining it. Although Denis had been known to follow her. In fact that was how they'd first met.

The Molly and Denis saga had begun almost twelve years ago. When Molly and Paige reached the ripe old age of sixteen they were finally allowed to take the train home from school – Loreto Convent in Killiney – on their own. There were one or two rules, of course. They weren't allowed to talk to strangers, including the boys from the neighbouring Christian Brothers' College, Killiney (CBC) and had to come straight home after their after-school activities. What their collective parents didn't know was that neither of the girls were actually members of the debating club, the school magazine, or the choir. They both played hockey all right for the Senior Thirds, and now and again Molly wrote articles for 'The Loreto Killiney News', usually detailed and somewhat hyperbolic accounts of hockey matches – *The crowd went wild as Paige Brady flicked the ball into the back of the opponent's net with all the grace and fury of an African gazelle . . .* – mainly to throw the parentals off the scent. Because after school all the Loreto girls congregated under the green bridge in the train station, on the southbound platform, shielded from nosy neighbourhood eyes, and smoked until they were green in the face, matching their putrid-coloured green uniforms perfectly. The station platform was also where they met the CBC boys – small in height compared to themselves, kitted out in purple and grey, and far more nervous of the girls than the convent girls were of them, however cool and together they seemed.

Molly always felt a bit of an outsider with the station gang. She didn't smoke for one thing – she didn't see the point really. It tasted nasty and made you feel ill – what was to like? Paige made it look cool of course. She could even French inhale, inhaling the smoke through her nose. The CBC boys were very impressed. When Paige learnt how to blow large smoke rings, she was considered the bee's knees.

Paige had lots of boyfriends – she changed regularly and was currently working her way through fifth year CBC after cutting her teeth on the boys her own age. Molly had never had one, apart from Garvan Evans, if you could count him. He'd only gone out with her for two hours in order to talk to Paige. But Paige had been so unimpressed with his treatment of her best friend that she'd completely ignored him when he'd introduced himself. But Denis was different.

Paige had noticed him first, not in the way she usually noticed boys though. Denis wasn't exactly what you'd call good-looking. Smallish and thin, with wispy dark brown hair that always looked as if it could do with a good wash, and eyes that were almost permanently fixed on the ground in front of him. The other boys pretty much ignored him at the train station but he always insisted on standing only a few feet away from them, as if some of their social skills with the convent girls might be transferred to him by osmosis if he stood close enough. Paige had also noticed him because, according to her, he was always staring at Molly. Molly refused to believe this of course. Why would he be staring at her for goodness sake? She was plain and didn't wear any make-up unlike the other girls. Her skirt was the regulation length, instead of hiked up towards her armpits, and even her shoes were boring – sensible brown lace-ups instead of the kitten-heeled black suede stilettos of her peers. Or, if you were very cool like Paige, flat black impossibly pointy winkle pickers with dinky fake silver zips adorning the toes.

One day when Paige was at the dentists getting fitted for a brace (which, to Molly's knowledge, she wore once then hid at the bottom of the kitchen rubbish bin, under some carrot and potato peelings and claimed she'd lost it) Molly was left to make the journey home alone. It was a nice enough day and she didn't mind too much to tell the truth. It meant she could go straight home instead of pretending to have debating. She'd just started a new Virginia Andrews novel and was dying to get stuck into the strange and warped world, which she found totally addictive. Her head was stuck in her book at the station and on the train. Two stops later she'd arrived in Burnaby, crossed the railway bridge and had started to make her way home, her nose still stuck in her book. She'd discovered many years ago that if she progressed slowly, she could read whilst walking. Once she'd walked into a concrete bollard and grazed her knees and she'd often narrowly missed being mowed down by a fast-travelling baby buggy, but generally she got home in one piece after managing to read a chapter or two of the current favourite.

Today, as she read, she could hear footsteps behind her. She waited for the person to catch up with her and overtake her plodding pace but it didn't happen. They stayed behind her. This began to unnerve her and she began to walk even more slowly, tucking herself into the side of the pavement, willing them to pass. But they didn't. Finally she'd had enough. She was nervous, scared and more than a little cross. Who was trying to keep her from her book? She took a deep breath and turned around.

'Oh,' she squeaked in surprise.

'Hello,' said Denis, blushing furiously.

'Are you following me?'

He coughed nervously. 'Um, no.'

'What are you doing then?'

'Um, I don't really know.'

She put her finger in her book to keep her place and stood up straight. 'Are you a stalker?'

'A what?'

'You know – do you follow people all the time? A stalker. Famous people have them.'

He still looked confused.

'Never mind,' she sighed. 'Do you live in Burnaby?'

'No, Bray.'

'So you are following me!'

'Maybe.' He shrugged his shoulders and stared at the pavement in front of him.

'Why?' she asked in amazement. She'd never been followed home before, except by a lost dog, but that didn't count. In fact, even Paige hadn't been followed home.

'Because I wanted to meet you,' he said still staring down. 'You look nice. Not like the other girls.'

'Oh!' Molly was completely taken aback. She hadn't expected that at all.

From that moment on they were inseparable – almost thirteen years in total.

Until April this year that was, when Molly had had a change of heart and Denis, in turn had his heart broken. She'd made the decision that there must be more to life than having a safe, comfortable relationship and a safe, comfortable job. She wasn't even sure she still loved Denis, and she'd stopped fancying him ages ago, so being with him had just become a habit. And encouraged by Paige, after several long, agonizing days she'd finally managed to convince Denis that she really meant it when she said she didn't want to be with him any more. When he'd called into her house and proposed in May after a month apart and daily phone calls, her heart had sunk to the pit of her stomach, leaving her even more convinced that she'd made the right decision. It was only then that he'd left her alone.

But last night he'd rung her mobile, knowing that it was rarely on in the evenings and had left an extraordinary message. 'Hi, Molly. Just to say, you don't have to worry any more, I'm completely over you. I've met a lovely girl called Carrie and things are going great. We're getting quite serious. I just thought I should tell you. Bye . . .' Bastard! He knew Molly had a jealous streak as green as the Incredible Hulk. But this wasn't going to make any difference this time, her mind was set. She was very happy that he'd met someone else and she wanted the best for him. And she was going to ring him later and tell him so.

'Molly, Molly.' Anita's voice rang out loud and clear as a bell from the shop floor.

She raised her head from the computer where she'd been reordering books for the crime department and looked at her watch. Ten to nine, almost time to open. Seconds later the office door swung open. She'd taken to rising earlier now that she was no longer in charge of the shop.

'There you are,' said Anita. 'Did you not hear me?'

'I did, I was finishing an order.'

'Already? How long have you been in?'

'A little while,' Molly admitted. 'We have a busy day ahead and I wanted to be prepared.'

'Milo and Sam are coming in this afternoon for the event. Just to warn you.'

'Checking up on us?' Molly saved her work, sent the order down the line and stood up.

Anita ignored her. 'They won't be here for the Book Club but said they'd both try to make the next one.'

She stared at Anita. 'Why would they do that?'

'I don't know, out of interest I suppose. What's wrong?'

'Reading is not a spectator sport. If they want to attend a meeting they'll have to read the book, same as everyone else.'

'Fine, I'll tell them. I won't ask what's wrong with you this fine morning as you'll only bite my head off.'

'Sorry. I didn't sleep very well, that's all. I'll be fine in a while, honestly.'

'You'd better be. I think I hear Felix at the door, I'll just let him in.' She turned on her heels leaving Molly in the office.

Molly leant against the desk. She thought of ringing Paige but didn't want to wake her up. Tom usually took the two boys for a walk to the shops on Saturday morning, leaving Paige to have a lie-in before the Book Club meeting. Still, she'd see her later and maybe they could have coffee together before the Rosemary Hamilton event kicked off at three. The phone rang, interrupting her thoughts.

'Hello, I wanted to find out about the event this afternoon. Is it booked out?'

'No, not quite,' Molly replied. 'Will I take your name and reserve you a seat? It starts at three.'

'Please.'

Molly scribbled down the woman's details. 'Thanks for ringing. See you later.'

The phone rang again almost instantly. She sighed. At least it would keep her mind off Denis, she thought.

'Is everyone here?' Paige asked the rest of the Book Club members, looking around the room.

'Harry's not coming, he sent his regrets,' said Anita. 'He has a wedding today and they want seven extra cactus arrangements for the tables apparently. He's doing his nut.'

'Cactus arrangements at a wedding?' sniffed Trina. 'Surely not? Whose wedding exactly?'

'No idea,' Anita replied.

Kate came flying into the side room where the Book Club meetings were held. 'Sorry I'm late, guys, have you started?'

'No,' Paige said. 'Out late were you? Another dummy date or a real one?'

'Dummy,' Kate said.

'She doesn't do the normal kind, remember?' added Trina who thought that Kate's other job was very peculiar indeed. She'd much prefer if the girl would commit to Baroque on a full-time basis but there was no talking to her on the subject. She'd threatened to leave completely if Trina didn't stop going on at her. And that was the last thing Trina wanted. Kate might be odd but she was a damned fine salesperson whatever way you looked at it, and she sure as hell knew her shoes.

Kate ignored her. 'I've only got halfway through the book, I'm sorry,' she admitted as she squeezed in between Molly and Anita.

'That's OK,' Paige said quickly before Trina had a chance to butt in. 'Let's get going, shall we? Who'd like to start?' She looked around the table. This month's choice had been a sweeping literary saga by Booker award nominee, Francesca Scata.

'I will,' said Cathy, 'as I chose it. I was a bit disappointed to tell the truth. I loved her other books, which is why I suggested this one. But it's not as strong. I found the main character Elena a little unbelievable. I mean, if she was as stunningly beautiful as the author portrayed her, why didn't anyone realize that she was a woman masquerading as a man? It didn't make sense.'

'You're right.' Anita nodded. 'It was a little unbelievable.'

'But in those times wouldn't it have been so unbelievable

that she would have got away with it?' Molly suggested. 'It would have been such an outrageous thing to do in the nineteenth century, especially in England, to pose as a man and work in a newspaper, maybe it just wouldn't have crossed anyone's mind to question it. Nowadays, yes, she would have been questioned, but perhaps not then.'

'But what about Oliver, her eventual husband?' Cathy demanded. 'Surely he would have copped? He said he was attracted to her from the moment he realized she was a woman – that's rubbish! How can he suddenly have feelings like that? It doesn't make sense.'

'Again, maybe not now, but this was set almost two hundred years ago,' said Molly. 'Things have changed. It wouldn't have been acceptable then to admit that you found a person who you thought was the same sex as you attractive.'

'Maybe,' Cathy allowed. 'But the way their relationship was described and the sex scenes . . . I mean really, what baloney.'

'I liked those,' Anita said. 'They were gentle and tender. We're just used to stronger stuff in modern books. But I thought the sex scenes were very much in keeping with the period. And I love her writing, it's so descriptive.'

'She has a way with words all right,' Paige said. 'Remember that scene set in the corn field – that was stunning.'

An hour and a half later they'd finished dissecting the book and were trying to decide on a text for the following meeting, which always provoked much discussion.

'Not Anita Shreve again, please,' Trina moaned. 'I know you like her, Cathy, but we've read her to death.'

'Trina has a point,' said Kate. 'How about Anne Tyler? She has a new one out.'

'Harry's not that keen on her, remember?' Molly said.

'But he's not here, is he?' Paige smiled. 'How about something different? Alan Frost has a new book out – *Stradbrook* – we could try it. It would be more literary than some of the books we read.'

'Wouldn't mind giving it a go,' Cathy said. 'He's a Booker winner, isn't he?'

'That's right – for one of his earlier books. *Stradbrook* sounds interesting, have you heard much about it, Anita?' asked Molly

Anita nodded. 'The book's been getting some rave reviews in the press all right, but that doesn't always mean much. The book's out in paperback next month but I might be able to get early copies off the rep if I ask nicely.'

'Excellent!' Paige looked around the table. 'Now are we all agreed?'

Everyone nodded.

'I'll order it and ring you all when it comes in,' Anita promised.

'How much will it be?' Trina asked.

'About ten euro, I think.'

'Fine.'

'You'll treat us all then, Trina, I presume?' Cathy said smiling. Rich as she was, Trina was known for her Scrooge-like tendencies.

Trina kept quiet. She knew Cathy was only teasing her.

'Who's coming for coffee?' asked Paige. 'It's on me.'

'We have to get back to the shop,' Cathy said, looking at Trina pointedly. 'We're supposed to open at twelve.'

'Only on Book Club days.' Trina sniffed. 'Otherwise it's strictly ten o'clock, that's what we agreed.' Although if she'd had her way she would have made Kate miss Book Club and open up on Saturdays without them. Kate had Cathy wrapped around her little finger.

Molly turned to Anita. 'Is it OK if I pop out for a few minutes?'

'Of course,' Anita said. 'But don't be too long. Milo and Sam will be here soon.'

'Don't remind me,' Molly groaned. 'I'll be back before one, I promise.'

'So, how are things at home?' Molly asked Paige as they walked into Coffee Heaven. 'Tom has the kids, I presume.'

'Yes, poor man. Callum's being rather difficult these days. He was like a devil this morning. He took a swipe at me with his shoe earlier and really hurt me.'

Molly's eyes widened.

'Don't look at me like that,' said Paige. 'He's five. Five-year-olds do that sort of thing, it's quite normal.'

'But maybe you should . . .'

'Drop it,' said Paige. 'I'm not bringing him to see anyone, especially to some child psychologist who will make him even worse. He'll grow out of it.'

Molly wasn't so sure. He was due to start school this September and she pitied his poor teacher.

'How are my favourite Saturday customers?' Alex smiled at the small group. 'I've booked a table for you in the back.'

'Thanks, Alex,' said Molly.

'No Harry today?' Alex asked.

'Busy with a wedding,' Molly explained.

'I see. And what can I get you all?' Alex pulled out her small notepad and pencil.

'The usual, I'd say,' Kate said, 'two cappuccinos and a latte, is that right, ladies?'

They all nodded in the affirmative.

As soon as they'd settled into their coffees, Paige heard a familiar shrill voice behind her.

'I need to talk to you urgently, Paige,' Connie Calloway mock whispered. 'It's about . . . well, you know.'

'The refugee centre,' Paige said, trying not to sigh.

'The *proposed* centre,' Connie corrected her.

'Would you mind terribly if I finished my coffee? I'm with my Book Club friends you see.'

'Not at all,' Connie replied. 'I'll just sit behind you here and wait.' She pulled a chair over and did exactly that – sat directly behind Paige, Kate and Molly, tapping her fingers together impatiently. After a few minutes Paige admitted defeat and moved to a table at the far side of the shop to talk to her in private.

'Poor Paige,' Kate said to Molly after she'd gone. 'Does that happen a lot?'

'Unfortunately yes.' Molly drained her coffee cup and placed it back down on the table. 'She's far too nice to people like that if you ask me. I'd tell them where to go.'

Kate laughed. 'You wouldn't go very far in politics then, my girl. Paige is contesting the next election, isn't she?'

'How do you know that? It's supposed to be a secret.'

'Cathy told me. Her husband is backing Annette thingy apparently and Annette thinks Paige will be her main opposition.'

'Annette Higgins? Wasn't her dad done for tax evasion a few years ago?'

'I believe he paid it all back, according to Cathy anyway.'

'Let off by his political cronies more like.'

'Shush, someone will hear you.'

'Don't care if they do. Paige is so decent and hard working. It makes my blood boil that someone like Madame Higgins can swan in and win elections on her father's rather dodgy name.'

'She was a councillor for a while, like Paige,' Kate pointed out.

'Yes and a pretty terrible one from all accounts,' Molly snapped.

'I didn't realize you felt so strongly about politics,' Kate said. 'It's a whole new side of you.'

'I don't really, except when it comes to Paige.'

'Fair enough. Listen I'd better get going or Trina will have my guts for garters. Will I see you this evening?'

'I'm having dinner at Paige's but I won't be too late. Have you anything planned?'

'If you're going to be out I'll probably call into Granny Lily and make her dinner.'

Molly smiled to herself. Kate was so good to her gran, it was quite something. 'Why don't I get a video and we can watch it when I get back. Something lame and girly.'

'You're on. But to be honest I'd prefer a thriller if you don't mind.'

'Not at all. I can pick something up from the video shop later. See you around tennish, OK?'

'Perfect, see you later. Tell Paige I said goodbye.'

'Will do.' Molly watched her housemate leave. She'd known Kate vaguely when they were both teenagers as they'd played hockey against each other, and Kate and Paige had liked the same boy at one stage. Luckily there had been no hard feelings when Paige had won the particular boy's heart, as usual. Molly had been pleasantly surprised when Kate had arrived at her doorstep one evening after answering an ad for a housemate – Molly thought she'd recognized the voice on the phone but hadn't been sure at the time as she hadn't asked for her surname.

They'd hit it off from the very beginning – it was nice to have someone to do things with, especially after breaking up with Denis. But Molly always felt there was something that Kate wasn't telling her – there was something about her return from Boston that didn't quite fit. Molly wasn't one to meddle and so she'd let it lie and Kate was very private and rarely volunteered any personal information about her past, or her present for that matter – especially when it came to men. And as time went on she'd almost forgotten about it. Until now. Because Molly had had a rather strange phone call from someone with a decidedly American accent. Someone looking for a 'Cat'. It was only afterwards that she'd realized that maybe the

'Cat' he'd been looking for was actually Kate. But as she hadn't even got a name from him it would be foolish to even mention it to Kate – wouldn't it?

As Molly walked back into the bookshop she was surprised to find Sam and Anita behind the front desk.

'I'm just showing Sam how to work the till,' said Anita. 'Then maybe you could show him how to take a special order.'

'Um,' Molly murmured noncommittally. He still looked stunning. His hair was falling foppishly over his face and he was biting his lip in concentration. She walked past them towards the side room where Felix was unstacking the folding chairs.

'Hi, Molly.' Felix looked up. 'How do you want the room set up? How many are you expecting?'

'About sixty, I think, but there could be a few extra late-comers who haven't booked. If you put the lectern at the far end of the room and curve the chairs around it in a semi-circle. It will look less formal that way. Rosemary said she'd like a comfortable chair for signing afterwards, one with arms.'

'I'll get one of the chairs from the office for the signing, will I?' asked Felix. 'No need to take it out yet.'

'Perfect.' Molly surveyed the room. Felix had adorned the room with pink and purple balloons and large banner-style posters advertising Rosemary's new book, and he had also placed a large glass vase of white lilies on the table beside the lectern.

'Is it OK?' Felix asked. 'Anita said just to fire ahead with the posters and balloons.'

'It looks great,' Molly replied. 'Couldn't have done better myself. I'll do a display of her books on the front table as you come in the door and then we should be pretty much set.'

'Is she a Ripley Barker do you think?' he asked nervously. 'Or is she normal?'

Molly smiled. Ripley Barker was an American crime writer, one of three writers who had taken part in last year's 'Murder on Burnaby Street' crime event. The other two authors had been charming but Ripley had been an eye-opener. Arriving in a black stretch limousine, wearing an Armani three-piece suit and a black Stetson, he looked like a Hollywood film star. He'd had three minders with him – two from the publishers and one from the film company who had optioned his latest book – and had demanded ultra-special treatment from the minute his silver-tipped cowboy boot had stepped in the door of the bookshop. Felt tip pens in dark blue only, no biros – he couldn't write with them; no flowers – he was allergic to them; French mineral water, not Irish, and only in blue bottles, not green – he hated the colour green; and vegetarian food with no mushrooms or peppers.

'And M&M's with all the brown ones taken out, I suppose,' Anita had quipped to his American publicist, who had not been amused.

'No,' Molly smiled at Felix. 'Not another Ripley. Rosemary's lovely apparently.'

'Good.' He breathed a sigh of relief. It had been his job to source the vegetarian food and the French mineral water in a blue bottle and he'd never forgotten it. Ripley hadn't even said thank you and had asked Felix not to look at him while he was eating as it interfered with his digestive system.

Molly felt a tap on her shoulder and jumped.

'Sorry,' Milo beamed. 'Didn't mean to startle you.' His eyes lingered on the balloons and the posters. 'Very pink, isn't it?'

'The cover of Rosemary's new book is pink,' Molly explained. 'They tend to use the same image and colour scheme on the posters and display material.'

'I was talking about the shelves. Have they always been pink?'

'Not always. They were natural brown to start with but

Anita updated them several years ago when the shop started specializing in romantic fiction.'

Milo nodded slowly, a thoughtful expression on his face. 'I see. What type of bookshop was it previously?'

'A general one really. It stocked a bit of everything. But we decided it was a good idea to specialize, as most of our customer base was female. It made sense really. So we have a large range of fiction mainly aimed at the female market plus most things you'd expect in your average bookshop as well – books on gardening, health, reference books, children's books and a very strong crime section of course.'

'But the figures have been slipping slightly in recent months, do you think it's time for another change?' he asked. His thick black eyebrows rose. 'Say a crime bookshop for example, or a literary bookshop?'

She hesitated for a moment. Was he fishing for a reaction or was he serious? 'There's already a crime bookshop in Dublin – "Murder Books" on Callow Street.'

'Is there a literary bookshop?' he asked.

'No, for very good reason. It's not . . .'

'Molly, are you ready to show Sam how to take a special order?' Anita interrupted. 'I have to help a customer with children's books.' She looked from Molly to Milo and back again. 'Sorry, were you in the middle of something?'

'Milo was just asking me what I thought of changing the shop into a literary bookshop. You know, Anita, lots of serious hardbacks, Booker novels, IMPAC nominees, black shelves, jazz music, that sort of thing. What do you think?'

Milo put his hand on Molly's shoulder before Anita had a chance to reply. 'Now, Molly, it was only a thought. No need to get hot under the collar, my dear.'

She shrugged off his hand. 'I'm glad to hear it.'

'As long as the figures start improving you have no need to worry,' Milo continued.

'And if they don't?' Anita demanded. He hadn't said anything about drastically changing the shop when he'd made his offer.

'We'll have to see, won't we?'

'I think we need to talk, Milo,' Anita said gravely. 'There are one or two things about Happily Ever After that you don't seem to understand.'

'Ah, yes,' Milo smiled a little too widely, showing two large gold-capped wisdom teeth, "Happily Ever After", now as names go . . .'

'We'll talk later, Milo,' Anita snapped, interrupting him midflow. 'Right now we have a shop to run. Why don't you help Felix and Declan with the chairs?'

'As long as I don't get dirty, I'd be happy to.' Milo brushed his hand over the front of his black polo neck. 'Cashmere does have a habit of picking up dust.'

'There are several publisher's T-shirts in the back,' Anita said. 'I can get you one if you like. Save your good clothes.' She emphasized the word good, trying not to wrinkle her nose in the process. Milo might be an attractive man for his age and most charming when he wanted to be but today he was seriously starting to annoy her.

He held up his hands. 'That won't be necessary.'

'Then let's get back to work, shall we?'

Molly led Sam towards the back desk where the second computer lay waiting.

'Customer orders are an important part of our business,' she began. 'We can order books from America or the UK in a matter of days but you have to be careful not to promise too much.'

'I'm sorry about Dad,' Sam said, not really listening to her spiel on special orders. 'When he gets an idea into his head he can be quite bullish.'

'I just hope he doesn't change the bookshop for the sake of

it,' she said. 'We've spent the last few years building the business up and tweaking things to get it just right.'

'I understand, really I do,' Sam said. 'But he's got it into his head that the figures should be better.'

'What line of business was he in before he retired?' Molly asked.

'Property. Money isn't a problem. He's just a stubborn old businessman who wants the shop to be as profitable as it can be.'

'I see. He's the owner. And you're his son. And to be honest, I don't feel all that comfortable talking about this with you. Can we just drop it?'

'Of course. But one last thing.'

She looked at him with interest. Damn, he had the loveliest eyes. But maybe in time she'd become immune to his physical charms. 'Yes?'

'Stand up to him. He likes a challenge.'

'OK.' And his son? Does he like a challenge? Please tell me I didn't say that out loud, Molly begged. Please, please. 'OK,' she said again, realizing that blessedly she hadn't. 'I'll stand up to him.'

'Good. Now what were you saying about special orders?'

'Do you really want to know?'

'Honestly?' he asked.

She nodded.

He smiled broadly, his eyes wrinkling most attractively around the edges. 'Not today, if you don't mind. I'm sure it's all very interesting and everything . . .'

'It's not,' Molly laughed. 'Why don't I show you around the different sections instead and how to tell if a book's in stock or not. You'll need to be able to find the books if you're going to be working here, won't you?'

'Absolutely! And you can tell me all about yourself in the process.'

'Another day,' she said. 'First, the crime shelves.'

He felt deflated but he tried not to show it. He was only trying to be friendly. Molly Harper was proving to be the Brazil nut of all nuts to crack.

'How did your event go?' Paige asked Molly that evening while standing over the sink. 'Sorry I couldn't make it, I had council business.'

'Not to worry, it was packed,' said Molly. 'Just over eighty people in total. And Rosemary was a pet. She stayed around for ages after the talk – signing people's books and chatting to them.' She picked a black olive from the bowl on the table and popped it in her mouth.

'Good. And how's Anita? It must be strange for her working in the shop when she's no longer the owner.'

'Especially when the new owner's the spawn of the devil.' Molly licked her fingers.

'Molly! You don't mean that.'

'Yes, I do,' she said. 'He's terrible. A big greasy lump of a man, in his cashmere polo necks and his bloody literary bookshop.'

'Hold it right there, what are you talking about?' Paige stopped washing the cherry tomatoes and turned around.

'He wants to change Happily Ever After into a literary bookshop.'

'You can't be serious?'

'He said unless the figures improved he was going to make changes. I'm telling you. Ask Anita.'

'Unless the figures improve?'

Molly nodded.

'Are they bad?'

'Not especially. The whole book trade is in a bit of a slump at the moment – it happens sometimes. There haven't been as many big titles as there usually are in the first half of the year and people are spending their money on other things, that's all.'

'No new Harry Potter or footballer spilling his guts you mean?' Paige asked.

'Exactly!'

Paige for silent for a few minutes.

'Paige?' Molly asked eventually. 'What are you cooking up in that brain of yours? I know you.'

'Nothing.' Paige smiled broadly. 'Absolutely nothing. Now let's eat. Tom!' she shouted out the door. 'Dinner's ready!'

'Coming!' he shouted back. A minute later he joined them in the kitchen. 'Callum's locked himself in the bathroom and I can hear all the taps running. Can you talk to him? I've tried till I'm blue in the face but he won't listen to me.'

'I'll give it a go,' Paige sighed. 'What's wrong with him?'

Tom shrugged his shoulders. 'I have no idea. And I'll kill him if he wakes up Alfie, I've just got him to sleep again.'

Paige kissed him on the cheek. 'You're an angel and I don't deserve you, do you know that?'

'I do.' He flopped down on the kitchen bench beside Molly.

'Keep an eye on the lasagne,' Paige said. 'I'll be as quick as I can.'

As soon as she'd left the room Molly turned towards Tom. He was slumped over the table, his head in his hands.

'You have to talk to her about Callum,' Molly began. 'He's getting worse and it's draining you both.'

Tom sat up and rubbed his eyes with his knuckles. 'I know, but she won't listen to me. Why don't you try again?'

'It won't do any good. What about her mum?'

'She said she doesn't want to get involved. And mine's as bad. Sometimes I think Paige is right – maybe he will grow out of it – but he may send one of us to an early grave in the process.'

'Tom! Don't say that.'

'You haven't had the day I've had. First he punched Alfie in the stomach on the way to the shops, then he had a tantrum in the supermarket, and then he ran across the road without looking and nearly got himself killed. It's no joke looking after him, Molly, believe me.'

She put her hand on his. 'I know, I understand, honestly. But unless Paige is prepared to do something about it nothing will change, you know that.'

'I know.'

'And I don't really want to be having this conversation with you for the rest of his childhood.'

'I'll talk to her again.'

'Promise?'

'Yes.'

'Good. Now you'd better check the lasagne. I'm the guest, I'm not allowed to move. I have to sit here and eat all these delicious olives.'

'Do you now?'

'Yes. And I'd love another glass of wine while you're up.'

'You're early. How was dinner?' Kate asked as Molly walked into their small sitting room.

'Great. Except for Callum.' She sat down in the armchair, flicked off her runners and curled her feet under her body.

'What did he do this time?'

'Flooded the bathroom. Paige had to break the lock to get in.'

'Poor Paige.'

'No kidding.'

'I hope you don't mind but I mentioned Callum to Granny the other day. I thought she might know someone who could help.' Granny Lily knew everyone in Burnaby and the surrounding area, and was a fountain of knowledge when it came to almost every subject from gardening to psychology.

'I don't mind at all. But don't tell Paige for heaven's sake. You know how touchy she is about Callum.'

'I know. But Lily would never say anything to anyone, you know that. She's the soul of discretion.'

'Did she have any ideas?' Molly asked hopefully.

'Not really, but she said she'd have a think about it.'

'Tell her thanks.'

'I will,' Kate replied. 'Now are you ready to watch Ben Syles?' Ben was the latest Hollywood hunk.

'Always. Bring on the eye candy.'

Chapter 5

Kate

On Wednesday evening, Kate checked her profile in her full-length mirror, and was satisfied that she looked presentable. Her Dummy Date clients always made a huge effort to spruce up and she saw no reason to let them down. This evening she was wearing a plain white cotton wrap-around shirt, neatly ironed and starched, and a dark pink silk skirt, which clung to her slender frame in all the right places. She was also wearing her favourite pink shoes – delicious leather and canvas sandals with sky-scraper heels that had cost her two week's wages even with her generous discount. But they were worth it – she always felt like a million dollars when she wore them and they were exceptionally comfortable for such a high shoe. She was a little over-dressed for the local but to hell with it, she thought as she looked in the mirror again, who cares?

It was only ten minutes on foot to Burnaby and, as it was a dry and reasonably warm evening she decided to walk, heels or no heels. She clicked her way towards the village, past her Granny's ambling Georgian cottage with its slightly haphazard-looking front garden. Her Granny did have an on-off gardener who was almost the same age she was, but he was decidedly more off than on these days because of a clicky hip. She'd have to find someone else or the garden would go to pot, Kate thought. Maybe Harry would have some local contacts.

As she walked into O'Connor's pub she looked around. There were several couples sharing drinks, a group of men and women in suits – an office crowd no doubt – but no men on their own, apart from one with very short hair and his head buried in a newspaper. She sat down at one of the tables overlooking the street and ordered an orange juice from one of the lounge girls. From experience, she needed all her wits about her this evening if she was to be of use to her client and even one glass of wine had a bad effect on her as she had no tolerance for alcohol. To tell the truth she was a little tired – Trina had been her usual obstreperous self this afternoon and they'd had several disagreements about the winter stock.

Trina wanted to stock leather boots in all colours of the rainbow for the winter season. Kate was trying to reason with her – all women really wanted was the perfect black or dark brown boot. They didn't want purple, cream, pink or green. It would be a waste of time stocking the whole colour spectrum. Trina wouldn't see reason. Eventually she'd said 'we'll see what Cathy has to say' and Kate had dropped it. She happened to know that Cathy had already bought most of the entire winter collection – including lots of different styles of brown and black boot as suggested by Kate – while Trina was on holiday in South Africa for three weeks in the spring, and she couldn't wait to see the sparks flying when Trina found out.

Kate pulled out her Filofax and checked her appointments for the following week. She had a Monday morning meeting with Ralph, a new client who worked with animals and sounded all right; and two evening dummy dates, one on Wednesday and one on Thursday. She was going to be busy. She looked at her watch. Angus was now officially late. She looked around the room again, her gaze settling on the man reading. As if sensing her, he raised his head. She recognized the eyes, even if they weren't hidden this time behind Germanic frames. It was Angus. He smiled over at her and waved.

'Stay there,' she said loudly. 'I'll come over.'

He nodded and folded up his newspaper.

She put her Filofax back in her bag, picked up her drink and made her way towards him.

'I didn't recognize you,' she said, standing in front of him. 'You look very . . . um . . . different.'

'Different good or different bad?' he asked, an anxious edge creeping into his voice.

'Good,' she said decidedly. 'Nice haircut.'

He ran his hand self-consciously over his head. 'I asked the hairdresser what she'd recommend and she scalped me. I'm not sure about it at all. I look like I'm in the army.'

'You're lucky, you have an evenly shaped head. Some men have lumpy heads and they can't carry it off. But you're head isn't bumpy at all.'

'Thanks, I think,' he said smiling.

'Now, aren't you forgetting something?' she asked.

He thought for a second. 'My glasses?'

'No, not your glasses, although now that you mention it, you look much better without them. You have nice eyes, there's no point in hiding them.'

He thought again. 'A drink, I haven't offered you a drink.'

'No you haven't. But that would come next. You need to greet me first. Pretend this is a proper date, remember?'

'I'm so sorry, how rude of me.' He stood up suddenly. 'Lovely to see you Kate, won't you sit down?'

'That's better. Standing up was a nice touch.'

'Now would you like a drink?' he said, relieved that he'd got over the first hurdle, albeit retrospectively.

'I already have one, thanks, but you can get the next one.'

'Do I have to pretend you're my date right now or can you just be Kate for a while?'

'I'm your date from the very beginning,' she said firmly. 'You can call me Betty if you like, would that make it easier?'

'Not really. I'd prefer Kate if you don't mind. Can I start again then? You've caught me a little off guard.'

'OK, if you think it would help. Pretend you've just greeted me and I've just sat down. Start from there.'

'Have I offered you a drink yet?'

'Yes.'

'So we're actually at exactly the same place as we were before I asked could you be Kate for a while?'

She looked at him intently. It was going to be a long evening if he insisted on analysing every little detail as they went along. 'OK, how about this? I'll be Kate for a few minutes, you can get any pressing questions out of the way and then I'll be your date again.'

'Great!' He beamed. 'First of all, what do you think of the clothes? I took your advice.'

She looked him up and down. White shirt tucked loosely into faded Levis, dark-brown lace up boots, dark brown leather belt. He was slim and toned, she noticed, with a real waist. She wondered did he work out? Most men of his age were starting to lose their waists unless they were actively fighting against it. 'So I see,' she said finally. 'The belt is a nice touch. It matches your boots perfectly.'

'So the lady in the shop said. It cost me an arm and a leg but she said it was a good investment.'

'She was right.'

'So you approve?'

'Yes, quite a transformation. As I said, I didn't recognize you.'

'And you look lovely too. I like the sandals.'

She smiled. She loved it when people noticed her shoes and it didn't happen that often, especially not with men. 'Thank you. Now do you have any other questions or will we press on?'

'If I think of more can I ask them as we go along?'

'Not really, it would interrupt the flow of the date.'

He seemed disappointed. 'Oh, I see.'

'But you can save them up and ask me at the end.'

'I might not remember them all.'

'Well, they can't be important if you can't remember them.'

'I don't know, I haven't thought of them yet.'

Kate said nothing. She couldn't win.

'You're annoyed with me, aren't you?' he asked. 'I'm doing everything wrong.'

'No, you're not,' she said kindly. She hadn't meant to make him feel ill at ease. 'Let's just have a conversation. And if you have questions ask away as they come to you. How's that? I don't normally allow it but I'll make an exception for you.'

'Thanks, Kate,' he said. 'I appreciate it. So how will I start?'

'Ask me something about my day. About work, or if I don't work how I've spent the day.'

'That's a good one. Will I tell you what I did first?'

'No, Angus, ask *me* first. It's much more polite.'

'Oh, right. How was your day, Kate?'

'It was fine thank you, Angus.'

He looked at her intently. 'That's not a great answer. What am I supposed to ask now? I expected you to go on for at least a few minutes. I haven't even thought of my next question yet.'

'No, you're right, it wasn't a great answer. But I'm testing you. Try saying – tell me a little about your work, Kate.'

'OK.'

'Well.'

'Well, what?'

She sighed. 'Say it.'

'Again?'

'Yes, again.'

'The thing you've just said about telling me about your work?'

'Yes, Angus!' She was trying not to get exasperated but he was starting to wear her down.

'OK, tell me about your work, Kate. Do you meet many interesting people during the day or is it boring?'

'It's boring.'

'But there must be something interesting about it. Sure, aren't you working there? There must be some redeeming factors. Sorry to interrupt the flow, Kate but do I know where you work or not?'

'Yes, I work in a shoe shop and you met me at a party and we talked briefly. Does that make it easier?'

'Yes, thanks. Will I continue?'

She nodded.

'What are your favourite shoe designers?' he asked. 'I've heard of Manolo Blahnik all right, do you sell his shoes?'

'Good,' Kate said. 'I love Manolo, these are actually his.' She couldn't help raising her foot and pulling up her skirt slightly.

'You have lovely feet,' he said admiringly. 'Very dainty. And I like the pink nail polish.'

'Thank you. Do you like shoes yourself?'

'Um, not particularly.'

'What do you like?'

'Books, films.'

'Anything else?'

'I thought I was supposed to be asking the questions.'

'At first, to get things going. After the first few minutes conversation will hopefully just come naturally. But don't worry if it doesn't. Just keep talking and letting her talk.'

'OK. What do I say next?'

Kate looked at the table for inspiration. This was one of the hardest dummy dates she'd ever had. Usually her clients got the swing of it much more quickly and treated her as a real date.

Angus seemed to be having problems getting his head around the whole concept. Her eyes fell on his newspaper. 'Tell her about something you read in the newspaper.'

'Her?'

'Me! Tell me! Your date!'

'Sorry. Are you annoyed with me again?'

'No,' she lied. 'So was there any interesting news today?'

'A man in his eighties swam the English Channel for charity. Is that interesting?'

'Yes, very,' she said. 'Go on.'

'Um, I only read the headline, I'm afraid. But he's someone famous's grandfather, I remember that much. Um, do you have any grandparents?' he asked, floundering for something to say.

'Yes, actually I do. One granny – she's nearly eighty. And she swims in the sea every day. She's never swum the Channel though.'

He whistled. 'Impressive. I don't have any unfortunately – more's the pity. They all died quite a few years ago. I always felt closer to them in a way than to my own parents. I could really talk to them, you know, without being judged.'

'I know exactly what you mean. It's an easier kind of relationship, isn't it?'

'Yes. Do you get on with your own parents?'

Kate drained the last of her drink and put it back down on the table before answering. 'Sort of. I don't see them that much to tell the truth. Dad took early retirement and they moved down to Connemara.'

Angus leant forward, his head on his hands. 'This is going well, isn't it?' he said in a low voice. 'Do I ask you for dinner now or later?'

Kate laughed. 'Angus!'

'Sorry, have I annoyed you again?'

'Stop asking me that! Please!'

'OK. But what about dinner?'

'Honestly?'

'Yes.'

'If I was your date, yes, this is a good time to ask. We are getting on well. But as for me, I'd have to say I'm not so sure.'

'Why?'

'I don't know if I have the energy to continue counselling you all night.'

'Are you suggesting I need counselling? Am I that bad?' He seemed a little upset by her comment.

'No, of course not. It was the wrong word to use. I should have said helping, advising.'

'I'm tiring you out.'

'Yes. I'm afraid you are.'

'Oh.' He stared at the table, his hands clasped together in prayer position, the tops of his fingers touching lightly.

'Angus, I'm sorry. I didn't mean to upset you. I shouldn't have been quite so direct.'

'You didn't upset me, not really. I was coming on too strong, wasn't I? You don't like me, do you?'

'That's not it at all. You were doing great. I do like you – as a client. And as I said, if I was your date I'd definitely go for dinner with you.'

'Really?' He looked up, his brown eyes catching hers and reminding her of something. 'How about we just go to dinner as friends?' he suggested eagerly. 'We could drop all the dummy date thing and . . .'

'I don't think so, but thanks for the offer.' She was often asked out by her clients and she made it a policy not to meet them outside 'office hours'.

'Have I overstepped the line again?' he asked.

'A little.'

'I didn't mean a date. Just dinner.'

'Stop right there,' she said. 'Please. I can't have dinner with you, OK? I have other plans.'

'That's OK. I'm a complete loser, I know. Why would you want to have dinner with me?' He stared at the table.

'Ah, Angus, you're not a loser. You're just a little different. Tell you what – let's meet again next week and talk – for coffee this time. What do you think? I'll give you your report and we can talk it through. Usually I send the report out in the post but I'd be happy to meet you if you think it would help.'

'Thanks,' he said. 'That would be great. I do appreciate your help, really I do. I'm finding this a bit difficult, that's all. Maybe dummy dating isn't for me. Please be nice about me in your report.'

'I'll be honest,' she said evenly. 'That's all I can promise.'

'Can I ring you to set up a time? I don't have my diary on me.'

'Of course.' She stood up. 'It was nice to see you again, Angus. And you did well.'

'Thanks. I'll see you next week.'

'Yes. Ring me.'

A bushbaby, Kate thought as she walked home. That's what his eyes remind me of, an African bushbaby – dark, chocolatey brown. All wide-eyed and innocent.

The following night Kate had an even stranger dummy date experience. She was sitting in O'Connor's pub again, this time with another client, Clive, chatting about cars and four-wheel drives (he was a car salesman who was trying to get his dating confidence back after coming out of a long relationship) when, out of the blue, a red haired woman poured a pint of cider over her head.

'What the hell!' Kate exclaimed standing up and leaning forward, her head dripping onto the carpet.

'Bitch!' the woman screamed. 'I should have known there was some reason Clive was going off me.'

'Going off you?' Clive demanded, standing up. 'I loved you.

You broke up with me, remember? Eight years and then wham, you said it was over.'

'Only because I thought you didn't love me any more. You never told me, how was I to know?'

'Excuse me,' Kate interrupted. 'I'm going to the bathroom to dry off. Clive talk to . . . sorry what's your name. Tell her how you feel.'

'Linda,' Clive said.

'What are you talking about?' the woman demanded. 'How do you know how he feels?'

'I'm his counsellor,' Kate lied smoothly. 'The electricity is off in my office so we had to meet here instead. He was just telling me how much he missed you at our session, weren't you Clive?' She stared at him, willing him to agree.

'Yes,' he said, rather convincingly. 'Kate has been great. A real professional.'

'Shit, I'm so sorry,' the woman said looking genuinely shocked. 'I saw you both over here together and I realized how much I missed Clive. I thought . . .'

'Never mind,' Kate said quickly. 'No harm done. Now I'll leave you both to it, shall I?'

'Thanks, Kate,' Clive said sincerely. 'Thanks for everything.'

'My pleasure. It's all part of the service.'

The following morning there was a knock on the door and as Kate answered it she was almost knocked out by the heady smell of lilies.

'Kate Bowan?' the man holding the huge bouquet asked.

'Yes?'

He thrust the flowers towards her. 'For you.'

'Thanks.' She stepped inside and managed to wrestle the tiny card out of its envelope.

'To Kate,' she read. 'Who's no dummy. Getting married to Linda in the spring. Thanks for everything, Clive.'

She smiled to herself. Another happy customer. The same

morning she got another surprise delivery – this time from the postman. She started as she recognized the familiar sharp, angular writing on the envelope and the American stamp. Her immediate reaction was to tear it up, but curiosity got the better of her. She walked into the kitchen, sat down at the table and stared at the envelope in her shaking hands. Just then the phone rang. She let the answering machine take it.

'Hi, Kate, hoping we could meet up on Tuesday at lunchtime. Say half twelve in Coffee Heaven? Give me a ring if it doesn't suit. Oh, this is Angus by the way. Your mad but keen client. Remember to say nice things about me in your report. Bye.'

She put her head on the table and let the solid wood cool her brow. Angus and a letter from America. She didn't know which was worse.

'What's wrong with you?' Trina asked as soon as Kate had stepped in the door of Baroque that afternoon. 'You have a real sourpuss face on you.'

'Thank you very much, Trina,' she said evenly. 'Nice to see you too.'

'Out late last night, were you? Had a few tequilas too many?'

'No, I just have a lot on my mind. Where's Cathy?'

'She'll be back in a minute. She's gone out with Flames for coffee and then I'm off. There's this charity lunch in aid of some local arts thingy that Connie's running. I promised I'd go for a while.'

'You can go now if you like, I'll hold the fort. But don't forget we all have to finish talking about the summer sale and the winter collection later.' Kate would be glad to see the back of her for a while – sarky cow.

'I won't forget.' Trina grabbed her black leather coat and Gucci bag. She kissed her hand and blew it at Kate. '*Ciao*!'

'Bloody *Ciao* to you too,' Kate said as soon as Trina had breezed out the door in her wafts of Gucci perfume. She looked at the desk and on the floor. As usual there were at least twenty assorted shoeboxes to be put away. Trina never cleared away after herself, leaving Kate and Cathy to do all the real work. She got stuck in, replacing the toe-stiffeners and foam in all the shoes and wrapping them back into their tissue cocoons before closing them into their boxes. At least it would keep her occupied. The letter this morning had really unnerved her.

At half past four Trina flung open the door and staggered in. Her eyes looked wild – her pupils dilated and the whites blood-shot. She was a terrible drinker – she couldn't take a glass of wine without looking like the mad Lady Macbeth.

'Uh-oh,' Cathy whispered. 'I'll run out and get some black coffee. Want anything?'

'No, thanks. But don't leave me with her in that state,' Kate said. 'I'll go.'

Cathy patted her arm. 'She'll be fine. She's a pussy cat really.' She turned towards Trina who was tottering towards them. 'Sit down, darling. I'm going on a coffee run. Back in a tick.'

Trina plonked herself down on one of the two large red-velvet covered sofas which ran down the centre of the shop, back to back.

'That's better,' she said, kicking off her impossibly high gold sandals. 'My feet are killing me.'

'Don't say that if any customers walk in,' said Kate. 'Those sandals are one of our best sellers.'

'Crappy things.' Trina ignored her. She began to massage the ball of her right foot. 'What have you been doing all afternoon anyway? Talking on your phone as usual, I suppose. Anyone would think you had a boyfriend the way you carry on.'

Kate stared at her but said nothing.

'Oh, no, too high and mighty for that sort of thing, aren't you? Think you're so superior with your vamps and your uppers and moulded soles – who gives a damn how shoes are made as long as they fit? I certainly don't.'

Kate ignored her again. She'd seen Trina drunk before, but she'd never been this bad.

'Answer me, girl!'

Kate had had enough. 'Don't speak to me like that, Trina, I have no intention of answering you, you stupid woman. Look at the state of you, it's embarrassing. You should go home.'

'No, I won't go home. And don't *you* speak to *me* like that. I'm your boss, remember? Now get me some water, I want some water.'

'Get it yourself, you know where the cooler is.'

'How dare you! Get me some water.'

Kate turned away and began to price some sale stock.

'Damn you!' Trina shouted.

Kate felt something hit the back of her head and then her shoulder. 'Ow!' she looked down. Trina's shoes were lying on the floor beside her. She turned around and glared at the woman angrily.

Trina had a nasty smile on her lips.

'Did you just throw your shoes at me?' asked Kate angrily.

Trina threw her head back and laughed manically.

'What's going on here?' Cathy asked walking in the door with two large cups of coffee in her hands.

'She threw her shoes at me and hit me on the head,' Kate explained.

'What?' Cathy stared at Kate in amazement. She looked down at Trina. 'Did you?' she asked crossly.

Trina nodded, still smiling.

'What's got into you? I'm ringing Farrell.'

'Don't do that. He'll be cross. I'm not supposed to be drinking – the injections . . .' She tailed off sheepishly.

Cathy stared at her again. 'Are you having fertility treatment again?' Silence. 'Answer me!'

Trina looked down at the floor.

'You stupid thing, you know you can't drink when you're having treatment, you know that. I'm ringing Farrell.' She put the coffee down on the counter, pulled out her mobile and had a quick conversation with Trina's husband. 'He's coming straight over. Could you get her some water, Kate? I'll lock the door and put the blinds down. I don't want anyone to see her like this. I'm sorry I left you, I hadn't realized how bad she was.'

'Yes, get me some water,' Trina cackled.

'Trina!' Cathy scolded. 'Not one more word out of you, do you hear?'

'OK.'

Kate felt like refusing but she knew none of this was Cathy's fault. She went into the office and came back a minute later with the water.

'Thanks, I appreciate it. Would you like to go home now? You look a little shell-shocked if you don't mind me saying. And take tomorrow and Saturday off.'

'Are you sure?'

'Yes. I'll be fine on my own in the morning and Trina will be in in the afternoon whether she likes it or not. And all day Saturday.'

Trina groaned beside her. 'Don't feel too well,' she said.

'I'm not surprised,' Cathy handed her the water. 'Drink this.'

''S'not alcohol is it?'

'No, most certainly not.'

Trina drained the cup. 'Didn't know you designed shoes, Kate,' she slurred. 'Lady at the lunch told me you used to work for Sin in Boston. You were one of their top designers.' She hiccupped loudly. 'And then you left suddenly to come back to Ireland.'

'She must have me confused with someone else,' Kate said calmly. She walked into the back room and collected her jacket and bag.

'Ring me if you need me tomorrow, Cathy,' she said before she left. 'Otherwise I'll see you on Monday.'

'See you then,' Cathy said to Kate's back. A shoe designer at Sin, the most cutting-edge of the American shoe design houses, now that was interesting, Cathy thought. And it made sense.

'So, Angus, how are you?' Kate asked after they'd sat down in Coffee Heaven.

'Good thanks. And what did you get up to over the weekend?'

'This and that.'

He cocked his head to one side. 'Why don't you answer the question? It wouldn't kill you.'

She shrugged her shoulders. 'Would you like some coffee?'

He nodded.

She caught Alex's eye. 'Two coffees,' she said loudly. 'Thanks, Alex.'

Alex smiled. 'Coming up.'

'You're very evasive,' said Angus, picking up a sugar packet from the table and playing with it, rolling it backwards and forwards in his fingers. 'What are you hiding?'

'Angus! I'm not hiding anything. We're here to talk about you, not me, OK?'

'Fine. I was just trying to be friendly. That's all.'

'Sorry . . .'

'Sorry what?' he asked.

'Angus!'

'I thought you were going to say something else there,' he explained. 'You know, like sorry but I don't find it easy to open up to people. Or sorry, but I prefer to keep my private life to myself, or sorry . . .'

'I get the picture. And if you must know I was going to say – sorry, I'm not in great form today.'

'Why?' he asked gently. 'If you don't mind me asking.

Although I know you probably do. But I'm asking anyway because I like you, Kate and I'm genuinely . . .'

'Stop! OK, I'll tell you if you're really interested.' Anything to shut him up, she thought. 'There was a bit of an incident with my boss on Friday – I work in a shoe shop some days, did I tell you that?'

'Yes, on our date.'

'Dummy date.'

'Sorry, of course, dummy date. Although I wasn't sure if it was you who worked in the shop or Betty.'

'Betty?' What is he talking about, Kate wondered.

'You know, you asked me did I want to call you Betty.'

'Right.' Kate was losing patience. 'Do you want me to tell you or not?'

'Yes, sorry. Go on.'

'Well, she's been trying to contact me all weekend. It's been driving me nuts. She sat in her jeep outside my house for ages on Sunday waiting for me. I had to get my housemate to go outside and tell her I was away for the whole day.'

'What did she do on Friday?' Angus asked, intrigued.

Kate sighed. 'I shouldn't really tell you.'

'I'm not likely to know her,' he pointed out. 'And I'm very discreet, honestly.'

She studied his face. For some reason she trusted him – he was kooky, said all the wrong things and was most inappropriate with his questions – but she had a gut feeling that he wouldn't betray a confidence.

'OK then. She threw a pair of shoes at me and hit me on the back of the head. Oh, and she verbally abused me.'

'Wow! Supermodels eat your heart out. Welcome to the spicy and vindictive world of Kate's shoe shop. Why did she do that?'

'A heady cocktail of alcohol and fertility drugs apparently. Gets them every time.'

'Are you serious?' he asked.

She nodded. 'The lives of Burnaby's rich and famous – who needs Hollywood?'

'No kidding. And are you all right? It must have really shaken you up.'

'It did,' she admitted. 'But I'm OK now.'

'And you haven't talked to her since – allowed her to apologize?'

'No, I'll see her later though. Unfortunately.'

'I presume you're not going to sue her. You don't seem the type.'

'No, I'm not. Life's too short.'

Alex put two large mugs of coffee on their table.

'Sorry about the delay,' she said. 'We're pretty short staffed at the moment. Rona's just gone on holiday for the whole month and Peter's out sick.'

'Not to worry.' Kate smiled up at her.

Alex leaned towards her. 'Heard about the shoe incident. Cathy told me. Are you all right?'

'Fine,' she said shortly. She hoped Trina didn't think it was *her* spreading the gossip. She would have to have words with Cathy. 'I think it would be best if you kept it to yourself, Alex, if you don't mind. For Trina's sake.'

Alex looked at her for a second. 'You're a good person, Kate. I won't say a word.'

'Thanks.' As Alex walked away Kate focused her eyes on her coffee cup – adding milk and sugar and stirring furiously.

'You should talk to Trina,' Angus said, breaking the silence. 'Clear the air.'

She raised her eyes. He was smiling gently at her. 'It would make work easier. You need to allow her to atone and to make amends.'

'You're probably right. I don't know why I'm worrying about it, it's her who should be embarrassed, not me.'

'I'm sure she is.' Angus picked up the small ceramic jug on

the table and poured more milk into his already very white coffee.

Just then, Molly came in the door and bustled over towards their table.

'Thank goodness,' she said breathlessly. 'I thought you might be here. I couldn't get through on your mobile and I've been home already in case you weren't answering the phone.'

Kate gestured towards Angus. 'I'm having coffee with Angus. Angus, this is my friend, Molly.'

He smiled up at her. 'Hi, Molly.'

'Hi, Angus. Nice to meet you. Sorry to interrupt, Kate, but you need to get to St John's Hospital as soon as you can. It's Lily.'

'Granny?' Kate asked faintly.

Molly nodded. 'Yes. She fell over this morning after swimming and she broke her ankle. But I think she also bumped her head.'

'Is she all right?'

'I'm not sure. They seemed a little concerned about concussion and wanted you to get there as soon as possible.'

'Why did the hospital ring you?' Kate asked in confusion.

'Lily suggested it when they couldn't get through to you. Your mobile was off apparently.'

Kate pulled her phone out of her bag and was greeted by a blank screen. 'No wonder, stupid thing is out of juice again.' She banged the phone ineffectually on the top of the table.

'I can get an hour off if you need a lift over,' Molly said, aware that her friend was in a bit of a state. 'I'll call into Anita – I'm sure she'll cover for me.'

Kate stood up and picked up her bag. 'OK. Thanks.'

'Listen, I'll take her,' Angus offered. 'I'm not working at the moment and I wouldn't mind, honestly.'

Molly looked at Kate. She was pale and seemed very shaken, but she didn't protest at the man's offer. Molly didn't recognize him but she presumed he was a good friend of Kate's to offer his services like that. Maybe even a new boyfriend. As Kate never shared her private life with Molly she had no idea if Kate had met someone recently. 'Is that all right with you, Kate? I'll call over to the hospital straight after work. Would you like me to call into Cathy for you and tell her what's happened?'

'Yes, if you wouldn't mind.'

'Not at all. And, Kate, ring me if you need anything later, understand,' said Molly. 'Anything.'

'Thanks.'

Molly looked at Angus. 'And you're sure this is all right?'

'Honestly, it's fine. I'll drive her over and stay with her for a little while to check she's OK.'

'Great, I appreciate that. Kate, I'll see you later.'

After Kate and Angus had left Molly ordered three coffees from Alex.

'He seems nice,' Molly said as she watched Alex pour. She was fishing for information and felt sure that Alex would know something. 'Kate's friend. Haven't met him before.'

'He's actually one of her clients,' Alex said. 'They left very suddenly. Everything all right?'

'Kate's granny's been taken into hospital with a broken ankle. She might have concussion too.'

'Granny Lily? I hope she's OK. Lovely woman. Mum knows her from the church flowers.'

'I should have driven Kate to St John's myself,' Molly said a little anxiously. 'I hadn't realized he was a client. But she seemed happy enough to let him drive.'

'Then don't worry. He seems sweet. He's been in here a lot over the last two weeks. Must have moved into the area.'

'You're right. I'll stop fretting and get back to work.' She paid and picked up the tray of paper cups. 'Thanks for the coffee.'

'Any time.' Alex smiled. 'Give my best wishes to Lily when you see her.'

'Will do.'

It was only a twenty-minute drive to St John's Hospital in Sandybay but Kate worried the entire journey. Angus tried to talk to her and keep her mind off her granny's fall but she was so preoccupied that he gave up after a few minutes and flicked on the radio instead. The presenter was discussing people who had strange collections – the lady he was talking to collected ceramic toads.

'Do you collect anything, Kate?' Angus asked as he negotiated a large pothole on Burnaby Hill Road. The hill between Burnaby and Sandybay, nicknamed 'Swiss Cheese' by the locals, was notorious for its lumps and bumps. He may as well give conversation one more go – he had nothing to lose.

'Sorry?' she murmured.

'Do you collect anything?' he repeated. 'You know – like model cars or cacti?'

'Shoes,' she said absent-mindedly.

'What kind of shoes?'

'All kinds,' she replied, still staring out the passenger window.

'Like what? New shoes, old shoes. Borrowed shoes, blue shoes? Blue suede shoes, dancing shoes?' he was trying to lighten the mood but it didn't seem to be working.

'Old ones,' she said after a long pause. 'Foreign ones. I pick them up on the internet and at car boot sales and sales of work.'

'What's your favourite pair?'

'I have some nineteenth-century Lotus shoes my granny gave me for my birthday a few years ago.'

'Lotus shoes?'

She sighed. 'Do you really want to know or are you just making conversation? Because if you're not really interested I'd prefer not to talk if you don't mind.'

'I was just making conversation to begin with,' Angus said,

ignoring her short tone. 'But now I'm interested. Very interested. Please go on.'

'Fine. Lotus shoes were worn by Chinese women. You've heard of foot binding?'

'Yes,' said Angus. 'Mao banned it in 1949.'

'Did he? How do you know that?'

'Read it somewhere. I'm a mine of useless information. Go on anyway.'

'A "Golden Lotus" was a foot measuring three inches or less. That's where the name of the shoe came from.'

'So they're basically tiny shoes.'

'Mine are tiny black shoes covered in pink and white embroidery to be exact.'

'Where did your granny find them?'

'In an antique shop in town. It was pure luck.'

'How long have you collected shoes for?'

'Years.'

'How many pairs do you have?'

'I'm not sure really. Lots.'

'What is your second favourite pair?'

'Angus! Enough! Stop the questions, please. I'm not in the mood for talking this morning, I'm sorry.'

'Worried about your granny?'

Kate said nothing.

'Sorry, stupid question.' He kept quiet until they drove into Sandybay.

'You can drop me outside St John's,' said Kate evenly. 'I'm fine from there.'

'I'll bring you in, it's no trouble.'

'But . . .'

'Kate, you might need me to go and get something for your granny. You probably won't want to leave her.'

'Like what?'

'Coffee or a newspaper.'

'Angus, she might have concussion, and if she has, she'd hardly be able to read a paper, would she?'

'Sorry, I wasn't thinking.' He sounded subdued.

'That's all right. I shouldn't have snapped at you. You're only trying to help.'

'I'm coming in with you whether you like it or not. You're in shock. I insist.'

'Fine.' She didn't have the energy to argue.

As they walked into Lily's ward Kate thought she could hear her granny's laughter from behind some drawn flowery curtains which encircled one of the hospital cubicles.

'Excuse me, I'm looking for Lily Bowan,' she said to a nurse.

The nurse pointed to the curtains. 'In there, love, talking to Dr Martin.'

'Thanks.' Kate pulled back the curtains and looked in. A white haired doctor was sitting on a stiff-backed hospital chair. Her granny was sitting upright in the bed, a blue cotton hospital gown covering her tanned chest.

'Hello, love.' Lily beamed. 'Coming to join the party? This is nice Dr Miles Martin. He'll be operating on my ankle in a few days. Isn't that right, Miles?'

'You must be Kate,' Miles said. 'Lily was telling me all about you.'

'That's right,' Kate faltered. 'And is Granny all right? I was told she might have concussion.'

'Not me.' Lily knocked her knuckles against the side of her head. 'Tough old nut, I have.'

'We think your granny passed out from the pain of breaking her ankle. We can't find any evidence of concussion but we're keeping an eye on her just in case.'

'That's a relief,' said Kate. 'And her ankle?'

'Cooee, I'm still here,' Lily reminded them, 'you can ask me, you know.'

Miles stood up. 'I'll let Lily fill you in on all the details. She knows almost as much about the procedure as I do from all accounts. Who was it had the same operation, Lily?'

'Old Mr Carmody from swimming,' Lily replied. 'Old fool slipped on seaweed a couple of years ago. Went into all the details at the time, let me tell you.'

'Thanks, Doctor,' Kate said.

'No problem. I'll be back to check on her later. Your granny is a great friend of my mother's, you know.'

'From the chess club,' Lily explained. 'See you later, Miles.' She waved at him.

'Granny, were you flirting with that poor doctor?' Kate smiled as she sat down on the bed.

'Ow,' Lily squealed sharply.

Kate jumped up immediately. 'Oh, my God! Did I sit on your bad ankle?'

Lily winked at her. 'Only joking,' she said, her eyes twinkling mischievously.

Kate frowned. 'I'll sit on the chair just in case.'

'What's ailing you, love?' asked Lily. 'You seem a little out of sorts.'

'I was worried about you. I thought you were concussed. I wasn't sure what to expect.'

Lily patted her hand. 'Sorry to disappoint you, chicken, but apart from my ankle I'm as fit as a fiddle.'

'And what will they have to do with it exactly – your ankle I mean?'

'Put pins in it,' Lily said. 'I'll be like the bionic woman. When you cremate me you'll have to take out the pins before you sprinkle my ashes on the sea.'

'Granny, don't talk like that!'

'Why not? Everyone dies in the end. Not much we can do about it. Might as well just enjoy ourselves while we're here. Kate, is there someone outside the curtains? I can feel something. Can you have a look?'

Kate got up and pulled the yellow and pink curtain open. Angus was standing patiently against the wall at the far end of the ward. She'd forgotten that he'd followed her up.

'One second, Granny.' She walked towards him. 'What are you doing?' she asked a little crossly. 'I'm here now and everything's fine. There's no need for you to wait for me.'

'I'll go then,' he said. 'I just wanted to make sure . . .'

'Bring the lad over,' Lily said in a loud voice. 'I'd like to meet him.' Kate hadn't closed the curtain behind her and she and Angus were in full view of Lily's hospital bed.

Angus immediately made his way towards Lily.

'You can't stay,' Kate hissed following closely behind him. 'She's very weak.'

'She looks it,' Angus said just before he reached the curtain. 'Hello, you must be Lily.' he smiled. 'I'm Angus. I'm . . .'

'Angus is a friend of mine,' interrupted Kate. 'Before you ask, he's a primary school teacher and he's on his summer break. He very kindly drove me over and he's just about to leave, aren't you, Angus?'

'No, I can stay for a little while.' Angus beamed angelically at Kate.

Kate felt like hitting him. Why was he being so obstinate? This was her granny, her hospital visit, her life for goodness sake. What the hell was he doing interfering?

'That's nice,' Lily said. 'I'm a bit bored to tell the truth. The nurses are pets but they're much too busy to chat. And all the other old dears in the ward are a bit doddery if you know what I mean.'

Angus stayed standing. 'Sit down, Kate. I'll go downstairs and fetch us all some tea, will I? Make myself useful. I'm sure you'd like to talk to your granny on your own.'

'I've tea coming out my ears. Do you know what I'd love, young man?' asked Lily.

'A nice big gin and tonic?'

Lily laughed delightedly. 'Apart from that. Some nice cold bottled water. The water they give you in here is lukewarm and tastes mouldy.' She pointed at the plastic water jug by her bed. 'And I'd love some sweets, toffees if you can find them.'

'Your wish is my command.' He bowed. 'And for you, mademoiselle?' he looked at Kate.

Really he was too much. 'I'd like a bottle of water too. Still please. And Granny likes sparkling.'

'Matches my personality,' Lily winked at him.

'I think you're right.' He laughed.

As soon as he'd left the ward, Kate sensed that the second interrogation of the day was about to begin.

'He's adorable!' Lily enthused. 'Such a thoughtful lad. Very endearing and such good manners. Where did you meet him?'

Kate thought quickly. 'Tell me about the operation, Granny. All the gory details.'

Lily was torn – she wanted to find out all about Angus but she knew she wouldn't get another chance to tell her usually hyper-squeamish granddaughter about her operation. She opted for the blood and guts.

'I won't bore you with too many details – but first of all they give you some sleeping pills, then the anaesthetist puts you to sleep,' Lily began. 'An injection. Hate them. They can never find my veins. I'm too slim you see, my toned figure is a curse.' She snorted and Kate smiled. 'They'll be paranoid putting me under, of course – convinced I won't wake up again on account of my age, you see.'

'Granny!'

'Then they'll cut through the skin and the . . .'

Kate tried to block out the procedure her gran was describing while still appearing interested. Maybe she should have told her about Angus after all and got it over with. But what was there to say – he's a lost cause, Granny, and I'm trying to help him get a girlfriend. Still, he had brought her to the hospital and he was doing an errand for them. But it didn't redeem his peculiar behaviour. And it wasn't lovable or endearing, not one little bit.

'Are you listening, Kate?' Lily asked. 'You seem a bit away with the fairies.'

'I'm fine, just a bit preoccupied with things at work, that's all. Please, continue. We got to the bit where the doctor was fitting the pins.'

Chapter 6

Paige

'Hi, Molly, you'll never believe what happened at the council meeting this evening,' Paige began. She was picking up Callum's clothes from the kitchen floor, the portable phone jammed between her shoulder and her ear. He'd insisted on warming his naked body in front of the aga before putting on his pyjamas and had dumped his clothes unceremoniously on the tiles. 'Davorka Ferata arrived.'

'The Bosnian opera singer?' Molly asked intrigued.

'The very same. Apparently she's also an award-winning photographer. She's in Ireland for the Wexford Opera Festival and one of her old friends, Besnik something or other is living in a B&B just outside Burnaby. He's a famous tenor in his own country.'

'What's he doing here?'

'He's an asylum seeker. He and his family were forced out of their home by the Serbian army.'

'Was Connie Calloway at the meeting?'

'She was.'

'You are infuriating sometimes. Where is all of this leading?'

'It was amazing. Davorka stood up and . . . Shit! What's that smell? Hang on a second, Molly.' Paige ran up the stairs and sniffed the air in the upstairs landing. The strong, heady odour was coming from Callum's room. She put her hand over the receiver. 'Callum, what are you doing in there?' There was no answer.

'Paige!' Molly protested.

'I have to go,' said Paige. 'There's a really strong smell coming from Callum's bedroom, suspiciously like Chanel No 5. I'll kill him if it is. He's supposed to be asleep.'

'Paige, you can't leave me hanging like this. Tell me what Davorka said. Please.'

'I'll ring you back in a few minutes,' she promised. 'I really have to go.' She put down the receiver, took a deep breath and walked into Callum's room.

He was nowhere to be seen. There was a telltale puddle of dark yellow liquid on the floorboards and as she bent down to investigate she was nearly knocked out by the fumes. It was her Chanel all right, but where was the bottle?

'Callum? I know you're in here. Are you under the bed?' She pulled up his duvet which was hanging over the side of his lower bunk bed and looked underneath. He wasn't there. However she did spy the pieces of broken glass and the plastic spray insert and metal top amongst the dust balls, once her perfume bottle. He'd obviously kicked them under there to hide the evidence. She stood up and pulled open his closet, another of his favourite hiding places. He smiled up at her nervously, knowing he'd done something very bad this time, but at the same time shocked at his own audacity and bravery.

'Get out,' she said in a dangerously low voice. She pointed at the pool of perfume on the floor. 'What happened?'

'I was on the top bunk and the bottle kind of slipped out of my hand,' he explained. 'It wasn't my fault.'

'And whose fault was it then exactly?'

'Um, Alfie's.'

'Why was it Alfie's fault?'

'He was annoying me.'

'But he's in his room asleep, Callum.'

'He was still annoying me. He's a shit.'

'Callum! Don't use that language in this house.'

'You do. I just heard you on the phone.'

'That's different.'

'Why?'

'It just is.' She sighed deeply. 'And what were you doing with my perfume anyway? You know you're not allowed to take things from Mummy and Daddy's bedroom, don't you? And why does the hall smell of perfume too? Tell me the truth. It'll be a lot better for you if you do. I know when you're lying to me, young man.'

He had the good grace to look a little contrite. 'I was using it as a magic potion. You know, like Harry Potter. I was making myself grow bigger. I put some on my head. It didn't work. I was standing on the stairs so I could listen to you on the phone, then I came up to my room. I dropped the bottle when I was climbing onto the top bunk.'

She leant down and smelt his hair. It reeked of perfume. 'Oh, Callum, what am I going to do with you?'

'Smack me?' he said nervously.

'No, I'm not going to smack you. We don't smack in this house, you know that. But you have to understand that you can't take things without asking and then break them. Or listen in to my phone calls.' She sat down on the side of the bed. 'I'm tired of all this, love. Can't you just be good for a change?'

'I'll try, Mummy.'

'You need a bath and a hair wash. Your hair stinks.'

'Can we use Fruit Alive Shampoo for Kids – "Makes hair washing fun for all the family"?' He sang the shampoo's distinctive jingle loudly.

'No, we'll use the normal shampoo. You watch too much telly, Callum.'

'No, I don't!' he shouted.

'Why did you just shout at me?' she asked in exasperation. 'You said you were going to be good.'

'Sorry, Mummy.'

'Now, I'm going downstairs to get some kitchen roll and a plastic bag to put the glass into. And then you can help me mop up the perfume, OK? Now sit on your bed and wait for me like a good boy.'

He nodded eagerly.

When she walked back into Callum's room three minutes later she found him crouched over the perfume puddle.

'What are you doing?' she asked.

'Helping.' He smiled up at her.

She looked down at the floor and to her horror saw that he'd been mopping up the perfume with his new white towelling dressing gown.

'Callum! What the hell are you doing? You'll ruin your dressing gown, you idiot.' She knelt down on her hunkers and put her head in her hands.

'Are you crying, Mummy?' he asked with interest.

'No! But I will be in a minute. You're driving me mad! Get out of here.'

'Where will I go?'

'I don't care. Out!'

'I'll go and watch telly, will I?'

'Yes, whatever. Just get out!'

'You shouldn't really shout at me, Mummy. Daddy doesn't like it.'

'Daddy isn't here. He's at the gym. And if you know what's good for you, you'll get out right now, Callum and stop annoying me. And stop answering me back, do you hear? Go!'

Callum skipped down the stairs to the television room. His

mummy got a bit tired sometimes, she didn't mean to shout, that's what Daddy said.

Paige sat on her son's floor, moving her legs from beneath her as they started to get pins and needles. She heard a faint cry coming from Alfie's room, then a stronger one. I know exactly how you feel, Alfie, she thought. She pulled some kitchen paper off the roll and began to mop up the perfume. She'd become immune to the strong smell by this stage. But as for Callum, she was far from immune to his fatal charms at the moment. As soon as Tom got home their son would get a strong talking to, she'd see to that. She didn't have the energy to do it herself. Besides, after cleaning the mess up and soothing Alfie back to sleep she'd be fit for nothing except her bed.

Paige rang Molly back an hour later.

'Is Callum OK?' Molly asked gently.

'No comment,' said Paige. She explained what had happened to her favourite bottle of perfume.

'Is he asleep now?'

'Yes, Tom gave him a bath and settled him down.'

Molly took a deep breath. 'It might be time for you talk to someone about Callum. For your own sake if not for his. He's wearing you down and it's not right.'

Paige didn't reply.

Molly broke the silence. 'I'm sorry, I shouldn't have said anything, you're probably exhausted. Bad timing.'

'No, you're right,' Paige said finally. 'It's getting beyond a joke and he doesn't seem to be growing out of it, in fact he's getting worse.'

'I hope you don't think I'm interfering because I'm not. I just care . . .'

'Stop! Honestly, it's all right.'

'Good. And you never finished the story about Davorka,' Molly reminded her.

'OK. To cut a long story short, she's going to hold a fund-raising concert in St John's Church next month to raise funds for the refugee centre.'

'I bet Connie is only too thrilled.' Molly snorted.

'No kidding. But she seems to have had a bit of a change of heart.'

'Oh?'

'Davorka's no fool. Apparently her friend Besnik filled her in on the details. Davorka called into Connie's gallery and offered her the very first showing of her photographs in Ireland. Connie was delighted and accepted immediately. But Davorka had one condition.'

'Let me guess. That Connie drops her objections to the refugee centre.'

'Darling,' Paige drawled in her best 'posh' Connie voice, 'now that a famous tenor is involved in the arts centre how could I refuse?'

'Arts centre?'

'Gas, isn't it? Connie agreed on the condition that the refugee centre be called the Burnaby Arts Centre and that Davorka be its patron.'

'Brilliant! But they'll still be teaching English and helping the refugees find jobs, like you wanted.'

'Yes. As well as holding multicultural music and drama evenings, exhibitions, festivals and events for children. So everyone wins.'

'Including you.'

'Exactly!'

'Another triumph for Councillor Brady.'

'Why, thank you, Molly.'

The following day Paige visited Lily in hospital.

'Hi, Lily, I hear this place is driving you bonkers.' She

smiled, leant down and kissed Lily's cheek. 'I thought I'd come in and say hi.'

'How lovely to see you, Paige. And how is your mum? Still teaching the flower arranging? I haven't seen her for a while.'

'She's great, thanks. And yes, still teaching, mainly evening classes these days. It keeps her out of trouble.'

'I took one of her classes last year, it was a one-off thing in the church hall for the Flower Festival. She was very good. Very organized. Perfectly symmetrical arrangements – amazing. I was useless of course, mine kept drooping to one side.'

Paige sat down on the chair beside Lily's bed. 'So how are they treating you in here?'

'Very well. My doctor is a dear – Miles Martin – do you know him?'

Paige shook her head.

'Lovely man. His mother is an old friend of mine.'

Paige smiled to herself. Lily knew everyone in Burnaby and had more friends than anyone she knew.

'And how are you, Paige? You look a little tired.'

'Things are busy enough, Lily. Alfie was teething last night so I didn't get much sleep to tell the truth.'

'And how's Callum?'

'Fine. Still a handful.'

Lily looked at Paige carefully, tapped the tips of her fingers together and then smiled knowingly. 'And when's the next one due? Kate didn't say anything to me so it must be early days yet. No wonder you're tired.'

Paige could feel the blood drain from her face and she became suddenly lightheaded. She swayed dangerously in her chair.

'Put your head between your knees and take deep breaths,' Lily commanded. 'That's it, good girl, take it easy.'

Paige sat back up after a few minutes and Lily handed her a

glass of water. 'I'm sorry, I shouldn't have said anything,' Lily said. 'Forgive me.'

'No, it's not your fault, really. I just . . . I hadn't realized to tell the truth. But I think you're right. No, I know you're right. It all makes sense. I've been really tired in the last few weeks and I've had to eat all the time or I've felt faint and sick. How could I have been so stupid? What lousy timing!' Fat tears began to roll down Paige's cheeks.

Lily pulled some tissues out of a box on the cluttered bedside table and handed them to her. 'It will all work out, you'll see.'

'But the elections are coming up soon and I've no one to mind the children in August and . . .' She began to cry, her sobs catching in her throat and making it hard to breathe.

Lily patted her on the shoulder. 'There, there, love. Things are never as bad as they seem. Stop crying now and we'll see if Lily can help, will we? I know a lovely primary school teacher who might be available. A young man called Angus who would be wonderful with Callum I think, from all appearances a kind and gentle soul. Don't cry, Paige, we'll sort it all out, you'll see.'

Paige looked at Lily, her eyes still full of tears. 'A primary school teacher. Do you think he'd be interested? It would be a godsend, really it would. I've interviewed all kinds of people, mostly college students, and older women, but none of them were quite right. Some had no experience of children at all, and there's no way they'd be able to cope with Callum. Mum has offered to take Alfie, but . . .'

'Let's just see, will we?' Lily smiled. 'God moves in mysterious ways. Leave it with me.' She patted Paige's hand. 'Now you go home and have a little lie down. You've had a bit of a shock. Ring that nice husband of yours.'

A couple of hours later Kate rang Paige on her mobile.

'Granny says you're looking for Angus's number,' she said, a slight edge to her voice.

'Are you OK, Kate? You sound a little strange,' Paige asked.

'It's nothing.' Kate had had a flaming arguement with Lily less than an hour ago and it was still affecting her. She couldn't believe that her granny wanted to ring Angus. She knew it was in a good, no an excellent cause, and she knew in her heart that her granny was right – Angus could be just what the doctor ordered for Callum – but Lily had no right to involve Angus in their lives. He'd actually had the nerve to visit Lily off his own bat the previous day – bringing her grapes and two bottles of sparkling water. It wasn't on. He was a paying client – nothing more and nothing less and she was damned if she was going to start treating him as a real person. 'Here's the number. Granny's already had a chat with him and apparently he is available in theory. But he said to give him a ring.'

'Brilliant! Kate, Lily is an amazing woman. If you see her this evening tell her how much I appreciate this.'

'I will.' Kate put down the phone, her blood boiling. Yes, Granny was amazing – amazingly interfering. And she'd had almost enough. She had a good mind not to visit her this evening out of spite. Her mobile phone beeped. It was a text message from her. She should never have bought Lily a phone in the first place – it was a bad idea. But after her fall, she'd been worried, and had presented her with a brand new mobile the day after her ankle operation and making her promise faithfully that she'd carry it whenever she left the house. Now she was using it to harass her – typical.

Can u bring in your posh moisturizer this eve? Skin drying out – bloody hospital. Granny.

That evening while lying in bed, Paige filled Tom in on all the events of the day. Callum and Alfie were both asleep, much to their parents' relief. She had tried to ring Tom earlier but he'd been in meetings all afternoon and evening. She'd decided to save the momentous news – the news about the baby – till last. She had no idea how he was going to take it and she was afraid that he'd be annoyed and upset. After all, it did have huge consequences for both of them, and the way things were at the moment, they were just about hanging on to their sanity by the thinnest of threads.

'So you talked to this Angus guy and he's agreed to come and meet Callum?' Tom asked with interest.

'Yes. He said it was up to Callum. They would spend some time together and if Callum liked him he'd do it.'

Tom smiled and shook his head. 'The man has no idea what he's letting himself in for, does he?'

Paige glared at him. She didn't appreciate Tom's flippancy. 'Callum's not that bad. I'm sure he'll be on his best behaviour when Angus meets him.'

Tom said nothing. In his opinion, Callum was likely to play up when confronted with Angus – he'd be Denis the Menace and Just William all rolled into one just out of mischief.

'And he'll bring over his references. He was working in the local national school in Killiney last term and has several character references – including one from the priest in Sandybay.'

'Sounds good,' said Tom. 'You'll check them all out, of course.'

'We'll check them all out, you mean,' Paige said, her voice dangerously low. Tom had a habit of leaving things for her to do and she wasn't in the mood for his passing the buck, not today. 'You can't be too careful. And he is a man after all.'

'If I'd said that you would have accused me of being sexist,' Tom pointed out.

'You're right, I probably would.'

'Did he sound nice on the phone?'

'Very.'

'Well, I'm happy if you're happy. And it certainly solves the babysitting problem for August. Mum's already agreed to take Alfie, bless her. And Paige, I heard on the news on the way home that they announced the date for the general elections. I would have rung you but . . .'

'I know, I know. You don't like using the phone in the car. As I keep telling you, you have a handset, Tom, it's legal you know. Anyway I heard about the elections earlier.'

'And as I keep telling *you*, I still prefer to concentrate 100 per cent on my driving. There are an awful lot of nutters on the roads these days and talking on the phone while driving is a distraction no matter how legal it is.'

Paige sighed. When Tom got an idea into his head there was no budging him on it. Besides, he was probably right. 'We'll have to start getting organized,' she said. 'I've already ordered the printing of the posters and flyers. And I'll have to start the doorstepping next week if I want to get around the whole neighbourhood by early September.'

Tom nodded. 'You're probably right. At least we've drawn up the provisional plan of action so we're fairly on top of things. And the Arts Centre issue has been a bonus. You managed to keep everyone happy and come out of it smelling of roses in the process, clever woman.'

'And I have a few more tricks up my sleeve which should keep the media interested,' she added.

'Really, and they would be?' Tom asked. This was news to him.

'I'll tell you tomorrow. I don't have any energy left right now.'

'No energy at all?' He smiled wickedly at her, his blue eyes flashing.

'Well, maybe a little,' she admitted. She flicked off the reading light on her bedside table and turned towards him. She had hoped to tell him about the baby but that could wait until tomorrow.

He kissed her firmly on the mouth and she responded instantly. No matter how often she kissed Tom she never tired of it. She was lucky she'd found him – a best friend and a lover all rolled into one. And what a lover. He was kind and considerate, yet powerful and strong when she wanted him to be. This evening she wanted to feel loved and cherished and he sensed this – taking things slowly and languorously, his hands moving expertly over her smooth skin with lingering, caressing touches.

Suddenly they heard something.

'What was that?' Tom asked.

'I don't know, it sounded like a thump.'

Tom sighed. 'I'd better go and see.' He pulled on a pair of boxer shorts and went into the hall.

'It was only Callum,' he told Paige as he got back into bed a few minutes later.

'Did he fall out of bed?'

'No, he'd pulled his mattress onto the floor so that he could play magic carpets.'

'What?'

'Don't ask. I remade his bed on the floor and told him he could stay there as long as he went straight to sleep.'

Paige smiled despite herself. 'Let's hope he stays there. Now where were we?'

'Right about here, Councillor,' Tom said, kissing her again.

The following day Molly rang Paige just before nine. 'Have you seen the local newspaper yet?' she asked.

'No, why?'

'I think you'd better take a look. Ring me back as soon as you've bought a copy. And try not to worry, it's only a newspaper. I have to run, the shop's about to open. Bye.'

'Molly, what are you talking about?' But her friend had cut her off.

Paige was intrigued. She made two pressing phone calls – one about rubbish collection or lack of it on one of Burnaby's cobbled pedestrian side streets, and the second about a gas leak on Collins Avenue – and then she walked down to the newsagents to buy a copy of the *Burnaby News*. She could have sworn that the young girl behind the till smirked at her as she bought her copy but Paige decided she was just being paranoid. She flicked through the pages as she walked home. The banner headline read 'Proposed Burnaby Rubbish Dump – Local Councillor Says No'. Was this what Molly was talking about? She stopped on the path and read on. No, this article was all about Paddy Burns, the local People's Party councillor and election candidate. Paddy was a decent man and Paige had a lot of time for him. He was a little 'old school' for her taste but he wasn't easily swayed and was a good ally to have. She was standing as an independent candidate and as soon as Paddy had heard the news he had rung to wish her good luck. 'We could do with some fresh blood in the constituency,' he'd said. 'But is there any chance you might stand for the People's Party, Paige, do you think? Any chance at all? A woman like you would live long and prosper in the party, mark my words.' She'd been flattered but unmoved.

Paige turned the page. Immediately the offending photograph struck her straight between the eyes. She felt like she'd been slapped in the face – her cheeks began to burn and she turned around her to see if anyone was staring at her, feeling distinctly paranoid. This was what Molly had been talking about. She closed the newspaper quickly and had to stop herself from running home. Once back in the house, she closed the hall door behind her, hurried into the kitchen, opened the newspaper on the table and stared at page three. How could this have happened and where on earth did they get that photograph? She felt sick to the stomach. She sat down and forced herself to read the tabloid-like headline. *Councillor and Election Candidate in Flashing Shocker.*

> Local County Councillor and independent election candidate, Paige Brady, has quite a checkered past as this recent photograph clearly shows. Is this the type of person we want representing Burnaby at national level? Councillor Brady was unavailable for comment when we contacted her last night, but Councillor Annette Higgins, another independent election candidate, had this to say – 'I think it's a disgrace, Ms Brady exposing herself like that. I have no idea where the picture was taken but I just pray there were no children present.' Ms Brady who lives in Burnaby has two young children and Ms Higgins feels that she should not be putting herself forward as a candidate in the September election in light of this exposé.

Paige stared at the photograph. It was her all right. Football shirt pulled up, showing a rather nice lacy white bra. She remembered the occasion only too well – the UCD team, under her captaincy had just won the all-Ireland university title and had been chosen to represent their country in France the following month. The whole team was over the moon and had pulled their shirts over their heads in true football fashion to celebrate. Unfortunately the shot had been taken as her shirt was on its way to her head and not covering her face. But why had they printed only her mug shot – where was the rest of the team? And why had they given so much space to Annette Higgins' rants? And most importantly – where had they got the photograph?

Paige sat down at the table and took a deep breath. This is only the beginning, she thought. I've put myself on the line by becoming an election candidate. I have two choices – I can fall at the first hurdle or I can fight back. Her mobile phone rang and she pulled it out of her pocket. It was Tom.

'Oh, Paige. It's all my fault, they rang last night. You were working on the computer and I never gave you the message, I'm so sorry,' he said all in one rush.

'The newspaper you mean?'

'Yes, they rang and I forgot to give you the message.'

'It's most certainly not your fault, Tom,' she said firmly. 'Who rang exactly?'

'The editor – Millie thingy.'

'Millie O'Shea?'

'Yes.'

Paige knew Millie from way back. She was a decent enough sort but very ambitious. Paige knew she'd do anything to sell papers but she hadn't expected this. She made a quick decision. 'I'm going to ring her. Tell her the real story behind the photograph. Insist that she print the whole photograph and not just the cropped version. That will put everything in context. I have a strong feeling that Annette is behind this whole thing, Tom, mark my words.'

'You're an amazing woman,' Tom said in admiration. 'And if Annette is behind this she'd better watch her back. No one messes with my wife and gets away with it.'

'Thanks, Tom. Now I'd better get moving 'cause I want them to run a front page retraction tomorrow.'

'Are you sure you're all right, Paige? Is there anything I can do?'

'No. I'm fine, honestly. For a brief moment there I was a bit upset to tell the truth, but I've decided not to let this get to me. I'm stronger than that. And this is only the start of it, Tom. I intend to win a place in the elections – I deserve it – I've worked bloody hard for this constituency and no one is going to deny me the chance.'

'Good woman, I'm proud of you. And Paige?'

'Yes?'

'I love you.'

'Love you too.' She clicked the phone off with a smile on her lips, walked into the sitting room which she also used as a study, bringing the copy of the *Burnaby News* with her. She dialled calmly.

'Hello, is that the *Burnaby News*? I'd like to speak to Millie O'Shea please. Tell her it's Councillor Brady and that it's urgent. She's in a meeting? Well you can tell Ms O'Shea that it's in her best interest to talk to me right now, or she can deal with my lawyers instead. Because I'm sure she doesn't want a libel case on her hands now, does she?'

Chapter 7

Molly

Molly smiled widely as she read the lead story in the following day's *Burnaby News – 'Councillor Brady All-Ireland Soccer Hero'*, which was accompanied by the large and extremely striking photograph of the UCD Ladies' Soccer team, each team member with her shirt lifted over her face in celebration of their all-Ireland victory. She read on:

> Councillor Brady is proud of her impressive sporting achievements, including three all-Ireland medals and one European silver medal. At only twenty-two she was awarded the most prestigious college sporting award in existence – the Golden Griffin – for her dedication and tireless promotion of the sport. Councillor Brady, an independent candidate in the forthcoming election, says she will wholeheartedly support all the local GAA and soccer clubs if elected, and might even be cajoled into coaching the ladies' youth team. We think that Councillor Brady is just the sort of politician needed to represent Burnaby on a national level, and we apologize unreservedly for any embarrassment caused by yesterday's unfortunate photograph, which had been cropped in error, and the corresponding article. Ms Brady has graciously accepted our apology.

Molly immediately rang Paige. 'Paige, that's a brilliant article –

how on earth did you get them to print it? You're a miracle worker.'

'I threatened them with a libel suit, no more and no less. Millie O'Shea is no fool – the paper isn't exactly rolling in it and a libel suit is the last thing she needs on her CV.'

'You'll make some politician,' Molly said with respect. 'There'll be no messing with you.'

Paige laughed. 'That's what Tom said. Let's hope I get in. So, are you free for lunch? I feel like celebrating.'

'I surely am. Coffee Heaven at one, or would you like to go somewhere more swanky, you sports hero, you?'

'Coffee Heaven is perfect. See you later.'

As Molly put down the phone and folded up the paper which was lying on her desk, she murmured jauntily 'Hi ho, hi ho, it's back to work we go'. As she walked out of the office and onto the shop floor she found Sam on his hands and knees in the small children's section at the back of the shop, sorting through picture books. He looked up at her.

'What are you smiling about?' he asked. 'Must have been a good joke.'

She told him all about Paige's article.

'Phew.' He whistled. 'She sounds like a tough cookie, your friend. But she's dead right – the press shouldn't get away with printing things like that. Good on her.'

'And what are you up to?' Molly asked. 'Are they not a bit young for you?' She nodded at the picture books fanned out on the floor.

'I'm alphabetizing them,' he explained. 'I wouldn't have started if I'd realized what a big job it was.'

'No kidding. Now you see why it doesn't get done as often as it should.'

He smiled. 'At least I now know what we have in stock. So it hasn't been a complete waste of time.'

'I wouldn't tidy them too well or you'll be stuck doing it till kingdom come. Unless you like children's books, of course.'

'I like all books. To paraphrase the late, great Dr Seuss – "a book's a book, no matter how small."'

Molly laughed. 'Not bad, Mr Devine, not bad. And how are you settling in? I'm sorry I didn't have much time to spend with you over the weekend, but it was pretty hectic.'

'Hectic but fun,' Sam said. 'And I liked Rosemary, she was a real lady. Are there any more events lined up?'

'Loads,' Molly said. 'So keep your diary free.'

'Are they always at weekends?'

'Not always, why?'

'Weekends can be difficult for me, that's all.'

Molly looked at him. Was he being funny? Weekends didn't exactly suit *her* either but she just got on with it, along with the rest of the staff. She hoped he didn't expect special treatment just because he was the owner's son. Just when she'd started to like him too – typical.

'Sorry,' he said after a moment. 'That came out wrong. I know working weekends is part of the job. It's just . . .' The bell rang on the front door.

'Excuse me,' Molly said to Sam as she broke away and strode towards the front of the shop.

'There you are!' It was Anita – looking in buoyant form – a huge grin plastered on her face. 'How's my favourite bookseller?'

'Not too bad. And to what do I owe this honour? It's not often I see you so early on a Monday morning. Especially as Monday is now officially one of your many days off, you lady of leisure, you.'

'I have news, my dear, good news. Paige tells me you're meeting her for lunch. I'll be joining you and we're going to talk about . . .' she leant towards Molly and whispered conspiratorially in her ear 'our plan.'

'What plan?' Molly asked in her normal voice. She refused to whisper. Anita was being very Nancy Drew-ish and she wasn't having it.

'Shush!' Anita hissed.

'Anita, what are you talking about? There's not a soul in the shop.'

'What about Sam?' Anita whispered.

Molly stared at her. This time she did lower her voice. '*What* about Sam? What are you talking about?'

Anita put her finger to her lips. 'Don't tell him a word.'

'I can hardly tell him anything as you haven't exactly told *me* anything now, have you?'

Anita winked at her. 'See you at one in Coffee Heaven.' She walked towards the door.

'Oh, no, you're not leaving,' Molly protested. 'That's so unfair. Tell me what's going on. I want to know.'

'See you later,' Anita said breezily, completely ignoring her.

'Anita!' It was no use, Anita was strolling down the road, swinging her shopping basket at her side.

'Who was that?' Sam asked.

'Anita. She just called in to say hi.'

'Nice woman.' Sam smiled broadly but said nothing else.

'What?' Molly asked.

'Nothing.'

'Why are you smirking?'

'Am I smirking? I don't mean to. Ignore me, it's nothing.'

'Sam! Go on. It's something about Anita, isn't it? You'd better tell me or I'll jump to all sorts of conclusions.' She studied his face carefully. He looked a little flushed. 'You don't . . . no!'

'What?' he asked. 'I don't what?'

'You know – like her.'

'Me!' he spluttered. 'Of course not. Not me. No offence, but she's at least twenty years older than me.'

'So? Some men like older women. She's very attractive.'

'I agree – she's just not my type.'

'Really? And what is your type exactly?'

'How did I get myself into this?' He laughed. 'You're a pretty straight shooter, aren't you, Molly?'

'Straight shooter?'

'You ask very direct questions.'

'Does it bother you?'

'No, not really.'

'So are you going to answer my question?'

'No, not today. Maybe some other time.'

'Fair enough. But at least tell me about your father's crush on Anita.'

'Molly! I never said that.'

'Do you deny it? It's true, isn't it? If it's not you, it must be him. It's hardly Felix, he's very happily married.'

He smiled. 'I'm saying nothing. My lips are sealed.'

'I'm going to be keeping a good eye on your dad, just in case,' she said. 'Smooth operator that he is.'

'Promise you won't say a thing to Anita,' he pleaded. 'Dad would kill me.'

'I promise. But you owe me one.'

'I do not.'

'You so do.'

'OK, I'm not going to argue about this. Now shouldn't we do some work?'

'*You* should,' she said. 'The Panda rep is due in at any minute and we'll be in the office for about an hour ordering the new titles.'

'Can I sit in?'

She shook her head. 'Sorry, someone has to keep an eye on the shop and Felix won't be in until twelve.'

'Fine.' He seemed a little put out.

'Tell you what,' Molly said. 'You can sit in on the session with Dunwoody Press this afternoon? How about that?'

'Thanks. Is there anything you'd like me to do in the meantime?'

'Tidy the tables and put out the stock titles. They're on the trolley in the Romance room.'

'Will do.'

'I have a few things to do in the office, so can you send the Panda rep in when she arrives?'

'Sure. How will I know her?'

'She's tall with blonde hair. She's called Mona.'

Molly sat down at her desk and stared straight ahead of her. Sam was definitely growing on her. Now if he hadn't been late this morning and given such a feeble excuse she might even . . . no, that was stupid. He was Milo's son for goodness sake. Just because Sam didn't wear cashmere polo necks it didn't mean that he wasn't another charmer. Like father like son. Still, he was nice and she missed having a man around. She liked her independence and enjoyed her evenings in with Kate or Paige, but it wasn't quite the same. She missed having someone to snuggle up to on the sofa, someone to bring her chips and bottles of wine, someone to watch videos with, someone . . . Stop it! She told herself. You're a disgrace to modern women. You are perfectly fine on your own and much better off without a man to complicate things. She turned her attention to the computer screen and checked her e-mails. One new message in her in-box jumped straight out at her. It was from Denis and the subject was 'Missing You'. She knew she should delete it immediately without reading it but curiosity got the better of her. As she opened the message she heard a gentle knock on the door.

'Come on in, Mona.' She smiled up at the rep as she entered. 'You're bang on time as usual.'

'Creature of habit,' Mona replied.

'Sit down,' Molly said. 'Make yourself comfortable.'

'In this place?' Mona laughed. 'Never!'

Molly liked Mona very much. She was a no-nonsense kind of

woman with a razor-sharp mind and she was damn good at her job. Meetings with her were always a pleasure. Molly dragged her attention away from her e-mail and concentrated on the job at hand.

'Who's the new assistant?' Mona asked with interest. 'Not bad.'

'That's Sam Devine. The new owner's son no less. You've heard the news I presume?'

Mona nodded. 'Patricia told me. I hope they don't change the shop – it's perfect as it is.'

'Thanks.' Molly smiled gratefully. 'You say all the right things.'

'That's my job, honey buns. What's he like – the new guy?'

'Sam? I haven't quite decided yet. I'll tell you when I have.'

'He's a good-looking man. I wouldn't mind working with him myself, let me tell you.'

'You're welcome to visit any time.'

'Better get back to business,' Mona sighed. 'I have some crackers for Christmas too. Wait till you see.'

'That's terrible!' Molly groaned.

'What?'

'Crackers for Christmas, Mona, I expect more from you.'

'I'll try harder next time,' Mona grinned. 'Now, let's talk food – de-da!' She pulled a large hardback out of her large black-leather rep's bag. 'The new, all singing, all dancing *Panda Sinful Chocolate Cook Book*.'

As Molly walked towards the till a little later, passing several customers who were happily browsing, Sam was standing beside one of the front tables. 'What do you think?' he asked as she approached.

She looked at the table. He'd changed the books around so that they faced the front of the shop, not all four sides as they usually did. He'd created a raised area in the center of the table with one of the most popular hardbacks of the week. 'It looks great. Thank you.'

'I quite enjoyed it. It's a bit like building, isn't it?'

'I suppose it is.'

'Mona seemed nice. She introduced herself.'

'Oh, really?' Molly said. 'Your sort of woman, is she?'

He sighed deeply. 'Molly! Stop. I was just saying she was nice, that's all. I'm not in the market for a girlfriend at the moment, thank you very much. And I'll keep my observations to myself in future.' He looked at her with a serious expression on his face.

Molly felt that she'd overstepped the line and was mortified. She hadn't meant to embarrass him. 'Look, I'm sorry, I promise I won't ask you any more personal questions, all right?'

'No, I'm sorry, I didn't mean that to come out the way it did.' He stopped for a second as if deciding what to say next. 'I had a bad experience with someone last year to tell the truth and I haven't quite got over it. That's all. So, go easy on me.'

'I'm sorry,' she said, contrite. 'I really am. I don't know what to say.'

'It's no big deal. Let's talk about something else. Where do you live, Molly? Is it near here?'

She smiled at him gratefully. She told him about the townhouse she rented in Burnaby Grove and about Kate, making sure she kept the whole conversation on level ground. They were interrupted once or twice by customers asking questions or paying for books but it didn't seem to interrupt the flow.

'And where do you live?' she asked him after she'd wrapped a book in gift paper for a customer.

'In Sandybay, near the beach. I own a little cottage – it used to be a railway worker's cottage – it's small but fine for one. I've spent the last few years doing it up, it was in a complete state when I bought it. It's handy for Burnaby too – I can walk or get the train if I'm feeling lazy.'

'You're so lucky,' Molly said enviously. 'I love Sandybay beach. I often walk along it in the evenings.'

'So do I. Maybe we'll bump into each other one of these days.'

'Maybe.' Another customer walked in. Molly smiled at them and then looked at her watch. 'Listen, I have to fly. Felix said he'll come out onto the floor to give you a hand. I'm off for lunch with Anita and my friend, Paige. I'll be back in an hour.'

'See you later.'

Molly stopped outside Coffee Heaven for a moment. She turned around quickly. She could have sworn someone was staring at her, she could feel it, but that was stupid – there was no one there. She looked across the road. There were a few people on the far pavement – a young woman pushing a buggy and a well-dressed older man talking to Connie from Halo – none of whom were paying her the least bit of attention. She pushed open the door to the coffee shop, breathed in the familiar warm, coffee smell and felt better instantly Paige and Anita waved at her from their favourite table at the back of the shop. She smiled and made her way over. I was just being stupid, she told herself. But the sensation of being watched had unnerved her and it took a few minutes to shake it off. But as she listened to the two women's plan unfold she forgot all about it. Their startling idea for the bookshop was quite something – but could they pull it off?

After their heady and productive lunch Paige walked Molly back to the bookshop.

'Come in and meet Sam,' Molly insisted.

'Can't – I have to run. I've a meeting with . . . hang on, this is Sam Devine, the owner's son? Anita says he's very attractive. Maybe I'll just stick my head in for a minute. Just to be polite. Why didn't you tell me he was good looking?'

'It wasn't relevant,' Molly sniffed.

'Since when are good-looking men in Burnaby not relevant?'

Paige laughed. 'Get a grip. It's not as if the place is exactly crawling with them.'

'You're a married woman,' Molly reminded her.

'Doesn't mean I can't admire a nice bod when I see it.'

'Paige!'

Paige ignored her and waltzed in the door. She went straight to the front desk. 'You must be Sam.' She smiled warmly and held out her hand. 'I'm Paige, a good friend of Molly's. Nice to meet you.'

'Hi, Paige.' Sam smiled back. 'You're the "Sport Billy". Molly was telling me about the article this morning. Good on you – I like your style. Newspapers get away with too much these days. It's good to see someone fighting back.'

'Thanks. Listen, I have to run. But welcome to Burnaby. Are you a local?'

'If you mean can I vote, then the answer is yes. And you have my vote, Councillor Brady.'

'Fell straight into that one, didn't I?' Paige grinned. 'You'll have to excuse me, it's election time after all.'

'Best of luck with it. Hope you get elected.'

'Thanks.'

Molly had been listening to the whole exchange with interest. She walked Paige out. 'You're shameless,' she hissed at her outside the door.

'And he's lovely,' Paige whispered back. 'If I were you . . .'

'I don't want to hear it.' Molly glared at her. 'Talk to you later, Councillor.'

'Later, lover.' Paige winked at her.

'I wouldn't be winking at me like that. Annette Higgins might have you outed as a lesbian.'

'Wouldn't put it past her. I wonder what she'll come up with next.'

'Next?'

'Who do you think sent the *News* the photo?'

'No!' Molly exclaimed. 'Really? How did you find out?'

Paige tapped her nose. 'I have my sources.' She glanced at her watch. 'Now I really do have to go. Later, Babe.'

As Molly turned towards the door she felt a hand on her shoulder and jumped.

'Sorry,' a familiar voice said, 'I didn't mean to frighten you.'

'Denis,' she said, staring at him in astonishment. 'I thought we'd agreed . . .'

'I had to see you, Molly. It was a matter of life and death.'

'Hardly. And I'm working, Denis. This is not a good time.'

He looked at her carefully. 'Tonight then. It's important, please.'

'No, Denis. Not tonight and not any night, understand? We have to get on with our lives. We can't go backwards.' She sighed. 'We've been through all this. And anyway, I thought you'd met someone.'

He looked sheepish. 'Yes, well that's over now.'

Molly stared at him in amazement. 'That was quick.' She narrowed her eyes. 'Hang on, Denis, there never was anyone, was there? You were just trying to make me jealous.'

'There was!' he protested. 'It just didn't work out.'

Molly knew better than to argue with him. 'I have to go,' she said firmly, walking away as she spoke.

'I'll drop in tomorrow.' He turned on his heels and scooted away quickly before she had a chance to say anything.

'Denis,' she called after him. 'Don't come into my work again, please.'

But to no avail. He'd rounded the corner and was now out of sight.

'Shit!' she muttered. Her hands were shaking. She leant against the shop front and took a deep breath. A few minutes later, when her heart had stopped thumping quite so hard in her chest, she went inside.

'Everything all right?' Sam asked. He'd seen her talking to a man outside and the exchange didn't seem too friendly. He didn't like to mention it, as he shouldn't have been spying on her.

'Fine,' she lied. 'Just fine and dandy.'

Later Molly opened yet another e-mail from Denis. *Darling Molly, why don't you stop this madness? You know we belong together. Don't fight it. I won't give you up. I love you with all my being. Denis.* She shivered. It was all going to start again, she could feel it. But this time would be different – this time she'd have the strength to say no. She'd made a promise to herself, not to mention to Paige. There was no way in high heaven she was going to get back with him. No way! It was time for her to move on – finally.

'Callum, please stop kicking my seat,' Molly said crossly. She glanced at Paige. 'Sorry,' she mouthed at her. She didn't want to get him in trouble but it was getting annoying and she had asked him several times.

Paige swiftly pulled into a parking spot. 'Callum, you'd better behave in the puppet show, I'm warning you,' Paige turned around and told him. 'Do you understand?'

'Yes, Mummy,' he said with an angelic smile and nodded his head vigorously.

'I'll get you a treat afterwards if you're good,' Molly said. Paige had been through a busy time in the last week, what with the unsavoury exposé in the *Burnaby News* and the corresponding aftermath and Molly was determined to make this afternoon as easy for her as she could. Paige had had to be convinced to come out in the first place – she was exhausted but felt guilty that she hadn't spent any time with Callum this week.

'Can I have Skittles?' he asked hopefully. His mummy never let him have Skittles and they were his favourite sweets.

'No,' Paige said firmly. 'They're full of E numbers, they

always send you up the walls. You can have some popcorn or crisps.'

'Pringles are crisps,' he said firmly. 'Aren't they, Molly?'

Molly said nothing. Most of the time it was best not to interfere when it came to Paige and Callum.

'We'll see how good you are,' said Paige.

A few minutes later they were entering the large red wooden gate of the Hayward Puppet Theatre in Blackrock.

'I haven't been here since I was a child,' Molly reminisced. 'It's changed quite a bit but I remember it clearly. Dad used to take me every Christmas until I was seven. Then he said I was too old for puppets and he stopped. I remember being really upset and Mum having to comfort me. He didn't replace the trip with anything, you see, and I didn't understand. I thought I'd done something wrong and that he was punishing me.'

'That's a shame,' Paige said. 'He can be quite . . . how will I put this – black and white, your dad.'

'Tell me about it.' Molly frowned. She didn't much like talking about her dad. Fergal Harper was a strong, overpowering man who had been deeply disappointed that his only daughter hadn't followed him into the family printing business. Even though she was twenty-eight, he still made Molly feel like a child when he talked at her. She got on well with her mother, Laura, but had never really forgiven her for not standing up to him more and for never taking her side when she was growing up. Molly, rightly or wrongly, blamed her lack of self-confidence and her feeling of inadequacy on her childhood.

'Have you seen your folks recently?' Paige asked as she paid for three tickets.

'Not really. I spoke to Mum last week, she seems fine. I sent her out the list of books we've read in the Book Club. She's just started one up with some of her Mothers' Union friends.'

'I didn't think she was a great reader,' Paige said, watching

Callum, who was walking in front of them, like a hawk as they made their way towards the puppet theatre.

'She used to read a lot apparently, before she had me. Then she kind of got out of the habit.'

'Callum!' Paige said loudly. 'Sorry, Molly. I'll be back in one second.' Callum had run on ahead, bumping into a tall man and his son and sending the young boy flying sideways. He came to a halt at the theatre door and leant against the wall to wait for his mother, oblivious to the trouble he'd caused.

'I'm so sorry about my son,' Paige said to the man. He turned towards her. 'Oh, it's you,' she said in surprise.

'Sorry?' he asked.

'We met briefly last week in the bookshop. I'm Paige, Molly's friend. Molly's just . . .'

'Here,' Molly finished for her.

'Of course. Paige. I didn't recognize you out of your suit. So this is what you do on your days off, Councillor.' Sam smiled at Molly. 'And Molly, not what I would have expected from you at all – going to puppet shows.'

'I'm here with Paige and her son, Callum,' Molly explained. 'He's the one who knocked . . . um . . .'

The boy had been watching and listening to the adults with interest. He was small, with white-blonde hair and steel-rimmed round glasses, but from his face Paige reckoned he might be five or six.

'This is Hugh,' Sam said. 'My son. Say hello Hugh.'

Hugh said nothing, clutched his dad's hand and hid behind his legs.

'He's a little shy.'

'You didn't tell me you had a son,' said Molly. She was more than a little taken aback to tell the truth. She'd presumed from what Sam had been saying over the last week that he was single. She was confused. Hadn't he said he lived on his own? She'd obviously got the wrong end of the stick. Still, it did explain some of his late mornings she figured – he was probably dropping his son to school. It also explained why working weekends might be difficult for him.

'You didn't ask,' he said evenly in answer to her question.

Paige snuck a look at Molly. Molly seemed a little flushed and flustered.

'What age are you, Hugh?' Paige bent down and asked the boy.

Still no reply.

'He's nearly six,' Sam answered for him.

'Mum!' Callum shouted from the doorway. 'Hurry up.'

'Sorry, I'd better go and get him,' Paige said. 'But we might see you both afterwards.'

She and Molly walked towards Callum, excusing themselves to the people queuing in front of them.

'Mum!' Callum beamed as she reached him. 'Who's the little boy you were talking to? I've been waiting ages.'

'That's the little boy you knocked down when you dashed over here,' she said sternly. 'He's called Hugh.'

'Sorry,' he murmured, knowing from her tone of voice that he was in trouble again.

The woman taking the tickets smiled at Paige. 'Go on in,' she said. 'The lad's dying for the show to begin. Can't wait, he told me, didn't you, pet? He's been as good as gold waiting for you.'

Callum smiled up at his new friend.

'Thanks,' Paige said gratefully, handing the woman the tickets.

'Enjoy the show, young man,' the woman said to Callum.

As they sat down on the small wooden seats in the dim auditorium Paige leant over to Molly.

'You never told me he was married,' she whispered.

'I didn't know he was. He's not wearing a ring and I could have sworn he told me he lived alone. Still, it makes no odds to me.'

'Really?'

'Yes, really. And stop looking around. He'll think we're talking about him.'

'We are.'

Molly sniffed. 'Not any more we aren't.'

'Message received and understood.' Paige smiled at her knowingly.

'My Action Man says that when you pull the string in his back,' Callum said.

Paige grinned at Molly. 'Little pitchers,' she said.

'Have big ears,' Callum finished for her.

'Yes, thank you Callum,' said Paige. 'That's what your daddy always says too. Now you tell me when the curtain opens, will you?'

'Do you not have eyes, Mum?'

'Just watch the curtain, Callum, OK?' Paige said curtly, ignoring his rudeness.

'OK, Mum. But can I go . . .'

'No!'

'OK, OK.' He sat slumped with his arms folded in front of him and pulled his face into a huge scrunched-up frown. He started jiggling his feet up and down on the floor.

'What's wrong, Callum?' Paige asked with a sigh.

'I only wanted to ask could I go to the loo. I really need to pee. It's an emergency. If I don't go I'll wet —'

'Yes, thank you, Callum,' Paige interrupted. 'We get the picture.'

'I'll take him,' Molly offered quickly.

'Are you sure?' Paige asked. She could do with a few minutes' peace.

'Not at all. Come along, Callum.'

'Tell her I'm allowed in the boys' loo, will you, Mum?'

'Is he?' asked Molly.

Paige shook her head. 'Bring him into the Ladies with you, if you don't mind. He has a habit of talking to strangers and you wouldn't know . . .'

'I understand,' said Molly. 'You can't be too careful. Now, hurry up Callum or we'll be late for the show.'

On the way back, Molly saw Sam and Hugh sitting on the right-hand side of the auditorium. Hugh had his head on his dad's knee and Sam was talking to him or telling him a story, she couldn't make out which. He noticed her and waved over. She waved back and took her seat again.

'Was Callum OK?' Paige asked.

'Fine,' Molly replied biting her lip. He'd actually tried to soak her with water from the tap but her friend didn't need to know that.

After the show, they met Sam and Hugh again in the foyer.

'Did you all enjoy that?' Sam enquired.

'It was great,' Callum answered. 'I want to be the prince.' He stood with his two hands together in front of him. 'Look, I can cut down that forest for the princess lady, no trouble.'

'Sleeping Beauty,' Hugh said quietly. 'She was called Sleeping Beauty.'

'That's right,' said Paige. 'Did you like the show, Hugh?'

He nodded eagerly. 'I have a puppet theatre at home. Daddy made it for me. It's wood.'

Paige and Molly looked at Sam with interest.

'You made a puppet theatre?' asked Molly.

Sam shrugged his shoulders. 'I like woodwork. I'm good with my hands.'

'He made my bed too,' Hugh added proudly. 'And my desk and my shelves.'

'Yes, well, we'd better be going.' Sam put his arm around Hugh. 'Have to get you home, young man.'

'Do you need a lift?' Paige asked kindly.

'No, it's only around the corner, we'll walk. But thanks for the offer.'

'Not at all. See you around.'

'Yes, and see you tomorrow, Molly.'

'Yes,' she replied distractedly. 'Tomorrow.' She could have sworn he said he lived in Sandybay. How could they walk that far? It would take hours. It was all very strange.

'What's up?' Paige asked as they got onto the car. 'You seem a little out of it.'

'Nothing,' Molly said. She had no intention of telling Paige that she'd been thinking about Sam. 'Just work stuff, you know.'

'Don't let it get you down. As I told you, once our plan is in action there'll be absolutely nothing to worry about. Honestly.'

'Thanks,' Molly said gratefully. 'I'll stop worrying, I promise.' Easier said than done, she thought. 'And how are you?'

'Fine, well almost fine. We're a right pair, aren't we?'

Molly laughed. 'That we are.'

'At least I don't have to worry about Callum this month. Angus starts tomorrow.'

'Kate told me. I don't think she's too thrilled to tell the truth. She doesn't like to mix business with pleasure.'

'Is there something going on between them?' Paige asked. 'Is that what you mean?'

'No! Sorry, pleasure was probably the wrong word to use. Angus is one of her dummy dating clients and . . . oops, you knew that, didn't you?'

'Not exactly. Lily said they were friends. She didn't say how they knew each other.'

'Trust me to put my foot in it. I'm sorry, I should have kept my mouth shut. Kate is very particular about client confidentiality. Don't say anything to Angus, please?'

'I won't,' Paige said. 'And if Kate and Lily like him that's all that matters to me. The fact that he can't get a date and resorted to using Kate's help has no bearing on my views of him. No, none at all.'

'Paige! Promise me you won't say anything.'

'I already have. It just seems kind of sad though. Sad and funny at the same time.'

'I guess it does,' Molly said thoughtfully. Although the way her own arid love life was looking, she could probably do with a helping hand herself.

Chapter 8

Kate

Kate stood on the doorstep and put the key in the lock. She heard a noise behind her – a slight rustle in the bushes and she swung around to have a look. Nothing. Must have been a cat or something, she reasoned. Then she heard it again. It sounded bigger than a cat, more like a person moving through the leaves.

'Hello?' she said nervously. 'Is anyone there?'

There was no reply. She turned the key quickly, let herself in and closed the door firmly behind her. Safely in the hall, she leant her back against the door, her breath catching in her throat and her heart thumping. Was there someone out there? She left the living-room light off, tiptoed towards the window and looked out. She gasped as she saw a shadowy figure crawl from under the rather scraggly hedge and walk towards the gate. Who the hell was that and what were they doing? The figure paused for a moment before walking out the gate and down the road. Kate watched him in astonishment. Because it certainly was a him and not a her. She noticed the lenses of his glasses flash under the street lamp as he sloped away.

'Molly?' she shouted upstairs. 'Molly, are you in? Quick!'

She heard a muffled noise from upstairs. 'Coming!' Molly

yelled. She appeared at the top of the stairs, resplendent in her dark pink towelling dressing gown, her hair caught up in a clashing light pink towel. 'I was washing my hair. Is everything OK?'

'Not really. There was a man hiding in the front garden. I opened the door and he went away. I saw him from the living-room window.'

'A man?' Molly asked with concern. 'Where exactly in the garden?'

'Behind the big straggly bush.'

Molly looked at her blankly.

'The one beside the gate.'

'Oh, that one.' She walked down the stairs and looked carefully at Kate. 'Nothing happened did it? He wasn't a flasher or anything?'

'No, I don't know what he was doing. Just watching the house, I think. He just gave me a fright, that's all.'

'And you're all right?'

'Fine. I think I should ring the guards though. He might be dangerous. He could be a burglar or something.'

'Maybe,' Molly said, a thought coming into her mind. 'What did he look like? Did you recognize him?'

Kate shook her head. 'No. He was quite tall and thin and wearing glasses, that's all I know.'

'I see,' Molly said slowly.

'What?' Kate demanded. 'Do you know who it was?'

'I might,' she replied slowly. 'I'll find out. Give me one second.' She walked quickly back up the stairs.

'Molly . . .' Kate shouted after her but it fell on deaf ears.

'I'll kill him,' Molly muttered as she picked up her mobile from her dressing table and punched in the familiar number. 'Denis, is that you? Where are you?'

'Um, nowhere,' he said a little nervously. 'Where are you?'

'You know damn well where I am. Just answer me this one

question – are you spying on me? Were you outside the house a few minutes ago?'

'Um, no.'

'What do you mean, no?' she asked, her voice rising to a dangerous level. 'I know you're lying. And before you say anything you may like to know that my housemate saw you and is able to identify you.'

'But I've never met her,' he protested. 'How could she . . .'

'Got you,' Molly screamed. 'Don't you ever, ever scare her like that again, do you hear me?'

'But I was just dropping in a letter,' he said meekly. 'Then I just thought I'd wait for a little while to see if you came out. I wanted to talk to you. You haven't been answering my phone calls and . . .'

'Too right I haven't, you nutcase. And if I ever catch you stalking me again I'll report you to the guards, do you understand?' She didn't wait for his answer.

She sat down on the bed and took a deep breath. Men! There was a knock on the door.

'Molly? Are you all right?' It was Kate.

'Come on in.'

'I heard the shouting and I was worried.'

Molly looked up at Kate. 'I should explain – that guy in the bushes earlier was my ex – Denis. I'm so sorry he frightened you. I wouldn't say he'll do it again in a hurry. I gave him a right earful.'

'At least it wasn't a burglar, I suppose. But he gave me a real fright. My heart is still thumping.'

'I'm so sorry.'

'It's OK, it's not your fault. And this was on the hall floor. It's addressed to you.' Kate handed her a red envelope.

Molly handed it straight back. 'It's from him. Bin it for me.'

'Are you sure?'

'Positive.'

Kate took it back, sat down on the bed beside her friend and cleared her throat. 'Is Denis, how will I put this, a little highly strung?'

'As in totally crazy?'

Kate nodded. 'Does he often do this kind of thing?'

'I'd have to say yes. But hopefully it's all over now.'

'Hopefully,' Kate murmured. She didn't want any more unnerving experiences – she got quite enough of those at work, thank you very much.

'I'm sorry about all this,' Molly said. 'I don't know what to say. He's a strange one.'

'And I never even had the pleasure of meeting him,' Kate said. 'Listen, don't worry about it. I'm going to bed now. I'm tired to the bone.'

'How was your date?'

'Brutal. He was a total male chauvinist and kept calling me babe.'

'That good?'

'Sad thing is he'll probably have no problem finding a date – some women love that kind of thing. Plus from all accounts he's rolling in it.'

'Always helps.' Molly smiled.

'No kidding. The more I learn about men the less I like them.'

'You don't mean that,' Molly said. 'You must have met some decent ones along the way. What about that Angus – Callum's nanny? Paige has been singing his praises.'

'I'm sure he'd be delighted to be referred to as a nanny,' Kate said. 'I must tell him that. He's OK, I suppose.'

'Only OK?' Molly looked at Kate, a smile lingering on her lips.

'What are you implying? Stop looking at me like that.'

'Like what?'

'You know.' Kate stood up abruptly. 'I'm going to bed.'

'Sweet dreams,' Molly said, still smiling.

'Yeah, Yeah,' Kate muttered. She walked into her room, the red envelope still in her hand. She threw it into her waste paper bin and stared at it. Men! What a waste of time and energy. She walked over to the window and stared out. No one lurking under the street lamp or in their garden as far as she could tell. She closed the curtains and sat down on the bed. Angus! As if she'd be interested in someone like Angus – what a joke!

The following lunchtime Kate called into Coffee Heaven before work. She'd had a blissfully free morning with no client meetings and was making the most of it. She'd gone for a long walk this morning up Killiney Hill, followed by a shower and some yoga and she hadn't felt this good in a long time. Last night's date was long forgotten and she even had a whole evening to herself – one of her clients had cancelled his date and she'd tried not to sound too delighted when he'd rung with his apologies.

'You look happy,' Alex said as she placed a steaming bowl of carrot soup in front of her. She raised her eyebrows. 'Anyone new on the scene?'

'Alex!' Kate scolded. 'I don't need a man to be in a good mood.'

'Sorry.'

'Don't worry about it. So how are things? Any news?'

'Well actually,' Alex leant down and lowered her voice, 'I did want to talk to you about something, are you free in a few minutes? I won't keep you long.'

'Sure.' Kate was a little taken aback. She didn't know Alex all that well and wondered what on earth she wanted to ask her about.

'I'll be back in a minute. I'll just get Matty out of the kitchen to cover for me.'

A few minutes later Alex sat down at Kate's table and smiled nervously at her. 'How's the soup?' she asked.

'Good.' Kate smiled back. 'Is that what you wanted to ask me?'

'Um, no, not exactly.' Alex blushed and leant forward. 'I wanted to ask your advice on, um, dating, I suppose. There's this guy I like and I don't know what to do about it.'

Kate put down her soup spoon and looked at Alex carefully. 'I don't know if I'm the right person to ask. I normally help men, you see. I've never helped a woman before.'

'I'd pay you,' Alex said quickly. 'What's the going rate?'

'Don't be silly.'

'But you're a professional, Kate,' Alex said firmly. 'I insist.'

'How about a month's supply of free coffee? And the odd bowl of soup?'

'Done!' Alex grinned. 'So, will you help me?'

'I'll try. Tell me about this man. What's happened so far?'

'Well nothing's happened really. Nothing at all. In fact he never seems to notice me at all. He's very busy and . . . um, I'm sure I don't make much of an impression on him. He's only ever seen me in my apron.'

'He's a customer?'

Alex nodded. 'If I tell you will you promise to keep it a secret?'

'Of course, everything you say is completely confidential, you have my word.'

'Thanks.' Alex looked around to check there was no one listening and then whispered, 'It's Harry from the plant shop.'

'Harry Masterson?' Kate asked in amazement.

'Shush, lower your voice. Yes, that Harry. He's amazing and I'm totally mad about him. And Kate, he doesn't even know I exist.'

'But he will,' Kate said and patted her hand. 'He most certainly will.'

Ten minutes later, after arranging another meeting with Alex, Kate put the first germ of her plan into action. This was going to be an interesting one. Because just the previous day she'd taken on a new client – none other than Harry himself. Alex and Harry would be a rather unlikely couple – he lived his life at breakneck pace and personally Kate found him rather spiky. Alex was far more laid back, a nice girl with a good heart, if a little nosy – but stranger things had happened.

Swinging open the door of Slick Harry's after lunch she was greeted by a shout.

'Watch the bloody cactus!' Harry came running over. 'Sorry, Kate. But I need it for the *Des and Shelly Show*. They are holding some sort of Western Special and I have to talk about cacti. That cactus is the centrepiece. So what can I do for you?'

'Two things,' Kate said coming straight to the point, knowing how busy Harry always was. 'Firstly, I'm looking for a new gardener for my gran, she's coming home from hospital next week but she has to rest her ankle for six weeks. I wanted someone to look after the garden for her. Someone who wouldn't mind being watched and advised.'

'Might know the very woman,' Harry said. 'Cecily Hammond. She's from Bray – nice woman and very sensible.'

'A woman? That would be great. Do you have a number for her?'

'Certainly.' He strode towards the large stainless steel desk, flicked through his large Filofax and scribbled a mobile number on the back of one of his cards.

'Thanks,' said Kate, pocketing it. 'I appreciate it. And the other thing was that Alex in Coffee Heaven was looking for some new plants for the shop. I suggested she called in on Thursday morning to have a look. Will you be here?'

He flicked through his Filofax again. 'Should be, yes, I think so. Is Alex the blonde girl?'

'Yes,' Kate said, hoping she didn't sound a little too eager. 'Lovely girl, great cook too.'

'Thought it was her brother who did all the cooking?' asked Harry.

'In the shop, yes. But she trained at Dunmore House, with Rena Travis.' Rena was a well-known Irish celebrity chef who ran her own cookery school.

'Really?' he seemed to be losing interest so she didn't push it.

'And I'll see you on Thursday evening for our, um, meeting,' she said moving towards the door.

'Yes, indeed,' he said a little nervously. 'See you then.'

As soon as she'd left he stared after her. To tell the truth he was a little embarrassed about using Kate's services, but as he'd had nothing but disasters on the dating front recently he'd decided that it was time to take matters into his own hands and do something positive about it. All he seemed to meet were models, television presenters and would-be actresses. And what he was really looking for was someone like his mother – a kind, decent girl who could take care of him and slow his life down. It had got far too fast for his liking and at times he longed to retire to the country with a Range Rover and a couple of dogs. And a nice, pretty wife and two adorable children – a boy and a girl. Not that he'd ever admit this to anyone of course. In everyone's eyes he was Harry Masterson, plant genius, daytime-television darling, and man about town.

'Hello, Kate,' Cathy said looking up from the desk in Baroque. 'Mind if I go on my lunch straight away? Trina's at the doctor's and I'm starving.'

'No problem. Just give me a second to dump my bag in the back.'

'You look well today,' Cathy said to Kate she returned onto the floor. 'I like the suede skirt.'

'Thanks, it's Molly's. She claims it's too tight on her so she gave it to me.'

'Listen Kate, Trina is a little, um, upset. She says she keeps trying to apologize to you but that you won't . . .'

'I don't really want to talk about it,' Kate said firmly.

'I understand, but Trina is my friend. She may be an old boot some of the time but she's not that bad really underneath it all. She's been very good to me over the years.'

'But she hasn't been good to me, has she Cathy? In all honesty?'

Cathy looked at the ground. 'No, I suppose not,' she admitted. 'But people change. Give her a chance.'

'That's just it, I don't believe they do. Not really.'

'Just let her apologize properly, please? It would mean a lot to her. And it would make working here with the two of you a damn sight more bearable.'

'Has it been awful?' Kate asked, suddenly realizing that it had probably been no picnic for Cathy over the while with the two of then sniping at each other.

'Yes, to tell the truth, it has.'

Kate sighed. 'I'll see what I can do. I'm not promising anything, mind.'

Cathy smiled. 'Thanks, Kate.'

As soon as Trina opened the door of Baroque that afternoon Kate made a decision. What both Cathy and Angus had said had made her think. She stood just inside the door waiting in case she changed her mind. Trina looked pale and slightly frazzled. She looked at Kate expectantly.

'Yes?' Trina demanded. 'Are you going to have a go at me already? Can you not wait till I'm in the door?'

'I want to talk to you,' Kate said mildly, ignoring the barbed questions. She flicked the sign on the door from 'open' to 'closed' and pulled down the blinds.

'Oh? What about?' Trina asked, her interest piqued.

'Sit down,' Kate replied firmly.

Trina did as she was told for once, without comment.

'I accept your apology,' Kate began. 'I know all about the fertility treatment – Cathy told me. The injections sound horrible and I'm sorry you have to go through all that.'

Trina nodded, too stunned to say anything.

'I want to declare a truce,' Kate continued. 'I've had enough of the bickering, it's tiring and neither of us needs it right now. So can we agree to be civil to each other?'

Trina nodded. 'Yes, absolutely.'

'And no smart comments from either side?'

'Agreed. On one condition.'

'What's that?' Kate asked.

'That you think about designing a shoe collection for Baroque.'

Kate began to protest. 'But . . .'

Trina put her hands up. 'I just said think about it, OK? I have a contact in Italy who runs a shoe factory. They specialize in soft leathers. I know you were good, Kate, one of the best. I talked to my contacts in Boston and they remember you well. Let me know when you're interested.'

'Don't hold your breath.'

'And last thing,' Trina added.

'Yes?'

'I think there's definitely a market out there for Irish designer baby shoes – soft leather ones. "Baroque for Babies", what do you think?'

'I don't think it would work,' Kate said calmly. She opened the blinds and let the sun back into the shop. Designer shoes for babies, now that would be a fun project – if she were interested, of course, which she was most certainly not. She hadn't designed a shoe for a very long time. Not since Boston. Not since . . . she blocked it out of her mind. No point thinking about the past, she had to move on.

Later that afternoon Cathy was delighted to find the two

women working together at the desk at the back of the shop – putting the final touches to the sale banners and showcards.

'Looking good, ladies,' Cathy said surveying the assorted dark pink signs. They'd had them printed in the local printers – dark purple lettering on a rich pink background, all in 'Baroque'-style lettering of course – to which Kate and Trina were adding pink feathers and assorted sequins and plastic jewels. 'How many more are you going to do?'

'We're almost finished,' Kate said with a smile. 'Thank goodness. I've glue all over my fingers.'

A customer walked in the door. 'I'll get it,' Cathy said. 'Councillor Higgins, how are you? How can I help?' Cathy knew that Annette Higgins liked to be referred to by her proper title and she tried not to smirk as she said it. It had been plain old Annette up until a year ago, before she'd gone all high flying. And now that she was on the verge of being elected to the Dail, the Irish government (in her own mind at least), Annette was becoming unbearably pompous.

'I'm looking for something comfortable but smart for canvassing,' said Annette. 'With a low heel, I think.'

'I have just the shoe,' Cathy said. 'What colour – black, dark brown . . . ?'

'Navy,' Annette said firmly. 'All my suits are navy.'

'Fine,' Cathy said. 'And you're a size . . . ?'

'Six.'

'Right then. Give me a moment and I'll pull out the shoe I'm thinking of.'

'Rather her than me,' Trina murmured to Kate as Cathy walked past them into the small storeroom. 'I bet her feet smell.'

'Trina!' Kate giggled. 'I'm sure they don't.' She smiled to herself – maybe being nice to Trina wasn't going to be as difficult as she'd thought.

*

'Hi, Angus, thanks for coming.' Kate gestured at him to sit down.

'Two coffees please, Alex,' she shouted over.

'Coming right up,' Alex shouted straight back.

'My pleasure.' Angus sat down, nudging the table a little and spilling some milk from the small white jug. 'Oops, sorry. So, am I in trouble? What does my report say – "will never amount to much", "if Angus spent as much time at his work as he did clown-acting he might do better in class"?'

'Report?' Kate murmured in confusion. Then she remembered. Of course – that was why they'd arranged to meet for coffee last week – before Molly had found them and they'd rushed off to hospital. She'd forgotten all about it. 'Sorry, I left it at home. I'll send it to you in the post. Is that all right?'

'Fine,' he said. 'So, you decided you couldn't live without me, it that it?'

'Not exactly.' Kate stifled a laugh. 'I wanted to talk to you about Paige. I understand she's asked you to mind Callum.'

'Yes, I'm going over to meet him tomorrow. I hope he likes me.'

Kate smiled. 'I'm sure he will. But do you think it's such a good idea? I don't feel all that comfortable with it to tell the truth.'

'What do you mean? Thanks,' he mouthed to Alex as she put down their coffee. He added milk and four spoons of sugar to his cup.

Kate wrinkled her nose. 'How can you drink it so sweet?'

He took a slurp and smiled. 'Easy. But stop trying to change the subject. Why does it bother you? Because Paige is your friend? Because in some strange convoluted way you've got it into your head that it compromises your position? Because you're scared that if you see too much of me you actually might start liking me?'

'No!' she protested. 'Nothing like that. I'm just thinking of *you.*'

'Oh really?' He raised his eyebrows. 'How's that?'

'As I'm sure Paige has pointed out, Callum is a bit of a handful. I just think you should know what you're letting yourself in for, that's all.'

'That's not it, is it, Kate?' he said gently. 'I know you better than that, even though you won't believe me. I know you care about Paige and Callum, too. And from what Lily told me the little lad could do with some attention right at the moment. And maybe I can help. Would you begrudge him that just because you feel uneasy about having me around?'

'I don't feel uneasy . . .' she began.

'Face it, Kate, you're beginning to like me and it scares you.'

'Angus! That's not it at all. You're being ridiculous.'

'Am I? Think about it, Kate. I'll see you around.' He stood up, pushed the chair towards the table, spilling both cups of coffee in the process and strode away.

Kate watched him leave, dumbfounded.

'Is he coming back?' Alex asked a few minutes later as she wiped the table down.

'Um, no,' Kate said. 'I don't think so.'

'Right, I'll take away his coffee so. Anything wrong, Kate? You look a little perturbed.'

'Just thinking.'

'Any news on Harry?' Alex asked in a low voice.

'Yes, actually. I forgot to tell you. He's expecting you to call in on Thursday morning about some plants for Coffee Heaven. So be sure to slap on some lip-gloss. Maybe put your hair up. You could bring him some muffins or biscuits or something. And make sure to tell him you made them yourself.'

'That's a little extreme isn't it?' Alex said. 'Bringing him food. He doesn't even know me.'

'Ah, but he does,' Kate corrected her. 'He said some very

complimentary things about you and he was most impressed when I told him about your Dunmore House training.'

'Really?'

Kate could see this gave Alex confidence and made her more sure of herself. She nodded firmly. 'Play it cool. Ask his advice on new plants for the shop, but don't decide on anything. That way you can call back another day.'

'Great, thanks. I hope I don't go all red and get tongue-tied.'

'If you do, just take a deep breath and smile at him. You have a lovely smile. No man minds a little blushing. In fact, they think it's quite sweet.'

'Really?'

'Really. And it would do no harm to drop into the library and take out a few books on plants. Drop in a few Latin names to impress him. Show him you have a shared interest.'

'I quite like gardening to tell the truth, and that's a great idea.' She leant forward and kissed her on the cheek. 'Thanks, Kate. I appreciate it.'

On Thursday Kate had two unexpected visitors to Baroque.

'Harry,' she said, surprised to see him as he walked in the door. 'You know we only do ladies' shoes. Unless you're looking for something in a larger size.' She winked at him.

'No, I'm not here for shoes. Although I'd love to try some on for the giggle. But someone might see me. You know how small Burnaby is.'

'Don't I just.'

'Are Trina or Cathy here?'

'No, I'm on my own this afternoon.'

'Good.' He sat down on the red sofa. 'I think I'll cancel our meeting this evening, if that's OK with you.'

'Fine,' she said. 'I'll refund the money.'

'Why don't you just hang on to it, I might need you at a later date.'

'And, if you don't mind me asking, what has changed your mind?'

'Um, I kind of met someone.'

'Really?'

'The girl from the coffee shop, you know, Alex. She called in this morning and I haven't been able to get her out of my head.'

Kate beamed. Yes! she thought. Instant success. You're good, Kate Bowan, damn good.

'She called into the shop and she looked so different. Her hair was pinned up with curly bits hanging around her face and she has the loveliest smile, Kate. I was trying to rush her through choosing some plants but she offered me one of these amazing chocolate bun things that she'd cooked – they'd just come out of the oven and they were still warm. I started to eat it on my feet and she said it wasn't good for my digestion to eat that way and that I should sit down.'

Kate stifled a grin. Alex telling Harry what to do – now there was a first.

'She waited until I'd finished eating and then we talked about plants,' he continued. 'She's quite into gardening, you know. She's just signed up for an evening course in Sandybay Community College on indoor plants.'

'Really?' Kate asked, most impressed. Alex had done her homework impeccably.

'And she even knew the Latin name of one of my favourites – the *Citrus mituis*.'

'Sorry?' asked Kate.

'It's a small tree that grows baby oranges. I suggested it for the coffee shop. She was a real breath of fresh air to tell the truth. I wanted to ask your advice. Do you think she might like to go to the Burnaby Flower Festival with me? It's on over the next weekend. Do you think I should ask her?'

'Yes, I definitely think you should.' Kate put her hand on his. 'If she's interested in plants she'd really enjoy it and it would give you both a chance to get to know each other better. The Flower Festival sounds lovely.'

'Thanks, Kate. I'll ask her tomorrow.' He jumped up. 'Must dash. Radio tomorrow morning and I haven't got anything prepared. I'm supposed to be talking about bushy succulents and their medicinal properties. Don't ask. See you.'

'See you.' Kate smiled to herself. Her plan had worked like a treat. Maybe she should take on more female clients. Pity she couldn't fix her own love life while she was at it. She popped herself onto the stool behind the desk to lodge the last two sales in the stock book – one pair of pink strappy sandals and a pair of red size three boots left over from last spring that they thought they'd never get rid of. Cathy and Trina would be delighted. Another customer came in the door. Before she had a chance to raise her head she heard a familiar voice. 'Cat? Cat?' She recognized the soft American accent instantly and her heart began to pound in her chest. She leant towards the desk, her eyes fixed on the stock book. The numbers and letters swam before her eyes. Was this some sort of elaborate nightmare? Would she wake up any second now sweating and head thumping.

'Cat?' The voice drew nearer.

She forced herself to look up. There he was, standing in front of her, smiling – the man who had almost ruined her life. Still as damn attractive as ever.

'Jay?' she whispered. 'What the hell are you doing here?'

Chapter 9

Paige

Paige lay in bed wide awake. It was only six o'clock in the morning but she couldn't get back to sleep.

'Tom?' she whispered. 'Are you awake?'

No answer. She nudged him in the side. 'Tom. I need to talk to you.'

He grunted.

'Tom!' she said again, a little louder this time.

'What's wrong?' he asked groggily. 'Have we slept through the alarm?'

'No, it's still early. But I have to talk to you.'

'Can't it wait?'

'No.'

He sighed and rolled over to face her. 'What is it then?'

She looked at him in the half light and wondered how he was going to react to the news about the baby. It was nearly a week since she'd visited the doctor and had had her home test confirmed and she'd been putting it off ever since. But she couldn't keep it to herself any longer.

'I'm pregnant,' she blurted out.

'What?'

'Pregnant. We're having another baby.'

Silence again.

'Tom? Say something.'

'I can't. I'm in shock.'

She started to cry. Getting the news off her chest was a relief but she'd hoped he'd be pleased.

'What's wrong, love?' he asked putting his arms around her. 'Are you not pleased? It's great news. I know it's a bit quick after Alfie, but it'll be fine.'

'Do you really mean that?' she asked. 'You're not annoyed?'

'Annoyed? Why would I be annoyed? Of course not. I'm delighted. You know I want a big family. It's a bit of a surprise, that's all.'

'No kidding.' She sniffed. 'Think of how I feel. What with the elections and everything.'

'It doesn't change a thing,' Tom said evenly. 'How many months gone are you?'

'Three, I think. I'm not sure of the dates.'

'So you're over the worst of the tiredness and the sickness, aren't you?'

'Yes, Dr Spock. Since when are you the great expert?'

'I've been through it twice before, remember? You won't be all that big for a while yet. And there's no reason to mention it to anyone until after the elections.'

'Is that not lying by omission?'

'Not at all. Your health is your own business. If anyone asks you directly you can answer them honestly. If they don't ask don't proffer the information. It's as simple as that.'

'Spoken like a true campaign manager.'

'Absolutely. Speaking of which, in the circumstances, are you really up to doorstepping this week, love?'

'Yes,' she said firmly. 'I'm going to do everything I can to win this election, Tom. Everything. Including drawing the raffle at the Burnaby Flower Festival, opening the new library in

Sandybay National School, and holding an open questions and answers session on my policies in the new Burnaby Arts Centre in the spirit of openness and transparency, as suggested by my campaign manager.'

'Are you really sure?' Tom asked again.

'Yes, positive.'

'Then I'm behind you all the way.'

'Thanks,' she said gratefully. 'I love you, Tom. You're so good to me.'

Tom held her hand to his lips and kissed it. 'Anything for the mother of my soon to be three children. Now seeing as we're up so early, Councillor.' He moved his hands over her arms and she could hear the smile in his voice. 'And we don't have to worry about time, let's make the most of it.' He nipped her ear playfully with his teeth.

'How about a big cuddle?' Paige asked. 'I'm not really up to anything else this morning, to be honest.'

'A cuddle it is.' He smiled warmly. 'Come here you.' He put his arms around Paige and hugged her tightly.

She hugged him back and smiled to herself. Maybe Tom was right. If she could just get through the next few tense and superhumanly busy pre-election weeks, then everything would be fine.

Paige and Tom started their first day of doorstepping at nine o'clock that very morning. 'Come in, young lady, come in. I've just put the kettle on,' said Mrs O'Brien, an elderly Burnaby Grove resident as they stood in her hall at ten o'clock. They'd already covered the High Burnaby estate and were now moving down Burnaby Avenue towards the village. 'Would you like a cuppa?'

Paige looked at Tom who shrugged then nodded.

'That would be lovely, Mrs O'Brien,' he said. 'But we don't want to put you to any trouble.'

'Not at all. I insist.' She showed them into the sitting room, then toddled slowly out the door.

Tom smiled at Paige when Mrs O'Brien had left the room. 'This doorstepping is taking longer than I'd planned. I hadn't realized how much people like to talk.'

'I know. But it means a lot to some of them, especially the older ones.'

'Next week Molly and Kate have promised to help. And I've roped in your mum too. And Lily's going to ring as many of her friends as she can. She said if she wasn't incapacitated at the moment she'd be burning shoe leather with us.'

'Lily's such a sweetie. I must give her a ring.'

After a few minutes, Mrs O'Brien returned carrying a tray. 'Here we go,' she said.

Tom jumped up. 'Let me help you.'

'It's fine, young man. But thank you anyway.' She placed the tray carefully on a small coffee table in front of them and began to pour tea from the elegant light blue china pot with matching tea cups, sugar bowl and milk jug.

'What lovely china.' Paige smiled. 'Where did you get it?'

Mrs O'Brien beamed. 'How kind of you to ask. My late husband gave it to me for our fiftieth wedding anniversary. I use it whenever I have special guests over. He was a wonderful man you know, such a gentleman. Let me tell you about our wedding day. When I saw him standing at the altar waiting for me I thought I'd pass out. He looked so handsome . . .'

As they left the house forty minutes later Tom smiled at Paige. 'You only managed to tell her about one of your policies but she adored you. You've definitely got her vote.'

'Wasn't she sweet? Imagine, they were married fifty-seven years, isn't that just something?'

'It is, quite something.' Tom looked at the list on the wooden clipboard in his hands. 'Burnaby Manor next. Should be interesting.'

As soon as they walked in the door of the old people's home, they heard loud piano music which sounded suspiciously like 'Knees Up Mother Brown'.

'That's Lily Bowan playing.' The matron smiled warmly. 'She's here every Monday morning running the weekly sing-song. The residents love it.'

'Isn't she supposed to be resting?' asked Paige. 'She's just out of hospital.'

'You try telling Lily to rest,' the matron snorted.

Paige laughed. 'I know what you mean.'

'Paige!' Lily cried as she and Tom entered the large front room. 'How nice to see you. I hope you're all voting for Paige, ladies and Mr Fowler. She's an old friend of mine.'

'Give us a song and we'll vote for you,' a woman with pink hair quipped.

'Yes, go on, give us a song,' another added. 'That Annette one refused. Said she didn't know any. But you do, don't you, Paige?'

Tom pushed her firmly towards the piano. 'She's a wonderful singer,' he assured them.

'Tom!' Paige hissed.

'Do the one you do for the kids. The one about the moon.'

'"Moon River"?' she asked.

'That's the one.'

'I don't think . . .'

'I know that,' Lily surprised her. 'Audrey Hepburn in *Breakfast at Tiffany's*, wasn't it? Let me see.' She played a few notes on the keys. 'Got it. On you go, girl.'

Paige began to sing the opening bars, wobbling a little at first. She had a clear, low-pitched voice which suited the song perfectly. As she sang the residents began to sing along, some more than a little out of time but it didn't matter, they were obviously enjoying themselves. As she finished everyone gave her a rousing round of applause.

'Well done, Paige.' Lily smiled widely. 'That was great. And now Tom.'

'Oh, no!' Tom protested.

'Go on,' Paige said. 'Do "Summertime".'

'I know that one too.' Lily started to play.

'Go on,' Paige cajoled. 'Do it for the votes, please,' she whispered.

He smiled. 'Just for you.' He sang in his lazy, easy manner and many of the residents joined in.

'He's great,' the matron whispered to Paige as he began the second verse. 'Thanks for being such good sports, you've made their day. I think they found Annette a little dry. She kept droning on about her policies and bored them all stupid.'

'I'll have to remember not to do that.'

'I don't think you could bore people if you tried. You have a nice easy way with people. And Lily is always singing your praises.'

Paige smiled. 'That's lovely to hear.'

'I hope you get in. Burnaby could do with someone like you. Best of luck.'

'Thanks.'

Leaving the home an hour later after more tea and more singing Paige felt like she was walking on air.

'That went really well, Paige,' Tom said. 'If you keep that up you'll have the whole of Burnaby voting for you in no time.'

'Here's hoping,' she replied. 'Fingers crossed.'

The following morning Paige was one of the guests on Chat FM's political and local news programme, *What's Going On*. The presenter, Wella Davis was a tall, attractive blonde in her late twenties, who was known and loved by the listeners for her sharp tongue and her 'take no prisoners' approach to interviewing. She was also known in the radio world for being brutally ambitious – many young producers and researchers had been cut to the quick by her bruising criticism and downright rude manner. Her current researcher, Rita Farrell, rumoured also to be Wella's girlfriend, had rung Paige the previous evening to ask her to appear on Wella's radio show.

'Late notice isn't it?' Paige had asked.

'Wella likes to spring things on people – it's part of her style,' Rita explained.

'Who else will be in the studio?'

'Annette Higgins, Paddy Burns, Miles McGreinna, Mark Tine and Jackie Pile.'

Paige whistled. 'Bring on the heavy hitters. And you want me as well?'

'Wella likes some of your policies. She thinks you have a good chance of winning a seat if the liberal vote comes through for you.'

'Really?' Paige was flattered.

'So we'll see you tomorrow at quarter to ten in the studio? Do you have the address?'

'Yes, I've been in a few times before. See you then. And thanks, Rita.'

'No problem. See you tomorrow.'

As Paige drove towards Dublin city on the way to the studio, she listened to Wella laying into a representative from an Internet company who had been less than scrupulous with their on-line competitions. The show started at nine, and Paige and her fellow politicians were on at ten. Apparently, the Internet company had been making quite a habit of giving their top prizes to friends and family, angering many of their on-line customers who, by all accounts, had really won the competitions and had documentary on-line proof of the same. Paige was impressed by Wella's technique. Her legal training obviously served her well – she cleverly extracted enough damning information from the interviewee to sink them and then stuck the knife in – making them admit to their wrongdoings. By the end of the piece the company had promised to recompense all the aggrieved parties and had given an unconditional apology to all their clients into the bargain.

Paige gripped the steering wheel tightly. Wella was not to be trifled with. She decided there and then that the only way to deal with Wella was to be open and honest – completely transparent – and to hope to goodness that Rita was right and that Wella really did like some of her policies. She wasn't going to get into any slanging matches no matter how tasty the bait.

Paige parked the car on Merrion Square, luckily finding a spot almost straightaway. She fed coins into the parking meter and stuck the ticket onto the inside of her driver's window. Bending down, she contorted her upper body to check her lipstick in the wing mirror. As she suspected – telltale dark cherry red stains on her teeth. She rubbed them with her finger, then popped a finger in her mouth, pursed her lips around it and drew it back out. That should deal with the rogue lipstick, she thought, shouldn't have put it on so hastily. She brushed down the front of her slightly wrinkled black pencil skirt and began to walk towards the radio station's building.

'Hello,' she said a little nervously into the intercom.

'Chat FM. How can I help you?' A disembodied female voice asked.

'Paige Brady. I'm on Wella's show at . . .'

The intercom gave an almighty screech and Paige heard the door lock click open.

'Push the door. We're on the third floor,' the voice said crisply.

Standing in the dimly lit lift Paige stared at her reflection in the grimy mirror. She looked pale. She ran her hands over her stomach. It was starting to take on a gently rounded shape. Soon she'd be in maternity clothes but hopefully not too soon. Luckily it was looking hopeful – with both Callum and Alfie she'd never got huge. She always felt sorry for the women who looked like baby elephants – their swollen bellies causing them to waddle in a most ungainly fashion, their breath short and laboured.

As the lift door opened she walked into the hall and looked around. There was no obvious indication of where she should go. Wooden swing doors led in three different directions. Then she spotted a small Chat FM sticker on one of the doors. She took a deep breath and pushed it open. Sitting on the lurid green sofas in front of her were Annette, Paddy, Mark and Miles.

'Hi, Paige.' A young woman with short dark hair came rushing towards her, her hand outstretched. 'It's lovely to meet you. I'm Rita. I spoke to you on the phone.' She turned towards the other guests. 'And you know everyone, I presume?'

Paige nodded. 'Yes, thank you.'

'Would you like a cup of coffee before we start? We're just waiting for Jackie and then we'll move into the studio during the news.'

'I'd love one,' Paige said gratefully. She could feel her hands begin to shake.

'Come and sit down, Paige.' Paddy smiled up at her. 'Take the weight off your feet. Not that you have any weight of course. Young slip of a thing like you.' He looked around the room. 'Or am I allowed to say things like that in this day and age? Annette will probably accuse me of being sexist.'

Annette scowled at him. 'And are we allowed to make comments about your weight, Paddy?' she asked.

'You can if you like,' he said mildly, holding his stomach in. He was fond of the good life and this had taken its toll on his girth and his jowls over the years.

'How's the anti-dump campaign coming on?' Mark Tine asked, aware that Paddy and Annette didn't exactly see eye to eye at the best of times. Mark was the local Green Party representative, an idealistic young man in his late twenties. This was his first time to contest an election.

'Good, Mark, good. And thanks for all your support, and

yours, Paige.' Paddy nodded at her and ignored Annette and Miles who had both deemed local environmental issues beneath them.

'I saw an interesting photograph of you in the paper last week, Paige,' Miles said, his sharp nasal voice cutting through the air. Miles McGreinna was the local Irish Party representative and Paige didn't like him one little bit. He was fixated by 'family values' and the destruction of morality by the liberal agenda. He'd spoken out vehemently against both divorce and abortion when the relevant referenda had come into play and he was firmly right of centre, a die-hard conservative and vocal Roman Catholic. His policies were positively prehistoric and Paige hated his creeping anti-working woman stance. Annette also took this stance. Which was unsettling since she was one in theory, although her children were grown up.

'Would that have been the one of my team winning the all-Ireland?' Paige said feigning innocence. She knew damn well which one he was referring to.

Before he had a chance to answer, Rita came flurrying back. 'Everyone ready? Let's get you all into studio. Jackie rang to say she was stuck in traffic. We'll have to go ahead without her.'

Miles led the way, followed by Annette and Paddy. Mark and Paige brought up the rear. The studio was small and they all had to clamber over wires, old jugs of water and discarded ring folders to get to their places around the large table. Rita handed each guest headphones.

'I hate these things,' Paddy complained. 'They always pinch my ears.'

'Me too,' Mark agreed.

Wella smiled at them. 'Welcome. They're playing the ten o'clock news at the moment and we'll go into our slot straight afterwards. I'm going to ask each candidate a question on their policies and there will be a little time for open discussion at the end. Please try not to hog the air space and give everyone a chance to speak.'

They all nodded.

'Here we go,' Wella said. She leant in towards the large furry grey microphone in front of her. 'Welcome back to *What's Going On*, the topical news programme on Chat FM, with myself, Wella Davis. This morning in the studio we are privileged to have the leading Dun Laoghaire Rathdown candidates in the forthcoming September election – Deputy Paddy Burns from the People's Party; Councillor Annette Higgins, Independent; Mr Miles McGreinna, from the Irish Party . . .'

Miles interrupted her. 'Doctor Miles McGreinna,' he said pompously.

'Ah, yes, I'd forgotten about your Open University doctorate in ancient history,' she said cuttingly. 'Sorry *Doctor* McGreinna.'

'London School of Arts,' he corrected her. 'And it was in philosophy not ancient history.'

Paige caught Mark's eye. He winked at her. She looked down at the table and tried not to laugh. Miles was so annoying.

'To continue,' Wella said, 'Mr Mark Tine from the Green Party and last but not least, Councillor Paige Brady, also Independent. I'd like to start with Deputy Burns. Deputy, there has been a lot in the papers recently about the proposed Burnaby dump, can you fill the listeners in on some of the issues please?'

'Certainly, Wella,' Paddy said warmly. 'Be glad to.'

As Paddy explained the risks involved in locating a dump near a residential area, Paige's mind began to drift. She was dog-tired today and she could have done without the mad dash into town to tell the truth. She was due back in Burnaby in two hours to talk at a Lady's Lunch in the Burnaby Golf Club and then Angus was calling in that afternoon to meet Callum and she was a little worried about it. She so wanted them to get on and . . . She was brought back to earth with a bump when Wella asked her a question.

'What do you think, Paige?'

Damn, she thought, what were they talking about – the dump? Or had they moved on from that? Openness and honestly, she reminded herself.

'Can you repeat the question, Wella?' she asked with a smile.

Wella looked at her for a second, and noticing Paige's drawn, pale face and dark shadows around the eyes decided to cut her some slack. 'Of course. Do you think you are a good role model for young people? I was thinking specifically about the recent photograph in the *Burnaby News*.'

Paige had been dreading this question, but figured if Wella hadn't asked it, Miles would have weaseled it in somewhere anyway.

Paige took a deep breath. 'Interesting photo, wasn't it?' She smiled at Wella.

Wella laughed. 'Yes, it was.'

'To answer your question in one word – yes. I am an excellent role model for young people. I was introduced to sport from an early age, thanks largely to my father, Lorcan Brady, who also played soccer for his country, and who set up the local Burnaby Soccer Club in his time. I've played soccer at the highest level and have also been involved in both college and school coaching. I am very involved in the community and was instrumental in setting up the new Burnaby Arts Centre.'

'And you have two young children I believe, Councilor Brady, is that right?' Wella asked.

'Yes. And one of my key policies is to lobby the government to provide affordable childcare for all working women in the country. At present Irish parents pay out over twenty per cent of their wages on childcare, way above the European average of eight per cent.'

Miles snorted at this.

'Do you have a problem with women working, Dr McGreinna?' Wella asked, knowing full well that he did.

'I have no problem with women working *per se*,' he said smoothly. 'It's women with young children who work I object to. Children shouldn't be abandoned to strangers for large portions of the day. It's causing huge problems in our society – teenage drinking, delinquency, rise in crime rates . . .'

'I agree,' Annette interjected. 'Women should take full responsibility for their offspring.'

'What about men?' Mark asked. 'Surely they should take equal responsibility.'

'Quite,' Miles said with a sneer on his face. 'But you wouldn't know anything about taking responsibility, Mr Tine, would you?'

'Sorry?' Mark asked. 'Would you care to explain that last comment?'

'Yes, Dr McGreinna,' Wella said, delighted with the way things were heading. Nothing like a whiff of scandal to boost the ratings. 'Please explain what you're trying to say. I for one would like to hear it.'

'Mark Tine is having a baby out of wedlock with a married woman.' Miles stared at Mark with an evil glint in his eye. 'Deny it if you can.'

Mark was silent for a moment. His eyes were flashing and there were two angry red spots on his cheeks. 'Of course I don't deny it. I *am* having a child with my partner of four years, it's true. And for your information, Miles, she's divorced . . .'

'An English divorce,' Miles said snidely. 'Not recognized by the church in this state.'

Mark stared at him. 'She's Protestant, so her divorce is recognized by her own church. But of course you don't believe there is any other church in this country except for the Roman Catholic one, do you Miles?'

'The Roman Catholic church has a very important role to play in —' Miles began.

Wella held her right hand up. 'We're not really interested in the church's role this morning, thank you. Now let's get back to Mr Tine. Is there anything else you'd like to say on this matter, Mr Tine?'

'Yes, Wella, there is. I'd like to say that I am overjoyed at the prospect of being a parent. My partner suffers from polycystic ovaries and she didn't think she'd ever have children, so it was a delightful surprise for both of us. And we hope to get married next year when we've found a new house.'

'Thank you for being so honest, Mr Tine.' Wella smiled at him.

'If I were you, Mr Tine . . .' Miles began.

'And do you have children yourself, Dr McGreinna?' Wella asked quickly.

'Um, no.'

'Or a wife?'

'No.'

'Then you're not really in a position to give advice are you, Doctor?'

'But . . .' Miles was livid. How dare that young pup speak to him like that?

'Can I cut in here?' Paddy Burns said.

'I haven't finished . . .' Miles blustered.

'Yes, you have,' Wella said, glaring at him. 'Please allow Deputy Burns to speak.'

'I'd like to congratulate Mr Tine on the news and wish him and his family all the best in the future.'

'Thank you,' Mark said gratefully.

After the slot had finished, they all walked through into Chat FM's hall together.

'Outrageous,' Annette said. 'Call that a radio show? I only got to talk about my garden winning a prize in the Tidy Towns competition for a brief moment and didn't get to mention the new computer call centre I have planned for Dun Laoghaire borough at all.'

'Terrible woman, that Wella,' Miles grumbled. 'Most unprofessional.'

Paige put her hand on Mark's arm. 'Well done,' she said in a low voice. 'You handled that very well.'

'So did you,' he said. 'Exhausting, wasn't it?'

She nodded.

There was an awkward silence as they all waited for the lift in the small hallway.

'So, who's for the Burnaby Flower Show on Saturday?' Paddy asked in a jovial voice, breaking the atmosphere. 'You're doing the draw, aren't you, Paige?'

'That's right.'

'Hardly fair,' Annette muttered.

'Sorry, what was that, Annette?' asked Paddy.

'They should really have asked me you know. After all, my garden did win a prize . . .'

'At the Tidy Towns, yes, I think we all know that by now, Annette. But I'm sure you're going to go along anyway, aren't you? Shame to miss an opportunity to meet the punters.'

'I might,' Annette admitted sniffily.

'And I'm running the bottle stall for my sins,' Mark said.

'Well, I'll definitely see you then, Mark.' Paddy laughed and rubbed his hands together. 'Hope you have some nice Irish whiskey. I feel a lucky streak coming on.'

Paige opened the front door and smiled at Angus. She felt decidedly nervous. Callum was in high spirits and was currently dashing around upstairs with no clothes on, nothing new. 'Come in.' She led Angus into the kitchen. Bright sunlight was flooding in the windows and she gestured towards the small flowery sofa. 'Please, sit down. Would you like tea or coffee? Or a soft drink?'

He smiled. 'Nothing for me, thanks. I'm fine. This is a lovely house, is it Georgian?'

'Yes. It was in rag order when we bought it but Tom's a bit of a DIY nut – he did a lot of it himself. And luckily he works in a mortgage company or we never would have been able to afford it. This part's an extension. They weren't mad into big kitchens in those days. The one we replaced was small and didn't get much light.'

'Liked keeping the servants in the dark, did they?' He grinned. 'I'm sure they would have had servants in a house this size.'

'You're probably right.' She was beginning to feel more at ease. Angus had a nice calm manner and a wonderfully warm smile. It was impossible not to smile back. 'I'll just go upstairs and get Callum.'

After she'd left the room Angus looked around. The kitchen was country-style wood complete with dark blue Aga and had a warm and homely feel. In front of the sofa where he was sitting was a large Victorian dresser crammed full with books of all shapes and sizes, framed photographs, a jar full of coins, plastic toys in various states of distress and candles in wooden and wrought iron holders. There were larger framed photographs on the walls, along with an attractive oil painting of Burnaby's coastal Martello tower, the sea stretching out shimmering blue in the background. The most striking photograph on the wall was of two laughing teenage girls in scary eighties outfits – one in a pink and blue ra-ra skirt, with legwarmers, lace-up boots, and a string vest over a yellow T-shirt; and the second fashion victim in a tiny stonewash denim miniskirt, her slim legs in fishnet tights and her hair piled up on top of her head and fastened with some sort of bright blue netting. Hang on a second. He got to his feet and walked towards the photograph. Leaning forward and looking even closer, he snorted. It was Paige and the girl from the bookshop, Molly.

Just then he heard a noise behind him and swung around. 'Great, isn't it?' Paige asked.

'Sorry, I didn't mean to . . .' Angus stammered.

'Don't worry, it catches everyone's attention. Molly gave it to me for my birthday last year. It was taken when we were thirteen. We thought we were the bee's knees.'

'Mummy looks silly, doesn't she?' a little voice piped up.

Angus smiled at the little boy who was holding his mother's hand tightly. He looked angelic with his white blonde hair and open, round face. 'You must be Callum. I'm Angus.'

'Mummy told me there'd be no telly if I was bold so I have to be nice to you,' Callum said. He then gave an almighty sniff and wiped his nose on the sleeve of his red sweatshirt.

'Callum!' Paige glared at him. 'That's nasty. If you need to wipe your nose go and get a tissue.'

Callum let go of her hand and toddled off into the hall.

'Sorry about that . . .' Paige began.

'Paige, I'm here to help. I'm well used to it, remember? I usually have twenty five or so of the little darlings at the one time.'

'Thanks,' she said gratefully. Callum came back into the room pulling a long tail of toilet paper behind him. 'Callum, what are you doing?' she asked in exasperation. 'I told you to get a tissue.'

'Couldn't find one. And the loo paper wouldn't break off.'

'That's just not true, is it young man?' she asked.

'It is, honestly, Mummy.'

She said nothing. What must Angus think? She tore off a piece of the white tissue paper, handed it to Callum with a stern look on her face and began to pick up the remainder of the roll off the floor. 'I'll be back in a second,' she said to Angus as she followed the paper out of the room.

As soon as she'd gone Angus looked at Callum. 'Do you like the Andrex ad where the boy gets the toilet paper stuck in his jeans and runs it all around the house?' he asked calmly.

Callum smiled knowingly and nodded. 'Are you going to give out to me?' he asked after a few seconds.

'Not at all,' Angus said. 'Sure, why would I? I'm only here to play with you, not to give out to you.'

Callum's eyes widened. 'Is that right?' he asked. 'That's not what Mummy said. She said you were here to mind me and that I was to be good.'

'You don't have to be good,' Angus said. 'Except at our games. You have to be good at them.'

'What sort of games?' Callum asked with interest, cocking his head to one side.

'All sorts – hide and seek, mountain climbing, making a tree house, making a camp fire, bungee jumping . . .'

'Bungee jumping!' Callum was amazed. 'I've seen that on telly. They jump off bridges and stuff. Mum would never let me do that.'

Paige, who was standing in the hall listening to the conversation with interest, stiffened. Bungee jumping? Callum was quite right. What was Angus thinking of?

'It's not real bungee jumping,' Angus explained. 'It's a bungee trampoline. You're attached to these rubber pulleys and you can jump up and down and go amazingly high. They have one on Sandybay seafront.'

Paige who suddenly realized that she'd been holding her breath, felt a huge wave of relief flood her body. For a second there she'd begun to wonder about Angus's suitability.

'Cool!' Callum grinned. 'Can we go now?'

'So you want me to play with you when your mum and dad are at work?' Angus asked.

Callum nodded firmly. 'Yes.'

'There's just one thing, Callum. Every morning you'll have to tidy up your room before we play and do one nice thing for your mum and dad.'

'Like what?' Callum asked suspiciously.

'Nothing major. Give your mum a kiss, pick up Alfie's toys

for him, blow your own nose, get up and dressed yourself like a big fellow, that kind of thing.'

Callum thought about it for a minute – it didn't sound too bad really. 'And then you'll take me bungee jumping and all the other cool things?'

'Yes, I promise. Bungee jumping or one cool thing every day. I'll make up a star chart and every morning I'll ask your mum and dad to put a star up if you've been helpful and nice. And then we play for the whole day. Is it a deal?'

'Sure,' Callum said. 'As long as Mum doesn't mind.'

Mind? Paige smiled to herself as she rested her forehead against the wall, the plaster deliciously cool against her skin. She felt weak with relief – had they finally found someone who understood how to deal with Callum?

Angus started on Monday and sure enough, encouraged by the idea of bungee jumping and other 'cool' activities, Callum behaved himself on Monday morning. After staring intently at the new star chart for several minutes, which Angus had dropped in over the weekend, he ran over and kissed Paige on the bottom.

'Callum!' Paige squealed and whipped around. She was rinsing the cereal bowls in the sink at the time and was taken quite unawares.

Callum smiled up at her. 'I kissed you, Mummy. Angus said that was being nice. Can I have my star now?'

Paige laughed. 'Yes, I suppose so, but next time try kissing me on the cheek. OK?'

'OK, Mummy.'

'He just got the wrong kind of cheek, love,' Tom grinned.

'Talking of cheek,' Paige said to Tom. 'Less of that, you. You're supposed to be showing your son a good example. How's Alfie getting on with his breakfast?'

'He's nearly finished. I'll drop him off to Mum's this morning if that would help.'

'That would be great, thanks. And you're all right for campaigning at the train station at five?'

'Grand, I'll meet you there. Looking forward to it.'

'Being belted by commuters' brollies, I'd say you are.'

'Surely it doesn't get violent.'

'Not usually, no.'

Tom looked at her and she broke into a smile. She walked over and kissed him on the cheek. She was feeling decidedly chipper this morning, all things considered. 'I'm going into the office to make some phone calls. See you later, alligator.'

'In a while, crocodile,' said Tom.

'Not too soon, you big fat baboon,' Callum joined in.

'Callum!' they both chorused.

'Have I lost my star?' he asked anxiously.

'No, but I'd watch it young man,' Paige said ominously.

'I'll go and tidy my room.' Callum ran out the door and thundered up the stairs.

'Whatever that Angus has done, God bless him,' Tom said.

'No kidding,' Paige agreed.

Chapter 10

Molly

'Who are we waiting for?' Paige asked the rest of the Book Club at the August meeting.

'Just Harry, I think. Trisha can't make it,' Cathy said. 'I'm not sure about Kate.'

'No, Kate's not coming. She sent her apologies, she's watching Lily swim,' Molly explained. 'She doesn't trust her on her own.'

'Is Lily's ankle better then?' Paige asked.

'Not quite. But there's no stopping her. She says she's having withdrawal symptoms from the lack of her daily swim.'

'Hello, everyone. This is the Book Club I presume?' Milo asked.

Everyone looked up.

'This is Milo Devine, the new owner of the shop,' Anita explained. 'He's going to be joining us today.'

'Have you read the book?' Molly asked a little too sharply.

'Yes,' he said. 'And I thought it was most . . .'

Paige put up her hands. 'Stop! We haven't started yet.'

'Sorry,' Milo said. Duly chastised, he sat down beside Anita.

Molly nudged Paige in the side. She'd already told her about Milo's crush. Paige smiled back at her and nodded discreetly.

Harry came blustering in. 'Sorry, sorry, last minute order came in. Sent the wrong bloody pots of course, idiots. Still, I'm here now.' He sat down beside Molly. 'And how are we all this fine day?' He looked around the table, his eyes stopping when they came to Milo. There hadn't been a new member of the Club for quite some time.

Paige noticed Harry's interested gaze. 'This is Milo, Harry. He's the new owner.'

Harry raised his hand and waved casually at Milo. 'Hi, welcome. Nice to have another man on board.'

'Will we get started then?' Paige asked. 'Who'd like to begin? Anita?'

Anita grimaced. 'I was hoping you wouldn't ask me first.' She sighed theatrically. 'I have to say I hated it. Absolutely hated it.'

'Thank goodness,' Cathy joined in. 'I thought it was just me. I couldn't make head or tail of it at all. What nonsense.'

'Pretentious rubbish,' Molly agreed. 'Practically unreadable in parts.'

'What I can't understand,' Harry added, 'is how the man won the Booker a few years ago. Had the judges gone mad?'

'The one that won the Booker – *Regret* – wasn't so turgid,' Anita said. 'In fact it was excellent in parts. But this one . . . *Mamma Mia*!'

'Tell us why you didn't like it, Anita,' Paige encouraged.

'Where to start? First of all – the plot was very weak. Nothing really happened the whole way through the book. It was supposed to be about the narrator revisiting the village he grew up in – a presumably fictional place called 'Stradbrook' which sounded like a small town in the north of Ireland. But it was so bloody boring. I couldn't stand the narrator – he never stopped moaning about how his life had stagnated in the place and how he'd never been able to make anything of himself because of his upbringing. And the other characters were completely wooden. I couldn't empathize with any of them, let alone understand them.'

'Old Mrs White was particularly unbelievable, wasn't she?' Cathy asked. 'She was like something out of *Ryan's Daughter* with the white lace shawl and the thatched cottage. I mean, please.'

'She was supposed to be the narrator's sort of surrogate mother, wasn't she?' Molly asked. 'But she wasn't a very pleasant character.'

'That's right,' Harry said. 'She had no time for her own children and when her youngest son died – what was his name?'

'Johnny,' Anita said.

'That's right, Johnny,' Harry continued. 'She didn't seem too bothered.'

'Another thing I can't understand is how the book got so many good reviews. It's complete hogwash,' Anita said. 'It would make you wonder what the reviewers were thinking about.'

'May I say something?' Milo asked Paige.

'Of course,' Paige said. 'Sorry, it is hard to get a word in edgeways at times. Fire away.'

'I thought the book was wonderfully written,' Milo began. 'So atmospheric. You could almost touch the mist on the bogs and smell the turf burning in the old hearths. I think Frost has a touch of genius when it comes to describing the way life was in Ireland in the last century.'

'Really?' Anita asked a little scornfully. 'Did you not think his descriptive passages went on a bit?'

'No, I enjoyed them. Some of the sentences were exquisitely crafted. You could almost smell the sweat that went into writing some of them.'

'But surely writing shouldn't be like that!' Anita cried. 'Over crafted and arty. Surely it should flow and be artless. I think the best writers are the ones who make writing look easy. Frost spends far too much time crafting perfect sentences and not enough time creating a strong plot and real, believable characters.'

'I agree with Anita,' Harry said. 'I found his writing most frustrating. I just wanted him to get on with the story, not waffle on about dew catching the light on spider's webs.'

'But this is literary fiction we're talking about here, not storytelling,' Milo insisted. 'Surely you see the difference. Maybe you're more used to reading popular fiction, that's all. Maybe your reading tastes are a little unformed, a little unrefined.'

'Rubbish!' Paige said a little more vehemently than she'd intended. 'We read all kinds of things in this Book Club, including some damn fine literary fiction.'

'Indeed,' Anita said angrily. 'All kinds of things. But we also read good popular fiction, we're not snobbish. A good book is a good book no matter what genre – crime, sci fi, historical saga, fantasy, whatever. Maybe you just haven't read enough good books to recognize *Stradbrook* for what it is, pretentious rubbish.'

'Well really!' Milo said looking a little red in the face. 'I'm not here to be insulted about my reading tastes. Maybe I should leave.'

'Please don't,' Paige said. 'And don't take anything personally. We often have quite heated arguments about books, it's quite normal. Stay. We'd all like you to. Please.'

Milo looked around the table. Everyone nodded. Even Anita.

'Sorry,' Anita mumbled. 'I got a little carried away there.'

'Yes, well . . .'

'Have I missed anything?' Sam asked, walking towards the table. Everyone stared up at him. 'Sorry I'm so late.'

Paige laughed. 'Not much, Sam. Please do sit down. Welcome. Did you get a chance to read the book?'

He nodded. 'Yes, but I only got about halfway through. There's not much of a story to it, is there? I got bored of it to tell the truth. Picked up *Lucinda's Tale* instead. Anita had recommended it to me when I started in the shop. Now, there's a book.'

Within minutes, the group was eagerly and noisily discussing *Lucinda's Tale*, which had been an earlier Book Club choice. Paige breathed a sigh of relief. She had enough squabbling children to deal with at home.

'So, what did you think of your first meeting?' Paige asked Milo after the meeting had finished.

'Interesting,' he said. 'Very interesting. I learnt a lot.'

'About books?' Paige asked.

'Among other things,' he said quietly. He looked over towards Anita who was deep in conversation with Cathy about next week's book. 'I don't think she likes me,' he said, gesturing towards the two women.

'Anita?'

He nodded.

'You'd be surprised,' Paige said. 'She just gets very passionate about books, that's all. I honestly don't think it was anything personal.'

He said nothing.

After lunch, Anita and Molly met in Coffee Heaven to discuss their plan for the bookshop. Paige had excused herself – she had an interview with one of the radio stations and a photo call for the Flower Festival.

'I'm worried about pulling off a Book Festival of this size,' Molly began. 'I know you and Paige are confident but there are so many things that could . . .'

'Molly, have some faith.' Anita smiled at her. 'It's going to be a lot of work but it'll all come together, you'll see. Especially now that we've found such a great second venue. Paige has arranged everything with Tara, the new arts administrator in the Burnaby Arts Centre and she's mad keen to get involved. She wants to run a special Love Bean event for the children with African storytelling and dancing. And best of all, she'll organize the whole thing herself.'

'What's a Love Bean when it's at home?'

'It's an African friendship token. It's literally a large, brown bean. You give it to someone you like.'

Molly sighed. 'I just don't . . .'

'Molly! What's wrong with you?'

She sighed again. 'I don't know. Sorry, I'm all over the place today.'

'Is that ex-boyfriend of yours pestering you again?'

'Not really. He's been fairly subdued this week to tell the truth.'

'Good. Don't let him get to you. Be strong.'

'I'll try.'

'And how's the writing coming along?'

'Not great,' Molly admitted. 'I haven't been able to concentrate for a few weeks now. Maybe I'm not cut out to be a writer.'

'Maybe not. But you should at least give it a go. You'll regret it if you don't.'

'I suppose.'

Anita put her hand on Molly's. 'Have some courage, Molly. Be brave for once in your life. You have it in you, I know you do. Reach inside yourself and find your inner strength. I really do think that there's a writer in there.'

Molly felt like crying. She had no idea why Anita believed in her but it was comforting to know that she did.

'Now, let's go over our list,' Anita said gently, sensing Molly's emotionally fragile state of mind. 'Who do we have for Saturday morning?'

Molly studied the sheet in front of her. 'We blast off with two of the biggies – Rose Lovett and Jennie Tracker.' Rose and Jennie were the American and British Queens of romantic fiction.

Anita whistled. 'That should draw the crowds. Followed by . . .?'

'The Literary Lunch.'

'Of course, that should be fun. And Matty and Alex have agreed to do the catering?'

Molly nodded. 'And Harry has offered to decorate the tables for free.'

'How sweet of him.'

'It is decent of him, isn't it? After lunch we have the panel discussion on "Getting Published – Tips from the Top".'

'Has Bonnie Evans agreed to sit on the panel?' Anita asked.

'She has.' Molly smiled. 'Should be interesting.' Bonnie was one of Burnaby's most famous locals – a flamboyant romantic saga novelist who spent most of her time in the South of France. She was well known for her strong opinions on everything from writing to poker and horse racing and always had something outrageous to say. The media loved her – a glamorous woman in her early fifties, she ate interviewers for breakfast and had rendered even Terry Wogan and Gay Byrne speechless in her day.

'Should be,' Anita agreed. 'It's going to be wonderful, really Molly. You and Paige have done Trojan work putting it all together.'

'Thanks, I hope it will work.'

'It will. No doubt about it. Especially now that Brenda Jackson's researcher has confirmed Rose and Jennie for the radio show the week before the Festival to talk about their work.'

'That's great news.'

'Isn't it?' Anita said. 'And talking about the media, did Millie from the *Burnaby News* get back to you?'

'She did,' Molly said. 'She agreed to run a short story competition to tie in with the festival. And she'd like you to be one of the judges, along with Bonnie.'

'No problem, could be a bit of fun. I hope you're going to enter, Molly.'

Molly wrinkled her nose. 'I couldn't. It might be a conflict of interests.'

'Perhaps. But think about it. Is there anything in the rules to say you can't?'

'Don't know,' Molly said thoughtfully. 'You haven't written them yet.'

Anita laughed. 'Then we'll have to see what we can do.'

'There's no need, I'm not going to enter.'

'OK.' Anita knew better than to push her. She looked at her watch and sighed. 'I suppose we'd better get back to the shop.'

'One last thing. Cathy and Trina have offered to sponsor Jennie's flights. And they said they'll do a window advertising the event in their shop. And Harry and Alex offered to put up posters in their shops too.'

'Excellent!' Anita beamed and put her hand on Molly's. 'It's all coming together. I knew we could do it Molly. Now let's see if the press will sit up and take notice, shall we?'

'And Milo,' Molly added.

'And Milo.' Anita nodded solemnly.

That evening Molly decided that some fresh air would do her good. She grabbed a fleece and headed out the door straight after her dinner. Kate was out on yet another dummy date and as it was a sunny, warm evening there was nothing to keep Molly in the house. As she walked down Burnaby Lane towards Sandybay beach she thought about a short story she'd been working on. It was set on a beach in West Cork and involved a chance encounter between a lobster fisherman and an American tourist. Molly wanted to use the Selkie story as a basis for her tale – the legend of how seals came out of the sea and became women on land. But she was having difficulties sewing the traditional strands into her own short story without it being too 'clunky' and obvious.

Crossing over the railway bridge, she stood for a moment

gazing at the sea stretched out in front of her. It glistened in the evening sun – the light dancing merrily on the tips of the waves. There was a good breeze which whipped at her hair, threatening to pull it out of its loose ponytail. She walked down the steps and her feet crunched onto the stony beach. She strolled down the beach at a brisk pace in the direction of Wicklow, swinging her arms by her sides and taking in deep breaths of the tangy, salty air.

After a while, she heard a familiar voice behind her.

'Hey! Molly! Wait up!'

She turned around and shielded her eyes from the sun. She smiled as she saw Sam being pulled along by a large black Labrador.

'Are you walking him or is he walking you?' She laughed.

'I'm not altogether sure.' The dog stopped at Molly's feet and began to jump up, putting it's wet paws on her thighs.

'Sorry,' Sam said. 'This is Tara, she belongs to my neighbour. She's just been playing in the waves, she's a bit wet.'

'So I can see.' Molly bent over and patted her head. 'Hello, Tara. Are you enjoying your walk?'

Tara wagged her tail eagerly and began to bark.

'I think she likes you,' Sam said. 'Sorry, are we interrupting your walk?'

'Not at all, it's nice to have the company.'

'In that case, mind if we join you?'

'Not at all.'

Molly began to walk and Sam fell into step beside her.

'You like going at a fair lick, don't you?' he asked after a moment.

'I know. Paige is always complaining. Sorry, I'll slow down.'

'Don't on my account. Tara likes it and I'll get used to it. I've been looking out for you when I'm walking but this is the first time I've seen you.'

'I've haven't been walking in ages,' Molly explained. 'Too busy. You know how it is.'

'Don't I just? But Hugh loves the beach. So we're usually here every weekend whether I like it or not.'

Molly said nothing. She hadn't asked any questions about Sam's private life since she'd touched one of his raw nerves in the shop – she'd been too nervous of annoying him again.

'You can ask me if you like,' Sam said, sensing her unease. 'I won't bite your head off this time, I promise.'

'About what?'

'About Hugh.'

'I'm sorry – you must think I'm awfully nosy.'

Sam laughed. 'You're not the worst. Must be the writer in you. I hear you're all a very curious bunch.'

'How do you know I write?' she asked quickly.

'Anita told me.'

'Anita?'

'Sorry, I didn't realize it was a secret. I'd love to read some of your work if you'd let me.'

Molly stared at the sea.

'Molly? Sorry, have I said something wrong?'

She shook her head. 'I just don't like anyone knowing about my writing, that's all. Anita shouldn't have said anything to you. Not that's there's much to know to tell the truth. I haven't written a word for weeks.'

'Why not?' he asked gently.

She shrugged her shoulders. 'Haven't felt in the right frame of mind I suppose.'

'Not centred enough? I have the same problem myself sometimes.'

She looked at him in surprise. 'You write too?'

He laughed. 'Me? Heavens, no. I make furniture, that's all. But I can only do it if I'm in a good mood.' He picked up a stone and kicked it into the sea.

'I remember now, Hugh said you made him a puppet theatre.'

'That's right. I make other things too. It's my hobby I suppose – I dabble in it. Not like your writing.'

'What do you mean?'

'Well, Anita told me you're quite serious about your writing. How many short stories have you finished?'

'Twenty-seven,' she mumbled. 'And half a novella.'

He whistled. 'That's really something. Twenty-seven. I'm impressed.'

'Don't be. It's won't come to anything.'

'Why do you say that?'

'I just know.'

'You should have some confidence in yourself. Maybe some of them are good.'

She frowned. 'I doubt it.'

'Let Anita read one or two. At least you'd know then.'

'Maybe I'm happier not knowing. Have you thought of that?'

Sam stopped walking and looked at her. She continued on without him, realized that he wasn't beside her, and stopped. 'What?' she asked sharply. 'What are you smiling at? Tell me.'

'You,' he said finally. 'You're one big mass of contradictions, Molly. Do you know that?'

'I have no idea what you're talking about.' Molly was getting more than a little uncomfortable at the direction this conversation was heading. She decided to change the subject. 'Tell me about Hugh.'

'What do you want to know?' Sam let Tara off the lead to play in the surf again, put the lead in his pocket and caught up with Molly.

'Are you married?' she asked before she could stop herself.

'Married!' He laughed. 'I suppose it's a fair enough question. No, I'm not married. I thought about it at one stage – to Hugh's mum in fact, but it wouldn't have worked out. What about yourself?'

'I was asked once,' Molly admitted. 'But like you, it wouldn't have worked out.'

'The guy outside the bookshop?' Sam asked astutely.

'You saw us?' she asked, embarrassed.

Sam nodded. 'He seemed a little upset.'

'That was my ex, Denis. He's all right really. Just gets a bit over-emotional at times.'

'I know the feeling, Brona is a bit like that.'

'Brona?'

'My ex, Hugh's mum.'

'What happened? If you don't mind me asking?'

'No, it's fine. We were in college together – Arts in UCD. She was in my philosophy class and we met on the very first day of term. She was wearing the most amazing yellow coat with a huge furry yellow collar – you could hardly miss her.'

'Love at first sight then?'

'You could say that. She sat down in the row in front of me during the very first lecture and I couldn't take my eyes off her. Afterwards I asked her for coffee and one thing led to another.'

'And Hugh?'

Sam was quiet for a moment. 'He wasn't exactly planned. Brona was in bits when she found out. Her family are quite strict Catholics and she was dreading telling them. At one stage she considered not having it but neither of us felt it was the right thing to do.'

'What age were you?' asked Molly.

'I was twenty-two and Brona was twenty-one.'

'It must have been hard.'

'It was I suppose, but we managed. We lived together for a while but things didn't work out. She moved back in with her parents nearly two years ago. She and Hugh live in a self-contained apartment in their basement now – so it's all worked out for the best really. He gets to see his grandparents every day while Brona's working and I get to see him every weekend.'

'What does she do?'

'She's an actress. She does voice-over work, radio ads mostly and she has a small part on *City Lights* as Jude's on-off girlfriend. You know, the soap opera.'

'Don't watch it I'm afraid.'

'Neither do I.' He took Tara's lead out of his pocket and walked towards the edge of the water. 'Here, girl!' he shouted. 'You've had enough now.' Tara barked and stayed in the water.

Molly laughed. 'You have great control over her.'

'I know. Still, she probably has the right idea.' He sat down on the stones and began to untie his boots.

'What are you doing?' Molly asked.

'Going paddling. Come on!'

'No way. It'll be freezing.'

'No it won't.' He pulled off his boots and socks and rolled up the bottom of his jeans. He walked boldly into the water, trying not to wince as the icy water lapped his ankles.

'Told you,' Molly said.

'It's not that bad,' he insisted. 'Come on. I dare you.'

Molly looked at the water which was rippling and bubbling over the shingle. It did look rather inviting. 'OK.' She joined him, dipping in one foot gingerly, followed by the other.

'You liar, it is freezing.' She grinned.

'Freezing but fun.'

After two minutes Molly's toes had had enough. She stepped out of the water and walked slowly towards her shoes and socks. 'My feet are practically numb,' she said. 'I blame you.'

'It's good for you,' he said. 'Toughen you up.'

She sat down on the shingle, waved her feet in the air to get rid of the drips and pulled her socks over her damp feet. As she tied the laces of her runners, Sam sat down beside her.

'When was the last time you paddled?' he asked.

She shrugged her shoulders. 'No idea. Ages ago.'

'You should do it more often, keeps you young.'

'Is that right? What happened to you then?'

'Very funny,' he grinned back. 'Um, what are you up to this evening?'

'Do you know, I think I might attempt to do some writing.'

'Good idea.' He jumped up and walked towards the sea. 'Here, Tara,' he shouted at the dog who was still enjoying the waves. 'Come on, girl. You'll freeze if you don't get out now.'

Molly watched him from her seated position as Tara ran towards Sam, her tongue lolling out of her mouth. He wrestled with her good-naturedly on the stones, Tara yelping enthusiastically as he held her down and rubbed her tummy. He looked over at Molly and smiled, his eyes crinkling attractively at the corners.

Damn, Molly thought. I do believe Sam was going to ask me out. And I blew it. She looked at Tara and back at Sam. Oh, to be a dog, she thought. Life would be so much simpler.

Chapter 11

Kate

'Hello. There are no free tables anywhere, mind sharing?'

Angus looked up in surprise at the attractive blonde woman in front of him. 'Um, no, not at all. Please sit down.'

'Thanks.' She said, placing her coffee mug on the table and sat down. 'It's busy in here today, isn't it?'

'Um, yes, very. Saturday shoppers, I suppose.'

'Yes, of course.' She looked at him and smiled. 'I've seen you in here a few times.' She held out her hand. 'I'm Patricia. Patricia Simons. And you are . . . ?'

Angus took a deep breath. Stay calm, he told himself. 'Angus Cawley.' He shook her hand firmly. 'Nice to meet you.'

'And you.' Patricia smiled again.

Angus smiled at her shyly and was about to go back to reading his newspaper when she asked him another question.

'Are you working today?'

'Sorry?'

'Working?' Patricia asked again.

'Oh, no. Just having lunch.'

'I see. I'm working.'

'Oh.'

'I'm a publisher's rep. Do you like reading yourself?'

'Yes, I suppose so. I don't get much time to read books though. Not whole ones anyway.'

'You are a scream.' She patted his arm playfully.

Angus wasn't sure why what he'd said was funny, but he played along with it anyway. He thought Patricia was a little pushy and there was something slightly off-putting about her perfectly set hair and immaculately made-up face but talking to her would be good practice. He was sure that Kate would approve.

'Your job sounds interesting,' he said, remembering Kate's advice on talking to women. 'Tell me about it.'

Patricia was only too pleased to oblige. She loved talking about herself. And Angus was really rather good-looking, with those lovely chocolate brown eyes. There was a Booksellers' Ball being held the following weekend and she just might ask him to escort her.

'What?' Kate asked incredulously. 'Angus is going out with who?'

'Patricia,' Molly said evenly. 'Patricia Simons. I'm sure I've told you about her before – she's one of my least favourite publisher's sales reps – she has a mouth the size of a car boot. She called into the shop this afternoon to drop in some catalogues and some car stock. Apparently she met Angus in the coffee shop, they got talking and she asked him to the Booksellers' Ball next weekend.'

'Are *you* going?' Kate asked.

'I wasn't planning to. Why?'

'No reason.' Kate was silent for a few moments. She tapped her teaspoon against the side of her mug. They were sitting at the kitchen table, having just finished sharing a Chinese takeaway.

'You're not jealous, are you?' Molly asked, trying not to smile.

'No!' Kate insisted. 'Of course not. What's she like anyway? This Patricia woman.'

Molly described the elegant, blonde sales rep.

Kate listened in stony silence. 'Good for him,' she said curtly before standing up. 'I'm glad he's met someone.'

'Where are you going?' Molly asked. 'I thought you were staying in this evening.'

'I've changed my mind. There's something I have to do.'

'But I rented a video.'

'Sorry. We can watch it tomorrow evening. How about that?'

'Fine.' Molly folded her arms across her chest. Kate had been in a funny mood all week. Molly had blown out dinner at Paige's to stay in with her this evening in the mistaken belief that Kate might like the company. Kate was a strange one sometimes. There was obviously something bothering Kate but she didn't seem to want to talk about it. 'Whatever,' Molly sighed to herself.

Kate strode into the lobby of the Killiney Arms appearing a lot more confident than she felt. She'd made a special effort to look nice – light brown on-the-knee suede skirt, brown leather high-heeled boots, fitted black shirt. Her hair was freshly blow-dried and she'd carefully applied a layer of foundation, glittery gold eye shadow and strong, red lipstick – her 'war paint'. Because this evening, above all other evenings she was certainly going to war.

She sat down in an armchair where she had a good vantage point of the whole lobby and glanced at her watch. Good, she was five minutes early, enough time to collect her thoughts. Because she knew exactly what she was going to say – she'd been rehearsing it over and over for the past week. But as a familiar dark suited figure walked down the stairs, caught her eye, smiled and walked towards her, she was rendered speechless. Damn, she thought, he always does this to me.

'Cat.' He grinned at her, his impossibly white teeth gleaming. 'You look a million dollars. Let me look at you.' He held both her hands firmly and looked her up and down. He whistled softly. 'Still a beauty.'

'Um, thanks,' she managed to say.

'Would you like a drink? A glass of white wine?'

She nodded wordlessly.

'Wait there,' he commanded her.

Kate watched as he walked towards the bar to the right of the lobby. His suit was immaculately cut, his smart black leather boots shone as if they'd just been polished, and his dark-brown hair was freshly shorn. As always, Jay Sweetman looked good, too damn good.

One of the top American fashion promoters, Jay's job took him all over Europe and he always dressed to impress. In fact, he was so stylish if you didn't know him you'd think he was Italian or Spanish, not Boston-Irish. Kate had first met him two years ago in the Diva, a glitzy hotel in Boston, at the launch party of a new range of Sin 'streetwear for feet', which included several of her designs for funky pink, light blue and moss green sneakers. She'd caught his eye across a crowded room and had blushed as Jay had smiled and winked blatantly at her.

Later that evening, to her delight and after several hours of heavily loaded exchanged looks, he'd asked her to dance. They hit it off immediately. He was her ideal man – charming and polite, strong-willed and intelligent. They had talked all night and once he'd kissed her in their shared taxi home, her fate was sealed. He kissed like an angel. Or should that be a devil? Either way, he kissed too well to be strictly human.

'Here you are.' Jay put a full glass of wine down in front of her. He sat down beside her, put the bottle in its silver cooler and his own glass on the table and put his hand on hers. She pulled it away quickly.

'Don't be like that,' he said. 'It's good to see you again. I've missed you, Cat.'

As soon as he uttered his pet name for her again, the way he always said it, lingering over the 'C' and caressing it with his tongue, Kate knew she shouldn't have come here this evening. Her stomach was already full of butterflies. She tried to keep calm and looked at him squarely in the eye.

'What are you doing here, Jay?'

'I came to see you.' He lifted his glass and took a long sip of wine.

'And?'

'And I have a couple of business meetings in Dublin.'

'Why did you want to see me?'

He raised his eyebrows, his normally baby-smooth forehead wrinkling slightly. 'Why do you think, Cat?' His eyes bored into hers, dark pools of intensity, burning straight into her soul. She looked away quickly and stared at the table.

'I'll cut the bullshit and get straight to the point. I still love you, Cat. Surely you know that. We had something, something real, something . . .'

'Stop!' Kate insisted. He'd always had the gift of being able to throw himself full force into every conversation and completely catching her off guard. 'We can't go back, Jay. You know that.'

He was silent for a moment. 'But things have changed. I've changed.'

'No you haven't.'

'How would you know? You vanished off the face of the earth. Never even said goodbye. I was distraught.' He ran his finger up the stem of his glass. 'I had a terrible time trying to find you. But I'm here now and . . .'

'How did you find me exactly?' she asked.

'Reena at Sin. You asked her to forward on your last pay cheque. It took me months to get your new address out of her.'

Kate winced. She thought she could trust Reena but obviously she'd been wrong. Although knowing Jay, he'd woven Reena some elaborate tale to cajole the address out of her. He had a way of doing that as Kate knew only too well.

'You shouldn't have bothered.' She gulped back the last of her drink.

Jay poured her another glass of wine. She didn't protest – she sure as hell needed some Dutch courage right now.

'I haven't been in Ireland for nearly two years,' Jay said ignoring her last comment. 'I've missed it.'

She said nothing.

'Would you like to go for a walk?' he asked. 'It's a beautiful evening. We could climb Killiney Hill.'

'I'm not really dressed for it.' She nodded at the heels on her boots.

'Why don't we go somewhere a little more private then? I have a hot tub on my balcony – and it has fantastic views.'

Kate stared at him. Had he been listening to a word she was saying? She wanted nothing more to do with him – couldn't he get that into his thick skull. 'I don't think so,' she muttered. 'I'm going.' She stood up abruptly.

'Leaving without saying goodbye, Cat?' he asked smoothly. 'Again? Your manners are appalling.'

'Don't talk about my manners.' She'd had quite enough of his arrogant behaviour. 'Manners! I'll give you manners.' She picked up her glass and poured the contents over his head.

'Cat! What the hell!' He grabbed her wrist, his hair and jacket soaked. 'What's all that about? You left me, remember? Or have you conveniently forgotten?'

'Yes, I did. And you remember why of course?' her voice was raised to a dangerous level.

'Let's take this upstairs,' he said calmly. 'People are beginning to stare.' He brushed his wet hair back with his hand, tendrils beginning to cling around his flushed face. Even soaked in wine he still looked good and remained poised and composed. Typical, Kate thought.

'Let them.' She looked around. He was right, the two women at the table beside them were staring wide-eyed and the reception staff had also noticed the commotion. It would be just her luck if someone she knew was listening. She suddenly remembered that Trina's husband owned half the hotel and she was reluctant to have her personal life gossiped about all over Burnaby Village but she hadn't finished with Jay quite yet. 'OK then,' she decided quickly. 'Let's go. Your room, now! I have one or two things I want to say to you, Jay Sweetman, in private.'

He strode ahead of her towards the stairs, drips of wine still falling from his head, and powered up them at break-neck speed. Kate found it difficult to keep up in her heels and tight skirt but she was determined not to let him get the better of her. That was Jay, always too impatient to wait for the lift. On the third floor, he stopped outside a door and opened it with a card swipe. Kate was relieved; her heart was pounding in her chest both from the exertion and from the bubbling anger she felt.

Jay held the door for her. She walked in and looked around. It was a stunning room, dominated by a huge bed dressed in sparkling white linen, with a mountain of different sized velvet and satin cushions in shades of gold and beige, and a luxurious fur throw draped over the foot. The dusky evening light bounced off the white walls and Kate could see the large sunken hot tub on the balcony, steam rising in swirling snakes from the top of the water.

'Great view, isn't it?' Jay asked calmly. He gestured towards the balcony. 'I'm going outside for a smoke. Care to join me? Then you can lay into me.'

Kate looked at him incredulously. Was he serious? She followed him out wordlessly.

'You're some piece of work, Jay, you know that?'

He nodded but said nothing. He took a rolled cigarette out of his inside jacket pocket, lit it and inhaled deeply.

'What's that?' Kate asked, smelling the air suspiciously.

'Don't act the innocent.' He smiled at her. 'Would you like some?'

'No! You know I don't smoke.'

'Sometimes you do. At least the old Cat used to. Or have you become a cheerleader, *Kate*?'

She ignored him, folded her arms in front of her chest and stared out at Killiney Bay, stretching out in front of them as far as the eye could see. The hotel was practically on the beach and Kate could smell the tang of salt in the air. Jay handed her the joint. She looked at it for a few seconds before deciding what the hell? She took it from him without looking at him, and took an almighty drag, the thick smoke hitting the back of her throat, making her cough.

Jay patted her on the back. She felt the smoke fill her lungs and she immediately began to feel a little lightheaded.

'So what did you want to say to me?' Jay asked mildly.

She shook her head, took another calming drag, then began. 'I hate you. You fed me a long line of bullshit and like a fool I believed you. I left Boston because I had to. I wanted to have people I could trust around me, decent people. Honest people.'

'I never treated you badly, Cat, it's just . . .'

'It's just what?' she asked. 'You were married, Jay. Married! And you never told me. I had to find out the hard way.'

'I never meant to hurt you, Cat. My marriage was over, *is* over. Cindy and I were never meant to be but I couldn't leave her. Not just then. You never let me explain.'

'Explain what?' Kate demanded.

'Cindy was pregnant. She broke the news to me soon after I'd met you and I didn't know what to do. We'd been trying for kids for a few years but it looked as if it was never going to happen. I knew even before I met you that I didn't love her any more. I was on the verge of telling her about you and me, but after she broke the news about the baby – what could I do, Cat? It's what she'd been dreaming of all that time – a baby of her own. I couldn't leave her, not then. I'm not that big a bastard. But I loved you so much, not seeing you would have broken me. I had no choice, I had to keep Cindy and the baby a secret. Don't you see?'

Kate listened to him, staring at the sea and not knowing what to think. All kinds of things were racing through her mind.

She looked him in the eye. 'So, as I keep asking, what are you doing here, Jay? What about Cindy? What about your child?'

Jay stared at his hands. 'She lost the baby,' he whispered. 'Just after you left Boston. Things were difficult after that. Cindy was distraught. I couldn't help her get through it, although I did try. She moved back to Maine to be with her family and met up with her childhood sweetheart, a dentist. They fell in love and the rest is history. I lost my baby and I lost you, all in one fell swoop. I was completely alone.' He paused for a moment to compose himself and swallowed. 'As you can imagine I was devastated.'

Kate didn't know what to say. Whatever explanation she'd expected, it hadn't been this. She was bowled over by anger and something else, something bordering on sympathy. He'd made her feel sorry for him and she hated him for it. How dare he?

'Why are you telling me all this?' she demanded. 'Are you

under the impression that I still care about you, Jay? Because as you've probably realized by now, I don't.'

Jay looked at her. 'You've asked me what I'm doing here. Well, I could ask you the same question, Cat. If that's true, what are *you* doing here? Why did you come here?'

'That's easy, Jay!' Kate said, her voice raised to a dangerous level. 'I loved you, really loved you. When you asked me to marry you I was so happy. And then that Christmas Eve . . .' She took a deep breath. Tears threatened and she was damned if she was going to let him see her cry. Not like this. 'I came here this evening to tell you to keep away from me. Pure and simple. I never want to see you again, do you understand? I didn't think I could do it on the phone. Not properly.'

She looked at Jay and was shocked to see that he was crying. Unashamedly. Tears were pouring down his face and he wasn't even bothering to brush them away. 'I'm sorry.' He shook his head. 'I'm so sorry you had to find out the way you did, it was unforgivable. But Cat, don't give up on us, please. I beg you. I love you. I've missed you so much.'

'How can you say that?' She stubbed out the joint in a plant pot and sat on the edge of the hot tub as she was feeling decidedly strange – hot and light-headed. 'You asked me to marry you when you had a wife already! That's bigamy, Jay. What were you thinking? You don't love me. You don't know the meaning of the word. And you certainly never respected me, or your wife for that matter.'

'Yes, I do,' he whispered. 'I love you, honestly.' He put his head in his hands. 'But I've lost you, haven't I?'

'Yes. I'm afraid you have.'

'The one person in the whole world who means the most to me. How could I have been so stupid? If only I'd met you earlier, before, things would have been different.'

'But you didn't,' Kate pointed out. 'Did you? And then you lied to me.'

He shook his head. 'And now that I've given up everything to be with you, you don't want me. How ironic is that?'

'What did you just say?' Kate asked.

He looked her straight in the eye. 'I'm in the middle of a divorce settlement and I'm selling the apartment. I came over here to tell you. In a few weeks, I'll be a free man. My meetings in Dublin are about moving over to Ireland. I thought that we could buy a house, be together, get married as we'd planned. Maybe have a family. Start again. I know how much you want to be near your granny and I respect that, Cat. Family means everything and I thought we could start our own family here in Dublin.'

Kate felt as if she'd been hit by a train. How dare he bring Lily into this? And what the hell was he talking about? She hadn't contacted him since coming home and now this. Was he mad? 'What?' she cried. 'I don't understand. Is this some sort of sick joke?'

'It's not a joke. You heard me. I'm free to marry you now. And I'll move to Ireland to be with you.' There was a strange intensity in his eyes. 'So I'm asking you again, Cat – will you marry me?'

'Are you serious?' she asked furiously. 'After everything you've done, you still think I'll come running? Are you crazy? We haven't spoken for almost a year, did it not occur to you that I want nothing more to do with you? Well, Jay?'

'Don't be like that, Cat.'

'Like what? You're some piece of work.'

'Cat, I know you're scared and you have every right to be angry with me. But this time it's different, trust me. I'm a free man. No more deceit, I promise. Just you and me, we were made for each other, you know that. I love you.'

Kate stared at him. 'Don't,' she whispered. She put her hand into the hot tub and moved her fingers through the clear warm water. She should never have come here this evening, it was a mistake.

He walked over and sat down beside her. 'I know you still love me, Cat. I can see it in your eyes. And I love you so much. Why can't you trust me?'

Kate sighed deeply. She felt suddenly exhausted. 'Jay, stop! I can't do this again. It nearly broke me the last time, but I'm OK now. Please, just let it go.' She could feel her defences weaken. He always had this effect on her, Jay was her one big weakness. But she wasn't going to give in, not this time.

He put his arm around her shoulders but she immediately shrugged it off.

'Cat,' he said softly, brushing her hair back with his hand.

'Don't touch me!' she insisted tetchily.

He ignored her and continued stroking her hair. 'Let me take care of you. It could be like it was in Boston, the way it was before. We belong together. Do you remember what you used to call us, "soulmates"?'

'I remember,' she murmured, feeling her resistance starting to fade even more. The joint and the wine weren't helping. Why didn't I refuse it and stay clear-headed? she chastised herself. Stupid, stupid, Kate. Always so stupid. Her mind raced. Wouldn't it be easier just to give in to him? I think about him all the time, from the moment I wake up, to last thing at night. I thought I was over him, prayed I was over him, but who am I kidding? And what does it matter anyway? He's going to win in the end, she thought woozily, he always does. Or why not have one last night with him, get him out of my system? She laughed out loud.

'Why are you laughing, Cat?' he asked.

'I'm laughing at you,' Kate replied woozily. 'At us.'

He ran his hand along the side of her face. 'My beautiful Cat.' He kissed her on the cheek.

She felt her heart somersault. 'Don't,' she said softly.

He silenced her with a firm kiss on the lips.

'Jay!' she protested and pushed him away. But he wasn't giving up that easily.

'Let me love you, Cat,' he said. He cupped her head in his hand, and smiled at her. 'Don't fight it.'

The next time he leant forward to kiss her, Kate couldn't help herself. She could feel her lips respond to his kisses, and a delicious warmness spreading from her lips, down her neck and suffusing through her body.

He put both arms around her and held her tightly. 'Cat,' he whispered in between kisses, 'my lovely Cat.' She felt powerless to resist, overcome by her own pent-up emotions. At that precise moment she didn't care about anything other than Jay's hands and lips, both sending her whole being into divine ecstasy and leaving her wanting more. God, how she'd missed him. He was right – she'd never stopped loving him – no matter what he'd done, the lies he'd told, the fool he'd made of her. And she still wanted him – more than anything. But she certainly didn't trust him.

While still kissing her, he gently and expertly pulled her top over her shoulders and undid her bra.

'Jay,' she said nervously, crossing her arms over her full, naked breasts. 'We can't do this. Please . . .'

'Just getting into the hot tub, my sweet, that's all,' he promised her. 'It will relax you, then we can talk some more.' He slipped off his own jacket and shirt, took off his boots and socks, leant over and kissed her bare shoulder. She felt a delicious shiver down her spine. As if in a trance, she pulled off her boots, socks and skirt, feeling exposed in just her black lacy G-string. Although it was a warm evening, she still shivered.

'Everything off.' Jay grinned at her. 'That's cheating.'

'What about you?' she asked.

He shrugged his shoulders, dropped his trousers, stepped

out of them and whisked off his pristine white boxers. 'As naked as a jay-bird.' He laughed.

He moved towards her, lifted her up in his strong arms and dumped her unceremoniously into the tub.

'Jay!' she spluttered.

He laughed again and stepped in. 'Come here.'

She stayed where she was, the water suddenly sobering her up. 'Jay, this isn't right. I can't . . .'

He moved towards her and kneeled in front of her. Cupping her face in his hand once more he kissed her on the forehead, on both cheeks and then ever so gently on her lips. She could feel them tingle beneath his.

'You know you want me, Cat. Let yourself go. Just concentrate on how you feel right now. Let go of everything else. Just let go.' He put his hands on her shoulders and pressed her against the back of the hot tub. 'Lie very still,' he whispered. He pressed a button behind her and jets of warm water began to fill the tub, snaking upwards and hitting her back, her buttocks and the tops of her thighs. 'Now open your legs.'

'Jay!' she cried.

'Just humour me, it'll be worth it. Please?' He kissed her again, this time his tongue caressing and teasing her lips and tongue and making her gasp. Her heart was racing and her whole body felt warm and on tenterhooks. As he nuzzled her neck, he moved his hands down her body, removed her G string and spread her legs. Then he lifted her up slightly in the water and repositioned her over a firm, strong jet of water. Kate could feel the warm, forceful jets against her most sensitive area. She closed her eyes and gave in to the delicious sensations. Jay held both her hands in his and kissed her all over her face and neck, whispering into her ears.

'That's it, Cat,' he crooned. 'I knew you wanted me. Just like I want you.'

After a little while the jets began to feel stronger and

stronger, warmer and warmer, until Kate's body had taken its fill. Her back arched and then she flopped forwards as limp as a rag doll, completely sated.

She opened her eyes and Jay smiled at her. Without saying a word he turned to sit, lifted her body onto his knee, light in the warm water. She wrapped her legs around his torso, pulled him close and began to kiss him ravenously, clutching and massaging his muscular shoulders and back in her hands.

'Cat!' he said. 'You're back.' She'd always been the most passionate and exciting woman he'd ever been with.

'Yes, I am,' she murmured. 'Now, shut up and kiss me.' For old times sake, she thought as she kissed him passionately, there's no way I'm letting Jay back into my life, no way in high heaven.

'Cat, I have to go now, I have a meeting in town.'

Kate opened her eyes and rolled over. Jay was standing in front of her, fully dressed in his signature dark suit. He looked fantastic as usual.

She looked up at him, rubbing her eyes. They hadn't had much sleep the previous evening and she felt a wave of regret that she had let things escalate to such an extent. She should have left straight after the hot tub. In fact she should never have been in the hot tub in the first place. Or in the hotel for that matter. What was she doing? She should have been stronger – the joint and the fact that she hadn't had sex since the last time she'd been with him in Boston were some excuse, but Kate was ashamed of herself. 'What time is it?' she asked.

'Eight,' he said. 'Don't get up. I'm sorry I can't stay but you know how it is. I have a breakfast meeting in The Morrison Hotel at nine.'

'On a Sunday?' she asked.

'I know, tell me about it,' he said, ignoring her suspicious tone. 'But I'm only over for the next three days and you know what us Americans are like about breakfast meetings.'

'It's fine, I understand.'

'I'll see you this evening. Dinner here at eight? I'll book the restaurant.'

'I don't think so, Jay.'

'Please, Kate, it would mean a lot to me. I know what happened last night wasn't . . .'

'I don't really want to talk about it, Jay, OK? Just leave it.'

'Can I at least ring you later?'

She sighed. 'I suppose so.'

He pulled out his mobile and stood waiting, his fingers hovering over the keys.

She dictated her mobile number.

He smiled at her. 'I'll see you later.'

'Jay . . .'

He kissed his fingers and lay them gently on her lips. 'Just humour me,' he said with a grin.

Soon after he'd left, Kate fell into a deep dreamless sleep. When she woke she felt deliciously refreshed. Standing in the shower, powerful jets of hot water spiking her body, she thought about Jay and about the previous night. And much to her disgust she felt happy. Happy that he still loved her, happy that he still wanted her. Because she knew deep down that she'd never stopped loving him. Lies or no lies. What was she going to do?

'You're in good form,' Lily said as she and Kate walked down the steps towards Forty Foot bathing place in Sandycove that afternoon. 'You haven't stopped smiling all day. What's up?'

Kate shrugged her shoulders. 'Nothing in particular.' She looked at the greyish-blue water stretched out in front of them. 'I can't believe you've talked me into this.' She laughed. 'I must be mad.' There were several people of all ages in the water – from young children with their parents to groups of teenagers and older swimmers. Some were jumping and diving in and others were sitting on the edge of the steps, chatting amicably in bathing suits with towels draped around their shoulders. The sun was hiding behind thick cloud cover but the air was warm.

'You'll enjoy it once you're in,' Lily said. She led them towards the right where there were concrete seats. Several people nodded or said hello to Lily as she walked past. She sat down.

'How's the ankle today?' Kate asked, sitting down beside her.

'Not too bad. Healing nicely. I should be able to go naked in the next week or so.'

'Naked?' Kate asked with interest.

Lily smiled. 'Without a bandage.' She opened her bag and pulled out her togs and towel. 'Come along,' she said to Kate. 'Don't just sit there. Unless you intend to swim in your clothes.'

'Maybe I'll just watch,' Kate said uncertainly. 'It looks a bit cold and . . .'

'A bit of cold never hurt anyone,' Lily said dismissively. 'Now that you're here you may as well try it.'

'I suppose so.' Kate was still very reluctant. To tell the truth her legs were still a little shaky after last night. She tried not to smile as she thought of Jay but it was proving difficult. Jay had held her in his arms and promised her that everything would be all right. Last night Kate had blocked out the voices in her head telling her that she was mad to get involved with Jay again. That he was a liar and a cheat, and a danger to her mental health. That he'd hurt her again, just like he did the last time. Today, as the afternoon had progressed the voices were becoming dimmer and dimmer. In fact she almost couldn't hear them any more. And one more evening with him couldn't hurt, could it? He was hardly serious about moving to Dublin and, after all, he was single this time – if he was telling the truth about his ex-wife and the loss of his baby. But Kate was sure that even Jay wouldn't lie about something like that.

'Kate? What do you think?' Lily asked again.

'Sorry, I was miles away. What did you say?'

'Would you like to go out for dinner this evening? To Bistro Nova?'

'I have to meet an old friend, Gran. Maybe next weekend.'

'Who?' Lily cocked her head. 'Anyone I know.'

Kate shook her head. 'No.'

'It's not that nice Angus is it?' Lily persisted.

'No!' Kate laughed. 'What made you think that?'

'He's a decent young man. And he seems very keen on you. Whenever he calls he always asks all about you.'

'He still calls in?'

'Yes. This week Callum was with him. Lovely child – he's really growing into himself. Angus is working wonders with him.'

'Well, I'm certainly not dining with Angus.'

Lily smiled gently. 'You could do worse. He's a good lad. You could trust him, Kate. He wouldn't break your heart like that American. What was his name again?'

'Gran!' Kate wanted to change the subject right now. She didn't feel at all comfortable with the direction this conversation was heading. 'You know I don't like talking about him. Just drop it, OK? It's all in the past.'

Lily looked at Kate carefully. 'Is it?'

'Gran! Are we going swimming or not?' Kate pulled her togs and towel out of her bag and began to get undressed, using her towel to protect her modesty. She winced as her bare feet hit the concrete but decided it was her penance for last night's excesses. They'd polished off three bottles of champagne between them, although a large part of the third bottle hadn't been drunk – it had been liberally sprayed over each other and over the sheets.

'We most certainly are,' Lily said. As she changed, Lily thought about Kate. She had a strong feeling that the American was back in town. She noticed a couple of fresh scratches and bruises on her granddaughter's arms, back and inner thighs. She wasn't born yesterday. And if it was the American and she was under his spell again – it spelt trouble for Kate. Trouble with a capital 'T'.

Chapter 12

Paige

Paige lowered herself onto the sofa. The house was blissfully quiet and, if she was lucky, she could catch a few minutes shut-eye before Callum and Angus arrived home. She rested her head against the side cushions and let her weary eyelids droop closed. A little while later she was wakened by a loud bang in the hall. It was the front door being slammed shut.

'Callum!' she heard Angus scold. 'What did I say?'

'Close the door gently,' Callum replied.

'And was that gently?'

'No,' Callum admitted. 'Please don't tell Mum and Dad. I've been really good today, haven't I?'

'Yes. And I'll let you off this time. But run upstairs and hang your coat on the back of the door, there's a good lad. And change your trousers, those ones are filthy.'

Paige heard Callum scamper up the stairs. Angus walked into the living room.

'Sorry,' he said, noticing her stretched out on the sofa. 'Did we wake you?'

'That's OK.' She yawned. 'I have to get up anyway. More

doorstepping this evening, I'm afraid. Are you still all right for babysitting?'

Angus nodded. 'Fine.'

Paige sat up slowly, rubbing her eyes. 'Thanks. You've saved my life. Mum was supposed to do it but . . .'

'It's no trouble, honestly. I could do with the money to tell the truth.'

'So what did you both get up to today?' asked Paige.

'We went to Bray on the train. Walked along Bray head and then had a few dodgem rides at the amusement park. Callum got a bit muddy rock climbing so I sent him upstairs to change.'

'Callum was rock climbing?'

'Sure. Rock scrambling more like. He's pretty talented – he has great balance and he's very agile.'

Angus looked at Paige's face. She looked a little anxious.

'It's good to stretch him, Paige. Don't look so worried, I'd never take him anywhere that wasn't safe, honestly.'

'Sorry, I know you wouldn't. So what's the plan for tomorrow?'

'The waterfall at Powerscourt. Thought we could do some dam building in the stream. There's a great playground there too – should run off some of Callum's steam.'

Paige smiled. 'You're full of great ideas, Angus. We were lucky to find you. Callum hasn't been so easy to deal with for I don't know how long. We really appreciate it, you know that.'

'I know. And he's a good kid – lively but bright. Just needs some one on one attention.'

Paige sighed. 'I wish me and Tom had more time to spend with him, but with the election coming up, and Tom's work . . .'

'It's difficult to juggle everything but . . .' Angus began.

'But what?' asked Paige.

He shook his head. 'Nothing. Forget it.'

'Please. Tell me what you were going to say.'

Their conversation was interrupted by Tom. 'Hello, everyone. How's my favourite councillor? Ready to visit some mad constituents?' He strode into the room and kissed Paige on the top of her head.

'Are you all right, love?'

'Fine. Just resting.'

Callum came bounding down the stairs and threw his arms around his dad's waist. 'Hi, Dad!'

'Hi, Callum. Have you been good today?'

'Very. Angus promised to show me how to use the washing machine this evening. How to put in the cleaning stuff and everything. All by myself. So I can help Mummy with the washing.'

Tom looked at Angus. 'Is Callum serious?'

Angus nodded. 'He's really interested in machines. I'd be surprised if you didn't have a little engineer on your hands, mate.'

'Sounds good to me,' Paige said. 'They're never too young to learn. I'll show you how to put on the dishwasher next young man, if you're good.'

'Thanks, Mum!'

Tom glanced at his watch and sighed. 'We'd better get something to eat, Paige. We need to leave in twenty minutes or so. The Killen Estate is huge – it will take us all evening to cover it.'

'Molly and Kate offered to cover some of it with us. And Molly said that Alex and Harry have also offered to help.'

'Harry from the plant shop? The guy from your book club?'

Paige smiled. 'Gas, isn't it? We should send him round the houses with the big gardens. Maybe he'd hand out some free gardening tips – that might win us some brownie points.'

Tom smiled back. 'No kidding, he's really popular on the

radio. I wouldn't have thought he was the political type though.'

'Molly was saying it has more to do with Alex's influence than anything else. Kate worked some sort of magic there apparently. I'll tell you all about it when we're walking.'

'Sounds interesting.' He turned towards Angus. 'You know Kate, don't you?'

'Yes.' Angus blushed slightly. 'Yes, I do. Lovely girl. I haven't seen her for a while but I called into her granny's a few days ago with Callum. I hope that was all right.'

'Of course,' Paige said. 'Lily's a pet, isn't she? And Callum adores her.'

'I'm hungry,' Callum interrupted. 'What's for tea?'

'Callum!' Angus, Paige and Tom said in unison.

'Sorry,' Callum replied meekly.

'How about we make some toasted sandwiches for everyone?' Angus suggested kindly. 'And then your mum and dad can have a sit down for a few minutes.'

'OK,' Callum said. 'Can we use the whirr thing to grate the cheese?'

'The food processor?'

'Yes!' Callum said eagerly.

Angus looked at Paige, who nodded assent. 'I suppose so. But you'll have to help me wash all the bits afterwards, deal?'

'Deal.'

The doorbell rang shrilly.

'That must be Mum with Alfie,' Paige groaned. 'No rest for the wicked.'

'I'll get it!' Callum ran out of the kitchen, past his parents and towards the door.

Tom patted Paige's hand and smiled at her. 'And we're having another? Are we quite mad?'

She laughed. 'I think we just might be.'

*

'You take this side of the road and I'll take the far one,' said Tom. 'Try not to spend too much time with each person. We have a hell of a lot of houses to call on this evening.'

'Right,' Paige replied. 'I'll try to keep focused and not get sidetracked.' She looked at the number of the house in front of her and checked her clipboard. 'I'll start with the Kavanagh household.'

'Good luck. I'll wave at you from across the street.'

Paige walked up to the door and rang the bell. A thin, dark-haired girl of about nine answered the door.

'Yes?' She stared at Paige suspiciously. 'What are you selling?'

'Um, nothing. I'm Paige Brady, one of your local councillors. I'm looking for your support in the forthcoming general election.'

'I'll get Mam. Mam!' she shouted into the house.

'Coming.' A dark-haired woman appeared at the door from a doorway at the back of the hall. She looked at Paige. 'You're the one who's campaigning for childcare, aren't you?'

Paige nodded. 'That's right. Among other things.'

The woman said nothing.

'Do you have any questions for me?' Paige asked evenly.

Again nothing. The woman was completely tongue-tied.

'Anything at all?'

Her daughter nudged her mother. 'Ask her about a playground,' she hissed. 'Go on.'

'Oh, yeah. We need a playground in the estate. The kids have nowhere to play since the green was taken over by the council for new housing. I have five kids and the garden is tiny.'

Paige jotted down a note in her diary. 'I'll certainly check it out for you, Mrs Kavanagh. As they haven't started building yet, maybe some sort of arrangement can be made with the builders. Insurance is usually the big problem with playgrounds, but I'll do my best. I promise.'

'Fair enough.' The woman was about to close the door when Paige stopped her.

'I'll make some enquiries and I'll ring you back within the next two weeks about it. Maybe in the meantime you could talk to some of the other parents, and if they feel the same way you could start a petition.'

'Good idea.' The woman looked a little taken aback. 'You're really going to ring me?'

'Yes,' Paige promised. 'I really am.'

'I'll vote for you if you do.'

'Thank you,' Paige said. 'But you don't have to.'

'No, you're grand, I will. And I'll make sure my husband does too. He works nights but he votes before he comes home.'

'Thank you, Mrs Kavanagh.'

As Paige walked away from the house she put two discreet ticks beside 'Kavanagh' on the list. She knocked on the door of the next house as the bell seemed to be broken.

'Jeeze, would you give me a chance,' she heard a voice mutter in the hall. Through the safety glass she could see a tall shadowy figure. 'Who is it?' a male voice asked.

'Paige Brady, one of your local councillors.'

'What do you want?'

'Would you mind opening the door, Mr Cole? I could explain then.'

'How do you know my name?'

'I have a list of all the registered voters in the estate. Your name is on my list.'

'It's like fecking *Big Brother*,' he shouted at her. 'Go away.'

'If I could just . . .'

He opened the door and glared out at her. 'Did you not hear me? I said go away. I have nothing to say to the likes of you.'

'What do you mean – the likes of me?' Paige asked in

astonishment. 'I'm an Independent candidate, Mr Cole. I don't belong to any political party.'

'I'm not talking about politics. I'm talking about women!' he practically spat at her. 'No bloody good – the whole lot of you. Spawn of the devil. Go to hell!' he slammed the door in her face.

Paige stood on the doorstep for a moment in complete shock. He was obviously quite barmy. She shook herself, took a deep breath and crossed a heavy line with her pen through his name. 'Mad!' she wrote to the far right of the line.

The next few houses had more normal occupants thankfully – even if two of them were staunch People's Party supporters and had already promised their votes to Paddy Burns.

'How's it going, Paige?' Tom crossed the road to talk to her.

'Not too bad.' She looked down at her clipboard. 'Five definite yesses, two for Paddy, seven undecided and one mad man.' She told Tom about her experience with Mr Cole.

'Take care of yourself, Paige,' Tom said with concern when she'd finished. 'There are a lot of nutters out there. Maybe we should do the next set of houses together.'

'It would take twice as long that way,' Paige pointed out. 'I'll be fine, honestly.'

'If you're sure.'

She nodded. 'And how are the others getting on? Have you heard from them?'

'Harry rang to find out about your policy on the proposed "Educate Together" school for Burnaby. Oh, and Molly got several requests for a playground for the estate. Apparently they're building on the green where the kids used to play.'

'Interesting,' Paige said. 'I got the same request. There might be something I can do about that.'

He linked her arm. 'You're going to make a great Deputy, Paige. Do you know that? You really care, don't you?'

'Of course.' She widened her eyes. 'What are you suggesting, Tom? That not all politicians care?'

'Not at all.' he winked at her. 'Would I?'

'No comment,' she smiled. 'Now let's get back to work. We have a long evening ahead of us.'

Paige sat down at the kitchen table the following morning. Tom had already got Alfie and Callum up and was feeding Alfie in his highchair.

'Morning, Sleepyhead.' Tom smiled at her as she poured herself a bowl of cereal.

'Thanks for letting me sleep on,' she said. 'I just couldn't get out of bed this morning.'

'How are the feet?'

'Not the best,' she admitted. 'I could do with a foot rub. Any offers?'

'I'll do it,' said Callum, immediately jumping under the table and crawling to his mother's feet.

He took her left foot out of its slipper and held it in his small hand.

She winced. 'Callum, your hands are freezing. Warm them up, please.'

'How will I do that?' he asked from under the table.

'Blow on them and rub them together,' Tom suggested.

'OK.'

Tom looked over at Paige and smiled. She smiled back, put her chin in her hands and waited. A few minutes later she felt a slightly warmer hand on her foot.

'Is that better, Mummy?'

'Yes, thanks, Callum.'

'Now what do I do?'

'Rub your mum's foot gently but firmly from the heel to the toes,' said Tom. 'Don't tickle her, OK?'

'OK.'

Callum stroked his mother's foot as directed. Paige was surprised, he was actually quite good.

'How is it?' Tom whispered.

'Not bad,' she whispered back.

'Will I pull your toes a little, Mummy?' Callum popped his head up from under the table. 'Kind of stretch them. I saw a lady on *Richard and Judy* doing that to someone's toes.'

'*Richard and Judy*?' Paige asked. 'When were you watching that?'

'When Angus and me were making toasties last night. They were talking about modern art and Angus told me to watch and tell him what I thought of the pictures.'

'Really?' Tom asked. 'Did you like them?'

'I liked the one of the snail by the French guy. The one made from all the bits of paper. Angus said the man did it like that because he was sick and his fingers couldn't hold a paintbrush properly. I think his name was Massey something or other.'

'Matisse?' Paige asked.

'That's it,' Callum said. 'Matisse.'

Tom shook his head. 'Amazing,' he murmured. 'Our son the art critic.'

'We're going to go to the gallery next week,' Callum continued. 'Angus said there's lots of pictures of animals and a cool computer thing that explains the paintings. Have I been to the gallery before, Mum?'

'No, I don't think so. But you've been to the stuffed animal museum and it's right beside it.'

'Maybe Angus will bring me there too. How's your foot, Mummy?'

'Better,' Paige said truthfully, wiggling her toes. 'You're doing a great job.'

'I'll do your toes.' He popped back under and after pulling Paige's toes gently for a moment asked 'Will I do the other foot now?'

'Please.'

'And will this get me an extra star, do you think?'

'It just might.' Paige laughed.

While Tom dropped Alfie over to his mother's, Callum sat on the end of the double bed watching his mother dress. She was currently standing in her bra, pants and tights, trying to decide what to wear.

'When will Angus be here?' he asked impatiently.

'Soon,' Paige promised. She looked at her watch. 'Very soon, hopefully.' She was due in the *Now TV* studios at half past nine and it was now five past. With Dublin traffic the way it was, she'd be lucky to get there on time. She breathed a sigh of relief as the doorbell rang.

'I'll get it!' Callum ran out the door and thundered down the stairs.

'It's a man,' he shouted up to Paige. 'He says he's your taxi driver. What will I do?'

'Nothing!' Paige shouted back. 'I'll be down in a second.'

'I'm here too, Paige,' Angus shouted up. 'Sorry I'm late. I asked the driver to wait in the cab for two minutes. Is there anything I can do to help?'

'No, thanks. I'm almost ready.' She looked in the mirror again. 'Thank goodness Angus is here,' she murmured. She quickly pulled a black top out of her wardrobe, held it up against her body, decided it would be too much with her black suit and threw it down on the bed with the other tops. 'Why didn't I choose my outfit last night?' she asked herself as she rummaged through the tops hanging on the rail. 'Damn, damn, damn!'

She picked up her mobile and keyed in Molly's number.

'Hello, Paige?'

'Molly. You've got to help me. I'm on *Now AM* this morning and I'm running late. What the hell will I wear?'

Molly thought for a second. 'Is your dark pink trouser suit clean?'

'Yes, but is it not a bit . . .'

'Wear it with a plain white top and some heels. You don't want to wear black on the television – everyone does and it's instantly forgettable. You want people to sit up and remember you.'

'I suppose.'

'What time are you on at?'

'Ten.'

'I won't keep you, so. Are you taping it?'

'Yes.'

'Cool, I'll be over later to watch it this evening. Good luck.'

'Thanks.'

Paige pulled a plain white top over her head, and stepped into the dark pink trousers. She hoped Molly was right. Paige usually wore this suit at parties, not for work. Still, she didn't really have time to think about it. She threw on the pink jacket, wiggled her feet into her matching dark pink court shoes, grabbed her large brown leather bag, ran into the bathroom and swept her make up and hair brush into it.

'Mobile, wallet, keys,' she muttered as she collected them all together and threw them into the bag. She looked at herself in the mirror. Her cheeks were flushed from all the rushing around, matching her suit. But she had to admit she looked pretty good. Luckily her stomach was still reasonably trim, otherwise she'd never have been able to wear the closely fitting trousers.

She walked quickly down the stairs into the kitchen, her heels clicking noisily on the tiled floor.

'You look nice, Mummy,' Callum said, looking up from the table-top.

'Thanks.' She smiled at him and ruffled his hair. He was

playing a game of Junior Scrabble with Angus. 'Be good now. I'll see you later.'

'*Now TV* this morning, right?' Angus asked.

Paige nodded. 'Ten o'clock.'

'We'll be glued. Hope it goes well.'

'Thanks. I have to run. See you later.'

'We'll be watching you, Mummy!' Callum shouted as she closed the hall door behind her.

She opened the door of the taxi. 'Sorry to keep you.'

'Not at all, love,' he said, folding away his paper. 'We'd better get going though. We have to pick up Ms Higgins on the way.'

Paige's heart sank. That was all she needed. She pulled her bag onto her knee and rummaged through it to find her foundation and her powder compact. She didn't want Annette to see her looking like a dog's dinner. She carefully poured some creamy base onto her fingers and holding the small compact mirror in front of her face, she began to smooth it onto her skin, taking care to cover the pasty, greyish skin around her eyes. Heavens she looked tired. She pulled out her tube of liquid concealer, dotted it on the dark circles and patted it in gently. Then she finished with some powder, mascara and lip-gloss. She looked at herself critically. She'd do – thank goodness for make-up. She knew she'd be given the full treatment in the make-up room of the studio, but she didn't want to go in there looking like death warmed up. Now at least she looked slightly presentable.

'Feel better now?' the taxi man asked.

'Sorry?'

She caught the taxi man's eye in the rear-view mirror.

'A lot of my fares do their make-up in my cab.' He smiled kindly. 'I think it helps them to wake up. Must be important in your line of work too. First appearances and all that. You're standing in the next election, aren't you?'

'That's right.'

'My wife says she's voting for you. She likes your policies on childcare.'

'And what about you?' Paige asked. 'Who will you be voting for?'

'Haven't really decided yet. Paddy Burns has always been a decent sort. Says what he means. I like him.'

'Would you think about giving me your second preference?' Paige asked directly.

'Sorry?'

'Putting me in as number two.'

'Ah, I might. I'll certainly consider it.'

'Thanks.'

'But what would you be doing for the average working man like myself?'

'That's a good question,' Paige said, wishing she'd never started this conversation. 'A lot of my policies relate to child-care, funding for schools, improved services – water supply, upgrading roads . . .'

'Upgrading roads?' he asked. 'Like making the roads better to drive on?'

'Exactly. Some of them are in a right state and I think it's unacceptable. And something positive has to be done about traffic congestion.'

'I think you're dead right. Let me tell you a story about traffic congestion . . .' he began. Paige sat back against the seat to listen. She'd obviously hit the right note. After a ten minute monologue, he pulled up outside a red brick townhouse and beeped the horn.

'The wife's not that keen on your one Higgins,' he admitted. 'She thinks she's stuck in the Dark Ages. And she wouldn't be my choice either.'

Paige smiled to herself.

Annette opened the door and walked towards the taxi. She

was immaculately turned out in a sombre navy suit with a frilly white blouse underneath. Her hair was perfectly set in a static halo around her head.

She climbed into the front seat of the car. The taxi man said nothing. He knew this one all right – she was the old boot who had called taxi drivers 'lazy' last year. How could he forget? He pulled swiftly out into the Dublin traffic.

'How are you this morning, Paige?' Annette asked crisply, turning around to face her.

'Very good, thanks.'

'You look a little tired. Not sick are you?'

Paige could have hit her. 'No, I'm fine. Just canvassing until late last night, you know how it is.'

'Oh, I leave a lot of that door-to-door stuff to my supporters,' Annette said breezily. 'Too busy myself. Far more important things to be doing.'

The taxi man grunted.

'Sorry?' Annette asked him icily. 'Did you want to say something?'

'No,' he muttered. He didn't like this one's attitude at all. Snooty cow. Too busy to meet the common people – like himself.

'Who else is in the studio, do you know?' Paige asked Annette.

'Jackie and Hilda.' Hilda Murphy was another Independent. She wasn't expected to win a seat, but had appeared on many radio chat shows expounding her rather extreme right wing views. She could always be relied upon to get under the listeners' skin.

'Just the women?' Paige asked.

'Just the women.'

'Should be interesting.'

'Quite.'

Paige looked out the window as they approached Dundrum,

where the studio was based. As they pulled up outside the buildings, she rubbed her finger over her teeth to check for any stray lip-gloss and pulled the hairbrush through her hair.

Stepping out of the taxi, she thanked the driver.

'Not at all,' he said. 'And I'll give you my number two,' he promised her.

'Thanks,' she smiled.

'And I'll get your number one, I presume?' Annette asked arrogantly, listening in to their exchange.

'Are you joking?' he snorted. 'You're the one who was giving out about taxi drivers, last Christmas in the *Southside Sentinel,* remember?'

Annette's face reddened. 'That was a long time ago. Besides, you can't believe everything you read in the papers,' she said sniffily.

As they walked into the lobby, Paige could feel butterflies in her stomach.

'Those taxi drivers,' Annette muttered as they approached the large curved desk. 'Not to be trusted.'

Paige ignored her and smiled at the receptionist. 'Paige Brady and Annette Higgins. We're here for *Now AM.*'

'Please, take a seat. A researcher will be out to you in a moment.'

'Thanks.'

Fifteen minutes later, Paige was sitting in the brightly lit *Now AM* studio, her lips sticky with freshly applied gloss and her short dark hair neatly stuck down by a generous soaking of hairspray, which had nearly asphyxiated her in the small make-up room. Her eyelashes felt heavy with mascara and her hands were hot and clammy with nerves. This was the very first time she'd appeared on national television. Jackie leant over and squeezed her clasped hands.

'Don't worry,' she said kindly. 'Once we're on air you'll forget your stage fright. Anyway, a bit of adrenaline never hurt anyone. Better than being as cool as a cucumber and dead on the screen.' She gestured towards Annette pointedly who was sitting calmly on the sofa opposite them.

'Thanks,' Paige said gratefully.

A moment later the presenters – Frank Ryan and Dee Kelly arrived and sat down.

'How are you all this morning?' Frank asked, smiling at the four would-be politicians.

'Fine, thank you,' Hilda replied for them all. 'And I hope this is going to be a fair and equal debate. I know this station is very left-wing and I want to —'

'This station isn't left wing, Hilda,' Dee cut in. 'Or right wing for that matter. It has no political allegiances whatsoever.'

'And we're not really having a debate, Hilda,' Frank explained. 'This is breakfast television after all. We'll be keeping it light.'

Annette muttered something under her breath.

'Sorry, Annette?' Dee asked. 'I didn't quite catch that.'

Just then the female floor manager strode over. 'We'll be on air in two minutes, after the news headlines. Is everyone set?'

They all nodded.

'And everyone's been wired for sound?'

More nods.

'Good.'

'They're all very young in here,' Jackie whispered to Paige.

'And mostly women,' Paige replied. 'Great isn't it?'

'Absolutely!' Jackie said. 'Wish more companies were like that.'

Dee looked at Jackie and put her finger to her lips.

'Oops, better be quiet,' Jackie said to Paige.

Paige stared at the coffee table in front of her which held two bright yellow *Now AM* coffee cups. The weather had just come on and she knew their slot was next. She raised her head and tried to stay calm. Her stomach was doing somersaults and she could feel a dull flush spreading down her neck and face. Hopefully the heavy television make-up would stop it being too noticeable. Damn, her cheeks would clash with her suit. She should have worn black – it would have been safer. What was she thinking of?

'And welcome back.' Dee smiled at the camera. 'We are very privileged to have the four women who are standing for election in the Dun Laoghaire Rathdown constituency in the forthcoming general elections – Deputy Jackie Pile of the New Alliance, Councillor Annette Higgins of the Democrats, Ms Hilda Murphy, an Independent, and Councillor Paige Brady who's also an Independent. Welcome to you all.'

'Thank you.' They all smiled and nodded.

'Let's start with Deputy Pile,' Frank said. 'Deputy, you've held a seat in the government for the past ten years, is that correct?'

'Eleven years,' she corrected him.

'Eleven years,' he continued. 'And in that time you've seen a lot of changes, especially for women. Could you tell us a little about your work on the Women's Health Bill and what that will mean for the women of Ireland?'

'Certainly, Frank,' Jackie said.

As Jackie explained the proposed bill, Paige's mind drifted. She watched Jackie as she talked and wondered if she'd ever be so poised and so confident in front of the cameras.

'And Councillor Brady, many of your policies involve women's issues of various sorts. Am I correct?'

Paige took a deep breath and looked at Frank. 'That's right, Frank. Ireland is way behind most other European countries when it comes to the provision of childcare facilities. If I win a seat, I intend to lobby the government to provide affordable childcare for all those women who wish to work. I also intend to lobby for funding of the "Educate Together" schools. I think it is important, especially in this day and age, that our children are educated with other children of different religions and different cultural backgrounds.'

'That would be a complete waste of money!' Hilda Murphy interrupted. 'We already have a fine network of primary schools in this country who all could do with extra funding. It would be foolish to start funding new schools.'

'But most of the traditional schools are run by the churches,' Paige pointed out calmly. 'Both Catholic and Protestant. I'm talking about a different sort of education – where all children can be taught together, no matter what religion they are.'

'What's wrong with religion?' Hilda spluttered. 'Do you have something against it, Councillor Brady?'

'Of course not,' Paige said, sounding calmer than she felt. 'But just because something has always been done in a certain way, it doesn't mean it's right.'

'Quite.' Jackie nodded. 'I think Councillor Brady has a good point. There is certainly a place for "Educate Together" schools in Ireland and her ideas on childcare are spot on.'

'Two opposing candidates agreeing,' Dee said. 'How unusual.'

'Well I don't agree at all,' Annette said firmly. 'I think Councillor Brady should stop trying to encourage mothers back into the workforce. A lot of Ireland's current social problems stem from mothers going out to work.'

'That's ridiculous!' Paige said. 'There are no approved statistics to back that up. How can you say that?'

'Look at your own son, Callum,' Annette looked Paige straight in the eye. 'I hear he has a lot of behavioural problems. Am I right?'

'That's unfair!' Paige raised her voice. 'There's nothing wrong with my son, how dare you?'

'Ladies,' Frank interrupted. 'I think this is all getting a little personal. Let's concentrate on your polices, not on your private lives. Oops, it's time for a break. We'll be back in a few minutes with more of this election special on *Now AM*. Don't go away now.'

As soon as Paige heard the ads come on she glared at Annette.

'How could you, Annette?' she asked. 'How could you drag my son into this? There's nothing wrong with him.'

'That's not what my contact at his crèche said. She told me all about his terrible record at Little Orchard. Calling the teachers names and running riot. Oh, I know all about Callum's behaviour, Paige, believe me.'

Paige was dumbstruck.

'That's all a bit below the belt,' Jackie said. 'Let's keep this clean. I have no time for dirty politics and I don't wish to be associated with them.'

'I'd have to agree.' Hilda nodded.

Annette pulled herself up bolt upright on the sofa. 'All's fair in politics, ladies.'

'If you don't mind me saying, I don't think it shows you in very good light, Annette.' Dee joined in.

'Really?' Annette raised her eyebrows and said nothing further.

As soon as they were back on air, Paige's heart sank.

'Now we have a viewer on the line who'd like to ask Councillor Brady a question.' Frank looked at Paige. 'Will you take the question, Councillor?'

'Um, I suppose so,' said Paige nervously.

'Hello, my name is Peggy and I wanted to ask the Councillor if she's having a baby. I saw her in Holles Street last week and I was just wondering.'

'Um, well . . .' Paige took a deep breath. Tom has told her to be honest and open if this ever came up, so that was how she was going to play it. 'Yes, yes I am. I haven't made the news public yet because . . .'

'I think it's a disgrace,' Annette piped up. 'Mothers should be at home with their children, not gadding about the place looking for votes. She's putting the baby's life in danger.'

'Yes, yes,' Hilda agreed. 'Women of Ireland, listen to me. I'd like to talk about the rights of the unborn child. In my day . . .'

Paige felt like crying. First the comments about Callum, now this. It was most unfair.

'I'd like to say something.' Jackie leant forward, interrupting Hilda's rant. 'We are not here to discuss Councillor Brady's personal life. What's Irish politics coming to if that's all we think the voters are interested in? Let's not insult their intelligence. Let's talk about what really matters – how we can get this country back on its feet. How we can improve the standard of life for the large percentage of the country who are living below the poverty line. How we can educate our children better. These are the things that matter, not the Councillor's personal life.'

'Well said, Deputy,' Frank said. 'And now we have another call. This time for Councillor Higgins. And I believe it's someone you know, Councillor.'

'Hello, Mum,' came a voice down the line. 'It's Chantal, your daughter. Remember me?'

'Um, yes, hello Chantal. And what are you doing, dear? Why are you ringing?' Annette's face began to pale and her eyes flicked around the studio nervously, before settling on her knees.

'I've been watching the programme and I'm ashamed of you, Mum.'

'Chantal!' Annette said. 'What are you saying?' She looked at Frank. 'I think you should cut her off. This is not my daughter. This is an impostor.'

'Mum, it is me. You know it is. And how can you be such a hypocrite? You worked the whole way through both your pregnancies and we never saw you when we were small because you were always at some meeting or other. Dad brought us up. And how could you say that about that woman's little boy? What kind of person have you become? We don't even talk, Mum. You haven't said one word to me in over two years, maybe you'd like to tell everyone why.'

'Um, yes, well, I've learnt from my mistakes, haven't I? And I don't think they'd be interested at all in our little stand-off. Goodbye, Chantal.' Annette looked visibly shaken.

'But —' Chantal said.

Frank stepped in, worried about the legal implications of what she might say. 'I'm afraid we'll have to leave it there as it's time for a commercial break. Thank you, ladies, for coming into the studio this morning. It's been most, um, interesting.'

'Join us after the break for the amazing story of Gina, the surrogate chimp mother.' Dee smiled broadly at the camera.

'Talk about getting personal,' Jackie whispered to Paige as soon as the ads had come on. 'I've never known an election like it. Remember Miles laying into Mark on the radio the other week?'

Paige nodded. 'How could I forget?'

Frank looked at all the candidates. 'That was quite something. I don't know what to say really.'

Annette stood up. 'You should never have accepted my daughter's call. It was most unprofessional of you. I'm, I'm . . .' With that she stormed out of the studio.

Hilda, looking almost as pale as Annette for some reason, followed her out.

'Phew!' Dee said. 'I wouldn't be surprised if some of that ends up on this evening's news. Explosive stuff. What do you think her daughter was going to say?'

'Who knows?' Frank shrugged his shoulders.

'Thank you for having us on,' Jackie said. 'Sorry it all got a little heated.'

'Not to worry, it's good for the ratings,' Frank said.

I'm sure it is, Paige thought to herself. But it's not good for my nerves.

Chapter 13

Molly

'Are you expecting someone?' Paige asked Molly who's eyes kept flitting towards the door of Coffee Heaven.

Molly looked at her. 'No, why?'

'You keep staring at the door, that's all.'

'Oh, do I?' Molly drained the last of her coffee. 'Would you like another cup? I'm getting one.'

'Please. And a chocolate muffin if there are any left.'

Molly pushed her chair out and made her way to the counter. Alex flew past her with two heaped plates of salad and a steaming bowl of soup.

'Back in a second,' she told Molly. Alex placed the food in front of its owners and bustled back to Molly. She blew a stray piece of hair out of her flushed face.

'Busy?' Molly smiled.

'No kidding. I hate lunchtime. Especially when it's raining and everyone wants to eat in. What can I do for you?'

'Two coffees and a chocolate muffin.'

'No problem.' Alex glanced over at the door, looked back at Molly and grinned.

'What?' Molly asked.

'Nothing. I'll bring your coffees over in a few minutes.'

'Thanks.' When Molly turned around, she understood why Alex had been smiling. Sam was now sitting at the table with Paige. Alex had it in her head that there was something going on between herself and Sam. Try as she may, Alex just wouldn't believe Molly when she explained that they just enjoyed having lunch together, that was all, nothing more.

'Oh, yeah?' Alex had asked. 'Every day? And coffee too?'

'We just get on well as friends, that's all!' Molly had protested. But it hadn't done any good. Alex still had the two of them pegged as the next Rhett and Scarlet. She just wouldn't listen.

'Hi, Sam,' Molly said as she sat down beside him. 'I thought you were on a day off today.'

'I am, but I got these this morning and I knew you'd want to see them straight away. But I don't have long I'm afraid, I have to collect Hugh soon.' He patted the large brown envelope which was resting on the table.

'What's that?' Molly asked.

'The designs for the Book Festival,' Paige said excitedly.

'Have you already seen them?' Molly asked a little miffed.

'No, we were waiting for you, of course,' Paige said. 'Will you show us now, Sam?'

'Certainly.' He opened the envelope and pulled out three sheets of A4 paper. 'My friend, Dora did three different designs. She said there's no problem changing anything you're not happy with – the colour, lettering, lay-out, that kind of thing.' He spread the three sheets on the table. 'What do you think?'

Paige looked at Molly. Molly was smiling broadly.

'They're great!' Paige said. 'Just what we wanted. Bright and fun, with a romance theme. Which one do you like best, Molly?'

Molly studied the three designs carefully. They were all very different. One was an old fashioned design in the shape of a heart with a lacy border and filled with what looked liked pink and red pick and mix sweets. The next was more modern –

another heart, this time filled with tiny books, all spilling over each other. The third was very striking – little pink cherubs flying up and down the page, their hair highlighted in gold, each holding a book.

She pointed at the cherubs. 'That one.'

'My choice too.' Paige nodded.

'What do you think, Sam?'

'I'm not really your target market, am I?' he said. 'But I'd have to agree with you. The cherubs are really eye catching. And the lettering and the slogan in the cloud is a great idea.'

Paige read it aloud. 'The Burnaby Book Festival in association with Happily Ever After Bookshop. Bringing Books Alive.'

'And best of all,' Sam said, 'Dora showed the designs to her boss in the design house who turned out to be a dedicated reader. Her boss offered to sponsor the printing of the posters and flyers for the event if we bung some free tickets her way and put their company's name on all our promotional material. And Ink Press offered to print the programmes for free as part-sponsorship.'

'Really?' Molly asked. 'That's excellent news. Thanks, Sam.' She felt like kissing him but thought against it.

'How can we thank you?' Paige said. 'That's the best news I've had all day. No, all week. You're an angel.'

'A cherub?' Molly laughed.

'Exactly.' Paige smiled. 'A cherub.'

After Sam had left, Molly and Paige finished up their coffee.

'He's so nice,' Paige commented.

'Sam?'

'Yes, Sam.'

Molly looked at her and smiled. 'I know. He's lovely, isn't he?'

Paige leaned closer towards her. 'Has anything happened that you haven't told me about?'

Molly shrugged her shoulders. 'Unfortunately not. But we're

going out to the cinema on Saturday, so you never know. Fingers crossed.'

'How did that happen? Did he ask you out again?'

'Not exactly. He mentioned there was a film that he'd like to see and I said I'd love to see it too but that no one would ever go to subtitled films with me. Not even you.'

'Liar!' Paige snorted.

Molly laughed. 'I had to think of something.'

'What are you going to see?'

'A new French film. It's supposed to be really romantic.'

Paige raised her eyebrows. 'Did he choose it?'

Molly nodded.

'Sure, you're away on a hack, girl, in that case. I look forward to hearing all about it.'

On Saturday night, Molly started getting ready early. She wanted to look her best but she didn't want to look like she'd put too much effort into it. If only men knew how long it took to apply 'natural looking' make-up, they'd be shocked. She'd fake tanned her body earlier and had spent most of the last hour walking around the house half-naked, worried that it would streak if she got dressed. Luckily, Kate was out for the night, though she'd been very coy about where she was going. All that she'd divulge was that she was meeting an old friend and wouldn't be back until the following afternoon. Molly was intrigued but try as she might, she couldn't get any more information out of Kate.

'I'll tell you when I can.' Kate had kissed her on the cheek, her eyes dancing with happiness.

'It's good to see you in such flying form,' Molly had conceded. 'But could you not just tell me his name, please?'

Kate had smiled and shaken her head. 'You'll be the first to know, I promise. OK?'

Molly smelt her arms. They still reeked – the sweet acidic

smell of flesh turning golden brown she hoped. She'd wait for a little while longer, then have a shower. She studied her legs carefully, turning them this way and that. They seemed a little browner all right, but it was hard to tell really.

Striding down the stairs two hours later in a flowery summer skirt, dainty slip-on sandals which flattered her feet, a white vest top and her fitted denim jacket she felt great. She'd piled her hair on top of her head, allowing a few tendrils to falls down on either side of her face to soften the effect, and her make-up was deceptively natural.

She waited for Sam in the living room. He'd kindly offered to collect her at home. Molly was delighted with this – it made it seem like a real date, not just two friends going to the cinema together. After spending a few minutes watching television, the doorbell rang.

Molly jumped up and went into the hall to answer it. As soon as she opened the front door she instantly regretted not checking through the tiny security peep-hole first.

'Hello, Molly,' said Denis. 'Can I come in?'

'What are you doing here?' she demanded, still holding the door half open.

'That's no way to greet an old friend.'

'Denis, I'm sorry but I'm on my way out. I'll ring you tomorrow, how about that? We can talk.'

'Why not now?' he asked persistently. 'I miss you, Molly. I can't get you out of my head. I'm so sorry things turned out the way they did. But if you'll only . . .'

'Denis, please stop.' Just then a car pulled up outside the gate. 'I think this may be my lift. It's better if you . . .'

Sam walked in the gate. Molly waved at him. 'I'll be with you in a second,' she said loudly. 'Denis,' she said, turning her attention back to him, 'you have to go now.'

'I see,' he stared at her, and she felt as if his cool, blue eyes could cut her in half, they were that sharp. 'Am I that easily replaced?'

'It's not like that,' Molly said. 'Sam is a friend from work. We're going to the cinema together, that's all.'

'Why are you so dressed up then? You never wore skirts when we were together.'

'Yes I did, you're being ridiculous,' Molly said. 'Now I have to go, I'm sorry.' She closed the door in his face, not knowing what else to do, grabbed her bag and waited a few seconds. Denis was still there when she opened the door again. 'I'll walk you to the car,' he offered.

She said nothing. There was no point in arguing with him, it would only make things worse. As they approached the car, Sam stepped out and held the passenger door open for Molly.

'Quite the gentleman,' Denis observed. He held out his hand formally. 'I'm Denis, I don't think we've been introduced.'

'Sam,' Sam said without betraying any emotion at all. 'Nice to meet you. And that's my son, Hugh, in the back of the car.'

Molly looked into the car in surprise. 'Oh,' she said waving at Hugh who waved back in reply. 'I didn't realize he was coming with us.'

'A family outing,' Denis said, an unpleasant look on his face. 'How sweet.'

'We'd better get going, Molly,' Sam said glancing at his watch. 'Nice to have met you, Denis.'

'And you.'

As the car drove away, Molly breathed a sigh of relief.

'Sorry about all that,' she said.

'Not to worry.' He lowered his voice. 'And I'm sorry I had to bring Hugh. His mum was called away on a voice-over job unexpectedly. Some ad she'd recorded got accidentally wiped by the studio and they have to re-record the whole thing. And his grandparents are away. I did try Dad but he's busy.'

'It's OK. But he won't be able for the subtitles, will he? And the film's not really suitable anyway.'

'Um, no. I was hoping we could go to the new Harrison Ford action film instead. Would that be OK? I know I should have rung you first but we were in such a rush and . . .'

'Sam, that's all right, honestly. We can go to the French film next week or something. I'm quite partial to Harrison Ford to tell the truth.' She turned around. 'Do you like Harrison Ford, Hugh?'

'Is he the old guy who plays Indiana Jones and who was in *Star Wars*?'

'Yes, that's right. I wouldn't have thought of him as old though.'

'He's got white hair, like Grampa.'

'But with a much younger girlfriend,' Sam added.

'Grampa has a girlfriend?' Hugh asked with interest.

'No! Harrison Ford.' Sam laughed. 'You have to watch what you say with Hugh,' he whispered to Molly.

'So I see,' she whispered back.

'What are you saying?' Hugh asked.

'Just talking about the film.'

After dropping Hugh back to his mum's, Sam drove back to Burnaby along the coast road.

'How's the writing going?' Sam said. 'Or am I allowed to ask?'

'You are this week.' She smiled. 'Because it's actually going all right, fingers crossed. I've almost finished the story I've been working on. I just have to get the ending right. I always find endings so difficult.'

'They are kind of important, aren't they?' He smiled back. 'But I'm glad it's going well.'

'Thanks.' Molly looked out of the window. Sam was very easy company. She never felt she had to fill the silences with him.

If they didn't feel like talking they didn't seem to need to. 'Look at that moon,' she said staring up. 'Isn't it amazing? So bright.'

'We should take a walk along the beach,' Sam suggested. 'It's such a beautiful evening.'

Molly's heart leapt. 'Yes, why don't we?'

Sam drove down the slip road to the beach and parked the car. 'You won't be too cold, will you?' he asked as they stepped out of the car. 'I have a jacket in the back if you like.'

'That would be great. Thanks.' He handed her a dark blue fleece and she put it on. The sleeves were much too long for her so she rolled them back. 'I look huge in this,' she laughed.

'No you don't, it suits you.' He locked the car and took her hand. The steady heat of his skin against hers made her feel safe and warm.

They crunched down the shingle towards the edge of the sea and walked along the firmer, damp sand. The waves were lapping at the shore, with gentle wet swishes, and the moon illuminated the water, giving it an otherworldly, unearthly glow.

'About Denis,' Sam began nervously. 'I'm not causing any problems there am I?'

'Not at all. He's having problems accepting that it's over between us, that's all. We were together for ten years on and off and I guess he figured we'd end up together eventually. But it's definitely over.'

'If there's anything I can do – talk to him for you, keep out of the way . . .'

'There isn't, but thanks for offering. He's harmless, just annoying. Anyway, let's not talk about him this evening. Did Hugh enjoy the film do you think?'

'Yes. He was a bit freaked out by the giant spiders, I think. He was gripping my hand so hard I thought he'd break my fingers at one stage, but he seemed to like the rest of it. Thank you for being so nice to him.'

'He's easy to be nice to,' Molly replied. 'He's a good kid.'

'He really took to you. He's not always that chatty with people. Actually he's usually quite shy.'

'We were talking about books mainly. He's quite the little reader, isn't he?'

Sam nodded. 'He started reading at four and he's been flying through them ever since. He's reading *The Hobbit* at the moment.'

'So he told me. That's quite some child you have, Sam.'

'I know, I'm very lucky.' He lifted her hand towards his face and kissed it softly. 'But thank you. And you're quite something too, you know.'

Molly didn't know what to say. She could feel her face redden but hoped Sam wouldn't notice in the half-light. 'Um, thanks.'

'You're not used to compliments, are you?' he asked.

'I suppose not.'

He stopped walking. 'Come here,' he said quietly.

Molly's heart leapt. His eyes were warm and kind and they drew her in, encouraging her to move towards him. He put his arms around her, touched her cheek tenderly, then ran his arms up and down hers, warming her through the fleece. 'You're cold,' he said. 'We should go back to the car.'

'I'm OK,' she protested, not wanting him to stop. 'Really.'

He smiled at her. 'Really?' he cocked an eyebrow.

I could drown in those eyes, she thought, staring into them. His blonde curls were falling over his face and he looked edible. Kiss me, she urged. Go on, kiss me.

He stroked her face again and ran his fingers over her lips. Molly thought her legs would melt from under her. She couldn't take much more of this. She could feel her breath becoming faster, and her heart skipped a beat as he planted a tiny kiss on the edge of her mouth. That was it – she'd had enough. She put one hand behind his head and pulled his lips towards hers. They kissed gently at first, exploring each other's mouths, growing more passionate with each lingering lip caress. Molly pressed her body against Sam's and felt him respond instantly, tightening his grip on her. They kissed for what seemed like hours, before drawing away and holding each other, Sam's firm hands cupping the hollow in Molly's lower back.

'You really are something,' he whispered into her ear.

'You're not so bad yourself,' she whispered back.

They walked back towards the car, lingering to have one final look at the beach before driving away.

'My house is just up the road,' Sam said as they pulled out of the side road. 'Would you like some coffee or something?'

Or something, Molly felt like saying but she refrained herself. 'Sure,' she said instead. 'That would be nice.'

As soon as they stepped into his house she knew he wasn't like other men. For one thing, from what she'd seen of the house so far it was incredibly tidy, except for an area of toys to one side of the living room, and shelves and shelves of slightly disorganized-looking books of all shapes and sizes. Children's books, Molly decided on closer inspection.

'Sorry, that's Hugh's play area,' Sam explained. 'It's always a bit of a mess.'

'It's a lovely room,' Molly said. She unzipped the fleece, pulled it off and handed it to him. He hung it on the back of the sofa. 'Sit down,' he said. 'I'll put the kettle on. Or would you like a glass of wine? I've a bottle of white open in the fridge.'

'I'd love a glass of wine.' She smiled up at him. 'Thanks.'

After he'd left the room, Molly had a good look around. The black fireplace had an intricate boarder of patterned tiles to either side of it and above the mantelpiece was a most unusual mirror, framed in what looked like driftwood. On either side of the fireplace were white wooden built-in shelving units, filled with all manner of objects – small wooden sculptures, a silver tankard, silver candlesticks, framed photographs of Sam and Hugh, some ornamental glass paperweights and a small block of wood decorated with painted-on primroses and forget-me-knots.

Sam came back in holding two generous glasses of wine. He handed one to her, put his own down on the wooden coffee table between the two cream sofas and sat down on his hunkers in front of the fireplace. He began to build a fire, placing firelighters on the grate and putting pieces of wood and small logs around them.

'I love real fires,' he said as he worked. 'They're a bit of a pain, but worth it.'

'We don't have one in our house, and I do miss it,' Molly said. 'We have a gas one in the living room but it's not really the same, is it?'

'It's a good substitute.' Sam stood up, brushed his hands on his jeans and picked up his wine.

'I love your mirror,' Molly said as he sat down beside her. 'Where did you get it?'

'I made it,' he admitted. 'I made most of the furniture in the house.'

'Really?' Molly said in surprise. 'Even the coffee table and the shelves?'

'Sure.' He nodded. 'They were quite easy. Hugh's bed was the hardest. He had a very fixed idea of what he wanted.'

'What did he want?'

'Harry Potter's castle.' Sam grinned. 'Complete with spiral staircase and turrets.'

'No! And you made it? Hogwarts isn't it?'

'That's right. I did, my impression of it anyway.'

'Can I see?'

'OK.' Sam stood up and held out his hand for her. He led her down the narrow hallway, opened a door and flicked on the light.

'Sorry it's such a mess.'

Molly stepped over the Lego pieces and walked towards

Hugh's bed. It was one of the most incredible things she'd ever seen. It reached from the floor right up to the ceiling, two dark green towers with purple turrets and a bed perched in between. Below the bed was a desk and a wardrobe, and against the far wall was a wooden puppet theatre, the puppets in an adjacent open wooden box.

'It's amazing!' Molly said. 'I've never seen anything like it. Are the towers hollow?'

Sam nodded. 'One has steps and the other has a spiral slide. Hugh loves sliding down it in his pyjamas when he's supposed to be in bed.'

'I'm not surprised, what fun. And you made all this?'

Sam nodded and shrugged his shoulders modestly. 'It took me a while, but yes, yes I did. I'm quite good with my hands.'

'I'm impressed.'

'Thanks. Now let's go back into the sitting room. Knowing my luck, the fire will have gone out.'

They sat back down on the sofa and Sam put his arm around Molly's shoulders. The fire hadn't gone out, as Sam had feared and they sat in companionable silence gazing into it and sipping their wine.

'Thank you for a lovely evening,' Sam said after a while.

'My pleasure.'

He leaned over and kissed her again, trailing his hand down her cheek and caressing her neck and shoulder.

Sam's right, he really is good with his hands, Molly thought as they kissed. Damn good.

The following afternoon, Kate still hadn't arrived home. Molly tried her mobile but she wasn't answering. Molly had also rung Paige this morning, bursting to tell someone all about her evening with Sam, but Tom had answered the phone and said Paige was writing up some report for the County Council meeting on Monday evening and had asked not to be disturbed.

Molly toyed with the idea of visiting her parents – but why spoil a great weekend she decided. She would have loved to have spent the day with Sam but he was working in the bookshop. They'd have to start getting their rotas in synch, she thought. Thinking about Sam she smiled. She could still feel his lips against hers. He had dropped her home at four in the morning, after waking her up. She'd fallen asleep on the sofa, head resting on his shoulder, lulled to sleep by the warmth of the fire, the wine and the heady passion of the evening. He'd offered her a bed, but she wasn't quite sure what he'd meant by this and had opted to go home instead. She hated waking up in someone else's bed after spending the night unexpectedly, last night's make-up sunk into her pores, yesterday's stale clothes, no clean underwear. She never felt at ease in someone else's shower either – if it worked that was – she liked things to be clean and had had horrible experiences of standing on the slimy, hair ridden shower tray in Denis's house. She always ended up cleaning out that particular shower before daring to step into it. Yes, boys' bathrooms could be a downright health hazard, although Sam's, from what she'd seen of it, was remarkably clean, except for some toothpaste residue on the sink and the mirror which were only minor hygiene crimes in her book.

After having a shower in her own, ultra-clean bathroom and getting dressed in her most comfortable grey tracksuit bottoms and an off-white fleece, she walked to Burnaby Village to pick up a bagel and the papers.

Sitting down at the kitchen table half an hour later, she started flicking through the *Sunday Times* supplements while munching on her cream cheese and salmon filled bagel, washed down with some freshly squeezed orange juice. After she'd finished eating she looked at her watch – three o'clock. Still a large part of the day to fill. She thought about catching the afternoon showing of the French film at the Cineplex in Dun Laoghaire, but she had promised to go with Sam. She could always see it twice she supposed – no, that would be stupid. She knew damn well what she really should be doing and going to the cinema would just be a delaying tactic. She stood up, cleared away her plate and stacked the papers neatly on the table. She poured herself a glass of water, and made her way out of the kitchen, up the stairs and into her bedroom. She stared at her desk for a few seconds before sitting down.

As she turned on her computer and waited for it to boot up, she thought of Sam again. Sam walking on the beach, the wind in his curly hair, Sam paddling in the sea, Sam on his hunkers, building a fire, Sam's lips on hers . . . If she wanted to get any work done, she'd really have to stop. Think of your story, she admonished herself, not Sam.

She clicked on Microsoft Word for Windows and opened the short story she was working on – 'The Fisherman'. She read over what she'd written, changing words or sentences here or there and trying to get into the story. It was almost finished but she was having problems with the ending. For almost an hour she tried to think of some sort of logical and fitting conclusion, but ultimately failed once again.

She sighed deeply, began to bite at the skin around her thumb before picking up a pen and fiddling with that instead. 'Come on,' she told herself. 'Think of something.' She was about to turn off the computer in disgust when an image came into her mind, an image of a laughing, smiling man. Who is he? She asked herself. What does he look like? He's called Arthur, she decided. Arthur, um, Arthur, what? She tapped her teeth with a pen. Arthur Logan, Art for short. And he's tall, with messy black hair and dark blue eyes. Well built. She began to form his character in her mind. He works in the local library but he's also a painter, no a sculptor. A girl joins the library staff, Lisa. She's extremely quiet and no one can get much out of her, except for Art. They become friends and gradually he finds out why she's so quiet – her daughter died over a year ago and she hasn't even started to deal with it. Art helps her to come to terms with her loss and they fall in love.

Molly smiled to herself as she typed her notes frantically onto the keyboard. The story seemed to flow out of her from nowhere. The story of a woman and her road to recovery through the love of a good man. Sure, it was sentimental and maybe a little over optimistic, but hell, why not? People needed a bit of light relief and a little hope. Life was hard enough without having to read depressing stories all the time. There was definitely a place for some optimism in the world. Not to mention love.

She jotted down some more notes on her characters and her plot and then began to launch into the opening paragraph.

Molly read over what she'd written and smiled. Not a bad opening if I say so myself, she thought. She continued typing, drawing out Lisa and Art's story. By the time she looked up again, she was astonished to find it was almost seven o'clock in the evening. Over the last while she'd found writing a bit of a chore to tell the truth, but today the story had just told itself. Once she'd started, the characters had simply taken over, telling their own tale. Something that hadn't happened to Molly for a long, long time. She stretched her arms over her head and yawned. She saved her work and shut down the computer, happy and content. As she collected up her laundry – one of her usual Sunday chores – her mobile rang. She checked the screen – it was the shop. Sam was closing up today – she hoped there wasn't any problem.

'Hello?' she answered tentatively.

'Molly,' Sam said warmly. 'It's me, Sam.'

Her heart leapt. 'Hi, Sam.' She sat down on the bed, all thoughts of laundry forgotten.

'Sorry I didn't ring earlier,' he said, 'but it was really busy in here. You know how it gets on a Sunday.'

'Don't I just. Are you only closing up now?'

'Yes, unfortunately. Listen, what are you up to? Can I call over?'

'Sure, that would be nice. Would you like something to eat? I was just about to start making something.'

'If it's not too much trouble.'

'No trouble at all.'

'I've been thinking about you all day,' Sam said.

'I've been thinking about you too,' Molly admitted, surprising herself. 'See you in a while.'

'Would you like me to bring anything?' he asked.

'Just yourself.' She smiled as she put down the phone. Sam was delightfully straightforward and didn't seem to believe in playing games which was refreshing after Denis, who seemed to think that their relationship was a protracted game of Snakes and Ladders with a little Poker and Cluedo thrown in for good measure.

Chapter 14

Kate

On Sunday morning Kate woke up and opened her eyes. Feeling the unusually firm mattress beneath she remembered where she was – in the Presidential Suite of the Killiney Arms with Jay. Jay was lying beside her, on his back fast asleep and snoring gently. The previous week had gone by in a blur and she couldn't think when she'd last felt so happy. After a remarkably civilized dinner the evening after the hot tub incident – where she and Jay had talked and talked all night, ending up in bed together again – Kate had decided to take each day as it came and, after some initial reservations, concluded that maybe Jay had changed. She'd decided to give him the benefit of the doubt and to enjoy the short time they had together. Because once he left, it was over for good. They would just have this one last week, that was all she promised herself. Just one last, very final fling. To get him out of her system.

Jay had stayed in Dublin for four extra days just to be with her, and he'd already asked her to spend Christmas with him in Boston, which she had no intention of doing, of course. Christmas. As Kate lay in bed, thinking about Jay her mind drifted back to last Christmas Eve, a day she'd tried to block from her memory and had almost succeeded.

They'd intended to spend last Christmas together but on Christmas Eve things had taken an unexpected turn. On that fateful day, Kate had finished up work early and joined her colleagues for drinks in the local watering hole. She'd tried ringing Jay several times as they were due to meet that evening, but his mobile had been turned off. Up until then they'd always met at her house, and looking back on it of course it seemed strange to Kate, but caught up in the romance of their relationship, it was one of many signs she hadn't spotted until it was too late. Her place was nearer where they both worked and it suited Kate well – it meant she didn't have to remember to bring fresh underwear and toiletries in her bag every time they met. But that particular evening, tired of waiting for him and sensing that something was up, after some dithering she made up her mind to call into Jay's apartment. It was a good half an hour's walk away from the bar but it was a fresh, crisp night and she decided she could do with the fresh air after the hectic day she'd had and the smoky atmosphere of the bar. She said goodbye to her colleagues and left, looking forward to seeing Jay.

Kate approached his apartment, her cheeks tingling from the cold and pressed his bell. No answer. She tried his mobile again – it was still off. Where the hell was he? A tall dark-haired woman approached the communal door and opened it with a key. She looked at Kate for a moment as if deciding whether she was dangerous or not.

'Are you all right?' the woman asked Kate.

Kate nodded. 'Visiting a friend. He's late.'

'Wait inside, it's a chilly night.' The woman held the door open for Kate.

'Thanks,' Kate said gratefully. She was beginning to get cold.

Kate walked inside, took a seat on the red couch in the lobby and watched as the woman's back disappeared into the lift. All around her was deathly quiet. She pulled out her mobile and tried Jay's number again. Nothing. She sat there for a few minutes turning over the mobile in her hands, hoping it would ring at any moment, not knowing quite what to do if it didn't. Since meeting Jay she hadn't seen much of her other American friends and now she was beginning to regret it. She could always go back to the bar, she supposed, but she knew she wouldn't.

Just then, she heard a car pull up and voices outside the door. She looked out. A dark-coated man was stepping out of a yellow cab. It was Jay! Kate jumped to her feet to get the door for him as his arms were laden down with multi-coloured shopping bags. So that's where he was – shopping – of course! She was relieved and delighted to see him. As he approached the door he saw her and his face froze. He stared at her and then looked behind him at the elegant blonde woman, also holding several shopping bags, who was leaning over, paying the cab driver. Kate's heart sank. Who was the woman and why was Jay frowning like that?

Kate opened the door and held it for him as he walked through into the lobby.

'Jay?' she said quietly. 'Are you all right?'

'No.' He looked at her intensely. 'I'll explain everything later, I promise. Right now please don't say anything to . . . um . . .' He gestured towards the woman. 'Stay right here and I'll be down in a moment, OK?'

Kate was too shocked to answer.

'Sit down,' he commanded. 'I'll only be a moment.'

Kate was so dumbfounded and so confused, she did as he requested. Surely there was some rational explanation for all this – an out of town college friend back for the day, a long lost sister . . . but why hadn't he introduced them? Kate feared the worst. Still, she just sat there, silent as stone.

As Jay and the woman walked past her, Kate watched them like a hawk.

'I'm exhausted,' the woman said in a strong Boston accent. 'I could fall asleep on my feet, honey. No more shopping, ever, OK?' She put her head on his shoulder as they stood and waited for the lift.

'Sure,' Jay replied. They both stood with their backs to Kate and it suddenly all fell into place. He had another girlfriend. He'd replaced his little 'Cat' with a more glamorous model. How could she have been so stupid? Jay was much too good for her, she'd known that all along.

She strained her ears, trying to hear what Jay and the woman were saying, but to no avail. She watched them both step into the lift and as they turned towards her, Kate looked at Jay's face. It was betraying no emotion whatsoever. Kate felt a sharp stabbing in her chest. How could he ignore her like that? What was she doing sitting there, watching him when he had another woman by his side? She stood up abruptly, determined to say something. But it was too late, the lift doors closed just as she was galvanized into action. She waited for the lift to come back down, determined to follow him up to his apartment. But as soon as the doors opened again she realized to her surprise that Jay was still in the lift.

As he stepped out she began to flood him with questions.

'Where were you, Jay? I've been trying to ring you all afternoon. Who was that woman? Why is she in your apartment? What's happening? You were supposed to —'

'Cat,' he interrupted. 'There's a perfectly good explanation for all of this. Let's take a walk.' He put his arm around her but she shrugged it off.

'No! I want to see your apartment. Do you realize in all this time that I've never been inside it? You've always had some excuse or other for me not to see it.'

'You're being silly,' he said smoothly. 'Let's go outside and get some air. Have you been drinking?'

'No, not really. Stop trying to twist things. Jay!' He was walking towards the door.

He turned around and smiled at her. 'Come on,' he said. 'Join me.'

She followed him, not knowing what else to do.

'Who's the woman?' she asked again as soon as they were outside. 'Tell me now, Jay, I need to know.'

Jay said nothing for a few minutes, just kept walking towards the end of the block. Kate walked beside him.

'Jay?'

He stopped and looked at her, his eyes dark and restless, unable to focus on hers for more that a brief moment. Kate knew immediately that it was over. He was smiling but his eyes were cold. 'I don't know how to tell you this . . .' he began. He put his hands on her shoulders and rested them there. Kate could feel them pressing down on her, like a dead weight. 'She's my wife.'

'What?' Kate could feel the blood draining from her face and she began to feel quite faint. She shrugged off his hands and took a step back from him. 'I don't understand. You never told me you were married.'

'It never really came up.'

'What do you mean?' she said again. 'Never came up. You're joking, right?'

Jay shook his head. 'I never meant to fall in love with you, Cat. But I did. And it's changed everything. My marriage was rocky before I met you but now it's practically over. But I can't leave yet, Cindy's . . .'

'Cindy?' Kate demanded sharply. 'Is that her name? Cindy?' She snorted. 'As in Sindy doll?'

'You're overreacting, Kate. As I told you, my marriage is over, we haven't been close for a long time. But this week she . . .'

'I don't want to hear it,' Kate said icily. 'You're married and your wife is waiting for you. It's Christmas Eve, why wouldn't she be waiting for you? God knows where you've told her you've gone, you lying bastard. So go on, go back to her.' Kate turned to walk away from him but he held on to her upper arm tightly.

'Cat, please let me explain.'

'No! Get your hands off me!'

'There's no need to be like that. If you'll just listen . . .'

'I've been listening to your lies for quite long enough. I don't want to hear another thing from you.'

'I understand that you're annoyed with me but . . .'

'Annoyed? Annoyed doesn't even begin to explain how I feel. I'm so angry, Jay I could hit you.'

He looked at her in alarm.

'Don't worry, it's not really my style. I just want you to leave me alone.' She turned away from him again and began to walk quickly down the street, not looking back.

'Cat! I can explain,' he shouted after her. 'Cat! Don't leave like this.'

But she ignored him. As soon as she'd turned the corner of the block she stopped and put her back against the cold grey concrete wall of an anonymous apartment block. Only then did she allow herself to cry in huge, heaving sobs, engulfing her whole body.

Kate sat alone in her Boston apartment that evening, staring at the large package wrapped in jaunty Christmas paper still sitting under the small artificial tree. It was Jay's carefully chosen present – a simple but hideously expensive black cashmere scarf. Jay had rung both her mobile and her apartment several times but she'd eventually turned the mobile off and taken the other phone off the hook. Her eyes were red and swollen from crying and her heart felt torn to shreds, so torn that it would never heal. She wanted to go home. Back to Dublin, back to people she could trust.

'Cat?' Jay murmured and her thoughts were dragged back to the present.

'Hi, Sleepyhead,' she said, trying to forget what she'd been thinking about. 'I was just about to have a shower.'

'I'll order breakfast and then I might join you.' He grinned. 'What would you like?'

'I'm pretty hungry,' she admitted. 'I fancy some scrambled eggs with salmon and some toast. And coffee, lots of it.'

'Your wish is my command.'

As she stood under the shower she heard Jay talking on the phone but she couldn't quite make out what he was saying. Must be ordering breakfast she mused, putting her head under the hot jets of water and letting it stream down her face and hair. God, she loved hotel power showers. Moments later Jay joined her, his tanned naked skin a sharp contrast to her paler body.

'Hello, stranger.' She smiled through the steam.

He moved towards her, a bar of soap in his hands. 'You look a little dirty,' he smiled back. 'Let me fix that.' He lathered up the soap and began to smooth it all over her shoulders and her upper arms, moving slowly downwards towards her chest and stomach.

'Turn around,' he said, 'I want to do your back.'

She did as requested and gasped as he ran his soapy hands up and down her legs, lingering deliciously on the tops of her thighs. He stood closely behind her, so close that she could feel his breath on the back of her wet neck.

'You're amazing,' he whispered. 'Do you know that?' He began to caress her stomach, moving his hands in tantalisingly slow circles on her skin. She began to turn around but he stopped her with his strong arms and pressed her gently against the white tiled wall in front of them. She put her hands against the tiles, feeling the damp coolness on her palms. He held her firmly, one hand circling her waist and resting on her stomach, the other free to caress her most intimate area. She surrendered to the sensation, her heart beating faster and faster and her legs almost buckling weakly beneath her.

He took his hands away, turned her around smoothly and entered her, making her gasp in surprise.

'Did I hurt you?' he asked tenderly, wiping water away from her face.

'No, don't stop,' she whispered back.

'I won't,' he promised. He was as good as his word.

'That was amazing,' Jay said as they tucked into breakfast, wrapped in the hotel's fluffy towelling bathrobes. 'I can't believe I have to go this evening.'

'Then don't,' Kate suggested. 'Stay another night.'

'You know I can't.' He took her hand and stroked it gently. 'I have to get back to Boston – I have a big meeting with one of the sports wear companies tomorrow. I'm sorry. But I'll be over as soon as I can.'

'Jay!'

'I'm coming back to see you, you know I am. I keep telling you . . .'

Kate groaned. 'And I keep telling *you*, this has to stop. I want to get on with my life and you're just confusing things.'

'Really?' he asked with a smile. 'You didn't seem too confused in the shower, Cat.'

Kate blushed and ignored him. 'I'm serious, Jay, OK. I don't want to see you again after this week. We've both had our fun and now it's back to real life.'

'Is that really what you want, Cat?'

'Yes,' she said definitely. More definitely than she felt. 'It is.'

'I'm going to ring you every day,' he said. 'You'll change your mind, I know you will. I know you.'

'No, you know the old Kate, not the new one.'

'Kate?' He laughed. 'I guess my little kitty Cat has all grown up then?'

'Don't make fun of me!'

'I'm not. You're just being so serious.'

'Life is serious, Jay, for some of us at least.'

'It doesn't have to be.' He leant over and kissed her on the cheek. 'Life with me would be a whole lot of fun, Cat, sorry, Kate. You'll miss out.'

'I'm willing to take that risk. I don't just want fun, Jay, I want something more.'

'Like what?'

Kate looked at him and then looked away. She wasn't quite sure. But being with Jay didn't feel safe, she could never really relax around him. 'I can't explain,' she said finally. 'Just something.'

'OK, I'm not going to push you. Let's just enjoy the remainder of the time we have together.' He kissed her hand. 'What will we do this afternoon? I have a few presents to buy, but apart from that, I'm all yours.'

'Presents? For who?'

'My secretary, she's expecting another baby in a few weeks. And I might even get you one if you're good.'

'Oh, I'll be good,' Kate said seductively, glad that he'd stopped grilling her about the future.

'Really?'

Kate nodded. 'Oh, yes.'

The following day, Kate was lying in her own bed again, in the doldrums. Jay was gone, her whole life had been turned upside down and being on her own again was a huge anticlimax. The previous week seemed like a distant dream. Had she done the right thing by letting him go? Her head said yes, but her heart . . . she was trying not to think about it.

Molly had been sweet to her this morning, bringing her a cup of tea and toast in bed. Kate still hadn't told Molly about Jay and she was sorely tempted to, but she didn't want to talk about it in her current fragile state. She missed him so much and they'd only been apart for mere hours. How was she going to cope? She began to think. What if she'd made a huge mistake? What if he had changed? He wouldn't be single for long, not a man like Jay. In a few months' time he'd probably be married again, or engaged at the very least. She had to know for sure. Maybe seeing him on his home territory in Boston would help her decide. She'd never met his family for goodness sake, or his friends for that matter. If he really was serious about loving her, surely he'd introduce her to them all – it stood to reason. Then she'd know for sure. Kate sat up. That was it. That was how she'd know if Jay really had changed. He'd bring her to visit his family. Ha! She'd book a flight for the very next weekend and surprise him. She began to feel instantly better.

'I saw you yesterday,' Lily said, looking at Kate carefully.

'Oh, really? Where?'

'On the main street, you were coming out of Presents of Mind.'

'Oh.' Kate knew that if Lily had seen her she'd also seen Jay, as they were holding hands at the time. He'd just bought a gorgeous silver picture frame for his secretary and a wooden toy for her little son. They should have been more careful – shopped in Dun Laoghaire or Bray – she should have known someone would spot them in Burnaby.

'The man with you – was that Jay?' Lily asked calmly.

Kate sighed. There was no point lying to her granny and besides, she was dying to tell someone. 'Yes.'

'You looked very happy,' Lily observed. 'Is he still here?'

Kate shook her head. 'No, he left yesterday.'

'Missing him?'

'Yes.' Kate stared out of the window. It was the early evening and they were sitting in her granny's kitchen, drinking tea.

Lily said nothing.

'Before you say anything, he's changed, Gran, he's not the man he used to be. He's so much more caring, more considerate . . .'

Lily snorted. She couldn't help herself. 'Is he still married?'

'Don't be like that, Gran, please.'

'Well, is he?'

'He's almost divorced. His wife moved back to Maine, she's with someone else, a dentist actually. Does that satisfy you?'

Lily again said nothing. She wondered why her perfectly reasonable granddaughter was so blinded by love.

'Gran! Don't look at me like that.'

Lily sighed. 'Be careful, Kate. I don't want to see you hurt again, that's all.'

Kate smiled. 'I won't be, Gran. I'll make sure he's serious this time, before I get involved.'

Lily felt uneasy. Why would a man who had just come out of a bad marriage want to get involved again so quickly? It didn't make sense. Lily had a bad feeling about all this, a very bad feeling. But she held her tongue. Kate had to find her own way in the world. She wasn't a little girl any more and Lily couldn't protect her.

'Say something, Gran, please.'

Lily reached out her hand and placed it on Kate's. 'I just want you to be happy.'

'I am, very happy.'

'Good.'

'In fact, I'm going over to Boston next weekend to see him. It's pretty quiet in the shop and I'm going to ask Trina and Cathy for a few days off and cancel my dummy dates.' Kate seemed so elated that Lily didn't have the heart to caution her.

'I hope you have a lovely time, dear,' she said instead. 'Take care of yourself. Boston's a big place.'

'Gran,' Kate smiled, 'I lived there, remember? Don't worry, I'll be fine.'

I hope so, Lily thought. God I hope so.

*

'I'm worried about Kate,' Lily said to Angus the following morning, handing him a mug of tea. They'd become firm friends in the last few weeks, and this week Angus had taken it upon himself, with Callum's 'help', to repaint her hall in a glowing yellow, replacing the rather drab white which had become decidedly off-white over time. He'd decided this was a good project for his young ward to undertake and a nice thing to do for Lily, who he'd become terribly fond of.

Callum was delighted with this of course, he'd never been allowed near the walls when his own house was being painted, in fact he'd been banned from the house outright when he'd trod in the paint tray and walked red footprints all over the beige carpet on the stairs. But today he had his own small paintbrush and mini-roller and he was dressed in an old dress shirt of his dad's, an old pair of ripped-at-the-knee jeans and a baseball cap, turned backwards to protect his hair. He was merrily and carefully applying the primrose yellow paint to the edges of the walls and the corners, taking extreme pains to 'stay within the lines' as Angus called it – on the walls and not on the skirting boards.

Angus sat down on the stairs and gingerly took a sip of the steaming hot tea. 'Why?' he asked. He glanced over at Callum to check he wasn't listening.

Lily sat down beside him.

'It's a long story,' she said. 'But I think she's involved with a less than honest man.'

Angus raised his eyebrows. 'I didn't know Kate was seeing anyone.'

'She wasn't until the last week or so, from what I can make out. Then this man reappeared, a man from her past. But I'm afraid his intentions are not honourable.'

Angus tried not to smile at her old-fashioned phraseology. 'Is there anything you can do about it?' he asked kindly.

'I don't think so. Just be there to pick up the pieces I suppose.'

She told a little about Jay and what had happened on the previous Christmas Eve in Boston.

'Poor Kate,' Angus said when she'd finished. 'Maybe it will all work out this time, you never know. Maybe he has left his wife.'

'Maybe,' Lily agreed. She didn't believe it for one second. 'Oh, I'm sorry, I shouldn't have burdened you with all this. And I know you like Kate, I can see it in your eyes. What was I thinking of?'

Angus shrugged his shoulders. 'That's all right. Anyway, I don't think she's ready for someone like me,' he said evenly.

'Someone decent you mean?' Lily said astutely.

Angus shrugged his shoulders.

'Maybe not quite yet,' she agreed. She looked over at Callum who was still stuck into his painting. 'So, have you any spare rollers? I thought I might give you a hand.'

'Lily, you're supposed to be resting.' Angus smiled.

'Resting, pah!' Lily swatted the air. 'You're only young once. Besides, I've my old worn-out tracksuit on, you don't think I'm dressed like this for nothing, do you?'

He laughed and handed her a fresh roller. 'OK, but take it easy. You'll have to share a paint tray with Callum though.'

'That's just fine. And how was your date last weekend? The ball?'

'How did you know . . .?'

She tapped the side of her nose. 'I know everything that happens in Burnaby.'

'It was terrible to tell the truth. Patricia is stunning looking but she's . . . how will I put this? Difficult.'

'Selfish and demanding?' Lily asked. 'I remember her as a small child – always terribly spoilt. I'm afraid she hasn't really changed.'

'It was an experience anyway,' Angus said. 'The meal was

nice and I had fun dancing with some of the other book trade people. They're a nice gang.'

'Were Molly or Anita there?'

'No, but the guy who owns Happily Ever After was – Milo. He was sitting at our table. Interesting man.'

'Yes, so I hear.' She rolled her brush in Callum's paint tray. 'That's great, Callum,' she said, studying the work he'd already done.

'I'm being real careful, like Angus said,' Callum said.

'Yes you are, poppet,' she ruffled his hair affectionately. 'You're doing great. I'll tell your mum and dad what a good little painter you are the next time I see them.'

After painting a large section of one side of the hall, Lily took a break and made more tea for her and Angus. He followed her into the kitchen to collect it, glad of the break. His shoulders had started to ache from lifting his arms over his head to reach the high spots.

'Would you like me to talk to Kate?' he asked as Lily put fresh tea bags in their mugs.

She looked over. 'About Jay?' she asked.

'Yes.'

Lily thought for a second. Her first reaction was to say no, but something made her change her mind. Maybe this gentle man would be able to get through to Kate. It couldn't do any harm – could it?

'You could try,' she said finally. 'I'm not sure if she'd listen to you though.'

'You never know.'

Kate opened the door early that evening and was surprised to find Angus standing there smiling at her.

'Hi, Kate, have you got a second?'

'Um, yes, sure. Come in.' She stepped back from the door, let him in and closed it behind them. 'Would you like some coffee?'

'Thanks.' He followed her into the kitchen and sat down at the table.

She flicked on the kettle and stood leaning against the counter. 'So, what can I do for you? More dating advice? I hear you've been seeing Patricia. How's it going?'

'I went to a work do with her,' he said evenly. 'That's all. We didn't really click to be honest.'

Kate felt strangely relieved. 'Oh, I see.'

'I'll get straight to the point, will I?'

She nodded, her curiosity piqued.

'Your granny is worried about you and the American guy. She told me a little about last Christmas. She doesn't want to see you get hurt again you see and —'

'The American guy, as you so delightfully call him, is called Jay,' Kate interrupted. 'And what right do you have to come here and lecture me about my choice in men? So Gran put you up to this. I can't believe she told you about me and Jay.'

'No. It was my idea. I just thought you might want to talk about it, that's all. Sometimes it's easier to talk to someone on the outside . . .'

Kate looked at him incredulously. 'I know damn well what you're doing here and it won't work. Coming over here all kind and caring. Trying to muscle in on another man's territory. You're just as bad as the rest of them. And I thought you were different.'

Angus was taken aback. That thought hadn't even entered his mind. He really did just want to help. 'No, Kate, you've got this all wrong. Lily was worried about you, that's all. I thought I could help. I'm sorry if . . . maybe I should leave. But I'm always there if you need to talk, remember that. I'm there for you no matter what.'

'Isn't that a boy-band song?' she asked disparagingly. 'I can look after myself thank you very much. I'm going over to see Jay this weekend and . . .'

Angus raised his eyebrows.

'Don't look at me like that,' she continued. 'You'll see, you'll both see. Now I think it's best if you do leave.'

Angus stood up. 'I'm sorry if I upset you. I didn't mean to question your judgement.'

'Yes, well, that's not what it sounded like to me. And you can tell Gran to keep my private life just that in future – private.'

After she showed Angus out, Kate leant her back against the door. She was furious with both Angus and Lily. She grabbed the phone from the hall-stand and dialled Jay's mobile number. His mobile was turned off. Typical! She dialled her gran's number instead but cut it off after two rings. She was too annoyed to speak to her. Still, at least she only had three more days until she saw Jay again. Three long, lonely days.

Chapter 15

Paige

'And this morning I'd like to welcome Finbar White, Chief Political Correspondent of the *Irish News* for our election special,' Wella announced on Chat FM.

'Shush, Callum!' Paige hissed. He was singing 'Twinkle, Twinkle Star' to Alfie at full volume.

'Sorry, Mummy. I'll go up and get dressed, will I?'

'Yes, good lad,' she said distractedly, trying to listen to the radio.

Tom turned the volume up, sat back down beside Alfie and began to spoon mashed apple and banana into his eagerly waiting mouth. Finbar White was the single most important and most highly respected political commentator in Ireland and his opinion counted. With only one week to go until the election, what he said this morning could sway the public's vote. Paige hadn't been able to sleep last night and was on tenterhooks this morning, waiting for his verdict on her possible election result.

'We'll start with the North Dublin constituency. Finbar, who's in the running there?'

Paige turned towards Tom. 'This is agony,' she said.

'Don't take what he says as gospel,' Tom advised. 'He's only one person. You have thousands of supporters out there, you know that, Paige.'

'I know, but so many people listen to him.'

Tom nodded. 'But at least he tends to be fair. And he has no bias towards the male candidates like some of the commentators. Or towards the People's Party.'

'I suppose so.' Paige chewed the skin around her thumb and listened again.

'And Dublin West, Finbar?' Wella asked.

The doorbell rang. Paige stood up quickly. 'I'll get it.'

Angus was on the doorstep.

'Hi, Angus,' she said.

'Are you all right, Paige? You look a little anxious.'

'I'm listening to Finbar White on the radio. He's predicting the outcome of the elections.'

'Phew!' Angus said. 'Are you sure you should be listening?'

'I don't know. At least this way I'll hear it from the horse's mouth. It'll be all over the evening papers later and I'd prefer to know the worst before that.'

'Or the best,' Angus pointed out. 'He might say that you're bound to get a seat.'

'He might,' Paige said doubtfully.

'I'll help with doorstepping this week,' he offered. 'And I could galvanize a few others too.'

'That would be great,' Paige said. 'Thanks. It all helps.'

'Paige!' Tom shouted from the kitchen. 'Dublin South after the ads.'

'Coming!'

'Welcome back,' Wella said. 'And this morning I have Finbar White from the *Irish News* with me, making his election predictions.'

'Get on with it,' Paige muttered under her breath.

'Dublin South next,' Wella said. 'Now that's an interesting one, isn't it Finbar?'

'Yes, certainly, Wella. Some changes could well be seen there.'

Tom looked over at Paige. 'Breathe,' he told her.

She smiled at him.

'There are four seats to be filled there and the first two, in my opinion, will certainly go to Deputy Paddy Burns, the People's Party stalwart and a very popular man. And Deputy Jackie Pile, another popular name with the punters. They have both been good, solid representatives and I can't see them losing their seats.'

'And Miles McGreinna?'

'I think Deputy McGreinna has had his day to be frank. From what I've observed over the last year, he's lost a lot of his support. I can't see him being re-elected.'

'And of course, Deputy Ryan, of the Green Party is retiring so he's not standing this time around,' Wella observed.

'Quite. I'd be surprised if Mark Tine didn't win the Green seat back. A bright young man, and a popular politician. The Green Party could do very well in this election if they play their cards right.'

'So that leaves McGreinna's seat,' Wella pointed out. 'Who's in the running?'

'Well there's Annette Higgins of the New Democrats, already a well-known Councillor in Burnaby. She is, of course, Ray Higgins' daughter. She has a good chance on the back of that alone.'

'Even after her father's tax scandal?'

'Yes, he's still fondly regarded by most, even after the revelations in the last tribunal.'

'And Rex Reximus?'

'Ah, good old Rex is back again, on his usual "Legalize Cannabis" ticket,' Finbar said. 'I don't think so, Wella. Do you?'

'I'm sure you're right,' she laughed warmly. 'And Hilda Murphy?'

'Again, she's not a runner. Too right wing for most people's taste.'

Paige looked at Tom. 'They've forgotten me.'

'No, they haven't,' he said reassuringly. 'Keep listening.'

'And finally, Paige Brady,' said Wella. 'Another Burnaby Councillor, running as an Independent. What do you make of her chances?'

'Reasonably good,' Finbar replied. 'She's very popular on the ground, she's not afraid to voice her opinion and she will certainly be in line for a good chunk of the liberal vote. I'd say she has a good chance of taking the fourth seat. It's between her and Annette Higgins.'

'Interesting. Now let's move out of Dublin and on to Tipperary South. Feelings on that, Finbar?'

Paige unclenched her hands and sat up.

'That was great!' Angus said. 'Your man said you have a good chance of getting elected. You must be pleased with that, Paige.'

'I suppose,' Paige said thoughtfully.

'What is it?' Tom asked. 'There's something on your mind.'

'If Finbar's calling it correctly and it is between me and Annette, I just wonder . . .'

'Yes?' Tom said impatiently.

'Whether she had anything else up her sleeve,' Paige sighed. 'I'm not sure if I can cope with any more surprises.'

Tom noticed that Paige's face looked pale and drawn and she had dark circles etched under her eyes. He put down the small plastic spoon he'd been feeding Alfie with and put his arm around her. 'Don't worry,' he said. 'It'll all be over soon. Just one more week to go – hang in there.'

Paige gently shrugged off his arm. 'I'd better go upstairs and get ready. I'm presenting the prizes for the Ladies' Cup at the Burnaby Sailing Club today. And I have a meeting with Connie before that.'

'She's not still on about the Art's Centre is she?' asked Tom.

'No, she wants a word about environmental waste charges apparently.'

'Exciting stuff.' Tom grinned. Just then, Alfie started to grizzle.

'Will I have a go at feeding him?' Angus offered.

'That would be a help, if you don't mind,' Tom said gratefully. 'I have a few things to go over for Paige in the office.'

'Not at all. Where's Callum? Is he still in bed?'

Paige smiled. 'He's upstairs getting dressed. He's been rather a long time though. Heaven knows what he's getting up to.' She walked towards the kitchen door and shouted up the stairs. 'Callum! Callum! Angus is here. Come down, please.'

A moment later she heard him dash across the landing. 'Slowly, please,' she said firmly.

As he appeared at the top of the stairs Paige had to hold back her giggles. He was wearing the most mismatched outfit she'd seen for a long time. Stripy blue and white trousers, with a red and white short-sleeved gingham summer shirt over a long sleeved black T-shirt.

'Angus is waiting for you in the kitchen,' she said and followed him in.

'Hi, Angus,' Callum ran over. 'Can I help you feed Alfie?'

Angus nodded. 'If you're careful.'

'I got dressed all by myself this morning,' Callum said proudly. 'Mum hadn't left any clothes out like she normally does so I got them out of the wardrobe all by myself too.'

'Well done,' Angus beamed. 'And you didn't pull everything else out too, did you?'

Callum looked a little worried. 'Um, not really. Some shirts fell down but that's all.'

Angus said nothing and continued to feed Alfie.

'Do you think I should put them back in the wardrobe?' Callum asked after a moment.

'Are they still on the floor?' asked Angus.

'Yes,' Callum admitted sheepishly.

'I think you should,' Angus said gently. 'That would be very helpful.'

'I'll give you a hand, love,' Paige said, smiling gratefully at Angus. 'I have to go up and get changed anyway. I can hardly go out in my pyjamas now, can I?'

'You could, Mummy.' Callum laughed. 'Sometimes I leave my pyjama bottoms on under my tracksuit bottoms if it's very cold.'

'Do you now?' Paige smiled grimly. 'I didn't need to know that. Come along, young man. Let's go upstairs and sort out these shirts, will we?'

Callum nodded solemnly.

After a brief tidy-up in Callum's room and another type of wardrobe crisis in her own room, Paige was finally ready to leave. She'd decided to play it safe and wear a plain black suit today – she didn't want to upstage any of the lady sailors after all. Unbeknown to Tom, she was actually squeezing in a trip to her GP, Dr Adams, this morning before meeting with Connie. She didn't want to worry Tom, but she'd been having sharp pains in both her sides and she wanted to get it checked out.

Dr Adams, or 'Jilly' as Paige called her, having been in school with her, gave Paige a thorough examination – blood pressure, weight, glands, stomach – before sitting her down in the old-fashioned dark red leather chair.

'Now, Paige, I don't think there's anything to concern yourself with. As there don't seem to be any other symptoms like bleeding or nausea, the pains sound to me like your pelvic muscles moving and stretching. It's perfectly natural during pregnancy. It's caused by the pregnancy hormones surging around your body at the moment, and it can cause some discomfort. But as long as you take it easy and don't go overdoing things, you'll be fine. Are you taking your iron tablets?'

'When I remember.'

'Well, remember,' Jilly said firmly. 'It's important or you'll become anaemic. Your iron count is quite low as it is. And have you been getting enough rest? Or should I ask?'

'Probably not,' Paige admitted.

Jilly looked her in the eye. 'I know it must be hard, what with elections coming up and everything, not to mention Callum and Alfie, but you must take it easy. Promise me you will? You'll put the baby's health in danger otherwise, not to mention your own health.'

'I promise.' Paige smiled.

'Good. And if the pain moves or gets worse, or you have any other worries ring me immediately.'

'Thanks, Jilly.'

As Paige walked out of the surgery and unlocked the door of her car she sighed. Take it easy, Jilly had said. How on earth was she going to take it easy over the next week? Let alone after that. Maybe Annette was right, maybe she was wrong to be contesting the election when she was pregnant. She tried to block the thought out of her mind as she stepped into the car. As she drove towards Burnaby Crescent to meet Connie, she listened to Wella's morning show.

'And after the news we'll have more details of the shock exposure which will appear in this evening's papers. Orla Murphy, daughter of the election candidate Hilda Murphy has given an exclusive interview to the *Evening Tatler* on her relationship with the daughter of another candidate, Councillor Annette Higgins and their foreign adoption hopes. This is not good news for either of the candidates.'

Paige couldn't believe her ears. If it was true, no wonder Annette and her daughter didn't get on. She pulled the car over and dialled Tom's mobile number.

'Did you hear the news?' she asked.

'I'm just listening to it on the radio. It's unbelievable, isn't it?

This country gets stranger and stranger every day. What possessed the girl to talk to the papers?'

'Who knows?' Paige asked. 'Sick to the teeth of her mother's piety probably. But it might mean Annette will stop digging up my past. From all accounts she has plenty of her own skeletons to contend with.'

'No kidding. How was the meeting with Connie?'

'I'm just on my way. I got talking to an old school friend in the street. You know what Burnaby's like.'

'Don't I just. I'll ring you if there's any more news.'

Paige felt bad about lying to Tom but there was no point worrying him unnecessarily. She'd tell him about her visit to the surgery later.

That afternoon Angus brought Callum to the park. Burnaby Park was in an idyllic location at the bottom of Burnaby Hill, stretching down to the sea. The playground in the park was a credit to the community council who funded it, recognizing the need for such a facility in the child-packed constituency. There was a wooden adventure playground for older children, and a brightly painted metal climbing frame, a set of miniature swings and a snake-like curving slide for the younger ones. It was a fine, if cloudy day, and they'd brought marshmallows to roast over the campfire that Angus had promised to help Callum build on the shore.

While collecting driftwood to make their fire, Callum saw a boy sitting on the steep rocks down by the sea. Callum was most impressed, he wasn't allowed to climb on those rocks alone as Angus said they were too dangerous. The boy looked familiar – white blonde hair and little round glasses. I've seen him somewhere before, Callum thought.

'Hello,' he called over. 'Want to help me collect some wood? We're making a campfire.'

The boy stared at Callum for a few moments, then nodded and climbed carefully down the rocks towards him.

'Are you here on your own?' Callum asked as they gathered up driftwood in their arms.

The boy shrugged his shoulders.

'Are you here with your mum and dad?' Callum tried again, not one to be ignored.

He shrugged again and then shook his head.

'I'm here with my friend, Angus.' Callum pointed up the beach where Angus was putting the fire together. 'Well, he's my minder really but he's not bossy like normal minders. We do cool things together like bungee jumping and snorkelling.'

The boy stared at him. 'Bungee jumping?' he asked in a quiet voice. 'Really?'

'Yes.' Callum chatted away as they collected more wood, stopping every now and then to make sure the boy was listening. After their arms were full, he started walking towards Angus.

'Come on,' he said to the boy who seemed reluctant to follow him. 'Are you not hungry? We have marshmallows and sausages and bread for toasting.'

The boy's eyes lit up. He was rather hungry. He hadn't eaten since this morning and his stomach was starting to make strange gurgling noises. He nodded at Callum.

'Come on then!' Callum powered on ahead, dropping some of his wood as he ran.

The boy bent down, collected up the wood and walked slowly towards Angus.

'Hello,' Angus said, sitting up on his hunkers. 'What's your name?'

The boy said nothing.

'This is my friend,' Callum explained. 'He was on the rocks over there. All by himself too.'

'Really?' Angus asked. He looked at the boy carefully and

then looked around. There didn't seem to be anyone in the park except themselves. 'Are you on your own?'

The boy said nothing, nodding slightly and staring at Angus, his light blue eyes shining a little behind his rather severe glasses. Angus decided not to push it. Maybe the child was lost.

'Can he have some of our campfire food?' asked Callum.

'Of course,' Angus said. 'I've started building the fire, we just have to light it now.'

'Can I do it?' Callum asked hopefully, fearing the answer.

'Yes, if you're very careful with the matches,' Angus said. He knew Callum would want to impress the other boy and he wanted to build his self-confidence.

'Cool!' Callum grinned. 'I'll be real careful.'

Angus showed him how to strike the match safely away from his body and how to light the firelighters. He knew fire-lighters were cheating a bit, but the kindling he'd found was a little damp and he knew only too well how short Callum's attention span was. If the fire wasn't lit within minutes, Callum would lose interest.

When the fire was burning successfully, Angus turned his attention to Callum's new friend.

'Do you like this beach?' he asked the boy.

The boy looked at Angus, nodded and went back to staring at the fire.

'Are you lost?' Angus tried again.

He shook his head.

'Do you live near here?'

The boy thought for a moment. 'Daddy does. He lives near the other beach.'

'Sandybay beach?'

Another nod.

Callum was watching the boy with interest. 'I met you at the puppet show,' he said, suddenly remembering. 'You were there with your dad. Molly works with your dad, doesn't she?'

Another nod.

'Molly from the bookshop?' Angus asked Callum. 'Molly who lives with Kate?'

'Yes, silly.' Callum laughed. 'I don't know any other Mollys.' He knew he'd been a bit rude but luckily Angus didn't seem to notice.

Callum smiled. 'Hugh! Your name is Hugh. I remember now.'

'Is your name Hugh?' Angus asked gently.

Hugh nodded and stared at the fire.

Angus could sense that something was wrong. The boy was practically on the verge of tears. Had something happened to him? Why was he on his own – he couldn't be much older than Callum.

'Before I ring your dad,' Angus said gently, 'is there anything you'd like to talk about? Did someone upset you?'

Hugh scrunched up his eyes. He wouldn't cry, he wouldn't. But tears began to cloud his eyes and he pushed up his glasses and brushed them away.

Angus put his arm around the boy and gave him a gentle hug. 'It's OK,' he whispered. 'You're safe with us now. Let's have something to eat and then you can tell me what's wrong.'

Hugh looked at him gratefully. 'Do you have anything to drink?' he asked. It was a warm day and his throat was parched.

'We have fizzy orange,' Callum said, oblivious to the boy's tears. 'I'm not normally allowed it, Mum says it makes me hyper. But Angus said I could have it today as a special treat. I'll share my can with you if you like.'

'Thanks,' Hugh said quietly.

Angus smiled at Callum. 'Good lad. Let's start cooking the sausages. I think Hugh could do with something to eat.'

'Me too!' Callum grinned. 'I'm starving!'

Paige winced. Her right side was aching badly and she couldn't do a damn thing about it. That was one of the downsides about being pregnant. She normally relied on heavy doses of pain killers to see her through her aches and pains, but this time she could take nothing. Stress headaches were her body's speciality, those and an occasional searing pain in her right knee from an old soccer injury.

She put her head in her hands and tried deep breathing for a few minutes. It didn't help. She stood up, went into the kitchen and flicked on the kettle. Maybe a hot water bottle would help. She pulled it out of the cupboard under the sink and put it on the counter. Waiting for the kettle to boil, she bent over the kitchen counter and put her forehead on the cool surface, which gave her some relief.

'Paige? Are you all right?' Tom walked into the room and stared at her. 'What are you doing?'

She straightened up a little too quickly, causing blood to rush to her head, making her feel dizzy.

Tom looked at her in alarm. She was very pale and seemed wobbly on her feet. He put his arms out and guided her firmly into a chair.

'Sorry, I just feel a little faint,' she said, trying a smile. 'Nothing to worry about.'

'If that's the case,' he said, 'why did you just wince?'

'I didn't,' she lied.

'And why is your hot water bottle on the counter? Do you have a stomach ache?'

She shook her head. 'I'm fine, honestly.'

'I'm not convinced.' The kettle boiled and clicked itself off. 'Will I make you some tea?' he offered kindly.

She nodded. 'That would be nice, thanks.' The pain came again and she took a sharp intake of breath.

Tom looked at her in alarm. 'I'm not stupid, Paige! What is it? Please tell me.'

'It's nothing, just a little twinge. The doctor said . . .'

Tom stared at her. 'What doctor? Jilly?'

Paige sighed. 'I didn't want to worry you . . .'

'Well, now you are worrying me. When were you at the surgery?'

'This morning,' Paige admitted. 'I've been having this pain in my side off and on the past few days and I wanted to talk to Jilly about it.'

'And?' Tom asked impatiently.

'She said there was nothing to worry about, it's hormonal. My pelvic muscles are stretching apparently – it's quite normal in pregnancy.'

'What else did she say?'

'Nothing really.'

'Paige, you're keeping something from me, I know you are. If you don't tell me I'll just ring Jilly and ask her myself.'

Paige sighed. 'OK. She said to try and get more rest, that's all.'

'And?'

'To remember to take my iron tablets.'

'Anything else?'

'No, OK, that's it,' Paige snapped. 'Now could you please stop harassing me? I have enough on my plate without this.'

Tom raised his eyebrows but said nothing. He made her a mug of tea and put it down on the table in front of her. 'Drink this. Then I think you should lie down for an hour or two, Paige,' he said evenly. 'The dinner this evening will be easier to deal with if you get some rest beforehand. I can deal with Callum and Alfie when they get back.'

Paige glared at him. 'As I keep telling you, I'm fine. I don't need a rest. Just leave me alone.' She shoved the mug away from her and stood up, slopping some on the table in the process. 'Stop treating me like some sort of invalid. I'm not sick, I'm just pregnant.'

'I know that,' Tom said gently. 'Sit down, love, and drink your tea.'

'No! I'm going to the study and I don't want to be disturbed. OK?'

She strode out of the room leaving Tom staring at her back in disbelief. Paige was prone to the odd mood but she hadn't snapped at him like that since Alfie was a few weeks old and she was over-exhausted.

'Paige!' he said loudly but she ignored him. A few minutes later he decided to check that she was all right. As he opened the door to the study he heard a strange noise. He stepped in. Paige was collapsed over her desk, sobbing as if her heart had broken.

'Oh, Paige. What's wrong?' He walked towards her and began to stroke the back of her head.

She looked up, her eyes red, puffy and full of tears. 'I can't do this any more,' she wailed. 'I'm so bloody tired all the time. And I never see Callum or Alfie. I'm a bad mother.' She began to cry again, heavy tears falling down her cheeks.

'Don't be silly,' Tom said. 'You're a great mother. You're just under a lot of stress at the moment. Things will get better after next week, you'll see. You'll get elected and . . .'

'That's just it!' Paige interrupted. 'I don't know if I want to get elected. What about the boys? And the new baby? Maybe I'm not being fair to all of them. I'm a selfish person and I don't deserve children.'

Tom thought for a few moments before saying anything. 'Paige, I understand what you're saying, really I do. But you've worked so hard over the last few years to make this happen. Being a Deputy is all you've ever wanted. Burnaby needs you. Hell, the country needs you.'

Paige smiled at him through his tears. 'I know, Tom. But

Callum's been so happy over the last few weeks. Maybe all he needed was some one-on-one attention, like Angus said. I'm scared he'll go back to Little Orchard in the autumn and he'll regress.'

'That's not going to happen,' Tom put his hand on hers. 'Because we won't let it. Politics is part of who you are. You can't abandon it because you feel guilty. I'm sure a lot of working mothers feel just like you. Think about it. The kids will be fine.'

'I just don't know,' Paige said. 'I'll be working such long hours and it will put a real strain on our family life.'

Tom said nothing. He stared straight out the window, a strange look on his face. He had a habit of staring into space when he was thinking.

'Tom?' Paige asked gently. She wiped the tears from her eyes. 'What is it?'

'I was just thinking,' he said, then smiled at her. 'No, ignore me, it's nothing.'

'What?' she demanded.

'It doesn't have to be you,' he began tentatively. 'I have equal responsibility for this family. I could take leave of absence for a year – the building society are quite flexible that way. I've been thinking about it for a while now. I could look after the baby and Alfie, bring Callum to school . . . no, it's a stupid idea, forget it.'

'Why do you say it's stupid?'

'It would never work. We'd be completely broke for one thing.'

Paige shrugged her shoulders. 'Money isn't everything. Besides, Deputies get paid reasonably well.'

Tom smiled. 'So you've come around to the idea?'

She shrugged again. 'Maybe. If I do get in, would you really take a year off?'

Tom nodded. 'Yes. If we could afford it, I think I would. Do you think I'd be able for it? I've never really looked after a baby on my own before.'

'Of course you would. You're great with Alfie.' Paige smiled. She was beginning to feel a whole lot better. Her tears had stopped and the heaviness in her heart had started to lift. Maybe there was a way they could make things work. 'And you'd take over all the household jobs too?'

'Like what?' Tom asked.

'The washing, cleaning, cooking, gardening . . .'

He laughed. 'Paige, give me some credit. I already do a lot of those – the cooking and the gardening anyway.'

Paige considered for a moment. 'I suppose you do. Except cleaning the bathrooms of course.'

Tom grinned. 'I keep telling you, you're far better at that than I am.'

'Excuses, excuses.' She smiled back. 'Tom?'

'Yes?'

She threw her arms around him and gave him an almighty hug. 'I'm lucky to have you. You're a wonderful man.'

'Why thank you, Deputy.'

'I'm no Deputy yet.'

'You will be, Paige. Trust me.'

She smiled at him. Suddenly everything began to click into place.

'What do you think Callum will say?' Paige asked. 'About you staying at home.'

'I'm not sure. I hope he'll be pleased. Angus has news for him too. He rang me this afternoon as soon as he heard.'

'What news? Why didn't you tell me?'

Tom smiled. 'I didn't exactly get the chance.'

'Sorry,' she said, contrite.

'Not to worry. Angus has just been appointed as a teacher in Burnaby National School. And guess what class he'll be taking?'

'Not Junior Infants?' Paige asked in amazement.

Tom nodded. 'Callum's new class. Isn't that great?'

'It's bloody brilliant! The best news I've heard all day. And it's been quite a day. Callum will be over the moon. He adores Angus. We're blessed.' She looked up at the ceiling and put her hands together. Tears threatened her eyes again, this time tears of joy. 'Thank you, God. I don't know what we've done to deserve this, but thank you.'

Chapter 16

Molly

Molly looked up from her computer screen for the first time that morning. She wasn't due in to work until after lunch as she'd taken a half day to try and get some writing done. Luckily her phone had been quiet – up until now that was. She reached down, grabbed it from the floor beside her and answered it.

'Hi, Molly, it's Sam,' said the familiar voice.

She felt a warm glow in the pit of her stomach. 'Hi, Sam.'

'I'm not interrupting anything, am I?'

'No, not really. I'm writing but I should probably take a break.' She glanced at her watch. 'I've been at my desk for almost three hours.'

He whistled. 'That's impressive. It's only half nine. That means you must have got up at about six o'clock. There's dedication for you.'

'Don't remind me,' she groaned. 'It nearly killed me. But I was fine once I'd had some coffee and toast. How's the shop?'

'Grand. I was just ringing to say that a researcher from the Pat Bolan radio show rang to ask about the Book Festival. Her name's Julie. They want to interview some of the authors and talk about romance books in particular. She wants you to ring her back this morning. I hope you don't mind.'

'Not at all, that's great news. I'll ring her back right now. Do you have the number?'

He read it out to her and she jotted it down.

'I'll see you at one in Coffee Heaven,' Sam said. 'And Molly?'

'Yes?'

'Are you dressed yet?'

'Mind your own business,' she laughed. She was still in her pyjamas. 'See you later.'

After talking to Julie, a lovely woman and a huge Rose Lovett and Jennie Tracker fan, Molly went back to her short story. She found it difficult to concentrate after the interruptions, her mind was jumping all over the place. She read over what she'd written earlier that morning and noticed several spelling and grammar mistakes, highlighted on her screen by green and red squiggly lines. It was funny, she never noticed them when she was writing, only afterwards. She clicked on the spell check and began to correct them.

Her short story, which she'd given the working title of 'Concrete Pictures', was really coming along. Her two main characters – Lisa and Art – had started to take over, telling their own stories almost without her help. Most importantly of all, for the first time in a long while, she was really enjoying writing. Her fingers clicked over the keys as fast as they could to keep up with the pictures and images that swarmed into her head. She had no idea where the story or the characters had come from. Often, listening to writers talking about their work she scoffed when they said that the characters just took over and told their own story. But in 'Concrete Pictures' this seemed to be exactly what was happening. Maybe she was finally discovering the secret of writing. Maybe not. Maybe Sam was spurring her on to achieve greater things with his gentle encouragement and support. Whatever was happening, she thanked her lucky stars for it.

She read over the second section one more time. It wasn't bad at all – pretty readable Molly thought. Although she might need to pick the pace up a little, it was dragging a bit. Heaven knows what anyone else would think of it though. Then she had an idea.

'Have you seen Hugh, Molly?' Sam asked Molly later that day in Happily Ever After's office. His face looked pale and his wild eyes scanned hers hopefully.

'Hugh?' Molly was confused. Why would she have seen Hugh? 'No. Is something wrong?'

'Yes. Brona dropped him off half an hour ago. I've just got off the phone to her. She said she was in a hurry and dropped Hugh outside the door. There was a tall man with glasses at the front of the shop and she presumed he worked there. She told Hugh to go inside and ask the man where I was. I must have been in here with you at the time.'

'Glasses?' Molly asked. 'Felix doesn't wear glasses.'

'I know.' Sam clutched the back of her chair as if he was about to fall over.

Finally Molly clicked. She gasped. 'You don't think the man . . .'

'Don't,' Sam said. 'I'm already thinking the worst.'

'Maybe the man was a customer and Hugh just wandered off.'

'That's what the guards said. They're on their way. I've already tried Burnaby main street but there's no sign of Hugh. Can I take Felix and try the back streets?'

'Of course.' She stood up. 'I'm coming with you.'

'What about the shop?'

'I'll close it. This is far more important. Your dad will understand.'

Sam nodded curtly.

Molly grabbed her bag. 'Let's go.'

They walked out and Molly immediately spotted Denis loitering outside Coffee Heaven. As soon as she saw him a terrible thought crossed her mind. It was him – the tall man with glasses. What had he done with Hugh? She ran towards him. Sam and Felix followed her.

'Where's Hugh?' she asked angrily. She held both his arms and began to shake him. 'What have you done with him? It was you in the shop, wasn't it?'

Denis stared at her in alarm. 'What are you talking about, Molly?'

'Were you in the shop about half an hour ago?'

Denis said nothing and stared at the pavement in front of him.

'This is serious, Denis, were you?'

He nodded nervously. 'I just wanted to see you. I only stayed a . . .'

'Did you see a small blond boy with glasses?' Felix asked calmly.

Denis looked at Felix. 'Actually I did. He walked in and then . . .'

'You bastard!' Molly shrieked, thumping Denis on the chest. 'I knew it was you as soon as I saw you out here. Where is he? I can't believe you've stooped this low. You evil . . .'

Denis put his hands in the air. 'Hold on just a minute. What are you accusing me of? Child abduction? Molly, are you mad? Is that what you think of me?'

'Well, you've been stalking me for weeks now, you creepy shit,' Molly said angrily, unable to stop herself.

Denis looked at her in alarm. 'Stalking you? But . . .' He broke off and stared at the ground again. 'I've been out of order, haven't I?'

Yes!' Molly said. 'Way out of order.'

'Listen,' Sam interrupted. 'This isn't really helping us find Hugh, is it?'

'Sorry,' Molly said quickly. 'Of course, what am I thinking?' She turned towards Denis. 'You said you saw Hugh.'

'Hugh was the blond boy in the shop?' Denis asked.

'Yes! What happened exactly?'

Denis thought for a moment. 'He walked in the door, waited until the car outside had driven away and then walked straight out again. I thought it was a bit strange at the time so I watched him out the window.'

'And?' Sam asked impatiently.

'He started walking down the main street and off to the right, towards the sea.'

'Did you follow him?' Molly asked.

'No, of course not. Why would I follow him?'

'Thanks,' Sam said. He turned towards Molly and Felix. 'We'll try the Strand Road area.' They both nodded in agreement.

'I'll come with you,' Denis added.

Molly glared at him but said nothing. They could use all the help they could get. As they split up to search around Strand Road – Felix and Denis went to the left and Molly and Sam to the right. Molly was glad Denis hadn't insisted on going with her. She'd finally had enough of his erratic behaviour. It had to stop. He was lucky she hadn't shopped him to the guards yet. Speaking of which, a squad car pulled up alongside Molly and Sam.

'Are you Sam Devine?' the guard asked levelly.

Sam nodded.

'We haven't had any luck with your son' yet but we'll keep looking.'

'Thanks. Someone saw him walk down this way,' Sam explained. 'Maybe he was headed towards the sea.'

'There's not much we can do at this stage, I'm afraid,' the

guard said, 'except keep looking. We'll keep you posted on your mobile. If you hear of any other sightings please ring us.'

'Of course,' Sam nodded.

As the squad car drove away Sam looked at Molly and ran his hands through his hair. 'This is hopeless,' he said. 'We'll never find him. And it's all my fault.'

'It's no one's fault,' Molly said. 'Things just happen sometimes. We'll find him, don't worry.'

'What if we don't? You hear such awful stories . . .'

'You've got to stop thinking the worst. He's a smart boy, he'll be OK. We'll find him, I know we will.'

They walked down the road, scanning every garden and every car that drove past. In less than five minutes they'd reached the sea, which stretched out in front of them, winking in the sun, as if mocking them with its beauty.

'I suppose we'd better try the beach,' Sam said, despair creeping into his voice. There were miles of it to comb – from Sandybay right down to Wicklow.

Molly didn't like to ask if Hugh could swim.

As they stepped onto the beach, Molly's phone rang in her bag. She was tempted to ignore it but something told her to answer it.

'Molly?'

'Yes?'

'It's Kate. Angus just rang me. He was looking for Sam's number. Do you have it? He's got Sam's son Hugh with him.'

Molly almost fainted with relief. 'Wait one second,' she said to Kate.

She turned to Sam. 'Hugh's with Angus, a friend of Kate's. He's safe.'

Sam began to cry. 'Thank God,' he whispered.

As Molly hugged him tightly, she could feel the tension melting away from his body.

'I'd better ring Brona,' he said, pulling away after a few

minutes. 'She's worried sick.' He looked at Molly before punching in Brona's number. 'Thanks,' he said, brushing away the last of his tears.

'For nothing,' she smiled at him. 'I'm just glad that Hugh's safe.'

They ran the whole way back to the bookshop where Angus had arranged to meet Sam. As soon as Sam saw Hugh he ran towards him and threw his arms around him.

'Where were you?' Sam asked, drawing back and looking at his son severely. 'We were so worried about you. Why did you go off on your own like that?'

Hugh looked up at Angus who was standing beside him. Angus nodded at him and smiled.

'Hugh asked me to talk to you on his behalf,' Angus said. 'But let's go into the coffee shop first and have something to eat. The boys ate all the sausages and marshmallows and I'm starving.'

'Good idea,' Molly said.

'But . . .' Sam began. Molly took his hand. 'The shop can wait. Everything can wait. Come on.' She led him inside.

A few minutes later Brona rang Sam. 'I'm outside the bookshop but it's closed. Where are you? Have you found him yet?'

Sam explained everything and a moment later Brona came bustling into Coffee Heaven.

'Hugh! You naughty boy!' she said walking towards him. 'How could you put your dad and me through this? Have you no sense? We were worried sick.'

Hugh looked at her nervously.

'Sit down, Brona,' Sam said levelly. 'Apparently Angus has something to tell us.'

Brona stared at Sam. 'Who's Angus?'

'I am.' Angus smiled at her. 'I found your son on the beach. Actually Callum did to be precise. To cut a long story short, he's a bit worried himself. Aren't you, Hugh?'

Hugh nodded solemnly.

'Would you like to tell your mum and dad what's worrying you?' Angus asked.

Hugh shook his head.

'Would you like me to tell them for you?'

Hugh nodded, staring at the table.

'Tell us what?' Brona asked.

'Why don't you go and play with Callum at the next table?' Angus suggested to Hugh. 'Look, he's making a pie with all the sugar sachets. That looks like fun.' Normally he'd stop Callum from making a mess on the tables, but today he was glad of the distraction.

'Callum? What are you building?' Angus asked.

'A sugar igloo,' Callum replied. 'But I need some more napkins.' Angus passed him some. 'I'm going to soak the napkins in milk and stick them on the top of the cup and cover it in sugar, like an igloo.'

Hugh looked on with interest and then got up and joined Callum at the adjoining table.

'Well?' Sam stared at Angus impatiently.

'To get straight to the point,' Angus said, 'Hugh is worried that he won't be able to see you any more, Sam, now that his mum's boyfriend has moved in. That's why he ran away.'

'Moved in where?' Sam asked Brona in confusion. 'What boyfriend?'

'Glen,' Brona said quietly. 'You met him a while ago, remember? He only moved in last week. I was going to tell you but . . .'

'But what?'

'Oh, I don't know. I thought you might be funny about it, that's all.'

'If it affects Hugh then you should have told me.'

'I know and I'm sorry. But nothing will change. You can still see Hugh whenever you like. He needs you around.'

'Have you told him that?' asked Sam.

'What?'

'That nothing will change.'

'Not exactly. I didn't think I needed to.'

'I see.' There was silence for a moment.

'And he's also worried about you and Molly,' Angus said to Sam. 'He thinks you like her more than you like him.'

'That's just ridiculous!' Sam said. 'I love Molly but he'll always come first. He knows that. Why would he think that?'

'He's young,' Angus said evenly. 'You both need to talk to him and tell him how much you love him. Reassure him that he's important in both your lives. He notices a lot more than you think and he's feeling a little left out at the moment. He needs more stability, I think.'

Brona nodded. 'You're right. Angus, you talk a lot of sense. Thank you. Are you a psychiatrist?'

Angus laughed. 'No, I'm a primary school teacher.'

'Thanks, mate,' Sam said. 'Now I think we have some talking to do with our son.'

Angus smiled. 'Why don't I take Callum home? I think he's caused enough mess for Alex to clean up already.'

'And I'd better reopen the bookshop,' Molly said glancing at her watch. 'Ring me later, Sam.'

'I will. And thanks, Molly. Thanks for being there.'

'Talk to you later.' As Molly walked out of the shop her mind was racing. Sam had said he loved her. He'd also said that Hugh was the most important person in his life, more important than her. She wasn't sure how to feel about that.

'Molly!' a familiar voice called her from outside the book shop. It was Denis. The last person she wanted to see right at this moment. She walked towards him.

'Hello, Denis,' she said, resigning herself to the fact that she'd have to talk to him sooner or later. 'I have to open up.' She put the key in the lock.

'I won't keep you,' he said following her inside.

'I'm not really in the mood for talking —' she began.

'I understand,' he interrupted. 'I just wanted to tell you that from today on you won't be hearing from me. I've decided to move on. I still love you, I probably always will, but it's time I found someone else. Sam seems like a decent man. I hope you'll be happy together.'

Molly stared at him in shock. 'Um, well, thanks Denis. I appreciate that.'

'I'm sorry I wasn't more helpful with finding Hugh. Maybe I should have followed him but I wasn't thinking.'

'You weren't to know,' she said kindly.

'Did you really think I'd abducted him?'

Molly shook her head. 'Not really. I was upset and worried. I shouldn't have said that.'

'It's OK. I've put you through a lot recently and I'm sorry.'

'That's all right, Denis.'

'Bye, Molly.' He leant over and kissed her on the cheek. 'Have a nice life.'

'You too,' she said as he walked away.

She sat down on the stool at the front desk, leant forward and put her head in her hands. All in all, it had been quite a day. And next weekend was the Burnaby Book Festival. She had so much to do it was scary. But right at that moment all she could think about was Sam.

Chapter 17

Molly

'Why do they have to make these book posters so damn big?' Molly complained to Anita as she fought to keep another Bonnie Evans poster on the wall of the Burnaby Arts Centre.

'Blu-tack won't hold it,' Anita said trying not to smile. 'Here, try these.' She handed Molly some drawing pins.

'Is it OK to use them? They'll make holes in the walls, Anita, maybe . . .'

'Stop fussing, I'm sure Tara won't mind.'

'Tara won't mind what?' Tara, the arts administrator of the centre asked as she walked in the door of the lecture room.

'Sticking drawing pins into your newly painted walls,' Anita explained.

Tara shrugged her shoulders. 'Go ahead. The walls are there to be used. I'd love to get notice boards put up eventually but money's quite tight at the moment. Is there anything I can help you with?'

'Yes,' Anita said. 'The PA system. You'd better show me how to use it in case it acts up. In my experience, microphones never work when you want them too. Especially those clip-on ones.'

'You shouldn't have any problems with ours,' Tara said. 'Touch wood.' She touched the back of a chair and smiled. 'They're all brand new.'

'Excellent!' Anita said. 'One less thing to worry about.'

As Tara showed Anita how to work the PA system, Molly finished putting up the posters and resting the show cards on the windowsills and on the long speaker's table which was on a raised platform at the top of the room. Tara had already put all the chairs out, facing the platform, and had decorated the table with elegant flower arrangements. With the posters and balloons, all provided by the various speakers' publishers, the room was starting to look pretty good.

Sam and Felix were setting up the mini bookshop in the smaller room next door. Down the corridor, a journalist from *Sunday Ireland* was waiting patiently to interview Bonnie Evans who was currently on the way back from the RTE radio studios where she'd caused quite a stir on one of the morning radio shows. Molly and Anita had listened to it while setting up, horrified yet delighted with the controversial things Burnaby's most famous daughter was saying.

In the space of twenty minutes Bonnie had managed to criticize just about everyone in Ireland – from crooked business men, to politicians, publicans, farmers, housewives, working mothers, students and rude children – the whole gauntlet of Irish society in fact. Not to mention other writers. She hadn't made herself popular on air, the average listeners ringing in to complain about her harsh views attested to that. But it was compulsive listening and great publicity for the Book Festival.

One besotted man had even rung in to ask Bonnie to marry him. He admired her fiery temper and her outspokenness, he said. Bonnie had thanked him but then gone into a tirade against marriage and why it was a raw deal for any woman. The man, give him his due, took it all in his stride and said he'd happily take her on if she changed her mind. It was quite a show!

As Molly placed the last show card on the table, her phone rang.

'Molly?'

She recognized the voice immediately. 'Paige, where are you?'

'Don't ask, I'm sorry but I'm running incredibly late and the battery's gone on my mobile. I'll be there in ten minutes.'

'Not to worry, we've done almost everything now, so don't rush.'

Paige sighed. 'I'm so sorry, I really did mean to be there to help . . .'

'Paige, get a grip. The election's in three days, you're not Superwoman. See you in ten minutes. I'll be in the cafe helping Alex set up the table for the literary lunch.'

'See you then.'

'Was that Paige?' Anita asked.

Molly nodded. 'She's on her way.'

'I'm now fully trained to work the PA,' Anita said. 'So what's left to do?' She glanced at her watch. 'Maybe I should get back to the shop. I'm sure Milo's fretting by now, stupid man.'

Molly stifled a smile. They'd bullied Milo into looking after the shop for the afternoon, well Anita had anyway. His soft spot for her hadn't abated, which was coming in quite useful.

'You do that,' Molly said. 'He's probably dying for some designer coffee at this stage. I'll stay here. If we need you I'll give you a ring.'

Anita kissed her on the cheek. 'I'll be back once we've closed up the shop. See you later.'

Molly walked her out, then strode into the Arts Centre cafe. It looked fantastic. Tara had hired tables, chairs and all the table settings from a local catering company, who had kindly given them everything free of charge. All they had to do was get the table linen laundered before they returned it. Harry was pottering amongst the tables, putting finishing touches to the simple yet stunning central arrangements.

He smiled at Molly as soon as he spotted her. 'What do you think?'

Each round table was covered with a simple white cloth and set with gleaming cutlery and starkly white plates. The glasses had been polished to perfection, and shone as if they'd been lit from inside. In the centre of each table was a glass bowl surrounded by brightly coloured exotic flowers in mini vases. As Molly looked closer at the bowl beside her, she realized that each bowl had a healthy looking goldfish in it, swimming away merrily in the clean water.

'Fantastic!' she beamed. 'Where did you get the goldfish?'

'From the pet shop in Sandybay. They're on loan. We have to take very good care of them, I gave my word.'

'Where's Alex?'

Harry smiled. 'Where do you think? In the kitchen. She's checking out the facilities for tomorrow.'

'What's on the menu?'

He thought for a second. 'Let me see – soup made by Matty, I'm not sure what kind, smoked salmon, salads, home-made bread and lots of delicious looking sweet things.'

'I can't wait,' Molly said feeling decidedly hungry. She'd brought a cheese sandwich for lunch but had forgotten to eat it in the end. It had been such a busy day. But everything was almost in place. 'Do you need any help?'

'No, I'm almost finished.'

'I really appreciate all your hard work. You and Alex have been fantastic.'

Harry shrugged his shoulders. 'Thank Alex. She bullied me into it. She's got a good heart and she likes helping people.'

'She's a great girl, isn't she?' Molly smiled. Kate had told her all about Harry and Alex's romance and she was delighted for both of them. Even though they were like chalk and cheese they seemed to get along famously and Harry had calmed down a lot since meeting Alex. She was obviously having quite an effect on him. Molly had always found him a little difficult to talk to, but he'd been positively charming all day. He'd even turned down a television appearance to help.

Molly stretched her arms over her head. 'I'll go into the hall and set up the registration table and the notice board then. Call me if you need me.'

'Will do.' Harry went back to his beloved flowers.

Molly met Tara in the corridor.

'There are masses of calls on the answering machine about the festival,' Tara said. 'I've checked some of them and they are all asking if the event's booked up. What will I tell them?'

'We have room for about twenty more at the talks but the lunch is completely full,' Molly said proudly. 'Would you like me to ring them back for you?'

'Not at all, I'll do it,' Tara said kindly. 'It's going to be some weekend, isn't it?'

'It sure is,' Molly agreed.

'There you are, Molly,' Paige interrupted them. 'Hi, Tara.'

'If it isn't the Councillor herself,' Tara said. 'How's tricks?'

'Good,' Paige said. 'Busy but good. Now put me to work.'

'Gladly,' Molly said. 'What are you like at photocopying? We need some more programmes.'

'A whiz.' Paige laughed. 'Lead on.'

'Who is that?' Anita asked Milo, gesturing towards a tall, blond man at the back of the shop. He was wearing black trousers, a black long-sleeved T-shirt and trendy steel-rimmed glasses and was talking notes on a palm pilot. 'He doesn't look like a customer.'

'Oh, pay no attention to him,' Milo said, drawing her attention away from the back shelves. 'He's from the council. Something about moving a water mains. Um, Anita, an order just arrived. It's waiting to be priced in goods-in. Would you like to see the new titles? There's a beautiful looking hardback Margaret Atwood.'

'I've been waiting for that.' Anita smiled. 'Thank you, Milo.'

He led her towards the goods-in area and followed her in. 'I'll see you in a few minutes,' he promised. 'I'll just finish with the council guy.' He went back out onto the shop floor and shut the door firmly behind him.

'Fine,' Anita said absently, her hands stroking the deliciously cool blood-red matt jacket of Atwood's new book. She couldn't wait to read it again. She'd been given a proof copy but it hadn't looked nearly as elegant as this finished product.

'Well?' Milo said, approaching the man, his voice low. 'What do you think?'

'It has possibilities,' the man replied. 'Distinct possibilities.'

'Any sign of Rose?' Molly asked Kate the following morning. Kate was manning the Book Festival registration desk, with the help of Cathy and Trina.

Kate shook her head. 'Nope. But Jennie's in the office with Tara and Anita.'

'Well, that's something I suppose.'

'Don't worry, she'll be here any minute,' Kate said. 'I'll come and get you as soon as she does.'

'Thanks.' As Molly walked back towards the lecture room, where Paige was waiting patiently to launch the event and introduce the speakers, she saw many familiar faces among the crowds and nodded and smiled at them in recognition – regular customers from the shop, two librarians from the local library, Connie Calloway and some of her cronies. As she made her way past the on-site bookshop she spotted Sam talking to Angus.

'Hi, Sam, hi, Angus.' She smiled at them both. 'I didn't take you for a romance fan,' she said to Angus.

'I'm not really. Lily mentioned it and I thought I'd come along just for the morning as it sounded interesting. She knows Bownie from way back.'

'Of course she does,' Molly said. 'Lily knows everyone.'

'How's everything going?' Sam asked. 'Will you be starting on time?'

'I hope so,' she said. 'We're still waiting for Rose to arrive from the airport.'

'I think she may just have arrived,' Sam said gesturing with his head to the doorway. Kate was standing there waving at them, the tall, red-headed Rose to her side.

'Thank goodness,' Molly said with relief. 'Let the show begin. See you both later.'

'Call into the shop when it's all over,' Sam said. 'I'll be there this afternoon to help Dad. Felix said he'd hold the fort here.'

'Great, see you later then.' She gave him a wide smile. He really was lovely. She walked towards the door.

'Rose, I'm Molly, one of the organizers, and you've already met Kate.' Molly held out her hand politely.

'And I'm Rose.' Rose smiled warmly at her and shook her hand firmly. 'And I met Anita and Tara in the office. And Jennie of course. I believe you're anxious to start. So lead on, I'm ready when you are.'

'Are you sure?'

'Absolutely.'

Molly felt a surge of adrenaline rush through her body. 'Right. Let's get started then.'

'That was brilliant!' a woman enthused to Molly after Rose and Jennie had received their second standing ovation. 'Such interesting women, and such accomplished speakers.' She touched

Molly gently on the arm. 'Thank you, my dear, for arranging this Festival. I'm having such a good time.'

'I'm glad. And are you staying for the lunch and the afternoon session?'

'Of course, my dear, I wouldn't miss it for the world.'

Molly looked around the lecture room and was delighted to see so many smiling faces.

'They were great,' Paige said, stepping down off the platform where she'd been sitting with Rose and Jennie. The two authors were surrounded by fans, signing books like there was no tomorrow.

'Weren't they?' Molly agreed.

'It seems to be going well so far. Who am I sitting with at lunch?' Paige asked.

'Millie from the *Burnaby News*,' Molly replied deadpan.

Paige groaned. 'You're not serious. I was hoping never to meet her again after all that photograph business.'

'I'm joking,' Molly replied. 'You're sitting with Connie Calloway.'

Paige stared at her. 'You're not funny, you know that?'

'Sorry, couldn't resist. You're at the top table with me and Anita.'

'Good.' Paige smiled and took Molly's arm. 'I'm starving.'

'How's the bump today?' Molly asked.

'Fine. I was feeling a little ropy yesterday but I cancelled a dinner last night and went to bed at eight.'

'Good woman, you have to take care of yourself, Paige.'

'Don't you start. You're as bad as Tom.'

'It's only because we love you.'

'I know, I know. Now where's the food?'

Molly led her to their table and they sat down. The room was already filling up with people, almost exclusively women, and there was a buzz of excitement in the air. A little while later, when Rose and Jennie walked into the crowded room, followed by RTE television news cameras, everyone stood up and clapped again.

'Hey, we might be on the telly.' Paige laughed and nudged Molly. 'Smile!'

Sure enough, the cameraman swung the camera around the room and rested the lens on Paige's smiling face. As an election candidate, with a fair chance of a seat, she was certainly worth capturing on film.

As everyone settled down into their seats, Anita stood up and addressed the room. 'Welcome to the first Burnaby Book Festival Literary Lunch,' she began. 'As you'll notice there is a vacant seat at every table. As the lunch progresses, you'll get the chance to meet different authors as they take that seat. The authors will move anti-clockwise around the room every fifteen minutes. At least that's the idea. Whether it works or not remains to be seen.' Everyone laughed politely. 'And now I'd like to introduce the authors and ask them to take a seat at a table. In no particular order – you've already met Rose Lovett and Jennie Tracker.' Another deafening round of applause and many cries of 'Sit here, Rose', 'Over here, Jennie'. 'And our very own Bonnie Evans.' More applause. 'All the three C's – Clare Connolly, Ciera Donald and Catriona Reilly.' Applause and whistles. 'Tina Laycock and Antonia Ash .' More applause. 'Cleo Holmes, Nancy Dealy and Peggy Walsh.' More applause. When Anita had finished her introductions she sat down again.

'Well done,' Molly said. 'Do we not get an author?'

'We already have one,' Anita replied. 'You.'

'I'm not an author,' Molly snapped.

'You will be,' Anita said, ignoring Molly's sharp tone. 'Now let's eat. Paige had already demolished all the bread rolls on the table. She must be famished.'

'Sorry,' said Paige, 'blame the baby.'

*

Molly sat between Paige and Kate for the afternoon session on 'Getting Published', with Anita to Paige's left, who was ignoring Milo Devine to a spectacular degree. Milo had arrived just in time for coffee and had found a spare chair and squeezed himself in beside Anita, much to her chagrin. He had then followed her like a puppy dog into the lecture room and sat down beside her.

'Who's on the panel?' asked Kate.

'You could read the beautifully and tirelessly photocopied programme,' Paige suggested.

'Or you could tell me and save me trouble. I'm feeling very lazy after that glass of wine at lunch.'

'Are you sure it was only one?' Molly smiled. 'I distinctly saw you order another bottle for your table.'

'Well, it might have been more like three,' Kate grinned back. 'But no more, mind.'

'Did you enjoy meeting the authors?' Molly asked her.

'Yes! Some of them were a riot. And others were really smart and well read. And so nice. You'd never think they were famous authors. Cleo Holmes has a real thing about shoes too, so I was talking to her for ages. In fact, I think she missed a table change because of me. It was a great success, well done to all of you. Now will you tell me who the speakers are or do I have to batter it out of you?'

'I think they're about to tell you themselves,' Anita said jumping to her feet. She was supposed to be introducing the speakers who were seated on the platform waiting patiently to begin.

'Welcome back, everyone,' Anita began. 'I hope you all enjoyed your lunch. Now I have the great privilege of introducing the panel who will talk to you this afternoon on the subject of "Getting Published – Tips from the Top". From Trinity Publishers in Dublin we have Maggie Stevens who is the Sales and Marketing Manager; next up is Bonnie Evans, who I'm sure you all know is originally from Burnaby and now lives in the South of France and is one of the world's best selling romance novelists; Cleo Holmes, another highly successful writer from Dublin; and last, but certainly not least, the only man on the panel, Gerry Begley, from the highly respected Begley Literary Agency. And first up will be Cleo.' Anita sat down as everyone applauded.

'Phew,' she whispered to Paige. 'I'm glad that's over.'

'You were great,' Paige whispered back as Cleo stood up and began to talk.

'Hello, everyone, I'm Cleo Holmes and I'm delighted to be here today with so many readers. I met some of you at lunch and it was lovely to talk to the people who appreciate my work. Writing is quite a solitary occupation and I don't get to meet many readers face to face. So I'd like to quickly thank the organizers here today for this fantastic Book Festival.' Everyone clapped enthusiastically. 'Now getting published can be a very frustrating business for new authors,' Cleo continued. 'Many of you here may be writers interested in seeing your own work in print, members of writers' groups or simply readers who are interested in the whole book world, including publishing. I hope you all find this session on getting published interesting and stimulating.' Cleo then went on to talk about her own experience – how she found an agent and got her first book published by Trinity Publishers in Ireland.

Paige turned to Molly. 'She's a good speaker isn't she?' she whispered. 'Very clear and easy to listen to.'

Molly nodded. From what Cleo was saying, having your first book published was pretty miraculous considering the competition. In fact, Cleo was making Molly feel downright despondent. What chance did she have if it was so difficult – less than none, she figured.

Cleo continued. 'You have to enjoy what you're writing and your heart must be in it 100 per cent.' She went on to explain the different genres and which genres were particularly popular at the moment.

'She's very thorough,' Kate whispered to Molly. 'I never knew there was so much to it.'

Molly nodded in agreement and went back to listening.

Anita was watching Molly with interest. Molly was totally focused on what Cleo was saying and was even jotting down some notes on her programme. Anita smiled to herself – maybe Molly was finally taking her talent seriously. Unbeknown to Molly, Anita had read several of Molly's short stories which had been stored on the computer at work. Molly's home printer was always playing up and she often saved and printed out her writing in the Happily Ever After office. Anita knew Molly had the potential to be a great writer, if she'd only believe in herself enough. But she knew Molly would have a fit if she thought Anita had betrayed her trust and read her stories, so Anita could say nothing.

'I wish all the writers in the audience the best of luck,' Cleo said, concluding her talk. 'And the best advice I can give you is don't give up. If you really want to be published you will. You just have to believe in yourself.'

'Hear, hear,' Anita murmured.

Everyone clapped enthusiastically. As the applause died out Maggie stood up.

'Hello, I'm Maggie Stevens, from Trinity Publishers, Cleo's Irish publishers. I'm going to explain what Trinity are looking for from new writers and how prospective writers should submit their book. Practical things like presentation of manuscript, how to send it in, how long you can expect to wait for a reply and so on.' Maggie was as good as her word and gave a slick, well-prepared talk.

Next up it was the agent, Gerry Begley. 'Most UK publishers expect writers to have an agent. In fact, the odds on getting published from what we call 'the slush pile' in the trade –

the unsolicited manuscripts sent in by authors directly to the editor of a publishing house – are tiny. So that's where I come in.' He explained his role in the whole publishing business.

'Seems like a nice man,' Paige said to Molly when Gerry had stopped talking. 'Maybe you should ask him to be your agent.'

'Get real!' Molly laughed. 'He wouldn't be interested in me.'

'You never know,' Paige replied mildly.

'Shush, it's Bonnie next,' said Molly.

Paige studied Burnaby's most famous daughter with interest. She was wearing a flamboyant wine-coloured cardigan, over a floor-sweeping black velvet dress. Her thick, rich dark red hair was piled on top of her head in an elaborate chignon.

'Attractive woman,' Kate whispered to Molly and Paige. 'Great cardigan.'

'Shush,' someone behind them muttered.

They grinned at each other and stifled the laughs.

'I'm Bonnie Evans,' she began, then snorted. 'As if you needed to be told. I am one of the world's best-selling authors and I think most of what is published today is unadulterated crap.' Several members of the audience gasped. The journalists at the back of the room began to scribble furiously. 'I think any writers out there who want to be published need to think long and hard.' She stared at the audience intensely, making eye contact with some, making them jump. 'Are *you* good enough? Is *your* work crap? Because if it is, don't bother trying to get published. And I think writers' groups are evil.' More gasps. 'Filling people's heads with silly notions of grandeur. Most people *can't* write. And you cannot be taught to write – I believe it's something you are born with. It's as simple as that. I have the gift, a very special gift. But most don't.'

A woman at the back of the room stood up, collected her things together and walked out, banging the door behind her.

'I've offended someone!' Bonnie clapped her hands together with glee. 'Excellent! Now what I have to say is very important so please listen carefully.' She looked around the room again. 'If you do have the gift, you must use it. Indeed, if you have any creative gift you must use it. If you can write you must put your whole being into your writing and produce the very best book that you can. I will now tell you how I discovered my own talent and how it has changed my life.'

'Powerful stuff,' Paige said after she'd finished and Bonnie had received a rapturous standing ovation. 'She's some woman.'

The three women watched as Anita stepped onto the platform and began to thank all the speakers, shaking their hands warmly. Within seconds the platform was surrounded by people, most wanting to meet Bonnie. She'd made quite an impression.

'No kidding.' Molly smiled at Paige.

'I found her quite inspirational,' Kate said thoughtfully. 'And she wasn't afraid of upsetting people, was she?'

'Quite the opposite,' said Molly. 'Most refreshing. And speaking of which, who's for a drink? There's a press reception in the cafe now to announce the winner of the writing competition and you're both invited of course. I'd better stay here and see if Anita needs anything done.'

'Is there food?' asked Paige.

'You've only just eaten,' Molly pointed out.

'It's not for me, it's for junior,' Paige said, rubbing her stomach gently.

Molly smiled. 'Good excuse. There's finger food and wine. Will that do you?'

'It will,' Paige replied.

'Excellent!' Kate stood up gingerly. 'My bum's killing me. These seats aren't exactly padded.'

'Maybe it's you who isn't exactly padded,' Paige pointed out with a smile. 'So quit complaining.'

An hour later, Anita stood in front of the crowd at the reception. She tapped the microphone head softly to check it was working and took a sip of water before starting. She stood up tall and addressed the crowd. 'I'd like to welcome you all to the prizegiving of the Burnaby Short Story Competition which has been run in association with the *Burnaby News*. Beside me are the two other judges, Millie O'Shea, the Editor of the *Burnaby News* and Bonnie Evans. The winner gets their story published in the newspaper as well as five hundred euro, kindly sponsored by Star Insurances in Burnaby, and just this very afternoon Gerry Begley has also kindly offered to represent the winning author. Quite a prize for a new writer. Judging this competition was very difficult. The standard of entries was very high.' She half-expected Bonnie to snort at this, but thankfully she didn't. Anita continued swiftly. 'But there was one story which really stood out from the rest. It was a story about starting again, about getting one's life back after a terrible tragedy – the death of a young child.'

Molly caught her breath. Did Anita just say the death of a child? Surely not? She listened to Anita carefully.

'The writer's prose style draws you into the story and the characters are extremely well rounded. I'd like to ask Bonnie to announce the winner.'

Bonnie cleared her throat theatrically. 'The winner is Mary Parker with her story "Concrete Pictures".' Everyone began to clap and looked around the room for Mary Parker.

'Could Mary Parker please come up and collect her prize,' Bonnie continued.

'What's wrong?' Paige asked Molly who had lurched sideways into her, spilling the last of her drink. Luckily Kate had gone to the bar for more. Molly's face was as white as a sheet. 'Molly?'

Molly looked at her, a strange expression on her face.

Suddenly Paige clicked. 'It's you, isn't it? Mary Parker. Molly, how exciting! Go up and collect your prize!'

'I can't,' Molly hissed. 'They've made some sort of mistake. I can't have won.'

'Is your story called "Concrete Pictures"?'

Molly nodded.

'Well then, it's not a mistake. Go on.' She pushed her gently towards the stage.

At that moment Kate came back, two glasses of red wine and one of sparkling water balanced in her hands. 'Have I missed anything?' she asked. Paige gestured towards the top of the room.

'What's Molly doing up there with Bonnie and Anita?' Kate asked in confusion.

'She only won the writing competition.'

'But they just said someone called . . . Oh, I see . . . Mary Parker *is* Molly Harper. You think she could have made a bit more of an effort with the pseudonym.'

Paige laughed. 'She never expected to win. I wonder what she's saying to Anita.'

'Let's get closer and see,' Kate suggested.

They wound their way through the crowd, towards the top of the room.

Molly was actually trying to persuade Anita to give the prize to someone else. Anita was having none of it.

'You won it fair and square,' Anita said firmly to Molly's protests. 'In fact, it was Bonnie who insisted that your story won the prize. She said she'd leave the judging panel if you didn't win.'

'But . . .' Molly protested.

'Is this Mary Parker?' Bonnie asked.

'Yes, and she won't accept the prize. She says she doesn't deserve it.'

'Don't be silly, girl. Some of the stories were rubbish. Yours wasn't. You have real potential. In fact, I think you may have the gift.'

Molly looked at Bonnie in surprise. 'Really?'

'I always tell the truth,' Bonnie said evenly. 'I'm renowned for it. Now stop being so stupid and accept what's your due.'

Whatever she felt about Anita, Molly was far too scared to say no to Bonnie.

'OK,' she said quietly.

'Excellent.' Bonnie stood beside her and faced the audience again. The room became quiet.

'And here is Mary Parker.' She handed her an envelope. 'Well done, Mary. Would you like to say a few words?'

'Um, no, thank you.' Molly's hands were shaking and she felt very faint. She hated public speaking and hated all those upturned faces watching her.

'Go on,' Paige encouraged from the floor.

'You can do it.' Kate smiled up at her.

Molly looked at them both and smiled back. She took a deep breath. Maybe she could.

'Um, I'd just like to say thanks to the judges for choosing my story. I've been writing for a few years now but I thought I was one of the crap ones, as Bonnie so succinctly calls them.' Everyone laughed. 'But I guess I'm not. And as some of you will know, my name is not Mary Parker, it's Molly Harper and I work in Happily Every After. I used another name because I didn't want anyone to know I'd entered the competition. I just wanted some feedback on my writing. But I never expected to win. But, um, thanks very much. I'm, um, delighted. And in complete shock to tell the truth. Thanks.' Everyone clapped warmly.

Anita stepped up to the microphone. 'Well, done, Molly.

And now I'd like to ask Councillor Paige Brady to close the Burnaby Book Festival for us.'

'Oh no!' Paige whispered to Kate under her breath and handed her her glass. 'I forgot I was doing this. I've nothing prepared.'

'Not you as well.' Kate laughed. 'You and Molly really are a right pair.'

Chapter 18

Kate

Kate gazed out the window at the fluffy, candyfloss clouds, illuminated by the blazing sun – the whole scene like something out of a Hollywood movie about heaven. The pilot had just announced that they were less than twenty minutes from Boston's Logan Airport and Kate could hardly contain herself. Her stomach was fluttering in anticipation at seeing Jay again. The fact that he didn't know she was coming only added to the drama. She rested the back of her head against the headrest and closed her eyes. In less than two hours, she'd be safely in his arms, cocooned by his love, basking in his admiration. She couldn't wait. She dozed off, into a deep dreamless slumber.

As the plane landed smoothly on the Boston tarmac, Kate let out a sigh – she'd never been the world's greatest flyer and was always relieved to be on solid ground once more. As soon as they'd pulled into the terminal, she gathered together her jacket, handbag and compact travel suitcase. As she was only flying over for a long weekend, she'd decided to travel light.

Walking smugly through the terminal with her hand luggage, past the poor souls in the huge, bustling baggage reclaim hall, and out through one of the entrance doors, she hopped straight onto one of the 'Massport Shuttles' like a real native. From here she was swiftly delivered to the Airport 'T', where she sat and waited for an underground train to take her safely to downtown Boston. As always she sent up a prayer for the efficient city transport network. It was one of the things she'd missed after moving back to Ireland.

It was Saturday afternoon and as she sat waiting for the train, she rang Jay's mobile. He tended to be busy at weekends – catching up with friends, shopping (unlike Irish men Jay liked to shop), and taking day trips out of the city. He was also a big Boston Red Sox fan and liked nothing better than to spend time in Boston's famous baseball park, Fenway Park, watching his favourite team compete. His mobile rang out. He probably can't hear it, Kate thought. Or maybe he's left it at home. His home number had changed recently and he hadn't remembered to give the new one to her yet, so she couldn't try there.

Kate tried to remember their exact conversation the previous evening. He'd said he had no definite plans but would probably meet a friend for lunch and go shopping for the afternoon. Then he might go out for dinner in the evening. It seemed a little strange to Kate who happened to know that his weekends were usually planned weeks in advance, but as he kept impressing on her, he'd changed. Maybe this weekend spontaneity was part of the new Jay. Perhaps she should have told him she was coming over, he could have met her at the airport, but, no, Kate thought, that would have spoiled the surprise.

A little later, after a pleasant enough 'T' ride and a ten-minute walk, Kate stood outside his apartment building. She rang his apartment on the huge brass intercom board beside the front door. There was no answer. Damn! She tried his mobile again – again no answer. Well, he's bound to be back at some stage, she reasoned, thinking again that surprising him might not have been the best idea in the world after all. What was she going to do now? She was overheated from walking in the early afternoon sun, and her hair had begun to stick to her forehead. In fact, she could do with a shower. Failing that, she needed to go somewhere cool and spacious, somewhere with a good air conditioning system, somewhere with a left luggage department so that she wouldn't have to drag around her wheelie suitcase all day. Not that it would be all day, she hoped.

She racked her brains for inspiration. She'd love to browse the clothes shops on Newbury Street or even visit Filene's Basement, but both would be incredibly hot and crowded on a Saturday afternoon. She could visit one of the huge bookstores – Barnes and Noble or Borders but that wouldn't keep her occupied for more than an hour or two. Then she had a thought. All the time she'd lived in the city she'd never visited the famous art gallery – the Boston Museum of Fine Arts. Well, she had no excuse this time – it was cool, spacious and air conditioned; they would look after her suitcase while she was there and it also had a cafe and toilets. Plus it was only two stops away on the 'T'.

Delighted with her decision she tried Jay's mobile one more time. Still no answer. Half an hour later, stepping through the doors of the rather grand museum building, she tried once more with the same result, then turned her own mobile off and plunged it into her handbag, determined not to try Jay again until later.

As she strolled through the huge exhibition rooms, unencumbered by her bags and jacket, she drank in the art and ancient objects surrounding her. Mummies, hieroglyphics and Old Kingdom sculptures in the Egyptian rooms, Buddhist sculptures, Chinese ceramics and the huge array of strikingly familiar Impressionist pictures from Monet to Renoir to Gauguin.

Several hours later, calmed and soothed by the art and the surroundings, and physically refreshed by a nice salad lunch and lots of chilled fruit juice, she collected her bags, promising herself that she'd visit again very soon. Maybe she'd even drag Jay along next time.

She walked out the door and tried his mobile again – still no answer. At this stage she was getting a little worried. Maybe he'd gone away for the weekend with friends unexpectedly. What would she do then? She rubbed her temples, feeling a tension headache coming on. I'll go back and wait for him outside his apartment, she decided. I don't have any other choice. He has to come back sooner or later.

Sitting on the steps of the apartment she felt a shiver of déjà vu which she tried to banish as soon as it wiggled its way into her head. This is just like last Christmas Eve, a voice said, waiting for Jay outside his apartment. Wondering where he was, what he was doing. Yes, but this time, she reasoned, it's totally different. Completely different. He's not married any more and he even offered to move back to Dublin to be with me. She took out the museum guide from her handbag and began to fan her face. She tried not to look at her watch but she couldn't help it. Almost six. He had to be home soon.

She heard voices behind her and swivelled around. A tall dark haired man was walking towards her. There he is! Kate grinned. That's Jay walking in front of that woman with the buggy. She felt a huge rush of relief spread through her body. Thank goodness! She jumped up and waved.

'Jay!' she shouted excitedly. 'Jay!'

He put his hand over his eyes to shield them from the sun. Then he stopped dead. He stared at Kate in amazement as if she was some sort of alien from another planet, complete with green skin and stun gun. The woman stopped beside him and said something. Kate couldn't hear the conversation as she wasn't close enough. He said something back to the woman. Kate began to walk towards them. Jay put up his hand as if to say 'stop', but Kate continued unabashed.

'Jay?' she said as she approached him. 'What's wrong?'

As soon as Kate looked at the woman's face she realized what was wrong. Because the woman pushing the buggy beside Jay was his ex-wife, Cindy. Kate recognized her immediately. And to top it all she looked at least four months pregnant, her rounded belly protruding proudly beneath a tight white T-shirt.

Kate stared at Jay in confusion.

'What's going on here?' Cindy asked. 'Who's this woman, Jay? She looks kinda familiar.'

'Just a friend from work,' Jay said, resting a reassuring hand in the small of his wife's back.

'Hi.' Cindy smiled at Kate uncertainly. 'I'm Cindy, and you are . . .?'

Kate looked at Jay. She felt her blood falling like a sheet from her face and upper body into her feet. Her palms began to sweat and she felt unable to say anything. 'Jay?' she managed finally in a weak, whispery voice before her body felt freezing cold and the whole world went blank.

'Granny, are you in?' asked Kate, gripping her mobile tightly. She'd turned it on as soon as the plane had landed on Irish soil.

'I am,' said Lily. 'And where have you been all weekend? I was looking for you yesterday but your mobile wasn't working.'

'Can I call over?'

'Of course, love. Is anything wrong? You sound a little strange. Where are you?'

'Dublin Airport.'

'The airport? But it's not even nine. What are you doing there?'

Kate gulped back the tears. 'I have to go, Gran. I'll see you in a while, OK?'

Lily sensed that this had to do with Jay but kept her thoughts to herself. What had the rat done now to upset her darling granddaughter? Had he stood her up?

'Take care of yourself, poppet. Granny Lily's here for you, understand?'

Kate clicked off her phone and immediately began to cry. It

was such a relief to talk to her granny. She felt such an almighty fool.

'Kate,' Lily said as she opened the door. 'Come here and give your old granny a hug.' Kate dropped her bags and lunged immediately forward, hugging Lily with all her might and breathing in the familiar scent of rose water.

Lily was shocked at Kate's appearance. She looked like she hadn't slept for days – her eyes were sunk into dark grey sockets and her face was red and blotchy as if she'd been crying for hours without stopping. Her breath was ragged and irregular and she was shaking.

'Come into the kitchen and we'll have a cup of tea. I'll put some brandy in it for you, pet, that'll help.' She led Kate towards the back of the house, sat her down at the kitchen, then went back into the hall, moved the bags and closed the hall door behind her firmly.

Back in the kitchen, Lily clicked on the kettle and stood waiting, leaning against the kitchen counter. She knew better than to ask too many questions. Kate would open up in her own good time. There was no hurry.

'He's still married, Gran,' Kate said immediately without prompting, unable to keep it in any longer. 'He's not separated at all. And they have a second child on the way.'

Lily stared at her in shock. After the episode last Christmas she'd thought she'd heard it all – but this was worse, much worse. How could a man behave in such a way?

'He lied to me, Gran. About his wife, his son . . . everything. He even told me that she'd lost the first baby – his son. How could he say such a thing?'

Lily stood behind Kate and put her arms around her and kissed the top of her head.

'It's all over now,' she crooned. 'You're safe with your Granny

Lily, now.' Kate gave a huge sob. 'That's it,' she continued. 'Let it all out, love.'

Kate cried for almost ten minutes without stopping, huge gut-wrenching sobs. Tears rained out of her eyes in a deluge, spilling onto the kitchen table in splashes. Lily rubbed her back, then held her firmly as she wept. 'It'll be all right,' she whispered to Kate. 'You're home now. Home with Granny Lily. Try to take deep breaths now, there's a girl.'

After a little while the sobs grew further and further apart and Kate's breathing began to go back to normal.

'I'm sorry,' said Kate, wiping her eyes and face with the large man's handkerchief Lily had given her.

'Sorry for what?' Lily asked gently. 'None of this is your fault. You've nothing to be sorry about.'

'But I feel such an idiot. How could I have let this happen? I should never have trusted Jay again. I'm so stupid.' She held her head in her hands and rocked backwards and forwards.

'Don't be too hard on yourself,' Lily said. 'It happens. Everyone makes mistakes, especially where love is concerned.'

'And she was so nice to me,' Kate said, starting to cry again. 'I feel so terrible.'

'Who was nice to you?' Lily asked gently. 'Maybe you should start at the beginning. Tell me everything.'

'I can't,' Kate whispered. 'I just can't.' Tears began to roll down her face again.

Lily patted her hand. 'Try. It will make you feel better. Then we never have to talk about it again.'

'Promise?'

'I promise.'

'OK.' Kate wiped her eyes and took a deep breath. 'I met him in the Killiney Arms the week before last,' she began slowly. 'He was over on business and he'd asked to see me. I should never have gone but I did.' She told Lily the whole sorry story – from that first heady evening with Jay, to fainting at his feet outside his Boston apartment block.

'Oh, Gran, I was mortified. I must have been out of it for several minutes. When I opened my eyes I found Jay standing over me and Cindy kneeling down beside me. She'd put the baby's blanket under my head and was wiping my forehead with a damp babywipe.' Kate cringed inwardly at the memory.

'What happened then?' Lily asked gently.

'They took me into their apartment. Once we were inside Cindy asked Jay to make some coffee. He seemed a bit reluctant to leave us alone together, but he wasn't really in a position to argue. When he was in the kitchen, she looked at me and asked me straight out was I having an affair with her husband. I nearly died. I didn't know what to say. I couldn't look her in the eye, I just nodded and stared at the carpet. I expected her to hit me or shout at me at the very least.'

'What did she do?' Lily asked.

'She started to cry. It was awful, Gran. She said she knew something was going on, that things hadn't been right between them for a long time – his mind seemed to be somewhere else. Cindy said he'd been carrying on with a girl from the office called Tammy for a few months but she'd confronted him about her and he'd stopped seeing her. She said she was sick of it and couldn't live with him any more. She'd stopped trusting him. I was so ashamed. I said I was sorry, that he'd told me he was separated. And then she said in this really sad voice, "They always say that, don't they?" Oh, Gran, I felt so bad. She was being so decent to me and then Jay . . .' She shuddered at the memory. 'He'd been standing at the door listening. He walked in and started telling Cindy how much he loved her right in front of me, how I didn't mean anything to him, how he couldn't live without her, how she had to give him one more chance. Cindy stood up and slapped him on the cheek. And then she told him to get out. At this stage the baby was crying in the buggy, I was crying,

Cindy was crying and all Jay could do was stare at me. "You've ruined my life," he said to me. "I'll never forgive you." Then Cindy said "Jay, you've no one to blame but yourself. This woman isn't to blame. You are. Now get out. You'll be hearing from my lawyers in the morning."'

'It's like something from a novel,' Lily said before she could stop herself.

Kate looked at her and then began to smile through the tears. 'Gran!'

'I'm sorry but you know what I mean,' Lily said. 'It's all very dramatic. What happened after he'd left?'

'Cindy made us some coffee and we talked while she fed the baby. She asked me what had happened with Jay and I told her everything. I reckoned I owed it to her to be honest. We got on pretty well, to tell the truth, in the circumstances. After we'd talked for a few hours she booked me on a late flight and I came home.'

'You must be wrecked,' Lily said. 'Would you like to lie down? The spare bed's all made up.'

Kate shook her head. 'I'm not tired. Maybe later. I slept a little on the plane. The air hostesses were so kind. I kept crying – I couldn't help myself. One of them sat with me for a little while to make sure I was all right.'

'The kindness of strangers,' Lily murmured.

'I really loved him, Gran,' Kate continued. 'He asked me to marry him only last week. He even said he'd move to Dublin to be with me but he was obviously lying the whole time. Just like he did before. I feel such a fool. How could I have trusted him?' She thought for a moment. 'But, you know, Gran, in a strange way, I don't feel as bad as I did the last time he crushed me. It's as if my heart will never hurt as much after that. Jay hardened it last Christmas.'

Lily smiled at her. 'Your heart isn't hard, Kate. Believe me, I know. But that Jay has a lot to answer for. At least you weren't married to him and suffering all those affairs. Poor Cindy. What's she going to do now?'

Kate shrugged her shoulders. 'She said she's going to divorce him. But who knows? They may be able to patch it up. There are children involved after all.'

'Sometimes it's not in the children's best interest for the parents to stay together,' Lily said thoughtfully.

'I guess not.' Kate yawned. 'Maybe I am a little tired. Can I take you up on the offer of a bed?'

'Of course. And when you've had some sleep I'll make us some lunch. How about that?'

Kate gave Lily a hug. 'Thanks. I don't know what I'd do without you.'

'Go and get some rest now,' said Lily. 'You've had a right old shock to your system.'

'Thanks, Gran.'

As Kate made her way upstairs, Lily drained her tea, by now a little cold. She put her elbow on the table and rested her head on her hand. For some reason she wasn't worried about Kate this time. Kate was right – she was in a far worse state last Christmas. She'd been so distraught then that she couldn't talk about what had happened for days. Kate was in a much better place now. If only she'd find a nice young man, someone who'd care for her and nurture her. Someone she could trust. Someone like Angus. Lily had done all she could to help things along. If it was meant to be they would find each other. But maybe they both needed just a little more assistance.

'Did you have a nice break?' Molly asked as soon as Kate walked in the door on Monday night.

'Yes, thanks.' Kate replied evenly, dumping her suitcase at the bottom of the stairs. She'd spent most of the previous two days wrapped in a duvet on her granny's sofa watching television and eating junk food. But considering everything that had happened she felt remarkably all right. Jay had rung her mobile countless times but she'd switched it off eventually. She had absolutely nothing to say to him. She'd listened to the first of his messages – saying how Cindy really was out of the picture now and how he and Kate could be together forever. Obviously Cindy really had given him the boot and he wasn't prepared to be alone for longer than a minute. Still there was always Tammy in the office, Kate thought wryly after she'd deleted the message. I'm sure she'll take you back you creep. It had hurt her to know that there had been other affairs, that hers wasn't 'special'. But however much it hurt her, she kept thinking about Cindy. It was a thousand times worse for her. Kate swore that she'd never so much as smile at a married man again, even if he had separation or divorce papers to prove that he was 'available'.

'You missed all the drama on Saturday,' Molly said as Kate flopped onto the sofa.

'Really? What happened?'

'Sam's little boy went missing. It was terrible. Sam was in bits.'

'I can imagine. With all the child abductions on the news, I'm not surprised. They found him though?'

'Yes, thank goodness. Your friend Angus found him on the beach and brought him back. The poor child had got it into his head to run away.'

'Angus?' Kate asked with surprise.

'Yes, he was quite the hero. Managed to convince the little lad to come back home of his own accord. Poor mite had it in his head that no one wanted him around.'

'I know the feeling,' Kate murmured.

'Sorry, I missed that,' said Molly. 'What did you say?'

'Nothing, don't mind me. It's good to be back. How was your weekend apart from the drama?'

'Good thanks. But you have to tell me all about your holiday.

I've never been to Boston. What was the weather like? Was it hot?'

Kate nodded. 'Yes, very. Makes a nice change. I wasn't out in the sun much though. I spent a lovely day in the museum and um, saw my friend.'

'How did that go? Was it fun?'

'Not exactly,' Kate admitted. 'It was a bit of a disaster to tell the truth.'

Molly sighed. 'I'm really sorry to hear that. I know you probably don't want to talk about it but I'm here if you need me.' She was quite used to Kate's obsession with privacy.

Kate thought for a second. She felt bad. Molly was a good person and seemed genuinely sorry for her troubles. It wouldn't hurt to tell her what had happened, in fact, it might be just what she needed. Granny Lily had been great and she'd made her realize that talking to a sympathetic ear really was the best therapy. 'You know, Molly, I do want to talk about it this time. I know I haven't always told you everything in the past.' Kate smiled gently. 'In fact, I'm sure I've been more than a little evasive. But if you have the time I'd like to tell you all about Jay.'

'Is Jay your American friend?'

'Yes. At least he was.'

Molly smiled back at her. 'Kate, I've all the time in the world. Why don't we open a bottle of wine and settle in for the night?'

'You know, I'd like that,' said Kate. 'I'd like that a lot.'

'Does this mean I can borrow your Jimmy Choo boots?' Molly tried her luck.

'Don't push it,' Kate laughed. 'Those boots are sacred. But we'll see.'

Chapter 19

Paige

Paige woke up. She felt terrible – her neck was stiff and her buttocks were numb. The inside of her mouth felt dry yet sticky and she had a desperate urge to clear the gunge by brushing her teeth. Her suit jacket had fallen off her while she slept, leaving her cold and shivery. She should never have taken Tom's advice to have a nap in the car. She wondered what was going on inside the polling station, the large town hall in Dublin city. When she'd left the election count it was two in the morning and it was now almost five. She stretched her arms over her head, as much as she could in the confined space and flexed her feet and buttocks. She'd better go back in. She flicked on the inside car light and studied her face in the rear-view mirror, wincing as she saw the pale, unkempt reflection. She licked her two index fingers and removed the black mascara stains from underneath her eyes, rubbing gently so as not to pull and redden the delicate paper-thin skin. She then pulled her bag from under the car seat and found her emergency make-up kit. A few minutes later she felt a little more presentable. She braced herself for the scramble through the crowds at the count. At least Tom and her supporters were easy to spot – to the very far left of the hall, against the wall and beside Jackie Pile's gang.

'How are you feeling, love?' Tom asked after he'd given her a huge smile and hug.

'Groggy,' she said truthfully. 'I'm sure I'll be fine in a few minutes though. What's been happening in my absence?'

'Mark's in and they're counting his second preferences as we speak.'

'How's it looking?'

'Hard to tell. Annette seems pretty confident – she's already given RTE an interview about what she'll do when she's in government.'

Paige bit her lip. 'Really?'

Tom smiled. 'Yes. But she'll look pretty stupid when you win the seat, won't she?' He squeezed Paige's hand.

'I can't bear all this tension,' Paige said. 'It's excruciating.'

'I know,' Tom said gently. 'But it'll be all over soon.'

'And we have a final count in Dublin North,' a voice boomed over the PA system.

Paige and Tom listened as the official read out the final results.

'In the Dun Laoghaire Rathdown constituency,' another official read a moment later, 'we have eliminated Hilda Murphy, Miles McGreinna and Rex Reximus.'

Tom nudged Paige. 'There's just you and Annette left.'

Paige's face was pale. She said nothing.

'I think you should sit down,' he said. 'I'll go and find you a chair. Back in a minute.'

'Thanks,' she said gratefully. She was feeling rather faint.

He pushed his way through the crowds.

Jackie Pile appeared beside Paige and touched her on the shoulder. 'How are you bearing up?' she asked Paige kindly.

Paige shrugged her shoulders. 'OK, in the circumstances. I'm delighted you got in again. Well done.'

'Thanks. And I look forward to working with you.'

'If I get in,' Paige sighed. 'It's going to be close.'

Jackie smiled. 'I have every confidence in you, Paige. You've worked hard and you deserve it. If there's any justice in the world, you'll be elected.'

'Thanks.'

'And we have a recount for the last seat in Dun Laoghaire Rathdown constituency.'

Jackie whistled. 'You were right about it being close, Paige. I hate recounts, I don't envy you.'

'You're an old hand at all this,' Tom said, overhearing Jackie's last comment. He opened the plastic folding chair he was holding and smiled at Jackie.

'It never gets any easier though,' Jackie said. 'Would you like some tea or coffee? We have some at our table. And some sandwiches I believe, although I can't vouch for their freshness.'

'That would be great, thanks,' Paige said gratefully. Although sitting down now, she still felt faint and something to eat might help her blood-sugar level.

An agonizing hour later, Tom put his hand on Paige's shoulder. She'd been dozing in the chair, leaning against his side.

'They're about to announce the result,' he said.

Paige raised her head, looked over to the right and tried to pick out Annette in the crowd. It wasn't hard. She was standing on a chair, craning to the see the stage, one steadying hand on her husband's shoulder. At that moment Annette looked over towards Paige, as if sensing Paige's gaze. She nodded in recognition, no emotion showing on her face, her eyes lingering on Paige for a few moments before swivelling back towards the stage.

'Annette looks very confident,' Paige said to Tom in a low voice.

'That means nothing,' Tom assured her, staring at the stage.

'There's our official. He's been handed the result sheet. Here we go.' The man walked towards the microphone. Paige took a deep breath and braced herself for bad news.

'And in the Dun Laoghaire Rathdown constituency on the second and final count, Councillor Paige Brady has one hundred thousand and fifty-six votes. On the second and final count Councillor Annette Higgins has one hundred thousand and forty-two votes. I hereby elect Councillor Paige Brady to the fourth and final seat.'

A roar of approval swept the hall and all around her people clapped and cheered.

'Well done, Paige.' Jackie kissed her warmly on both cheeks.

'Where's the new Deputy?' Paddy Burns boomed as he made his way towards her. 'Congratulations, my dear.' He gave her a huge bearhug.

Paige was overwhelmed. She clung to Tom's hand, the tears freely flowing down her cheeks.

'Have you anything to say to us, Deputy Brady?' An RTE radio journalist thrust a large grey woolly microphone in her face.

'Um, yes,' Paige said. 'I'm delighted and I'd like to thank everyone who voted for me.'

'Are you surprised that Councillor Higgins didn't get in?'

'Yes,' Paige said honestly. 'I suppose I am.'

'How do you feel about her comments about you this evening?'

Paige raised her eyebrows and looked at Tom. He smiled at her and shrugged his shoulders.

'I wasn't aware that she'd made any,' Paige replied evenly, refusing to be baited. 'And it's all a little irrelevant now, isn't it?'

'I suppose it is,' the journalist said reluctantly. 'But I think you should know that she called you . . .'

Paige put her hands in the air. 'I honestly don't want to hear, thank you very much. I think Councillor Higgins has her own problems to be getting on with, don't you? And I'm sure what she told you was said in the heat of the moment. Now would you like to talk to Deputy Pile? She's right beside me.'

'Um, yes, sure,' the journalist said and left Paige alone.

'Well handled,' Tom said.

Paige smiled at him. 'Hey, I won. There's no point in rubbing her nose in it.' She yawned. 'Now, let's go home. I'm exhausted. We can celebrate tomorrow night. Right now, me and the baby need some sleep – in a bed!'

'Anything you say, Deputy.' Tom put his arm around her protectively. 'Home it is.'

The following morning Paige woke up and remembered instantly. A warm feeling flooded her whole body – she'd won the election and she was now a full-blown Deputy. The enormity of the situation began to sink in. She glanced at the clock radio beside the bed – almost eleven o'clock – she should have been up hours ago. It was all very quiet downstairs – maybe Tom had taken the boys out for a walk.

She pushed herself up in the bed. She was still exhausted, exhausted but elated. She wondered if everyone had heard the news yet. She'd texted Molly last night but she must ring her mum and Tom's mum this morning. Although by this stage they'd probably have heard on the news. She got out of bed, slipped her feet into her slippers and wrapped her towelling dressing gown around her. Her stomach was starting to round out now – soon she'd be in fully-fledged 'preggy' gear, but for now her looser clothes sufficed.

'Tom?' she called as she walked down the stairs. 'Hello? Anyone home?'

She heard a muffled giggle from the kitchen and smiled. Callum was probably in hiding – waiting to jump out at her from under the table or behind the curtains.

As she walked into the kitchen she was met by a host of smiling faces – Tom, Callum, Molly, Kate, Lily, Angus, Tom's mum and dad, and her own mum. And Alfie looked on with interest from his highchair in the corner.

'Surprise!' Callum said. 'We're having a party for you, Mum.'

Paige laughed and looked down. 'But I'm still in my pyjamas.'

'It's my fault,' Tom said. 'I invited everyone over. I thought we should celebrate now as I have a special surprise arranged for you this evening.'

'What sort of surprise?' Paige asked with interest.

'You'll have to wait and see.' He smiled.

'Have some cake, Mum,' Callum insisted, pulling her towards the kitchen table by her dressing gown tie. 'Come on. Granny made it this morning and it's still warm. It's chocolate!'

'Well in that case.' Paige looked at the large rectangular cake which was sitting on the table. 'Congratulations,' it read in white icing surrounded by little silver balls.

'Thanks, Mum.' Paige smiled at her mother.

'We're all very proud of you,' her mother said. 'I'm afraid the icing isn't quite set, but I'm sure it will taste fine.'

Tom handed Paige a knife. 'You do the honours,' he said. 'We're all dying for a slice.'

'I can't believe you're a Deputy now.' Molly grinned. 'Does this mean we have to watch what we say around you?'

'Not at all,' Paige said. 'It won't change me one little bit.'

'Will you be famous, Mum?' Callum asked.

She ruffled his hair. 'No, Callum.'

'But you'll be on the telly?' he asked hopefully. 'On *The Den* children's show?'

She smiled. 'Doubtful. Unless Dustin the Turkey invites me.'

'I'll write to him and tell him all about you,' Callum promised. 'I'll tell him what a good mummy you are and then he'll have you on.'

'You do that,' Paige said.

Everyone laughed.

Tom organized coffee and tea for everyone while Paige talked to Molly, Kate and Lily about the nerve-wracking night.

'How did you feel when they announced the final count?' Lily asked.

'I was in shock to be honest, I was convinced Annette had pipped me at the post. And it came as a huge relief I suppose, after all the hard work.'

'We all knew you could do it,' Lily said.

Paige smiled. 'Thanks.'

'Sure didn't Gran cajole all her friends to vote for you,' Kate quipped. 'Which must be practically half of Burnaby.'

Lily laughed. 'At least three quarters, please.'

Paige smiled. 'I couldn't have done it without all of you. And without Tom of course. And Angus.'

'I did nothing,' Angus insisted, handing Alfie back his soggy Liga biscuit.

'You kept Callum entertained,' Paige pointed out, 'and helped with Alfie. That's hardly nothing.'

Tom tapped his coffee mug with a tea spoon. 'I'd like to propose a toast. To Deputy Brady. May God protect her and all who sail in her.'

Everyone laughed.

'I think he's calling you a ship, Mummy!' Callum said delightedly.

'Tom!' Paige protested.

He grinned at her and winked.

'To Deputy Brady,' he repeated. They all raised their mugs and clunked them together. 'To Deputy Brady.'

*

That afternoon Tom met with his boss in the building society. He'd been working for Hannah Brookes for over five years now and they'd always got on well. She was a kind, if somewhat formidable woman who kept her staff firmly in line and had a habit of being a little more abrupt than most would like. Walking into her office, Tom felt a little nervous. He had no idea how she would react to his request.

'Hello, Tom.' She looked up from her computer screen and smiled. 'Please sit down.'

'Thanks.'

'How's Paige? I believe she's our new Deputy. Do congratulate her for me.'

'I will.'

'Now what can I do for you?'

'I'll come straight to the point, Hannah. Paige and I have been discussing the coming year and we feel that the children need one of us around. Callum will be starting school next year and we'd like to be able to collect him every day and do his homework with him – that sort of thing. And as you know, Paige is expecting again next year.'

'Go on,' Hannah said evenly.

'Well, um, I was hoping to take a year's unpaid leave to stay at home with the kids. Paige will be working all hours and um, we thought this might be a solution.'

'I see,' said Hannah. She said nothing for a moment. 'Have you taken parental leave before?'

Tom shook his head. 'No. If I've needed any extra days I've taken them out of my holidays.'

'You're a good manager, Tom. I'll be sorry to lose you.'

Tom caught his breath.

'I'll rephrase that,' Hannah said quickly. 'I'll be sorry to lose you for the year, but I understand completely. My own are all teenagers now, but it's still a struggle to keep the house running smoothly. I know how hard it is when they're younger, believe me. Besides, according to European Law you're entitled to several months unpaid parental leave if you have children under four or five. I can't quite remember the details but one of the women in the Bray branch has just started three months' parental leave.'

'Really?' Tom asked. 'And my job is safe even if I take as much as a year off?'

Hannah smiled. 'Of course, we'd hate to lose you permanently. And maybe you'd consider doing some consultancy work for us at home?'

'I'd be happy to,' Tom said eagerly.

'You're a good man, Tom,' Hannah said thoughtfully. 'There's not many husbands who would put their wives' careers before theirs. I admire you.'

Tom blushed. Hannah wasn't usually renowned for her compliments. 'Thanks,' he murmured.

That evening Tom arrived home early from work.

'Anybody home?' he shouted as he walked into the hall.

'Daddy!' Callum came careering towards him and threw his little arms around Tom's waist.

Tom picked him up and threw him in the air. 'How's my best boy?' He grinned. 'Have you been good for Angus today?'

'Yes! And he told me about being my teacher. Isn't it cool?'

'Very cool.' Tom smiled. 'But you'll have to be extra good for him in class.'

'I will,' Callum said solemnly. 'Angus has already told me that I have to be a good mample.'

'Mample?' Tom was confused.

'You know, show the others how to be good.'

Tom clicked. 'A good example.' He tried not to laugh.

'Yes,' Callum nodded solemnly. 'A good mample.'

They went into the kitchen where Angus was feeding Alfie some sort of mushy goo.

'Hi, Tom,' Angus said. 'Want to take over?'

'Sure.' Tom pulled off his jacket and hung it over the back of one of the kitchen chairs. Tom removed his tie and shoved it unceremoniously into a jacket pocket. Won't be needing one of those soon, he thought. He took the plastic bowl and spoon off Angus and sniffed the bowl's contents. 'Banana?'

Angus nodded. 'Banana and apple. Paige made it.'

'Where is Paige?'

'Upstairs having a rest. She was looking a little worn out so I took over Alfie's tea.'

'Thanks,' Tom said gratefully.

'No worries. So how was the office, dear?' Angus asked with a grin.

'Fine, thanks.' Tom laughed. 'Actually it was good. I asked my boss for a year's parental leave and she said yes.'

'That's great! Callum will be thrilled to have you around more. He's always saying how he'd love to do more things with you.'

'Really?' Tom asked. 'You never mentioned it before.'

Angus shrugged. 'You and Paige have been under a lot of pressure recently. You didn't need any extra guilt trips.'

'I suppose not. I look forward to spending more time with him. He's growing up so fast. And I believe you told him about being his teacher.'

'Is that OK? I hope you didn't want to tell him yourselves.'

'No, it's fine. And he's delighted.' They both looked at Callum who was colouring in a picture of Spiderman with chunky crayons.

'He's a good kid.' Angus smiled. 'I look forward to teaching him.'

Tom coughed. 'Um, I know we've never really said it to you before, not properly anyway,' he began, 'but we really appreciate all the time and effort you've put into his nibs this summer.' Tom gestured towards Callum with his head. 'It's made all the difference. We really are very grateful.'

'I know you are.' Angus smiled at Tom. 'And it's been a pleasure, really. He's a real little charmer.'

'Well, thanks anyway.' Tom punched Angus gently on the shoulder. 'And are you sure you're OK to babysit this evening?'

'Yes, positive. I'm sure it'll be useful to the school to have Deputy Brady owing me a favour.'

Tom laughed. 'You're probably right!'

Later that evening Paige had her usual wardrobe dilemma, except this time it was worse. The dark brown suede trousers she'd intended to wear were far too tight around the waist. She'd tried leaving the button and zip undone and pulling a black jumper down over her stomach but that made her look bulgy and made the seat of the trousers bag unbecomingly. Besides, what if her trousers fell down during the night and she didn't notice? She sighed and put the outfit back in the wardrobe.

'What's up?' Tom was lounging fully dressed on their bed, watching her. He'd already changed out of his work gear, showered and shaved and was rearing to go. He hadn't had much for lunch and his stomach was starting to complain loudly.

'I can't find anything to wear,' she complained.

'Can I help?'

She smiled at him. 'I don't know, can you?' She put her hands on her hips provocatively and raised her eyebrows.

'I think you should go out just as you are,' he said. 'You look great.'

She smiled at him and looked down at her black lacy bra, matching G-string and hold-up stockings. 'I think I might get a little cold. Besides, unless we're going to a lap dancing club I don't think it's quite appropriate.'

Tom got up and walked towards her. He stood behind her, wrapping his arms around her waist.

She flinched. 'Your hands are freezing!'

'They'll soon warm up,' he promised. He moved them up her body, lingering over her breasts. He unhooked her bra and deftly removed it, throwing it onto the floor.

'Tom, we have to go,' Paige protested. 'We'll be late. Besides, Angus is downstairs.'

'There's no mad rush,' Tom said. 'And Angus has taken the kids out to the park, bless him.' His hands caressed her breasts and he began to kiss the nape of her neck gently. She turned around and smiled at him. She was actually feeling quite good all day and Tom seemed to be in flying form, it would be a shame to stifle him. Besides, they hadn't had sex for weeks as she hadn't been feeling up to it. And once the baby came . . . she shuddered to think how tired they'd both be. They should grab every opportunity they could, especially if Callum and Alfie were otherwise occupied. 'In that case . . .' She kissed him firmly on the lips, put her arms on his shoulders and pushed him backwards towards the bed.

'Deputy Brady.' He laughed, as they fell onto the bed. Paige silenced him with another kiss.

'I had an interesting meeting with Hannah today,' Tom said later that evening after they'd ordered their food. They were sitting at a secluded table in their favourite restaurant, Fallon's in Burnaby.

'Oh?' Paige took a sip of her wine and smiled at him. 'What about?'

'Things.' He smiled mysteriously.

'Go on,' she said impatiently. 'What things?'

'About taking a year off to look after the kids.'

'Really? What did she say?'

Tom smiled again. 'She said yes. She's going to promote Annie Jones on a temporary basis and take on a new trainee manager to replace her.'

Paige looked at him with a strange expression on her face.

'What?' he asked. 'Are you not happy? It's what we'd discussed, Paige, before the elections.'

'I know. But we didn't really go over the details – the financial end of things for example.'

'I've had a look at the figures and as long as we don't go wild we should be fine. It'll mean no foreign holidays for example, and we won't be changing the cars, but we'll manage.'

She was quiet for a moment, her fingers running up and down the stem of the wine glass, her eyes fixed on the dark red wine.

Tom allowed her time to collect her thoughts.

'I guess I haven't had time to take it all in,' she said finally. 'I didn't expect it all to happen so quickly I suppose.' She looked him straight in the eye. 'To tell the truth, it makes me feel a little inadequate as a mother. I feel like you'll be taking over and that I'll just be in the background, plodding away at work.' She sighed. 'I'm sorry, I'm not being fair. It's what we'd agreed, I know. I just didn't expect to feel like this.'

Tom put his hand on hers. 'Paige,' he said softly. 'You'll always be their mother. Nothing can change that. You'll always have a special relationship with them. I'll just be the one doing the school run and changing Alfie's nappies, that's all.'

Paige snorted. 'And you're more than welcome to Alfie's nappies. You're right, I know you're right. But I just feel kind of, oh, I don't know – left out, I suppose.'

Tom smiled at her warmly. 'Paige, you won't be left out of anything, I promise you that.'

'I'm sorry, I'm being really ungracious,' she said. 'Most women would be delighted to have such a supportive husband.'

'That's what Hannah said.' Tom smiled.

'I really am very lucky.' Paige leant over and kissed him on the cheek. 'And I do love you, Tom.'

He stroked her hand. 'And I love you too. More than ever.'

Paige felt a warm sensation in the pit of her stomach. She knew the next year was going to be hard for both of them, but as long as they were together they'd get through anything.

Chapter 20

Molly

'Before we get started I'd like to apologize,' Milo began as soon as the other Book Club members had settled into their seats and stopped discussing their favourite event at the book festival, which they'd unanimously declared a huge success.

'Why?' Paige asked.

'Yes, what have you done now?' Anita asked with a sigh.

Molly tried not to laugh. Anita was sitting beside Milo and from what she could see the cold war between them still hadn't thawed.

'I recommended *Bright Light of My Soul,*' he said picking up that's month's book choice and turning the elegant-looking matt grey paperback over in his hands. 'It got some great reviews in hardback and I thought it would be an interesting read.' He stopped for a moment.

'Milo, are you saying that you didn't like it?' Paige raised her eyebrows.

'No I didn't, not really,' Milo admitted. He put a finger under the collar of his trademark black polo neck, as if letting some air in. 'It wasn't the easiest read, was it?'

Anita snorted. 'But I thought you informed us at the last

meeting that we should all be reading more literary fiction, that our tastes were too, how did you put it, ah yes, "unformed" and "unrefined".'

'I didn't say that, did I?' Milo asked, getting a little red in the face.

'I'm afraid you did,' Harry said, smiling broadly at him.

'Dad!' Sam hissed at him. 'I must have come in after that,' he said to the table. 'It's not as if he's the world's greatest reader himself. In fact up until he bought this shop . . .'

Milo coughed loudly. 'Um, yes, well, I'm sorry if I caused any offence at the last meeting. I was wrong.'

'We won't be reading any more of your recommendations for a while anyway,' Cathy laughed. 'I hated *Bright Light of My Soul* – it was so depressing. I don't mind depressing as such, but there was absolutely no hope shining through at all. It was a weep fest from start to finish. Nothing of any interest happened to the main character, Hoppy. And what kind of name is "Hoppy" for a woman anyway?'

'I thought it was supposed to be a kind of twist on the word "happy" myself,' Trina said. 'But that's probably a bit too obvious. It's her first book though, isn't it? Una Franklin's. Maybe she'll cheer up a bit in the next one.'

'Let's hope so,' Anita nodded. 'She can't get any worse. And what about the men in the book? They were all totally nasty characters – from your man Frankie, her first husband, to that guy who killed her at the end, Joe. I know as a gender men are not perfect,' she looked pointedly at Milo, 'but they're not all bad.'

'I agree,' Sam said. 'It was a pretty bleak reflection on men. But some of the women weren't any better. Didn't her own mother practically sell her to Frankie for a piece of land?'

'That's right! She was horrible to Hoppy,' Molly agreed. 'And her so called "friend" Susan wasn't much better."

'The one who told the guards that Hoppy was a prostitute?' Kate asked.

'Yes.' Molly nodded. 'She was a nasty piece of work.'

'What are you doing after this?' Molly whispered to Paige an hour later. The debate on *Bright Light of My Soul* was beginning to wind down and the group were now discussing choices for next month's book. 'Going for lunch with you.' Paige smiled.

'Great!' Molly squeezed her friend's arm. 'I wasn't sure if you'd be free, Deputy.'

'What do you think, Molly?' Anita asked her, interrupting them.

'Sorry?' Molly replied. 'I missed that.'

'Cathy was asking if we could order copies of an American title in time for next month's meeting?'

'Depends on the book,' Molly said. 'But it shouldn't be a problem if the American wholesaler we use has it.'

'Well then, I vote we take a break from literary fiction,' Anita glanced at Milo and he winced.

'Hear, hear,' said Cathy.

'I agree.' Trina nodded. 'Let's have something with a real story this time. And a happy ending please, if it's not too much to ask. Optimistic at the very least.'

'Well then, I nominate Bonnie's new book,' Cathy said. 'It's only available in the States at the moment so we'll be the very first people to read it. It's based in Burnaby apparently and we might even recognize some of the characters. She told me about it at the festival.'

'Excellent!' Anita clapped her hands together. 'Any objections?'

Everyone shook their heads.

'Back to decent fiction then,' Anita said, her eyes lingering on Milo. 'And about time too.'

*

The following Monday, Molly lingered outside the Begley Literary Agency, her stomach twisted with nerves. She looked up at the imposing Georgian Merrion Square building and fished in the small pocket of her oversized red leather bag for her powder compact, flicked it open and checked her face. She hoped she was dressed appropriately. She'd spent ages last night deciding what to wear, with Kate and Paige's patient help, and had finally settled on a pair of old reliable black trousers, a white shirt (Kate's) and a dark red fitted cashmere cardigan (Paige's). She completed the outfit with a black beaded choker (Paige's), the red bag (hers) and killer Jimmy Choo black high-heeled boots, Kate's pride and joy, which she'd insisted on lending to Molly for good luck. She'd popped a pair of runners in the bag just in case her feet were crippled from the heels on the way home as she'd taken the Dart train to abate the extra stress of driving in the Dublin city traffic, not to mention finding an elusive parking space.

The three of them – Molly, Kate and Paige – had had a delightfully girly evening in the end and Kate, usually dismissive of 'girliness' had really got into the spirit of things. Kate had turned out to be a dab hand at making pink cocktails complete with authentic blender-produced slushy ice, slices of orange and lemon, and tiny multi-coloured paper cocktail umbrellas that she'd discovered in the cupboard under the sink, left over from some party or other. Molly and Paige had been most impressed. Molly regretted drinking quite so many of the 'Deputy Brady Delights', as Kate had christened one of her dark pink concoctions, not to mention the 'Milly Molly Mandys' which were blood red and full of vodka, or the baby pink 'Catikins' but it had been a great evening.

Molly glanced at her watch. It was just after ten and if she didn't go in now she'd be late. She smoothed her trousers down her legs, checked the eye and hook fastenings on her shirt, as Kate had warned her they had a habit of coming undone at inopportune moments, and walked up the steps towards the imposing red front door. She rang the intercom beside the discreet 'Begley Literary Agency' brass nameplate and waited. A moment later, a friendly woman's voice answered.

'Hello? Begley Agency. Can I help you?'

'Um, it's Molly Harper.'

'Hi, Molly, Gerry's expecting you. Push the door and go up the stairs. Our offices are at the back of the first floor, in the return.'

'Thanks.' Molly stepped inside and looked around. The hall was amazing – it had soaringly high ceilings, complete with what seemed to be original plasterwork. A large, ornate crystal chandelier hung from the middle of the space, dangling weightily from the most organic ceiling rose Molly had ever seen. It was made up of huge fronds of fern-like leafy foliage, all curving and twisting down from the horizontal plane as if growing towards the floor. The hall was painted creamy white and the black and white tiled floor set it off beautifully. As Molly walked up the stairs, she could feel the thick pile of the cream carpet under the thin soles of her boots. The Begley Agency was obviously a huge success judging by appearances and Molly was distinctly impressed and overawed.

'What would Mr Begley want with me?' she asked under her breath. 'He obviously has more than enough clients to be going on with.'

'Hello.' As Molly reached the top of the stairs she was greeted by a small, dark haired young woman. 'You must be Molly, nice to meet you.' She held out her hand and smiled.

'Hi,' Molly said, shaking her hand firmly. She followed the woman through a doorway and into a small, bright office, furnished with a simple mahogany desk, an armchair and an antique-looking coffee table stacked high with book trade magazines – *The Bookseller*, *Publishing Ireland*, *Inis*, and *Dublin Books*.

'Gerry will be ready for you in one minute. He's just on the phone to an editor at the moment. He spends most of his day on the phone – he gets hundreds of calls every day.' She gestured at the chair. 'Please, make yourself comfortable. Can I make you some tea or coffee?'

'No thanks, but I'd love a glass of water,' Molly said.

'No problem.' The woman came back a few minutes later with a tall glass and handed it to Molly. 'I'm Julie by the way, Gerry's assistant and general dogsbody.'

'Nice to meet you, Julie.' Molly smiled shyly. 'Quite some offices you have here.'

Julie laughed. 'Most of this building belongs to the accountancy firm Gerry used to work for. We just rent this bit off them. It's not as glam as the rest of the building but it's in a great location. We get to impress clients with the address,' she lowered her voice, 'and the accountants get to namedrop the literary agency to make themselves sound more interesting. Plus we recommend a lot of our clients to them. So, everyone wins.'

Molly smiled again.

Julie noticed how tightly Molly was clutching the bag on her knee. 'You're probably nervous, but don't be. Gerry's a lovely man and he's very easy to talk to.'

'What were you saying about me?' The door opposite Julie's desk opened and Gerry himself stepped out. He smiled at Molly. 'I hope it was nice.'

'Of course it was, Gerry.' Julie winked at Molly. 'Sure why wouldn't it be? Great man like yourself.'

'Indeed.' Gerry laughed. 'Sorry to keep you waiting, Molly. I'm sure Julie was keeping you entertained. Please come in.' He held the door for her and Molly stepped into his office. Julie was right – it wasn't as glam as the rest of the building but it was still an impressive room. The end wall was made up of richly coloured stained glass depicting a phoenix rising from vivid orange flames. In the centre of the room was another large mahogany desk and to the left and right there were filing cabinets and shelves and shelves crammed with books of all shapes and sizes.

'Do sit down,' Gerry said. 'Have you ever talked to an agent before, Molly?'

Molly was taken aback. 'Um, no,' she murmured. 'Never.'

He looked down at the sheets of paper in front of him. 'Am I the first person to read some of your stories?'

She nodded shyly. She hoped she wasn't blushing too noticeably, her cheeks felt decidedly pink.

'Your work has a lovely fresh feel,' Gerry said. 'I think you have real talent. Unfortunately there's no real market for short stories at the moment. And I think your *Price of Gold* saga is a little too ambitious for a first book.'

Molly's heart dropped. He didn't want her. Of course he didn't – a highly respected man like Gerry Begley. What was she . . .?

'How would you feel about that?' he asked. 'Could you try it?'

'Sorry?' she'd missed what he'd said.

'Writing a contemporary novel. What do you think?'

Molly looked at him in surprise. 'Um, I could give it a go.'

'Your short stories are excellent and I'm sure Julie could place them for you in magazines, say *Trend* for example and *Dublin Books*.'

'Really?' Molly asked with delight. 'That would be great.'

'I liked "Concrete Pictures" very much. How would you feel about expanding that story into a novel? The two main characters were very strong and I think there's a lot of meat to them.'

Molly smiled. Meat? She wasn't quite sure what to make of that but it sounded like a compliment.

'How about writing five or six chapters and a plot outline and then we could put a proposal together for a publisher? How does that sound?'

'Fine,' Molly said. 'Great, I mean. I think I could do that.'

'I'm sorry, I never asked if you wanted me to represent you. You may like to look around for someone else. There's Josie O'Hara of course, and Phelim . . .'

Molly didn't have to think. Gerry seemed like someone she could trust, plus he genuinely seemed to like her work. 'No, I'd like you if you'll have me.'

'Of course I'll have you, my dear.' Gerry's eyes twinkled. 'I'd be delighted to be your agent. I think we'll get along just swimmingly.'

'So do I.' Molly smiled back. 'And I'll get writing straight away.'

'That's what I like to hear,' Gerry said. 'Welcome to the family, Molly. I'll ask Julie to draw up the official papers allowing me to act as your agent. Maybe you could come in next week and sign them?'

'I'd be happy to.'

'Good, and you can tell me all about your progress on "Concrete Pictures".'

Molly skipped down the building's steps after the meeting, almost twisting her ankle in the process and causing her to lurch ungainly against the dark blue handrail. She straightened herself up, rubbed her side where she'd hit the solid metal and smiled. Nothing could dampen her mood at this moment, not even a large bruise

'So how did it go this morning?' Sam asked as soon as she'd stepped foot in the bookshop. He was sitting on the stool at the front till, keying some customer orders into the computer. There were a few customers browsing the shelves but all in all it was pretty quiet.

'Really well.' Molly smiled and dumped her bag on the counter to the relief of her poor shoulders – she always carried too much junk 'just in case'. She hadn't bothered changing into her runners either and was starting to regret it. Kate's boots were killers in more ways than one. She was dying to take them off and give her soles and insteps a rub. 'Gerry was nice, he wants to be my agent. He's going to place some of my stories with magazines, well, his assistant Julie is, and he asked me to try writing a book based on "Concrete Pictures".'

Sam laughed. 'Try stopping for breath, Molly!'

She smiled at him again. 'Sorry, was I gabbling? I'm just so excited about the whole thing. I can't believe it's all happening. First winning the short story competition, now this.'

He jumped off the stool, walked around the counter towards her and gave her a huge hug. 'If anyone deserves it, you do,' he kissed the top of her head. 'Well done, you.'

Molly felt on top of the world. Not only did Gerry want her, she had the kindest and nicest boyfriend in the world.

'Thanks,' she said.

'Ahem,' a customer coughed beside them. 'Can I pay for this?'

'Sure.' Sam grinned and winked at Molly. 'Why don't you go into the office and put your feet up for a few minutes. I'll deal with this.'

'That would be great if you don't mind. I'll be back out in a while.'

Once in the office Molly flopped down in a chair and rang Paige again. She'd tried her on the walk down to the train station, positively hopping to tell her the good news, but Paige's mobile had been turned off.

'Molly, I was just thinking about you. How did the meeting go?'

Molly told her all the details.

'Fantastic!' Paige said enthusiastically. 'He sounds like just the man you need. So, I guess you just have to get writing now.'

Molly bit her lip. The reality of the situation was only starting to kick in. 'What if I can't write a whole book? I've tried before and I've always come unstuck about halfway through. I've never finished a whole one before.'

'This time it's different,' Paige assured her. 'You've just won a prize for you work and you've got an agent. Everything's changed. You're a real writer now and it's your job to write. Just like it's my job to stop dog owners from allowing their dogs to poop on the beach. I know which job I'd rather do right at this minute.' Paige laughed. 'And I thought being a Deputy would be much more glamorous than being a Councillor. How wrong can you get?'

'Right now, alleviating dog poop sounds much easier to me.' Molly sniffed. 'Paige, what have I done? I can't write a book. Who am I kidding?'

'Listen to me, Molly.' Paige's voice sounded firm and unbending. 'You most certainly can and you most certainly will. I want you to go home this evening, have dinner, go for a walk and then sit down at your computer. Read "Concrete Pictures" again. Read it over and over as many time as you have to.'

'Why?'

'To get it into your thick skull that you can write, dummy,' Paige said. 'I know you have a book in you and I bet Sam thinks so too. And Anita. And Gerry has confidence in you, and he's a professional who doesn't know you from Adam. It's about time you had a little confidence in yourself, Molly. Do you hear me?'

Molly nodded.

'Molly?'

'I was nodding.'

'So you'll stop thinking negative thoughts?'

'Um, I suppose so.'

'And you'll sit down this evening and write?'

'I will,' Molly said.

'Promise?'

'Promise.'

'I'll ring you later. Now, smile, Molly. You *can* do it, don't forget that.'

'Thanks, Guru Brady.' Molly laughed. 'I feel much better now. Talk to you later.'

Molly smiled as she clicked off her phone. Just then Sam popped his head round the door.

'Dad's here for the meeting. Are you ready?'

'Damn, I'd forgotten all about it. Is Anita here yet?'

'Yes, she's talking to Dad. From what I managed to eavesdrop, they're going to the theatre together this evening.'

'Really?' Molly raised her eyebrows. 'I thought she couldn't stand him.'

'I know.' Sam smiled. 'Wonders will never cease.'

'Give me two minutes. I presume the meeting will be in here?'

Sam nodded. 'And Felix is covering the shop floor for an hour or so.'

'We'd better get going then I guess,' Molly sighed. 'Lambs to the slaughter and all that.' She looked at him carefully. 'What has your Dad said to you? What do you know? I know you know something.'

'As I keep telling you,' he put on a feeble Italian accent, 'I know nothing. Nothing I'm at liberty to tell you anyway. Trust me.' Sam looked down at his hands. Molly sensed there was something he wanted to tell her but for some reason he couldn't.

Molly sniffed. 'He's going to change the shop, I know he is. He's never liked the pink and purple shelves and quite frankly I think the whole "romance bookshop" thing is just an embarrassment to him. I can see it now – "Milo's Cool Literary Bookshop" – all black and grey shelves. Black leather sofas, jazz music, poetry readings . . .'

'Hello, are you ready for the meeting, Molly?' Anita walked into the office, interrupting Molly in mid-flow.

'Um, yes,' Molly said. She looked at Sam who was trying not to laugh. 'Ready, Sam?' she asked pointedly.

'Sure, whenever you are.'

They all sat down in the small office, Molly behind the desk, Anita and Sam on the sofa and Milo beside them on a fold-out chair. It was decidedly cramped.

'So, Milo,' Anita began, 'why are we all here?'

Milo cleared his throat theatrically. 'As you all know the bookshop figures haven't been the best in recent weeks. But I'm delighted to say that the festival was a huge hit and . . .'

Anita stared at him, her eyes narrowing. 'And what?'

'The figures in the last two weeks since the festival have been very strong. So, I've changed my mind. The bookshop can stay as it is for the moment.'

Sam looked at him in surprise. This wasn't what he was expecting.

'No jazz music?' Molly asked.

'Well, maybe a little jazz,' Milo said. 'But no black shelves and you can keep the name.'

'Thanks very much,' Anita muttered. 'Milo, what do you mean – "for the moment"?'

'For the foreseeable future, does that clarify it?' said Milo.

'No,' Anita said firmly. 'It does not. I want you to guarantee that you won't change the shop, not now, not ever. Like you promised me when you bought it.'

'But I can't do that!' Milo protested. 'Something might happen, romance might go out of fashion.'

'Romance will never go out of fashion.' Anita glared at him. 'Not that you've ever read any of it. So how would you know?'

He looked straight back at her. 'For your information, I read one of Bonnie's books only last week.'

'Really?' Anita was genuinely surprised.

'Yes, really. And I liked it. I'll be reading her next book, for the reading group. After that I thought I'd give Rose Lovett a go.'

Molly looked at Anita, who had a strange expression on her face, Molly couldn't quite read it.

Sam whistled. 'Three books in one month, Dad. You'd want to watch that. Reading's a dangerous thing. Addictive. So when are you going to tell them, Dad? Are you going to play at book-selling for another few weeks, another year, another two years? That wasn't exactly the plan now, was it? Your architect was on the phone yesterday. He asked for Mr Devine so I took the call. I can't believe you've been lying to me, your own son. How could you?'

Milo looked at Sam in shock, his face growing pale. 'I don't think this is the time or the place, Sam. Why don't we discuss this later. I think . . .'

'The plan?' Anita asked Sam, steel in her eyes. 'What do you mean?'

'Ask him,' Sam gestured at his dad. 'I had nothing to do with it, Anita, believe me.'

Milo looked sheepish. 'Ignore Sam,' he muttered. 'He doesn't know what he's talking about.'

'Milo,' Anita said firmly, her voice dangerously low. 'Go on.'

'If you won't, I will,' Sam said, a threatening edge to his own voice.

'But . . . ' Milo looked at Sam. There was a dangerous glint in his son's eyes.

'I mean it, Dad.'

Milo sighed. There was no way out, he'd have to come clean. 'I bought the bookshop to knock it down and build offices and apartments. The architect was ringing to discuss the planning application. He needs to make one or two small changes to the plan. So it'll take a while to get the application passed. But in the meantime the bookshop will stay as it is, of course. At least that was the plan. But now . . .'

Anita slapped him across the face. 'You nasty little man. How could you?'

Milo put his hands to his face. 'I'm sorry, Anita. But I'm a businessman. At least I was.'

'That's no excuse, Dad,' Sam said. 'Why didn't you tell me at the very beginning? You're unbelievable.'

'I knew you'd never manage to keep it a secret. You'd too damn nice for your own good, Sam, that's your problem.'

'And once the building started, you'd fire me, along with the rest of the staff, was that it?' Sam demanded.

'Of course not, I was hoping you'd manage the whole project. You did do two years of engineering, after all. I thought it would work out for the best. Your brother, Miles, is very happy working for me.'

'I'm nothing like Miles,' Sam said with icy calm. 'I was happy, am happy working in the bookshop. I don't need a high-powered job like you or Miles, working all hours, never seeing my family. I'm ashamed of you, Dad. How could you dupe Anita like that? You promised her that the bookshop wouldn't change.'

'And it won't,' Milo said.

'What?' Anita cried. 'Spit it out, man!'

'That's what I've been trying to tell you all,' Milo said. 'I've changed my mind. I'm not going to develop this site at all. It'll stay as a bookshop. I'm going to sign the deeds over to Sam. I want you to own it, son.'

'I don't want your charity,' Sam said angrily. 'How dare you?'

Milo smiled. 'I knew you'd say that. Which is why I'm going to take a good chunk of the profits for the next ten years until you pay back every penny.'

'Sounds reasonable,' Anita said. 'Don't be stubborn, Sam, take his offer. Stupid man's trying to make amends for what he's done. Idiot that he is.' She shot a withering glare at Milo. 'And don't think you'll be taking me anywhere this evening, you damn fool.'

'But Anita . . .'

'Don't but Anita me. You'll have to do a hell of a lot of grovelling to get out of this one, Milo Devine.'

Milo stifled a smile. 'Yes, Anita,' he said meekly.

'So you'll accept your dad's offer?' Anita asked.

'I'll think about it,' Sam said. 'I'll have to discuss it with Molly first. If she'll manage the shop with me I'll consider it. It would have to be what we both wanted.'

Molly's heart melted. 'Oh, Sam,' she said before she could stop herself. 'I'd love to.'

Anita looked at Molly and smiled warmly. 'Good, that's settled then.' She glared at Milo. 'Count yourself lucky Milo that you're still standing. Now let's get back to work. We have a bookshop to run after all.'

'I'm exhausted.' Molly flopped onto Sam's sofa that evening and kicked her runners off. Her feet were still hurting. 'What a day.'

Sam handed her a steaming mug of peppermint tea and sat down beside her.

'Thanks.' She smiled at him. 'But I still can't believe you didn't tell me about that architect.'

Sam shrugged. 'Sorry, I thought it was for the best. He only rang yesterday and I thought you had enough on your mind to be honest, what with meeting your agent and everything.'

'You're probably right, speaking of which,' she looked at her watch, 'I can't stay long, I have to go home and write. I promised Paige.'

'Not to worry.' Sam reached over, took the mug out of her hands and placed it on the floor. 'But you have to do it for yourself, not for anyone else.'

'I know.'

He smiled. 'But before you go there was something I wanted to ask you.'

'Yes?' she said immediately.

'Don't be so impatient, woman. Follow me.' He stood up and offered her his hand.

She took it and followed him out the door and down the corridor. He pushed open the door of the spare room.

'What do you think?'

Molly looked around. The late August sun shone through the windows, illuminating the new empty pine bookshelves and matching desk.

'Did you make all this?' she asked.

He nodded. 'What do you think?' he asked again.

She smiled. 'It's great. A home office. Now you can mull over all those exciting bookshop invoices from the comfort of your own home.'

He said nothing for a moment, looked at her and smiled broadly. 'It's not an office, it's a study. It's for you. To write your book in. I thought, um, in time, when things settle down with Hugh, that you might like to live here with me. So this will be *your* study, not mine. Well, say something.'

Molly could feel tears prick her eyes. She looked up at him. 'Are you sure?' she whispered.

'Yes, positive.'

'I'd love to live here with you. I understand about Hugh, so whenever you think he's ready that's OK with me. Until then, you might even let me use the study. I think I could write a book here, in fact, I'm sure of it.' She ran her hands over the smooth surface of the top of the desk.

'Of course, it's your room now.'

'And this is the nicest thing anyone's ever done for me.' She threw her arms around his neck. 'Thank you, Sam.'

'It's a pleasure,' he said as she covered his face with kisses.

Chapter 21

Kate

'What are you doing here?' Kate asked Angus suspiciously as she walked into her gran's living room.

He looked at her, red paintbrush in his hand. 'Same as you, I presume, painting – or are they your normal clothes?'

Kate looked down at her ancient navy tracksuit bottoms, complete with holes in the knees, paint-splattered runners and an inside out light grey sweatshirt.

'Of course not,' she replied archly. 'Won't you excuse me?' She flounced out of the room.

'Gran!' Kate said walking into the kitchen where Lily was having a cup of tea. 'What's Angus doing here?'

'I must have forgotten to tell you,' Lily said mildly. 'He offered to help paint today.'

Kate glared at her.

'Don't look at me like that,' Lily said. 'He's a nice lad and very easy to talk to.'

'I have no intention of talking to him,' Kate said sharply.

Lily tried not to smile. Her granddaughter really was very stubborn. But still, it was a good sign if she felt so strongly about Angus. Much better than apathy. 'Why ever not?' Lily asked.

'Just because.' Kate didn't feel like explaining right at this minute. Besides, she wasn't sure if she understood why Angus always managed to get under her skin – it didn't make sense. She'd had quite enough of men in the last while and however 'nice' Angus was she had no intention of becoming involved with anyone ever again. It was time to start concentrating on her career. She had a lot of dummy dates to catch up on – that would keep her busy. She was far too busy to think about anything else. And she'd had a couple of ideas for leather baby shoes – not that she intended to do anything about them of course – but it was nice to know that her talent hadn't completely deserted her as she'd feared. After breaking up with Jay the first time around, Kate thought she'd never design again. Maybe finally her heart was finally starting to heal.

Lily watched Kate's face. She seemed lost in thought. 'Would you like some tea?' Lily suggested. 'Or coffee? Sit down and have a break before you get started with the painting.'

Kate stared at her. 'I'm not painting with *him* in the same room.'

Lily laughed gaily. 'Listen to yourself. You sound like a petulant teenager, Kate. It'll take half the time with the two of you and you can keep each other company. Give it a go and if it's really awful you can leave after lunch, OK?'

Kate muttered something under her breath and walked out of the kitchen.

'I presume that's a no to tea, then,' Lily said to herself. She smiled and hummed softly as she washed down the sink and the kitchen counter tops. Some days she liked cleaning, she found it cathartic. As she wiped down the cooker, she thought about Kate and about Kate's parents. It was no wonder that Kate found it hard to talk intimately to people – her own parents had spent their early married life screaming and shouting at each other. Billy Bowan had never been a nice man. Luckily his fiery temper had abated with age and nowadays he and Cleo, Lily's daughter and Kate's mother, seemed to live a reasonably stable life all things considered. About time too. Lily sighed. It was all in the distant past but Lily feared it had all left an indelible mark on her only grandchild, one which she'd carry for life. It was no wonder she'd always been drawn to attractive, powerful, older and bullying men who ultimately always treated her badly in the end. Men like her own father.

'You're back,' Angus said looking up at Kate. He was kneeling down on the floor, painting carefully around one of the plug sockets with a small brush.

'Let's just get this done,' she said shortly, not wanting to encourage small talk. 'Where are the brushes or will I make a start with the roller?' She surveyed the walls. Angus had already painted the corners, edges and around the plug sockets of three out of the four walls.

'The roller, I think. I'll finish what I'm doing and then I'll join you. What do you think of the colour?'

Kate considered for a moment. Lily had chosen a rich, warm red, very different to the previous creamy white. 'I'm not sure, it's difficult to imagine the whole room red. Won't it make the space seem very small?'

'Maybe. But it's a decent-sized room so it shouldn't matter too much. And the light is very good.'

'I'll guess we'll have to wait and see.' Kate moved towards the paint tins which were resting on a large white dustsheet, aka one of Lily's old bed sheets, and crouched down. She levered the lid off one of the tins and moved the paint tray beside it.

'Let me help,' Angus said. 'Those tins can be a divil to pour.'

Kate was about to refuse his offer but he was beside her before she could open her mouth. He gently took the heavy tin out of her hands and poured a generous amount of the viscous liquid into the tray.

'Thanks,' she murmured grudgingly. She pushed back some stray hair behind her ears and stood up. Tray in one hand and roller in the other she began painting the opposite wall to Angus, as far away from him as she could get.

'How was Boston?' Angus asked after a few minutes. 'Paige told me you were over there for a holiday, lucky thing. I spent a summer working there in college on a J1 visa. I loved it.'

'Really?' Kate left it at that. She had no intention of discussing her trip to Boston with him but she didn't want to completely ignore him – she wasn't that rude.

'Lily told me you used to live in Boston,' he continued unabashed. 'How long were you there for?'

'A while.'

'I see.' Angus wasn't one to be put off easily. He soldiered on. 'I stayed in an apartment near Fenway Park. Mad place. Underneath the apartment block there was a pizza restaurant – very handy, and this second-hand shop which only opened when the owner felt like it. But it had amazing things for sale, dirt cheap too. Old clothes from the '40s and '50s, records and tapes of really bizarre bands and weird hats and shoes. Hundreds and hundreds of pairs.'

'I think I know the place,' Kate said before she could stop herself. 'I used to go there to buy shoes.'

'I forgot about your strange collection.' Angus laughed. 'You'll have to show me it one day.'

Kate went silent again. She hadn't meant to talk to Angus at all. She was letting her resolve slip. She loaded the roller with some more paint and concentrated on covering the wall.

'Little Callum will be in my class this year,' Angus said, still unwilling to give up. 'Did Paige tell you?'

'No.'

'He seems to be really looking forward to school. When I was there on Friday he dressed up in his uniform for me. He was dead funny, parading around the house like a male model. You should have seen him, Kate. His grey trousers were far too big for him – Paige hadn't had a chance to take them up yet. He was tripping over the ends.'

Kate smiled. Callum really was a hoot. 'I hear Tom's taking a year off to mind the kids,' she remarked.

'I know, isn't it great? I think more fathers should do it. It makes sense if their other half has a good job. What do you think?'

'I suppose you're right,' Kate said thoughtfully. 'Although Irish men aren't exactly known for their love of childcare and housework.'

'Hey, that's unfair!' Angus laughed. 'We're getting better. I'd have no problem minding my own kids. I'd love spending time with them. It would be a privilege.'

'You'd like your own then?'

'Of course, wouldn't you?'

'I'm not sure.'

Angus stopped painting and looked at Kate but her back was still towards him. 'Why ever not?' he asked gently.

'Not everyone wants them you know,' she said quietly. 'I suppose you had a happy childhood?'

'Yes. Most of the time. Didn't you?'

Kate said nothing. She continued to move the roller up and down the wall. Angus noticed that there was no longer any paint left on it. He walked over and lifted the tray off the floor for her.

'You might need some of this,' he suggested.

'Thanks,' she murmured, dipping the roller into the tray.

Angus noticed that her eyes were glittering. Surely he hadn't made her cry?

'Um, did you hear about Sam's boy, Hugh running away?' he said, changing the subject.

Kate nodded. 'Molly told me the story. Sam must have been in bits, poor man.'

'He was. But Hugh hadn't gone far, thank goodness. It all worked out all right in the end.'

'And you were great,' Molly said. 'Talking to the lad and making him feel better.'

Angus shrugged. 'Anyone would have done it.'

Kate considered this for a moment. 'No, I don't think they would have. They might have brought the boy back to his parents but they wouldn't have stuck around to help sort everything out.'

'Maybe not. But as I said, I like kids. I just wanted to help.'

'Here,' Kate thrust the roller into his hands, 'I'm just popping out to the loo. Be back in a minute.'

Sitting on the edge of Lily's bath and staring at the white tiled floor, Kate wondered why she was feeling so strange. Lily was right, Angus was a nice man. A very nice man. Not as charismatic as Jay maybe, or as good-looking as some of her previous boyfriends. But he had other qualities. Deeper qualities. Damn it, he was a kind man who cared about other people and he liked her. He'd as much as told her so, over and over again. So what was her problem? She put her head in her hands. Maybe it was finally time to break the habit of a lifetime. She took a few moments to collect herself and then walked back down the stairs to the living room.

'Angus, I've got something to say to you.'

Angus looked over at Kate who was still lingering in the doorway. 'Really?'

Kate smiled. He had red paint splattered in his hair and a large red stripe on his forehead where he must have brushed a painted hand. 'Yes. I'm sorry if I've been a bit . . . um, funny towards you. But you were one of my clients you see.' She stopped, feeling decidedly awkward. 'Anyway, I'm sorry. You're a nice guy.'

Angus sighed. 'I see.' He sounded disappointed. He began to paint the wall again.

'What?' Kate asked. 'What did I just say?'

He raised his eyebrows. 'Are you serious?'

She nodded.

'You called me "nice".'

'So?'

'Kiss of death. Believe me.'

'I really don't have a clue what you're talking about, Angus.'

He snorted. 'Yes you do. Let's just paint.'

'No, I'm trying to talk to you. But you're not making any sense.' She walked towards him. 'You have paint on your forehead.'

He reached his left hand up to touch it.

'It's worse now. Look at your hands.'

Both his hands were covered in red paint. 'What can I say, I'm a messy painter.' He wiped both his hands on his jeans, leaving dramatic red smears all down the denim.

She put her fingers in his paint tray and touched his forehead gently. 'You looked better with the red stripe.' She smiled, backing away from him.

He stared at her, grabbed her hand and forced it onto her own cheek, leaving a blob of red paint.

'Angus!' she shrieked loudly. 'What are you doing?'

'And you look better with red cheeks.' He laughed.

She looked up at him. His eyes twinkled back at her. He was smiling broadly and still holding both her hands, his grip firm. Her breath began to quicken. Was he going to pull her towards him and kiss her?

'What are you thinking about?' he asked. 'You have a funny look on your face.'

'Do I now?' she asked, cocking her head to one side.

'Are you flirting with me, Kate? Because if you are . . .'

'Of course not.' She shook her head. 'Sure, why would I do that? But come to think of it, I do owe you a date.'

'Really?'

'Yes. How about tonight?'

'Are you serious?'

She smiled at him.

Angus smiled back. 'I think that could be arranged.'

Lily backed away from the door. She'd been standing there listening since she'd heard Kate shrieking and had hurried up from the kitchen to check that they weren't killing each other. But from what she'd heard, killing each other was the last thing on their minds.

'So, how was your date with Angus?' Lily asked Kate on the phone the following evening.

'How did you know? Did he tell you, I'll murder him!'

Lily laughed. 'I'm psychic, you know that. And to tell the truth, I also have a bad habit of listening through doorways.'

'Gran!'

'Tush, child. Anyway, are you going to tell me about it or not?'

'I suppose so,' Kate said reluctantly. She knew what Lily was like – she'd go on and on at her if she didn't spill the beans so she might as well. Besides, part of her wanted to tell her gran everything. She'd already told Molly all about it after all. She felt she had to after she and Angus had woken Molly up at one in the morning with their tipsy giggling in the hall.

'It went really well, Gran. We went out for dinner in Cicero's and then went for a walk by the sea. And that's all I'm telling you.'

'Are you seeing him again?'

'Maybe.' Angus was calling over that very evening as Molly was going to the pub with Sam, but she was damned if she was going to tell Lily that.

'I'm glad, he's . . .'

'Nice. I know.' Kate laughed. 'Now I have to go, Gran. I've something in the oven.'

'Dinner for Angus?' Lily asked astutely.

'Gran! Goodbye.'

*

'You look great,' Angus said as Kate opened the door. 'New shoes?'

Kate looked down at her precariously high-heeled strappy silver sandals, peeping out from under her denims. 'Like them?' she asked. 'You don't think they're too much with the jeans?'

'Not at all, they're great.' He handed her a clinking bag.

She peered into it. 'Three bottles!' She laughed. 'Are you crazy? It's a Monday night.'

'We're celebrating.'

'Celebrating what?'

'The full moon.' He grinned.

'You're quite mad, you know that?'

'I'll take that as a compliment.' He looked through the open door into the sitting room. 'Is Molly here?'

'No, she's already left.'

'So just the two of us then?'

Kate smiled. 'Yes. But don't go getting any ideas, young man. Follow me.'

She led him towards the kitchen, plonked the bottles down on the counter, took two glasses off the already-set table and grabbed the corkscrew.

'Red or white?' she asked.

'Red please. Can I open the bottle for you?'

'No, I've got it, thanks.'

Angus sniffed the air. 'Something smells good.'

'It's pasta with meatballs. I hope you like it. I'm not much of a cook but it's fairly difficult to mess up pasta.' She pulled the cork out of the bottle with a resounding pop and poured out the dark red liquid.

'I love it,' said Angus.

'Sit down, it'll be a few more minutes.' She gestured towards the table.

'Thanks.' He looked at the dark pink tulips in the vase at the centre of the table and the candles in their tall silver candlesticks. 'You shouldn't have gone to so much trouble.'

Kate blushed a little. 'It was no trouble, really.' She handed him a glass of wine and tipped her own glass gently against it. 'Cheers! To the full moon.'

'To the full moon and to us,' he said.

After dinner, they slumped onto the sofa in the sitting room, bringing a fresh bottle of wine with them. They'd already shared one bottle and Kate was feeling comfortably relaxed. She'd kicked off her heels and was rubbing the ball of her foot with her fingers. She loved her new sandals but they weren't the kindest to her feet.

'Let me,' Angus offered, putting down his glass.

'No, honestly, I'm fine,' Kate began, but before she knew it he had her foot in his lap and had begun to massage it expertly.

'I used to give my mum foot rubs,' he said, working his thumbs into the ball of her foot and almost making her groan with relief. He really was very good at this, Kate thought. She lay back and closed her eyes. 'Tell me if I'm hurting you.'

'No, that's great.'

After a few minutes he moved onto the second foot. When he'd finished, Kate's feet felt wonderfully rejuvenated. She opened her eyes and smiled at him lazily. 'Thanks, you're a star.'

'No problem.' He brushed a piece of hair away from her face. 'You're beautiful, do you know that?'

Kate smiled. 'And you're very good for my ego. You're not so bad yourself.'

He leant towards her.

Kate's heart gave a tiny leap. He'd given her a gentle kiss on the lips last night while saying goodbye, but she wasn't sure how she'd feel about . . . He leant over again and gave her a firm yet tender kiss. She tried to block all her preconceptions out, and kissed him back, gently at first, then more strongly. To her surprise, he seemed to know exactly what he was doing. To be honest, she'd expected him to be an average kisser at most, but he was actually supremely talented. A little less forceful than Jay, which wasn't a bad thing. In fact, she thought, as he began to stroke her back through her cotton top, Angus was a bit of a natural.

'Are you OK?' he murmured into her neck. 'Should I stop?'

She pulled him closer towards her. 'Don't you dare!'

'You look very happy,' Molly said the following morning over breakfast, instantly noticing Kate's wide smile. 'Good night?'

'Very good thanks.'

'And was that Angus letting himself out earlier?'

'I'm sorry, did he wake you up?'

'It's fine, I was already awake. So he stayed the night then?'

'Might have.' Kate spooned a large amount of cereal into her mouth and crunched away.

'That's great.' Molly smiled. 'He's a lovely guy. Really cute too. Patricia will be livid. She's asked him out several times since the Booksellers' Ball but he's always said no.'

'Really?'

Molly nodded. 'Must have been saving himself for you.'

'Must have, poor man.'

Molly laughed. 'Listen, I bumped into Alex last night in the pub. She said to ask you to drop into the coffee shop first thing, she has news for you.'

Kate glanced at her watch. 'I have a meeting with a client there at nine, so I'll call in a little early to say hi. I wonder what's up.'

'Who knows? She was in flying form though. Harry was there too. They make such a darling couple, don't they?'

Kate nodded and stood up. 'I'd better get a move on then.' She rinsed her breakfast bowl in the sink and dumped it in the dishwasher. 'See you later.'

The coffee shop was quiet and Kate spotted Alex as soon as she walked in the door. She was making sandwiches behind the counter, her back to the room.

'Alex?' Kate said.

Alex turned around and beamed. 'Hi, Kate. Give me one second.' She rinsed her hands under the tap and dried them on her apron. 'Would you like a coffee?'

'Love one.'

'I'll join you if you don't mind. You sit down and I'll be over in a minute.'

Alex brought two large mugs of coffee over with her and sat down beside Kate. She placed her hands on the table in front of her.

'So how are things?' asked Kate. 'Molly told me you had news.'

'I sure do.' She picked up her mug and Kate suddenly noticed the large, sparkling ring on her ring finger.

'You're engaged!' Kate smiled. 'I don't believe it. When did this happen?'

'On Saturday night. We haven't really told everyone yet, so I'll have to take the ring off now, but I wanted you to be one of the first to know.'

Kate leaned over and kissed her warmly on the cheek. 'I'm delighted for you both.'

'And it's all thanks to you,' said Alex. 'I hope you'll come to the wedding.'

'I'd be honoured. But you know, it had very little to do with me, Alex, honestly.'

'But you gave me the confidence to talk to Harry. I would never have approached him without your help. I must recommend you to all my single friends.'

'But remember I don't normally do girls, so to speak.'

Alex laughed. 'That sounded bad, but I know what you mean.

But maybe you should. You have a gift for bringing people together, it's your duty to use it. Us Irish girls need you.'

'Maybe you're right,' Kate mused. 'It might be fun. I'll certainly think about it. Now I think my client has just walked in. If you'll excuse me . . .'

'Of course.' Alex stood up. 'And thanks again.'

A small, red-cheeked man with a receding hairline walked towards Kate. He was wearing a plain navy sweatshirt over what looked like billowing multi-coloured pyjama bottoms. She had her work cut out with this one. She smiled as he approached the table. 'Paddy, I presume?' She stood up and held out her hand.

He nodded shyly, blushed and took her hand in his. He had a surprisingly firm handshake and kind eyes. Maybe there was hope.

'Nice to meet you,' she said. 'I'm Kate.'

Kate swung open the door of Baroque and sauntered in. She'd had a very productive morning, managing to squeeze in three client meetings and a quick lunch with Molly. And Alex's news had put her in a great mood too.

'Hi, Cathy. How was your morning?'

'Fine, thanks. What has put you in such a good mood?'

'Just life in general,' said Kate, dumping her bag on the counter at the back of the shop. 'Beautiful day, isn't it?'

Just then Trina came bustling in the door. 'I have news!' she shrieked. 'I was just at the clinic and I'm pregnant. And the doctor says everything seems to be all right this time. I think I'm going to have a baby!'

Cathy shrieked with joy and immediately gave her a huge hug. 'I can't believe it, that's fantastic!'

Kate watched a little shyly before moving towards Trina and kissing her on the cheek. 'That's great. Well done. When are you due?'

'Around Valentine's Day – can you believe it? I'm so happy.'

'You deserve it after everything you've been through,' said Cathy.

'Thanks.' Trina wiped the tears from her face and sat down. 'Now you'll have to get on with those baby shoes,' she smiled at Kate. 'You have no excuse.'

'Actually I did come up with a few designs,' Kate said casually. 'Would you like to see them?'

'Of course!' Cathy said immediately. 'You're a dark horse, Kate.'

Kate pulled her sketch book out of her bag. She'd intended to work on them a little bit more before showing them to Trina and Cathy but it felt like the right time to share them. It was turning out to be quite a day.

Chapter 22

Epilogue – A Year Later

Paige

'How's my favourite god-daughter? Behaving yourself, Jess?' Angus rubbed the baby's cheek tenderly and gently with his fingers. 'How's she been?' he asked Tom.

'Pretty good, touch wood,' Tom said still standing in the doorway. 'Come in, Callum will be delighted to see you.'

'Mr Cawley!' Callum tore down the hall and threw himself at his favourite teacher.

'You can call me Angus now,' Angus laughed. 'Except in school, of course.'

'But you're not going to be my teacher in September, are you?' Callum asked dejectedly.

'No, you'll have Miss Peters. She's lovely. I hear she gives treats on Fridays to the best table.'

'Really?' Callum couldn't hide his interest. 'What kind of treats?'

'Special pencils, I think. And stickers.'

'And sweets?' Callum asked hopefully.

'I don't think so,' Angus said. 'But you never know.'

'Would you like a cup of tea?' Tom asked him.

'If you're not busy . . .'

'Not at all. It gives me a good excuse not to hang out the baby's washing.'

Angus followed Tom into the kitchen. 'Here, give me Jess while you put the kettle on.'

'Thanks.' Tom handed her over and began to rub his right shoulder. 'She's getting really heavy.'

'Where's Alfie?'

'At Granny's,' Callum interrupted. 'It's just me and Daddy today.'

'And Jess,' Tom reminded him.

'But she doesn't really count,' Callum said patiently. 'She doesn't do anything. Just eats and cries and poos.'

'Callum! He's very taken with his new baby sister as you can see.' Tom laughed.

'After I've had my tea, why don't I take you out for a while, Callum?' Angus suggested. 'Give your dad some peace. What do you think? If that's OK with you, Tom.'

Tom grinned and gave him a thumbs up. 'That would be great.'

'Cool!' Callum practically jumped up and down on the spot. 'Can we go to the zoo, Angus, please?'

Angus looked at his watch. 'Sorry, Callum, we'd never get across the traffic in time. But what about the pet farm in Bray?'

'Yes! I'll just go and get my wellies.' He dashed out of the room. 'And don't worry. I'll tidy up my toys before we go.'

'Hasn't lost any of his energy I see.' Angus smiled at Tom.

'No kidding.'

'So, how are things? Still enjoying being at home? I haven't seen you since the summer holidays kicked in. Sorry I haven't called in sooner.'

'Not to worry,' Tom said. 'Things have been busy but I'm enjoying being with the kids. Most of the time at least. Although I'm not sure about next year. We may need extra help then.'

'Really?' Angus was curious. 'Why so?'

Tom grinned and pushed his hair off his face. He really did need a haircut but with the three kids to keep under control it was hard to find a slot. 'We haven't told many people yet, but Paige is expecting again.'

'No! Are you serious?'

'Couldn't be more so. It's a little sooner than we might have liked, but hey, four is a good-sized family. And they're opening a crèche in the local government offices in Dun Laoghaire which will make life much easier. We've already put Jess and the baby down for it next year. I'm hoping to work in the mornings and look after the gang in the afternoons.'

Angus whistled. 'You'll be busy.'

Tom nodded in agreement, poured boiling water from the kettle into two large mugs and added tea bags. 'Milk and sugar?'

'Both. Two sugars.'

Tom put the steaming mug down on the table in front of Angus.

'Thanks.'

Just then Paige walked into the kitchen. 'Is there enough water for another mug, I'm dying for a cuppa?'

Tom smiled at her. 'Of course, Deputy.' He prepared her a mug, added a dash of milk and handed it to her.

She kissed him on the cheek. 'You're a honey. Hi, Angus. A natural with Jess as always. Would you like to keep her?'

Angus laughed. 'What would you do if I said yes?'

'The way she's been sleeping, I might take you up on the offer.'

'How's work?' Angus shifted Jess a little as his cradling arm was starting to go dead.

'Will I take her for you?' asked Paige, noticing his discomfort.

'Not at all, she's grand.'

'To answer your question, work's great. Busy, but great. I

have a meeting in Blackrock this evening so I'm only home for an hour or two.'

'Tom told me the good news,' said Angus. 'About the baby. Congratulations.'

Paige looked at Tom and back at Angus, grinning ruefully. 'In for a penny, in for a pound as they say. We must be mad.'

'Mad but happy.' Tom wrapped his arms around Paige's waist.

She turned a little and kissed him on the cheek. She felt truly blessed.

Kate

'Do you want them painted?' asked Angus, staring at the new shelves on Kate's living room wall.

Kate thought for a moment. Molly had recently moved in with Sam, leaving Kate with the lease, so she'd decided to live in the townhouse on her own for a while. Her new dating cum matchmaking service for men and women – 'If the Shoe Fits' was doing very well, her baby shoes for Baroque had been a great success and rent money wasn't a problem. Angus was angling to move in with her, but she was enjoying living alone and being self-sufficient. Still it might be nice having him to cuddle up to when the nights got longer. Maybe she'd ask him to move in at Christmas. A new beginning for them both and a good way to banish any lingering Christmas Eve skeletons.

'What about white?' he asked.

'Against the blue? Do you think?'

He nodded. 'Might be quite striking.'

'I think I'll leave them plain wood for the moment. I'll put the shoes out and then we can see.'

'So I'm finally going to see this famous shoe collection,' he said. 'I'm most privileged.'

'Better believe it, Buster.' She smiled. 'I might even let you see my own designs. I won an award for my green "Emerald City" trainers I'll have you know.'

'No!' he joked. 'Not the "Emerald City" trainers!'

She elbowed him in the side playfully. 'Stop slagging me.'

'Ow,' he protested, grabbing her around the waist and pulling her towards him. 'That's how you treat me, after my long weekend of hard work.'

'And Sam had nothing to do with it?' Kate laughed.

'Well, he might have helped a little,' Angus conceded.

'You couldn't have built the shelves without him,' she said. 'Admit it.'

'You're probably right. But I was the one running all the errands to the DIY store when we ran out of things.'

'You were, pet.' She patted his hand.

'I think we should christen the new shelves,' he said, kissing her firmly on the lips and pushing her towards the sofa.

'You don't christen shelves, that's beds.'

'Who says?'

'I suppose you could have a point.' She kissed him back enthusiastically. Angus Cawley had been a revelation to her. Not only was he kind and considerate, he was also passionate, spontaneous and fantastic in bed. To top it all he'd proposed marriage every day since last New Year's. One day in the not too distant future she could even see herself taking him up on the offer.

Molly

'And this is my office,' Molly said proudly to Paige. 'Sam built all the units for me, and the desk.'

'It's fantastic,' Paige said enthusiastically. 'What a lovely place to write. And what a view.'

They both stared out the window. The early evening sun was bouncing off the waves and the sky was still eggshell blue.

'Would you like a glass of wine?' asked Molly.

'Love one.' Paige followed her into the kitchen.

'Sam and Hugh won't be back for ages,' said Molly. 'They've taken Leon for a long walk on the beach to try and tire him out a little. Puppies are a lot of work. But Hugh adores him.'

Paige laughed. 'Wait till you have a baby to contend with.'

'At least babies don't chew the legs off your furniture,' Molly pointed out, 'and you can put them in nappies to avoid all those delightful "accidents".'

'True.' Paige laughed.

Molly handed her a large glass of red wine. 'Cheers!' she said lifting her glass to Paige's. They clinked glasses gently.

'Cheers,' Paige said. 'To you in your new house.'

'Thanks.' They sat down at the kitchen table.

'How's the book doing this week?' asked Paige.

Molly smiled. 'It's doing well from what I can gather. And there were nice reviews in *Dublin Books* and in *Taste*.' Molly's first book, the extended version of her 'Concrete Pictures' story had been published at the beginning of the month. Renamed *Just in Time*, with a show stopping red and white cover, it had already sneaked into the bestseller lists at number five and was the talk of Burnaby. It was hard to miss the dramatic window displays in Happily Ever After, Baroque, Slick Harry's and in Coffee Heaven. Alex and Harry were now married and living in domestic bliss in Wicklow with two black Labradors and a huge black Land Rover and were delighted to support their friend's book.

'And Anita loves it,' Paige reminded her. 'She told me yesterday – I saw her at that new Irish art exhibition in Halo.'

'Was Milo with her?' Molly asked with a smile.

'He most certainly was. Following behind her like a puppy dog, as per usual.'

Molly laughed. 'She still claims she can't stand him.'

'They're as bad as each other,' Paige said. 'And speaking of Milo, how's his son, your other half?'

'Don't call him that!' Molly protested. 'It sounds awful.'

'OK, then, how's your partner?' Paige said in a terrible fake American accent.

'Stop!' Molly giggled. 'Sam's just fine.'

'Good.' Paige smiled at Molly. 'I'm glad you found him. He's a lovely guy.'

'I know.' Molly smiled back. A moment later she gazed into her wine glass. Paige is right, she thought, I am lucky. I found Sam and somewhere along the way I also found myself. I'm Molly Harper, and I'm a writer.